A NOTE FROM THE AUTHOR

Dear Reader,

First, I so appreciate you and I'm thrilled that you've chosen to spend time with me in Rodhlan. No matter how long we've been together, know that you mean so much to me.

As the third installment in a series of four planned novels, *Vow of Magic* explores the "dark night of the soul" that is intrinsic to the human experience. It's not an easy story. However, since the beginning, my goal has been to bring to life flawed characters who misstep and make imperfect decisions just as we do. I have dearly loved bringing their journeys to life, and I hope you enjoy reading this story as much as I have loved writing it.

This book has been hard-fought and hard-won through a global pandemic, major work & life challenges, and my own private struggles with illness and trauma. It has served as both an escape and a healing modality in its own right.

To Lira, Aidryn, Eremon, and Caitir - thank you for leading me through my own dark night.

- Haley

VOW OF MAGIC

THE WITNESS TREE CHRONICLES, BOOK 3

HALEY WALDEN

MORAVON PRESS

Vow of Magic is an epic fantasy set in a medieval-reminiscent world. Learn more about its themes and tropes at authorhaleywalden.com.

ISBN: 978-1-7353431-7-4
(Paperback Edition)

Published by Moravon Press

Developmental Editor: Allison Martin
Copy Editors: Jolene Perry; Ashley Olivier
Proofreader: Elyse Grothendick

Cover Illustration: Saint Jupiter
instagram.com/saintjupit3rgr4phic

Additional Illustrations: Danaye Shiplett
danaye.com

Map Artist: Cartographybird Maps
cartographybird.com

Author Headshot by Jessica McIntosh Photography
jessicamcintosh.net

BOOKS BY HALEY WALDEN

◞◟

Stay up-to-date on bookish news and happenings:
www.authorhaleywalden.com

Follow the author on Instagram, TikTok, and Facebook:
@authorhaleywalden

THE FROZEN ISLANDS

LA'HAYN

THE IMMORTAL WATERS

RIV'ANA

SVA'CERA

ITELORIA

PORT OF RASU

◎ CAPITAL CITIES

◉ CITIES AND TOWNS

◯ MINOR SETTLEMENTS

THE SALTSWEPT LANDS OF THE

OLYRAN SEA

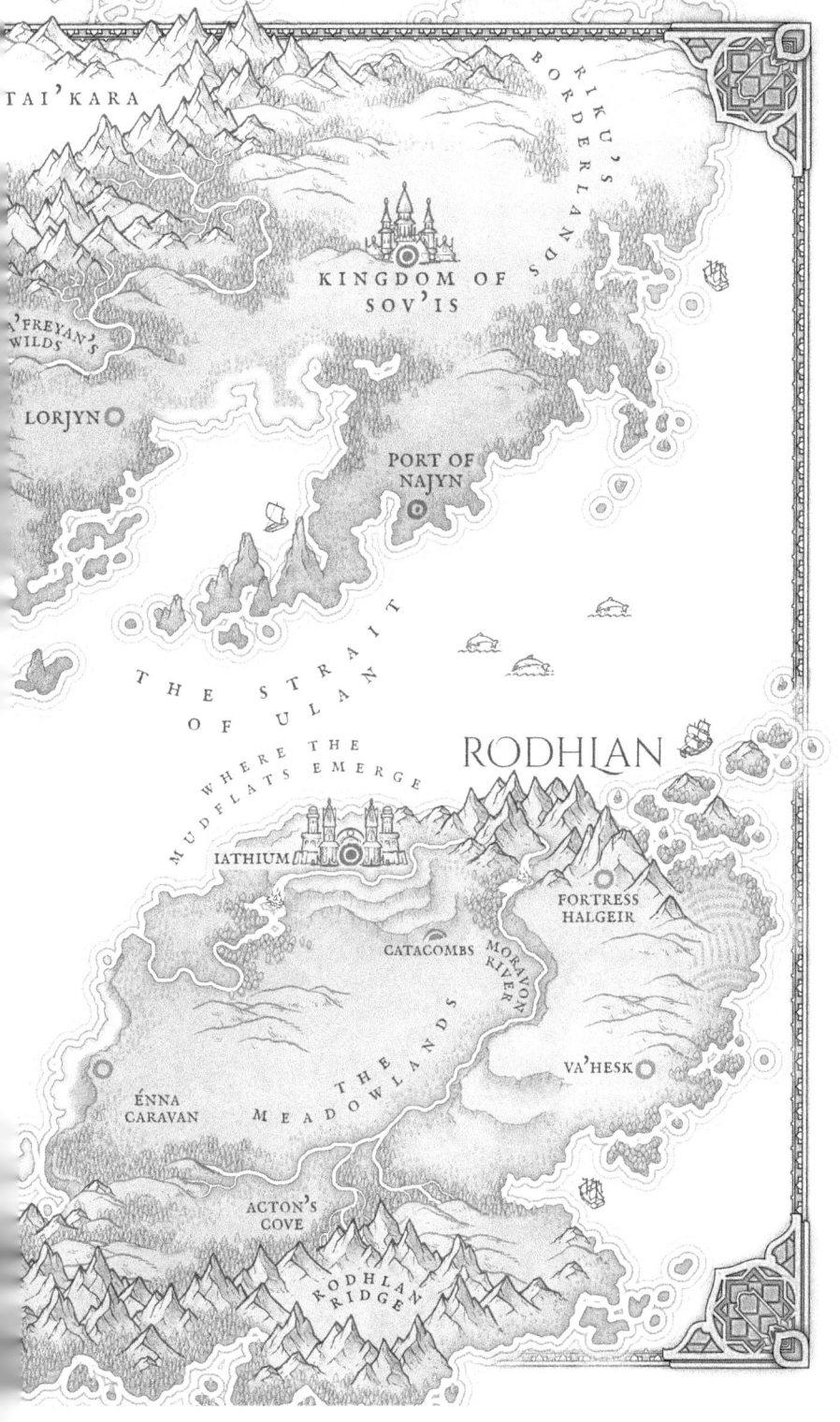

For Marcella. Peasant insisted.

CHAPTER 1
EREMON OF TATHIUM

Meadowlands
Noon

"Stay alive."

Eremon could scarcely hear his own voice over the pounding of Edan's hooves. Silira Mór's body was dead weight against him as the black stallion raced toward Rodhlan's eastern coast.

"Stay alive, Lira," he chanted against the meadowlands' lashing wind. "Please, just stay alive."

This was the work of powerful dark magic. If Eremon indulged its implications for too long, despair would overcome him. If he truly wanted to save her, he would keep moving.

Gritting his teeth, Eremon tightened his hold on Lira and urged Edan on. The stallion, descended from a long line of magical horses, would have been swifter if Eremon had known its incantation. But without the right words, Edan was no better than an ordinary mount.

If only Lira had been able to tell him what to say.

If only her husband, Aidryn Tarlach, wasn't on the other

side of the continent, the stubborn beast would have been able to answer him, too. Those words were imbued with Aidryn's magic, after all.

Days ago, Aidryn had ridden out to Va'hesk, the remnant of Clan Tarlach in the east. Now that the tent settlement had been set ablaze, it wasn't clear whether Aidryn had survived. From here, Eremon's immortal sight could make out the large plume of black smoke in the distance.

Lira groaned, the sound a long, low rumble against Eremon's chest. He held his breath, slowing the horse gradually until it halted in the meadowlands' tall grasses. The warm wind stirred Lira's rich brown curls around her face, and her pale skin was slick with sweat. Eremon bent over to study her, giving her shoulder a light jostle.

"Lira?"

Her lips parted, and she took a shallow inhale, stirring slightly as her dark lashes fluttered. But then she sighed, settling back into that unnerving slumber.

He tried again. "Lira, wake up."

When she remained still and silent, a swell of hopelessness rose in Eremon's throat. What had his healer, Ljós Beran, done whenever Eremon fell ill? He laid his palm over Lira's brow; she felt clammy despite her heavy tunic and the warmth of their proximity. When he pressed his fingertips just below her jawline, her pulse felt alarmingly weak.

"You can't die," he said in a low voice, gathering her close and kissing the top of her head. "Not like this."

With a click of his tongue, Eremon nudged Edan into a canter, then finally, a gallop. The late autumn sun was hot on his back, his black tunic absorbing its rays as he pushed the stallion harder. When Edan's pace plateaued, Eremon growled in frustration.

"*Move*, damn you!" He pressed his calves harder into the stallion's sides, to no avail.

This far from Iathium, Rodhlan's terrain was beginning to look unfamiliar. A pang of doubt crept into Eremon's mind, but he shoved it down. It had been so long since he'd navigated the continent's sprawling wilderness, and he had never done it without a contingent of sentries and advisors surrounding him.

So much had changed since Eremon's death in the way of clan loyalties and alliances. He wasn't sure where to go except toward Clan Tarlach's land. Clan Mór's southern mountain range might be safe, but Gerallt the Usurper had once held their loyalty as its former master. Eremon had no way of knowing where Clans Beran and Énna had placed their loyalties, either. He would need to make himself known to them all, one step at a time. For now, he hoped they might somehow encounter Aidryn between here and Va'hesk.

Surely, that plan wasn't too foolish.

They rode eastward for another hour before gradually turning their path toward the south. In order to cross the Moravon River with ease, they needed to ride in the direction of Acton's Cove at the base of Rodhlan Ridge. As the river flowed southward, it grew shallow and split into cool, rushing streams that fed the Cove's lush green foliage and mossy undergrowth.

Eremon didn't slow their pace again as he guided Edan toward the river crossing, as deeply as he dared. They were still miles from the cove, but he didn't want to waste time going too far south, and the stallion was large enough to weather the rapids. With one arm cradling Lira's body, hand on the reins, Eremon hooked his free arm under her knees and lifted her, turning her so she sat sidesaddle across his lap.

As they moved slowly to the other side of the river, cold water filled Eremon's boots. Curiously, he perceived the change in body temperature—the transition from dry feet to wet—yet remained unfazed. He remembered how the elements, and even how riding a horse, had affected his mortal body, and he couldn't help but appreciate the total lack of discomfort. This immortal form would have its advantages, at least once he got acquainted with it.

A rush of guilt pulled his attention back to Lira. She could be dying, and he was ruminating on the upsides of immortality. After all that Eremon had done in hopes of shielding her—from giving her that useless protective ring to forging the magical Binding that had irrevocably connected her to Aidryn—he had failed miserably.

Lira had been unresponsive for hours. That wretch, Fiadh Énna, had attacked her with dark magic. Fiadh's brother, Faolan, had died in Iathium's crypt just after Eremon's resurrection. Afterward, Eremon had donned Faolan's swords in a show of respect. But then they'd encountered Fiadh and the would-be usurper, Caitir Tarlach, outside the crypt.

Fiadh had taken one look at those swords and launched herself at Lira. During the scuffle, she had managed to take hold of Lira's bronze tree pendant. Unbeknownst to Eremon, his ring's stone had cracked, rendering its protective magic powerless against what had happened next.

Unchecked dark magic had blasted through the pendant and into Lira's body. It seemed as though Fiadh's peculiar power had turned the pendant into some sort of conduit—something Eremon had never believed possible. Then again, he had never believed the dead could be resurrected, either.

Eremon's thoughts drifted to Caitir, whom Fiadh had appeared to be serving. If Fiadh was a wretch, then Caitir was a far worse creature. He shuddered, recalling the Itelorian folk tales his mother had once told to frighten him into submission. Caitir's pale eyes had been reminiscent of the Tai'ceru sorceresses he'd feared in those days—powerful mages with the ability to reduce a man to a shredded carcass with a mere look.

If only his father had told him he'd had every right to fear. That his own mother, the late Raní Macha, had been one of those mages. That Caitir's mother, Aila, was one as well. They had been hiding in plain sight, and there were likely more in Rodhlan.

Eremon sighed bitterly, shaking his head. As Rí—supreme ruler of Iathium—he had once been a capable figurehead. He would have made a strong politician if his mother and her council had not undermined him at every turn. At age twelve, he had been too young to take the throne in his father's stead. His coming of age had made no difference to the established politicians at court, so Eremon had taken it into his own hands to establish alliances in secret and seek ways to sidestep his mother's chokehold on power.

Secret allies like Aidryn, Lord Irem Énna, and later, Lira, had given Eremon hope that he might one day be able to right Iathium's wrongs. For centuries, Eremon's ruling ancestors had painstakingly erased and rewritten history, stealing magic from Rodhlan's people until its existence was eventually erased from common knowledge. Magic-wielding descendants of the continent's four clans had skillfully hidden what remained of their power, and until Eremon's death, knowledge of this power had been successfully contained.

Generations of Eremon's ancestors had accumulated stolen clan powers, passing the immeasurable mass of magic down the bloodline to each ruling Rí. Mingled with Eremon's own birthright abilities—dark magic and a mysterious cobalt power his father had instructed him to suppress—the magical disarray had built into an immense, thunderous pressure that had gradually weakened his mortal body. In the end, the magic had killed Eremon, and the clan powers had returned to the people of their own accord.

Eremon wasn't sure what had become of the city-dwellers after his death, and there had been no time to ask. Without Eremon, Iathium—and by virtue, Rodhlan as a whole—had fallen into the hands of an enemy mage. It hadn't been difficult to conclude that Aila sought to yield the continent to neighboring Iteloria in exchange for a secure throne. The implications, and the danger to Rodhlan's people, were dire.

Selfishly, Eremon returned his focus to Lira. Waking to realize he'd lost his own future with her had been a devastating blow. He had taken for granted that she would live to clash with him about Rodhlan's future. Now, they might all lose her.

Eremon dreaded the moment he would have to look Aidryn in the eyes and admit it.

On the horizon, he spotted a copse of willow trees—a bit out of place for this terrain, if he remembered correctly. The breeze shifted, and Eremon could feel the unmistakable essence of magic wafting around them like a fine mist. It felt like Lira's power, so he steered Edan in its direction.

The willows reminded him of the foliage Lira had created to protect Talfryn and Oda this morning. Before Eremon's death, she had not yet embraced her clan's earth magic. It had been jolting to watch her wield it, even for a moment.

He slowed Edan to a trot as they approached the willow grove and eased the stallion through the canopy of leaves. The land's vibration shifted so profoundly that Eremon could feel it in his bones. Lira's magic hung in the air like moisture, clinging to the insides of his nostrils as he breathed it in. Although he couldn't perceive a scent, as some magic-wielders could, it felt crisp and cold like winter wind.

She had discharged an obscene amount of power in this place.

"What did you do here?" Eremon murmured to her, halting the horse and dismounting. He shifted Lira's body carefully, hefting her from the saddle with ease. Her head lolled against his chest as he padded across the soft grass.

Eremon crouched beneath the largest tree, lowering her to the ground. He took a moment to study her lovely face, brushing his fingertips over her cheek reverently before he returned to Edan in search of a blanket. The horse was still hauling camp supplies from wherever he'd traveled before.

Attached to Edan's saddle was a bedroll. Eremon unbuckled the strap and tugged it free, unfurling it and spreading it out beside Lira. Carefully, he moved her body onto it and covered her. Then, he leaned against the trunk of the nearest willow, heaving a sigh and staring up into the leaves. He tipped his head back against the rough bark, letting his eyelids flutter closed, and reached for the magic Lira had poured into this place.

"Mortal gods," he groaned. "Rodhlan. Nameless immortals. Help me—*someone.*"

A surge of her power pulsed from the tree, reverberating into the earth around them. He whirled toward the willow, pushing onto his knees and pressing his palms to its trunk. Magic thrummed within it, so potent that he let go in alarm.

Next, he pressed his fingertips into the grass. Every blade was saturated with Lira's magic.

Her breathing was shallow and erratic. Beneath her lids, her eyes darted, lashes twitching. She gave a little gasp as though surprised, and her lips began to move.

Eremon whirled, hope flooding him at her response. "Lira?"

She groaned, the sound low and weak. "I am memory," she said on a breath before settling into stillness once again.

Roughly, he shook her shoulder. "Silira." His voice was sharp. Panicked.

Lira turned her head in his direction, as though considering an unfamiliar word. Her eyes remained closed, but her body tensed, her hand scrabbling in the grass for purchase. Eremon grasped it and squeezed.

Her fingers tightened on his. "I know your voice; I won't forget it," she said, the near-incoherent words slurring as she uttered them.

"Don't do this," he breathed, his body trembling. "Rodhlan needs you. I need you."

With a gasping breath, Lira's lashes fluttered. She opened unseeing eyes, and Eremon recoiled with a sharp breath.

The magic shining in her irises should have been a vibrant emerald. Instead, twin storms of sickly green power churned in her eyes. She closed them tightly, succumbing again.

Eremon's mind raced with the overwhelming implications. Fiadh's dark magic had done this, which meant that beyond Lira's life, her anointed power was in grave danger. But if this land—this place—was teeming with Lira's magic, was it possible to counteract the damage?

The desperate scrap of an idea seemed plausible. If the magic in the earth had responded to Eremon's call a moment ago, surely he held some sway over it. What good was being an immortal if he had no command over the outside world?

Intent, he thought. *That's all I need. I'll figure out the rest later.*

He took Lira's hand again. Instinctively, he pressed her palm into the grass.

"Rodhlan, help her," he pleaded. If the land could hold memories, perhaps it had sentience enough to obey its immortal and wake its Witness Tree.

For a moment, the world was silent. Desperation crept into Eremon's throat, tightening it. His eyes stung with tears. But then, he heard a low sound.

It began as a rumble in the earth, far below them. As the sound approached, tendrils of emerald magic burst from beneath the dirt, winding around Lira's body like vines. Eremon yanked her blanket back, allowing the magic access to her. It wrapped around her, warping and swirling, illuminating the little clearing in the dusk as it finally settled on her skin and sank into her pores. She lay still, silent and luminous as the magic did its work, then gradually faded.

Eremon reached for her wrist, feeling for a pulse. Already, her breathing seemed steadier—more peaceful.

Sitting up on his knees, he watched her carefully for any sign of movement, taking her hand in his own.

"Silira Mór," he whispered, squeezing her hand. "Witness Tree, wake up."

This time, her fingers tightened around his, and slowly, she opened her eyes—clear, brown, and familiar, much to Eremon's relief. First, she looked up at the sky as though dazed. Then, her gaze slid to him, and her brows rose in surprise.

"Eremon," she tried to say, but her voice was a gravelly rasp. She grimaced and swallowed hard.

"Wait, don't talk," Eremon answered softly. "We're in the meadowlands, traveling east."

He remembered how he'd taken Oda's pain on instinct back at the crypt. Pressing his fingertips to Lira's throat, he willed away her pain with a flash of cobalt magic. Her expression relaxed, and she swallowed with a sigh of relief.

"But Va'hesk was burning." Lira's voice was hoarse, though a bit stronger. "Aidryn could be dead out there."

Eremon's breath caught in his throat, but he straightened, keeping his gaze steady. "Can you feel his magic through the Binding?"

"I can try." Lira's lids fluttered closed for a long moment, and her shoulders sagged before she opened her eyes again. "I—I think he's alive."

Lira slowly pressed her fingertips to the side of her head and hissed, gingerly touching the gash she'd received from her clash with Macha in the crypt. Gently, Eremon took her wrist and lowered her hand, pouring more of his magic into the wound. To his dismay, it didn't close, but Lira gave him a tired smile as she withdrew from his grasp. "Thank you."

"You need a skilled healer, which I am not," Eremon

replied, his gaze flicking to her hands. She covered Aidryn's silver ring with her right hand. "That wound is still open."

"At least it doesn't hurt for now," Lira replied, suddenly taking a keen interest in the lush grass beneath them. She ran her open palm lightly over the blades. "When I was buried in that power, I could hear your voice, but I couldn't answer."

"Buried." Eremon followed the movement of her fingertips, noting the absence of the archival ink that had once stained them. "What was it like?"

"It was like a storm; consuming. All I could see, taste, touch, and feel was dark magic." Lira withdrew her hand from the grass and met his eyes. "How did you wake me?"

"Rodhlan woke you with your magic," he said. "There was a lot of it concentrated here."

She pulled her knees to her chest. "It's lucky that Skelly gave me all that power, or it wouldn't have been here when I needed it."

Eremon stilled, scrutinizing her. "What do you mean, 'all that power'?"

Her gaze drifted toward the eastern horizon. "It's a long story."

When she didn't elaborate, he shifted uncomfortably. "It feels as though I returned to a completely different world."

"You did." She looked back up and forced a half-smile. The evening breeze stirred her dark curls around her face. "I don't know where to begin."

Eremon shrugged. "You don't have to yet."

Lira rested her chin on her arm. "Someone has to, and it's just us."

Just us. Just us and a Binding and your husband somewhere out there, waiting for you. Just nothing. Nothing left.

"Eremon?"

He'd drifted, snagging on his thoughts. Blinking, he focused on her. "Sorry."

Lira shrugged dismissively, still staring into the distance. "Are we making camp here or riding for Va'hesk?"

"That depends," he answered, studying her carefully. "What do you want?"

Her chin quivered. "I want Aidryn."

CHAPTER 2
CAITIR OF IATHIUM

Dome Courtyard
Morning, Four Hours Prior

"Give me the pendant, Fiadh."

Caitir stretched her empty hand toward Fiadh Énna expectantly. For a long moment, Fiadh didn't acknowledge the request. Instead, she stared into her bloody palms like a dumbfounded simpleton, wincing as she attempted to flex her fingers.

"I need bandages," Fiadh replied absently, flicking her gaze toward the Dome.

Caitir stared down into her own scarred palm as though she could will the bronze tree pendant to appear. She had once attempted to take the ancient charm from Silira Mór herself, and this old wound was hers to bear for it. Dragging the faint scar over her loose, black silk tunic, she bit back a wave of nausea.

"Not before you hand over Lira's necklace," she said, trying her best to fix a hard stare on Fiadh. Her eyes began to water, and she let her lashes flutter shut. Her next words came out in a winded rush. "Then you can do as you please."

The *turas* traveling spell they'd used to return from the meadowlands had aggravated the perpetual sickness Caitir had felt for the past two months. She pressed a palm to her lower belly, centering herself around the thought of the babe growing within her. But any comfort she might have drawn from it was shattered by the memory of Lira's voice, soft with surprise.

Eremon, she's with child.

Images of Lira—of *Eremon*—rose before Caitir, and she snapped her eyes open. Sickness was preferable to seeing their faces again. It had been unpleasant enough to encounter Lira in the meadowlands, but to come face-to-face with Eremon had stirred a deep pool of emotions that Caitir wasn't prepared to explore.

Once, Caitir had loved Eremon from afar. While he was Iathium's Rí and her path to the throne, she had done everything in her power to capture his attention. Instead, he had perpetually overlooked her in favor of Lira, Caitir's former friend and the bane of her current existence.

Apparently, Eremon had spent years quietly pining for Lira before embarking on a short, but scandalous, love affair with her. He had maneuvered her into a title—Defender of Histories, the master of Iathium's historical archive—then set about pursuing her like an addlepated courtier. The debacle appeared to have culminated with a marriage proposal just before Eremon's untimely death.

The ring he'd given Lira had been the subject of long-forgotten myth, hidden away for generations by the heirs in his bloodline. Of all the unworthy people to inherit it, a lowly daughter of the clans had been the worst. It had been a protective token from the mortal god Riku to his wife, Rhona—the first rulers of Iathium.

Over the centuries, the ring had been handed down to the

Rí's rightful heir, usually the eldest son, although a ruler could legally select someone from outside the bloodline if they chose. Eremon's family had managed to secure the throne for almost two thousand years, and he had carelessly thrown it away on Clan Mór's Anointed. Lira—the bookish little shrew—could have never fully appreciated the gravity of that gesture, let alone the trust she had gained from Eremon with so little effort.

Eremon had clearly wanted to keep Raní Macha from ascending, and Caitir could understand that. Macha had been notoriously domineering and was generally disliked among the populace during her son's reign. Since Eremon had no children of his own, he would have wanted someone to protect the inheritance. But *Lira*?

Choosing Lira as his heir had been both emotional and foolish. What Eremon hadn't realized was that the ring's protective magic had been tethering him to his mortal existence. Once he'd transferred that protection to Lira, he had forfeited it for himself.

"Giving that ring away spelled Eremon's doom," Caitir's mother, Aila, had said when they'd learned the Rí's fate. "He might have lived longer, had he not given it to Silira."

Caitir had spent the following months in a daze, her chest aching and hollow. She'd followed Aila in a rage, using the continued promises of more magic, more *power*, to numb herself in the face of her mother's increasing demands.

"Silira is to blame for every misfortune that has befallen us," Aila had raged the night after they'd fled Iathium. "If it had not been for her miserable existence, you would hold the inheritance to Eremon's throne, and we would have no need to conquer it.

"We would not have to bind ourselves to her repulsive uncle, and we would be free to rebuild our lives anywhere we choose: Iathium, Rodhlan's wilderness, or even Iteloria's shining capital if we so desired. The world would be ours.

Instead, Silira destroyed it all."

Aila had gripped Caitir's chin roughly, rage crystallizing in her dark eyes as she added, "If you wish to prove your wisdom and worth to me, you may start by remembering that—and by helping me destroy her."

Her mother's words had emblazoned themselves on Caitir's heart, and they'd inspired a string of spiteful mantras she recited to herself whenever she felt weakened by grief or longing or pain.

Eremon died because of Lira.

Lira stole my chance at the throne.

My brother followed Lira and left me behind.

I'm here because of Lira.

I'm broken because of Lira.

"Did you hear me, Caitir?"

Caitir blinked, clearing her thoughts to focus on Fiadh's indignant expression.

"I did not," Caitir answered.

"You used the pendant for *turas*," Fiadh repeated, crossing her arms and widening her stance as she surveyed Caitir. "Did you lose your grip on it?"

Strands of raven hair lashed Fiadh's face, whipped by the morning wind, and the scrapes on her forehead from her fight with Lira had already begun to bruise. In her black uniform—a richly woven doublet, leggings, and glossy leather boots, with a sword sheathed at her side—she embodied the authority she had so obviously coveted.

Caitir took a slow, steady inhale through her nose, willing her nausea to pass. "No. I *had* it."

She distinctly remembered gripping the heavy, warm bronze tree in her hand as the spell had dissipated. The emerald glow of Lira's magic had been tinged with a sickly green haze, like the angry sky before a cyclone. Caitir had puzzled over the magic's odd hue for exactly half a minute before doubling over to retch.

"Are you going to be sick again?" Fiadh asked, taking a tentative step closer.

Caitir held up a hand, silencing her. After a long moment, the sensation eased enough for her to answer, "It's possible."

"Let's get inside." Fiadh jerked her chin toward the great glass Dome. "You need to rest, and I need to bind my hands. I'll come back and look for it later."

Caitir's body went rigid. Even shaking her head caused her stomach to roil as she bit out one word: "Árchú."

Her eldest half-brother, and Aila's most trusted brute, had been overseeing her every move in the days since her mother had set sail for Iteloria. Now that Caitir and Fiadh had lost the family's remaining Itelorian horses, Edan and Senga, Árchú would make her suffer for it. She cursed Eremon and Lira inwardly; the two had stolen the horses on the meadowlands this morning.

As though reading Caitir's thoughts, Fiadh said, "Árchú is strong, but you're more powerful. If he lays a hand on you, melt that scowl right off his face."

Caitir remembered the last time Árchú had struck her. It had happened two weeks prior, when she had attempted to flee Gerallt's chamber in the middle of the night. Árchú had been standing guard in the hall, and he'd seized her by the arm, shoving her back into the chamber and barring the door. The commotion had roused Gerallt from his drunken stupor and stoked his rage anew—the very thing Caitir had been trying to escape in the first place.

She clenched her fists, gritting her teeth and willing the unwelcome memory to pass. *Dead*, she reminded herself. *Gerallt is dead.*

"Come on, Caitir," Fiadh urged, drawing her sword from its scabbard. She winced as she wrapped her fingers around its hilt. "Stay behind me."

Fiadh headed toward the Dome, and Caitir followed. She didn't acknowledge the gratitude that swelled in her chest.

The Dome was silent as they entered. They crossed its wide, marble-laid corridors toward the western tower's chambers. Sentries deemed disloyal to Aila had been barred from the grounds and relegated to the city streets to earn their way back into the barracks through demonstrated obedience. True loyalists—what few were left—guarded the Dome's exterior, with some occasionally patrolling indoors.

Caitir's footsteps faltered as they approached Gerallt's chamber, where she had been forced to sleep these past months. Fiadh left her by the door with a meaningful look, as if to say, *Now, you have the power.* Then, she peeled off in search of dressings for the blisters on her hands.

At the door, Caitir braced a hand on the frame and took a breath, steeling herself. With one slippered foot, she stepped over the threshold, then froze, heart racing.

I can't go in.

This horror of a marriage had been her mother's political scheme. Aila had coerced Caitir into the arrangement under the guise of protection, binding both herself and her daughter as wives to Gerallt. As Master of Clan Mór, the corrupt, power-hungry Gerallt had been more than willing to accept the deal in exchange for dark magic and the promise of political influence and riches in Iathium. Marching on the city in Lira's name had given the opportunistic beast the prestige he'd craved for so long.

"Gerallt will give us asylum from Raní Macha's wrath," Aila had promised, and Caitir had believed it. "He is our only hope now. Do what I ask of you, and when we rise to power, you will have your crown."

Although Aila gave Gerallt the magic and political ends she had promised him, that was where her side of the bargain had ended. Aila had crowned herself Raní, and Caitir was expected to gratify Gerallt's lust and give him heirs. A brood mare—that's what she had been lured here to be.

Once Aila had secured the throne and surrounded herself with loyalists, she had set sail for Iteloria, leaving Caitir under Gerallt and Árchú's supervision. Aila had been desperate to secure her new position as Raní through her longstanding acquaintance with Iteloria's King La'hiran. She had tasked Caitir with locating Lira and having her captured, and had given Gerallt enough coin for the bounty.

Gerallt had not planned to ride out with his fighters to defend Iathium from Lira and the clans, but Caitir had persuaded him. She'd hoped to steal the reward money and hire someone to follow her husband, but Árchú had stolen the coin first, spending it on drink for himself and his companions in the barracks. Caitir had fallen into despair, believing that, at best, she would only have a few days of freedom from Gerallt.

The news of his demise had given her hope. There was something wonderfully poetic about death by his own daughter's arrow. If Caitir ever encountered Ellwyn Mór again, she would thank her for the favor.

Her thoughts eddied for a moment, then sharpened at another realization. Lira and Ellwyn had been together on the coast when the archer had loosed that fatal shot. Was it so far-fetched to think that Lira had ultimately enabled Gerallt's death? She shook off the thought. *It doesn't matter. She also enabled Eremon's.*

Again, Caitir attempted to enter Gerallt's chamber, and again, she halted just over the threshold. Her gaze flicked from Gerallt's vacant armchair to the cold hearth, then to the rumpled bedclothes. The heavy canopy was tied back on all sides, crimson curtains spilling generously into the floor at the bed's four corners. Its sturdy, ornate mahogany frame shone as though newly polished.

Hatred seared outward from Caitir's chest, down her arms and legs, and into her hands and feet. Almost unbidden, dark magic pooled in her palms, near effortless in its conjuring. Vaguely, she noted that there was no pain, which was unusual, though perhaps well-deserved. If she was going to wield this magic, putting herself and her child at risk, she might as well feel nothing in the process.

"My lady?"

Caitir's power fizzled out as she whirled toward the voice, chest heaving. Behind her stood Deghan Mór, one of the red-haired archers who had occupied Iathium with Gerallt. Unlike the other archers who had defected with Gerallt's eldest son, Artagán, Deghan had become a sentry, proving himself loyal from the day they conquered the city onward. He was one of the few whom Caitir could trust.

Deghan's speculative stare pinned Caitir to the spot, and he didn't feign disinterest at the open chamber door behind her. Instead, he craned his neck, peering inside. "D'you need something?"

"I need my possessions," she answered, setting her shoulders and raising her chin. "Have my clothing moved to another chamber, then destroy the rest."

He chewed the inside of his cheek and adjusted the sleeve of the black fatigues he usually wore beneath his armor. "What of Rí Gerallt?"

"Dead," Caitir answered flatly.

A spark of glee ignited within her when Deghan took a step closer. "By whose hand?"

She leaned forward conspiratorially. "His own daughter's."

Deghan swore under his breath. "Didn't know Ellwyn had it in her." His gaze flicked down the corridor before he added, "The mistress know?"

"No," Caitir said, too quickly. "Just Fiadh."

"I'd watch that one," Deghan replied, rolling a shoulder and giving Caitir a wry look.

She returned a delicate snort. "Duly noted." She nodded in the direction of the bedchamber. "Do you mind? I'm going to the garden."

Deghan gave her a little bow. "I'll get Aeron and we'll move your belongings out. Where do you want your things?"

"I don't care where you put them. Just burn everything of Gerallt's," Caitir said. "Make a bonfire in the corridor for all I care. Just clear it all out—furniture, clothing, drapes. Come fetch me when it's done."

She turned before Deghan could see her bottom lip wobble, then moved swiftly down the wide corridor in the direction of the Rí's garden. Her heartbeat pounded in her ears as the true weight of the situation settled over her.

Gerallt was dead.

Aila was in Iteloria.

And Caitir was as free as she had ever been, at least for the moment.

She had rarely escaped Aila's watchful eye, and certainly not for this long. Still, there was no time to enjoy the freedom. For once, Caitir's most pressing problem was not her mother, or even the fact that Lira could rightfully seize power at any time. It was the fact that Eremon was alive—and it was only a matter of time until he reclaimed his rightful place.

He could return in hours, days, weeks... Caitir wasn't sure. If she wanted to gain a foothold in this city, she would have to think and act quickly.

Eremon had been disarmingly familiar when they'd come face-to-face this morning. Everything about him, from his lithe, willowy form to his silken black hair, had been the same—except for the color of his angular eyes, which had changed from gray to silver since his resurrection. Seeing him dressed in black from neck to feet had been unsettling; he had always donned brightly colored silks and stylish robes in his mortal life.

Before this morning, Caitir had never seen his hair unbound. It had tumbled down over his shoulders, and the wind had whipped strands of it around his face as he'd held his blade to her cheek. Raising a hand, she pressed her fingertips to the shallow cut he'd left on her skin to find that the blood had since dried.

Eremon is alive.

The thought was a jolt, as though she didn't already know. As though she hadn't seen him with her own eyes.

Caitir neared the large indoor garden, a place she, Eremon, and Lira had frequented in the old days. Usually, Caitir had paraded through when she'd known Eremon would be here. Other times, she had persuaded Lira to take a turn about the garden with her while she pretended to be interested in the various species of native and foreign foliage the gardeners cultivated.

Lira had played a hand in so many of the past year's events, from ruin to resurrection. It had become easy to loathe her. Still, a nagging thought had been playing at the edges of Caitir's mind since their morning encounter, and it threatened to upend the resolve she'd worked so hard to maintain.

Eremon is alive because Lira brought him back.

CHAPTER 3
AIDRYN TARLACH

Rodhlan Ridge
Morning

"Lira!"

Aidryn Tarlach threw the door of Skelly's cottage open so hard that it might have splintered. He crossed the little house in a few strides, noting the disarray Lira and Talfryn had left behind. The home was deathly silent, just as he'd expected it to be.

He paused in the middle of the kitchen, heaved a sigh, and surveyed the room.

The wood in the hearth had been burned away to nothing but soot and charred fragments, as though a fire had been left to burn itself completely out. Mugs and bowls had been left on the table after their last meal, the basin crowded with dirty dishes they hadn't bothered to wash. A half-full pot of stew hung cold in the fireplace, its contents long ruined.

Aidryn had hoped Lira would be here waiting for him. On the ride from Va'hesk, he'd imagined that she might have used *turas*, her traveling spell, to come back to the cottage as though she'd never left. But she had been seen in a skirmish with her uncle, Gerallt, and his men. She'd used her power to topple a manor on the western coast.

If Aidryn's instincts—and the magical key he now possessed—were any indication, Lira had gone from the coast to Iathium's crypt to resurrect Rí Eremon.

It was tempting to be angry with her for going against his wishes. After all, they'd agreed to go to the crypt together. But clearly, something drastic had spurred her on without him.

Heartbeat quickening, Aidryn stepped into the tiny bedroom. Talfryn had left a rumpled bedroll on the floor beside the bed, and the sparse blankets were haphazardly piled on the mattress. The room smelled putrid, and when Aidryn circled the bed, he found vomit on the wood floor.

He pulled his tunic up over his nose, his panic rising. A glint from the bed caught his eye, and he leaned over the mattress to find Lira's familiar leather pouch splayed open, her heirloom trinkets from Skelly scattered as though they'd been hastily dumped out. With trembling hands, Aidryn gathered Lira's things and placed them back in her pouch, his breaths now coming in short gasps.

What happened here?

His mind raced, grasping for something—anything—that might explain what he was seeing. The fastest route to Clan Énna's territory on the coast would have been *turas*, and that was what Lira used these trinkets for. Rifling through the bag, he noted that the gray pearl from Clan Énna was indeed gone. But that didn't explain why Lira had become ill.

Aidryn felt the urge to try using Lira's magic again. He'd attempted to tap into it through the Binding once, back at Fortress Halgeir, but had failed. Perhaps being here in Lira's ancestral home would help.

Aidryn sat on the bed and felt for the thread of Lira's power, seeking a memory. He recalled Ljós's admonition to try asking the continent for its memories, so he said, "Rodhlan, show me: What happened to Silira?"

A feeling of deep dread washed over him as her magic responded, but he witnessed nothing. An odd smell filled his nostrils, like the scent of the air after a lightning strike. The hair on the back of his neck stood on end.

He tried twice more, waiting long moments between each attempt. The quieter Lira's power was, the more alarmed Aidryn became. Frustrated, he pressed the palms of his hands to his eyes. "Show me Silira Mór's last visit to this room."

He lost his sight as the witnessing overtook him.

Lira is lying on the bed, panting, her right hand trembling violently.

"What did you see?" Talfryn cries, alarm etched into his features.

"Fiadh is allied with Caitir." Lira clutches her hand, attempting to steady it. "Since before Halgeir. She was there to gather information."

"By Numi..."

Lira grips the pendant in her hands, and her eyes go emerald again; she's diving back into her power, no doubt rifling through memories that might tell her something more about the alliance between the other two women. When she emerges from the witnessing moments later, she hauls herself over the side of the bed to be sick, her tremors more pronounced than before.

"Lira, stop this," Talfryn begs. "Please, tell me what you've learned so far. You could—"

"Once more. Just once more." Again, she is gone.

The witnessing released Aidryn, and he found himself sitting in nothingness, panting, his head pounding. He blinked several times, to no avail. This wasn't night; there was no moonlight filtering in through the window, no shadows stretching across the worn floorboards.

Aidryn patted the rough spun blanket he'd been lying on, lifting the fabric in a fruitless attempt to study it. He could feel his surroundings, but this depth of *nothing* felt like the first time he'd ventured past Umhan Cavern, the entrance to a vast network of caves below this room. Skelly had climbed down behind him and extinguished the torches, plunging him into a void that could drive a person mad in just a few days' time.

He rubbed his eyes, blinking furiously once, twice. When he opened them again, he perceived a gray haze. A moment later, the shapes in the room around him began to take form again. He turned toward the window, which was now a bright patch of light.

Tapping into the memories of others, rather than asking Rodhlan for its memories, carried grave consequences. Lira's memory magic could easily be used for great evil, and it had been wisely balanced to dissuade such tampering. When she had misused it, she had grown ill and developed a tremor in her right hand.

Had Aidryn's tampering cost him his sight?

Fear clenched his throat. Taking the Witness Tree's memories must have been a more significant infraction—worse than Lira delving into others' minds. Even though he was bound to her, Clan Mór's Anointing was not Aidryn's to do with as he pleased.

Just as he was preparing to make his way outside and call for help, his sight suddenly began to sharpen. Light and color poured in rapidly, sending shooting pains through his head and face. He swore and closed his eyes, pressing his fingertips gingerly against the lids. Then, he lay back on the pillows, gradually adjusting to the light before looking up to study the heavy wooden beams on Skelly's ceiling.

He intended to rise again—truly. Lira was out there somewhere, and Aidryn needed to get to her. But exhaustion weighed on his limbs, his chest. His breathing slowed of its own accord. Before he could force himself to move again, sleep swept him under.

"WHAT IN BLAZES ARE YOU DOING?"

The unwelcome voice sounded from the bedchamber door, and Aidryn scrubbed a hand over his face, groggily opening his eyes. He hadn't meant to go to sleep at all, and now the afternoon sun was high. Panic and awareness flooded him as his vision adjusted to the figure scowling down at him.

Terovi Tarlach stood by the bedside, arms crossed. Awareness flooded Aidryn, and he sat up abruptly from where he'd been sprawled across the mattress, still covered in traces of soot from the settlement fire.

"Mortal gods," he swore, swinging his legs over the side of the bed. His head throbbed, and he reached back to knead a knot in his neck.

Terovi's gaze fell to where Lira had been sick. "Are you drunk?"

"I don't get drunk," Aidryn replied.

"Good. The assembly looks down on it."

"That mess has been there a few days," Aidryn said, jerking his chin toward the floor at the beside. "I think Lira was ill here."

The older man cocked his head. "Well, why were you asleep? You should have gone to find out what happened."

"I used—" Aidryn shut his mouth. Terovi and the council didn't know about his Binding with Lira, and he wanted to keep it that way for now. "I suppose I didn't realize how exhausted I was."

Terovi grunted, then disappeared into the kitchen before he returned with a basin of water and a cloth. He knelt by the bed and began cleaning the mess. Aidryn retrieved his own cloth and joined the older man, pulling his tunic up over his nose to ward off the smell.

"What does the assembly have to do with anything?" Aidryn's voice was muffled beneath the fabric.

Terovi sniffed. "Eiren wants to offer you a seat."

He paused his scrubbing for the barest of moments before continuing with a shake of his head. "Thank you, but I'll forgo that."

"Why?" Terovi sneered.

Aidryn sighed.

He had more important issues to worry about than serving as a member of Clan Tarlach's council. Besides, he had only known Terovi and the clan's elderly adviser, Eiren, for a few days. He had traveled to Va'hesk, the clan's settlement in Eastern Rodhlan, hoping to secure magical horses and fighters to assist the clan army. Instead, Terovi had taken him captive. Worse, Aidryn's magic had been cut off, and he'd been unable to prove his anointing at first.

Mentally, he ticked backward over the past few days, and suddenly, it made sense: Lira had tampered with her magic around the same time as Aidryn's had been snuffed out. He filed the realization away for later, a sinking dread filling his stomach.

"I asked why, boy." Terovi snatched Aidryn's cloth from him and dropped both into the basin of murky water. He adjusted the leather patch over his right eye and scowled.

Aidryn's shoulders tensed, and he forced himself to breathe. "Clan Tarlach has made it clear they want no involvement with the clan army," he answered. "My highest obligations are to my wife, to Thorne Beran, and to securing Iathium. The assembly would be a competing priority."

"You put the clan's needs first during the fire," Terovi pressed, the edge dropping from his voice. "Instead of leaving, you stayed—protected our people and horses."

"And that's why Eiren wants me?"

"Not just Eiren." It must have pained the older man to come

a hair's breadth from admitting that *he* wanted Aidryn on the assembly, too. "You're the anointed. Do you know how many years it has been since Clan Tarlach had its Key Keeper on council?"

Aidryn was finding it difficult to remain apathetic. "No."

"Neither do I." Terovi stood abruptly, taking the basin back into the kitchen. "Your mother was the last, and she had no care for us, either."

Aidryn bristled at the insult to his birth mother, whom he'd never known. "Perhaps I inherited my ambitious streak from her."

Terovi snorted. "Call it what you want, if it makes you feel better."

Magic was all Aidryn knew of his mother. Her name had been Eiren, too, after the adviser. But she had died in Aidryn's infancy, and his late father, Emyr, had quickly remarried. Aila had raised Aidryn as her own, relatively speaking, until Caitir's birth three years later.

When the two were still children, Aila had tricked Aidryn into giving most of his power to Caitir, and he had done so willingly. At the time, he'd believed himself to be Caitir's rescuer—until she had plunged so far into darkness that he'd had no choice but to leave her there.

He heard the front door open, but he remained motionless on the floor. Terovi's persistence had surprised him. The man had done everything in his power to humiliate Aidryn back at Va'hesk. Clearly, he only cared now that he'd seen Iuchair.

Aidryn summoned the great golden key into his palm, hefting its weight before running his fingertips over the ornate bow. Iuchair had been buried in Iathium's crypt with Eremon's father, Rí Corlan, for nearly eight years. It was a master key imbued with Clan Tarlach's magic, which only the Key Keeper's power could summon.

This key granted its bearer access—not only to any structure in Rodhlan, but to the magic of its mortal gods, too. Centuries ago, it had been used to lock away their power. But if Aidryn's instincts were correct, Lira had used it to unlock Eremon's magic and resurrect him.

A few moments later, Terovi's footsteps sounded through the cottage again. Aidryn tucked Iuchair into his magic and met the older man in the kitchen.

"I came here to ask for your help," Terovi admitted, shifting as though he was uncomfortable saying so. "Mór's people know you, but they're putting up quite the resistance to Tarlach moving in. Tensions are high, and I don't want blood spilled before we can get shelters built."

Coming back to the mountain territory had been a gamble. Aidryn wasn't sure that he, Lira, or the other clanspeople who opposed Gerallt would be welcome here. But the valley was sparsely populated these days, and the people who had stayed behind were largely women, children, and the elderly—all of whom had no choice but to welcome more able-bodied folk to help tend the fields, gardens, and livestock.

"I told them what to expect," Aidryn said, following Terovi out the front door. "Half of Clan Mór left, anyway. There's plenty of room to house Tarlach for a little while. They should be able to handle themselves."

"They still look at us like invaders." Terovi spat in the grass. "As though we'd want to confine the Seanlaoch to the top of a mountain forever."

Aidryn grunted but didn't respond. Clan Tarlach had confined itself and its magical horses already, limiting its power in favor of a life in the wilds of Rodhlan.

"I want you to think about Eiren's offer." Terovi's hard stare was unnerving. "You've no idea how powerful you really are, or what good you could do for this world if you weren't tethered to the Witness Tree."

"I am *not* tethered," Aidryn said through gritted teeth. The moment the words left him, he felt a deep sense of uneasiness in his gut. But he pressed it down and headed for Gerallt's keep. Terovi grunted, keeping pace beside him. "Keep telling yourself that."

Although ire rippled between the two men, neither spoke again. Terovi peeled off as they approached the keep, where a silver-haired woman was engaged in a fierce argument with a soot-smudged settler from Va'hesk. The settler was stocky and dark-haired, and she was wagging a finger in the older woman's face.

"I shouldn't be surprised that you're up here with this lot." Her cheeks grew red as she dropped her hand and clenched her fists at her sides. "You harbored their anointed, Nevala, and now Va'hesk is gone!"

Aidryn's ears perked at the name, and he picked up his pace as he strode toward the them. This silver-haired woman was Nevala Tarlach, the healer who had nursed Lira after Aila and Gerallt had imprisoned him.

"Clan Mór gave us shelter when no one else would," Nevala answered, her voice steady and calm despite the anger that roiled in her eyes. "You should be grateful, Delory."

"They have no choice," Delory snapped. "We're greater in number. We—"

"Enough!" Aidryn halted before Delory and held up a hand. Although the woman closed her mouth, she narrowed her dark eyes at him. "We can't afford to fight amongst ourselves."

"You're the one they called Key Keeper," Delory said with a slow nod. "I saw you and your stallion this morning. You saved my son from the fire."

Delory's gaze darted across the sparse courtyard, where a little boy and his older sister sat huddled beneath a horse blanket. Aidryn remembered the boy's terrified cries as he'd grasped his small arm and wrenched him up onto Fannin's back. The tent the child had been hiding in had gone up in flames, and he had emerged just before it collapsed.

"I did," Aidryn said. "Clan Mór's Anointed is also my wife, and I believe I have Nevala to thank for harboring her."

Nevala whirled to face him, her hazel eyes wide. Her hair fell over her shoulder in a long plait, and up close, she looked younger than he'd expected her to. He reached for her hand and she took it, giving it a squeeze.

"I—forgive me," Delory cut in, backing away a step. "I'm going to see to Hamel."

"I think that's a wise choice," Aidryn admonished.

Delory dipped her head, cheeks pink, and headed toward where her children sat.

"Aidryn Tarlach." Nevala broke into a wide smile. "Your name has become legend."

"Something's happened to Lira," he said in a low voice. The smile dropped from her face. "Come with me."

Concern creased Nevala's brow, but she didn't reply. Instead, Aidryn led her into the bustling great hall. Members from Clan Mór were doling out bowls of porridge, and it appeared that some of Tarlach's people were trying to help feed the masses that gathered within and outside the hall.

They took seats at the end of one of the long dining tables, where Aidryn explained what he had been able to piece together. Nevala listened intently, a hand pressed to her lips.

"I need to find her," he said, resting his forehead in his hand, "but—"

"You can't leave the clans like this," Nevala cut in. "Thank Rhona there aren't many Mór men here, or we'd have a real problem. There's so much tension, but I think you'll be able to help keep things stable."

Aidryn's heart sank. "What about Lira?"

Nevala smiled wanly. "I very much doubt she's alone this time. You said her brother went with her?"

Aidryn nodded. "And she was seen in a skirmish."

"Which means she's likely among friends," Nevala answered. "I know you want to be near her, but..." She glanced around the hall, where members of Tarlach and Mór had divided themselves between tables. "These clans know you. They'll listen to you before they listen to me or Mytr. Or anyone else."

Nevala tilted her head toward where her husband stood doling out afternoon porridge alongside two of Clan Mór's women. The dark-haired, younger man cast a wary glance their way, then nodded when he met Aidryn's gaze. According to Nevala, they'd been living in the valley since shortly after she'd cared for Lira.

With a heavy sigh, Aidryn said, "I wish there were two of me. My heart's out there, not here."

"Sometimes, you have to ask your heart to wait while you do what must be done in the moment." Nevala reached across the table to pat his hand. "We have few allies here, so Mytr and I will go in your stead."

Aidryn straightened. "I can't ask that of you."

"You didn't." Nevala cast another look toward her husband. "We'll leave tonight, and if we find Silira, we'll bring her back to you."

CHAPTER 4
SILIRA MÓR

Meadowlands
Afternoon

"I want Aidryn."

Eremon's expression sent a pang through Lira's chest, but he nodded and stood, offering his hand and pulling her to her feet. She swayed, still weak. He led her to one of the willows, and she braced herself against its trunk while he packed the bedroll she'd been lying on. The chill that skittered through her body set her shivering.

He crossed the clearing to Edan and attached the roll to the stallion's saddle. She watched as he fastened the buckles with deft fingers, then ran his hands over the horse's smooth coat.

"Are you sure you feel like traveling?" he asked, lingering over Edan's tack. "You gave me quite a scare."

Lira wrapped her arms around her middle. "Of course not."

"Of course not," Eremon echoed absently. He stood before Edan, stroking the stallion's velvety nose as he checked the bit. "Forgive me; that was a stupid question."

She shrugged. "It was considerate."

His silver gaze flicked to hers. "And your answer, as always, was disarmingly honest."

Tension coiled between them. Nothing about this felt natural, and Lira found herself missing the easy companionship they'd shared before.

"You admired my honesty once," she said quietly. "Why is it suddenly a bad thing?"

Eremon was taken aback, and a look of horror crossed his face. "I didn't intend—" He closed his mouth, considering his next words. Standing up straighter, he said, "I *do* admire your honesty, Lira. I do."

He schooled his expression into a mask of neutrality. Lira didn't miss the way the corner of his mouth twitched downward, as though he would rather be frowning. Turning his back to her, he fiddled with one of Edan's stirrups.

Lira approached the horse, clasping her hands behind her back.

"Well," she said with a tight smile, "now that I'm awake, we can use Aidryn's incantation, and you'll be rid of me."

He draped an arm over Edan's saddle and paused. His shoulders rose and fell once as he released a harsh breath. Then, he turned his head enough that she could hear him say, "I don't want to be rid of you."

She gaped at him. Thoughts of their time together in Iathium flooded her, followed by that moment they'd shared in the crypt, when Eremon had noticed Aidryn's ring. Her cheeks ignited as she tried to suppress the sudden memory of Eremon embracing her, kissing her—

"I—I was trying to be lighthearted," she stammered.

"There is nothing lighthearted about this." Eremon turned to face Lira fully, his eyes shining with an emotion she wished she didn't recognize. "I still love you."

Lira's breath escaped in a whoosh, and she took a step back, curling her fingers into tight fists. What was she supposed to say to that? How did Eremon expect her to respond? She couldn't comfort him, and there was no reassurance to give.

She tried to calm her racing thoughts long enough to form a constructive reply. Instead, she blurted, "What's wrong with you?"

He had the audacity to look wounded, which sent a wave of anger shuddering through her body. She tried to shake it off, but she wasn't sure what else to focus on: her embarrassment? Fear? The guilt she felt at her memories of them together?

What's wrong with me? Her heart began to race, and her ears burned as she added, "You mustn't say things like that. *Ever.*"

"You value honesty." A muscle in Eremon's jaw tightened. "It's the truth."

"You married me to Aidryn. You. *Bound. Us.*" Lira's voice trembled. "You can't just return and upend what I have with him."

"I know, I just..." He turned his back again, pressing his face to his arm. "I lost *everything*," he finally said, his voice muffled against the fabric.

"So did I," she retorted, hugging herself tightly, "but everything you need now is in Iathium."

He bristled, straightening. "And what if I disagree?"

"Unbelievable," Lira scoffed, pressing a palm to her forehead. "You would leave your throne at Aila's mercy?"

"I need time," Eremon mumbled, crossing his arms and looking at the grass.

"There *is* no time!" The wind whipped a few stray curls against Lira's face. "Take Iathium back from the usurper. Then you can abdicate, if that's what you want. But the people need you. You can't abandon them now—not when we risked everything to bring you back."

"Oh." His eyes lit as he stepped away from the horse and began to circle her. "So that's what I am to you now—a means to an end. A weapon to be wielded against our enemies.

Perhaps you should dispense with the niceties and start calling me Trebuchet."

Lira recoiled. "Eremon, you're being ridiculous."

He ran a hand through his hair, barking a hollow laugh. "No, you are! You ran right into Aidryn's arms the moment I was gone. How did I not anticipate that?"

She pointed a finger at his face, narrowing her eyes. "You know that's not true."

"Isn't it, though?"

"Don't change the subject," she said. "My marriage has nothing to do with your responsibility to the throne."

"Did you mourn me at all?" Tears shimmered in his silver eyes. His words were laced with an agony so palpable, Lira could feel it in her chest.

The wind rustled the leaves in the willows as they stared one another down. Her first instinct was to tell Eremon everything: how bitterly she had grieved his death, how reluctant she had been to accept the Binding with Aidryn, and how she had feared Eremon's resurrection for exactly this reason. She and Aidryn had known that bringing him back would likely give rise to emotions better left buried, but Eremon deserved to live. Deserved to embrace the power long denied him in every way.

"Well?" Eremon's whisper cut through her thoughts.

Lira blinked slowly, her disbelief mounting at his insolence. "If you can't answer that for yourself, then you don't really know me."

He leaned nearer, expression hard. "It's a simple question with a simple answer: yes or no."

"You know I did," she hedged, "but you want an answer that placates your tender feelings. If I say yes without holding you accountable for your manipulative question, you'll goad me more about Aidryn. Am I correct?"

Eremon rocked back slightly, so Lira pushed harder.

"I thought so," she sneered. "You mean to imply that it

wasn't possible for me to have fallen in love with him if I'd *truly* mourned you. You don't get a say in how I grieved, or in the choices I made after you were dead."

"I doubt you know how to grieve." He scowled like a petulant child. "I haven't forgotten how you keep busy to avoid your feelings. Aidryn was an excellent distraction, I'm sure."

Lira's eyes stung as his words cut into her. She didn't think before she closed the distance between them and slapped him. "Entitled brat," she hissed.

Eremon's eyes widened, his fingers splaying across his pale cheek. "How dare you." He took a step closer, clenching his jaw.

"How dare *you*," Lira challenged.

Her body quivered with anger as they stared one another down. Eremon had watched as she'd thrown herself into her archival work after their fathers' deaths—just as he had immersed himself in his new role as Rí. Making a mockery of how Lira had needed to cope was the lowest she'd ever seen Eremon stoop.

After a silent moment, he sighed. "I'm sorry, Lira. I only thought you would at least have the decency to wait out a proper mourning period."

"Did death strip you of discretion, or were you always this hubristic under the surface?" Lira's voice sounded ragged and hoarse as it rose. "If I had known this was what you were masking under all those pretty words, I would have never given you a second thought."

Eremon bent closer, his lips curling back. "I chose you because of your loyalty and dedication. Clearly, your virtues were limited to your own ambition."

An unfamiliar vitriol rose from Lira's toes to her gut. "Is this why you tried to corner me into marriage, so I wouldn't see who you really are? Selfish and envious and cruel." The words flew out before she could stop them. "Am I supposed to feel grateful that you chose me?"

He looked aghast as he raised his palms. "Stop, Lira. Just—
we should stop. We're making this worse by quarreling."

Pain flashed in his eyes, and Lira ached with the familiarity
of it. She wanted to embrace him, but instead she gripped her
forearm, pinning it to herself.

"I knew this would be distressing," she said, her voice quivering. "I've had a little time, but your grief is fresh. I can't expect
you to adjust to reality in a day's time."

"Reality." Eremon snorted softly. "You brought me back to a
wasteland of a life you think I should *adjust* to?"

"Yes," Lira said, "like I adjusted to the truth about the histories, and the magic, and the Binding—which you imposed on
us, by the way. If I can manage it as a mortal, you'll be fine."

Eremon glared at her. "Oh, so immortality is a cure-all. I
see."

"You should be grateful," she snapped, though she felt a
pang of guilt at the words. "I didn't have to bring you back.
There are people who didn't want an immortal Rí, but I fought
for you. Time will heal your pain, and you have plenty of it."

"Unlikely," Eremon answered, "since my memories of you
lingered, even in death." He tilted his head to scrutinize her,
and she wanted to disappear. "We were promised ethereal
comfort in the afterlife, but my solace came from thinking of
you, Lira—how you loved me until my last breath, and how I
would give anything to see you one last time."

An unwelcome tear trickled down Lira's cheek, and she
swiped it away with the back of her hand. She sniffed, fighting
the urge to reassure him of how much he'd meant to her, and
how much he still meant. Showing him that sort of tenderness
right now was dangerous.

"I'm right here," she answered. "You see me."

His shoulders sagged. "You know that wasn't what I
meant—"

"It doesn't matter what you meant." Lira threw her hands

up in exasperation. "What we had is in the past; we have to move on."

"So says the living vessel of history," Eremon snarled, though his eyes shone with hurt. "*In the past.* Is that what you say when your magic gives you an inconvenient memory?"

"*Stop it.*"

He ignored her, closing the last two steps between them. "Exactly how trustworthy is a Witness Tree who disregards the past?"

"That's enough! I'll find Aidryn on my own." Lira shoved past him and strode to Edan's side, gripping his saddle to haul herself up. She tried to ignore the sudden darkening in her vision. Once she was astride, she swayed a bit but blinked hard, shaking off the fatigue.

Eremon crossed the clearing to Edan in a few long strides and grabbed the reins, glaring up at Lira. "You can't do this; you're too weak."

"I'll do what I please." Lira tried to pull the reins from his hand. "Let go!"

"No," he growled, tightening his hold. "You're staying with me."

"I don't need you," she lied.

Eremon recoiled and let go of the reins, fury and hurt marring his beautiful features.

Lira sat up in the saddle, braced herself, and said, "*Ano je.*"

But the incantation had no effect. Edan cocked an ear, glancing back at her as though to say, *What do you expect me to do?*

She sucked in a breath. Aidryn's magic had never failed to respond to her before. Panicked, Lira looked down at Eremon with wide eyes.

"*Ano je,* Edan," she repeated, using her legs to gently squeeze the stallion's sides.

Edan began to walk. Heat flooded Lira's cheeks. Why had

Aidryn's magic failed now? She had felt it along the Binding less than an hour ago, unless something worse had befallen him since then.

Eremon walked briskly at Edan's side, a thumb hooked into his belt. "Magic troubles? How unfortunate for you."

Lira stared straight ahead, her breathing growing ragged as horror overtook her. "It's not funny. Something's wrong."

CHAPTER 5
EREMON

Meadowlands

"Wrong like what?" Eremon asked. "Wrong with Aidryn, or wrong with you?"

"If Aidryn's magic isn't working, something is *wrong*." Lira had shed all pretense, the full breadth of her frustration now on display. "My power was completely out of reach for a little while after I misused it. I would rather think he's done something foolish than assume he's dead."

"Well, how would you know?"

Lira threw Eremon an exasperated look. "I would ask my magic to show me his most recent memories."

Eremon stopped walking, his mouth dropping open. "What gave you that notion?"

"Desperation," she answered.

He remembered the odd exchange between Lira and Caitir earlier that morning. Lira had taunted Caitir, suggesting she might be capable of accessing the memories of living people—memories Rodhlan had not freely given to her.

My power is truth. As far as I'm concerned, your memories are fair game, Lira had said.

Sounds like someone's been tampering with her power, Caitir had replied coolly.

"And what were the consequences?" He wanted to tell Lira that her words had horrified him, but he had plenty of time to chastise her. For now, he needed whatever openness he could get.

"A tremor," she answered, holding up her right hand. "Loss of my magic. Illness."

Eremon glowered. "Do I really have to tell you to refrain from such tampering?"

"You've already demonstrated that you'll say whatever you want," Lira said. "Whether or not I heed it is my choice."

"Of course I'll say what I want; I'm the Rí." But the moment the words left his mouth, he regretted them.

"Are you, now?" Lira halted Edan, a smug expression on her face. The lilt in her voice grated on Eremon as she added, "That's convenient for both of us."

Eremon shouldn't have used his rightful position as leverage. Not when he'd just said he had no plans to ride into Iathium and reclaim the throne the way she'd envisioned.

"No, I mean—" He sighed when she gave him a heavy-lidded, expectant look. "I'm not going to parade into the city and declare myself savior. No fanfare. If I return—"

"*When* you return," she amended.

"*If* I return to the throne," Eremon pressed, "I will do it in my own time and as I see fit, once I've gathered enough information."

Lira sighed heavily. "Aila gains a deeper foothold with every day you waste."

"Exactly how many *days* have I wasted, Lira?" Eremon growled, taking long strides to keep up. Heat filled his body with his mounting anger, and a low, rumbling vibration began to spread from his feet upward. "Last I checked, I was dead until this morning. I've had mere hours to register the fact my body is *alive* again, with new powers I can barely comprehend, and you're already moaning about wasted time?"

Lira's lips parted in surprise, but she rallied quickly. "What if Aila brings Itelorian forces to conquer the continent? What if Caitir succeeds and the people start to love her? What if they turn against me and forget about you?"

"I can understand your fear, but the people want a ruler who is powerful and familiar, and I'm both," he answered, his mind boggled by the number of possible catastrophes she'd spun without taking a breath. "I'm the immortal here, I have the power, and I'll reveal myself when I'm ready."

"You've made yourself perfectly clear," Lira said sharply. "And as for wasted time, I need to get to Aidryn. If I look into his memories—"

"Absolutely not." Eremon glared up at her. The rumbling sensation had reached his stomach now and continued to climb. "You're not going to tell me all the terrible things that happen when you tamper, then resolve to do just that."

Lira set her jaw. "It would be worth the risk to find out where he is."

"No risk to you is worth it," Eremon replied curtly. "Come down off the horse, or at least let me ride with you if you're determined to go."

"After the things you said to me, I don't want you that close," Lira answered, her cheeks turning bright pink.

Eremon regretted putting his raw emotions on display when there was nothing either of them could do to change what had happened. His momentary guilt dulled the rumbling inside his body. "How am I supposed to keep up on foot?"

She shrugged. "Use your new magic. Sprout wings, I don't care, but you are *not* getting back on this horse."

Lira urged Edan into a trot, leaving Eremon standing alone

in the willow grove. He swore as he stalked forward, the rumbling in his body returning at full force and spreading up to his throat.

"Lira!" he shouted after her.

As he pushed his way out of the copse of trees, his shoulder struck a willow trunk. Though he felt no pain, he cursed the tree anyway. The rumble he'd been feeling pulsed outward unexpectedly, and every tree around him exploded in a shower of splinters and leaves.

Lira looked over her shoulder at the destruction, her face paling and her eyes widening with terror. Eremon shook his head frantically—a wordless, fruitless plea for her to *please* come back. But she did not. Instead, she turned her back on him and braced herself in the saddle as Edan sped to a gallop. Her long curls whipped behind her as the stallion picked up speed.

Panic and anger warred within Eremon, and he wasn't sure where to focus first: on Lira's retreating form, or the destruction he'd wrought. Turning his palms over, he studied them. A sheen of cobalt power had flared and was now fading back into his skin.

He hadn't meant to destroy the willow grove, but his anger had been powerful enough to communicate intent to his magic. This couldn't happen again. Losing control of his magic wasn't an option. There was no way to predict what or who he might destroy.

What if Lira had received the brunt of that power?

Eremon closed his eyes, willing himself to breathe evenly, feeling for the tendrils of magic that lived within him now. The cobalt power that had emerged was shot through with a current of the dark magic he'd tried so hard to suppress in his first lifetime. But now, it didn't feel as though it was trying to escape from his body. It felt malleable. Controllable.

Curious, to have this duality of power existing so quietly within him.

He held both of his palms out before him and tried summoning each. In his right palm, cobalt flame flared. Black lightning crackled and popped in his left. When it winked out, his skin was unmarred—no blood or blisters to be found.

Back at the crypt, his magic had acted on pure instinct. He had taken Lira's pain, directed Faolan's spirit into his vault, and reduced his mother's body to ash on little more than a whim. Though he did not regret killing Macha, he was surprised by his own detached resolve in retrospect.

He should have felt *something*, but he had not.

Eremon clenched his fists, straining toward the horizon. If this power acted on a whim, what were its limits? Did it have limits at all? Would he be able to control it?

He reined in his spiraling thoughts, focusing his intent on catching up with Lira.

Use your new magic. Sprout wings, I don't care.

The wind picked up, whipping around his body. In the distance, he heard the call of a falcon. An idea sparked, and he chuckled at the absurdity of it. Still, he closed his eyes, fixing his mind on the animal's form and what it might be like to soar eastward, as swiftly as Edan could run.

An intense, tingling surge of magic overtook him, starting on his scalp and quickly spreading over his body. His vision winked out, replaced by that bright cobalt power. For a moment, his awareness flickered, too—only to be replaced with keener senses than before.

The world shifted into an array of colors Eremon had never seen, sharper and more defined than his own eyes had ever beheld. His sight was beyond perfect, and he craned his neck to survey his form. He was covered in iridescent, silver feathers, and he stood on raptorial feet with gleaming silver talons.

Eremon's thoughts had eddied from words and emotions to

snatches of images. Flashes of pure instinct. So he focused on the image of a young woman racing across the meadowlands, setting his intent to catch up with her. To fly until she was once again within reach.

And then he spread his wings.

CHAPTER 6
CAITIR

The Rí's Garden

Late afternoon light poured into the Rí's spacious garden, glinting off the little stream that tripped and gurgled through its heart and spilling over the trees and flowers that bloomed there. Caitir sat on a stone bench beneath a floral archway, which was teeming with dark blue and teal ne'ala roses. Macha had commissioned the arch in Eremon's memory, and Caitir had avoided the reminder until today.

Now, the roses provided a much-needed focal point. If she was going to rethink her strategy, she must do it with Eremon and Lira in mind. For Caitir, the roses represented heartbreak. Grief. Hopelessness. They fueled her desire to rise above Eremon's dismissal and Lira's betrayal.

Just a few paces away, more of the Itelorian roses bloomed on a flourishing bush. Her late father, Emyr Tarlach, had been Eremon's ambassador to Iteloria, and he had brought the roses to the Dome as a diplomatic gift from the neighboring continent. The Rí had pampered those flowers the way Aidryn had always coddled the little white and yellow birds he'd kept as pets when they were children.

Caitir shivered at the thought of Eremon's eerie silver eyes. She could still feel his contemptuous gaze searing into hers. He had terrified her, yes. But something about the way he'd looked at her—truly focused on her for the first time—had sent a heady thrill coursing through her body.

With a sharp breath, she brought her thoughts back to the present. Caitir's aim was to inspire loyalty. She had solidified that plan months ago, before she'd sent Fiadh into Fortress Halgeir as a spy. But at the time, she'd believed that she would have Gerallt and Aila to contend with. Now that she was alone, Eremon was her greatest obstacle.

She wasn't concerned about Lira. Her former friend had already proven she had no desire to claim the inheritance Eremon had handed her. Lira posed more of an existential threat than a physical one, and Caitir was beginning to believe she could easily overcome that.

Lira had not returned to save Iathium. She had scarcely shown her face since Eremon's death and had not appeared to rally the clan army's morale. Soon, the people would see that their beloved figurehead was nothing more than an apparition.

Footsteps sounded along the wooden bridge that spanned the stream. Caitir looked up to see Deghan approaching. He gave her a little bow when he arrived by the bench.

"My lady, your new chamber is ready," he said. His ruddy cheeks were redder than usual. Caitir hoped it had to do with the blaze she'd asked him to set.

"Good." She raised her chin. "Now, I have additional tasks for you."

Before she could continue, Aeron Énna pounded over the little bridge behind Deghan, halting before Caitir. His normally buoyant demeanor was unusually subdued, his eyes red-rimmed. She assumed his cousin Fiadh must have told him of Faolan's death.

"A letter, my lady," Aeron said, extending a little scroll. "It's addressed to Gerallt. I think it's from the Itelorian king."

The last thing Caitir needed was to be under King La'hiran's scrutiny. She stood to accept the letter, wincing as she moved. A low, sharp pain gripped her belly, just above her hip, and she hissed, pressing her palm over the hurt.

"Are you all right?" Deghan asked.

Caitir straightened as the pain eased. "I'm fine."

The discomfort was a sign her baby was growing, Fiadh had said. They'd calculated that the child had been conceived three months ago, around the end of summer.

Caitir turned the scroll over to study its wax seal. Sure enough, King La'hiran's coat of arms was stamped neatly into it. She drew a breath and broke the seal, unrolling the small piece of parchment to skim its contents.

The letter was written in Athi, but the handwriting carried the thin, sweeping style she had seen often in the Itelorian documents Aila had collected in her study.

Gerallt the Usurper:

We understand you seek to claim Iathium's throne, but the circumstances of your conquest are complex.

Riku's storied bloodline only ends when Eremon's magic returns to Iteloria. His mere existence violated our centuries-old treaty with Rí Ulan. If you are not familiar with its terms, now is the time to enlighten yourself.

We cannot—indeed, we will not—acknowledge your sovereignty until the treaty is fulfilled. Until then, we are holding your wife in our capital city of Sov'is. Seek diligently to meet our terms within six weeks' time, and no harm will come to her.

We hope to pursue a diplomatic accord in future.

"It's too late," Caitir murmured to herself, a hand drifting to her mouth.

There was no way to fulfill La'hiran's terms now. That meant Aila wouldn't be leaving Iteloria unharmed. The realization sent a giddy jolt through her body.

"Too late for what?"

Caitir started, tossing an irritated glance over her shoulder at Deghan. He was squinting down at the scroll, but no matter; he, along with the majority of Iathium's citizens, couldn't read. Aeron moved nearer, giving Caitir a wary look.

She rolled the scroll tightly and slipped it into her pocket, then clasped her hands before her. Willing herself back into focus, she said, "As I was saying before—additional tasks. Deghan, I want you to call the troops home."

"They'd have to retreat," Aeron protested. "Thorne Beran would declare victory."

"Then have them retreat. I need them back in Iathium," Caitir said, her voice firm. When Gerallt had stormed the city, many of Eremon's former troops had fled. "Keep the questionable sentries outside the Dome's gates, and bring the loyalists in. Close the city to all outsiders."

"Won't the clan army use the opportunity for a siege?" asked Deghan. "With trade halted, the city won't survive long. Resources are running out already."

She shook her head. "They wouldn't be that stupid; the clans need Iathium."

"Not now." Deghan crossed his arms, scowling. "With magic flowing freely, the clans can make their own way. If they can't create what they want, they'll take it by force."

A chill skittered along Caitir's skin, but she forced her demeanor into calmness. Deghan gave the inexperienced magic-wielders too much credit. Most of them would likely only succeed at destroying themselves or those around them before they accomplished anything productive. Still, the few experienced magic-wielders would have already begun teaching those who had inherited power after Eremon's death. They would be a force to be reckoned with soon enough.

"We won't invite a siege," she finally answered. "We'll send the clans home to their territories with a promise of peace and diplomacy. Rodhlan is small; no one here wants a drawn-out war."

"How do we get Clan Beran off our backs?" Deghan scratched the back of his neck.

Caitir chewed on her bottom lip, letting her thoughts flit from one to the next. "Give them their overlord, that's how. The clans disband, and Artur Beran goes free."

Lira's stepfather, Artur, had been foolish enough to attempt forming an alliance with Macha before Aila and Gerallt took Iathium. He had paid dearly, and Caitir had played a part in his suffering. They'd held him until the army marched out, then sent him out with sentries who had gone into the meadow-lands' war camp as bait.

"We should let them think they rescued him," Aeron said conspiratorially. "Give them a small victory."

"How about this." Caitir drew her words out, looking from Aeron to Deghan. She held the red-haired sentry's gaze, because he would understand exactly what she meant. "Ger-allt's beloved council—do you remember them?"

"Aye," Deghan answered. "Jón and Timms."

The vile men had been her late husband's closest compan-ions and co-conspirators. Gerallt had drunkenly threatened to give Caitir to them if she proved herself *uncooperative*. Neither had wasted the threat, leering at her as a reminder every time they were near.

Caitir paced to the rose-covered archway and cupped one of the soft blooms in her palm. "Offer them up as a sacrifice of sorts in this little victory you're planning to simulate."

"Cold-hearted," Aeron remarked. There was an amused lilt to his voice that made her want to pummel him.

"Practical," she shot back, "unless you'd rather volunteer."

Aeron held a hand over his heart and bowed his head in mock solemnity. "Of course not, Your Merciful Eminence."

Caitir rolled her eyes and refocused on Deghan, whose jaw was set in thought. His green eyes were hard as he watched her.

"How long do you think you can manage this?" he asked.

If she hadn't understood his concern, she might have grown angry. Between the threat of Iteloria raining terror on Iathium and Eremon returning to bring terror of his own, Caitir didn't know how long she really had.

"I won't announce Gerallt's death until I'm forced to." Giving Deghan and Aeron a timeline would make them ask more questions about the letter she'd received. "Until then, I will act in his stead. He dictated all his missives; I'll write under his name."

Deghan nodded. "Understood. I'll take a mount and make for the meadowlands."

"Full armor," Caitir said as he made his way toward the garden's exit. "Take Aeron and two others."

"Me?" Aeron blanched, hesitating behind Deghan.

"It'll keep you busy," Caitir said, waving him on. "Take your mind off your cousin."

Aeron pressed his lips together, staring at her for a long moment before he finally followed Deghan out of the garden.

With a ragged exhale, Caitir took out La'hiran's letter and read it again. She had thought herself incredibly lucky to be rid of Gerallt and temporarily separated from Aila. If she played her cards well, perhaps she could shed Aila for good. The thought was ambitious, to be sure; but was it any more ambitious than declaring to Eremon himself that she was going to take his throne for her own child?

She huffed a disbelieving laugh. Immortal Eremon had stood before her and simply allowed her to tell him exactly what she planned to do. He'd had the audacity to look aghast when she'd suggested that mortal subjects might not want an immortal ruler. Clearly, the notion had never occurred to him.

What do you think Iathium will have to say about an infinitely powerful immortal seizing its throne?

The look of shock on his face... the almost imperceptible widening of his now-silver eyes, the slight parting of his lips...

Her words had rung true. And Lira had not disputed them.

How impossible was it, truly, to think that Caitir had a chance at not only taking the city's throne, but also at gaining the people's love before Eremon gathered his wits enough to strike?

Caitir had known it was possible to take his power, but the idea of a mortal god ascending to immortality was long-dismissed ancient myth. It was certainly not an outcome Aila had predicted, nor had La'hiran, if his letter was any evidence.

What would the Itelorian king do when he learned what had really happened? Would Eremon possess enough power to protect Rodhlan from Iteloria, or were they all doomed before they began?

Footsteps sounded over the little bridge, and Caitir looked up to see a red-cheeked Árchú storming toward her, his large hands balled into fists. He was dressed in a midnight blue tunic, black trousers, and a black leather bandolier fully armed with an array of swords and knives. His dark hair was slicked back, sapphire eyes like their father's trained on her every movement.

When they locked gazes, Caitir's heart leapt into her throat, her palms breaking into a sweat.

Her eldest brother's eyes flicked to the letter in her hand. He pointed one large finger at it and said, "Give me that."

Caitir tilted her head up innocently and held the scroll where he could see it. "This?" She summoned a little spark of dark magic into her fingertips, and the parchment burned before Árchú's eyes.

Furiously, Árchú lunged for Caitir and grabbed her roughly by arm. He pinched the tender flesh beneath her upper arm, and Caitir tensed, trying not to let him see her wince. She had long since learned not to cry out.

"Get up," he snapped, hauling her to her feet. Another sharp pain lanced through her lower belly at the sudden movement, and this time, she hissed. This near, she could smell the stench of drink on his breath.

"Bit early," Caitir said through gritted teeth, trying to pull from his grasp, "to be half-drowned in mead already."

"Shut up," Árchú growled. "What did you do with the mistress's horses?"

The pain in her arm had begun to wane. "How am I to both answer and shut up?" she shot back.

A shock came without warning as he pierced her skin with dark magic. A barely noticeable spark of black lightning burned through the fabric of her black gown and into the underside of her arm. She tried to suppress a cry of pain but failed.

"You were seen riding." Árchú gave her a rough shake. "Tell me what you did with them."

"They were stolen," Caitir blurted before she could think. How was she supposed to explain Eremon's return to this oaf?

She wrenched her arm hard, failing to free herself from his tightening grip. Her eyes filled with tears.

"Who did you sell the horses to, Caitir?" he demanded. "Where's the coin?"

"We didn't—" Caitir gasped, struggling harder. "We didn't sell them!"

With her free hand, she released a burst of dark magic into Árchú's chest. With a roar, he let go of her, his fingers grappling at the fabric over his heart as the smell of scorched flesh reached her nostrils. His face turned ashen, and he pointed at the rose archway.

"One of the roses," he rasped, "*please.*"

Ne'ala roses could be used as a remedy for injuries inflicted by dark magic. Caitir stepped closer to the roses, letting her fingertips play over one of the velvety blooms. She met her brother's pained gaze for a lingering second before releasing a burst of dark magic into the nearest bloom. It spread over the archway in a blink, the roses sparking and burning beneath her power. The blue and teal blooms melted and withered in the heat.

Caitir ignored the painful tug of her heart at the sight. This was her chance to rid herself of all her keepers; not just Gerallt and her mother, but the brute of a half-brother who had answered Aila's every whim for Caitir's entire life. The one who had resented Caitir for holding their father's heart and gaining her mother's favor, however twisted it may have been.

She turned her attention to the rosebush Eremon had pampered for so many years and sent more magic flowing into it. In moments, the lovely blooms were reduced to ash.

"What roses?" she simpered.

Árchú swore, rising to his full height as though uninjured. He loomed over Caitir, closing in as she scrambled to escape his reach. But the former sentry was much swifter; he grabbed her by the throat and lifted her off the ground.

"Gerallt is dead," he said through gritted teeth. "Your mother is gone. That black-haired wraith of a girl can't get between us. Let's see you save yourself now."

Terror seized her, and she clawed at his hand, trying to gasp. "Please..."

His fingers tightened. They were as hard and cold as iron, and she could feel the tingle of dark magic rushing down his arm toward her throat.

"No," she ground out, pressure building in her face, shadows dancing in her vision.

With all the strength she could muster, she stopped fighting his grip, summoning her own dark power into her palms. She fought to stay conscious as he crooked his arm, bringing her inches from his face.

"A curse on your death." He spat in her face.

Caitir blinked at him, her sight hazing. In one swift movement, she lifted her hands to his face and forced a surge of scalding power into him. He cried out and released her abruptly. She fell hard, crumpling to the cobblestone pathway as she fought to draw breath.

Árchú's body hit the path across from her with a sickening thud. Caitir's head swam, and pain still reverberated through her bones. She thought she heard Fiadh screaming for Aeron, her voice distant and disembodied, before she blacked out.

CHAPTER 7

LIRA

Meadowlands

Fatigue weighed Lira's body down as Edan raced across the open meadow. Her chest felt heavy, and her eyelids drooped. Only the relentless pounding of the stallion's hooves kept her awake enough to grip the reins, one hand on his saddle to steady herself.

She had been finding it increasingly difficult to stay awake, much less maintain her sense of place. After Eremon had awakened her, she had thought herself on the eastern side of the Moravon. But now she and Edan were so far south that she was unsure what side of the river they were on. More than once, she'd nodded off in the saddle. Each time she shook herself to alertness, they were heading toward Acton's Cove again.

As though matching Lira's sluggish demeanor, Edan's gallop slowed to a canter, and then a trot.

"No, Edan," she said, groggily steering the stallion eastward. "We have to get to Aidryn."

The terrain around her blurred, and she reached up to slap her cheeks. Rather than making her more alert, the action only made her eyes water. She squeezed them shut, letting exhausted tears slide down her face. But closing her eyes was a mistake, because heavy sleep rushed in before she could stop it.

Lira felt her body slide off the horse. Felt herself hit the lush grass with a thud. Her breath left in a whoosh, and she curled onto her side, coughing until she could breathe evenly again.

She could hear running water nearby, and the cool air smelled of teeming foliage and clear mountain streams. Edan, the daft beast, must have defied her and turned back toward Acton's Cove again. When she could think clearly, she'd have words with the stubborn horse.

Lira's back ached, and after her fall, it hurt to draw a full breath. Her skin tingled, alert to the ancestral magic that saturated this land. Rather than sitting up, she rolled onto her back to survey her surroundings.

The moon was high now, and stars twinkled in a cloudless sky. Her view was partially obscured by the towering mountain range that rose to her right. Suddenly, the world felt too vast, and Lira felt vulnerable lying out here all alone. Had she not already learned her lesson about fleeing like this—many times over?

She shouldn't have left Eremon. No matter how much he'd upset her, no matter how frightened she had been of his power, she had risked everything to bring him back.

Stupid, stupid.

"Mortal gods, Lira," she murmured to herself, "you do have a knack for abandoning your companions and running headlong into trouble."

There was a rustle overhead, and Lira scanned the trees above. A silver falcon had alighted on a branch, eyes gleaming as it stared at her. Beneath its scrutiny, she felt exposed. Cold. She shivered.

Rolling onto her side, she pushed herself up into a sitting position, then forced herself to stand on shaking legs. Moving to Edan's side, she unbuckled the straps on his saddle that held her bedroll in place.

Lira felt the falcon's watchful gaze on her as she tethered Edan to one of the larger trees and chose a place to unfurl the bedroll. She slipped beneath the thin blanket, not bothering to remove her boots. Still, the raptor watched.

She stared back at it as it tilted its head curiously. There was something familiar in the intensity of its eyes. Strange, but she didn't feel afraid to lie down here. Being alone in the cove should have alarmed her, but somehow, it did not.

Sprout wings.

Lira laughed softly to herself as her lashes fluttered shut.

CHAPTER 8
CAITIR

Dome

Caitir curled her body into a large chair that sat in her new chamber. The sun had long since set, but she hadn't bothered to light the lanterns that hung on the walls. It was eerily quiet. Though the silence was unnerving, she was glad Fiadh and the sentries had left well enough alone.

Aeron and Fiadh had removed Árchú's body from the gardens before rousing Caitir. She had first demanded to know why Aeron had not followed Deghan to surrender the troops. Then Caitir had asked to see her brother, but they'd only managed to look ashen.

She'd thought killing Árchú might have helped her feel assuaged, at the very least, but she was disappointed to find that she felt nothing at all.

The chamber door clicked open, and Fiadh stepped inside, her face illuminated by the single candle she carried. For a moment, she hesitated by the door. Caitir heard her sigh just before her footsteps padded across the room.

"Why is it so dark?"

Caitir shrugged, as though Fiadh could see the gesture. She had killed her own brother without a second thought. Perhaps there was something empowering about the strength the act had required.

But what if it had been Aidryn in the garden? Would she have been able to do it then?

"Aidryn wouldn't have allowed what happened with Gerallt, and he would not have attacked you," Fiadh said darkly, resting her hand on the back of the chair. Her voice was tinged with bitterness.

Caitir started; she hadn't realized she was speaking her thoughts. "Funny you think that when he did nothing to help me before."

Aidryn's transgressions had always been passive. He had allowed Aila to control Caitir, hiding himself away in Iathium's archive with Lira instead. When he wasn't pining after Lira or sneaking off to meet with Eremon, he was out in the fields with his blasted horses, escaping everything Caitir had been chained to her entire life.

She wished she could say that she'd dreamt of Aidryn taking her away from the city on the back of his fastest stallion. But the truth was that Caitir had wanted the things her mother did. She'd cooperated with Aila's schemes, even long after realizing she was only a pawn.

"That's not entirely fair," Fiadh muttered.

"Oh, you're defending Aidryn now?" Caitir sniffed, shaking away the intrusive thoughts. Fiadh and Aidryn had once been intimately entangled to some extent, though Caitir found it difficult to believe Fiadh's claim that they'd been lovers. Aidryn had always been far too preoccupied with Lira to pursue anyone else with serious intent. "That's an interesting plot twist. And here I thought you were ready to skewer him."

"For my own sake." Fiadh was silent for a long moment

before adding, "The mistress does have dark magic, and she gave that magic to you. Aidryn would have been outmatched."

Caitir nodded but didn't reply. It was true; Aidryn had been forced to rely on his wit, his connections, and his impeccable secrecy in his attempts to protect himself and Lira. The situation had been well out of his hands for years.

Fiadh leaned nearer. "What was in the letter this afternoon?"

Willing her features into neutrality, Caitir said, "Nothing that concerns you."

It occurred to Caitir that Fiadh might have intercepted the letter before Aeron delivered it, but she reminded herself that neither of them would have been able to read it. Writing and reading had been widely banned in Rodhlan for many years, but Aila had skirted the law to ensure her daughter could do both. It was one of the few things Caitir felt grateful for, where her mother was concerned.

Those who were capable of reading or writing had hidden the skill for centuries, except for historians like Aidryn and Lira, who prided themselves on being allowed to gather and preserve knowledge. It was something of a popular trend to be willfully ignorant to the city's true past, and to scholarly learning in all its forms. Storytelling, theatre, the arts—those were the people's preferred methods of learning, and they had been heavily shaped and sanctioned by the ruling classes to fit the desired narrative.

"Are you going to tell your mother about Gerallt?" Fiadh asked.

Caitir shook her head. "She'll find out soon enough. Besides, I don't want to alert King La'hiran to that fact. It would be far too convenient for his ends."

Fiadh tilted her head curiously. "What ends?"

Idiot. Caitir had said too much.

"I just..." she trailed off, searching for words that sounded definitive, "believe it could put Mother in danger to broadcast that information."

"They'd certainly kill her if they thought themselves free to," Fiadh replied.

Caitir snorted. "One can only hope." She could hear Fiadh's soft gasp as the words left her lips, but she didn't care.

"I can't believe you would say that about your own mother," Fiadh said.

"So, you do have a conscience." Caitir's scowl deepened. "Not everyone had a perfect upbringing like you."

"If you think losing your mother at fourteen is perfect—" Fiadh's voice rose with each word.

"I don't," Caitir cut in forcefully. Then, she softened her tone, keenly aware that she'd struck a nerve. "I only wish I might have traded places with you."

Fiadh and Faolan had been born and raised in Iathium. Their father was a blacksmith, their mother a midwife. Though Fiadh's mother had died during the birth of a younger sibling, at least she'd had a good mother for a time. Caitir couldn't speak to the brother situation, though. Aidryn and Faolan had been the best of friends and had shared interests, which had been detrimental to both Fiadh and Caitir in the end.

All in all, the years Fiadh had spent with her family intact had been idyllic. In light of the happy memories Fiadh had shared, Caitir was finding it difficult to sympathize and effortless to envy.

Fiadh straightened abruptly, taking the candle with her and moving toward the door. "You should be making your move to take the throne instead of trying to wound me. You're wasting time."

Caitir's shoulders tensed. "If anyone has been wounded here, it's *me*."

It was crucial to keep steering Fiadh away from the conversation about Aila and King La'hiran's letter.

Fiadh glared. "What did I do to you?"

Now alert, Caitir sat up and fixed a hard stare on Fiadh. "I've been at a loss since you had Va'hesk burned."

"What does Va'hesk have to do with anything?" Fiadh demanded, stepping around in front of the chair. "I prevented Clan Tarlach from joining the clan army; you should be thanking me."

"I still need them to ally with me," Caitir answered, pressing a palm to her forehead. "You should have *known* that. The fact that they didn't fight alongside Thorne Beran should have meant that I had a clear opportunity to forge a connection. Now, I can't."

With a nonchalant shrug, Fiadh said, "There is always an opportunity for an alliance, if you know what to offer them. Perhaps they'd like new tents and provisions, or unspoiled pastureland."

There was a satisfied lilt to her voice that made Caitir's stomach do a sickening flip.

"Create both the problem and the solution?" Caitir scoffed. "I do *not* want to get allies that way."

"But it's effective, is it not?"

Caitir's jaw tightened, sending a spark of pain up to her temple. "It's devious. I want to inspire real loyalty."

Fiadh snorted. "As though you aren't the most devious person here."

"What *you* think I am is irrelevant." Now, Caitir stood and advanced toward her. "I have an opportunity to lead the clans out of Gerallt's chaos—"

"When you were a part of it: the problem and the solution." Fiadh stepped closer, the candle's flame glinting in her hard stare. "*You* occupied the city with Gerallt and Aila, and now you think you can end the tyranny? It's laughable."

Caitir was nearly nose to nose with Fiadh now. "*Occupied,*

Fiadh. Notice that we didn't burn our way in. We didn't leave a scratch on the Dome, and few died."

It had been easier to take the city than Caitir had expected. With the people weakened by unfamiliar magic and fearful in the wake of Eremon's sudden death, there had been little resistance. Although Eremon's mother, Raní Macha, had been fearsome and powerful in her own right, she, too, had been easily defeated. The last time Caitir had seen Macha, the deposed Raní been imprisoned in the crypt. It was unlikely she had survived long enough to see Eremon resurrected.

Fiadh nodded slowly. "So destruction is only justified when a throne is the end goal." Her words sliced through Caitir's thoughts, bringing her full awareness back into the moment. "I wish I was that talented at twisting my motives into some sort of—"

Dark magic buzzed through Caitir's body, and she felt the overwhelming urge to strike the other woman. "Stop it, Fiadh."

"—grand logic!"

Now, Caitir did stand and raise a hand. "Stop, or—"

"Or what?" Fiadh sneered. "You'll kill me like your brother?"

The words jolted Caitir, and she dropped her hand, clenching her fist instead. "I'll have you dragged from the grounds."

"By whom? My cousin?" Fiadh laughed, the sound hollow and emotionless. "You're not my superior. If you value your allies, you'll take care how you speak to me."

Caitir scoffed. "As though you have allies of your own, beyond me and Aeron. A veritable army."

Aeron had betrayed the clan army and followed Fiadh to Iathium, where he'd reclaimed his old post as a sentry. They left Faolan behind with the clan army.

A shadow crossed Fiadh's expression. "You know nothing of my allies."

Caitir folded her arms. "Who, the Beran warriors you paid to burn the Tarlach settlement?" She knew quite well that Fiadh had had little time to acquire real allies. "You were both so quick to turn on our brothers and what few friends you had before. You'll turn on me next, the moment I'm no longer useful."

Fiadh's dark eyes showed a hint of regret, but when she blinked, it was gone. "There's more to gain by working together."

Caitir set her jaw. "We can't work together if you're provoking the clans as revenge for my brother's stupidity."

She willed her body into a calm state, keenly aware of the thick tension that had filled the space between them. One breath. Two. Three.

Fiadh held Caitir's gaze, her posture relaxing a bit. Finally, she exhaled and gave a small nod. "You're right."

"I know." Caitir sat once more, carefully considering her next words. "You once told me that you wanted to make something great of yourself. What does that mean to you?"

The candle's wick drooped, its flame sinking into the steadily melting wax. What little light it had provided dimmed to almost nothing.

Fiadh took a few reluctant steps forward, as though unsure whether she wanted to answer. Finally, she sat too, angling her body so she faced Caitir. "Great used to mean magical," she mused. "I would have given anything to wield Clan Énna's water magic."

More than once, Caitir had tried giving that power to Fiadh —but their attempts had culminated in the death of its original bearer, and in Fiadh's own altered state of existence. Fiadh's heart had stopped beating the last time Caitir had transferred power to her. Though Fiadh's body now hummed with latent magic, she couldn't access it. Magic sustained her, but it seemed she might never wield it.

"Now..." Fiadh's voice cut through Caitir's thoughts, and the memories of the Énna girl who had died that day. "I think great means proving I'm worthy of something more than assisting at my father's smithy or delivering swords to ungrateful warriors."

Caitir straightened, assessing her. Fiadh had confided that Thorne and the rest of Clan Beran's warriors had refused to acknowledge her true skills as a blacksmith. Instead of helping to forge weapons for the clan army like she'd hoped to do, she had been made a runner. Expendable. When she'd foolishly attempted to win back Aidryn's affection—after he'd been bound to Lira, no less—she had truly understood how insignificant she was to the people she'd hoped to belong with.

But here in Iathium, Fiadh could remake her own legacy. And if Caitir could offer her ways to do that, she could solidify Fiadh's loyalty. Her thoughts ticked through the possibilities, swiftly landing on one effective notion.

"Do you want to be my armorer when I take the throne?" Caitir asked.

Fiadh's eyes lit. She clearly understood the significance of the offer. Years ago, Lira's father, Arlen, had served as armorer. Not only would the position carry prestige, but it would also deeply insult Lira for Fiadh to step into the role. The thought gave Caitir an inordinate amount of joy.

"That and more," Fiadh answered.

Caitir leaned nearer. "Then what about this: Be my armorer and my right-hand."

Fiadh's expression softened. The subtle rise of her brows told Caitir everything she needed to know. "You could be whatever you want, if we're remaking this place," Caitir added.

"Then there's much to think about," Fiadh mused, removing the waning candle from its stand and rising again.

Fiadh crossed the room and opened the glass facing of a lantern that sat on the sideboard, tipping the candle to light its wick. Then, she moved from one lantern to another, lighting each one as she went. The room was still dim, but the flickering light chased away the pitch-darkness that had engulfed the chamber's corners before.

Caitir fought against the way her insides warmed at the gesture. She hadn't intended on lighting her room tonight. The darkness suited her mood, and she had planned to sink into it.

"I wanted to keep it dark," she sulked.

Fiadh paused by the door, blowing out the candle she held. "Yes. But you're also with child. How will you feel if you stumble and fall because you can't see?"

She opened the door, and the chamber filled with the torchlight from the corridor outside. Fiadh stepped out but turned to Caitir again and said, "You're welcome," before pulling the door shut behind her.

Caitir heaved a sigh, crossing the room to lock the door behind Fiadh. Almost as an afterthought, she remembered Lira's lost pendant. She pulled the door open to call after Fiadh, but a gray-green haze passed over her field of vision. With a few blinks, it was gone—presumably one of the many bothersome effects of pregnancy.

She shook her head in a vain attempt to remember what she'd been doing just now but failed. Nervous laughter bubbled from her as she shut the door, smoothing her robe and returning to her preferred chair—not a comfortable one, by any means, but the best Deghan had managed to do.

Caitir pulled her thoughts back to the present, considering what should happen next. She would need to cull the sentries once they arrived home—find out who would stand with her against the rest of the city. Her thoughts swirled as she fought to wrap them around what, exactly, she could do to endear herself to them. The odds weren't good. She was sure word of Gerallt's death had already spread among them, so she would have to act quickly to gain their favor.

Until then, many of Gerallt's fighters were stationed around the Dome's exterior, the courtyard walls, and the outer walls of the city. They were men and women Aila had filled with dark magic, and the people of Iathium were too fearful to cross them. With the chaos Eremon's death and Macha's overthrow had unleashed across the city, its citizens weren't yet unified enough to be a threat.

But that time was coming, and quickly.

CHAPTER 9
LIRA

Acton's Cove

It wasn't clear how many hours had passed when someone shook Lira awake. The first thing she registered was a hand on her shoulder, then garbled words.

"Silira Mór."

She stirred, blinking the sleep from her eyes. Nevala Tarlach hovered over her bedroll, her cool palm on Lira's cheek. Her silver hair, slightly disheveled, fell in a long plait over her shoulder. "Let me look at you."

With much effort, Lira forced herself to sit up, rubbing her eyes. Her head ached from the wound she'd sustained in the crypt. Sunlight streamed through the canopy of trees overhead, and the soft sounds of trickling water and birds singing made her perk up.

Mytr, Nevala's husband, hung back on the edge of the tree line, holding onto their pony's reins, along with a large basket of herbs. He gave Lira a terse nod, his expression wary. The pony, Tudur, bobbed his head, almost as if he recognized her.

Nevala took in the dried blood, the bruises, and the gash on Lira's head. "What are you doing out here alone?"

Her first instinct was to blurt out the story of Eremon's return, but that would mean explaining their quarrel—and the fact that she had left him alone, just like she'd left Skelly the first time Nevala found her. Lira's encounters with the healer, apparently, had a theme. "It's a long story."

Nevala pursed her lips, inspecting the head wound more closely. "Your husband will be glad to see you."

Lira grasped Nevala's forearms, heart racing. "You've seen Aidryn?" Her voice cracked painfully.

"He's up in the valley with Clan Tarlach," she answered in a soothing tone. "He led them into the mountains after the burning."

"How bad was it?" Lira said, anticipation welling within her.

"They lost everything," Nevala answered, removing her satchel and rifling through it. "I told Aidryn we'd come to find you. Clan Mór doesn't trust the refugees, but they trust him."

"Did you lose everything, too? What about your remedies?"

"No." Nevala took several vials and a canister of ointment from her bag. "Mytr and I have been living in the valley with your kin for several months now."

"Why?" Lira tilted her head, curious.

"We were banished." Nevala smiled sadly. "Harboring fugitives is forbidden at Va'hesk."

Lira's cheeks burned. "Oh." The couple had taken her in before she'd traveled to Clan Beran's territory last spring. "I'm sorry."

Nevala brushed a finger under Lira's chin and coaxed her to look up again. "Do not apologize; it was our choice, and that isn't your fault. Besides, we might not have salvaged our possessions otherwise."

The healer applied ointment to Lira's wound before she mixed up a tincture for pain. Lira gulped down the bitter medicine. Then, Nevala coaxed Lira to lie back down as she produced a needle and thread from the satchel.

Nausea washed over Lira as she put the pieces together. She sat back up abruptly. "Wait, what's that for?"

Nevala's smile was pinched. "To stitch you up. Lie down; let the medicine work and it will be easier to bear."

Lira obeyed, though she began to shiver. With a glance up into the trees, she noted curiously that the falcon was still near. It leaned forward, as though to survey the healer's work.

After a few moments, she felt herself relax as the tincture took hold. Trying desperately not to think about the silver needle Nevala held between her fingers, she told herself she would be fine. She swallowed the bile that rose in her throat as the woman carefully threaded the needle, then looked back down at her.

"This will only hurt for a moment," Nevala said, reaching for her with gentle hands.

When the needle pricked her scalp, Lira fainted.

SHE PASSED in and out of consciousness after that, vaguely aware of the throbbing in her head, of strong arms draping her body over a horse's bare back, of a warm and steadying hand resting on her. Nevala's and Mytr's soft voices drifted in and out of focus, but Lira couldn't piece together what they were saying.

When she woke again, they were outside Skelly's cottage in the valley. Mytr helped Lira off Tudur's back and led her inside, where he stoked the hearth. He then went to work drawing a bath for Lira, hauling in water from a nearby spring to fill the tub.

"Where's Aidryn?" Lira said, looking around her grand-mother's small home. Nevala led her to sit before the fire. "You said he was here."

"He was going to help build shelters for the refugees," Mytr answered, setting his buckets aside. "I'll fetch him."

Lira remained before the fire as Nevala took her husband's place, heating a large kettle of water to warm the bath. Once Mytr was gone, she helped Lira undress, bracing her as she climbed into the tub. The warm water was a welcome comfort, and Lira sank into it with a soft sigh. She was too exhausted to fret over the older woman seeing her naked.

Using a rough sponge, Lira scrubbed the grime from her skin. Closing her eyes and tipping her head back against the side of the tub, she let Nevala pour water over her curls, rinsing out the dried blood. The healer worked gentle fingers through Lira's hair, carefully combing out the snarls.

"There was a falcon watching over you, back in the cove," Nevala said. "He followed us into the valley. Silver... Never seen anything like him."

Silver. Lira remembered the falcon's familiar gaze and sat up with a gasp, sloshing bathwater over the edge of the tub. "Is it even possible?"

Nevala rocked back, surprised. "Is what possible?"

"Can immortals change shape?"

The healer laughed and cocked her head. "So you *did* raise Eremon from the dead."

Lira sighed with relief. "I did." She'd meant to leave Eremon behind, but it seemed he had discovered a new talent. "Did you see where the falcon went?"

"I lost sight of it near the keep."

"Sneaky fiend," Lira muttered, reaching for Nevala's hand. "Help me out?"

Nevala obliged, wrapping a coarse robe around Lira once she'd stepped out of the bath. Suddenly, the door burst open, and Aidryn bounded inside, wild-eyed. He stopped in his tracks at the sight of Lira and Nevala by the fire, his eyes drifting over her form.

"Mortal gods, you're alive," he cried, closing the distance between them in a few long strides. He pulled Lira into his arms.

"Aidryn!" She warmed at his touch, keenly aware of her scant clothing and wet hair. "I've missed you terribly."

He cupped the back of her head and bent to kiss her with dizzying intensity. Lira clutched the front of his tunic, rising on her toes, returning his kiss. His lips were warm and soft, and she bit back a groan, keenly aware they weren't alone here.

Aidryn broke away, wrapping her in another tight embrace. "What happened?" he murmured into her hair, rubbing a warm palm over her back. "You were supposed to stay here!"

"Aila—she's in Iteloria," Lira answered.

Aidryn stilled, sucking in a breath and drawing back to look at her, a few loose strands of dark hair falling into his face. His cerulean eyes sparked with alarm. "What?"

"There is so much to tell; I hardly know where to begin." Lira's knees buckled, acute weakness suddenly washing over her. "Everything I did was absolutely necessary."

He nodded slowly. "I know." Concern washed over his face as he studied her more closely. "Your face and throat... how did you get these bruises?" His eyes drifted lower, widening a bit. "Where's your pendant?"

"Fiadh took it." The memory of Fiadh's magic burning through her was visceral, as though the power had etched itself into her insides. She squirmed uncomfortably at the thought. "She gave me the bruises. I—"

Black washed over Lira's vision, and she sagged. Aidryn gripped her elbows, then looped an arm around her waist, leading her into the small bedroom. Nevala, who had been sitting quietly beside the window, rose to follow them.

Aidryn helped her sit on the bed, then sat beside her. He wrapped the blanket around her shoulders before pulling her close. "Let's start from the beginning. I saw your last memories in this room, when you were ill. What happened after?"

Lira drew back. "You witnessed?"

His cheeks turned pink. "I broke the rules, but it was absolutely necessary." With a shrug, he added, "I didn't glean much, though."

Her vision darkened again. This time, roiling clouds filled the space behind her eyelids, crackling with lightning. *Black* lightning. She sucked in a breath and blinked the sight away, willing the bedchamber into view.

Aidryn turned to face her, gripping her shoulders, fear in his eyes. "What's wrong?"

Lira blinked several times, forcing her eyes to focus on his face. "I... I don't..."

"With all respect," Nevala said tentatively, leaning against the door frame, "she's incredibly weak. Perhaps we should let her rest for a little while before she shares the tale."

Aidryn looked down at Lira, frowning, then placed a kiss on her hair. "All right."

The healer brought another tincture to Lira. It was bitter going down, and she chased it with a sip of water from the spring. As drowsiness overtook her, Aidryn helped her lie down, covering her with Skelly's blanket. He and Nevala stepped out of the bedchamber, but she could still hear their voices.

"There's more to this than a head wound, isn't there?" Aidryn's voice was laced with trepidation.

"Dark magic, that's certain," Nevala answered. "She's been quiet since we found her. You need to find out exactly what happened."

"Gods..." he murmured. "Should I take her to Halgeir?"

"I wouldn't rush a journey," Nevala said. "Watch her for a little while."

There was a long beat of silence.

"She had a companion when we found her." The healer's voice seemed farther away now, and Lira strained to hear. "A silver falcon. He followed us up the mountain."

"Silver falcon?" Aidryn sounded incredulous now.

"Eremon," Nevala answered in a low voice.

Aidryn swore softly. "Will you stay with her? I'm going after him."

"Of course."

"Stay with me, Aidryn," Lira slurred as the medicine took hold.

When Aidryn didn't return, she opened her mouth to try again, but her pillow was far too comfortable and required her full attention.

CHAPTER 10

AIDRYN

Rodhlan Ridge

Aidryn left Lira sleeping in Skelly's cabin, near bursting with unanswered questions. Perhaps when he found Eremon, he could ask them.

The wind ruffled his hair as he stopped by the horses' pasture and scanned the tree line, searching for a flash of color or a bit of movement. He turned in a slow circle, his gaze sweeping the broad expanse of sky overhead.

Aidryn wondered how Lira had come to be alone, and why Eremon suddenly felt the need to pretend he was nowhere near the valley.

"Why are you hiding?" he said under his breath. "Don't be a damned coward."

Leaves rustled in the midday breeze. He could hear the nearby mountain stream trickling and tripping over the smooth stones that filled it. Birds sang in the trees. Horses grazed in the lush pasture, their tails swishing softly. Long moments passed, and still, there was no sign of the falcon.

Finally, Aidryn took a deep breath and shouted, "Eremon!"

His voice echoed through the valley, bouncing far into the mountain range. The call was met with silence, so he tried again, expanding his voice this time. Again, the name filled the sky, but no reply came.

Silence stretched on and on. Anger flooded him, and he clenched his fists. "I know you're out there."

The horses in the pasture watched Aidryn curiously. Fannin stepped to the fence line, and Aidryn reached for him. The stallion nudged his palm with its velvety nose.

There was a rush of wind, and suddenly, the falcon was perched on the fence post, staring at Aidryn. He watched the creature in wonder, waiting for it to make the first move. The raptor regarded him, tilting its head and blinking. Time seemed to still.

"Are you ready to save the world, my friend?" Aidryn heard himself ask. It was a question Eremon had once posed to him, on the cusp of all this chaos.

There was a bright flash of cobalt magic. Suddenly, Eremon stood before him: the same young man with silken black hair and angular eyes—silver now, instead of gray. Eremon regarded him without calculation, his expression unguarded.

Aidryn laughed in disbelief, his voice rasping. "It's a good thing your clothes came with you. Did you test that trick before the grand flourish?"

Eremon blinked, then looked down at the black tunic and trousers he wore, patting the fabric for good measure. "Come now, Tarlach," he said, one corner of his mouth tugging upward as he crossed his arms, "don't pretend you've never been the least bit curious about what's hiding under all this."

"A smug attitude the size of the Dome, I'm sure," Aidryn retorted with a wry grin. He surveyed Eremon, scarcely believing his eyes. "You don't look a day over nineteen."

"Apparently, I never will," Eremon replied, his silver eyes twinkling.

Aidryn stepped forward and pulled Eremon into a tight embrace. "By Nami, it's good to see you."

Eremon exhaled heavily. "And you."

Tears pricked Aidryn's eyes at the unexpected familiarity. Eremon clapped his friend on the shoulder and took a step back. "How is Silira?" he asked, concern impressed upon his features.

The pit of Aidryn's stomach bottomed out for a moment, but he shoved the anxiety away. "Nevala stitched her up and gave her a sleeping draught."

Eremon's gaze tipped downward for a moment—enough that cold dread crept back into Aidryn's belly. "Ah. That's a relief."

Aidryn crossed his arms. "What happened?"

Eremon shifted uncomfortably, suddenly more interested in a moss-covered stump than in holding eye contact. "We quarreled in the meadowlands."

"Mortal *gods*, Eremon!" Aidryn raked a hand through his hair, barely resisting the urge to shake him.

Eremon smirked, though pain flashed in his eyes. "At your service. Except immortal now, you know."

"This isn't the time to jest." Aidryn growled, frustrated. His jaw ached; he'd suddenly clenched it so hard. "She was hurt and alone, and she needed you! What sort of stupid thing did you say to her?"

Eremon's laugh was brittle. "You assume I'm the one who said something stupid?"

Aidryn couldn't help but enjoy the sudden surge of superiority. "If you felt the need to hide afterward."

"We both said stupid things," Eremon muttered, looking away again.

Taking a step closer, Aidryn said, "Lira risked everything for you. There are people in Rodhlan who didn't want you to return. If it hadn't been for her, you would not be standing here."

Eremon heaved a ragged sigh. "She made sure I knew about the perils she'd faced."

The wild, bitter edge in his tone gave Aidryn pause—but only a brief one. "Right, because of you."

Eremon's eyes flashed, and he straightened. "I was the one who *died*, Aidryn," he said through gritted teeth. "None of you can say the same. No matter what sacrifices any of you made to get me back, nothing compares to that."

"Oh?" Aidryn clenched his fists, anger rippling through him. "What about death with no hope of return? Some of us won't live to see the end of this war, and we won't have the chance to come back like you did."

Eremon's eyes widened, and he blanched, taking a step back. "I—forgive me. I spoke out of turn." Something akin to grief flashed across his expression.

"What happened?" Seeing him back down this way set off every warning in Aidryn's body. His thoughts raced as he considered what might have happened in the short time Eremon had been alive again. With a sinking feeling, Aidryn said, "Did someone die in the crypt?"

Slowly, Eremon nodded. Bile crept up Aidryn's throat.

The answer seemed so painfully obvious. It must have been the one person who had not returned with Lira. His throat tightened. "Talfryn?"

Eremon's expression shifted into infuriating neutrality. "No. Talfryn took Oda to Fortress Halgeir—she was wounded." His voice sounded vacant and hollow.

"Gods." He leveled his gaze at Eremon. "But who—"

"The sentry." Eremon flinched almost imperceptibly as the words left his lips. "Faolan Énna."

Even as the words landed, Aidryn tried to mask the utter horror that washed over him. Instead, he blurted, "You're wrong." But the moment the denial burst out, his body began to tremble. "That's not possible."

Eremon slipped into the familiar, regal tone he'd cultivated since childhood. "Why is it impossible?"

Aidryn resented the refined kindness in Eremon's voice. He tried to shake off the sudden chill that coursed through him. Instead, he doubled down, advancing on Eremon. "How do you know it was him? There are so many sentries. It could have been any of them."

Eremon looked wounded as the words found their mark. "You think I couldn't tell my own sentries apart?"

That was the problem; Aidryn knew he could. He halted, the world suddenly warping around him, and released a shaky breath.

Shoulders sagging, Eremon sighed resignedly. "If you don't believe me, let Lira's magic confirm it. I'm telling you the truth, and I'm sorry."

Aidryn didn't want to reach into that truth-telling power. He didn't want to know, because once Lira's power spoke, he wouldn't be able to deny it any longer. And he needed—he needed Faolan. His friend, his fellow warrior. His brother.

A terrible question filled his mind, roaring in his thoughts: *Is Faolan truly dead?*

The horrible truth curled itself around the Binding and tugged its confirmation.

CHAPTER II

EREMON

Rodhlan Ridge

Eremon felt raw and hollowed out by the time Nevala emerged from the cottage and called for Aidryn. The sun was setting, and the cool mountain air had dipped into something cold and vast. It caressed his skin without leaving the first trace of gooseflesh. He had always hated the cold before, but now he could observe it without discomfort.

He watched Aidryn jog toward Skelly's home, the weight of the past few hours settling onto his shoulders. Sharing his memories from the crypt had been a necessary pain. The visions had pulled Aidryn through the entire terrible sequence of events at lightning speed, leaving him reeling. He'd shown Aidryn memories of Lira drawing on Clan Tarlach's Anointed magic, Oda's injury, Faolan's death, and Macha's demise.

The sickening image of his mother's body, an axe sunk deep in her chest, flashed before his eyes again.

"What kind of monster kills his own mother?"

He hadn't meant to blurt the question to Aidryn when there was so much to process, but Aidryn had just tilted his head and replied, "You're not a monster, Eremon—just an immortal protecting his friends."

Eremon had almost laughed at that. *Just an immortal*, as though any of them really knew what horrors he might be capable of.

Aidryn had witnessed Fiadh's attack for himself and the way Lira's own power had awakened her in the meadowlands. Eremon hadn't spared many details—not even the hurtful things he'd said to Lira during their quarrel. He had flinched at Aidryn's disapproving glare after the *I still love you* bit, but thankfully, the Key Keeper was more prone to forgiveness than his wife was.

Evening wore on, and Eremon watched the little cottage for signs of life. Candles flickered in the windows, and he could make out Nevala and Aidryn moving about the kitchen. Loneliness gnawed at him. He desperately wanted Lira to ask for him, to be acknowledged as someone she wished to see. But the longer he waited, the more apparent it became that no one was going to call for him.

When the moon was high overhead, Nevala emerged, tightening a shawl around her shoulders and heading toward the keep. Restless, Eremon watched her go. Once the healer was out of sight, he made his way toward the cottage.

It might have been most appropriate to hang back and make himself scarce, yet Eremon needed to see for himself that Lira was on the mend. His care for her wellbeing had risen alongside his growing resentment at being ignored—both unbearable, if he was being honest. Besides, he'd conveniently neglected to tell Aidryn that Caitir was pregnant. That was a conversation best left to Lira, but Lira needed to know it was her responsibility.

Aidryn answered the door, hair tousled, feet bare. The laces of his tunic had been loosened, and his eyes were tired. A sudden pang of discomfort coursed through Eremon, so he took a step back. "Is she sleeping?"

"No. Come in." Aidryn moved aside so Eremon could enter. "We have tea and stew."

"Thank you, but I'm fine."

"Don't you need to eat and sleep?"

He shrugged a shoulder. Now that he was paying attention, he realized he hadn't felt any hunger pangs since awakening, nor the first wave of fatigue. "I don't need anything. Besides, there's nowhere to sleep here, unless you want me bunking at the foot of your bed."

Aidryn grinned. "Lira would kick you in the face."

"Before or after you kick me?" Eremon smirked, his gaze roving the cramped space. The kitchen was the only part of the cottage's main living area that wasn't cluttered with knick-knacks and trinkets. There was a generous hearth and a small worktable for cooking and eating.

"She's just through there," Aidryn said, pointing to a door off the kitchen. "Lira?" he called. "You have a visitor."

Eremon hesitated. Aidryn turned his back, fussing with a large soup pot that hung over the hearth. When it was clear the intent was for Eremon to go in alone, he took a few halting steps toward the bedchamber door, then entered.

Lira was sitting up in Skelly's bed, a blanket thrown around her shoulders and a large book propped on her knees. Several candles burned on the little table beside the bed, and she was squinting hard at the page in front of her. From Eremon's vantage point, the tome appeared to be rather old.

Shaking her head, she turned the page, paused, then sighed heavily before finally glancing up. She pursed her lips at the sight of him, but she busied herself with the book again. "Come to apologize?"

"Yes, actually." Eremon's voice sounded all wrong, and his thoughts began to race.

He hadn't thought this through, had he? He'd known it was late, and that Lira had been in bed all day. From the rumpled state of the pillows and sheets, Aidryn had clearly been in here with her. And why wouldn't he have been? He was her husband, after all.

Mortification washed over Eremon, and heat crept up his neck and into his cheeks.

Oh, mortal gods.

"I'm sorry," he stammered, backing up a step. "I should have waited till morning."

"Nonsense." Lira lay her book aside and pulled the blanket tighter, fixing him with a piercing stare. "It's better to make amends sooner rather than later."

He swallowed hard and nodded. "All right, then." Clasping his hands behind his back, he continued. "The things I said to you in the meadowlands were wholly inappropriate. I apologize."

She scrutinized him, then inclined her head. "I accept your apology." Her cheeks reddened before she added, "I'm sorry I slapped you."

He pressed his lips together. "I deserv—"

"Lira slapped you?" Aidryn's voice sounded from behind him, tinged with delight despite his obvious exhaustion.

Eremon whipped his head around to glare at Aidryn, who draped his arm over Eremon's shoulder and grinned like an idiot.

He closed his eyes and let out a long-suffering sigh. "I'm sure she left that detail out for a reason."

Lira covered her face with her hands, her ears turning a bright shade of red. "A very tall reason," she said, voice muffled, "who will never let it rest."

"And who is taking liberties with my personal space," Eremon added, shrugging Aidryn away and crossing his arms. "I thought this was a private conversation."

Aidryn's cheeks flushed. "I intended for it to be. I'll just..." He ducked back into the kitchen, doing a poor job of hiding his smile as he did so.

When Eremon looked at Lira again, she had a flabbergasted expression on her face. Their eyes met, and they burst into laughter. Lira covered her mouth with a hand, cheeks high with color. Eremon couldn't help moving nearer, until he finally took a seat on a stool beside the bed and took her hand.

"I'm truly sorry," he said again, giving her fingers a squeeze before drawing back. "I'd like to say we'll look back and laugh at all this one day, but it's just ridiculous right now."

"Isn't it?" Lira caught her breath, pressing a hand over her heart. "Of all the scenarios I imagined about bringing you back, quarreling never crossed my mind."

Eremon grew quiet again, lacing his fingers together. His voice dropped until it was nearly inaudible. "I lost myself, I think."

"You can find yourself again," Lira answered, a knowing glint in her dark eyes. "So much that was yours can still be restored. All you have to do is take Iathium back."

The magic within him stirred, as though it had infiltrated his entire being, from his deepest recesses to the space just beneath the surface of his skin. He remembered the way the tree in the meadow had splintered on contact, and his shoulders tightened. "Do you really think the people will have me again?"

"You know they will," she pressed. "Why do you doubt yourself?"

Eremon glanced out the window. The thin curtains had been left open, and his gaze found the moon, which shone silver in the night. "People fear what they don't understand."

"You mean *you* fear." His gaze snapped back to hers. She gave him a slow nod, appearing to realize the same truth that he felt in his bones. "You fear yourself."

Eremon shifted uncomfortably. Lira had always been astute and entirely too perceptive for her own good. "You saw what my power can do. I saw the look on your face; I know you were frightened of me. That's why you ran."

"Immortal magic is new to me. I..." She paused to gather herself, it seemed. "It's just unfamiliar, that's all. I'm sure you'll be able to control it in due course, and probably more quickly than you realize."

Rather than arguing with her, Eremon looked to the book she'd discarded. "What were you reading?"

She pursed her lips, then hefted the book and handed it to him. "Aidryn found it hidden in some of Skelly's things. There are several volumes."

Eremon accepted the book and ran his fingertips over the worn leather cover. "*Tales of Iteloria*?"

"The stories read like fictional narratives, but growing up, I believed Skelly's tales to be mythology." Lira sat up straighter and turned to face him, crossing her legs beneath the blanket. "I tested the book with my magic, and I think there are elements of truth to it."

"Itelorian myths?" Eremon said. "But it's written in Onnen, not Itelos."

"It's not Skelly's penmanship." Lira shrugged. "Actually, it isn't attributed to anyone. You might find something about other immortals in there."

"Maybe." He handed the book back to her. "You keep it; I'll look another time."

Lira scrunched her brows, as though puzzled. "But what if there isn't another time? Why wait, if you could glean more information now?"

"Because you're better at this than I am." He suddenly felt restless, as though he might turn himself inside out if he didn't leave this cramped room. "I trust you."

"There are more books," she offered. "I'm particularly interested in refreshing myself on the myths Skelly repeated often. There was one story about a winged horse that Ellwyn used to fancy. You could take this one, and I could fetch—"

"Not now." Eremon held up a hand and forced a pained smile, doing his best to ignore the overwhelming urge to take the tome back. He wanted to accept it simply to make her happy, which was precisely why he should not. "I'm going to Iathium tonight. I want to see what's happening with my own eyes."

She nodded in agreement. "And then I assume you'll want to make plans for ascension."

"As soon as I understand the scope of what's happened," Eremon hedged.

Lira set her mouth in a hard line. "If you wait too long to *understand the scope*, as you say, Caitir will have the throne, just like she's schemed for all these years. Aila is gone. Gerallt is dead. It's the perfect opportunity to sweep in and reverse the damage they've done."

"There is no reversing it," Eremon said. "All I can do is assess where we are right now, then decide what to do based on that."

She stiffened, her voice taking on a sudden edge. "I just told you where we are."

"*Silira.*" Eremon closed his eyes and pressed his fingertips to the lids. "We both know the situation goes far beyond surface details."

"But you can fix *everything*." Lira leaned forward, imploring. "I don't want to spend another day wondering whether Caitir will destroy my city before it can be saved. You can save it, so why not now?"

Her words grated against him in every possible way. Why couldn't she grasp what Eremon was trying to convey? Did she not understand that the people's collective experience with magic these past months would fuel their reaction to his return? Revealing himself must be done delicately, or he would spoil his chances of a peaceful ascension.

"We're wasting time arguing over it," he said sharply. "I need you to trust that I know what I'm doing."

"Ah, there's our supreme ruler." Lira assessed him, a sneer curling her lips. He recoiled slightly, a sick sensation creeping into his gut at the look on her face. The expression was wholly unfamiliar, even after their quarrel in the meadowlands. "Doesn't like being questioned. Can't stomach the thought of a commoner holding him accountable."

"That's enough." Eremon's tone was sharper than he meant for it to be. He stood, pushing the stool back, his muscles suddenly taut with frustration. "You have a head injury, Lira. It's time to rest."

"There isn't time for rest, only action," she said, curling one hand into a fist. "Do the right thing, Eremon."

A worried-looking Aidryn appeared in the doorway before Eremon could reply. "Is everything all right?"

Lira opened her mouth to speak, but Eremon answered for her. "She's not herself. And I think she and I have vastly different opinions of what *doing the right thing* means at the moment."

"I'm perfectly fine." She crossed her arms and raised her chin. "He just doesn't like what I have to say."

"And here I thought you'd made amends," Aidryn said with a weary sigh.

Lira blinked at him, waving in Eremon's direction. "Tell him, Aidryn. Tell him to do the right thing."

Aidryn chewed his bottom lip, eyes alight with concern. "That depends on what the right thing is."

Her mouth dropped open. Then, she closed it and scowled at them.

"There." Eremon nodded decisively. "We'll speak again soon, Lira. I'm going to Iathium."

Lira had barely managed to exclaim, "How dare y—" when Eremon clapped a hand on Aidryn's shoulder and spoke over her. "Have Lira give you an update on your sister while I'm away, will you?"

Aidryn's expression darkened, and then he whirled to look at his wife. "What about my sister?"

Lira made an indignant sound in the back of her throat. Eremon ducked out of the bedchamber and exited the cottage, leaving them alone with the uncomfortable truth. He didn't attempt to untangle his whirring thoughts before he shifted into falcon form and took to the sky.

CHAPTER 12
CAITIR

Dome

It was late afternoon before Caitir emerged from her chamber the next day. She'd spent the day lounging in bed, trying to ignore the gnawing in her stomach. With each passing hour, her mood had darkened.

Taking Iathium's throne felt more insurmountable than ever. It was easy to imagine it, but executing on effective plans was something else entirely. The idea she continually came back to was to gain the sentries' trust. With Aeron's help, it felt like the most realistic step forward.

She'd considered providing them with new armor or weapons, better supplies, or some way to make their living quarters more comfortable. When she'd pressed Aeron about it, he'd said they could use new boots. Without access to the Dome's coffers, though, it was impossible to buy the sentries' loyalty.

The Dome's treasurer, Tomis, was still in residence. Aila had treated him well, no doubt because of his access to

Eremon's gold. Caitir had attempted to puzzle out the best way to win his favor, but she found herself devoid of ideas.

Remaining in her room drained Caitir's energy, and by the time she was ready to stop ignoring her hunger pains, her head ached, and she felt nauseous. Before Aila had left, Caitir had been mostly confined to Gerallt's chambers, interacting primarily with the servants who brought her meals. Now that her mother and Gerallt were gone, the servants were nowhere to be found. Caitir had managed to talk Fiadh into bringing her a few meals the day before, but Fiadh had not come to her room today.

A wave of nausea clenched Caitir's stomach, and she pressed a hand to her belly, forcing herself to rise and make her way to the door.

"So demanding," she murmured.

Caitir hoped the baby was a boy—not so much to continue a bloodline, but because holding the throne for a girl seemed much less appealing. A daughter would be more likely to hand her power to a husband, who would eventually usurp by proxy, if not by force. Iathium had always measured eras and events by Rí, not Rani. But perhaps Caitir could break that tradition.

She had to seize the throne first.

Rising, she crossed her dimly lit chamber and opened the door. Her heart sped as she raised her chin and made herself step out onto the tiles, veering toward the corridors that led away from the western towers. Moving through the Dome alone sent a pang of anxiety through her these days, but she pushed forward, trying to ignore it.

She checked the timepiece on the wall, faltering outside the entrance to the kitchens. It was late in the day, but a low, humming sound was drifting up the stone stairwell. Carefully, she picked her way down the stairs in the near-dark.

The air grew warmer as she descended into a wide corridor, which forked into a large kitchen and dining hall. The voice she'd heard wasn't just humming; it was singing. Caitir recognized the old folk song.

When she rounded the corner, one of the cooks was kneading dough at the wide worktable, looking pleased with himself as he sang. He grinned as though he were protecting a happy secret, his round face jolly as he worked the dough over and over. Caitir stopped in the doorway to listen. When he'd finished his song, she cleared her throat softly.

The cook went rigid, angular eyes widening as his gaze landed on Caitir. "Yes, my lady?"

His voice was soft and quivered a bit. He looked a good two decades older than Caitir—late forties, at the youngest. She took in the tension in his posture, the guarded expression on his face, before she spoke. "I was looking for something to eat."

The cook visibly relaxed. "What would you like? I can have it sent to your chambers."

She felt a pull to remain where she was, so she pressed a hand to her belly and said, "Actually, I think I might like to stay here for a little while."

He looked surprised but answered, "Of course."

Caitir dragged a stool over to the worktable and sat, resting her forehead in her hands.

"I have fresh bread from the oven and two different types of stew—cabbage and beef," the cook said.

His warm, genuine nature was disarming. Caitir liked how comfortable he made her feel, though he kept a wary eye on her.

"I need something bland," she half-groaned, swaying where she sat. "Bread would be nice."

Concern darkened his expression. He crossed the kitchen, took a large loaf of bread from beneath a cloth, and cut a large slice. When he returned, he placed the bread on a small plate and slid it across the table to her. "Are you ill?"

"In a manner of speaking." Caitir tore a piece off the bread, twirling it slowly between her fingertips. Saliva pooled in her mouth, and her stomach lurched at the thought of actually eating anything. She set the bread back down on the plate. "I'm expecting a child. I'm so nauseous I can't see straight."

"Ah," the cook breathed. "I'd heard the spare wife was with child."

A sheen of sweat broke across her face. "I'd prefer to be called by my name," she snapped.

"Caitir Tarlach. I remember your brother Aidryn well." He gave her a gallant nod. "I'm Kenji."

"Charmed." Caitir buried her face in her hands, still unable to consume the bread in front of her. She felt compelled to speak freely, so she followed the impulse. "It's just Caitir. I signed my clan surname over to the city. My late husband—"

"Late husband?" Kenji's question was barely audible. "You mean the new...?" He drew a circle in the air over the top of his head, indicating a crown, and mouthed, "He's dead?" She almost laughed at his expression; he looked as though his eyebrows might rise past his hair line.

"I only just learned. Mother doesn't know." Caitir shuddered. Kenji visibly relaxed as she continued. "If he survived somehow, I'll finish the job myself." She drew a finger across her throat.

Kenji hesitated before replying. "Most of us agree with you."

His voice was soft and kind, a bit like her father's. She found herself leaning forward, drawn in by him.

"As you should." Caitir gathered the nerve to take a bite of bread, willing the nausea away as she chewed slowly. "You know *she's* gone, too. To Iteloria."

"Hmm." Kenji went back to kneading his dough without answering. Every few moments, he glanced at her out of the corner of his eye, as though he wanted to say something else. Instead, he worked in silence for a long while.

After a few bites of bread, and Caitir's stomach began to settle. She felt her body relax a bit and kept her eyes on the cook as he lifted the lump of dough into a large bowl, then covered it with a cloth to let it rise. The reality of what she'd divulged settled over her, but curiously, she found she didn't regret telling him about Aila's absence.

Kenji stepped closer once again, eyeing her dwindling bread. "Ready for something else? Perhaps some soup?"

She shifted in her seat, wrapping her arms around her middle. "Yes."

He took an empty bowl from the stack of clean dishes and went to work dipping from a large pot that hung over the wide hearth. Before he set the steaming bowl in front of her, he sliced more bread.

"You'll want something to dip in your broth," he said, placing the bread on her plate. "Eremon always did."

Caitir froze at the mention of Eremon's name. For a moment, she wrinkled her nose, attempting to imagine him sitting down here in the kitchen in his ceremonial robes, sopping broth from the bottom of his bowl with a chunk of bread while Kenji bustled about. It would be unfathomable if she hadn't seen him dressed like a peasant just yesterday.

"Eremon," she ventured. "He came here?"

"Every day—sometimes twice." Kenji looked as though he wanted to smile at the memory, but his expression crumpled instead, and his eyes filled with tears. "He was so..." He looked up at the ceiling, collecting himself before spoke again. "I miss him terribly."

Caitir snorted softly. *Little do you know.*

"Did you ever hear what became of the girl he loved?" Kenji asked. "Silira, the new Defender."

An icy shard of contempt pierced the warmth Caitir had begun to feel toward the man, and she straightened. Always, the conversation turned to Lira.

"I don't want to hear her name from your lips," she replied curtly. "Besides, she's not the Defender."

He propped a fist on his hip and tilted his head. "Who will your mother appoint to the position?"

She straightened, willing her expression to relax despite the tension building between her shoulder blades. "She'll appoint no one. I'm taking the throne."

Kenji's eyes lit, bemused. "Ambitious of you."

Caitir held his stare, jaw tight. "It's not ambition, it's fact."

This time, the cook *laughed*. Anger flared within her when he said, "You'll never rule Iathium."

Her muscles tensed, the crackling sensation of dark magic rushing to her fingertips. "Careful, cook, or I'll—"

"You'll what?" Kenji leaned close, his gaze hard, though the pleasant tone never left his voice. "You'll kill me like Árchú? Torture me like Aidryn or Beran's overlord"

The magic fizzled out. She raised her chin, though every fiber of her body wanted to recoil. "I see my reputation precedes me."

Kenji scoffed. "And that"—he pointed a finger at her nose before pushing to stand again—"is why you'll never win us over."

"Who is *us*, the kitchen staff?"

"The kitchen staff are vitally important to your survival," he answered, bending to check on a covered tray of pastries on a low shelf. "And you're short on allies already."

Caitir picked up her spoon again, stirring the broth carefully. The spoon clanked against the side of the bowl once and she flinched, sloshing a bit of the broth onto the tabletop. She froze, but Kenji wordlessly tossed her a cloth to soak up the spill, then went about his business.

Gaze trained on the cloth, she swiped it across the tabletop. Aila had always hated for Caitir to make noise, especially during meals. She hated the sound of cutlery making contact with dinnerware. More than that, Aila hated for food to stray from its proper place. One splatter, one drip, one speck of food on the corner of Caitir's mouth, and her mother would launch into a tirade about etiquette and securing a husband.

She pressed her lips together and exhaled slowly through her nose, then released the tension that had bunched her shoulders. Gingerly, she lay her spoon down and refocused on Kenji. "If you're so skilled at diplomacy, cook, tell me: How do I win more allies?"

"Show people kindness without demanding anything in return," he answered.

Caitir ran a finger over her spoon's delicate handle. "And if I wanted to win over the sentries?"

"Make yourself a leader worth following. Find ways to improve their lives."

"All those ways involve coin," she grumbled. "A lot of it. Tomis isn't going to let me near the coffers."

He sniffed. "Why not intimidate him with that magic of yours? Seems effective."

"That's counterproductive. I want him as an ally."

She didn't miss the cook's smirk, or the subtle shake of his head.

"Then find an alternative," Kenji replied. "Something simple that will show the sentries you care about their wellbeing. Nami knows, no one has paid them any real mind since Eremon died."

"You speak in generalities," Caitir said. "I need specifics. Tell me what to do for them."

"Ah, there's the rub. A worthy ruler observes the world around her and sees what must be done."

"I don't have time for observation."

"A weak excuse," he said, holding her gaze. "Nearly as ineffective as asking a cook how to usurp a throne."

She clenched her fists, nails piercing her palms, and stood

abruptly. Pain spiked through one side of her belly at the sudden movement, and she suppressed a wince.

"This is a waste of my time," she bit out.

Kenji laughed again. "That it is."

Caitir whirled and marched toward the stairwell. An orange cat crept across the pathway, arching its back and hissing when it saw her. She stopped in her tracks, calling on her thread of Clan Tarlach's power as she glared down at the cat. "*Jox cheh.*"

The cat yowled and bolted, cowering in the corner across the room from her. Caitir cast a half-glance back at Kenji, who was now glaring at her.

"I hate cats," she said before exiting the kitchen, climbing the staircase, and heading for her chamber.

CHAPTER 13

EREMON

Iathium

Iathium was dark as Eremon approached. Where warm torchlight had once emanated from the structures and walkways, there was nothing but inky black. Even as a falcon, he felt alarm course through his body.

The city appeared to have sunken into deep despair and folded in on itself. Melancholy was thick in the atmosphere, rising from the homes, the streets, and the Dome itself. Its normally luminous glass was darkened from within, now only a faint glow, as though those inside had only bothered to light a portion of the torches that lined the interior.

He flew toward the western side of the Dome, mentally ticking off the possible reasons why lighting might had been reduced. Perhaps the usurpers were shorthanded. Or maybe they didn't have enough respect for the household to know that there should always be enough light emanating from the Dome to make it a beacon for all of Rodhlan.

This place—Iathium's palace—was meant to be a symbol of

hope. Whether it had always served as such was a different matter for another time.

Rather than perching near the Dome right away, Eremon swooped eastward, passing over the Drochaid and the roaring Moravon River. He skimmed the cityscape below, until his eyes rested on what should have been a familiar sight. Where Lira's cottage home had once been, there was now nothing but a pile of rubble.

His heart grew heavy, his body agitated. There must be something he could do for her to make up for everything she'd lost.

Caitir had made off with Lira's pendant. Perhaps Eremon could take it back while he observed the state of the city. That was a small bit of progress in the grand scheme of things, but it would be a significant victory for Lira.

Eremon thought of Caitir, and of her horrified expression as she'd laid eyes on him back in the meadowlands. Perhaps even more satisfying than taking Lira's pendant back from the little usurper would be the look on her face when he did it.

First, the necklace. Then, the throne.

A shudder wracked his body at the thought.

The notion of Caitir Tarlach scheming to rule his city was almost laughable. From what he recalled of her in his former life, she'd been a vapid, superficial ninny. Aila and Macha had attempted to throw her into his path over and over. Every time, he'd sidestepped her, his focus trained solely on Lira those last few years of his mortal life.

When he was younger, he'd dallied with some of the young women at court, sneaking under Macha's nose. He'd used his father's secret passages to slip into their chambers, and for a little while, he'd enjoyed the sense of rebellion it brought him. The heady sensations and the rush of secrecy had never failed to distract him from the increasingly frustrating situation at court. It was one of the only things he had been able to control.

But then he'd set his sights on Lira. He had stopped pursuing other women, stopped sneaking into their rooms in the dead of night. As his magical illness progressed, he'd only found comfort in the idea of Lira, the one person he'd thought might be able to save him. It didn't hurt that she was brilliant and beautiful and kind.

Stop it. He shook away the memories of what she'd once been to him. There was no going back.

Eremon hadn't been able to ignore the rush of revulsion he'd felt when Lira had insisted he *do the right thing.* As though he didn't know himself. Iathium was the beginning, middle, and end of his identity. He had never even borne a family name; for generation after generation, his bloodline belonged solely to the city.

Since its earliest days, Iathium's rulers had abstained from taking surnames to demonstrate their dedication to the city-state above all else. They were raised in service to Iathium, groomed to carry on a bloodline saturated in stolen magic they had no right to wield. But Eremon had been freed of that ill-gotten power. And, for the first time in his existence, he realized he was restless for an identity of his own. Something beyond Rí.

The problem was, he didn't know where to begin. Nothing felt like *his.* He had defeated death—not singlehandedly, but with the help of his friends. He had a seemingly endless well of power that he had no idea how to use. He had been reunited with his truest love, only to find she longer belonged to him.

Eremon forced himself to refocus on the idea of finding Lira's pendant, gliding toward the southwestern tower and swooping low to glance through its narrow windows as he passed. He reached out with his senses, feeling for the presence of Lira's magic, but felt nothing, so he moved on to the north-western tower. As he passed the second window at its base, he caught a glimpse of dim lantern light, golden hair, and a flash of fabric the color of pearls.

He circled and returned to the window, landing quietly on its stone sill. The door had been left ajar, and the room was empty. But the lanterns that lined the walls had been lit, so he watched and waited, making himself as still as stone.

This chamber had once been reserved for diplomatic guests who were staying at court for a time—all cold, white marble, dark wood paneling, and crimson curtains. There was a large bed near the window, which was normally concealed from the rest of the chamber by one of the heavy curtains. Against the left wall was a cherry wood sideboard the delegates had often used to enjoy a drink after dinner in the banquet hall.

A settee was pushed against the far wall beside the door, and several mismatched, plush chairs were scattered throughout the room, as though they'd been haphazardly dragged inside. The wardrobe that sat against the right-hand wall stood partially open, yards of lush fabric spilling out.

His gaze darted to the chairs and the few small tables that had been arranged between them. Their surfaces were bare, with no sign of the bronze tree that he could see. He was preparing to take flight again when Caitir entered the room, her expression stricken. Fiadh was at her heels.

Eremon bristled at the sight of them.

"—always about Lira," Caitir was saying, gesturing wildly. "I'll always be in her shadow; there's no overcoming it."

"That's only true if you want it to be," Fiadh answered, crossing her arms. "She hasn't shown her face here in months, and people will remember that."

"No, they *only* remember her," Caitir seethed, "falling all over Eremon and begging him to stay alive, like a pathetic heroine in a tragic performance."

"It *was* tragic," Fiadh ventured.

"How would you know? You weren't there!"

"Neither were you," Fiadh snapped. "If I recall, you'd been banned from *Nami Mostari* for accosting her."

Caitir threw up her hands in exasperation. "Why are you defending Lira? You hate her."

"I'm being objective," Fiadh said, mirroring Caitir's gestures. "You can't let your hatred for her or anyone else dictate your next moves. Be strategic."

Caitir's disgusted expression would have made Eremon guffaw had he not been in his falcon form.

"How are you suddenly the diplomat?" she demanded. "You're the one who burned a settlement out of jealousy—the classic jilted lover with more fire power than brains."

The corner of Fiadh's mouth turned up, as though she was trying to suppress a smile. "I never claimed to follow my own advice."

Caitir crossed her arms, stepping closer to the dark-haired woman. "You're pleased with yourself."

Fiadh shrugged, the light in her eyes brightening. "It was only a small settlement—poor outliers. They mean nothing to the city."

"The outliers could break this city if enough of them band together," Caitir seethed. "I don't care how small the settlement was. Five people, or two thousand five, it makes no difference. I cannot afford to be labeled as a conqueror who brings the people of this continent to heel. I wish for them to comply, but because they want to. I can *make* them want to."

Fiadh scoffed, backing toward the door. "Good luck," she drawled. "From what I hear, you couldn't even make the Rí look at you twice. What makes you think the whole of Rodhlan will care?"

With an angry cry, Caitir snatched a crystal glass from the sideboard and threw it at Fiadh. She had terrible aim; the glass struck the wall next to the chamber door, shattering as it hit the tile.

"Get out!" she screamed, veins of dark magic gathering around her fists—the black lightning that had killed Eremon.

But her knees buckled, and she released her power, bending over to brace herself on the nearest chair. Her back was to Eremon, but he could see the leer in Fiadh's expression.

"Careful," Fiadh said, backing out into the corridor. "Wouldn't want to harm the heir apparent."

She pushed the door shut, leaving Caitir alone in the chamber.

The young woman started to sink toward the floor but stiffened, her shoulders rising and falling with her heavy breaths. Slowly, she turned toward the window, face pale, thin hands pressed to her belly as she walked toward the bed, her gaze focused on the soft pillows. As she reached for the blanket, her hands were trembling. She climbed into the bed, painstakingly lowering herself onto her side.

Eremon struggled not to tilt his head curiously. She'd barely begun to show; in fact, anyone who hadn't been told she was with child would never know. But she moved as though she was already heavily pregnant—and in an incredible amount of pain.

He remembered the way she'd dismounted her horse in the meadowlands. She appeared to have been in pain then, too.

If Eremon had not been wearing a falcon's form, he might have felt some semblance of pity for her. It was a good thing he didn't have to think about how her obvious discomfort made his insides twist. Or about the bits of strategy she'd revealed—a strategy that, for all intents and purposes, was a good one.

Eremon remained perfectly still, hoping she wouldn't notice the silver falcon watching her as she slowly settled into bed, her golden hair splayed across the pillow. She curled onto her side and pulled the coverlet up to her chin. He remained on the sill until her breathing settled into the slow, gentle lull of sleep.

CHAPTER 14

LIRA

Rodhlan Ridge

"Caitir's with child, then." Aidryn sighed heavily. They were sitting side-by-side on the small bed in Skelly's cottage, Lira leaning into Aidryn's warmth. He nodded more times than he ought, as though trying to convince himself of the reality. Lira couldn't blame him for his apparent shock. As vile as Caitir had chosen to become, they had both loved her once. Deep down, Lira knew Aidryn loved his sister, still.

Lira rested her hand on his thigh. "We knew it was likely."

Of course, they'd known since Skelly had given them the news of Caitir's Binding to Gerallt; they had just never spoken of the inevitability. There had been no need. Now, though, it felt like anticipating a long-ailing relative's death but expecting to avoid the bitter sting of grief afterward.

Aidryn turned his head to look down at her, then pressed a gentle kiss against her curls. "We did. It is what it is, I suppose." He reached for her hand and laced their fingers together.

They settled into a tenuous silence. Lira studied the bright slice of moonlight that streamed in through the window and cut across the rough spun blanket they shared. She rubbed her thumb over Aidryn's and rested her head on his shoulder.

She closed her eyes and let herself drift, content to be this near to him again. But as her body begin to relax, images from the day before rushed in. Suddenly, there was the roiling storm lanced with dark magic, Fiadh's enraged expression, and that horrible burning she had unleashed into Lira's body.

With a gasp, Lira jolted awake, sitting upright to cover her face with trembling hands. Aidryn followed her movement, gripping her shoulders protectively.

"What's the matter?" he asked, tucking Lira's curls behind her ear. "Talk to me."

Lira scrubbed at her eyes and released a harsh breath. "I—it's nothing, just a sudden memory."

"A witnessing?" He coaxed her hands down and touched her chin with tender fingertips, drawing her face to look at him.

"No," she said, wetting her lips and swallowing. Her throat was so dry. "It was like reliving what Fiadh did to me."

"I know it was terrifying," Aidryn said. He gathered her close again, guiding her to lie down and rest her head on his chest. Pulling the blanket up, he tucked it over her shoulder, then wrapped his arms around her body and pulled her flush against his side. "But I'm here now. I won't let more harm come to you."

Two days ago, the declaration would have been comforting. Now, though, she found herself doubting his word. There were greater, wilder powers afoot than what Aidryn could ever hope to protect her from. Eremon himself hadn't been able to stop what Fiadh had done, and he was an immortal.

How was she to put her trust in Aidryn when a being infinitely more powerful than he had failed her?

"I'm afraid, Aidryn," Lira said in a small voice.

He was quiet for a moment. "Of?"

"Shall I make you a list?" She took a shuddering breath. "I'm afraid of what happened to my pendant. Afraid of what Fiadh did to me and what else she might be capable of. Afraid Eremon won't take the throne back. Afraid I'll have to ascend if he doesn't. Afraid of Caitir leading Rodhlan to ruin if I refuse any duty that falls to me. Afraid of Iteloria invading and sacking Iathium."

"All understandable fears," Aidryn replied. "Go on. Tell me everything."

Lira's eyes blurred with tears, and she poured herself out to him for what felt like hours. He listened intently, his hands roaming idly to stroke her hair, her skin. She talked herself into exhaustion until finally, her eyelids were drooping, and sleep felt unavoidable.

"I just can't..." Her words trailed off, but she shook herself awake again. "I can't see my way to reassurance."

"Try," Aidryn urged her, giving her shoulder a gentle squeeze. "Hear my words and tuck them away. You're safe from Fiadh, and so is your magic. That power Eremon used to wake you? I have to believe it played a part in your healing."

"I want to believe that," she whispered, "but I feel different inside."

"You're wounded and exhausted; give it time," he answered. "As for Eremon, he'll do what's right. I think that was grief speaking for him."

"One can only hope," Lira said.

"When he ascends, I believe that will set your other worries at ease. But whatever happens, Lira, I believe in you." Aidryn kissed her temple. She closed her eyes, her fingers wandering to clutch the fabric of his tunic. "I have always believed in you, and I know you're strong enough and wise enough to overcome anything—fear, enemies from within or without, dark magic. Whatever the future brings, I know you have exactly what you need to rise and stand firm against it. And I'll be at your side, wielding blade and magic to defend you and our people from harm."

"Mortal gods, I love you," Lira murmured against him, trying to ignore the doubt that rose within her at his words. She inhaled the familiar scent of springtime he'd always carried. "There will never be another Aidryn."

He laughed softly. "There will never be another Lira."

She pushed up on her elbow, reaching for a kiss. Aidryn turned to brush his lips against hers. But when Lira tried to deepen the kiss, he gently disentangled himself and tucked her head back against his chest. She whimpered in protest.

"I'm not letting you avoid sleep," he said, a stern edge to his rich tenor. "You need rest. Let me chase the nightmares away."

"That's precisely what I was trying to do," Lira grumbled.

"Perhaps tomorrow." Aidryn chuckled. "Sleep now, love."

With a sigh, Lira snuggled against him and closed her eyes, throwing her arm across his torso. As sleep crept back in, she couldn't help but think that Aidryn wasn't capable of doubting her. In the past, knowing how deeply he'd believed in her had bolstered her every step of the way—even helped her to trust herself more, if she was being honest.

After what had happened with Fiadh, though, Aidryn would say whatever he thought necessary to keep Lira calm. It was true, she was injured and exhausted, which was precisely why Aidryn had tried to soothe her fears. Though she lay still in his arms, her thoughts whirred back into motion. She revisited every point of fear she had poured out to him, deconstructing his responses and refuting each one until she had exhausted herself.

It was lovely to have a husband who would have gone to the ends of the world for her, if she had asked. But Lira valued truth above all. If she could painstakingly poke holes in every one of Aidryn's well-meaning arguments, then she was on the side of truth. She further confirmed these suspicions by reaching for her power's affirming tugs.

Night dragged on, and Lira sank deeper into her well of fear. Long after Aidryn's breathing had slowed to a steady cadence, her heart was galloping more swiftly than his prized stallion, Fannin. Where one terrifying thought spiral ended, another began. By the time sleep finally found her, she felt as alone and vulnerable as she had in Iathium's dungeon.

I just need to rest, she thought. *It'll be better in the morning.*

But as she drifted again, another thought crossed her mind, as though it had been whispered into her ear: *The fool mistakes wisdom for fear. Trust your magic. Trust yourself. In your fears, you will find your salvation.*

CHAPTER 15

AIDRYN

Rodhlan Ridge

Aidryn woke before dawn to find Lira curled on the opposite side of the bed, shivering in her sleep. Carefully, he rose, mindful of the rustling mattress and the creaking floor. He draped his half of the blanket over Lira's body to warm her, then stood back, watching until she appeared to relax.

On his way out of the room, he paused, his gaze lingering over Lira's sleeping form. The memory of the contempt she'd shown Eremon haunted him. As fiery as she could be, he'd never seen that look on her face before. It was as though some deep, long-suppressed hatred had hauled itself up from the darkest parts of her being and was straining to break free.

Beyond simply loving Lira, Aidryn had always looked to her when he needed reassurance that the world was still on its axis. He'd already lost one of the people who had tethered him to reality. Now, she was losing the sense of safety they'd worked so hard to restore during their time at Halgeir. It had pained Aidryn to hear how many deep fears she was harboring the night before, and he wasn't sure where to begin alleviating them.

He moved quietly into the small cottage's kitchen. The tub Lira had bathed in the day before still sat full, so he busied himself by hauling loads of water outside. He repeated the steps until his back and arms ached, the tub was empty, and the coming sunrise had turned the sky a dim shade of gray.

Aidryn's thoughts drifted back to his sister, and another wave of grief swept over him. He shouldn't have been surprised that Caitir was with child, but the news had bludgeoned him anyway. Aila's wishes had always ruled the day, and Caitir had been too worn down to resist the pressure.

Though he'd always tried, in the end, he'd never been able to protect Caitir from anything. Her fear of Aila had always outweighed her trust in Aidryn. It was horrifying to think that intimidation had led her into unthinkable abuse, not only at her mother's hands, but at Gerallt's, too.

His arms ached, and after dumping the last of the bathwater, he discarded the bucket by the front steps and headed for the pasture, where the horses were just beginning to stir. Fannin approached the fence, swishing his long, white tail and tossing his mane. Aidryn felt his body relax as the massive gray stallion leaned down to nuzzle and nip at his shoulder.

Aidryn's fingertips trailed over Fannin's soft, dark muzzle, and he leaned forward with a shuddering sigh. Wrapping his arms around the stallion's broad back, he rested his face against Fannin's mane and took in the lingering scent of ash and heat on his coat.

The horse's presence had always been a comfort to Aidryn, even on his darkest days in Iathium. Fannin had been with him through years of madness as Aila had plotted for the throne. He'd saved Aidryn from despair thousands of times over. And he'd protected Aidryn and Lira, freeing them from a city that had so abruptly been turned upside down.

After a long moment, Aidryn leaned back and pressed a kiss to Fannin's muzzle. "Thank you, old boy," he whispered, brushing his fingertips along the stallion's soft face.

"Just so you know"—Eremon's voice sounded beside him as he approached—"if I ever figure out how to assume the form of a horse, I will *not* be offering free comfort."

"That's valuable information," Aidryn muttered, turning to Eremon and leaning against the fencepost.

Fannin took the sleeve of Aidryn's tunic between his teeth and gave it a tug, eager to regain his attention. With a chuckle, he reached up to stroke the stallion's mane, his gaze fixed on Eremon.

"See anything interesting in Iathium?" Aidryn asked.

Eremon gave him a curt nod. "Your sister and that Fiadh woman, hissing like feral cats in a glass blower's shop," he said flatly.

"Oh, good." It was nearly impossible for Aidryn to keep his tone buoyant. Fannin grunted at the shift in his demeanor.

Eremon stretched his arms overhead, craning his neck to look at the brightening sky. Then, he sprawled out on the ground, his loose black hair splayed on the dew-damp grass, silver eyes fixed on the same focal point. He locked his fingers behind his head and breathed deeply. "They're making a valiant attempt at strategizing. Might succeed at running the place if they could retract their claws for long enough—which is doubtful."

It was so odd to see the Rí lying on the ground that Aidryn couldn't make himself look away. He understood what it was like to crave that sort of freedom, though, and he'd always centered himself outdoors. "So that's why you look so comfortable."

The Rí cut him a sideways glance. "Their pettiness was comforting."

Aidryn rocked back on his heels and crossed his arms. "If

they're so distracted, it might be a good time to make your move."

"I'm not ready to reveal my new power," Eremon said quickly. "Besides, the windows were sealed tightly, per protocol. I'm not eager to draw undue attention before it's time."

Aidryn had desired to give Eremon the benefit of the doubt, but suddenly, Lira's ire made more sense. This evasive attitude wasn't like Eremon at all. In fact, in his former life, Eremon would have jumped at the chance to undermine the usurpers once he'd observed their weaknesses. He patted Fannin's neck again and pushed off the fencepost.

"They say it has changed—Iathium," Aidryn said. "Did you find that to be true?"

Eremon rose, brushing blades of wet grass off himself as he began to walk the fence line. He pulled his long, straight hair over one shoulder. "The spirit of the place feels different. There's a sense of hopelessness I wasn't prepared for."

"Then you have the upper hand here, because you can offer renewed hope," Aidryn said, falling into step beside him. "Why don't you use your shifting powers to get inside the Dome? See who's still alive, who's loyal, and gather your allies. Find the pendant in the process. That way, you won't show yourself prematurely."

Eremon tilted his head and shrugged. "I'll think about it."

"For Nami's sake, Eremon," Aidryn exclaimed, tension bunching his shoulders, "it's a good idea. What do you have to lose?"

The Rí's expression darkened. "You should go back to Lira —see how she fares."

Before Aidryn could speak again, Eremon had shifted and soared northward. If Aidryn's own searing emotions compared to Lira's in any way, then he understood why she'd been so enraged before. But life as a ruler was all Eremon knew. It was unlikely many people had ever pushed against him, except for his mother and her loyalists.

Aidryn made the trek back to the cottage as the sun climbed higher into the sky. His melancholy deepened as he drew nearer, but he tried to shove it aside. Lira needed him, and he would do whatever he could to help her feel safe again.

CHAPTER 16
CAITIR

Dome

L ate-morning sunlight streamed into Caitir's chamber, warming the heavy blankets she'd cocooned herself in the night before. A sheen of sweat covered her forehead. She wriggled out from under the coverlet, throwing it aside and letting the cool air envelop her.

She'd always felt cold before, but now, carrying a child, she was often warm. Breaking out in an unseemly sweat at inopportune moments wasn't something she had bargained for. Then again, she'd quickly realized how little she'd understood about pregnancy. If she thought too long about the coming months, she grew fearful. So instead, she pushed the questions to the back of her mind.

There was a scraping sound outside her window, and she whirled to see what appeared to be a large raptor taking flight from the sill. Its wing swept around the side of the tower before she could get a good look. Last night, Caitir had drifted off to sleep with the distinct sensation that someone had been watching her. She assumed the creature was to blame.

Caitir slipped into the bathing chamber. She splashed her face with cool water from a large crystal basin, then applied a rose-scented cream to her face, scowling in the mirror as she did so. Pregnancy had riddled her once-clear skin with blemishes.

She leaned near to the mirror, scrutinizing a red spot on her chin. Before leaving for Iteloria, Aila had overseen Caitir's cosmetic routine, coaching her in the various methods of concealing her imperfections. Since then, Caitir had stopped wearing cosmetics and powders altogether, in hopes that their absence would allow the blemishes to heal.

Fiadh, whose mother had been a midwife, had insisted that Caitir should stop allowing anyone to treat her hair with the gold dust dye Aila had forced her to use since childhood. The substance was dangerous, Fiadh had said—both for Caitir and the baby. It hadn't taken further convincing.

Beneath the years of dye lay a color Caitir had all but forgotten: ash blonde. Its roots were beginning to peek out from her scalp. She'd always imagined the color to be a clash between her mother's Itelorian heritage and her father's Tarlach roots—as though the silvery white of the Tai'ceru tribe and the earth tones of Rodhlan had merged without overruling one another. Aila had always kept her hair dyed a pristine black to match what Macha's had once been, but beneath, it was a shade of silver so pale, it was nearly white.

It had been years since Caitir had allowed herself to think about the true color of her hair or the cosmetics she applied to her skin. Years since she'd had days on end without her mother dictating her every move. Now, with her own child on the way, Caitir was unnerved to realize that she could not imagine doing the same to her son or daughter.

She would never seek to control her child's life. Not for a marriage. Not for a crown. Not for a throne. Not for magic.

Not even for the idea of immortality.

Caitir looked at herself in the mirror, unsettled once again by the now-pale eyes that stared back at her. The one thing she'd been allowed to keep before, unaltered, had been the rich blue of her eyes—and now her mother's hunger for power, as well as her own, had almost entirely leached their hue.

"What did you do to my eyes?" she'd demanded on her wedding night.

"If one wants power, one must sacrifice superficialities," Aila had replied coolly. The answer had been a stark contrast to her usual preoccupation with Caitir's appearance. "Magical innovation has its consequences."

Magical innovation. Experimentation, more like. Caitir hated to admit that she'd lived as her mother's magical test subject all her life, but it was the truth. So, she had swallowed her protests and forced herself not to argue.

The idea had been to comply with her mother's demands for long enough to amass the power and the coin it took to free herself. But a chance at real freedom had never come, and Caitir had been forced to adapt to the cruelty and control. She had become like Aila in order to survive her. Now, she was scheming to defy Eremon—*immortal* Eremon, of all people. Perhaps she had truly lost her mind somewhere along the way.

Fear clenched her heart, and she braced herself on the marble counter, staring down at its hard, cold surface. *What is wrong with me?*

But she'd long since passed the point of no return, and there was no choice but to stay on the path she'd chosen. There were no other options.

She took several deep breaths to calm her heart's erratic pounding. Nausea gripped her throat, and she bit her cheek, pressing a thumb to the inside of her wrist. When the wave passed, she left her room and headed for the kitchens. The cook had been insufferable, but he'd offered her a meal, and she could use the company—anyone but Fiadh.

When she arrived, Kenji was bustling about, directing the kitchen staff as they worked to glaze the pastries he'd been making the night before. They froze in the middle of their work as she entered, averting their gazes. One of the girls' shoulders curled in, a fearful posture that made Caitir's insides squirm. Kenji noted the shift in the room, looking to Caitir, then glancing at his staff.

"Let's break early," he said. The cooks wasted no time clearing out.

Caitir sat at the same stool as the night before. Kenji cast another wary look her way, then bent down to rummage for a moment before emerging with a package wrapped in cheesecloth. "Here."

She peeled the cloth back just enough to peek inside. It was a large, dense pastry drizzled with thick frosting—the kind with sweet, soft cheese baked into the middle. She suppressed a groan at the sight of it. But her excitement quickly turned to dread; Aila had rarely let Caitir touch such a decadent sweet, much less devour an entire one like she wanted to now.

Her chest tightened at the sudden memory of Aila catching her with a little cake Aidryn had snuck home from the kitchens. She'd been eleven years old at the time.

"The Rí will never want you if you eat like a little piglet," Aila had hissed, snatching the cake from Caitir's hands before slapping her across the cheek.

The next morning, Caitir had risen to the news that her little white kitten—the last pet she'd ever loved—had died during the night. It wasn't the first time she'd lost a pet shortly after disappointing her mother, and the tragedies had taken on something of a pattern.

"Bad things happen when you disobey," Aila had always said. "When you're a naughty girl, no one has to catch you. No one has to tell. We only have to wait a little while, and *poof*— misfortune will find you out on its own."

There was rarely room for secrecy. Even though Caitir always got caught, misfortunes continued to occur. When Aidryn had come to bury the kitten for Caitir, a job he had always assumed without being asked, he'd sighed and given her a look full of pity. His blue eyes had shone with sorrow.

"Don't keep any more pets," Aidryn had admonished gently, embracing a trembling Caitir before disappearing back into the stables. "She'll only use them to punish you. Bring them to me, and I'll take care of them."

Caitir suspected that by *take care of them*, Aidryn had meant that he would quietly give them away. As much as she'd loved animals before, she learned to feign disinterest, waving off any living gifts and demanding gowns and jewels instead. Gradually, Aila turned to destroying Caitir's favorite garments to punish her—a great relief to both Caitir and Aidryn.

Blessedly, Aidryn had gotten away with pawning animals off on his friends and acquaintances. One of the hounds that loped alongside Faolan and Aeron in the city streets had looked suspiciously like a puppy Caitir had given to Aidryn on her thirteenth birthday. Yet another white cat took up residence at the Énna family's smithy, or so she'd heard. Its sooty appearance had served to hide it from Aila's keen eye.

Caitir's eyes stung as she pushed the thoughts from her mind. "Thank you," she said weakly, pushing the pastry away, "but I'm not hungry."

Her stomach rumbled loudly, betraying her lie.

Kenji took the kettle from the stove top and poured her a large cup of tea. "Then take it with you."

"I couldn't," she said as her mouth began to water. "I can't eat this. My mother—"

The cook set the tea before her. "She isn't here," he cut in, his voice barely audible.

Caitir startled, meeting Kenji's knowing gaze. She weighed

what to say next, her mouth going dry before she settled on, "I know."

"But it feels as though she is, doesn't it?"

She squeezed her eyes shut and nodded. Aila had controlled Caitir's access to food for years, as though every bite would add undesirable weight to her small frame. "Like she's always in my head, or just around the corner."

He reached across the counter and rested his hand on her clenched fist; she didn't realize she'd been clenching it. "Your mind and your body belong to you."

Do they? "I—I know." Her words sounded much more uncertain than she wanted them to.

Kenji kept his gaze steady and trained on her. "You can choose what you want to do. Eat what you like."

Caitir looked down at the pastry again, then unwrapped the paper. She tore off a piece and put it in her mouth, chewing slowly and sighing at the decadent flavor of it. Kenji watched her the way Aidryn used to—full of concern, as though he fervently wished to see her enjoy it—and for the first time in months, her heart ached for her brother.

"You know," he said, moving back across the kitchen to check on his roast duck, "you'll need to eat and drink plenty, for yourself and the babe."

"What do you know about it?" Caitir said, taking another bite of the pastry. "You're just a cook."

Kenji scowled. *"Just a cook,"* he mocked. "My wife Toryn is a midwife, and we have four daughters."

"Well, midwifery is *her* profession, not yours," she said around a mouthful.

"I care about her work," the cook shot back. "I attended all my children's births."

Caitir's eyes widened. "A man was allowed in the birthing room?"

"We didn't ask anyone's permission." He grinned and winked at her. "There's no law against it."

"But it's..." *Scandalous*. She couldn't square with what he'd just admitted. "Base and improper."

Kenji scoffed, throwing a towel over his shoulder and opening the oven. He picked up two thick potholders and wrapped them around the handles of a heavy platter.

"Why is that funny?" Caitir narrowed her eyes. "It wasn't a compliment."

"I didn't think it was," he answered. Slowly, he removed the meat from the oven and slid it onto the worktable to cool. "But I don't feel insulted. I didn't expect any better from you."

Caitir straightened. His words stung, and for a moment, she considered storming out again, like she had the day before. Instead, she fixed a hard gaze on him, which he returned without flinching. A long moment passed between them, the tension building until Caitir thought she might scream. But she considered her next words carefully.

"I'll say what I please," she said haughtily.

"Oh, no doubt." Kenji cracked a grin, which infuriated her all the more. "Perhaps, in time, you'll please to say kind things."

Caitir could engage this commoner in another verbal sparring match, or she could use her time more wisely. She glared at him, and dark magic crackled against the skin of her palms. For a moment, she considered burning up his precious roast duck, but his meals were infinitely more valuable than the momentary satisfaction of making him squirm.

"I'm wasting my time here," she said, snatching the half-eaten pastry from the table. "There's a throne waiting for me."

CHAPTER 17

LIRA

Rodhlan Ridge

Lira was stoking the fire in Skelly's hearth at midmorning when Talfryn burst through the front door, cheeks pink and eyes alight. She dropped the poker and cried out, rushing across the kitchen to catch her brother in a tight embrace. Ellwyn was right on his heels, and Lira moved to her next.

"Let me look at you." Her cousin took Lira's face in her hands and appraised her, strands of coppery hair falling down over one green eye. "By the mountain peaks, I'm so glad you're safe."

"Where is everyone?" Lira asked, gripping Ellwyn's arms. She turned to Talfryn. "How's Oda?"

"Completely healed already," her brother answered, ransacking the cupboard for something to eat. He withdrew some of the crusty bread Nevala had brought to go with their stew and tore a chunk off the loaf. "She's demanding news of you and Aidryn."

"D'you want to know who else is demanding?" Ellwyn said

in her sing-song lilt. "Skelly. And Thorne Beran. Poor Lord Irem; he's been sitting in the corner of that wagon biting his tongue for the better part of two days. I told him he'd have a room to himself when we arrived, but with Clan Tarlach up here, I may have to rescind the offer."

"Wait, Skelly and Thorne are coming? And Lord Irem?" Lira said in surprise.

"Talfryn met our traveling party on the way up the mountain," Ellwyn answered. "Everyone will be here soon."

Talfryn swiped Lira's mug and took a swig of the tea dregs she hadn't bothered to finish. "Ellwyn insisted on leaving them behind so she could be the first to bring the news."

All morning, Lira had felt on edge. Her fears from the night before had surged into her mind before she'd had a chance to wake properly. The unexpected visit had taken her mind off her grating restlessness, if only for a moment. She'd truly been happy to see Talfryn and Ellwyn. But now, her brother was adding to her frustration.

She sighed, exasperated, and reached for her cup. "I could have made you some tea of your own."

Her brother's brows rose, but he tipped his head back anyway. When he'd emptied the tea, he placed it in Lira's upturned hand. "Why, when yours was right there? Anyway, it was cold."

She huffed and turned her back to him, pouring more hot water into the mug. Then, she took two more mugs from the cupboard, setting them on the worktable with a loud clatter. Ellwyn and Talfryn were quiet as Lira steeped more tea.

Her cousin backed toward the cottage door. "I'm going to see about the traveling party's progress."

"At least stay for tea," Lira said, motioning toward one of the mugs. Her cousin had never been discourteous, and it was unconscionable as to why she'd begin now. "I went to the trouble of making it for you."

Ellwyn gave her a pinched smile. "Maybe Talfryn would like two cups."

Lira bristled, but Talfryn cut her off.

"I would," he said with a quick nod. He and Ellwyn exchanged a meaningful glance, though Lira wasn't sure what it meant. "Very much."

"Then it's settled. I'll see you at the keep." With that, Ellwyn slipped out the door and across the meadow at an easy trot. The door banged shut behind her, and Lira jumped, startled.

Talfryn rounded on her. "What was that, just now?"

Lira blinked at him, incredulous. "What was what?"

"The tea," he said, waving his hand in the direction of the mugs she'd set out. "You've never reprimanded me for finishing your cup—not once. And you looked ready to pounce on Ellwyn."

"I—" Lira faltered, face growing hot. She didn't think she'd been unreasonable, but the way Talfryn framed it made her sound almost belligerent.

He moved closer and wrapped his arm around her shoulders. "Are you all right?"

Talfryn's proximity reminded her of the left arm he'd lost in Iathium after Eremon had died. He'd sworn fealty to Lira before the late Raní Macha and a courtyard teeming with hostile sentries and citizens. Lira's little brother—who had left home at sixteen to become a sentry—had given up everything to show his loyalty to her. And Ellwyn had made sacrifices of her own, most recently by assassinating her father, Gerallt.

Lira had repaid that loyalty by spitting thorns about tea.

Slowly, she began to shake her head. "I didn't intend to seem cross," she said, pulling her hair back so Talfryn could see the stitches in her scalp. "Nevala said my injury might cause me to feel angry."

"Ah." Talfryn gave her a squeeze. "Pain and grief make terrible bedfellows."

Just then, Aidryn burst through the front door, dark hair windblown and cheeks high with color. "They're here—oh, hello, Talfryn!"

"I brought that bay mare Lira stole from your sister." Talfryn tossed a stray curl from his eyes and gave Aidryn an impish grin.

"Senga," Lira said, perking up. "Aidryn, she's *from* Iteloria."

Aidryn made a noise that Lira could only have described as something between a squeak and a contented groan. Although Fannin and Edan were almost certainly purebred, there was little question of Senga's lineage, particularly since Caitir had said she was a gift from the rival nation. "Truly? Is she in the pasture?"

"I'll show her to you later." Talfryn's dimples deepened with his smile.

"By Nami, this means I can breed the Seanlaoch myself," Aidryn said on a breathy sigh. "I've always wanted a mare."

"It's a good thing you never gelded Fannin and Edan," Talfryn replied with a laugh. "They're going to be stupid for Senga, you know."

"I'll have to give the boys a talk before we introduce her," Aidryn grumbled. He winked at Lira. "Commanding randy stallions is a special talent of mine."

"I wouldn't brag too loudly about that," said Talfryn. "Out of context, it sounds terrible."

"What?" Aidryn exclaimed in mock offense. "You've seen how well-behaved they are."

Lira burst out laughing, linking her arm with Aidryn's. The three left the cottage together, heading in the direction of the keep. Aidryn kept craning his neck to get a glimpse of Senga, coaxing smiles from Lira whenever he did so. He'd always been able to lift the darkness when it descended around her, and she loved him for it. She reached for his hand and laced their fingers together, tethering herself to the joy he exuded.

When they crested the hill that led to the main mountain road, Thorne's traveling party finally came into view. The large warrior walked alongside his bear, Yrsa, far ahead of the caravan. His blond hair was unbound and tumbled over his shoulders, his beard more unkempt than when she'd seen him last.

Thorne's warm amber eyes met Lira's, and he rushed toward her, closing the distance between them in what seemed like a few strides. Lira broke from Aidryn and trotted toward Thorne, throwing herself into his arms.

"*Sjeovi*," she cried.

He enveloped her in a warm embrace, bending low to level with her. "You survived." Pulling back, he surveyed her, brushing a curl out of her face and cupping her cheek with one of his large hands. "Talfryn told me what he knew."

Lira hooked her hands over his forearms and held his gaze. "Good. Then we understand one another already."

"I understand that you disobeyed orders," he said, voice gruff. He released her face and crossed his arms. "Where is the boy-king?"

"Iathium," Aidryn answered. Yrsa sidled up to him, leaning into his side, and he scratched behind one of her ears contentedly.

"That quickly?" Thorne asked. "When will we have an audience with him?"

With a sinking feeling, Lira realized his assumption. "He hasn't taken the throne back yet," she said in a low voice.

Thorne frowned. "Then what is he doing?"

Lira jerked her chin in the direction of Skelly's cottage. "Come with me. I'll explain everything."

"Not now," Thorne hedged. "We need a healer first."

"We have you," she said, puzzled.

"This is beyond my skill," he said, casting a furtive glance over his shoulder at the riders and wagons that approached. "It's your stepfather."

~

LIRA STOOD against the far wall of Nevala's chamber in the keep as Thorne and several of his men carefully laid Artur Beran on the bed. Her stepfather lay lifeless and gray, his once-muscular form now gaunt. A wave of weakness washed over her when she finally got a good look at him, and her knees suddenly felt as though they might give way.

"Oh, by Rhona..." Nevala groaned, pressing her hand against her mouth as she surveyed the overlord. "What happened to him?"

"Imprisonment at the Dome," Thorne answered. "Torture, illness, starvation—for too long."

"How did you manage to get him from Iathium's army?" Lira asked, her gaze fixed on the gruesome sight before her.

"We were allowed to take him," Thorne said. "They let us; there's no other explanation. It was too easy, and we picked off two of Gerallt's commanders while we were at it."

The healer went to work cleaning Artur's wounds. Thorne crossed the room to stand beside Lira and Aidryn, where he leaned against the wall.

"When we returned to the camp," Thorne continued quietly, "there were sentries from the Dome waiting to surrender. We gave them Gerallt's head to deliver to the city."

Lira kept her eyes trained on Thorne, afraid she might be ill if she watched what Nevala was doing. "You retrieved it from the estate?"

Thorne gave her a curt nod. "Yes. We went there looking for you first. We thought you were dead."

"What were the terms of surrender?" Aidryn whispered.

"Everyone returns to their territories," Thorne replied. "Iathium will show no further aggression toward the clans, and the fighting will end."

"Sounds like Caitir's putting her plan to work," Lira grumbled.

"No other terms for the clans to follow?" Aidryn pressed.

Thorne shook his head. "I think war is over as long as Eremon does his duty. The clans would agree."

From across the room, Artur groaned. A wave of nausea washed over Lira, and she pressed a hand to her mouth. Aidryn gripped her elbow. "Let's go. There's nothing more we can do here."

Lira led the men out of the room and down the hallway to Gerallt's old audience chamber, where she'd begged her uncle for asylum back in the spring. The air in the room was stale, as though it hadn't been used since then. Musty straw littered the floor, and Lira wrinkled her nose at the odor.

"We'll need to clean this place up," Aidryn muttered, his gaze raking from floor to ceiling.

"It'll do for privacy." Lira motioned toward the large chairs that sat near the back wall. "Skelly's probably back at the cottage by now."

She had caught a brief glimpse of her grandmother and Lord Irem in the back of one of the approaching wagons. In her haste to see to Artur's needs, she hadn't spoken to them.

Thorne was somber as Lira and Aidryn recounted the events of the past several days. His countenance dropped further when they explained what Eremon was doing in the city. He scowled, deep worry lines etching in his forehead.

"He shouldn't have wasted one day," the warrior said.

Lira sighed heavily and pressed her fingertips against her eyelids. Making excuses for Eremon would be fruitless. "I know."

"You will not want to hear this," Thorne ventured, "but you have the power to get Iathium under control. You need to use it."

Suddenly, Lira's blood was pounding in her ears. "I did use it," she answered. "I brought Eremon back."

His gaze flicked meaningfully to her hand. "I see he leaves his ring in your care, even now." She felt a fresh rush of rage at Thorne's knowing expression. "He must not intend to cooperate."

"For all I know, he could come here tonight and take it back," she said. Her thoughts raced, and she struggled to tame them. "I will not plot against him for the throne."

A smile ghosted the warrior's lips. "There is no plot, because you're his rightful heir."

"The city does love you," Aidryn mused.

She shot him a dirty glare. "Now that Eremon's back, I can't go near the throne." Heat rushed into her cheeks as she considered the implications. "The people associate me with him because of what happened in the spring. We'd be expected to rule together."

The color drained from Aidryn's face. "That's also true."

"As far as I'm concerned, this discussion is over, Thorne." Lira let the edge back into her voice and sat up straighter. She tried to ignore the wave of fear the swept over her as she added, "Eremon will do the right thing."

"We hope," she heard Aidryn say softly.

"You—" Thorne inhaled deeply, nostrils flaring. His gaze sharpened on Lira, and he leaned toward her abruptly. "Your magic smells different."

She wrinkled her nose, though she was grateful for a reprieve from the Eremon conversation. "How so?"

He and Aidryn exchanged a terse glance. Thorne extended his hand. "Will you show me exactly what happened with Fiadh?"

Mouth dry, Lira nodded and placed her palm in his. The witnessing rushed over them without warning, and when it was over, her vision clouded with a sickly green mist. She blinked, but the mist was stubborn, and it would not clear away.

It took her a long moment to realize that Aidryn was speaking to her, his voice distant. The familiar sound rushed in when he cupped her cheeks in his hands and knelt before her.

"Lira," he implored, "look at me."

Her vision rushed back into focus. Aidryn's expression was distraught, and there was a wild panic in his blue eyes.

"Are you all right?" He dipped close to press his forehead to hers. "You seemed lost in it for a moment."

She closed her eyes again, leaning into him. "I'm—"

A sudden spinning sensation stole her next words, and she pressed a hand to her temple, hissing with pain. It must have been her injury. Perhaps the witnessing had aggravated it somehow.

"Lira," Aidryn urged, "talk to me."

But the whirling had turned to a roaring inside her head, and she could not.

"We must get her to my father at Halgeir," Thorne said, his rich baritone cutting through the cacophony between Lira's ears. "Tonight."

CHAPTER 18
AIDRYN

Rodhlan Ridge

"What's happening?"

Aidryn followed Thorne into the great hall, then outside the keep. Lira had weakly insisted on walking, but the warrior had refused, hefting her into his arms and carrying her instead. She'd groaned and rested her head against his chest after that.

Thorne's voice was grim as he answered, "There's dark magic inside of her."

Lira whimpered. Horror surged through Aidryn. "You mean it didn't just injure her?"

"No. I think her birthright magic is being corrupted," Thorne said, "just like Eremon's. My father can slow it down."

Aidryn remembered the horror of watching Eremon's magic taking its final blow. The young Rí screaming in agony. His burning, black power ripping a gaping wound in the center of his chest.

"Your father couldn't stop Eremon from dying," Aidryn protested.

At the sight of Thorne's enraged expression, he regretted saying it aloud. "Nothing could have saved Eremon," Thorne said sharply. "That is what inheriting a power-hungry dynasty will get you."

Aidryn refrained from mentioning Skelly's own greed for Clan Mór's magic. No matter how any of them tried to frame it, she had also hoarded magic that wasn't rightfully hers. He wasn't sure where that left Lira, but the sinking feeling in his chest carried a foreboding he didn't want to examine.

He entered the cottage behind Thorne, who carried Lira straight to the bedchamber and ordered her to stay there. Then he and Aidryn readied Fannin, Senga, and Edan for the journey to Fortress Halgeir. Aidryn was inspecting the horses' shoes when Talfryn came bounding up to the fence.

"Aidryn," he called, "I need to speak with you."

The worry in his green eyes was as visceral as the dread in Aidryn's gut. He handed Fannin's reins to Talfryn, then led Senga and Edan out himself. Thorne tethered the horses while Aidryn followed Lira's brother a few paces away.

"What's wrong with her?" Talfryn asked.

Aidryn explained Thorne's theory, and Talfryn squeezed his eyes shut. "She was so angry over tea today, with no provocation. I've never seen someone channel their rage through a kettle the way she did. Everything down to the way she steeped the leaves—it was completely unlike her."

"It could still be from her head wound," Aidryn insisted, though doubt rose in the back of his mind.

"Yes, but..." Talfryn threw a glance over his shoulder. "I mean no offense, but she needs more eyes on her. Going with Thorne is really the best idea for now, because you'll keep making excuses for her. You don't want to think about the worst case."

Aidryn scowled, but Talfryn's words rang true. He inwardly cursed Lira's truth magic for tugging at the most inopportune times.

"So, you're to decide our next moves." Lira was squaring up against Thorne once again, fixing him with a hard glare. "Why?"

Aidryn emerged from the bedchamber, carrying her meager belongings. Thorne's towering height made the cottage's cramped interior painfully obvious. He'd folded himself onto a bench at Skelly's worktable, where he sipped a cup of tea. Lira's grandmother had yet to return to the cottage, and he assumed she must still be at the keep with Irem.

"I did not make this decision alone." Thorne set the mug down. "Tarlach agrees with me."

"What if I don't agree?" Lira said. "What if I would rather stay here in my ancestors' homeland than go back to Halgeir?"

Aidryn suppressed a snort. Lira had never argued in favor of staying in Rodhlan Ridge, for any period of time. They'd spent almost the entire summer at Fortress Halgeir this past year.

"We can either go to my father now, or you can wait to see what this dark magic does to you," Thorne barked.

"Who's to say I won't heal on my own?" Lira pressed. "We haven't given it enough time."

Thorne's jaw tightened. "Silira, I'm afraid." His voice was dangerously low. "Look me in the eye and tell me when you have seen me fear *anything*."

Aidryn watched their exchange, biting his lip to keep silent. Watched Thorne's steady gaze on his wife. Watched Lira's chin tremble almost imperceptibly when she answered, "I can't."

The warrior leaned nearer. "And you're going to stand there and tell me you aren't afraid?"

Lira dropped her gaze sheepishly.

Thorne grunted. "All right. I'll give orders to my men, and we'll go." The warrior stood but paused, looking as though he wanted to say something but wasn't sure how. "I want you to both limit the use of your magic for now. Silira, under no circumstances should you *misuse* yours. Who knows what the dark magic will do to the Binding—or through it."

She made a panicked sound, but Aidryn sat at the worktable across from Thorne and squared with him. "How could it have anything to do with the Binding?"

"You share magic." Thorne straightened and crossed his arms. "When Silira came to us at the war camp, half dead, her magic was nearly gone. She couldn't access it. So, what do you think dark magic would do?"

"That doesn't mean my use of power would affect Aidryn's," Lira insisted.

But Aidryn suddenly felt dizzy. "Yes, it does."

Lira and Thorne focused their attention on him. She slid onto the bench beside Aidryn, propping her elbow on the table and turning to face him. "What do you mean?"

"I put the pieces together yesterday—after you tampered with your power to learn Caitir's strategy, I couldn't access mine. Clan Tarlach imprisoned me at Va'hesk because I couldn't prove I was Key Keeper."

Lira's eyes widened, her voice tinged with panic. "Why didn't you tell me?"

"There has been little time to do so," Aidryn shot back. Suddenly, another realization washed over him. He rubbed a hand over his face, taking a steadying breath as Thorne and Lira looked on.

When I searched Lira's memories…

Thorne peered at him over the rim of his cup. "What is it, Tarlach?"

"When I arrived back here, you were gone, Lira." Aidryn heaved a shaky sigh. His words caught in his throat as he forced them out. "I was desperate—afraid you might've died. I tampered with your magic to learn what had happened."

"And there were consequences," Thorne filled in.

"Yes," he said, the words coming out breathy and wrong. "I went blind."

Lira pressed a hand to her mouth with a sharp cry. "Blind? For how long?"

"Only a few moments. It was terrifying."

She squeezed his hand, hard. "I don't think I felt any of that."

Aidryn shook his head. "You probably wouldn't have known. Did you use your magic on the journey back here?"

"No," Lira answered. "I didn't have the energy."

"Then we have to assume it affected you somehow," Aidryn said. He pressed his lips together, then looked to Thorne.

"No more protests, *sjeinga*," Thorne said. "Meet me in one hour."

"What about Artur?" Lira pulled her long mass of curls over one shoulder, twirling the end of one around her finger.

"We'll bring my father to him." Thorne crossed the room in a few long strides and pulled the door open. "One hour. Avoid using your magic at all costs."

With that, he was gone, and suddenly Lira was in Aidryn's arms, pressing her head to his shoulder. He gathered her closer, drinking in the faint scent of roses that had always clung to her hair.

"Blind, Aidryn?" She pressed a warm kiss to the side of his neck, then drew back to cup his face in her hands. Turmoil shone in her eyes. "Rhona, help us!"

"I'm fine—you see," he soothed. "It was only for a moment, and then it was over. But that's why we need Ljós."

Her shoulders tensed, and she wrapped her arms around herself, averting her gaze. "I would never forgive myself if I hurt you."

Aidryn shoved his rising terror down and took her hand. "You won't, because we're going to fix this." As the words left his mouth, though, a shard of uncertainty pierced him.

"I have the power of an entire clan in my veins," she said in a voice so low that it was almost unintelligible. "What if I've corrupted it all? Just another fear to add to everything else."

"Hush, now," Aidryn soothed. "There will be a solution."

The cottage door swung open and Eremon strode in, his silver gaze flicking between Aidryn and Lira. "What's going on?" he said, his movements as slow as gliding as he joined them in the kitchen. "What's the Beran warlord doing here?"

"Artur is near death," Aidryn answered. "He's being tended to in the keep."

Eremon's expression darkened, but he bowed his head and placed a hand over his heart. "I'm sorry to hear that. Berav be with him."

Aidryn straightened. He had never heard the name of Clan Beran's deity invoked, not even during the months he and Lira had lived at Fortress Halgeir. The few times he'd run across texts that addressed the clan's religion, he'd gotten the impression they had long since abandoned observing it.

He felt the room's energy shift when Eremon flexed his fingers and studied them more closely. "What else is going on?"

"It's my magic," Lira answered quietly, fidgeting with one of her sleeves. "Thorne says it smells corrupted."

The corner of Eremon's mouth twitched up. "Magic-sniffing? Now that's a lost art."

"Of all the times to jest, this isn't one of them." Aidryn jerked his head toward the table. "Sit."

The Rí pressed his lips into a thin line and nodded. He listened in grim silence as Lira and Aidryn described what was happening with their magic, particularly through the Binding. When they were finished, he held out an upturned palm. "May I see the ring?"

Lira grasped the golden band. For a moment, she looked hesitant to remove it. Aidryn felt himself lean in her direction, suddenly fearful she might refuse. He held his breath until she finally slipped it off and dropped it into Eremon's hand.

He held the stone up, scrutinizing it in the sunlight that poured in through the cottage window. "When I repaired this, I couldn't extend any of its protection to you, Aidryn. Its resonance was somehow affected by Fiadh's magic."

When the Binding had first taken hold of Lira and Aidryn, only a small amount of the ring's protective power had extended to Aidryn. But it had kept him alive.

"Thorne is afraid for us to use our power," Lira said.

Eremon closed his eyes for a moment and shook his head before he continued. "Did he forget that suppressing magic will make it turn on you?"

A conflicted expression crossed Lira's face, and she shrugged halfheartedly. "What am I supposed to do? I can't hurt Aidryn."

"It shouldn't hurt Aidryn for you to simply discharge your power," Eremon said. "That's irrational."

Lira shot him a dark glare, but Aidryn cut in, "He's right. We have to keep using our magic."

Her brown eyes looked wild. "But—"

Eremon reached across the table and lay a steadying hand on hers. She snapped her face in his direction, and the tension dropped from her shoulders. Aidryn couldn't help feeling a spark of ire at the contact.

"Why don't we try this?" Eremon's voice took on the smooth, calming tone Aidryn had heard him adopt during tense interactions in the past. "I can try infusing my protective magic into the Binding, just like it was before."

Lira rocked back a bit, furrowing her brow as she withdrew her hand. "Through the ring?"

Eremon pushed several loose strands of hair away from his face. "No, leave the ring out of it this time. I'll imbue the Binding itself. Then your protection won't depend on a physical object that can be damaged or broken."

"I think it makes sense," Lira ventured.

She closed her eyes for a moment, lashes fluttering. Aidryn could feel the tug of her magic along the Binding before she said, "There's nothing in the histories for guidance, but I don't think we have anything to lose."

"Then let's try," Aidryn urged.

They followed Eremon outside into a wide expanse of soft meadow grass near the tree line. Lira and Aidryn sat facing each other, and Eremon dropped to his knees beside them.

"I'll need to access the Binding," he said, summoning an orb of bright cobalt magic between his palms. He let it flow from one hand to the other, his fingers playing softly over the power.

Lira nodded. "Aidryn, we'll need to summon it the way we did at Halgeir."

She moved closer to Aidryn and lifted her hands, lacing her fingers together with his. A jolt passed between them at the contact, just as it always did, and he fought the urge to haul her into his arms and kiss her. Eremon raised a hand and laid it lightly over their joined ones.

Aidryn eyed Eremon warily, a sudden hesitance flooding him. "You sure you know what you're doing?"

Eremon gave him a shallow nod. "Call your magic together."

"But—" Aidryn cut in.

"It's all right, Aidryn," Lira said, her voice soothing. "Intent, remember?" She took a steadying breath. "I intend for our birthright powers to be protected from any dark magic that might threaten them."

Aidryn closed his eyes for a moment, willing the same intention. He felt their powers mingling as they had back at Halgeir, and he let himself sink into the sensation.

Suddenly, Lira's grip tightened on his fingers, and he felt a rush of darkly familiar magic skittering across the Binding, burning and tearing at his insides. He opened his eyes to see Lira's go from that familiar, bright emerald glow to something else entirely—sickly green tinged with sparks of black, like the sky before a cyclone.

Eremon uttered something in Itelos, and his cobalt power flared, instantly soothing the burn of the dark magic and spreading across the Binding. Aidryn released a shuddering breath as Eremon's magic flared, then settled between him and Lira, coating every strand of their power. Finally, the surge quieted, and Eremon released them, eyes filled with something akin to terror. When he did, Aidryn could see that Lira was trembling.

"What was that?" she cried.

"Let me see you," Aidryn drew nearer to her, pressing his palm to her cheek. "Are you all right?"

Tears gathered in her eyes. He pulled her to her feet, but there was a strange weight to her movements he'd never felt before.

"What just happened?" she repeated, leaning heavily into Aidryn's touch.

"I'm sorry," Eremon said. "I shouldn't have suggested—"

"Is it worse now?" Aidryn fought to keep his voice steady. "Did you just make this worse?"

"I protected your Binding," he said. "I know I succeeded in that."

"I felt that. But something else happened—her *eyes*. The

color!" Aidryn pressed a hand to the small of Lira's back and held her closer. He couldn't get her close *enough*. Couldn't shield her as he wanted to. "What did you see, Lira?"

"It was like a nightmarish witnessing," Lira said, her body trembling, "all green haze and a sharp pain behind my eyes."

"I—I let you call your own powers before I summoned mine," Eremon stammered. "Perhaps we did it all backward."

"And you didn't think of that before?" Aidryn shouted.

Now Eremon raised his voice. "I'm doing my level best, Tarlach! Mortal *gods*!"

Lira, who had grown still and tense in Aidryn's arms, broke away and turned on Eremon. "Your best got you killed."

She fixed a hard gaze on the Rí, and his silver eyes widened. He took a slow step backward as she prowled toward him, fists clenched. "Your best shattered with the ring you coerced me into accepting."

Eremon straightened, blinking incredulously. "Lira, what's the matter with you?"

Lira's entire body buzzed with rage. Aidryn could feel it from where he stood. Goosebumps pebbled his skin, and a chill snaked through him.

"Lira, stop," he said, his tone a warning.

She ignored him, focusing entirely on Eremon instead. "Your best got me thrown into the dungeon. It got me a Binding I never wanted."

The world slowed as the words left her lips. They felt like a gut punch, and for a moment, Aidryn couldn't breathe. He wanted to protest. Wanted desperately to hear her say she hadn't meant it.

But it was true; she hadn't wanted the Binding. That didn't mean she'd never wanted Aidryn.

Surely, it didn't mean that.

Lira's nostrils flared, her eyes so hard they were nearly

unrecognizable. Through clenched teeth, she said, "Your best ruined everything."

He was rooted where he stood, panic coursing through him so fiercely that he barely registered what Lira was doing with her hands. Her fingers moved, curling into fists before splaying wide. Aidryn snapped back into reality when the first sparks of black lightning danced between her fingertips, and she hurled a surge of dark magic toward Eremon.

CHAPTER 19

EREMON

Rodhlan Ridge

E remon threw a shield of bright cobalt magic between himself and Lira. Her dark power pummeled against his, but the immortal magic absorbed it easily, leaving nothing but weak sparks in its wake.

Lira froze, panting, eyes wild. She lifted bloodied hands and stared down at them in horror, then turned to face Aidryn, who had gone pale. Eremon thought he might lose his footing, as well. He let his eyelids drift closed as Lira's words tore through him once again.

Your best ruined everything.

Of all the things he'd been told in either of his lives, this cut him to the core like nothing ever had. Lira's words seared into his bones. His chest ached, an eerie echo of the magic that had torn him apart when he died.

When he opened his eyes again, Lira's focus was solely on Aidryn. They were whispering breathlessly, her fists gripping his tunic, his lips brushing against her ear as he pressed a steadying hand to her back.

Eremon took a step backward, careful to make no sound. Then another. If he could just shift, just get out of here—

"What happened?" a deep baritone voice demanded.

He whirled to see Thorne Beran stalking toward them from around the side of the cottage, amber eyes alight with panic. Thorne's gaze bored into Eremon, and for a moment, Eremon thought they might come to blows. But Thorne shifted focus abruptly, veering toward Lira instead.

"Silira," Thorne said, voice gruff as he pressed a large hand to her shoulder. He lowered his tone, murmuring to her, pausing to listen as she and Aidryn answered his questions. His expression grew darker by the minute. Eremon steeled himself against whatever might come next.

Suddenly, Thorne whirled. "Tell me exactly what you did to Silira's magic."

"You will not make demands of me, Beran," Eremon said coolly. He'd never come face-to-face with Thorne before, but already, he felt an overwhelming surge of disdain toward the brute. "I protected their Binding and the anointed powers."

Thorne's shoulders bunched as he clenched his fists. "You used magic to protect magic? Why not protect *them*?"

Lira and Aidryn seemed to realize the error at the same moment Eremon did. They exchanged a terse glance, and Eremon went rigid. Thorne's hard stare seared him to the core.

No, no, no, no...

But now wasn't the time to appear weak.

"I don't know what you're talking about," Eremon said sharply. "I protected the Binding, which should, in turn, protect them."

Thorne's cheeks grew red. "Should? Silira is overrun with dark magic," he growled. "Do I truly know more about what's happened than the one who inflicted it?"

Eremon's magic thrummed in his palms, begging for release. He held Thorne's gaze, challenging. The Beran warrior might try to leverage his brute strength, but he'd be no match for this infinite power. If Eremon untethered his magic, he could—

"What about Aidryn?" Lira's eyes grew wider. Her voice cut through Eremon's thoughts. Thorne broke from his staring match with Eremon to focus on her. "Does he have dark magic now?"

Aidryn cut in before Eremon could speak, "No."

"He's fine," Thorne said with a glower. "It's all within you, Silira—unchecked. Adding Eremon's power to the Binding drove it away from the magic and into your body. We'll just have to see how long it takes for the darkness to start eating away at the magic again."

Eremon's stomach dropped, and he looked to Lira, who had finally turned her attention to him again. Grief twisted her lovely features. Aidryn looked as though he might collapse.

"My power is more potent now," Eremon insisted. "The dark magic won't hurt it."

"Eremon, you're not thinking," Aidryn said, voice tinged with distress. Eremon bristled as he continued. "Without the magic as a focal point, the dark power will turn on *her*."

The full weight of Aidryn's words crashed into Eremon. He took a step back, shaking his head. After everything he'd done to protect Lira, she was more endangered than ever—at his hands.

"No." He blinked rapidly, as though he could clear the terrible scene from his line of sight for good. "No. I'm going to fix this."

"We won't waste any more time here, boy-king," Thorne said, reaching for Lira's injured hands. He cast a golden healing orb over her skin, and the blisters vanished. "We ride for Halgeir."

Aidryn cast a pained look at Eremon before trudging

toward the pasture. Lira's eyes filled with tears. Yet none spilled down her cheeks, and a moment later, she appeared to have suppressed them. She wrapped her arms around her middle, gripping her sides.

"Eremon," she said, though his name caught in her throat.

Your best ruined everything. He shut his eyes against her truth.

"I spoke harshly, Eremon. Forgive me," she said weakly. When he opened his eyes, her hand was extended toward him. He did not take it.

"Get her to your father, Thorne," Eremon said listlessly. "Quickly."

Lira's eyes clouded with sorrow and fear at the rejection, but Eremon could not bring himself to regret it.

"And you take your throne back," Thorne growled, "or Clan Beran will take it in Lira's name."

"Thorne, you will *not*." Lira's sharp reprimand reverberated through Eremon. Gratitude mingled with his anger, fear, and shame—a riot of emotions that grappled for dominance within him. "Eremon knows what must be done."

Eremon's jaw ticked. His building fury won out, setting him more keenly on edge as it overtook him. "Keep your clan out of Iathium, Beran." He kept his gaze trained on Lira as he said, "I'll do the right thing, Lira."

Thorne's deep, commanding tone held a promise that turned Eremon's stomach. "You had better, sovereign of clans."

Eremon pressed his lips together and nodded to the warrior. "I swear it." He took another step back.

"What about the ring?" Throne asked, jerking his chin in Lira's direction. "You'll need that."

Lira reached for the ring as though to remove it, but Eremon held up a hand to stay her.

"She needs whatever protection it can still offer her." At

Thorne's enraged expression, he added, "I'll come back for it; I swear."

He didn't give either of them time to speak again before he shifted into falcon form and fled the mountain range.

CHAPTER 20

LIRA

Rodhlan Ridge

Lira felt numb as Aidryn handed Edan's reins to Thorne. Yrsa stood at his side expectantly, the sun catching the flecks of gold in her fur. He placed a large, steady hand on her back and murmured something in her ear. The bear grunted and ambled toward the southern forest. There would be plenty of fruit in the woods and fish in the mountain streams to keep her well-fed while they were away.

Thorne mounted Edan, settling into the saddle and wordlessly steering his horse toward the mountain path. Lira lingered beside Senga as they watched him go, stroking the mare's mane.

Aidryn fussed with Senga's saddle while Fannin grazed at their side. Lira could feel the unspoken words that hung between them, a building pressure that begged for release. Her words to Eremon had been the harshest edge of truth, and though she'd felt remorse for her blunt delivery, she couldn't bring herself to take them back.

Still, she'd wounded Aidryn. His warring emotions were as evident as her own, his silence louder than if he'd spoken.

"What I said about the Binding," she ventured as he worked. He stilled, hands lingering over Senga's saddle, and turned his head toward Lira to listen, though he didn't look directly at her. "It was directed toward the arranged marriage aspect, not you."

He shrugged, going back to his work. "No one could blame you for that. You never wanted the choice made for you."

Lira caught the sleeve of his tunic, and he paused, finally facing her fully. He studied her face, his expression pained. Tentatively, she let her fingers play over the laces at his collar, then cupped the back of his neck. His skin was warm against hers, and this close, she caught the familiar springtime scent of him. He closed his eyes.

"I couldn't have asked for a better person to be bound to," she said. "If it had to happen this way, I'm glad it was you. I need you to know that."

Aidryn leaned forward and placed a soft kiss on her forehead. "I do."

She coaxed him down for a brief kiss, bracing her other hand on his waist to press their bodies close. Aidryn's fingertips grazed her cheeks before he gently broke away.

"We have to go." He pulled her into an embrace and whispered, "Everything's going to be all right."

She tried to ignore the sinking feeling in her gut. "I hope so."

They mounted Senga and Fannin, easing the horses into a trot. She'd left a note for Skelly back at the cottage, briefly explaining that they would ride to Halgeir and bring the healer back for Artur. There was no need to detail their other reasons for leaving without saying goodbye.

It was an unseasonably warm day in the valley, and the sun beat down on Lira as they headed for the main road that led down the mountainside. Fear had already rooted itself deep within her, but she took a steadying breath and willed herself not to dwell on it. If she let herself sink into despair, she might never emerge.

She and Aidryn led Thorne to Acton's Cove, the horses picking their way carefully down the rocky trail. Once they'd reached the cove, they let the horses canter toward the meadowlands. Aidryn signaled them to halt as they emerged once again into the afternoon sun, the wide sprawl of Rodhlan's grassy wilderness ahead of them.

"Have you ever ridden the Seanlaoch?" Aidryn turned in his saddle to look at Thorne, who shook his head. "Then you'll want to hold on. Brace before I use the incantation."

A wary Thorne adjusted his seating in Edan's saddle. Lira noticed his knuckles go white around the reins and suppressed a smile. Thorne hadn't adapted well to travel by *turas*; she hoped his experience with the Itelorian stallion would be easier for him.

"They're incredibly swift, Thorne," she warned, patting the side of Senga's neck. "You can't prepare for how it's going to feel."

Thorne smiled, his lips tight. "Then there's no reason to delay."

CHAPTER 21
CAITIR

Dome

The sentries beat out a metallic rhythm as they returned to Iathium, marching in formation along the cobblestone streets. They shouted in unison and beat their shields as they moved, their words unintelligible. Caitir strained to understand them, but they were still a mile from the Dome.

From her vantage point in the western tower, she could see all the way to the city gates. City-dwellers emerged from their homes and shops, lining the streets in eerie silence to greet the army's return. Aeron stood behind her, surveying the scene over her shoulder.

"You should've been down there," Caitir mused, staring toward the city's gate. "Why didn't you go with Deghan?"

She had asked Aeron before, but he'd evaded the question. Behind her, she felt him tense.

"A higher duty called," he finally answered. "Forgive me; after what happened in the garden with Árchú, I couldn't leave your side to meddle in lesser affairs."

"I fainted; that was hardly worthy of disobedience," Caitir said, waving him off and turning back to face the window. She ran her fingertips over the fine marble sill, squinting into the distance. "How does the Dome welcome returning forces home? I don't know the protocol."

In Caitir's lifetime, the sentries had never been sent outside Iathium on such a campaign.

"The remaining sentries are to stand at attention by the courtyard gate, as well as along the pathway back to the barracks and the training grounds," Aeron answered. "They will honor the dead, if any have fallen. Normally, the Rí would greet them and observe the proceedings."

Caitir tilted her head, eyeing him over her shoulder. "And the Raní?"

Aeron clasped his hands behind his back. "Not customary."

She gave a defiant little huff. "Macha interacted with the sentries."

"She was unusual—at least, according to the older fighters," Aeron said. "The chatter was that she stepped into Corlan's role to get between Eremon and the sentries."

"Not surprising." Caitir would have done the same.

"That's how Faolan played double agent, you know," Aeron ventured, taking a step closer. "He got close to Macha; he was quite diverting, if you take my meaning."

Now, he was a hair's breadth from Caitir, and she could feel the warmth emanating from his body. She felt herself go rigid at his proximity. The hairs on her arms stood on end, and a crawling sensation swept up her spine and into her hairline. It took every ounce of willpower to keep herself from squirming.

Eyes open. Back straight, she commanded herself. *This is not Gerallt.*

"Is that so?" Caitir forced herself to relax on an exhale, dropping her shoulders and moving to the side.

She pivoted so that she was facing Aeron again, whose dark

eyes were warm with desire when they met hers. Her stomach knotted.

It had been no secret that Aeron had admired her for years. Aidryn had teased her about it and even encouraged a match at one time. Her brother had hoped to disrupt Aila's plans for a noble arranged marriage.

"There was talk that they were lovers." Aeron flashed her a conspiratorial grin. "I don't know if it was true, but she always did seem strangely affectionate toward him."

"Macha had no lovers." Caitir let an edge creep into her tone as she spoke. She willed her gaze to harden. "If she had, Mother and I would have been the first to know."

A laugh burst from Aeron. "Were either of you in her rooms at night, monitoring the passageways? Rulers take all sorts of secret lovers, both common and noble. They're under such pressure all day." He lowered his head and canted his body toward hers, his voice dropping to a hush. "I'd argue they're most deserving of pleasure at night."

Caitir recoiled, her heart racing. She broke into a sweat, suppressing the ragged breaths that rose in her chest. Her eyes flicked to the stairwell that led downward. With a sinking feeling, she realized he was standing between her and the only exit.

Breathe. Think. She took a slow inhale, willing her thoughts to slow. *Make him move.*

She willed her expression into impassivity, igniting an orb of dark magic in her palm. "Distraction is the last thing a ruler needs."

Aeron drew away, his back hitting the wall as he gave her a wide berth. She smiled down at the popping, flickering power, ignoring the jolt of pain it sent skittering along her skin. Caitir stepped onto the spiral staircase, grasping the rail as she began the trek downward.

"Follow me down to the courtyard," she said over her shoulder. "I'll meet the sentries myself."

"GERALLT THE USURPER IS DEAD!"

Now, Caitir understood the sentries' chant perfectly. She stood at the Dome's entrance, flanked by Aeron and Deghan, both in full armor. Fiadh stood to the side in a black doublet and a flowing skirt, swords sheathed on each hip. Her dark hair hung loose, whipping around her face in the afternoon wind.

"So much for containing the news," Fiadh muttered.

Caitir rolled her eyes. She had wound her golden hair into coils that encircled her head, locks falling in a cascade over her shoulders and down her back. This would be her first chance to send a message to the people. She only hoped they could read her signals.

One of her father's most memorable lessons resounded in her mind: *Everything is a symbol, Caitir.*

She vividly remembered the day he'd said it. Caitir had been sitting at table with her parents one evening—a quiet dinner, just the three of them. She had been ten or eleven at the time and had sat in rapt attention as Emyr had described life in the Dome.

Aila had sat in silence, nodding sagely. It had been one of the only times she'd allowed her husband to speak to Caitir without commandeering the discussion.

"Among nobility, everything—from the colors you wear and the words you use, to the way you tilt your head or raise your chalice—is symbolism, a secret language. The highest nobles understand its meaning and nuance."

There was a childlike wonder in Emyr's voice, a sparkle in his eyes that had made Caitir's heart leap. "We navigate this life with decorum and turn of phrase, all the while sending signals to one another through the folding of a napkin or the subtle clink of silverware against a plate or glass. We learn to speak in veiled messages to survive, and if you want to survive in this world, then the language of symbols is the first thing you must master."

Her father had looked pleased with himself when Aila gave him a rare, genuine smile. He'd leaned nearer to Caitir and tweaked her nose. "And you must remember that this is a language commoners cannot understand. Not even working nobility. No, these secrets are reserved for only the worthiest among us, and they must be preserved for all time."

Though Caitir had tucked his words away, she'd always disagreed with his assessment of commoners. She had Aidryn, Aeron, and Faolan to thank for that, with all their quiet mockery of the elite over the years. Caitir believed the people understood far more than nobility gave them credit for, and she would test her theory today.

Caitir moved away from the Dome's glass exterior, signaling for Fiadh and the sentries to follow. She moved across the courtyard toward the gate, where the army was fast approaching. And from the way her presence snagged the people's attention—and the attention of the sentries on the front lines—she knew her instincts had been right.

Four of the sentries carried a large chest between them, one at each corner. They halted before the locked courtyard gate. The sentries deposited the chest on the ground and stood at attention. Caitir pressed a palm to her belly for a moment, gaze flicking from one sentry to the next.

"I welcome you back to our city," she said, squaring her shoulders and raising her chin.

"A welcome is not yours to extend," one of the sentries answered through the gate. He had dark hair and spoke with the thick brogue of the southern mountains. "We return with the head of Gerallt the Usurper and demand that his wife Aila meet us here at the gates."

Aeron straightened beside her, spear in hand.

"Aila has departed Rodhlan," Caitir answered, keeping her

voice steady. "I cannot say when she will return, but perhaps you'd like to wait there until she does."

When the sentry spat at her, she was grateful they'd remained a spear's distance from the gate. The spittle landed on the ground an inch from her hem. She pursed her lips and *tsked* him.

"I thought Rí Eremon taught you manners," she said.

The sentry sneered at her. "Rí Eremon would have thrown the likes of you into the dungeon without a second thought."

"Ah, but he is nowhere to be found." As quickly as the words left her lips, they curdled in her stomach. "Gerallt may have been a usurper, but he *was* crowned, and I carry his child."

A roar rose from the fighters as word spread among the ranks and along the streets. The clamor was chaotic, but the sentries made no move to advance on the gates. Iathium's public servants had been well trained to make noise, but they weren't inclined to take any action that might risk their position or social status.

"Liar!" a female sentry with bronze skin and green eyes shouted.

"Cursed spawn!"

"Trampling on Eremon's wishes!"

"Kill her!"

"Let us through," another called.

"I'd rather see the gift you brought me," Caitir said, jerking her head toward the chest that still rested on the ground.

"A gift to ourselves," the first sentry said, kneeling to unlatch the chest. "A curse upon you."

Rather than lifting the lid and tilting the chest to present its contents to Caitir, he yanked it open and dumped it out. Gerallt's head rolled from the chest's bloodstained interior onto the cobblestones, coming to rest before the gate. It was half-rotted, eyes already plucked out, perhaps by some carnivorous creature in Rodhlan's wilderness. The sentries gave the head a wide berth, forming an arc around it.

Caitir pressed the back of her hand to her mouth and took a slow, steadying breath. She tore her gaze from Gerallt's head and locked eyes with the dark-haired sentry.

"Good," she said. "A blessing, then."

A slow smile crept across his lips. "Then open the gates, and let's celebrate together."

"I think not." Caitir nodded toward Deghan, then Aeron. "Have bread and water delivered to them through the gate. I won't let them starve, but I won't have my life and the child's threatened, either."

The people gathered in the streets began to jeer and shout, enraged. Deghan and Aeron exchanged a wary glance.

"As though no one holds a key to these gates!" the sentry shouted. "The moment you move, someone will let us in."

Caitir gave them a slow, knowing nod, then held out a palm. "The key, Aeron?"

Reluctantly, Aeron produced the gate key and lay it in her hand. She briefly closed her eyes, then made herself move. Despite the rotting head that churned her stomach and the hostile fighters on the other side of the gate, she closed the distance. Those sentries closest to the gate immediately moved away from her.

Raising a hand, she lay her palm on the lock as though to brace it, then raised the key. Magic welled within her—a dormant power she had never attempted to access. With a wicked grin in the sentries' direction, she called on Clan Tarlach's metalworking gift to melt the gate lock into a molten mess, its keyhole disappearing entirely.

"You were right, sentry," Caitir said, moving backward and out of reach of the angry fighters' grasp. "No one holds a key to *this*."

She realized her fatal mistake when the men and women

on the other side of the gate pushed it inward, and the melted lock began to give way. They put their backs into it, trampling Gerallt's head in the process. With a panicked cry, Caitir unleashed a wave of dark magic, electrifying the gate with her black lighting and sending the sentries scrambling backward, shouts of horror on their lips.

The dark-haired sentry with the brogue did not let go of the gate. In fact, it appeared he *could* not. Caitir watched in horror as his eyes widened, his body convulsing while the dark magic burned through him. It melted skin and sinew, devouring until there was nothing left but charred bones and blackened armor on the cobblestones.

She suppressed a retch and pointed to Gerallt's head. "Put it on a pike, in full view of the street. I want Iathium to know his death pleases me."

The nearest female sentry gave her a shallow nod, her shock evident even beneath her helmet.

Caitir took a few more steps back until she was shoulder-to-shoulder with Deghan and Aeron. Fiadh shot her a wary glance, but she didn't meet the other woman's eyes. She struggled to suppress the images of Gerallt's severed head and the burning sentry that had been embedded into her mind. The nausea she'd been battling was beginning to overtake her.

Still, she raised her voice. "Honor my authority, and we may have an accord. Only then will you enter the Dome and resume your lives here."

No one replied to her offer. Instead, a horrified silence had swept over the sentries and city-dwellers alike. She counted it a good sign that they were no longer attempting to storm the gate. For now, that would have to be good enough.

Caitir turned on her heel, intending to lead the way back to the Dome. But she paused, swaying, then vomited onto the courtyard pathway.

CHAPTER 22
EREMON

Dome

If Eremon had been in his human form, he might have burst into laughter. Caitir's pathetic, albeit shameless, display had almost been impressive. The fact that she'd managed to hold her retch for long enough to give a speech was the only part of the whole debacle that had held his attention.

He'd assumed the form of a silver cat, perched atop the courtyard wall and cloaked by the tall trees that grew alongside its interior. As the long minutes passed, he'd found himself more preoccupied by when she might finally vomit than what she was actually saying. In the end, Fiadh and the loyalist sentries had all but dragged Caitir toward the Dome's entrance.

Eremon considered his next moves. Now could be the perfect time to shift, show himself, and command the sentries' attention. But the time still wasn't right, and the sentries weren't his only concern. There were still townspeople lining the streets; one look at a resurrected Eremon, and they would riot.

All nonsense would break loose, and the sentries would have to contain it. The troops were already exhausted from being on the march, and their judgment might be impaired. If Eremon haphazardly reappeared to his people, the spectacle alone could lead to unintended harm.

No; right now, it was best to follow Aidryn's plan. Shift, get inside the Dome, and start gathering information and allies. *Quietly.*

The red-haired sentry opened the heavy glass door, and Eremon moved. He sprang from the wall and descended the tree, tearing across the courtyard as fast as his lithe feline body could carry him. Just before the door shut, he slipped inside, where he hid at the top of the archival staircase. Once Caitir and her co-conspirators had made their way down the corridor, he followed at a distance, keeping near to the walls as evening fell outside.

CHAPTER 23

CAITIR

Dome

"The show of strength was somewhat impressive until you ruined my boots." Aeron wrinkled his nose as he wiped the worn leather with a soiled cloth. "They still stink."

"Don't stand so close next time," Caitir shot back.

Fiadh crossed a leg and flicked her flowing black skirts out. The fabric settled over the shiny leather of her boots. "I'm just glad it wasn't me." She smirked at her cousin.

Caitir tipped her head against the high-backed chair. "You try being pregnant and having a head rolled at you. And not just that—there was the idiot hanging on the gate, too."

"Oh, that was Tarba," Aeron said, his voice laced with disdain.

"He fit your description well enough," Fiadh murmured. "I remember hearing you and Faolan go on about that one."

Deghan looked a bit green. He shook himself, the movement somewhere between a shiver and a whole-body shudder.

"Tarba." The name rolled off Caitir's tongue, the smell of

his charred flesh lingering in her nose. She sat up, biting down on her tongue in hopes of abating the nausea that accompanied the memory.

"As a unit, would you say the sentries share his sentiments?" she asked, tapping her fingertips against the chair's plush armrest.

"More likely now than before you burned him up," Deghan answered flatly.

Aeron shrugged, letting his boot drop to the floor before pitching the cloth aside. "Why do you ask?"

"Ideally, I would like to let them into the barracks," Caitir said, "but also avoid a mutiny."

Aeron laughed at that. Caitir glared at him. From her other side, Fiadh snorted.

Aila had deployed Eremon's loyalists into battle, effectively separating them from the sentries who had pledged fealty to Gerallt. As it stood, the sentries left on the Dome's grounds were sworn to protect Caitir. Out in the courtyard, she'd realized—almost too late—that she couldn't afford to simply let all the returning fighters flood in. She needed some way to weed out the dissenters and identify those who would align with her, and she could only hope that word of her victory had spread among the ranks in the meantime.

"How d'you expect to open the courtyard gate now?" Deghan asked in his mountain lilt. He ran a hand through his wavy red hair. "Did you think of that when you melted the lock?"

"I'm sure we'll figure something out," she answered. "Fiadh knows her way around metal."

Fiadh made an indignant noise in the back of her throat. "I didn't volunteer my services. You made a right bloody mess of that gate. My father would fall over dead if he laid eyes on it."

Deghan sat up abruptly and leaned forward, peering across the corridor. "Where did that cat come from?"

"What cat?" Fiadh craned her neck. "How did you see anything back there? It's nothing but shadow."

"The cook keeps cats," Caitir said with a wave of her hand. "Probably one of his."

"Speaking of the cook, someone needs to tell him he's expected to feed the three thousand sentries you locked out of the Dome," Aeron drawled.

"He'd have to feed them inside the Dome, too," Caitir replied.

"Bread and water should be simple enough," Fiadh said. "Easier than a feast."

An idea began to form in Caitir's mind, and a giddy feeling spread from her gut into her limbs. "Bread and water will do for now, but we need a feast. A feast *and* a treaty."

"There goes her last shred of rational thought," Aeron said with a guffaw. "It ran down the corridor behind Deghan's imaginary cat."

"It's more than you've contributed," Caitir said, her voice sharp. "As it stands, the only reason we're all sitting here together is that we all betrayed someone. I think we need a unifying cause to keep us honest."

Fiadh lay across her chair, a dark laugh bubbling from her before she sat back up and fixed Caitir with a piercing stare. "Are we to believe you were ever honest to start?"

"I was under duress," Caitir answered coolly.

"Honestly..." Aeron trailed off, propping his chin on a fist "With a mum like Aila, I think we could all agree on that."

Caitir felt a warm sensation creep over her skin. She had assumed the others would consider the statement a weak excuse. The pleasant, though tenuous, feeling of camaraderie only lasted until Fiadh added, "You're still a terrible person."

Deghan grunted in agreement.

A rush of rage blazed to life in Caitir's chest. She stood angrily, gathering her skirts. "Then I'm in excellent company."

Aeron sat up, pouting. "Where are you going?"

"To speak with the cook," Caitir said.

She moved to leave the sitting area, but Aeron rose as well, blocking her path. Warning bells sounded inside her head, drowning all coherent thought. For a moment, she froze, unable to move or speak. He held up a palm, which she shrank from.

But he wasn't raising his hand against her. Rather, he looked as though he wanted her to stay where she was. That would not do.

When she'd finally regained some semblance of composure, she glared up at him. "Let me pass!"

"At least tell us what's supposed to unify us," he implored. A sly smile crept across his lips, and he rested his other hand heavily on her waist. "You can't tease but not deliver."

His touch was hot through the layers of fabric. She whirled from him to break contact, glancing from Deghan to Fiadh, keenly aware of the moment Aeron stepped closer to her. A rush of uneasy energy crept up her spine at his proximity. "Do any of you even care?"

"A real idea's better than sitting here all night, bickering with you lot," Deghan said sulkily.

Fiadh gave a little jerk of her head and a dismissive shrug.

"I care." Aeron brushed his fingertips along her shoulder, then gently kneaded the muscle. "Tell us: What's this glorious cause you speak of?"

Tension built beneath his touch, followed by sharp pain. Caitir jerked away this time, willing her face into an angry scowl. "Executing Aila," she said, curling her fingers into fists to hide their trembling. Her companions didn't have to know that King La'hiran might do the honors for them. "Piking her head beside Gerallt's."

Aeron paled and took a step back. Despite the momentary

falter, he smiled. "Merciless, my lady." The smoothness in his voice grated on her.

"Indeed," Deghan said.

"You'll need sentries to watch the strait, then, for when she returns." Fiadh tapped her chin. "We should station fighters along the sea wall. Send them with plenty of provisions and move them away from the Dome. Have loyalists oversee their movements."

"Anyone who signs the treaty must agree to strip dissenters of their weapons," Caitir mused.

"Put the disarmed sentries on lookout duty," Aeron added.

Fiadh gave him a nod. "Continue to provide for their basic needs, regardless of their sentiment toward you, Caitir."

"Yes." She folded her arms, unbridling her racing thoughts.

Caitir had less than six weeks to secure the city and gain the sentries' trust. With any luck, when that time ran out, La'hiran would do them all a favor and execute Aila himself. But her mother was nothing if not wily, and Caitir would be stupid to pretend that Aila would never figure out how to make her way back here.

She would hold her knowledge close but prepare the city as though Aila could return any day. It would keep the sentries and her companions on their toes, freeing Caitir to make whatever moves were required to secure her place in the Dome. There was no way to hand over the magic Iteloria wanted, so Caitir would have to find a way to guarantee Rodhlan's safety instead.

One step at a time.

She thought of the archers who had followed Gerallt to Iathium, then defected. Aila had given them all dark magic, and they could imbue their arrows with it.

"Fiadh, see if you can gather a few scouts," Caitir said. "Offer them a reward for locating the archers, and one to the archers themselves."

Fiadh scoffed. "From whose coffers?"

Caitir waved her off. "Macha's jewelry should be worth something; I don't want it. There's a whole trove of it in her old chambers."

"And when that runs out?" Fiadh stood up and stepped before Caitir, placing her hands on her hips. "The treasurer won't comply with your demands. How will we get access to *anything*?"

"We'll get it," Caitir said, holding Fiadh's gaze. "We have no choice."

"KENJI?" Caitir called as she reached the bottom of the kitchen stairs.

"In here," the cook called from around the corner.

A gray cat swept past her ankles, rustling her skirts, and she froze, cursing under her breath as she steadied herself. The cat —a gray hue, with strange, iridescent eyes—looked up, its wide, round stare meeting hers. It held her gaze in the most unnerving way, and she shuddered, nudging it aside as she brushed past.

"Since when do your cats loiter by the stairs?" she said, entering the kitchen.

"I have one cat," Kenji replied from where he worked, nodding to the ratty orange beast crouched in the corner, "and he never goes near the staircase. His name is Jolly, and he's a great lazy oaf."

Jolly nudged his empty dinner bowl with his nose and yowled. Rather than showing interest in the prospect of food, the new cat plopped down on its haunches and blinked up at Caitir again.

"Well, it looks like you have two now." She eyed the furry new addition with disdain. Down here in the torchlight, the little monster's coat gleamed as though it were shot through with silver. "You're an eerie one," she breathed. "*Jox cheh*—scat, get out of here."

The cat held her gaze unwaveringly. Caitir drew in a sharp breath. The incantation had worked on Jolly. In fact, she'd never seen an animal resist Clan Tarlach's magic before.

Kenji laughed heartily as he emerged from behind the worktable. "You've met your match, my lady." He looked down at the cat, eyes widening. "I've never seen his kind before, that's certain."

"It's beautiful," she mused, though the disgust she felt at the sight of it hadn't abated. "Silver beast."

The cat blinked at her and flicked its tail before turning its back and wandering into the shadows. Caitir curled her lip. "Good riddance."

"Why do you hate cats so much?" Kenji grabbed a cheese-cloth to cover a mound of rising dough. "I'm truly interested."

"A favor for an answer," Caitir ventured, sitting on her stool.

"That depends on the size of the favor, weighed against my level of interest." Kenji grinned and winked a dark eye at her. His plump face and deep dimples made him look two decades younger than his apparent middle-age.

"It's a big favor."

"And I'm significantly interested."

Caitir fought the urge to smile at him. Instead, she said, "First, there's an order of business. The sentries have returned from the battlefield, and they need bread and water. I trust you can bake for them in short order?"

Kenji shook his head. "No. The sentries have their own kitchen down in the barracks. You'll have to take those orders to their cook."

She sighed. "Then that's settled, I suppose. As to the favor, I want to hold a feast for them in a week's time. Those who are loyal to me will enjoy the best fare Iathium has to offer."

The silver cat emerged from the shadows and leapt onto a stool a few feet away from Caitir's. She suppressed a groan as a low whistle left Kenji's lips. "For the sentries? Unheard of."

"Why?" she demanded.

"It's not customary," Kenji said. "We don't serve delicacies to the lower ranks, just the generals on occasion."

"Well, who's going to oppose the change now?"

The cook's expression relaxed. "No one, I suppose." He pointed his wooden spoon at her before he turned back to his work. "But just so you know, giving them one fine meal won't earn their loyalty. You need to give them a better life."

"How am I supposed to do that?" Caitir demanded, bristling.

"Have you ever asked yourself why the sentries left behind have stood down?" Kenji gave her a knowing look. "Magic will change how they fight wars forever, and they know it. If I were a sentry, I think I'd want to master any magic I might have inherited. Finding a way to teach them will cost you little coin but pay large dividends."

Caitir hadn't thought of that. She'd never considered that the sentries might have been fearful of the clan magic, not to mention the darkness. The troops had never been trained as a unit to fight with or defend against magic, either.

"So, we train them to wield power in battle," she said. "I could put Aeron in charge; he was with Clan Beran for long enough. He knows clan army tactics."

"That could work." Kenji propped an elbow on the worktable, plated a dinner roll, and pushed it toward her.

"What about the people? Ordinary citizens." She tore off a piece of the bread and chewed it slowly, savoring the buttery flavor.

"They'll need the same things," he answered, then lowered his voice. "Eremon wanted to restore magic and the true histories, you know."

Again, with the histories. Caitir looked at the gilded ceiling, taking in its ornate details with a sigh. The last thing she wanted to do was immortalize Lira further in the people's minds. Her former friend had long since been deemed a martyr.

"I'm sure there's another way that doesn't involve the archive." She accepted a cup of tea from the cook. "What do you say about the feast?"

Kenji grew silent. He covered another mound of dough before he said, "I would gladly make a spread for the sentries, but we're short on supplies and ingredients. My funds haven't been replenished in weeks beyond necessities. I would need additional coin to do what you're asking."

"What will it take to get the money?"

"The treasurer's favor," Kenji answered with a little shrug. "He is willing to give me what it takes to serve basic meals to court, these days. Anything extra was always approved by the Rí or Rań." He snorted. "You can imagine how that's been going."

"I could ask on your behalf."

Kenji laughed, and Caitir's face heated at the sound of it. "That's absurd. Tomis will never grant you an audience."

She tensed. "Not even if you came with me?"

The cook's laughter faded, his smile vanishing. "What?"

Caitir extended her hand toward him, palm upward, inviting him to clasp it. "Come with me. Vouch for me."

Kenji just looked down at her hand before meeting her eyes again. "Why would I do that?"

There was a deep disappointment in his gaze, like that of a father looking down on his wayward child. Her face flushed. She wanted to crawl beneath the table and never come out.

Caitir drew back. "I suppose I asked the wrong person."

She turned to go, body trembling as the weight of what she'd asked settled over her. All of this was insurmountable. If she couldn't even convince a lowly cook to join her, she would never win over the people.

"Caitir."

Kenji's voice froze her in place. She stopped walking but did not turn. Instead, she dropped her head. "Yes?"

"I didn't refuse outright." The cook propped his forearms on the worktable and leaned toward her. "I won't engage in treason, but I will protect Iathium from traitors. What is it that you mean to do, once you engage the sentries' favor?"

"Take the throne from my mother," Caitir answered.

"A usurper and a threat." He tilted his head. "What makes you any different?"

She bit down on the entire truth, suddenly realizing she no longer knew what it was. When she was younger, she'd desired riches, power, and adoration. But now...

Caitir raised her chin. "If you can't see a difference, then we are at an impasse."

Kenji laughed. "I can see you were groomed for a throne, and I'm sure that feels like part of who you are."

"It is entirely who I am."

Challenge flashed in his eyes. "Is it?"

She was poised to lash out, but she stopped herself as the realization swept over her. Instead, she pressed her lips together, struggling to hold his gaze. There was no choice; she must make a move now, or Eremon would come back with the clans to pull everything out from under her.

Caitir gave him a shallow nod. "As a child, I was enthralled by the superficial lure of power. Now..." She bit her lip, willing a twinge of desperation into her voice. "I am no longer a child, and I understand the weight of duty a ruler has to her people. I can't help but hope that I have a chance to protect Iathium from the grave threat that is looming."

Kenji narrowed his eyes. "What are you playing at? What makes you bold enough to try taking the throne?"

Shrinking back, Caitir answered in a small voice. "The fact that King La'hiran is holding my mother prisoner. He wants Eremon's magic returned to Iteloria in six weeks."

Kenji's eyes widened in alarm. "Six weeks? After all this upheaval in Rodhlan, there's no way we can withstand a war with Iteloria. Why can't you just fulfill this treaty he's speaking of?"

Now, Caitir's desperation was real. It clawed within her, raging into a panic like none she'd ever felt. If she couldn't persuade someone so lowly as a Dome cook into helping her, she truly was doomed. So, she squeezed her eyes shut, released a shuddering breath, and whispered, "Because Eremon lives."

CHAPTER 24
EREMON

Dome

Kenji stilled, his jaw going slack. Then, he burst into laughter. "What?"

"It's true, and he's a monstrosity." Caitir's chin quivered—a practiced move, Eremon was sure. "I've never been so frightened. The power he holds now... it's unimaginable."

It was all he could do not to shift and turn Caitir to ash on the spot, but that would reinforce the monolithic lie she was spinning. So, he remained in cat form, still as a statue and perched on the stool he'd claimed moments earlier. His tail flicked and curled as he watched the exchange.

Perhaps he could get in a good swipe with his claws.

"That is the best one I've heard so far," Kenji said, wiping tears of laughter from his eyes. "I assume you're the one who started the rumors."

"What rumors?" She crossed her arms. "This isn't a rumor."

He waggled his fingers, to which Caitir's scowl deepened. "There *were* sentries found dead in the catacombs. You disappeared that day; you could've killed them yourself."

"I was dragged into the meadowlands by my family's horses, which Eremon and Lira stole," Caitir exclaimed. "We have my brother's magic to thank for that."

Eremon opened his mouth to agree but startled himself when a loud mew escaped instead. Jolly, that ruddy cat who'd been yowling for his dinner, paused to regard him warily, then bolted to hide under the stairs.

"Eremon and Silira, horse thieves?" Kenji broke into another giddy peal of laughter.

"You don't understand, Kenji. He is truly terrifying—an immortal. All powerful." Caitir's gestures grew wilder, her voice higher, as she spoke. Eremon blew a breath through his nose, a discontented purr rumbling through his body. "If he takes the throne, he'll never let it go. That's what Iathium should fear, not *me*."

Kenji raised his brows. "Interesting tale you're weaving. Wish I believed it."

Caitir pointed a finger at him. "You should."

"I can't imagine the Defender in league with a monster." Kenji's voice was clipped now, his exasperation undisguised. "I also can't imagine both Silira and Eremon leaving Iathium to the likes of you and your mother. If they were together, then they would have come back here to set things right."

Agitation burst through Eremon's body so abruptly that it was almost impossible to sit still. Kenji didn't speak for him; no one did. Not Lira, not Aidryn, not Thorne—not *anyone*.

"Lira's a beast all her own." Caitir adopted a more somber tone now, as though resigned to the fact that her prior tactic hadn't worked. "You haven't seen her since she fled, roaming the continent with Clan Beran's army of outliers, absorbing Nami knows how much dark magic from—"

The cook held up a hand to silence her. "Waste more energy if you like. I won't help you."

"But—"

"If Eremon has truly returned, then my loyalty lies with him." Kenji stood tall, crossing his arms. "If your claims are true, then I wish us all the luck in the world, because we're both going to need it, aren't we?"

Caitir sniffed. "Luck." She rose and turned to leave but paused at the foot of the stairs, gripping the railing and pressing her palm to her belly, sucking a sharp breath in through her teeth.

Eremon straightened, his gaze trained on her.

Kenji breezed past, rushing to her side like a doting father. He pressed a hand to her shoulder. "Here, let me help you sit."

"No!" she cried, withdrawing from him. "I don't need you. I'll make it on my own."

She gathered her skirts and started up the stairs, grimacing. Kenji stood at the foot until she'd reached the top, then swiped a hand over his face, his shoulders hunching.

"Jolly, what are we going to do with that one?"

The orange cat mewled from the corner and batted its dish. Kenji ignored Jolly's begging, returning instead to the work-table to check his rising dough. He sighed heavily, bracing on the side of the table.

Eremon peered at Kenji, torn between disappearing into the shadows and making himself known. Aidryn had told him to gather allies, and Kenji was one of them; that much was certain. But he felt the sudden, urgent need to reassure himself that he was *not* the monstrosity Caitir claimed.

Kenji had been like a second father to him. He had been the comfort Eremon sought when there was none to be found anywhere else. The man had been a friend and mentor, almost a surrogate after his own father had died. When he was exhausted by politics and court intrigue, Kenji always had time, sage advice, and a hearty meal for Eremon, often accompanied by a pastry or slice of cake.

He sat there watching his friend for a moment too long. The

cook nodded decisively to himself, then strode toward the staircase, scooping Eremon under one arm and hauling him along
before he had the chance to shift.

"Come on, you," he said. "We're going to get Toryn."

CHAPTER 25

AIDRYN

Fortress Halgeir

"I'm sorry you weren't able to bring Eremon here." Ljós Beran sent another orb of healing magic into Lira. It burst across her skin and settled, soaking into her. "Is he much changed?"

Lira sighed, her features relaxing beneath the warmth of the golden magic. "He's still Eremon, only he's not."

"Undesired dark magic has a way of altering what it touches," Ljós said, hands steady as he worked. "The longer it remains, the more destruction is left in its wake."

Aidryn bristled. "With all due respect, Eremon wasn't destroyed. But I do think death stripped away all pretense and exposed the man underneath."

"Now *that* is a thought I'd rather not explore," Lira mumbled sleepily.

She lay on a thin cot in the healer's chambers, fingers laced over her belly, eyes closed. Her long, dark lashes splayed over her cheeks, which were now high with color.

Ljós had healed her head wound completely, drawing the

thread out of her scalp afterward. He had worked on the bruising around her throat and on her face, too. Aidryn noticed that her voice sounded smoother, as though the healer had soothed the damage Fiadh had done.

"You have always been yourself, Lira," he replied. "I don't think you have to worry about the dark magic destroying some mask you were never wearing to begin with."

She grew quiet for a moment, seeming to relish the power Ljós poured into her. Then, she said, "What makes you think Eremon was wearing a mask?"

He opened his mouth to retort, but Ljós's glance was laced with warning. "A ruler must mask his weaknesses," the healer said in a calm, steady voice. "He fought his magic until the end. With no illness to contend with, it's no surprise he would be different."

A contented smile ghosted across Lira's lips at the answer. But no, that wasn't it at all. Inexplicably, Aidryn felt compelled to make his point, and damn what Ljós thought about it. "I meant that he was on his best behavior when he pursued you, not that he was fighting his illness. Though, that's valid."

Lira opened one eye to glare at him.

The healer set his jaw and fixed a hard stare on Aidryn. He'd never been able to see the family resemblance between Ljós and Thorne before, but here it was. Aidryn had to fight the sudden urge to flee.

"That was unnecessary," the older man said quietly.

"Thank you, Ljós," Lira snapped as she closed her eyes again.

It was hot in Ljós's chamber at Fortress Halgeir. In part, the healer's hearth was to blame. The stone fortress had long since begun to grow cool with the changing of the seasons, but the interior rooms could be made quite comfortable.

Now, though, this room was stifling.

Aidryn stood and stretched, abandoning the stool he'd been occupying at Lira's side. "I need a bit of fresh air."

"Please take it," the healer muttered.

He moved toward the door, but Lira said, "Ljós, I was thinking of something."

Aidryn paused, hand on the latch, waiting for her to continue.

"Before Eremon died, I came across a Tai'ceru remedy in the archive." She sounded wistful and far away, as though in a dreamlike state. "Do you think that could help me?"

"It couldn't hurt," the healer said. "Aidryn could retrieve the book while you heal."

"No," they said in unison.

Ljós started, looking between them with astonishment. Aidryn hadn't meant to be so forceful about it, but there was no negotiating. Apparently, Lira shared his sentiment.

"I won't be parted from her," Aidryn insisted. "The last time we were separated, it was a disaster. That's how all this started."

Lira nodded. "We're safer together until this is over," she said.

"Then it's settled. Eremon can take care of the remedy," Aidryn said.

The door swung open, and Oda burst in. When she spotted Aidryn, she grasped his forearm. "Where's Lira? Tell me everything."

Oda's green eyes sparkled, her dark brown skin rich in the glow of Ljós's amber stones. She'd tied her black hair, adorned in its usual twists, back at the nape of her neck, one lone white twist framing the right side of her face.

"Ask me yourself," Lira said, turning her head to grin at their friend.

Oda rushed to Lira's side, sitting on the stool where Aidryn had been moments before. She bent forward and placed a kiss on Lira's forehead, taking her hand.

"Look at you, on the mend," Oda said with an easy smile.

"Both of us," Lira replied, noting the linen bandage still wrapped around the warrior's side. "Did Ljós take all the moss out of you before he stitched you up, or are you growing a forest inside?"

Oda wrinkled her nose. "He made Talfryn take it out. That was unpleasant. Your brother was fine at packing wounds, but removing the moss was an entirely different matter."

"He ruined my favorite satchel," Ljós grumbled. "You can sit up, Silira."

Lira laughed softly, swinging her legs over the side of the cot and pushing herself up. She pulled Oda into a warm embrace. Aidryn leaned against the wall and smiled, though his gratefulness for their reunion gave way to his own grief. Thoughts of Faolan invaded his mind, but a moment later, Thorne's massive form was taking up the entire doorway, surveying the scene.

He'd trimmed his beard since they'd arrived back at the fortress and had wasted no time grooming himself. One side of his thick blond mane was braided tightly against his scalp, while the other flowed freely over one shoulder. He wore a fresh leather tunic and still smelled of the pungent herbs he'd ground for his father just hours ago.

"How is she?" he said, leaning against the door's frame and casting a brief glance at Aidryn.

Lira smiled at the older brother she'd chosen for herself. Aidryn couldn't help but feel envious of their bond, particularly since he'd never felt bonded to his own brother.

"Hungry," Lira said, brightening.

"Well, we have food." Oda pulled Lira to her feet and headed for the door. "Come on; you can tell me about everything I missed while we eat."

"Are you coming, Aidryn?" Lira's hopeful expression made Aidryn's heart twist.

Aidryn wanted to say yes, but he hesitated, casting a furtive glance at Thorne, then Ljós. "You go," he said, catching her free hand and pressing a kiss to her knuckles as she passed. "I'll find you soon."

Lira and Oda linked arms and strode into the outer corridor, then around the corner. Aidryn waited until they were gone before he spoke, hoping his helplessness wouldn't be obvious to the Beran men.

"She's not all right, is she?" The words came out in a rush.

To Aidryn's surprise, Ljós said, "No. I was able to slow the dark magic's effects for now, but I can't predict how long my power will last."

Aidryn broke out in a cold sweat, his heart pounding. Memories from the courtyard, the spring, and Eremon's gruesome death pummeled him. His throat tightened around his next words. "Will she die?"

"You have to remember that she is only experiencing an echo of what Eremon endured," Ljós answered. "I think there's still hope."

From where he stood against the wall, Thorne crossed his arms. He made a low sound in his throat.

Grasping the stool, Aidryn sat wearily. "How can I help her?"

"You can try to help her stay comfortable and calm," the healer hedged, "but she is responsible for harnessing her fear and rage."

"Transmuting," Thorne added in a quiet voice. "Not just harnessing."

Aidryn shifted uncomfortably. "What rage?" He felt like a filthy liar as the question left his lips.

Ljós looked at Aidryn the way Lord Irem used to when he was an apprentice. Once, Aidryn had rushed to transcribe a manuscript page in a race with Lira but had splattered it with ink instead, ruining a day's worth of quill work in one fell swoop. Irem's disapproving glare had kindled such a visceral humiliation in Aidryn that he'd wanted to crawl beneath the desk. The look Ljós was giving him now felt very much the same.

"The acute anger Thorne described when you brought her to me," the healer answered, glancing across the room at his son. "What you were too fearful to speak of."

Aidryn tensed. "I wasn't—"

"Yes," Thorne said, pushing off the wall and crossing the chamber. "You were."

He paused by his father's pit of amber stones, conjuring orbs of golden magic and sending them into it. The stones flared with his power, and the warrior sighed, flexing his fingers. Magic-wielders who failed to discharge their power grew ill, particularly the anointed with their extra measure of magic.

"Why are we talking about Lira's anger?" Aidryn asked, rubbing the back of his neck. "I thought this was about dark magic."

"They are interconnected," Ljós answered. "I suspect she has been suppressing anger since childhood, and now it's fueling the magic's spread. In turn, the dark magic is intensifying her emotions."

"So, until we find an answer for the magic, we have to address the anger." Aidryn crossed his arms.

The healer nodded. "She can do that through caring for her spirit, body, and mind."

"But what happens when the magic overtakes her?" Thorne said. "How long until she turns it on Tarlach, or one of the other anointed?"

The world slowed, and Aidryn blinked. "She wouldn't."

Thorne crossed his arms and shrugged a shoulder. "She already unleashed on Eremon."

"She was angry at him before," Aidryn protested. He could

feel his own anger building now, sweeping through him like the Moravon rushing over the falls. His body hummed with it, as though he might burst any moment.

"Do you want to know what I think, Tarlach?" Thorne turned to face him, his features illuminated by the glowing amber stones. "You should break that Binding."

"No." The ferocity in Aidryn's own voice surprised him. "Absolutely not."

"Who's going to protect Clan Tarlach's magic, then?" Thorne challenged. "When her birthright burns up, the darkness will come for yours."

The healer's gaze fell heavily on the two as they squared off. Tension rippled up from Aidryn's clenched fists into his forearms, biceps, shoulders. "It won't go that far."

"You are foolish," Thorne said, stepping closer and pointing a finger at his face. Heat rushed up Aidryn's neck and into his cheeks. "I thought no one could be as childish as Eremon, but you prove me wrong."

Thorne was the one who had jeopardized Lira's safety by separating them in the first place. His audacity to demand further submission was maddening. Aidryn felt tendrils of his magic drawing themselves from his palms, swirling around his hands. They warmed beneath his power, and he took a steadying breath, letting the crimson magic flare.

"You're talking about our Binding, Beran," Aidryn growled.

Thorne's gaze flicked down to Aidryn's hands, then back up to his face. His next words were calmer, more measured. "That spell means nothing."

But it meant everything. It was as good as a magical vow, and Aidryn would never—could never—break it.

Pounding, maddening fury roared in Aidryn's head, drowning out his thoughts before he rushed Thorne.

CHAPTER 26
LIRA

Fortress Halgeir

Lira halted in the doorway to Ljós's chamber just in time to see Aidryn take a swing at Thorne. She stopped short, jaw dropping open as Thorne easily dodged Aidryn's right hook. Oda, who had been at Lira's heels, slammed hard into her back.

Thorne grabbed a fistful of Aidryn's tunic and hauled him off his feet, slamming his back into the wall. Aidryn's head snapped back against the stone, and he blinked rapidly, dazed, though he fought the warrior's grip.

"Release him, Thorne!" Lira shouted.

Oda shoved past her and into the chamber, storming in Thorne's direction. Her muscles rippled with tension as she drew her axe from its sheath. "Enough, *sjovyn!*"

It was a Brylla word that Lira neither knew nor understood, despite Thorne's gifting them the language during the summer.

Thorne froze, fist raised as though to pummel Aidryn. He let go of Aidryn's tunic as though it had scalded him, letting the younger man's feet hit the ground. Though

Aidryn stumbled, he did not fall. Ljós crossed the room to him, keeping a wary eye on Thorne and Oda as he did so. The healer pressed his fingertips to Aidryn's temples and spoke to him in low tones, seeming to dull the pain of impact.

Aidryn sought Lira out, his gaze sharper than a moment before. The color was high in his cheeks, and he was panting, his body as taut as a bowstring.

When Thorne whirled on Oda, the ferocity in his expression made Lira shrink. But Oda widened her stance, adjusting her grip on the axe, and squared up to him.

"You dare—" he began, though she cut him off and took a step closer.

"You owe me a debt," Oda said through gritted teeth, voice low. "And you know I have never invoked it."

"Do not speak of that here," Thorne replied, a vein in his forehead bulging. The tension reverberating from his body was visceral.

Lira moved cautiously around the room's perimeter to where Aidryn and Ljós stood against the far wall. She pressed a hand to Aidryn's cheek. Although he gave her a silent nod, he kept his eyes trained on Thorne, who was still wholly focused on Oda.

"I'll say what I must," Oda answered. "If you threaten our friends, I will do whatever is necessary to call you down."

"He will stand down because a future overlord must let go of disruptive emotions." Ljós's voice was calm and steady, but there was a fury in his amber eyes that Lira had never beheld. The healer glared at his son as though wounded. "And now he will leave my chamber."

Thorne looked from his father to Oda, then stalked out of the room, yanking the door open. It banged against the wall with a reverberating boom as he rounded the corner into the dark corridor.

Silence fell over the chamber for a brief moment before the healer said, "Oda, I want a word."

She stood straighter, giving him a slow blink. Her green eyes shone in the amber light, her stony expression unreadable. "As you wish."

Aidryn and Lira exchanged a terse glance, then hurried from the chamber.

The moment they sealed themselves into their old chamber, Lira was fussing over Aidryn, inspecting him for signs of injury. "Are you hurt?" she asked.

Aidryn set a candle on the table at their bedside. "I was, but Ljós took care of it," he said.

So far, she'd had no luck getting Aidryn to tell her why he had attacked Thorne. It wasn't for lack of trying. The warrior must have said something egregious; it was not like Aidryn to throw the first punch. He was always the voice of reason—the first to calm others through his disarming wit.

Lira's stomach growled loudly, drawing Aidryn's attention.

"Eat your stew," Aidryn said, settling onto the bed with his bowl.

Lira looked down at her own steaming bowl. They'd wandered numbly to the Arthmael's Hall in search of food after leaving Oda with Ljós. Instead of eating supper with Oda, Lira had insisted on trying one last time to persuade Aidryn to join them.

She scooped up a spoonful of hot stew and blew gently, watching the steam sway before taking a bite. The savory flavor was both welcome and familiar. They'd eaten plenty of this stew over the summer, savoring hearty meat and root vegetables in the days after Lira and Thorne rescued Aidryn from captivity in Iathium.

Lira assumed the vegetables had come from the magical hanging gardens Talfryn and Iva, their mother, had planted during those months. Her heart swelled with pride at the memory.

When they were finished, Aidryn took their empty bowls and they readied for bed. When Lira emerged from the bathing chamber, he was leaning against the wall, his back turned to her. The sorrowful droop of his shoulders gave her pause, but she made herself keep moving toward him. She laid a gentle hand on his back. He flinched at the contact, the movement almost imperceptible.

"Please, tell me what happened," she said softly.

His shook his head. "I already told you. I can't."

Lira grasped his hand and guided him to face her, then drew his knuckles to her mouth. "The last time we were in this fortress, we kept so many secrets from one another. We can't do that again."

Aidryn's smile was gentle, yet sad. He ran a thumb over her lower lip. "What he said was so hurtful, Lira. It will stoke your anger."

"But—"

"Ljós said we need to soothe it, not make it worse." He closed his eyes for a moment, drawing in a long breath. "But I might feel safe telling you more when I've had time to consider it."

Disappointment rose in Lira's chest, but she nodded resignedly. "I suppose I can give you time."

"I won't hold it close forever." His blue eyes were soft in the candlelight as he studied her. "I swear it."

She rose on her toes to kiss his cheek. Aidryn drew in a short, shallow gasp—a sound that had become familiar, yet never failed to send a thrill through her. When Lira broke away and sank back down to her feet, Aidryn followed, lowering his mouth to hers.

His kiss flooded her senses, and for a long moment, she was drowning in him. He wrapped one arm around her waist to hold her against him and cupped her cheek with his other hand. She parted her lips to deepen the kiss, her fingertips digging into the hard, lean muscle of his biceps.

Aidryn guided them backward toward the bed, then sat, pulling her down to straddle his lap. Cupping her backside, he hefted her closer with a soft groan. Lira clutched him tightly, reveling in the torrent of sensations. She wanted only to focus on him, not the horrors of the morning. Not his fight with Thorne, or the things he'd refused to tell her.

An unwelcome thought forced its way into her mind, cutting through the haze of desire she'd been clinging to.

You let him lie?

She chased the thought away, kissing him harder. He hadn't lied; he was withholding information to protect her, and she was aware he was doing it.

There was no reason to be angry with him. Was there?

Sometimes truth demands rage.

A shudder wracked her body, and as though from far away, she heard Aidryn let out a sharp gasp. It wasn't his familiar sound of pleasure, but of pain.

Lira's eyes flew open, and she pulled away. The first thing she registered was the shocked expression on his face—his raised brows, lips parted in surprise. His head was tilted back at a sharp angle, blue eyes cutting down at her.

"What—"

She realized that her hand had wandered into his hair, still disheveled from their ride across the meadowlands. Sometime during the kiss, her fist had closed tightly around the dark strands.

And she had yanked.

"Easy, Silira," he murmured as she disentangled her fingers, rubbing along his scalp where she'd pulled his hair. He looked down at her, emotions warring in his eyes, and panic tightened her chest.

"I'm sorry," she whispered. "I don't know what happened."

But she *did* know. He had refused to share the truth with her, and her magic had resisted his omission.

"Just got carried away," he said, voice rough. "That's all."

The corner of his mouth quirked up. His smile didn't reach his eyes, though, and her stomach did a fearful flip. But a moment later, he tilted his head back of his own accord and bared his throat. He pressed a palm against her back and coaxed her body closer. "But you gave me some very good ideas."

"Did I?" Lira met his gaze, desperate to confirm the desire she still heard in his voice. His subtle nod and the canting of his body toward hers gave her the answer she sought.

Tentatively, she brushed her fingers along his warm skin, and his dark lashes fluttered closed. She lowered her head to press a kiss to his throat, drinking in his scent, and he shivered. His hand tightened on her thigh, and his pulse sped into a fury beneath her tongue.

He whispered to her then, the rich depth of his voice reverberating pleasantly against her mouth. "Finish what you began."

CHAPTER 27
CAITIR

Dome

Caitir lay on her side, her back to the door, knees curled to her chest. She shivered, cradling her belly. Tonight wasn't the first time she had bled during this pregnancy, and it certainly wasn't the first time she had felt pain. But tonight, the pain had been profound, and more alarming than before.

She thought about Kenji's steadying hand on her shoulder, and about Toryn, the midwife she'd neglected to meet for so many weeks. So much time had passed already—time without proper care, time spent not knowing whether she and her child would be safe.

Fiadh had told her to lie down the last time she bled, so she'd done that again. She lay in silence, listening to the sound of her own breathing, focusing on each inhale and exhale. The cramping in her lower abdomen gradually subsided, and she felt herself begin to relax.

Each time anger toward Kenji began to rise in her, she crushed it back down. His refusal to help her shouldn't have come as a surprise. Now, she couldn't afford to dwell on it. She would simply need to move on to the next idea.

Whatever that was.

Caitir had just begun to doze when someone quietly opened the door to her chamber. She held her breath as footsteps echoed from across the room, growing closer to her bed.

"You have visitors," Fiadh said.

Caitir sighed heavily before rolling over to see Kenji standing beside Fiadh, with a dark-haired woman by his side. She was round-faced and petite, with a kind expression. Toryn looked every bit the perfect match for the jolly cook.

Relief flooded Caitir, but she scowled. "Kenji, I told you—"

"I know." Kenji frowned down at her, though his eyes were warm. "You might not need *me*, but you do need Toryn, so I'll take my leave."

He took a step back and turned to go.

"Wait!" Caitir reached for him, and he froze, turning slowly to face her once again.

Kenji regarded her outstretched hand with a puzzled expression but stepped closer and took it anyway. "I'm listening," he said.

A lump rose in her throat, and she swallowed hard before she said, "You've been kind to me. I don't deserve it."

"Yes." He squeezed her hand and met her gaze. "You do. Good night, Caitir."

Kenji stepped back, bending down for a moment. When he stood again, he was holding the silver cat from the kitchen. He scratched it behind its ear, and the cat narrowed its eyes, emitting a low, agitated yowl.

"It followed *you*," the cook said, setting it onto the bed beside Caitir. "So you get to keep it."

"No!" she groaned. The beast immediately moved to the pillow beside hers, where it turned its back on her, curled up, and closed its eyes.

"And you still owe me that story." Kenji chuckled, heading toward the door.

"Not without a favor," Caitir called, watching him go. He closed the door without another word.

When she looked back to Fiadh and Toryn, the women were staring down at her, seemingly confused. She waved them off, trying to laugh. "I see Kenji put you up to this late-night visit."

"He said you were in pain," Toryn answered. She smiled warmly, though her expression was guarded. "Lie back, let me take a look at you."

Fiadh crept out of the room, leaving Caitir and Toryn alone. Seeing the opportunity to escape, the cat bolted too, slipping out into the corridor before Fiadh could shut the door.

Now that they were alone, Caitir felt a sudden jolt of panic, and she tugged the blankets up to her chin. "What does a midwife do? I mean... I know you deliver babies."

Toryn scoffed lightly. "No, *you* deliver the baby. I care for you during your pregnancy and help with baby after the birth." She sat on the edge of the mattress beside Caitir. "Sometimes I may ask to assess you, and that will be different each time, depending on what you need. We can talk about what you're feeling if you like."

"Can you tell me why I'm bleeding?" Caitir asked in a small voice. "Or if the baby is all right?"

"Most likely, yes." Toryn reached for her hand and grasped it. "You've never had a midwife visit you at all?"

Caitir bit her lip and shook her head. Toryn's expression softened further, and she nodded her understanding. "Then I'll explain everything as we go and do my best to help you feel safe."

∾

ALTHOUGH TORYN WAS patient and gentle, the process was harrowing for Caitir. Mingled with her fear for herself and her child was the surge of memories that rushed in unbidden. Horrific images of Gerallt's face—memories of what he'd done to her—flashed in her mind, though she tried to suppress them. She knew Toryn would see the final bruises he had left on her, and the realization set her more on edge than she had been before.

By the time the midwife finished her assessment, tears had soaked Caitir's cheeks, running down into her ears and hair. Her nose was stuffy, and her eyes were swollen as she cocooned herself in the blanket again. Toryn rose and crossed to the bathing chamber to wash her hands, then returned, handing Caitir a handkerchief.

"It looks like you have an infection, which can cause bleeding and pain," Toryn answered. "It's a common ailment; every woman experiences this at least once, to varying degrees. We have remedies for it, so you should begin to feel better soon."

"Is the child in danger?" Caitir asked, her voice muffled with tears.

"No," Toryn said, offering her a soft smile. "The baby is safe, but you need rest and better care. Kenji says you're not eating or drinking enough."

"Kenji *would* say that," Caitir mumbled.

"Well, if it's true," the midwife said, suddenly stern, "then you should take better care of yourself. I know it's difficult, but we're here for you. You don't have to do this alone."

Caitir raised an eyebrow, not bothering to hide the scowl that twisted her lips. "I appreciate the sentiment, but I've had to do plenty alone."

"I don't envy you," said Toryn with a sigh. "Breaking free from bondage and bringing new life into the world, all at once. It's difficult enough to free yourself from abuse, let alone become a parent while you're doing it. You need friends by your side."

Caitir scrutinized her. "What would you know about it?"

"I was married once, before Kenji." Toryn's tone had taken on an edge that sent a chill sweeping over Caitir's skin. The midwife's eyes were sharp, and she leaned nearer. "Let's just say the bruises I bore were mirror images of yours. I know the agony of keeping them hidden, and how long it takes for them to heal."

A sudden flood of questions rushed into Caitir's mind. More than anything, she wanted to ask Toryn about the wounds on her spirit, and whether those would ever heal. Instead, she kept her lips pressed shut as a new lump rose in her throat.

Toryn didn't break eye contact as she waited for an answer. When Caitir remained silent, she said, "The difference between us is that I had one tormentor to contend with. You have had many. Now, what will you do with the opportunity you've created for yourself?"

Still, Caitir didn't respond. Toryn gave her a little nod and gathered her things.

"There are few pregnancies in Iathium right now, and I have plenty of time," she said, standing and pressing a hand to Caitir's shoulder. "If you need someone to talk to, call on me."

Toryn turned, crossed the chamber, and left the room without looking back.

CHAPTER 28
EREMON

Dome

Eremon crouched low in the shadows near Caitir's chamber door until long after Toryn had departed. He had expected Fiadh to come back, but she hadn't, and he was growing restless. So he rose, moving back down the corridor toward the kitchens, from which voices were emanating.

As he made his way down the stairs, he could hear Kenji and Toryn quarreling—in the soft, gentle way they always had. Kenji's only clear sign of agitation was the moderately loud sigh he blew through his nose at random intervals. When Eremon was close enough to hear what they were saying, Toryn was making her case.

"I don't think it would be considered treason," she was saying. "She is nothing like them, and no one from Eremon's bloodline has even tried to claim the throne, because they can't. Silira Mór is the rightful heir. If Caitir invokes Silira's name, the people will pay attention."

"But there are rumors. I believe an uprising will come,

whether led by city-dwellers or clanspeople," Kenji replied. "I don't want to be caught in it."

"If an uprising comes, you'll be caught in it regardless." Toryn crossed her arms, her exhale matching her husband's. "We live and work in the Dome. Any of us who have remained in service could be considered traitors, depending on which way the wind blows. Or have you not realized that?"

"I hadn't thought of it," he said. "I don't know if it's true."

"Let's say that it is," Toryn pressed. "What then? Would you still refuse to help someone who wants to drive out people like Aila?"

"Silira would drive out people like Aila."

"But she has not," Toryn countered. "I wanted to believe that she would come back and save us, but three seasons have passed, and she hasn't shown her face here once. But Caitir is right in front of us, asking us to help her take the throne from Aila. Are we really going to hold out hope for someone who could not care less about taking the city back, or are we going to help the one who is here now?"

Kenji stepped closer to his wife, lowering his voice. "Caitir says Eremon is alive. Do you think it's possible?"

Toryn's eyes went wide, and she pressed a hand to her mouth. "He had the marking," she said softly. "So I suppose it is."

He paled. "Well, how can we find out for sure?"

"He will have to show himself to us," she answered. "We can believe it when we see it, don't you think?"

Eremon sighed. There was never going to be an opportune time to do this.

Toryn moved to survey Kenji's work, and for a moment, both their backs were turned. He crept away from the kitchen and into the shadowy dining area across the corridor. Before he could shift, though, Toryn was climbing the staircase.

"You need to come rest, Kenji," she called down. "Don't work all night."

"I'll try not to," he replied.

Eremon waited in the dark dining area after she'd gone, letting the cook settle back into his work. After a long while, he shifted, straightening his tunic and trousers. He pressed his back against the wall, listening to his friend's preoccupied humming.

Finally, he forced himself to cross the corridor. His eyes stung as he stepped into the kitchen and said, in a barely audible voice, "Kenji."

The cook stilled, then whirled to meet Eremon's gaze. A loud laugh burst from him, abrupt and harsh.

"What kind of cruel joke is this?" he cried, angular eyes widening as he took in Eremon's form. "I don't want any trouble!"

Eremon stood still, holding up his hands, too. "Kenji, it's me. I was listening. I—"

"How?!" Kenji cried, pressing his hands to his round cheeks. "She told me to rest; I must have fallen asleep at the work table again. This can't be happening—I'm dreaming!"

"You aren't dreaming, I swear it." Eremon took one careful step closer, then another. "I was going to do this before Toryn left, but I wasn't fast enough."

"How were you listening?" Kenji was pressing himself against the kitchen counter now, his entire body trembling. "There was no one else here!"

"The, ah," Eremon chuckled, shifting uncomfortably where he stood. "I... my magic is significantly different." There was no way to say it, except to say it outright. He felt a bit ridiculous. "I was the silver cat you just hauled halfway across the Dome."

Kenji shook his head as though trying to rattle something loose. "That's it. I've lost my mind," he murmured to himself, scrubbing a hand over his face. He threw his cloth down on the worktable. "I'm going to bed."

"I can help you with the pastries." Eremon's whisper was barely audible.

The cook barked a startled laugh. "Please! I'd love for my delusions to contribute something to this kitchen, if they're going to intrude on my work time."

"You taught me how to make them, once." He rounded the corner into the work area, moving closer to his friend, whose pallor intensified. "They were my father's favorite—sweet cheese and raspberry filling."

Kenji's eyes widened as he peered up at Eremon. "Your favorite, too."

Eremon gave him a slow nod and smiled. "Mine, too."

The cook's chin trembled, and his shoulders sagged. He screwed up his features in a stern expression, pointing at Eremon with his wooden spoon. "You remember everything I taught you? Missing a step ruins the entire batch."

"I remember every step. I also remember the flat end of your spoon." Eremon blinked away the stinging in his eyes. He extended his hand, praying Kenji would take it.

"As you should." Kenji looked from Eremon's face to his hand, then back again. Cautiously, he reached out and grasped Eremon's hand.

The warmth of the contact sent an overwhelming surge of emotion through Eremon. Kenji gasped, yanking Eremon into a tight hug and muffling his own shout of, "It *is* you!"

Eremon returned the embrace, pressing his cheek to the top of the cook's head. Kenji dissolved into loud sobs that made Eremon's cheeks burn. Hot tears gathered and pooled in the corners of his eyes before spilling into the shorter man's hair.

"Oh, Kenji, I've missed you."

Kenji had been the only person in the Dome who had allowed Eremon to weep after his father died. During

Eremon's agonizing seven-year reign, Kenji had been the one person he could turn to without fear of judgment. He didn't know if that was because the cook posed no political threat, like the others who surrounded him—or if it was just that he craved a father's love, and Kenji had offered it freely.

"But *how* is it you?" The cook clapped his hands onto Eremon's shoulders and pulled back to study his face.

"Magic I didn't even know existed, that my father protected after he died," Eremon said. "Leave it to Silira Mór to discover it and give me another life."

"So this *is* her doing." Kenji grinned, deep dimples accentuated against his splotchy cheeks. "Then the rumors are true; the two of you *will* be the salvation of Iathium."

Eremon's stomach tightened. "It's not that simple."

Kenji's expression darkened. "Why? What happened?"

"I need allies," Eremon answered carefully, dodging the questions. "I need your help getting them—quietly."

"And you're not going to tell me what's going on." The cook placed his fists on his hips and scowled. "You really are the same Eremon."

"Calm yourself, Kenji," he said, raising a hand to stay his friend. "One thing at a time."

"Let me look at you." Kenji grabbed Eremon's cheeks, scrutinizing him more closely. "Your eyes..." With a loud gasp, he exclaimed, "Then the old stories are true!"

"Which ones?" Eremon asked. He let Kenji turn his face this way and that.

"Itelorian legends about the immortals," Kenji replied. "My mother told them to me when I was a lad, and Toryn said—oh, turn around and move your hair!"

Eremon drew back, alarmed. "Whatever for?"

"You had the marking," Kenji answered, twirling a finger at him. "It was on the back of your neck."

"What are you talking about?" Eremon laughed nervously, fingers creeping to the nape of his neck. "When, what mark?"

"It's called Nami's Rune—barely visible except in the moments right after birth." Kenji stepped around him.

Eremon reluctantly pulled his hair over one shoulder, feeling for any sign of this rune. "Here?"

From behind him, Kenji gasped. "It's a bright blue now, glowing like magic itself!" Eremon whirled to face him again. Fresh tears were falling from Kenji's eyes. "Toryn hid the mark from your mother."

"A blessing, truly," he replied, voice wavering.

That was why Macha had never been able to confirm the true extent of Eremon's power. It was the reason he and his father had shared their secretive bond over his magic, and why there had been precious few to guide him through his final years as a mortal. There had been Ljós and Lord Irem, with what little they'd known.

And then there had been Lira.

As though reading Eremon's thoughts, Kenji said, "And what of Silira? Now that you're immortal, what will that mean for her?"

He shrugged numbly. "Simply that she is mortal, and I am not."

"But surely there is a way to extend that magic to her," he said, his features settling into a familiar, determined expression. "She is truly worthy of you. I could think of no one better suited to rule at your side."

Eremon tried to force a smile through the sudden surge of sorrow that overtook him. "Did the little usurper not tell you? Silira has married Caitir's brother, Aidryn Tarlach."

He sagged a bit at the admission and at the sudden, shattered look on his dear friend's face.

"Oh, my boy." Kenji pressed a consoling hand to his shoulder. "I am so sorry."

Eremon considered pulling away and defusing the tension that now filled the room. But instead, he merely answered, "I'm broken."

It was as much as he was willing to admit, and it was nearly enough to topple him where he stood.

"Sit down," the cook said gently, wrapping his arm around Eremon's shoulders, "and tell me everything."

CHAPTER 29

AIDRYN

Fortress Halgeir

Aidryn strode toward the pasture, his body thrumming with energy. Tension had coiled tighter within him since his standoff with Thorne the day before. He'd awakened before dawn, pressing a whisper of a kiss to Lira's hair and sliding out of bed.

The meadowlands were calling, and he needed to ride.

Fannin was waiting for him expectantly at the pasture's edge. Aidryn led him to the stables and saddled him, humming a low tune under his breath. He gave the stallion's shoes a look, then led him back out onto the pathway.

Thick, heavy fog descended as they ventured farther away from the fortress, so oppressive that Aidryn could taste it. He relished Fannin's quiet companionship, the stallion's warm body at his side as they walked together. When all else was askew, they had one another.

Aidryn hadn't been able to stop thinking about what had happened with Lira the night before—the rough way she'd exposed his throat, as though she'd been more interested in slitting it than... well, what she'd actually done. He shivered at the memory.

Her eyes had taken on a wild look before she realized that she'd caused him pain. That glint haunted him still.

In the distance, a figure emerged from the fog. A moment later, Oda came into view, her fighting staff and axe slung across her back. Her stony expression relaxed, and she raised a hand in greeting before trotting in Aidryn's direction.

"Did you take the night watch?" Aidryn asked.

"Aye." Oda reached out to stroke Fannin's muzzle. "For the same reason you're leaving before dawn breaks, I'd wager."

Heat rushed into Aidryn's cheeks. By all accounts, he should still be cocooned in bed with Lira. He shrugged. "I've always ridden at odd hours—sometimes overnight, sometimes before the sun."

"Particularly when something's amiss," she pressed. "What did Thorne say to rile you so?"

Aidryn raised a brow. "When you're ready to tell me how you stopped him from pummeling me, maybe I'll share."

"Not a chance." Oda pressed her lips tightly, focusing solely on Fannin. The stallion nudged at her hip expectantly.

Aidryn shifted his weight from one foot to the other, his boots pressing onto the hard-packed earth. A cold breeze stirred his hair, sending gooseflesh up the back of his neck. "Has Thorne asked about your anointing?"

She shushed him. "When I returned from the crypt, he said my magic smelled different. I told him that Macha had struck me, and that satisfied him."

Aidryn lowered his voice. "Not for long. Might as well pretend your Énna magic finally manifested, if you're not going to tell him."

He almost missed her few rapid blinks before she righted herself and said, "Leave it alone."

"You know," Aidryn pressed, "Lira was resistant to her birthright, too."

"Look at what's happened to her." Oda adjusted her staff. "If I embrace this, I'll lose my alliance with Thorne."

"Why?" The wind picked up again, ruffling the dark twists in Oda's hair. "You're both anointed. That should strengthen bonds among all four of us."

"He'll say my loyalty to Beran is compromised," Oda answered.

Aidryn couldn't suppress the surprised laugh that escaped him. "Oda, that's ridiculous. You're making him sound like a tyrannical husband." Oda abruptly cut her gaze back up to him, rage shimmering in her eyes as Aidryn barreled on. "I've never seen you cower like this."

She drew her staff with lightning speed and angled it at him. Her lip curled, nostrils flaring. "You think I'm a coward, Tarlach?"

"Of course not." Aidryn raised his palms, his heart pounding erratically.

Oda snapped her staff toward him, stopping short of his nose. "My forgiveness is costly."

Aidryn flinched but steadied himself. They squared off that way for a long moment. Beside him, Fannin gave a nervous huff.

Finally, Oda lowered her staff and pushed past Aidryn, knocking into him with her shoulder. The impact forced him back a step. "Get out of my sight," she said.

With an angry growl, Aidryn swung astride Fannin, nudging him into a canter, then a gallop. Oda wanted him out of her sight? That was fine. Aidryn didn't want to see anyone either, for a long while.

~

THE SUN WAS high overhead when Aidryn turned back toward the fortress, letting Fannin canter at an easy pace as they went. He'd long since expended his pent-up energy, riding at full speed down the eastern coastline, then returning to the north. It had been colder on the beach, and Aidryn's cheeks were chapped from the wind. But his spirits were higher as Halgeir came into view, and he was eager to see how Lira fared.

A shadow passed over them as they rode, stretching along the ground ahead of them. Aidryn heard the beat of wings at the same moment the shadow took their shape, and he looked up to see Eremon swooping overhead. Sunlight glinted off his silver feathers as he swept to the east of the fortress, and Aidryn followed.

Eremon alighted on the ground, then transformed in a burst of magic. He crossed his arms, leaning against one of Beran's pasture fence posts as he waited for Aidryn to join him. Something about the expression on his face stirred Aidryn's anger.

"You've made yourself scarce," he said coolly. "Come to survey the damage?"

Eremon scowled, then sighed. "That bad?"

"We don't know yet." Aidryn swung down from Fannin's saddle, then began removing the stallion's tack. "Thorne's already pressuring me to break the Binding."

When Eremon didn't answer right away, Aidryn spun to face him. His expression was contemplative, and Aidryn bristled. "You, too?"

"I said nothing," Eremon answered, "although it might not be the worst idea he's ever had."

Aidryn turned back to Fannin's tack, his fingers fumbling over the saddle's buckles. "Did you come bearing useful news, or are you just here to be insufferable?"

With a scoff, Eremon replied, "You never spoke to me this way when I was on the throne."

"Well, I wanted to." Aidryn hefted Fannin's saddle, setting it on the ground, then led him through the pasture's south gate. Next, he went to work on the bridle. "So I'm taking full advantage of the opportunity while I can."

Eremon's gaze was heavy on him as he worked. "Do you really hate me so much?"

"It's not so much hate as it is simmering resentment," Aidryn grumbled.

"Impeccable semantics." He heaved a sigh. "I already apologized for what happened to Lira. Are my apology and efforts not enough?"

Aidryn turned to Eremon, crossing his arms and widening his stance. "When your efforts produce results, we'll see."

"Then you won't be happy with what I've come to tell you." The breeze stirred long strands of his black hair, drawing them across his face. When he took a step closer, Aidryn's stomach did a nervous flip. "I've been searching for Lira's pendant, but I haven't found it yet."

"Just keep trying. In the meantime, there's something else. Did Lira have a chance to tell you about the nea'la rose remedy?" When Eremon blanched, Aidryn's heart sank. Still, he added, "We were hoping you could retrieve it."

"I do remember," Eremon replied slowly. "The problem is that the roses were destroyed. I noticed when I visited the garden—nothing but ash."

Aidryn's eyes pricked, and he took an unsteady breath against the disappointment that filled him. "Then I suppose that's that."

A mission to Iteloria's snowy western coast was entirely out of the question. It was the only place where the roses grew wild. They were often given to rulers as diplomatic gifts, so it was possible they could retrieve some from the Itelorian capital of So'vis. But it was imperative that they avoid calling King La'hiran's attention to them, so securing blooms from his palace would be a feat in itself.

"There may still be a way to retrieve them." Eremon's voice was infuriatingly gentle. "But we'll have to give it time."

The weight that had settled on Aidryn's chest eased slightly. "What news from Iathium?"

Eremon's expression was troubled. "Walk with me," he said.

They strode away from the pasture gate, moving eastward against the cold wind. It stung Aidryn's raw cheeks and lashed his hair against his face.

Eremon recounted everything he'd seen in the city so far, from the sentries left to sleep in the streets to Caitir's plan for Aila's execution. Today, he was roaming the meadowlands in search of Gerallt's disbanded archers, whom he'd planned to lure into Iathium with the promise of a reward.

Eremon cast a wary glance in the direction of the fortress. "I should go; someone's coming."

He took a step back but paused when Aidryn said, "Wait. What about Caitir? How does she fare?"

Eremon gave him a blank stare. "She seemed unwell last night. The midwife, Toryn, is caring for her."

Aidryn felt uncomfortably guilty for asking after Caitir; after all, she'd chosen her side. They were enemies now. "Do you know what's wrong?" he pressed against his better judgment.

A slow smirk spread across Eremon's lips. "Probably the tribulation of usurping a throne, not to mention her general unpleasant nature."

Aidryn's mouth tugged into a frown. "Eremon."

"Or perhaps carrying the mountain master's spawn."

Aidryn crossed his arms, shoulders tightening. "Would you have a care?"

Eremon's eyes flashed. "Why should I? Whatever she suffers, she brought upon herself."

"That's not true," Aidryn replied, glaring at Eremon, "And you know it."

The Rí had the audacity to look bored. He slid his gaze lazily toward the horizon, then brought it back to rest on Aidryn. "Then I suppose we'll have to disagree. At least we both know you're accustomed to that position."

Now, Aidryn could hear footsteps approaching from the main pathway. Eremon didn't say anything more before he transformed and took to the skies.

CHAPTER 30

LIRA

Fortress Halgeir

L ira spotted Fannin's saddle and bridle discarded on the ground at the far edge of Clan Beran's pastures. A flash of silver caught her eye, and she followed the movement to see Eremon soaring eastward over the meadowlands in his falcon form. Seconds later, Aidryn rounded the bend, faltering when he caught her gaze.

"Where've you been?" she called.

"Out riding," he answered, hefting the tack and crossing to her.

Indeed, his cheeks were pink from the biting wind, his hair tousled the way she loved. He leaned down to kiss her, and she took Fannin's bridle and saddlebag from him.

"What was Eremon doing here?" she asked as they turned down the long road toward Fortress Halgeir.

"Bringing news," Aidryn answered. "We crossed paths as I was coming in."

Lira wrinkled her nose. "He didn't bother to see the rest of us?"

"I suppose it was faster this way. He said he's on the way to find Artagán and the rest of the archers. Besides, I can relay the message."

"Fair enough," she replied.

They trekked to the stables, where Aidryn stored Fannin's tack, then returned to the pathway. Lira listened intently as Aidryn described what was happening in Iathium. When he told her of the nea'la roses' fate, she shoved down her hopelessness, focusing instead on each step she took along the road. Each breath. Reaching for his hand, she laced her fingers through Aidryn's, moving closer to his side to fend off the chill.

When he'd finished, he looked over to survey her. "How are you feeling?"

Her cheeks warmed beneath his gaze. "Restless." She rolled her shoulders, noticing the tension that had bunched her muscles since she'd awakened alone that morning. "Oda was supposed to train with me at dawn, but she never came."

"That's because she took night watch," he answered. "I saw her."

"Did you recognize that Brylla word she used yesterday?" Lira asked. "*Sjovyn.*"

"It sounds like a term of endearment to me." Aidryn shrugged. "Maybe it's fictitious."

She pursed her lips. "I couldn't find it in the histories."

Aidryn scrutinized her, chewing the inside of his cheek. "How did that go? Using your magic, I mean."

Lira raised a palm to conjure a violet. She handed it to Aidryn, who accepted it with a warm smile. "Well, I think." Pointing toward the cattle's pasture, she tugged him along. "Come; there's something I want to show you."

On her way to find Aidryn, Lira had spotted a new calf in the pasture with its mother. Now, she dragged him toward the heifer with her shaggy red hide, and the calf whose hide was perfect match. It nudged beneath its mother, craning its neck up to nurse as they approached.

"Oh," Aidryn breathed, leaning on the fencepost to get a better look. "Look at him."

"So lovely," Lira whispered. "Just like his mam."

With a smooth, lithe movement, Aidryn hoisted himself up and over the fence, landing on the other side with barely a sound. He sank into the grass, resting his back against the fence post. A dreamy grin spread across his lips as he watched the calf.

Lira climbed between the rails and joined him. "I knew you'd like this."

"I needed it," he admitted in a low voice, tilting his head toward her but keeping his eyes trained on the cattle. The calf fixed its curious, black eyes on him and took a few tentative steps in his direction. "You've no idea how much."

He turned his full attention back to the calf, murmuring to it in *Hes'ka*, Clan Tarlach's native tongue. After a few tenuous moments, the calf closed the distance between them, nudging his shoulder with its little snout. Aidryn sighed contentedly, petting the calf and scratching behind its ears.

"When all this is over, I want a home overflowing with animals," he said wistfully. "A pasture teeming with horses and cattle, a stable cat or two. Puppies rolling in the soft grass outside our front door."

Lira grew silent and let him chatter while he showered the calf with attention. Even though she felt his warmth emanating through her, she suddenly found it difficult to smile and even harder to respond. When the calf wandered back to its mother's side, Aidryn leaned toward her, dipping his head to brush his lips against her cheek.

"Mortal *gods*, I can't wait to have our own home together," he whispered. "And children one day."

The words landed like a lead weight in her belly, and the

fear she'd been ignoring surged. "We'll have to be safe before we can do any of that."

"We will be." Aidryn looped an arm around her waist.

"I never imagined living anywhere but Iathium." Lira grimaced. "Now even that feels impossible."

"Our home is together," Aidryn replied. "We'll figure out the rest in time."

"How can you be so optimistic?" Lira demanded. She wanted to tell him how terrified she felt, but he'd only try to soothe her again. What she needed was to face the facts as they were.

Aidryn grew quiet, making careful eye contact with Lira. She hated the caution in his gaze when he said, "Because dreaming of the future gives me hope."

She drew her knees to her chest, wrapping her arms around them. "If there's no hope in the here and now, then hope doesn't exist."

LATE THAT AFTERNOON, Lira poured her birthright magic into Clan Beran's hanging gardens, discharging the power into the soil until she relieved the crawling, restless sensation beneath her skin. Lira, Talfryn, and Iva had revived the dead garden together, replenishing it after it had been poisoned during the summer. Clan Beran's people were still working tirelessly to refill the food stores before winter's harshest months arrived, so adding magic to the plants now and again helped them to grow lush and plentiful.

Lira and her mother worked side by side, cultivating vegetable plants, fruit trees, and the plots of land they'd nurtured these past months.

"Any word from the mountains?" Iva asked, pouring a bit of

her emerald magic into the vines that curled up and along the stone columns.

"Not yet," Lira answered. "I've thought about going back for a little while."

Iva cut a dark glance toward her daughter. "You want to leave?"

"If we wait too long, we could be trapped here come winter," Lira answered.

Rodhlan's winters were normally characterized by rain and wind. But this autumn had been uncharacteristically cold, and the breeze already carried a bite that promised a frozen winter. Regardless of how severe it became, the terrain around Fortress Halgeir could easily become impassable with only a small amount of ice or snow.

"It's far easier to get out of Halgeir in the winter than to leave the mountain valley," Iva said, stepping closer to brush Lira's chin. "What's troubling you?"

Lira's shoulders sagged as she faced Iva. "I'm afraid Eremon won't do his duty. I *need* him to take away this horrible pressure."

With every day that passed, Lira's responsibility to Iathium weighed more heavily on her shoulders.

"Four emissaries visited this morning," Iva said abruptly. "One from Clan Énna, three from Iathium—unofficially appointed, of course. They want you to challenge Caitir."

Lira tensed. "Why would they do that when Gerallt marched on the city in my name?"

Iva gave her a sympathetic smile. "They're loyal to you, not to Gerallt. I think you should consider it."

The last thing Iathium needed was another corrupted magic-wielder on the throne. Why should Lira ascend, knowing she was at risk of a death similar to Eremon's? She pressed her lips together before she replied. "I don't care what they want."

"Thorne meant what he said." Iva stepped nearer and lowered her voice. "Clan Beran will step in if the Rí will not. You can prevent that."

"You're leading the clan, not Thorne," Lira said, gaze hardening. "*You* prevent it."

"The threat was entirely his," Iva said, keeping her voice steady, though fury simmered in her dark eyes—a mirror of Lira's. "But I will support it if I see fit."

"There will be no need." Lira set her jaw. "Eremon swore."

"Then we'll see whether his vow truly means anything." Iva gave her daughter a dismissive bow. "I'll take my leave."

Lira didn't watch Iva go. Instead, she clenched her fists at her sides, rage washing over her like the tide over worn stone. If it weren't for the dark magic, Lira would be capable of righting so many wrongs. She wouldn't have to hide among the clans. She could take the throne, if she chose to.

What would she do if Thorne *did* decide to invade Iathium? She would be forced to choose a side. Eremon, Lira, the anointed, and the clans were supposed to be united. Everything they had worked for after Eremon's death would be shattered.

Finally, she let the truth of the roses' loss sink in. That cure had been her only remaining shred of hope, and now it was gone, too. After all the time she'd spent ransacking Iathium's archive to find a cure for Eremon, the rose remedy was the only thing she'd found—and that had come too late.

Fear gripped Lira, tightening her chest and making her body tremble. There *had* to be a solution. She sank onto her knees, wrapping her arms around herself.

Like a gentle reminder, a thought that had come to her back in the mountains resurfaced.

Trust your magic. Trust yourself. In your fears, you will find your salvation.

As if in reply, her magic pulsed within her. The gardens that had engulfed Fortress Halgeir's courtyard teemed with it. She had helped to create the magnificence that surrounded her, and here, her birthright magic stirred from within and without. If she could create these gardens, then maybe she could grow the roses for the remedy.

Her heart swelled with hope, and she stood again, flexing her fingers.

"Why didn't I think of this before?" she murmured to herself.

With a deep breath, she closed her eyes and summoned her magic. It rushed into her palms, swirling around her body, stirring her curls before it plunged into the soft earth at her feet. She poured her intent into the magic, visualizing the blue and teal Itelorian blooms.

Thick vines laden with sharp thorns and bright buds burst from the ground, spreading rapidly across the open courtyard. They took hold of the columns, climbing up and across the stone railings, infiltrating the hanging gardens. One by one, the buds began to bloom. Lira's heart swelled with joy at the sight, until the roses began to burst.

Though her emerald magic winked out, the vines kept crawling, choking every living thing they touched. One after the other, each deep, rich bloom exploded with a shower of dark magic. The crops, fruits, and blooms they'd worked so hard to cultivate began to wither beneath the cursed power.

Panic drowned out all rational thought. What would her mother say when she inevitably returned to see this carnage? What about Thorne? Aidryn?

"Mortal gods," Lira whimpered, calling on her magic again.

She had to reverse the damage.

Lira let the power of the Witness Tree surge until it stole her breath, then dropped to her knees and sank her hands into the soil. Bright emerald light split the earth beneath her, then streamed back up through the fissures. The ground quaked, and from somewhere in the distance, she heard shouting. Crying.

But now she was engulfed in the power. Drunk on it. Drowning in it. Emerald mingled with the green of a stormy sky, and thunder crashed all around. She wasn't sure if she was holding her breath, or if the magic had sucked it from her lungs.

A strong pair of arms wrapped around her middle, lifting her from the ground and breaking her contact with the soil. She landed hard on her back, and as the magic finally settled around her, she was able to open her eyes. Thorne was standing over her, his own eyes wide with terror.

"What happened here?" he demanded as she pushed herself up to sit.

As her eyes regained focus, she could see that he was covered in blood from his palms to his elbows. Splatters of red had stained his face and beard. Lira's body began to tremble. "Are you hurt?"

"It's nothing I can't heal," Thorne retorted, showing her his palms. They were burned and bloody, as though he'd contacted the dark magic himself.

"Who else? Did I harm anyone?"

"No." He crouched at her side. "What. Happened."

"I tried to grow nea'la roses myself," Lira said, voice rasping. "I wanted to make the remedy. That's all."

"Come, *sjeinga*," he said, scooping her into his arms and standing with her. He cradled her body against his chest with a soft, resigned sigh. "Let's get you to Father."

CHAPTER 31

EREMON

Dome

Beneath the Dome lay a city in its own right. Aside from the archive, the barracks, and the catacombs, there was a vast and deep network of compact stone apartments where those who served the nobility lived. Eremon followed Kenji down to his home after the cook finished work for the day, keeping to the shadows as they moved.

When they reached Kenji's door, the cook unlocked it and Eremon slipped inside, transforming quickly. Kenji milled about quietly, kindling a fire in the hearth and putting the tea kettle on. Toryn and their daughters were sleeping, he'd said, so their business here must be brief.

They sat side-by-side on two stools before the small hearth, nursing steaming cups of tea. The flames danced and flickered, casting a warm glow through the small apartment.

"How many of my spies survived the siege?" Eremon asked in a low voice.

Kenji swirled his cup. His usual levity was gone as he

answered, "Eight, though only Biren and Luko still serve. The rest disappeared."

Eremon swore under his breath. "To where? Rodhlan is small; there aren't many places to hide."

"Iteloria, perhaps," Kenji said with a shrug. "Much of the nobility sought refuge from Aila and Gerallt. Imagine their horror when they learn Aila followed them there."

"What's happening with that?" Eremon asked.

"Luko's looking into it." Kenji sighed heavily before turning to face Eremon fully. "There's something you should know."

Eremon's brow furrowed. "What?"

"King La'hiran is holding Aila prisoner," Kenji said. "Caitir showed me his correspondence, and it's legitimate. I'd know his hand anywhere."

Eremon almost spat his tea across the room. "Prisoner?"

"He gave Gerallt six weeks to fulfill the terms of the treaty—to send your magic back to Iteloria, essentially," Kenji said. "Clearly, he missed the latest kitchen gossip."

Kenji had been raised in Iteloria before following Toryn to Rodhlan. More than being the head of the Dome's kitchens and Eremon's dear friend, he was a skilled spy. His disarming charm, nurturing demeanor, and prowess in the kitchen made him the perfect go-between because no one had any reason to suspect him. He had mentored most of Eremon's spies, teaching them the nuances of life in Iteloria and training them to blend flawlessly into the continent's society while they gathered information.

"Oh, he'll catch up," Eremon said. "Let's have a little bird tell La'hiran that the rumors of Gerallt's death are simply a testament to his cowardice. He's assembled a special team of magic-wielders to unearth the secrets of Eremon's magic, and he's in an absolute panic."

"Easy enough," Kenji said into his cup before he drained the dregs.

"This is a disaster," Eremon said, scrubbing a hand over his face. "Even if we had six months to prepare, we could never stand against Iteloria. They're too strong."

"Don't talk like that," Kenji chided. "Iteloria has always kept an underlying hold on Rodhlan's power, but that's because they fear us. Rodhlan has the potential to be mighty."

"No idea how we managed to squander that," Eremon said.

"You know the histories," Kenji shot back. "Millions of magic-wielders had to die before the power here could be properly suppressed. Iteloria's kings have coveted it ever since. Now, why do you think that is?"

"The magical imbalance in Iteloria, of course."

"Of course." Kenji took Eremon's empty teacup. "It's not hard to conclude why La'hiran is so desperate for your magic now. We just need confirmation."

"What kind of confirmation?" Eremon asked, leaning an elbow on his knee.

"Did your father not teach you about this?" Kenji rose and set the cups on the mantel, then stoked the fire.

"Why would he have?" Eremon scoffed bitterly. "Didn't even bother to tell me I was a mortal god."

"Ah, that's right; forgive me." Kenji ran a hand over his face, appearing suddenly exhausted. "When Iteloria's magic begins to wane, it disrupts the natural order of things. Crops wilt, animals die. It impacts the continent's ability to sustain itself."

"You mean when Iteloria can't siphon magic from Rodhlan," Eremon supplied.

"It's a little of both. I like to think of Rodhlan's magic as the underpinning—the stability," Kenji said. "It showed signs of weakness beginning last spring, if my spies are to be trusted."

"Can an immortal rebalance the magic?" Eremon asked. "Between Rodhlan and Iteloria, I mean."

Kenji laughed incredulously. "You're asking the wrong cook."

Eremon made a noise at the back of his throat. "I could trade Caitir to La'hiran in exchange for a new treaty and be done with it. She has magic; perhaps she'd make a decent holdover."

Kenji had the audacity to look shocked at the suggestion. He harrumphed. "I happen to like Caitir."

"You would; you attract feral beasts." Eremon smoothed the fabric of his robes, ignoring an impulse to fidget with the hem. "I admit, I was surprised Aila left her here alone."

"She most certainly did not." His friend's gaze slid to him. "Clever girl rid herself of her keepers."

Eremon raised his brows. "Ruthless."

Kenji's mouth formed a hard line before he said, "Decisive."

He thought of the wariness in Caitir's pale eyes when she'd encountered him in the meadowlands. The careful way she'd moved, her guarded posturing. "She's particularly valuable, carrying that child."

"Leave the babe out of this; it's innocent," Kenji countered.

With a smirk, Eremon said, "Perhaps innocent by virtue, but conceived in deceit nonetheless."

Kenji's expression suddenly grew stormy. "Conceived under duress."

"Mortal gods." Eremon rubbed a hand over his face, feeling suddenly ill. He had believed Caitir's pregnancy to be strategic, but he had wrongly assumed whose strategy it had been.

Kenji seemed to sense the shift in Eremon's demeanor, because he added, "Toryn said she's still healing from injuries Gerallt inflicted, if you take my meaning."

Eremon's fingers curled into a fist. "How severe?" he asked in a low voice.

"You know Toryn," Kenji hedged. "She held those details in confidence."

A long moment of silence passed between them. Eremon could no longer stomach the thought of handing Caitir's child over to La'hiran, no matter what its mother had done. Iteloria's king aside, he found he didn't want Aila getting access to it. If the pregnancy had indeed been forced on Caitir, then Aila would likely seize control over the babe once it was born.

He tapped his chin, then pointed at Kenji as a realization struck him. "I have an idea."

"You're wagging your finger at me," Kenji said.

Eremon narrowed his eyes, but Kenji just imitated the way he'd been pointing to emphasize his words. Although he tried his best to remain serious, Eremon couldn't help laughing. "What are the chances the people might actually grow fond of Caitir?"

Kenji wrinkled his nose. "Not good."

"But you just said you like her," Eremon protested.

"I'm a special case," said Kenji. "Why?"

"Because I overheard some of her ideas, and they're not bad," Eremon said. "With a little wise guidance, she could buy me time to operate behind the scenes."

"Why behind the scenes?" Kenji exclaimed. "We need you back *now*."

"I need to gain the sentries' trust as I am now," Eremon hedged, "and I need to rebuild a council that's truly mine. Besides, I don't really know how to wield this immortal magic yet. It's too powerful; I don't want to make myself infamous like Nami."

Nami, Iathium's second supreme ruler and Eremon's distant kinsman, had once destroyed the original Dome in a fit of rage toward the clans. Eremon imagined the potency of his power was similar, if not stronger.

Finally, Eremon clapped a hand to his knee. "I'm getting you the money for her feast."

Kenji rocked back in surprise. "What?"

"You heard me. I still have some coin stashed away in my old chambers; I'll get it for you tonight."

Eremon had been pleasantly surprised to find that Macha hadn't ordered his rooms plundered after his death. When he'd gathered the courage to return to them the day before, he'd found everything just as he'd left it—save for the thick, unseemly layer of dust that now coated the vast space. Six bags of gold coins still sat nestled in a hidden compartment of his wardrobe, and that was more than enough to satisfy Caitir's whims.

Kenji opened his mouth as though to challenge Eremon, but muffled sounds caught the cook's attention. The bedchamber door cracked open, and Kenji's youngest daughter, Kyra, peered out. Her dark eyes widened, and she let go of the door, stepping back as she clapped a hand over her mouth.

"Tiriya!" she shrieked, long and high-pitched. "There's a ghost!"

"No, no!" Kenji and Eremon hissed in unison, waving their hands frantically at the little girl, who had backed against the wall, wide-eyed.

Kenji rose from his stool and rushed across the room toward Kyra, who was rubbing her eyes, hair askew.

"Quiet, you'll wake everyone!" he whispered.

He picked Kyra up, shushing her. She peered over his shoulder at Eremon, her large, dark eyes fixed on him, unblinking.

A bleary-eyed Toryn peeked out from the bedchamber. Kenji moved to block Eremon from her view, drawing near to the door. "Sleepwalking," he said, patting Kyra's back. "You go back to bed. I'll settle her."

Toryn disappeared, latching the door behind her. Kenji pressed a finger to his lips, then let Kyra wriggle out of his arms. She made a beeline for Eremon, stopping to stand beside his stool. Raising a little finger, she poked his leg, then jumped backward, startled.

"I've never touched a dream," she whispered.

"I'm not a dream, Kyra." Eremon leaned forward and lightly tweaked her nose. She gasped with delight, a wide smile spreading across her face. "It's really me."

Kyra threw her arms out wide. "Emon, I want a hug!"

The sound of the pet name she'd given Eremon as a toddler sent an unexpected surge of emotion through him. He smiled broadly, dropping from the stool to one knee, where she launched herself at him.

Kyra had been born the year after Corlan died, during the first year of Eremon's reign. The then-thirteen-year-old ruler had doted on her, often sneaking down to Kenji's quarters to play with her and rock her to sleep. As Eremon's illness had progressed and he'd grown more preoccupied with Lira, he had seen less and less of Kenji's children. He'd forgotten how much he loved being in the cook's home.

The little girl shimmied her tiny arms and legs around his torso. "Stand up with me," she demanded.

"Kyra," Kenji scolded gently, though the emotion on his face mirrored the bursting in Eremon's heart.

But Eremon just smiled and obeyed, hefting Kyra and grunting as he stood with her. "You're heavier than I remember!" he exclaimed.

"What's this? You're supposed to have earth-shattering immortal magic." Kenji crossed his arms, scowling playfully.

Kyra giggled as Eremon shifted his hold on her. "I don't think that applies to carrying exuberant six-year-olds."

Placing her palms on either side of Eremon's face, Kyra screwed her expression into a scowl. "Papa said you died," she said in a stern voice.

"I did."

She tilted her head, scrutinizing him. "Did you see my Pampy and Renny anywhere?"

Eremon cast a frantic glance at the cook. *Toryn's parents,* Kenji mouthed.

"Well..." Eremon said, grasping for the right words. "I didn't see anyone. Not even my father, my grandparents, or my little sister."

He felt a sudden rush of pain at the memory of Miryn, the babe he'd secretly named years ago. She had not survived long after birth, and as Iathium's royal traditions demanded, she was given no name and no record in the city's histories. It was as though she had never existed at all.

"Kyra, it's late," Kenji admonished, stepping forward to reach for her. "I told your mother I would settle you."

"But I want Emon." Kyra lay her head on Eremon's shoulder and snuggled against him. "Tell me a story," she said on a deep yawn, "about Pampy and Renny and the afterworld."

"All right," he said.

"Can Tiriya and Fjella and Juri come hear it, too?"

Eremon chuckled. "I'll tell it to them later. Are you ready?"

"Yes."

He patted her back, settling back down onto his stool by the fire. "There were so many flowers there, and the sky was a brighter blue than any Rodhlan has ever seen. It was peaceful, quiet. No sound but the breeze rustling in the tall grasses and the leaves of the trees overhead."

Kyra took a deep, sleepy breath against him as he continued.

"I imagine your Pampy and Renny were sharing the wide meadow with me, surrounded by flowers of every color and looking up at that same sky. Had I remained longer, we might have found one another. But the Defender of Histories brought me back to life, and back here to see you again."

When the little girl was sound asleep, Eremon let her father take her to the bedchamber. He was standing by the door when Kenji emerged.

"What was that nonsense about the feast?" he said, crossing his arms.

"I said I'll get you the money for it," Eremon answered, his fingers drifting to the door's handle. Before his friend could object, he said, "Trust me."

But doubt plagued him as he moved through the corridors later that night, long after Kyra had drifted to sleep again and Kenji had bundled her back to bed.

Asking for others' trust was easy. It was the follow-through he wasn't so sure about.

CHAPTER 32
CAITIR

Dome

Caitir woke at midmorning to incessant rapping on her door. Groggily, she rolled over and sat up, stretching as the person outside continued to drum a beat on the heavy wood. She threw on a dressing gown and crossed the room, opening the door to reveal an energized Kenji, who was bouncing on his toes and looked as though he'd already steeped five cups of tea.

His grin only grew wider when he saw her, disheveled and scowling. "I got the funding for your feast," he said. "Do you know what that means?"

She blinked at him, head swimming. "You... did what?"

"That means you got your favor, and now it's story time." He shoved a paper-wrapped pastry into her hands and nudged his way into her chamber.

"No, it's chamber pot time," Caitir grumbled.

A hearty laugh burst from the cook as he bustled over to the sideboard and filled a glass of water from the pitcher. "Oh, I remember those days! Toryn always said I had sympathy symptoms. Every night, when she got up to use the chamber pot, I was right behind her."

"That's more than I needed to know." She pressed her lips together to suppress the smile that was forming—both from Kenji's ridiculous story and what he'd just said.

He'd really changed his mind? And he'd managed to get the extra coin?

When she shut herself in the bathing chamber, she did grin, pressing her hand to her mouth to suppress a little squeal. She emerged a few minutes later, refreshed and more confused than she'd been when Kenji arrived.

"What made you change your mind?" Caitir sat, and Kenji nudged the pastry and glass of water toward her.

"Toryn can be very persuasive," Kenji answered. "She helped me see a perspective I hadn't thought of before."

"Which was...?"

The cook leaned toward her conspiratorially. "That we can't wait for people outside the city—no matter who they are —to save us. We must save ourselves. And if there's someone among us who can do that, then we should let them try." He gave her a little shrug. "I think it's what Eremon would have wanted."

Caitir was taken aback. "I... yes, I think he would."

A flash of movement caught her attention. From the open door, the silver cat slipped into the chamber. It trotted toward Kenji and leapt onto an empty chair, its shimmering eyes flicking between Caitir and the cook.

"You again." Caitir's lip curled.

"I told you, he's yours," Kenji said merrily. "I'm not going to claim him. Between my four children and Jolly, I can't afford to feed another mouth, no matter how adorable."

He reached over to scratch the cat's head. It flattened its ears and narrowed its eyes at him.

She could appreciate its perturbed expression. It was an

exact mirror of how she felt about Kenji's suggestion. "What makes you think I want a cat?"

"Because pets are good for the spirit," Kenji answered. "And you, my friend, are in need of some joy."

"Fiadh could use some of that herself. Maybe she needs a cat," she muttered. But the cat hissed, and she jumped, peering down at it. "Don't like that, do you?"

"As miserable as you can be, Fiadh is worse," Kenji said.

"I won't keep my promise if you insist on insulting me," she shot back, leaning forward to unwrap the pastry that sat on the table before her. She tore off a piece and took a bite, sighing contentedly.

"I just said she was worse than you; that should be a compliment."

Inexplicably, she wanted to laugh at him. The insult should have made her angry, but she was too preoccupied with her sudden change in fortune to worry about it.

"That's relative." Caitir schooled her expression into a deeper scowl. The cat was still staring at her, looking righteously indignant. "Well, what am I supposed to call it?"

Kenji looked as though he might burst out laughing. "Something happy, like... Precious. Rosebud. Dainty." He chortled, his face growing red.

Caitir wrinkled her nose. "Why is that funny? Those are ridiculous names."

The cat shot a hateful look at Kenji, as though it understood the exchange.

"What, kitty? Do you find those options unacceptable?" Kenji laughed harder.

"Isn't it a male cat? He certainly is regal, and I don't think he likes your ideas." She scooted to the edge of the chair and leaned nearer to the cat, who sat up tall, though it kept its gaze fixed on Kenji. Tentatively, she reached out as though to stroke the cat's fur, but it hissed at her approach.

Caitir drew her hand back with a sharp intake of breath. "Thinks he's better than everyone, too. A proper royal. Perhaps his name should contrast his attitude."

Kenji propped his chin in his hand and leaned forward, grinning like a fool. "I'm listening."

She regarded the cat, who looked at her expectantly. Raising her chin, she said, "Peasant."

The cook dissolved into a fit of giggles. Peasant glared at her, then leapt onto Kenji's chair, settling into his lap. Kenji yelped when the cat began to knead his thigh with its claws, and he grasped it and set it on the floor, swearing under his breath.

"Is *that* why you don't like cats?" he said, now scowling as Peasant leapt up onto Caitir's bed and settled right in the middle of her pillow.

"The scratching, the hissing, the general unpleasantness— that's part of it," she answered. "The rest of the answer is more complicated, and not the best conversation to have over breakfast. Or any time."

"Was it a bad experience with a pet, then?" he pressed.

"I will say this much, and then I will ask you to let it go." She sighed. "If my mother was displeased with me, she saw to it that my pets died mysteriously. Aidryn started giving them away or selling them for me once he figured out what she was doing."

The words were acrid in her mouth. Kenji's expression darkened, a deep sadness filling his eyes. Her emotions echoed his, and she averted her gaze to the knots on the wooden tabletop. "I've never spoken to anyone about this, except for Aidryn."

"I'm sorry I pressed you for the story; I didn't realize," Kenji said sorrowfully. "You never deserved such cruelty."

The pendulum on the mantel ticked, and for a long moment, that was the only sound in the room.

"Couldn't Aidryn have gotten you away from your mother?" Kenji asked, his voice gentle yet hesitant.

"He tried, once or twice. I wouldn't hear of it." She ran her fingertips along the smooth wooden arm rest of her chair, lightly tracing its swirling pattern. "Besides, our parents had too much political power. No one would have harbored us for fear of them."

"So your path to freedom was taken away from you," Kenji said.

"It was." She rubbed a hand over her belly absently. "I can't imagine hurting my own child. I don't want him lured down the same path."

"Or her?" Kenji's lips wavered into a sad smile.

She shrugged, a wave of sorrow washing over her. "Boys have more opportunities. Fewer chances to be used."

Kenji pressed his fingertips together and looked down at his hands. "I think Eremon would have a lot to say in that regard. He knew what it was like to be used and wanted for power."

Caitir bristled. "Well, he's not here to make his case, is he?"

The cook pursed lips and reached for the cat, scratching the back of its head. Peasant shrugged away, only to leap into Caitir's chair and curl up in her lap. She went rigid, raising her hands to avoid touching him.

"Get off!" she cried, bouncing her knees in an attempt to bump the cat off her lap.

Instead, Peasant found one of her hands and butted his head against it insistently. With a sigh, Caitir gave in, relaxing her hand and letting the cat nudge her palm.

"There, you see?" Kenji grinned. "The best of friends."

Caitir glowered at him. "I will kill you in your sleep."

"I have no doubt of that," the cook answered, rising to go, "but who would bring you pastries first thing in the morning?"

"Perhaps I could train Peasant to do it in your stead."

A laugh burst from Kenji. "I'd like to see that." He crossed the room toward the door but paused. "A word from a lowly cook: Our sentries do not want to be seen as pawns, or as means to an end. They want to be proud of the city and the people they protect."

"I expect you at table when I call my first council," she replied, suppressing a smile.

"Oh, I'll be at the table, that's certain," he replied, grinning broadly. "But don't expect me to sit next to the courtiers."

You could sit beside me. She pressed her lips tightly together. Her own father hadn't loved her enough to talk with her like this. Help her. Guide her. Give her advice.

Against her better judgment, she blurted, "Where are you going?"

Kenji swung the already-open door wider. "To plan a feast." He stepped out, shutting the door behind him and closing Peasant in.

The cat looked up at her once they were alone, blinking its silvery eyes, its expression unreadable. "Do you want out?" Caitir said, nodding toward the door.

Peasant looked at the door, then at the warm chair Kenji had just vacated. He leapt into it and began kneading his claws against the cushion.

"Fine," she grumbled. "Just stay off my bed."

Bed. Lying down for an early nap seemed like an excellent idea, so Caitir rose and padded across the room, not bothering to remove her dressing gown before she dropped back into bed and pulled the blankets over her head.

CHAPTER 33
EREMON

Dome

I t took Caitir an agonizing half-hour to fall asleep. Eremon watched her from his vantage point in the chair, quiet as he could be, until her breathing was steady and she'd stopped twisting and turning in her bed. When he was satisfied that she was sleeping soundly, he transformed, stretching his arms and legs.

Jumping into her lap had been stupid and impulsive. He'd let her sad story lure him into it, but he'd be more guarded next time. She clearly hadn't wanted him there, but she'd been strangely gentle in the way she went about shooing him. It had given him pause, made him want to nudge her, just to see what she'd do. He had thoroughly enjoyed refusing to comply with her wishes.

Eremon slid his boots off and padded around the room, surveying the surfaces for any sign of Lira's pendant. Caitir's furniture was sparse, and there weren't many places where she could've hidden it. It wasn't tucked away beneath a cushion, under the bed, or inside the shallow drawer at her bedside. He crept to the wardrobe next, whose door was still mercifully standing open.

One by one, he rifled through the garments, checking their pockets for any sign of the bronze tree. He suppressed a frustrated sigh when he came up short yet again. Two passes through this chamber so far, and he still hadn't managed to find it.

Caitir groaned in her sleep, stirring a bit as she rolled over, turning to face him. Eremon froze behind the open wardrobe door, waiting until she settled before he moved again. He crossed the room, slipped his feet back into his boots, and moved toward the chamber door, praying the oil on its hinges was still fresh enough to prevent an inconvenient squeak. With a careful turn of the handle, he transformed, slipping through the crack in the open door.

Let Caitir think the cat was wily enough to open doors on its own. It served her right.

Peasant. He snorted, reminding himself to claw Kenji to bits later for suggesting a name in the first place.

Eremon's thoughts raced as he moved down the corridor, but unlike in his mortal life, he didn't feel overpowered by them. Now, he was free to consider each thought, one by one. He remembered a time when the crushing weight of responsibility often rendered him unable to function beyond attending council meetings.

Everything had been too heavy back then, especially for a mortal man who hadn't yet entered his twenties. He'd assumed the throne too young, then watched helplessly as his mother descended into cruelty and ruthlessness. His own political limitations, in addition to his magical illness, had rendered every day a battle. This time, when he reclaimed the throne, he would be a better Rí.

But that thought carried its own weight, and if he was being honest, it felt heavier than all the others.

Eremon moved silently, keeping close enough to the wall that his fur brushed against it as he moved. The building had been eerily silent since he'd arrived, and he hadn't yet grown accustomed to the lack of activity. His Dome had always been a grand city center. Standing almost empty this way, it felt like a lavish waste of space.

He turned into the narrow, darkened corridor that led to the chambers of the treasurer, Tomis Énna. A cousin of Lord Irem's, Tomis had favored Eremon because of his affinity for the histories and his relationship with the former Defender. But he was a man with a nervous disposition, and Eremon worried that revealing himself might be considerably frightening.

He transformed in the corridor, pressing into the shadows as he willed the thumping of his heart to slow. Was it possible that Tomis might have been more intimidated by Aila and Gerallt? Would it be a relief to see Eremon? Would he believe his own eyes?

Rapid footsteps echoed in the hall, drawing near to him. For a split-second, Eremon considered shifting again, except his magic would be conspicuous, and he would call even more attention to himself. Perhaps it was best to remain still; it was dark, after all, and he was dressed in black, and—

"What in Nami's name!" a voice cried out.

Suddenly, he was standing face-to-face with the archival curator, Iona, whose hazel eyes had gone wide with terror. She was only inches away from him, trembling, her gnarled hands clapped over her mouth.

Eremon held his breath and didn't move as Iona squeezed her eyes shut, then opened them again "That's it; I am too old to be doing this," she murmured to herself. "Seeing things is the first sign."

"Only if the thing you see isn't real," Eremon whispered.

Slowly, Iona leaned nearer, peering at him in the darkness.

"How?" she whispered. Eremon found himself at a sudden loss for words, and the question became a demand. "How?!"

She reached out and grasped his face in her hands, soft from years of tending to the archive's many artifacts. He closed his eyes at the contact, though his body went rigid, as though it remembered the discomfort of close proximity from his former life. Iona withdrew, falling to her knees before him.

"My Rí." She gasped, then began to weep. "How is it possible? Have you returned to save us all?"

Eremon knelt before her, shushing her as he pressed a reassuring hand to her back. "There, there," he soothed. "I wish I could answer that myself."

"Where are Silira and Aidryn? And Lord Irem, is he alive?" Eremon sat on the floor in front of her and mirrored her earlier movements, moving his palms to her cheeks and gently guiding her to look at him.

"They're all alive," he whispered, holding eye contact. "We must be quiet, or we'll attract attention."

"Is that not what you want?" Iona asked, her thin lips trembling. "For us to know you've returned?"

"Soon," he answered carefully. "I don't fully understand my immortal power, but perhaps you could help me with that. I want more control over it before I ascend."

Iona straightened, as though she'd been handed an ancient relic to piece back together. There was a determination to the set of her jaw that made Eremon's heart swell with pride. "Anything."

"There are Itelorian texts in the inner chamber," Eremon said. "We can start with those. At best, I have five weeks to set things right."

"Why five weeks?" Iona asked.

"I'll explain as soon as I can," Eremon said. "I'm going to reveal myself to the treasurer."

"You'll kill Tomis with fright," Iona replied.

"I wouldn't want to do that." Eremon stood and offered her his hand. She took it timidly, and he pulled her to her feet.

"If you're going to him, I do have a request," she ventured. "The archive is dark and low on supplies."

"Candles, lantern oil, quills, and ink, then," Eremon said with a nod. "Places of learning should never be shrouded in darkness."

They strode arm-in-arm down the dim hallway. Several moments of silence passed before Iona spoke again, her voice laced with hesitation. "We wasted so much time preserving lies."

"Nothing is a waste, Iona," Eremon replied gently. "When Lira returns, we'll set things right."

"Nothing would make me happier, my Rí," Iona said.

"Just Eremon, please," he said with a smile. "Blast the formalities. From now on, we call one another by our given names."

EREMON SLIPPED OUT of the treasurer's chamber and back into the dark corridor two hours later, quietly releasing the laugh he'd been holding in since he'd entered. As Iona had predicted, Tomis had gone into such a fright at the sight of Eremon that he'd collapsed in a near-faint.

After he'd calmed down, Tomis had listened intently to Eremon's ideas, agreeing to assist him. Tomis had had one condition: He'd asked that he and his family be moved to new quarters.

"That sentry, and—and the girl," Tomis had said, voice quaking. "They terrorized my family for Aila. I want a good night's sleep without having to fear."

Aeron and Fiadh, Eremon had thought when Tomis

described the two. When the time came, he would deal with them both.

Eremon transformed in silence, his cat form moving further into the Dome's interior. He headed toward the staircase that led to the sentries' barracks, which were nestled underground between the archive and the dungeons. Like the rest of the Dome, the meager torches burned low. The sharp, mingling odors of mold and sweat would make a mortal ill.

This place wasn't suitable for sentries; it was an abyss.

His eyes adjusted to the dim light, and he scanned the faces of the men and women who milled about, searching for someone familiar. There were few faces he recognized. He noted that quite a few of the sentries were red-haired, like Deghan, the man from the mountains who often lingered near Caitir. They must have belonged to the party that had raided the city with Gerallt.

His gaze snagged on a lean, dark-haired sentry who had discarded his tunic: Aeron. Three long, angry scars marred his chest, and his hazel eyes were worry-filled as they darted around the crowded room.

"Is it true, then?" a blonde woman was saying. She secured her long braid and tossed it over her shoulder, looking expectantly among the men who were gathered against the far wall.

Eremon thought he recognized her from before his death, but Aidryn had been right: Beyond the most prominent and visible guards near the Dome, he had never truly gotten to know his sentries. He couldn't easily separate the impostors from the veterans because he hadn't spent enough time among them to know.

"Why don't you go up and see for yourself?" Deghan drawled in Clan Mór's heavy brogue.

"Don't do it, Vela," Aeron piped up. "It's grotesque. I piked it myself."

Vela smirked. "You think I can't stomach it?"

"I couldn't," Deghan said with a shudder. "I right vomited my guts up after."

"You don't want vengeance for your... what did you call him? Clan lord?" A smug smile lit Vela's face.

Deghan scowled. "Master—and no. May the scoundrel rot."

"Are you going back to the mountains now that he's gone?" Vela asked, edging a bit closer. From the high color in her cheeks, it was clear she was attracted to the red-haired sentry.

He shrugged. "What's for me out there? I like Iathium."

"If you live long enough to enjoy it," another sentry said—a man who appeared to be nearing middle age, judging by the shocks of gray in his dark blond hair. The others turned to look at him. "Can't expect the ranks to keep protecting impostors."

"You need us in your ranks, Rej," Deghan growled, prowling toward the sentry.

Rej pulled out a blade and closed in on Deghan, who threw his hands up. "For what? You helped Gerallt Mór hand this city to Aila. Where is she now, eh?" He thrust the dagger to punctuate his words, and Deghan flinched. "Let us settle our score with her, and maybe we'll let you live."

"She's in the Dome," Deghan answered, too quickly. "No audiences."

"Lies!" Rej fisted the front of Deghan's tunic and angled the tip of his blade beneath his chin. "Vela saw her leave on that ship before Gerallt marched."

Vela nodded her affirmation. Deghan sneered, and dark magic encircled his closed fists. Aeron moved then, pushing between them, casting a wave of violet water magic to douse the other men.

"Enough!" he shouted. "Infighting does no good. Those of us in the Dome have to stick together. We don't want to be out on the streets, with what Caitir is planning."

"And what do you know about it?" Vela drew her own dagger, pointing it at Aeron.

Palms up, Aeron's gaze darted from Vela to Rej to Deghan. "Aila is gone," he said, casting a sharp look toward Deghan. "To Iteloria. Caitir killed her bodyguard, too."

Eremon perked up. A low whistle left Vela's lips.

"Then I say we kill the girl and the usurper's spawn while we have a chance," Rej snarled. "End the line before it starts."

An enraged glint lit Aeron's eyes as Rej's suggestion landed. "You won't lay a finger on her."

"Oh, what won't I do to her?" the sentry said in a low voice. "And after that, I'll—"

The rest of Rej's words were lost as inexplicable rage rose within Eremon, roaring in his ears. It was that rage that had him transforming in an intense flash, right in the middle of the barracks. The moment he'd regained his human form, he was driving a terrified Rej backward, forearm to throat, pinning the sentry against the wall with enough force to knock the breath out of him.

"No sentry of mine murders and rapes," he seethed, slamming Rej's back against the stone to punctuate the order.

Rej's dark eyes widened with horror. The sentries around them shouted unintelligibly. He could hear them scrambling backward, away from where he had the man pinned.

"Is that clear?" Eremon said, leaning closer.

Rej nodded, blanching. "Yes, my Rí," he rasped.

Eremon let go of the sentry so abruptly that he sank to his knees, coughing, a hand at his throat. Rapid footsteps echoed behind Eremon, and he whirled to see Deghan running at him, dagger raised. Eremon raised his hands, but his body erupted with cobalt magic, blasting the sentry across the barracks and against the far wall, where his head cracked before his body landed on the floor with a sickening crunch.

"Get a healer!" Vela cried, keeping her eyes on Eremon as she rushed to Deghan's side. The red-haired sentry groaned as the magic retreated and seeped back into Eremon's body.

The room erupted, some sentries scrambling for the stairs and others frozen in place, mouths agape. Still others pushed their way toward the place where Eremon stood, taking in his form.

"Who in Nami's name are you?" one of them said.

Eremon wanted to run—to transform, to find a place to hide. Let them forget him. Let him become a phantom, a figment of their imaginations. But he found himself rooted to the spot instead, heart pounding as he looked each sentry in the face, one by one. A hush fell over the room.

On the far side of the room, a small group of sentries was loading Deghan onto a litter. He cried out in pain as they moved him, and Eremon tried not to flinch as he trained his focus back on the men and women in front of him.

"You know who I am," he answered.

At that, sentries began dropping to their knees before him, bowing their heads. One after the other, they placed hands over their hearts and knelt.

"My Rí," they murmured in response.

"I wish to share my story with you, and the plan I'm forming. But first, I understand some of you came to Iathium with ill intent." He scanned the sentries' faces, noting which cheeks reddened, which eyes averted. "If you choose to stay and serve me with the utmost loyalty, you will be pardoned for your crimes. If not, then you will be rooted out, one by one, and I will turn you to ash—not even a head left to pike. And you are to tell no one you saw me here today. Am I clear?"

There was a resounding chorus of, "Yes, my Rí."

Motion from across the room caught his eye, and he saw Aeron sinking into the deepest shadows at the far end of the chamber. For a moment, their eyes met. And for that moment, Aeron looked terrified.

Eremon couldn't suppress the swell of satisfaction that rose in him as he turned his attention back to the fighters before him.

"Good." He gave a decisive nod and clasped his hands behind his back, straightening as he scanned their faces once more. "Now—listen carefully."

CHAPTER 34
LIRA

Fortress Halgeir
1 Week Later

Lira and Aidryn leaned on the heavy stone railing that overlooked Fortress Halgeir's courtyard, watching Iva and Talfryn repair the hanging gardens. After the incident in the courtyard, Thorne had sent Aidryn back to Rodhlan Ridge to fetch Talfryn. Although Lira hadn't wanted Aidryn to go, her magic had urged her to let him.

Aidryn's protests had been weak, which had baffled Lira after their agreement not to separate. The only logical explanation was that he'd wanted distance from her. To her dismay, her magic confirmed the truth. And now that Aidryn was back, he seemed painfully distant.

Pay attention. The thought entered her mind of its own accord, as though it had come in from outside. *You are right to fear his gradual detachment.*

"Have you spoken to your mother yet?" Aidryn bumped his boot against the base of the railing, looking over at Lira. He wore a heavy cloak of deep crimson, which Clan Tarlach's adviser had gifted him on his return to the mountains. It contrasted nicely with the deep emerald tunic he wore—a gift from Skelly, he'd said, to pay homage to Clan Mór.

From the courtyard below, Iva's gaze found them. Lira quickly looked down at her hands. She toyed with the lacing on the sleeve of her long, fur-lined dress.

"No," she said. "She came up while you were away, but I didn't answer the door."

Aidryn's brow knitted. "It's not like you to hide, Lira."

Lira shrugged and shrank out of her mother's view, trying to shake off her growing unease. "I humiliated myself; that's reason enough."

"The worst thing you can do is disappear," Aidryn said, drawing nearer to her. He cupped her elbow and coaxed her to look at him. "People need to see that not even dark magic can alter who you are or what you stand for."

"But it *is* changing who I am," Lira protested.

"It's only changing how you *feel*," Aidryn pressed, though a troubled expression crossed his face.

"I'm fearful and angry, and I'm *dangerous*, Aidryn. I can't just will those things away." Lira leaned into him, grasping a fistful of his tunic. "I'm lucky I only destroyed the garden that day. What if I'd killed someone?"

Whatever Aidryn saw in Lira's eyes made him pull her into a tight embrace. She went briefly rigid before relaxing into his arms, then finally sagging against him. "You didn't kill anyone, my love, and you *won't*. You're strong and courageous. Hold onto that. The feelings will pass."

"But what if they don't?" Lira's voice was muffled against his chest.

"They will." Aidryn nudged Lira back a step, then took her face in his hands and kissed her forehead. "Stay grounded in the truth; it's what you do best."

The problem was that her truth magic had consistently

confirmed every fear she'd put before it. Before she could point out this inconvenient truth, footsteps sounded up the path. A moment later, Oda emerged onto the walkway.

"Things are looking better," she said, halting at Aidryn's side. "Talfryn says the lightning parched the ground, though. If we don't see rain before first snowfall, late harvest could fall short."

"You could water the gardens, you know," Aidryn said.

"We already talked about this," Oda answered with a glare. "I really shouldn't."

Aidryn ignored her and pressed on. "Between my experience with Faolan and Lira's access to the histories, I'm confident we can teach you."

Oda heaved a resigned sigh, casting a doubtful glance at Aidryn. A long moment passed before she finally said, "If I let you talk me into this, Thorne *cannot* know about the anointing under any circumstances. As far as you're concerned, this is just the other half of my birthright magic. Understood?"

Aidryn grinned broadly. "Perfectly."

CHAPTER 35
CAITIR

Dome

"Do you still mean to go through with this?" Fiadh was waiting outside Caitir's chamber with Aeron when she emerged late in the afternoon, two blades strapped to her back in her brother's old style. Aeron was dressed down to his black tunic and trousers, the standard issue clothing he usually wore beneath his armor.

"Yes," Caitir answered, sweeping past them, her golden gown brushing like a whisper along the marble floor. It wouldn't be long before she would need the garment altered; it fit snugly around her middle, stealing her breath more often than not. Already, she was feeling winded.

"The sentries don't care a whit about your protection," Fiadh said. "I wouldn't be surprised if one of them lobs a spear at you while they've got a clear shot."

Fear tore through Caitir at the thought. She cradled her belly. No forward movement was without risk; gaining the sentries' loyalty was her best chance.

Aeron shrugged halfheartedly. "What they want is to know

how to get their comrades back inside the Dome and off the streets. And they want news of Silira."

"Why should they care about her?" Caitir snapped, raising her chin.

"She's a symbol of freedom now," Aeron answered. "They believe she'll come back to save the throne."

"She hasn't bothered yet," Fiadh grumbled.

Caitir wanted to let every bitter thought she harbored toward Lira come spilling out, but this was her chance to forge a path on her own terms. "I'll talk to them about Lira. Whatever they want to hear, so long as they help me convince their friends to sign my treaty."

Truly, that was what this feast was about. The sentries in the Dome had capitulated to Caitir's terms with no trouble. In fact, she'd been surprised at the ease in which she secured their signatures. The next step was bringing the rest of the army back into the Dome, and they would begin tonight.

Aeron raised his brows but didn't say anything.

"Is Deghan well enough to attend?" Caitir asked. Their companion had been injured in a training exercise, according to Aeron, and had been out of commission for a week.

"I don't know..." Aeron looked to his cousin. "Fiadh, could you check on him?"

Fiadh's dark eyes slid to Aeron. "Fine." Turning on a heel, she headed toward the eastern side of the Dome, where the barracks were housed.

Aeron and Caitir lingered in the sitting area together, watching Fiadh go. The ticking of the timepiece was uncomfortably loud, punctuating the silence and emphasizing their proximity. The sentry was near enough that Caitir could feel the warmth emanating from his body.

She smoothed her gown and sighed, taking a step back. It was too uncomfortable; she wouldn't last the night in such a constricting dress, and she couldn't stand another loaded moment beside Aeron.

Forcing a pinched smile, she said, "Would you excuse me?"

Without waiting for a reply, she slipped into her chamber and crossed to the wardrobe, selecting an ivory gown with laces up the bodice and silver embellishments on the long, wide sleeves. When she was satisfied with her comfort, she crossed the room once again, unlocked the door, and opened it.

Peasant shot through the door, catching her attention. "Scoundrel," she called as he settled on her pillows.

When she turned back around, Aeron was standing in the threshold, looking down on her with an oddly contemplative expression. She opened her mouth to speak, but he stepped inside the room, pushing the door shut behind him.

"I'd like a word," Aeron said in a low voice.

"You hem me in as though I already consented," she replied, nervous energy skittering along her skin as she forced herself to hold eye contact.

"Please, Caitir," he pressed. "There's something you need to know."

She raised herself to her full height, for what little good that did. He still towered head and shoulders over her. "Make it quick."

"Everything is changing so quickly, and I fear we're running out of time," Aeron said, reaching for her hand. Though she drew away, he leaned forward and caught it in his own, bending his head to press a kiss to her knuckles. "I can't let another moment pass without telling you how I feel."

Her insides turned to cold lead as she stepped back, pulling out of his grasp. "You've told me before."

"Then you know why I didn't go to surrender." His gaze softened despite her reluctance, his voice gentle. "I couldn't bear to be parted from you."

Caitir remembered the market alleyway two summers ago

—how he had so brazenly backed her into the shadows and stolen a kiss. He'd been hasty for fear of her brothers, and she had been surprised to feel nothing.

Her breath came in quick huffs. He was still blocking the chamber door.

"You stayed to save your own skin," she replied sharply. "It was never about me."

If he believed mere emotion would be enough to sway her after everything that had happened, he was a fool.

His lips curved into a seductive smile, as though her reluctance was appealing. "You've become so harsh. I like it."

"Let me out," she said, making a move toward the door.

Caitir attempted to push past him, but he caught her by the shoulders, whirled her around, and slammed her back into the door as his mouth crashed down onto hers. His kiss was possessive and rough, his lips pressed so tightly against her own that she was trapped. She shoved his chest, attempting to turn away from his mouth, but he followed her every movement, sealing himself to her.

Panic forced her body into unyielding rigidity. Caitir tried to summon magic, but darkness impeded her vision, alternating with bright flashes of cobalt and silver. Perhaps she was going to die pinned against this door with Aeron's mouth on hers, stealing her breath in the worst possible way.

Abruptly, Aeron jerked away, releasing her and stumbling back. Her knees buckled as she tried to blink the room back into focus. The reek of burning flesh reached her nostrils, and she gagged.

There was a flash of silver, and Peasant leapt toward her. Without thinking, she threw her arms out to catch him. Strange, but she thought she caught the scent of ozone wafting up from his fur.

When she got her bearings, she made herself look at Aeron. He had a horrified expression on his face, and his tunic was in shreds. Open, bloody wounds—*burns*—covered his chest, arms, and face. Maybe her magic had acted on its own.

"You monster," Aeron growled.

Caitir cradled the cat in one arm. Her shaking fingers found the door latch, and she swung it open. "Get out."

"Fine," Aeron replied, "but you'll regret this."

She tried to ignore the pounding of her heart. "I doubt it."

Aeron glared at Peasant, his lip curling in contempt. As he turned to cross the threshold, he muttered an insult under his breath.

With a piercing shriek, Peasant launched himself from Caitir's arms and latched onto Aeron's shoulders. Aeron let out a garbled cry as he tried to detach the silver cat, but it got several swipes in before it finally leapt down. The sentry covered the side of his face with one hand, but Caitir caught a glimpse of three deep slashes running from his left temple down to his opposite jawline. They were laid open so severely, he would need stitches.

Aeron drew away blood-covered fingers. When he looked back at Caitir, the horror in his eyes transformed into hatred.

"Curse you," he spat. "Curse that stupid cat!"

"Go see to your wounds," Caitir said coolly.

With a final glower, Aeron turned and stalked away.

Caitir turned her attention to Peasant, who was now rubbing against her skirts affectionately, as though he hadn't just mauled a grown man. She couldn't decide whether to feel frightened or grateful. It wasn't particularly comforting for an animal to behave so savagely.

Perhaps the beast had served its purpose. Caitir would need to have it put down before the babe was born—likely sooner rather than later.

Carefully, Caitir guided the cat outside her chamber door. She gave it a little nudge with her slipper, moving it further away from the threshold before ducking back inside and shutting it out. She felt its soft body thud against the door, and it let out a surprised yowl.

Caitir locked the door and exhaled, pressing a hand to her forehead. She listened to Peasant scuffle about at the door for a few minutes before silence finally fell outside.

CHAPTER 36
EREMON

Dome

Eremon left Caitir's chamber door and trailed Aeron to the barracks. He crept into the deepest shadows and waited while the medic tended the sentry's wounds, then departed. Waited as Aeron raged silently in the empty bathing chamber.

Evening was upon them, and the other sentries had long since filed out to the courtyard for the feast. They wouldn't be back for some time.

He waited until Aeron crossed to the dingy looking glass that hung on the wall in the communal chamber, wincing as he gingerly touched his stitches. Willing his rage to the surface, Eremon transformed and advanced on Aeron, his deliberate footsteps echoing through the barracks.

Aeron's body tensed as the Rí's reflection came into view in the glass. Eremon was pleased to find that his eyes glowed silver in the darkness, and his skin was illuminated with a cobalt sheen. The sentry's expression went slack as he met Eremon's eyes.

"So Rej can't lay a finger on Caitir, but you can force your-self on her?" Eremon's voice was smooth and low. "How does that work?"

Aeron whirled to face him, his eyes wide with terror. "My Rí —I don't—"

But Eremon's hand was at his throat in a flash. Aeron let out a surprised, strangled cry as he lifted him off his feet. "I saw everything," Eremon sneered.

Aeron struggled to escape Eremon's hold, but his immortal magic responded in kind. It rippled in waves over his skin, and the sentry arched his back as though in pain. For a moment, Eremon thought about turning him to ash and being done with it. He tightened his grip on Aeron's throat, magic searing beneath his palm.

The veins in Aeron's temples bulged, and he strained against Eremon with all his might. It would be so easy to simply end the wretch's existence.

"Please," Aeron gasped. "I'll do anything."

"If you want to live," the Rí said, releasing him and letting him crumple to the stone floor, "take no one and nothing with you, and leave my city. *Now.*"

CHAPTER 37

CAITIR

Dome

Caitir crossed the platform, her knees weak, her stomach doing flips as the sentries dining in the courtyard turned their attention to her. The moon was full, stars winking brightly in the clear night sky. She'd draped a heavy, fur-lined cloak of soft crimson wool over her gown to ward off the chill and noted that the sentries had donned extra layers as well.

Her breath caught as she paused to scan the crowd below. Aeron was nowhere to be found. But as much as he loved to preen over his appearance, he wouldn't have wanted to show his marred face tonight. That was a mercy, because she didn't think she could be near him without displaying open hostility.

Caitir thought of the bejeweled dagger that now hung in a sheath at her side, wishing she'd thought to wear it before now. Then she could have left those slashes on his pretty face herself. She'd found it in a trove of Macha's jewels weeks ago and had hidden it among her belongings.

She cleared her throat and paused center-stage, looking out

over the gathering. Most of the sentries, even those who had been locked out, had signed her treaty with no resistance. Tomis had read it to them in the barracks, as most commoners in Iathium still could not read. He'd then instructed them to leave their mark as a sign of their commitment to Caitir.

Those who had refused the treaty had been relieved of their posts and were not permitted to leave Iathium. Sentries guarded every city gate to ensure those who had not pledged their loyalty were confined within its walls. Caitir couldn't afford for deserters to leak information to the clan leaders, especially before she'd managed to secure the throne.

Thankfully, Iathium's people were accustomed to powerful and ruthless women ruling from the Dome. But they also had an innate craving for truth and righteousness. If she could paint a picture of ascendancy and genuineness for them, that would be half the battle.

As though someone had called for attention, the buzz in the courtyard died to a lull, and the sentries turned toward her expectantly. She locked eyes with Kenji, who stood at the end of a long serving table on the other side of the yard. He gave her a slow nod.

Go on.

She took a deep breath. "Thank you for being here," she began, her voice resonating in the otherwise quiet evening air. "I trust you find your supper pleasing."

Kenji and his cooks had prepared a spread of roasted meats and vegetables, sweet mead, breads, and pastries. His two eldest daughters, Tiriya and Fjella, stood alongside the cooks. Each had black hair and angular eyes like their father. Tiriya was short and thin, with a round, pleasant face, while Fjella was taller and broad-shouldered, her soft curves accentuated beneath the fitted, nondescript cook's uniform she wore. While Tiriya had been friendly and accommodating like her father, Caitir had become the target of Fjella's ire.

"I don't understand why Papa is helping you," she'd said under her breath as Caitir had inspected the menu two days prior. "You've made us all traitors."

An angry flush had spread over Caitir's face and throat, but she'd held her tongue, keeping her eyes trained on the chart Kenji had sketched instead.

Tiriya cut in, "He has his reasons. *Hush.*"

Fjella's gaze had sharpened, and she'd lowered her voice to a hiss as Caitir had moved away. "What would the Rí say? Papa was his friend; he would be crushed."

"I think he would consider the greater good," Tiriya had replied smoothly, "which is what we should be doing rather than goading the spare wife."

Spare wife.

Blinking, Caitir returned to the present. Now, she heard the offending term carried on whispers through the crowd.

"To all of you who signed the treaty," she began, setting her shoulders and projecting her voice across the courtyard, "you have my gratitude. Welcome."

Whispers died on the sentries' lips. A thick, unsettled silence descended over the crowd. Caitir inhaled tremulously through her nose, forcing her body to relax.

This wasn't the rapt attention Eremon had once received. Then again, she shouldn't expect it to be.

"You all know why we are here." Her mouth went dry. She bit down on her tongue, drawing just enough saliva so she could swallow. "I've given you my word."

Caitir's treaty had contained her sworn condemnation of Gerallt, Aila, and the harm they had inflicted on the city. In it, she had pledged to do everything in her power to ensure Aila's demise. She had also pledged more coin from Iathium's coffers for more essential supplies for the sentries. The bare bones of her plans to build tighter alliances with the clans had also been part of the agreement.

"I wholly condemn my mother's actions," Caitir said. "By now, you likely know she fled to Iteloria to seek King La'hiran's aid. If she returns, I will be ready for her. In the meantime, I want to secure our city.

"This is an Iathium I do not recognize, teeming with lawlessness, treason, and uncontrolled magic. Only through order and restoration may we rise to our former glory."

Caitir chanced a glance at the sentries nearest the stage and was disheartened to see that their expressions were unaffected. One of the sentries toward the back crossed his arms and snorted. She tried not to look directly at him.

"What makes you think you deserve our protection?" An unfamiliar sentry near the stage met her gaze, his dark eyes flashing with challenge.

"I never claimed to," she answered, raising her chin. "But I can guard the throne while we await Silira Mór's return. If you have no love for me, consider my love for her."

That garnered a low buzz from the fighters assembled before her. She'd considered painting herself the victim for sympathy or leveraging her pregnancy for support, but that would be ineffective. These people didn't care about the child in her womb any more than they cared about a pebble on the street. Instead, she must be a defender in her own right.

"You betrayed Silira," an older man said, chin jutting out defiantly. His amber eyes sparkled, a stark contrast to his dark skin and white hair.

Her heart hammered so loudly she could barely hear herself speak. "I did," she said. "But then I saved her from execution. It was I who took her from the western tower to safety. From there, she escaped the city with my brother."

The crowd rumbled in agreement. She'd correctly assumed they would have heard reports to corroborate her story—likely talk from the veiled handmaidens who had assisted Macha in the tower that day. None of them had been privy to what had occurred at the Tarlach estate afterward, before Aidryn had intervened and whisked Lira away.

A smile curled Caitir's lips when understanding lit the sentries' expressions.

"I understand my late husband used Silira's name in order to seize power from Macha. But I invoke her name for a very different reason. If you will trust me to guard Iathium's throne, then I will stand vigil in the Witness Tree's absence."

"And why would we crown you?" The voice came from the back of the crowd, though Caitir could not make out who it was.

"*You* won't," she replied. "I would never ask for the crown."

It was true; she would never ask. Whether she took the crown for herself later was no one else's concern.

"Then tell us what you will do for us." The man who'd spoken of Lira fixed Caitir with a hard glare.

"I plan to mend the city's relationship with the clans and rebuild the government here," she answered. Her eyes darted among the faces in the crowd before her. She could not find one reassuring expression among them, and her stomach tightened as she forced herself to recite the statement she'd prepared.

"In the coming weeks, I will appoint a new council, based on the support and recommendations of respected citizens. I will attempt to call back any surviving dignitaries and members of court who wish to resume their service. You will also witness changes to some of our long-held traditions.

"In accordance with the late Rí's wishes, we will begin offering literacy education to all in Iathium who wish to read and write. I also hope to organize magical education and history lessons in the immediate future, as Eremon and Silira wanted.

"And I invite Silira to return to Iathium, and to the many who love her," Caitir concluded. "She must leave behind her unlawful clan alliances and return to her rightful place."

There was a sudden jolt among the crowd, as though she'd cast a wave of dark magic and shocked them to wakefulness. They began to jeer at her, shouting obscenities.

Perhaps referring to Lira as the rightful heir had pushed the people a bit too far.

"Traitor!"

"Impostor!"

"Bring us Silira!"

"We want Silira!"

"We must unify—we cannot survive divided." Caitir raised her voice over the din. Although she expected to feel panic, she only found resolve in its place. "Silira has given you nothing; only a name and a tragic love story with your dead supreme ruler."

Her brazen lie must have rung true, for a tense silence fell once again. They rattled her as she said them, settling sour in her gut. She let a long moment pass as she made eye contact with each sentry before her, one by one. Where she'd hoped to find some shred of understanding, of connection, there was none. They each held her gaze with an infuriating impassivity.

"Iathium will know peace again," Caitir finally said, "and I swear to you, I will finish what Eremon started."

As she pivoted to leave, something in the air shifted, and she felt the change before she saw the motion from her periphery. There was a shout from the back of the crowd, and when she turned toward it, that's when she saw the spear. It sailed over the heads of the sentries, directly toward her. Though her mind told her to move, her body wouldn't budge, horror rising within her and holding her in place.

She squeezed her eyes shut, preparing for impact.

But from behind her closed lids, she saw a bright flash of blue light, and the crowd erupted. Her lids flew open just as the last of the cobalt-blue burst dissipated and the spear turned to ash in mid-air. As though appearing from nowhere, Fiadh grabbed her by the elbow and hauled her toward the Dome.

The sentry who had thrown the spear—a tall, blonde girl with a long braid thrown over her shoulder—was dragged from the grounds, screaming nonsense. In the chaos, Caitir could make out only the words *Eremon* and *Deghan*. One of her comrades stuffed a dirty rag in her mouth to muffle her screams.

Fiadh ushered Caitir down the wide corridor as quickly as they could move. Peasant passed them, trotting ahead, his silvery coat shimmering in the torchlight.

"What sort of magic was that?" Fiadh demanded. "How did you learn to shield yourself that way?"

"I—I don't—" Caitir was winded as she struggled to keep up. "It just happened. I didn't do it."

Her heart was pounding erratically by the time they reached the western side of the Dome.

"Stay in your chamber until we get the sentries cleared out of the courtyard," Fiadh ordered, opening the door for Caitir.

"Let them stay," Caitir insisted. Kenji and the cooks had gone to too much trouble for the feast to be wasted. "I'll retire for the night, but don't send them away."

Fiadh held up her palms. "No promises." At the door, she paused. "By the way, where is Aeron?"

"Peasant scratched him," she said. "Last I saw, he was going to the infirmary."

Fiadh glared daggers at the cat, who was loitering on the other side of the threshold. "Get rid of it, or I will." She slipped from the room, and Peasant slipped in.

Caitir shut and latched the door, too overwhelmed to shoo the cat out. She pressed her back against the cool wall and closed her eyes, letting her head fall back as she panted. Invoking Lira's name had been a stupid risk. Then again, everything she was doing was risky.

When she opened her eyes, the room seemed uncommonly dark. Strange; the moon was full tonight, and she should have been able to see more than a foot in front of her. Puzzled, she squinted—and that was when she finally noticed the tall, lean figure blocking her view of the window.

"Who's there?" She reached back to grasp the door's handle, scrabbling for her dagger with the opposite hand. Her heart hammered as the man moved toward her, closing the distance just as her fingers closed around the hilt. "Aeron, if that is you, so help me—"

Now he stood before her, fully blocking her view of the windows and the moon beyond. He was Aeron's height, but there was a smoothness and grace to his movements that Aeron had never possessed. In the shadows, she couldn't make out his features. But then, he tilted his head, and a shaft of moonlight caught the silver of his angular eyes.

A scream stuck in Caitir's throat as Eremon pinned her against the wall, pressing his palms on either side of her head. He leaned closer, his black hair glossy as strands of it fell around his pale face.

"What lovely lies," he said softly, his voice smooth as satin. "Tell me again how you'll finish what I started."

CHAPTER 38
EREMON

Dome

Caitir's blade stung when it sank into Eremon's left side. She was craning her neck up to hold his stare, eyes wild, nostrils flaring, strands of hair falling from the loose coils she'd twisted it into. He thought he'd seen one of his mother's obsidian pins securing the style, and he had half a mind to yank it out of those golden tresses.

Rage shivered through Eremon as the pain dissipated. "How dare you."

She faltered, blinking at him in surprise. He ground his teeth as he wrapped his fingers around hers and wrenched the dagger from where she'd seated it between his lower ribs. Though the blade sliced him again on the way out, it came away clean. He let go of Caitir and pressed his hand to his side. The wound burned briefly, followed by a tugging sensation as it closed of its own accord.

Caitir held the blade before her, pointing it toward Eremon's heart. "Get back." Though her voice quivered, she jabbed the dagger's tip in his direction for emphasis.

"Doubling down, I see," he mused, planting his feet and drawing up to his full height. "I suppose when you've run out of sympathetic stories and empty promises, repeating a failed strategy is as good an approach as any."

Her tone was stronger when she replied, "If you expected me not to retaliate, then you've never accosted a woman in her chamber before." The slight waver he'd seen in her hand vanished as she steadied herself.

Eremon didn't try to stop the sly grin that spread across his lips. "*Accosted* is a strong word, though I will say the occasional midnight ambush always went unpunished." He advanced on her and lowered his head, his lips hovering near the shell of her ear as he added, "Not that you would know."

Caitir fumbled, dropping the dagger. It clattered to the floor with a heavy, satisfying sound. Eremon bit down on his lip to suppress the laugh that threatened to burst from him, then moved back in time for her palm to connect with his cheek. The impact snapped his head to the side, and it took great effort to quell the sudden flare of rage that rose within him.

He raised his fingers to touch the spot, astonished that he'd felt no pain. "Is this the thanks I get for stopping that spear?"

She raised her hands to his chest as though to shove him, but she stopped short of making contact, her brow knitting in confusion. "Why would *you* have done that?"

The same reason why I spared you from that fool of a sentry, he thought. "Because if anyone is going to end you, it will be me."

A muscle in Caitir's jaw ticked. "Then why wait?"

She was preternaturally still, looking more predator than prey. He couldn't help noting that her free hand had drifted to her belly, so he gave it a pointed look. That was when she flinched.

"I have no intention of harming the spawn, no matter who is responsible for its existence," he said.

"So merciful." Her cheeks and full lips were warm with

color, a stark contrast to her icy, pale irises. "What will you do when the *spawn* threatens your rule?"

"That won't happen." He stretched his fingers toward where the dagger lay, and it turned to ash in a blink. Although Caitir held perfectly still, as though unfazed, he noted the way her skin pebbled across her collarbone. "It will be sent to live with your brother, none the wiser, after I've dealt with you."

She crossed her arms. "And how do you plan to deal with me?"

"Perhaps a timely execution," he answered. "I'm quite the swordsman, so I could do the honors myself. Wouldn't want to mar the spectacle with a dull blade or a quaking hand."

Caitir's gaze flicked to the floor for a split-second before returning to him and hardening. "And in the meantime?"

He dropped his voice. "I'll let you know what I decide."

"Hmm." She bit her bottom lip, her teeth sliding sensuously over the soft flesh. "Not the way I imagined commanding your attention, but I'll take what I can get."

A shocked chuckle burst from Eremon as he assessed her. How in Nami's name had Aila managed to control this sharp-tongued creature? "I suppose you never imagined sinking a blade into my side either, did you, Caitir?"

Her name rolled off his tongue with surprising ease. That would not do.

Caitir didn't reply, but instead continued to stare him down as though her gaze alone could incinerate him. He warmed his voice. "That is your name, isn't it? Caitir."

She blinked rapidly, color rising in her cheeks. "Of course it is."

"Ah." Eremon licked his lips, leaning nearer. "You were so inconsequential to my existence; it's a wonder I remembered."

Caitir's gaze drifted to his mouth, then flicked back up. "Your mistake." Her voice was soft, a stark contrast to the way she was staring—as though she might draw blood through sheer will.

Eremon blinked and took a step back. "Staring contests were always so dull. Let's sit."

He drifted toward one of the chairs and lowered himself into it. Caitir moved to a cushioned chair across from him and perched on the edge of its seat, the hem of her ivory skirts rippling at her feet. The small pendulum timepiece across the room ticked, the sound punctuating every tense moment that passed. There was something unnerving in the way she held herself, as though she had summoned him to this meeting instead of the other way around.

"Tell me something." Eremon stretched his arms across the back of the chair and kicked one up his ankles up over his knee. "You could have had your pick of the rooms here, yet you're sleeping in an old audience chamber with a puny bathing room and furniture that looks like you dragged it in from the hallway. Why?"

Caitir bristled, her back rigid. "What concern is it of yours?"

He shrugged, offering her a lazy smirk. "Well, if I was going to be an upstart throne-stealer, I would at least do it right."

She pressed her lips together tightly, finally breaking eye contact with him again. So he leaned in and added, "Ah, I see. You weren't allowed the privilege of taking something for yourself, after all you sacrificed."

Her head snapped up, eyes flashing. "You know nothing."

"Don't I?" Eremon tilted his head, leaning forward. "Caitir, we have a problem. Normally I might ask if you know what it is, but you're an intelligent woman."

"You want to know what I think I'm doing here, so I'll tell you." she said, smoothing her gown over her knees. "I'm taking action where no one else would. Not Lira, not Aidryn, and certainly not you." She pointed an accusing finger at him. "All of you, missing from Iathium while the city cries out for aid."

"To be fair, I was indisposed," he replied lazily, though unease tugged at him.

"Until two weeks ago. What have you been doing all this time?" Caitir sniffed and rose abruptly, crossing the chamber to the wardrobe to rifle through it. "If you're not planning on ending my life in the next hour, I'd like to rest. Your presence is exhausting."

His lip curled. "Then I suggest you get used to fatigue."

She remained by the wardrobe, lingering over her choice of rich fabrics and elaborate gowns. He watched her, his annoyance ratcheting up with every passing moment. No matter how he'd maneuvered tonight, he couldn't seem to keep the upper hand. It was obvious that she was intent on ignoring him now, which was wholly unacceptable.

"Don't pretend to be so indecisive," he called. "You like the soft gray dressing gown; the one I could never get my claws on. Pity, that. I would have loved to shred it to bits, just to see the look on your face."

Caitir froze, then turned slowly to stare at him, her mouth agape. The expression of pure offense on her lovely face was perfection. Eremon had to bite back a burst of laughter in favor of the cold, calculating demeanor he'd adopted.

Her cheeks were blazing red as she stammered, "Shred... you—you were—"

Eremon winked, inclined his head, and replied, "You can call me Peasant, my lady."

CHAPTER 39
CAITIR

Dome

Heat rushed into Caitir's cheeks at the expression on Eremon's face. What had he seen? How often had he crept through the shadows of her room while she dressed—or undressed? *Oh, mortal gods.*

"You degenerate rake!" she shouted.

Suddenly, he looked a bit sheepish. "I haven't seen you naked, if that's what you're implying."

Without thinking, she snatched a small mirror from the vanity and threw it at him. It sailed across the room toward his head. He dodged, and it shattered on the marble floor behind him. Next, she grabbed a heavy hairbrush from the tabletop and stalked in his direction. "Get out of my room!"

"Did you not hear me?" he demanded, clenching the arms of his chair. He looked as though he wanted to launch himself at her but was expending great effort not to.

She pointed the brush at his nose, suppressing the urge to scream. "You invaded my privacy!"

He held firm, silver eyes sharp. "And you invaded my city. I had a right to know what was happening here."

"Not in my bedchamber," she said, raising her arm to strike him.

He let her bring the brush down, catching her wrist at the last possible moment to stop the impact. His grip was warm and firm, and he pulled her down to eye level with him, baring his teeth. "You will not touch your Rí again." The smooth, warning tone in his voice set her knees quaking, and she fought to suppress her sudden rush of dread. "Are we clear?"

She swallowed hard. "Yes."

Eremon's eyes narrowed. "Yes, *what*?"

"Yes, Eremon." Her words came out on a reluctant rasp. He'd wanted her to call him *my Rí*, but she would not give him the satisfaction. She caught the faint scent of spice that clung to his tunic, then held her breath to block it out.

When he released her, she pointed to the door and repeated, "Get out."

Caitir took a step back as he rose, leering down at her. "I will give you leave to prepare for bed," Eremon said, moving fluidly toward the door, "but don't expect me to go far."

His long fingers wrapped around the latch, and he pulled the door open. With one last, contemptuous look at Caitir, he transformed into his cat form in a bright burst of cobalt. Before she could throw the brush, he slipped from the chamber.

She all but ran across the room, slamming the door and engaging the lock behind him. Panting, she pressed her back to the cool wood. Her body began to tremble.

He'd managed to catch her off guard tonight, and she'd had to fight to stay on balance. She had spent the last week imagining what his inevitable return might be like, but every possible scenario had involved certain doom, not to mention the fact that she'd already imagined the many ways he might dispose of her. At no time had she ever imagined that she would raise a dagger against him, much less stab him between the ribs.

Caitir shuddered, then prepared for bed. She spent the night staring at her chamber door, despite the exhaustion that weighed her down.

Eremon never returned.

CHAPTER 40
CAITIR

Dome

C aitir milled aimlessly about her chamber, bone-tired and scowling. At sunrise, she'd begrudgingly risen, expecting Eremon to return no later than sunrise. Now, as late morning light streamed in through the windows, she splashed her face with cold water from the basin before dressing for the day.

She was standing on the other side of the open wardrobe door when she heard the chamber door swing on its hinges. Relief surged through her. Finally, she could stop anticipating the Rí's return.

"Back to taunt me again, I see," she called, making a space to hang her dressing gown. "Couldn't wait one more hour?"

"...What?"

The responding voice was definitely *not* Eremon's. When she peeked around the wardrobe door, Fiadh was standing just inside the chamber, a puzzled look on her face. Caitir's cheeks went hot.

"Ignore me," Caitir said airily. "I barely slept."

Fiadh's eyes traveled along the haphazard parlor furniture. "You had a visitor last night." She nudged the small pile of ash with the toe of her boot—what was left of the dagger Eremon had destroyed. Next, her gaze landed on the broken mirror Caitir had hurled across the room. "Make you angry, did he?"

Caitir's heartbeat quickened. "Pardon?"

Fiadh rested her hands on her hips. "Don't play daft. The furniture is disturbed, too."

"Oh, the midwife was here," Caitir said, hoping her airy tone would be convincing enough.

"Caitir." Fiadh crossed her arms. "I know you didn't duel with the midwife. What happened?"

Resignedly, Caitir sighed. "Aeron accosted me in here last night."

Fiadh drew back, aghast. "My cousin would never."

"He's a man; of course he would," Caitir snapped. "They're all animals."

"Then why was Aidryn so fond of him?" Fiadh demanded.

"Probably the same reason he was fond of you," Caitir replied smoothly. "Pitiful judge of character."

Fiadh's chin trembled. "Aidryn made me like this, you know. I wouldn't be trapped here with you if it weren't for him."

"Pity," Caitir said sourly. "Since you feel so trapped, I rescind my offer of the armory. I would be better served giving it to Clan Tarlach as a peace settlement."

"I knew not to trust your word," Fiadh said, baring her teeth. "You're just like Aila, all charm and empty promises."

"Oh?" Caitir leaned nearer, alarm coursing through her. "What did you give my mother in exchange for empty promises?"

The silver cat came trotting from the direction of the kitchen, as though he meant to squeeze past Caitir and into the chamber. She bent and scooped him up, receiving a hostile hiss in response.

"Ask him," Fiadh said, nodding to the cat—*Eremon*. The strange truth of it sent a jolt through Caitir. "I'm going to find my cousin." With a dark glare, she turned and stalked down the corridor, white-knuckling the hilt of her sword.

Caitir slipped back into her chamber before dropping the cat to the floor. Eremon landed on his feet and transformed in a flash of magic, raking a hand through his black hair and straightening his tunic.

"Don't you dare pick me up like that again." His scowl was almost humorous.

"Don't behave like a pet, and I won't be tempted." Caitir answered, clasping her hands before her. "What can I do for you, dearest Peasant?"

He scowled. "The archers are here, seeking an audience. I saw them at the gate."

So Gerallt's son had finally received her message. "Then I suppose you'll want to meet them."

"This scheme to gain Iathium's trust is yours. I want you to follow through with it." Eremon looked her up and down, then made a disapproving noise in the back of his throat. "You need a different gown."

Caitir's hand flew to the bodice of the powder-pink dress she wore. He was standing so near that she had to crane her neck to make eye contact. "What's wrong with this one?"

Eremon tilted his head in thought, a strand of silken hair slipping out from behind his ear. "Nothing, but I have an idea. Just—" He nodded toward the wardrobe. "Choose a red one, and don't meet the archers without me."

He whirled, crossing the room and disappearing behind a tapestry. Caitir followed, pulling the fabric away from the wall just in time to see the hidden door behind it click shut. She ran her fingertips along the seam of the door, then stepped away and moved to the wardrobe.

Caitir's heartbeat thundered in her ears as she selected a

crimson gown and changed into it. She stayed within earshot of the doors so Eremon couldn't surprise her again, hastily fastening the stays and buttons. By the time he returned, she was before the mirror, securing her hair into elegant coils that framed her head like a crown.

Her throat tightened as he stepped closer, her palms breaking into an unseemly sweat. In his hands, he carried something wrapped in plum-colored velvet. "You're going to need this," he said, gingerly tugging back a corner of the material to reveal a crown.

The circlet was made of blackened steel, with dagger blades rising from the mid-point of the crown to the front, ascending in length. Between the center blades, heavy, blood-colored rubies were set. Caitir took a step back on a sharp inhale.

"That's gruesome," she said.

Eremon raised his chin. "It's fitting." He discarded the cloth and held the circlet up.

She flinched. "This is a trap."

"It's a ruse," he answered, drawing back slightly. "Now, be still."

She released a shaky exhale. Eremon raised the crown again, setting it gingerly onto Caitir's hair. A lump rose in her throat as its full weight settled and he withdrew his hands. She couldn't resist taking a peek in the mirror, and she was surprised to find that she cut a truly terrifying figure, clad in red and wearing a crown of blades.

"I told the sentries I wasn't asking for a crown," she said weakly, pulling her attention away from her reflection.

"Yes," Eremon replied, reaching to tuck a stray strand of her hair back into place. She tensed at the contact. "But the archers didn't hear that. You're going to establish your authority with them today. Leave the sentries to me."

Caitir drew back. "*My* authority?"

Eremon didn't reply. His shimmering gaze swept over Caitir,

from the hem of her dress to the tip of her crown. Her skin grew uncomfortably warm under his scrutiny, and she fought to keep her breathing steady. When he took a step closer and tipped her chin with his forefinger, she shivered.

"Shoulders back," he ordered softly, then nodded when she straightened. "Now you're ready."

Artagán Mór and a band of five archers were standing in the center of the throne room when Caitir entered, cat-Eremon at her heels. They parted as she passed through their ranks and ascended the dais. Her heart began to pound as she turned to face them, then sat on the cushioned edge of the throne. Eremon leapt onto its broad, intricately carved wooden arm and settled there, eyeing the archers with the same scrutiny as she.

The throne room was a wide-open space, its walls and ceiling made of ornate stained glass. Sunlight filtered through the glass in a spectrum of colors that stretched along its polished mahogany floors and drifted elegantly over the crimson-cushioned throne that sat on the far end of the room. Dust motes caught the colors, floating like tiny orbs of magic through every shaft of light.

She forced herself to focus on Artagán, who stood tall before her. His rich auburn hair bore a stark contrast to the Clan Mór green of his tunic, and he'd slung a heavy, fur-lined cloak over his shoulders that reminded her vaguely of the Clan Beran style. The archers were dressed similarly. Each wore a polished leather brigandine over their dark green tunics, with matching vambraces secured on their forearms. Their weaponry was new, as well.

Artagán gave her a small bow. "We received your summons from a falcon in the western meadowlands."

Caitir flicked her gaze to Eremon, who purred on the arm rest beside her. She suppressed a snort. "Silver, perchance?"

"It was," he answered, looking confused.

She bit down on the inside of her cheek, unsure whether she wanted to laugh or shove the cat from its perch. "I intended to ask how you fare, Artagán, but it appears you've done quite well for yourselves. Mercenaries, I take it?"

"Fighters for hire." He let a silent moment pass before adding, "We're not thieves."

"Neither are you loyal." Her voice reverberated so pleasantly through the room that gooseflesh rose on her arms. The sudden, heady rush of power was almost enough to make her forget that Eremon sat at her side. "Not that I blame you for abandoning your father's cause. Is it true your sister loosed the fatal arrow when you could not?"

"Aye." Another beat of silence as their gazes locked. "In the end, I think it was right. He would have brought her to harm, just like he did to you."

"And you would have left her to fend for herself either way." Caitir remembered how Artagán—how all the archers—had stood by and allowed Gerallt to harm her. "Just like me." The last words came out on a low murmur.

The cat leapt from the arm of the throne onto its high back, letting his tail dangle over the side. From the corner of her eye, Caitir could see it rhythmically curl and release.

"My lady, I am deeply—" Artagán began, but she cut him off.

"Your willingness to face me here is admirable," she said, reaching for the cat and stroking the back of its head. "You will receive a reward for coming, as promised."

Artagán blinked in disbelief. The archers who stood behind him exchanged bewildered glances. "My gratitude," he said.

Caitir inclined her head. "I want to know what it will take to keep you in the city. I need archers along the sea wall."

The other archers murmured to one another. Artagán's lips curved into a dark smile. "Why, when Aila is being held in Iteloria?"

"How—" Caitir's eyes widened. "Where did you hear that?"

"We have our sources," Artagán replied. "I wouldn't put it past Aila wriggling her way out of captivity, if you take my meaning. Best be on our guard."

"If you think that's possible," Caitir said carefully, "then you'll agree we need more eyes on the strait. How widespread is the news of Aila?"

"It's traveling on barely a whisper," said Artagán.

"Then what will it take to buy your silence?" she asked.

"You need more than our silence." Artagán's wily gaze slid to his archers, then back to Caitir. "You need us to silence those who know."

The cat sat up straighter, eyeing Artagán.

"No deaths," Caitir blurted. "Just a revision of the narrative. Can you make that happen?"

Artagán's eyes lit. His sharp gaze swept from her slippers to her crown. "For the right price; of course, there are no guarantees."

Caitir held still, mirroring his scrutiny. She noticed the tension in his stance, the rigid way he waited—as though holding his breath. "Try me."

Artagán answered without hesitation, "Five years' pay for each of us. We want double the sentries' wages and homes in the city, all provided by the Dome. And political immunity."

The cat hissed, but Caitir held up a hand. "Quiet, Peasant." She turned her attention back to the archer, ignoring the cat's low rumble. "That can be arranged. It's understandable, given your history here."

Artagán crossed his arms, his vambraces groaning with the friction. "Is it true you're with child?"

His question sent a jolt through Caitir, but she tilted her head in answer. "Your half sibling."

The archer blinked as through he hadn't expected the rumors to be truth. "Then I pledge my loyalty, and that of my archers, to the Clan Mór flesh and blood you carry." He made a fist, struck himself in the center of his chest, and bowed his head. His archers followed suit.

Caitir's heartbeat sped at the invocation of that name—that clan. No matter who had fathered it, this child would never be a Mór.

She jumped when the cat leapt into her lap, pressing its head beneath one of her hands and giving it a little push. It was only then she realized she'd been gripping the throne's arms so hard that her fingertips were turning white. When she released them, pain lanced through her fingers, and she suppressed a hiss. She scratched behind one of Eremon's silver ears and refocused her attention on the archers.

"I accept your loyalty," she said. "We'll arrange your rewards and payment with haste."

Artagán nodded. "Then tell us what we must do."

CHAPTER 41

CAITIR

Dome

An hour later, Caitir found herself locked inside Macha's audience chamber with Eremon, sorting through his mother's jewelry trove. There were pendants of gold, diamond rings, silver bracelets, and diadems weighed down with jewels. Just one piece alone would fetch a hefty exchange in the treasury, so she set aside a few pieces for each archer as Eremon looked on, occasionally commenting on her choices.

"Not that one," he said from his vantage point on his mother's sofa.

Caitir held up a glittering sapphire brooch. "Why?"

"I always liked that one." He lay across the couch cushions and draped his legs over one of its plush arms, turning his head toward her again. "Find something more garish."

She turned the brooch over slowly, examining its deep blue hue and the jewels' pristine cut. "The tackier the jewel, the more impressed they'll be with their spoils."

"Exactly." He laced his fingers together and rested his hands on his stomach. "We'll need to watch Artagán closely. I don't trust him; they got that new armor somewhere."

"He raided your coffers before he left Iathium the first time," she admitted, remembering the way Aila had raged when the archers were found to be missing. Gerallt had been to blame. His son had talked him into providing the archers with excessive coin for new supplies. "He's had little time to forge solid alliances anywhere."

"You'd be surprised how quickly alliances can form." Eremon studied the gilded pattern on the ceiling before he added, "Put them on night watch and I'll patrol. During the day, they could be given court duties. The best course of action will be to keep them contained and occupied."

"Then it will be done as you say." She glanced over her shoulder, wiggling the brooch so it caught the light. "Shall I set this one aside for you, Rí Messenger Hawk?"

Eremon rolled his eyes and waved her off. "No, but I *do* think I deserve a finder's reward. Perhaps you'll deliver me a pastry from the kitchens every morning."

"If I had known you were so fond of pastries, I would have been sneaking to the kitchens years ago," Caitir said. She wondered fleetingly whether she should be embarrassed by her candor but brushed the thought aside.

He turned his head to look at her again, his gaze resting heavily on her for a long, silent moment. Caitir tried to ignore him, instead studying a pair of emerald earrings before setting them aside. If the past day had been any indication, these quiet moments between them would be the hardest to bear. She couldn't reconcile the overpowering awe of being in his presence with the sharp-tongued banter they'd fallen into.

"How did Aila manage to hold such sway over you?"

Eremon's question made heat rush into Caitir's cheeks, and a heaviness settled onto her shoulders that made her want to shrink. Instead, she sat up straighter. "Probably for the same reason you couldn't bring yourself to banish your mother's council and assume your full power."

"That was careful maneuvering on my part," he said, his voice clipped. "I wasn't a puppet, and I certainly didn't need more enemies than I already had."

Caitir released the bracelet she'd been eyeing and let it fall back onto the jewelry case's soft cushion. "I would have done anything for Mother."

Eremon snorted. "You *did*."

"Short of murder by my own hand, though I would have killed Lira if she had asked me to—friend or no."

A slow smirk played across his lips. "I'd say that's a no."

Caitir glared at him. "I thought of her as my friend until she became a threat."

"Lira was a threat to exactly no one." Eremon's bemused expression twisted into a scowl. "It's clear your mother taught you to value yourself above all others, including benign archivists."

His words made her heart pinch. "On the contrary; she taught me to hate myself," she said.

Caitir turned to face him fully, shifting from her knees to her bottom and stretching her legs out in front of her. "I was never enough. Rouge for my too-pale skin. Golden dye for my mousy hair. Bindings for my breasts because—" Her cheeks suddenly grew warmer. "I shouldn't talk about my breasts."

The corner of Eremon's mouth turned up, though he kept his eyes on her face. "You have my attention."

Caitir glowered at him. "I was allowed to exist, but not to truly live. I was a brainless pawn. And the only person I was encouraged to openly love, value, and fear was her."

Eremon grew silent for a long while as she stared listlessly into the case of gold and jewels. When he finally spoke again, he said, "I think the first thing you need to learn is that your behavior wasn't brainless. It was the worst kind of self-preservation."

Caitir's lips parted, and Eremon's silver eyes lit knowingly as she straightened the chain of a heavy pendant that lay in the center of the spread she'd created.

"Speaking of Lira, I have to ask," he ventured, "whatever did you do with her pendant? I've looked everywhere; I could've sworn no one knew more hiding places in the Dome than I."

"What?" Caitir asked incredulously. Of course, she remembered the bronze heirloom tree from Skelly. A sickly green haze crept into her vision, and she shook her head, blinking it away. "What would I have done with it?"

"You stole it from her in the meadowlands," he pressed. "You and Fiadh used it to *turas* back here."

"I did use it for *turas* once," Caitir replied slowly, fighting through the sudden haze in her memories. "It was when I saved Lira from the tower chamber in the spring. You were lying in state up there; Macha had locked her in."

Caitir had been careful not to let her gaze linger over his lifeless body for too long. The thought of Lira being locked in that room with him still haunted her, though she'd tried and failed to suppress it. A brief wave of nausea rushed over her at the memory.

The color drained from Eremon's face. "Why was Lira being kept with my body?"

"We—the handmaidens—prepared her like a bride on her wedding night," she whispered. Sickening regret coiled within her, tightening around her heart. "The intent was to coerce Lira into suicide."

Lira's possession of Eremon's ring, and the protective magic that surrounded it, had deterred Macha from executing her. That ring, Caitir had learned, had been a quiet but essential part of inheriting Iathium's throne for centuries. Eremon's ancestors had been able to keep it secret, since it had never once departed their bloodline until Lira. It signified the supreme ruler's choice of heir, delegitimizing any other claim to the throne.

Eremon swore under his breath, bringing Caitir's awareness back into the present. "And you helped her escape?"

"Only the tower," she admitted, "for Mother. Aidryn got her out of the city."

Eremon swung his legs back down and sat up on the couch, propping his chin in his hand. His scrutiny fell heavily on her shoulders. "You changed the topic. Do you truly expect me to believe you don't remember taking that necklace?"

She squeezed her eyes shut, straining to remember. Broken images of that afternoon in the meadowlands rose to the surface. "I remember Lira wearing it, and Fiadh trying to take it. There was dark magic, but..." With an exasperated sigh, she looked at Eremon again. "I don't even remember returning to the Dome that day. Strange, since you stole our horses."

Eremon sat back and crossed his arms. "Could Fiadh have stolen it from you?"

Caitir shrugged. "Maybe."

The corner of his mouth quirked in amusement. "And if I asked you to help me find it, what would you say?"

"I would agree," she answered quickly. She would do anything to gain even the tiniest shred of his trust. "I'll do whatever you ask if it means keeping my child safe."

"And yourself." He pressed his lips together for a moment, then nodded. "Keep your eyes open, and I'll do the same. I don't understand your forgetfulness, but for my life, I believe you."

Caitir heaved a shaky, relieved sigh as he continued.

"If you find it, return it to me immediately," Eremon said. "If you learn its whereabouts, tell me right away. Do you swear?"

The intensity in his silver eyes was unnerving, and Caitir had to fight the urge to look away. "I swear."

Eremon gave her a slow nod, then rose from the sofa, crossing the room to look out the window, which faced the Dome's central oculus. He stilled, clasping his hands behind his back as another deep silence fell over the chamber. A flock of birds passed the window, migrating southward for the coming winter. Sunlight reflected off the array of stained glass on the oculus, and Caitir could almost see the splash of color that bathed the throne room below at this time of day.

Long moments passed before Eremon spoke again.

"Some believe I should take the throne back now and dispatch you." He didn't turn to face her, though she could sense his tension by the way his shoulders bunched. "But I think we may be able to benefit one another instead."

Caitir stilled. "What do you mean by that?"

"I mean—" Eremon pivoted, then perched on the window's wide, ornate sill. His gaze flicked to the ceiling, then back down to Caitir. "Today, you proved that you were willing to take my instruction. To be honest, that was unexpected."

She sniffed dismissively. "I assure you, I'm full of surprises."

"You know your priorities," he shot back, standing again and moving nearer. He ran his slender fingertips along the back of a beautifully carved wooden chair, whose plush, plum-colored cushions looked as though they'd never been touched. "Survival, your child—I can respect that."

"All base human instincts." Caitir shrugged, doing her best to appear nonchalant despite the wild flare of curiosity that blazed through her. She held still, bracing for Eremon's next words. Her palms began to sweat as he leaned forward.

"Well-deserved justice is never dull, and I think Iathium demands that." His silver eyes flicked just below her face—to her throat—for a moment before he met her gaze again. She swallowed hard. "So why don't we focus on ensuring Aila never returns?"

Surprise coursed through her, and her eyes widened. "I—" She echoed his earlier words. "You have my attention."

"She is our common enemy," he said. "I think the city may forgive you in time, if you work with me to save it from her."

Caitir sat up straighter, unsure whether she'd heard him correctly. "I want a pardon and a life with my child when this is over."

"Negotiating already?" Eremon gave her a wry smile. "You haven't heard my idea."

"I won't negotiate for anything less," she replied.

His eyes lit. "I'm sure something can be arranged."

"Indeed." She hoped he couldn't see her desperation. Until now, she had assumed that Eremon would return to Iathium in all his glory, dispose of her immediately, and ascend once again. Of all possible outcomes, this was one she had never imagined. "Tell me what you're planning."

"I'm going to draft a series of directives based on my plans for the city." Eremon leaned back in his chair. "You'll find them hidden in the archive—by chance, of course. The treasurer will verify my signature and enact these posthumous laws on my behalf."

Caitir had to fight to keep from gaping at him. "What kinds of laws?"

"Laws regarding magic and education," he said. "The people need to know the power they've inherited. We can use the archival texts to teach them to read."

The thought of the histories stirred an uneasy feeling in her stomach. These must have been the laws Eremon had originally intended to pass with Lira at his side.

"I want you to rebuild a council—with my blessing, of course," Eremon continued. "I'll help you correspond with La'hiran to hold him off. Our biggest challenge will be when he inevitably learns Gerallt is dead, and in truth, he may know that already."

He rose and began to pace, rattling off one idea after another.

"Your biggest advantage is the fact that you never *actually* took the throne. We'll make you Crown Regent and sidestep the usual punishment for usurpers that way. Maintain the narrative that you're guarding the throne for its heir. Meanwhile, start soothing the peoples' pain.

"We have four weeks, at most, to influence public sentiment here. After that, I'll take the throne and pardon you."

Caitir shoved aside a twinge of fear. "You would act as Rí from the shadows?"

"Yes." He stood again, this time closing the distance between them and extending his hand. "Finish what I started, like you promised. Do we have an agreement?"

She looked down at his waiting hand. By all accounts, he should want to be rid of her as quickly as possible. Yet, against her best judgment, she found herself trusting him without hesitation. Perhaps that was because he'd never given her a reason to believe him untrustworthy before.

Caitir hesitantly clasped his hand, and he helped her to her feet. When she touched his skin, she felt a buzz of tingling power beneath her palm that extended into her fingertips and raised the hair along her arms. Her breath escaped in a soft huff, and she resisted the urge to let go.

She looked into his silver eyes and nodded once. "We are agreed."

CHAPTER 42
AIDRYN

Meadowlands
1 Week Later

Oda flopped onto her back in the thick, dry meadow grass, heaving an exasperated sigh. "I can't do this!"

Aidryn turned to face her as she threw an arm over her eyes. The cold wind ruffled his hair, and he was glad he'd let his usually short beard grow thicker for the deepening winter. "Only because you think you can't. I need you to try again; we can't stay out here for much longer."

They'd taken Senga and Fannin out to the meadowlands beyond the fortress, far enough away to practice magic without the risk of Thorne catching them. But as the morning sun had risen higher and higher, Oda had grown increasingly anxious about her inability to summon water.

"How am I supposed to believe I can when all evidence points to the contrary?" Oda retorted.

"You have to be open enough to let the magic flow," Aidryn

said, "but something within you is blocking it. You say you've always wanted to wield Clan Énna's power?"

"In theory," she hedged. "I've said it often enough."

Aidryn cast a glance back at the fortress, the truth piecing itself together in his mind. He wasn't sure if it was Lira's magic at work, or pure intuition guiding his instincts. "But do you really want it?"

Oda sighed again. She seemed unbothered by the chill in the air, clad in her sleeveless leather tunic and training breeches as though it was still summertime. "You try living as half-Énna among Clan Beran, then tell me what you think my answer is."

"Ah." Aidryn's instincts had been correct. "I imagine suppressing part of yourself for so long might make it difficult to access."

"It's more than that," she murmured.

Aidryn didn't miss the way she peeked out at him before she sat up, drawing her knees to her chest and wrapping her arms around them. Her green eyes were troubled.

He treaded carefully as he ventured, "You do know that this power will grow beyond your ability to shove it down, don't you?"

Oda's attention snapped back to Aidryn. "And how long will that take?"

He shrugged, sensing her defenses rising. "I can't say for certain, but the longer you hide from your anointing, the more likely it will be to erupt on its own." With a pointed look, he added, "And that will be *much* harder to explain to Thorne."

"You're right, but I'm not ready for any of it." She laid her head on her arm.

The world around them was quiet as Aidryn weighed Oda's words and the emotions in between. Her unease nagged at him.

"I don't understand," he finally said. "You seemed to hold

such sway over Thorne in the healer's chamber that day. Why are you afraid of him?"

Her head snapped up, and she glared hard at him. "I saved your pretty face that day, but I'll damage it myself if you press me."

"Empty threats." Aidryn chuckled, ignoring the hint of promise in her voice. He leaned forward and nudged her boot with his own. "What does *sjovyn* mean?"

Oda lunged for him as though intending to clap a hand over his mouth. Aidryn dodged her outstretched arm as she growled, "Don't!" She jumped to her feet in one swift, fluid motion and drew the sword she'd worn for training.

"It's not in the histories," he said, rising to meet her. He wrapped his fingers around the hilt of his broadsword, which lay in the grass at his side, and lifted it, sinking into a defensive stance. "We can't find it with Lira's magic."

"You *won't*," Oda said, widening her stance and angling her blade as she slowly circled Aidryn. "It doesn't exist outside its intended use." Her eyes widened, and she pressed her lips together, as though she hadn't meant to say that much.

"That makes no sense," Aidryn protested. He braced for her to strike—which she did, with lightning speed.

Their blades met, reverberating with the impact.

"It does when you know," she said, drawing her blade back to thrust.

Aidryn dodged, blocking her next strike, then the next. She fought with control and focus, as though transmuting her emotions through each impact of blade on blade. Perhaps she needed to expel *this* energy before she could unlock the other half of her power. If that was the case, then Aidryn was willing to keep pushing.

He raised his blade to block her overhead strike, gritting his teeth against the impact. "So enlighten me."

"No." She angled her stance and swung at his side.

He dodged, turning to meet her blade again.

"This *is* Clan Beran," he quipped. "For all I know, even thinking it is a capital offense."

Oda tripped, dropping her weapon as she rolled, then rose, her back to Aidryn. He picked up her sword, and when she turned again, there were tears in her eyes. She snatched the hilt when he extended it, then sheathed it again.

"Exactly," she said, turning on the ball of her foot and heading toward where they'd tethered the horses. "We're done here."

Aidryn watched her go, a sudden surge of anger rising within him. With a snarl, he gripped his sword and stalked after her. "No, we are *not*."

"Why can't you leave me be?" Oda whirled on him. "I told you it was useless to try this magic, yet you persisted. I told you not to ask me about that blasted word, yet you pressed the issue. Who do you think you are?"

"Your friend," he answered firmly. "Anointed, like you. And I can't let you diminish your own strength to keep Thorne comfortable."

"Thorne has *never*—" she said through gritted teeth. She squeezed her eyes shut, took a deep breath, and began again. "Choosing how I want to appear to the world is my choice and no one else's."

"Because it gives you a false sense of control." Aidryn raised his brows knowingly. "You can't fool me, Oda; I can see through you. I spent most of my life managing everyone's impression of me because I was hiding my own power and trying to protect those I cared for."

Her shoulders went slack, and she took a step back, blinking as though stunned. Aidryn closed the distance between them again, crossing his arms as they leveled with one another.

"So tell me," he said in a low voice, "what are you protecting?"

CHAPTER 43
LIRA

Fortress Halgeir

Lira and Thorne took the long way back to the courtyard after a lengthy meeting with Iva, who was anxious to bring Artur back to Fortress Halgeir. She was beginning to buckle under the pressure of ruling the clan, and the latest correspondence from Skelly indicated Artur was recovered enough to travel.

"Bringing Artur back here is a bad idea," Thorne said in a low voice.

Lira hugged herself to ward off the chill. "It's likely to attract attention. Mam's concerned about snow, though, like I am."

"Do you still mean to leave soon?" Thorne asked.

"I think we'll have to," Lira answered with a shrug. "We've been here longer than I intended already."

"And look what happened," Thorne countered. "You've needed Father. It would be best to keep your ailment quiet for now. The more you're seen around Rodhlan, the more it will be noticed."

The worst thing you can do is disappear, Aidryn had told her.

People need to see that not even dark magic can alter who you are or what you stand for.

Lira's smile was pinched as she replied, "With all due respect, everyone is telling me something different. You and Mam think I should hide. Aidryn and Oda think I should show my strength. I don't know what to do; I just know I don't want to stay in one place."

"Don't think about what you want to do," Thorne said. "What do you think you *should* do?"

With a resigned sigh, Lira answered, "I should have greater access to Eremon. He's not keeping us well informed here, and I think it's because he doesn't want to see you."

"I don't want to see him." Thorne snorted. "It is mutual. But I don't need to see him."

"I assume you have spies, then," Lira ventured. Thorne blanched, and she laughed. "It's only logical."

"We do what we must," Thorne hedged. "I learned long ago that people will not always understand a leader's decisions, so you cannot worry about what they think. You simply lead. They can thank you another time."

The corners of Lira's mouth tugged into a grin. "*Sjeovi*, this is why we are allies."

He looked incredulous. "Flattery. Is it not good sense?"

"It is."

She paused when she heard several sets of footsteps rapidly approaching. Bard and two of the other Beravakt marched in Thorne's direction, shields up, battle masks donned. Thorne straightened, stepping past Lira to greet them. They pounded their spear staffs on the stone floor when they halted.

"Speak, Bard," Thorne commanded in Brylla.

"The traitor's in custody," Bard answered. "Arena."

"What traitor?" Lira asked.

Bard turned to her long enough to say, "Énna rubbish." His

eyes roved over her. "Not in the healer's quarters with your husband?"

Lira stilled. "Why would I be?"

"He took a nasty slice, sparring with Oda," Bard answered with a grin. "Best see how he's getting on."

Lira sucked in a breath. Thorne rested a large hand on her shoulder, and she felt a bit of his calming, healing magic pouring into her. "You should go to him," he said.

"Who—" She blinked, trying to shake away the haze Thorne's magic left behind. "Who is the traitor?"

Bard smirked. "Aeron Énna."

LIRA WAS PANTING by the time she arrived in Ljós's corridor. Aidryn was emerging from the room when she arrived, looking pale. He'd removed his tunic, and though his hands and the fabric were bloodstained, his skin was pristine. His cerulean eyes locked with Lira's, and he let out a ragged sigh.

"I swear to you, I'm fine," he said as she lunged, trapping him in a fierce embrace. *Fine* came out on a breathless choke as she squeezed the air out of him.

"What happened?" Lira pressed her palm to the center of his chest. This close, she could make out a faint, pink line where Ljós had healed the skin.

"It was an accident," he said, just as Oda pushed through the door from behind him.

"It was a *warning*," she corrected, straightening her shoulders as she walked away.

"What?" Lira let go of Aidryn, jogging to catch up to Oda, who didn't deign to respond. The acrid scent of ozone filled Lira's nose as her vision clouded, but she shook it off. "Why would you harm him?"

"We were sparring, Lira," Aidryn said from behind her as he closed the distance. "I overstepped."

Oda whirled on him. "You *did* overstep."

"I don't understand." A sharp flash of pain coursed behind Lira's eyes. She clenched her teeth against it, her body growing rigid. "You cannot harm him, Oda. I forbid it!"

"You forbid *me*?" Oda barked a laugh. "I do not bow to you, and I don't have to answer Tarlach's incessant questions."

Aidryn crossed his arms tightly. His dark hair was still disheveled, the strands falling from the leather band he'd used to secure it at the nape of his neck. "Oda, I was trying to—"

"I don't care what you intended," Oda retorted, baring her teeth.

Lira bristled, clenching her fists to suppress the sparks of dark magic that stirred in her palms. "You could have killed him!"

"I know my blade." Oda's fingers curled around the hilt of her sword. "If I had wanted him dead, he would be."

The warrior's eyes flicked down to Lira's fists, and her lips curled. "Stay your corrupt magic, Witness Tree. At least my damage was mendable."

Shock jolted down Lira's spine, followed by a wave of shame that left her mouth agape. Aidryn stepped between her and Oda, raising his hands in surrender. "That's enough, now. I'm sorry I offered help, Oda; it won't happen again."

Oda's green eyes flicked from Aidryn's boots to his face, and she blinked slowly. "No, it won't."

She turned her back on him and stormed away.

CHAPTER 44

AIDRYN

Fortress Halgeir

As soon as Oda rounded the corner, Aidryn sighed heavily. "I should have left well enough alone," he said. "She's not ready to wield her magic."

Lira shook her head. "No, we just want her to be."

He thought about what had happened in the meadowlands a mere hour earlier. Oda's self-restraint had snapped once Aidryn pieced together the hidden details of her story. Though she'd claimed his injury as a warning, truly, he had been so shocked to be right that he'd faltered.

Aidryn had continued pressing Oda for answers on her secrecy. He'd made his guesses deliberately absurd in the hopes that she might feel safe enough to answer. Instinct told him that her guarded nature was blocking her water magic, and he'd thought if he could just get her to talk—to trust him—that she might have a breakthrough. Instead, he'd almost gotten himself impaled.

"You look terrible," Lira said, wriggling out of his grasp. She scrutinized him, placing her hand in the center of his chest.

Despite the cool air, he warmed at her touch. "How much blood did you lose?"

He shrugged. "No idea. I feel fine."

"Liar." She bit her lip, gripping his forearm as she lowered her voice. "There's something I have to tell you. They've captured Aeron. Bard brought the news. They have him in the arena."

Horror seized Aidryn. "We need to get to him. They'll torture him within an inch of his life; we can't let them."

He grasped her hand, pushing through a wave of weakness to lead her down the corridor in the direction of the arena. Aeron, the bloody coward, had spilled Clan Beran's war council secrets to Fiadh, who had in turn passed them to Caitir, Aila, and Gerallt. In the end, he'd fled to Iathium with Fiadh and joined Caitir.

What was he doing here now?

"Did Beran capture Aeron, or did he come here on his own?" Aidryn asked, already winded as they moved.

"Bard just called him a traitor," Lira answered, taking long strides to keep up. "That's all I know."

Fear and anguish warred within Aidryn as they neared the entrance to the arena. Already, the place was teeming with Beravakt. Aidryn tightened his grip on Lira's hand and began to push his way through the crowd, tugging her after him.

They took the steps toward the training floor as quickly as they could move. When Aidryn finally got a clear view of the floor, he nearly stopped in his tracks.

Aeron was on his knees before Thorne, his body sagging, hands bound behind him. His exposed skin was marred with what appeared to be large, scabbing blisters, and his face had been sliced open and stitched up. Though he still wore his black, city-issued tunic and trousers, they were filthy and torn.

Beside Thorne, Bard stood, whip in hand, a hungry glint in his eyes.

"Thorne!" Aidryn shouted. He let go of Lira's hand and took the stairs two at a time. "You will not lay a hand on him."

"Halt, Tarlach," Thorne barked.

Slowly, Aeron turned his bloodied face toward Aidryn, hazel eyes empty and hopeless. He was nearly unrecognizable, and suddenly, it didn't matter what he'd done or who he'd betrayed. All Aidryn could think of were their years of brotherhood. The time they'd spent mastering their magic. How Aeron and Faolan had helped Aidryn and Lira flee Iathium.

Faolan—mortal gods. He couldn't bear to lose Aeron, too.

Thorne's voice cut through his roaring thoughts. "I said, halt!"

Aidryn ignored Thorne, instead picking up speed until he pounded onto the arena floor. He stopped only when four of the Beravakt stepped between him and Aeron.

"Let me pass!" he demanded.

Thorne held up a hand to stay Bard, then crossed to where Aidryn stood.

"You were not summoned," Thorne said, shoulders tensing.

Aidryn squared his stance, his hand flying to the hilt of his broadsword. "Let me go to Aeron." He made to move forward, but Thorne stepped closer, challenging him.

A muscle in Thorne's jaw ticked. "We have no need for you here."

"As an anointed, I have a right to be here," Aidryn replied. "So should Lira, but I won't have you torture someone in her presence."

He chanced a look back at his wife, who had frozen halfway down the steps, a hand pressed to her mouth. Her gaze was fixed on Aeron, and she was slowly shaking her head.

A fresh wave of rage rose in Aidryn, and he turned to face Thorne again. "She has endured enough." His body trembled with the effort it took to appear calm before the Beran warriors. "And from what I can see, so has Aeron."

Thorne scowled. "You want mercy for him now?"

I always want mercy. The thought rocketed through Aidryn, but he clamped down on it, shoving it deep inside. As long as Aidryn was at Fortress Halgeir, there would be no pleading. Thorne would only understand dry logic.

"Let me ask you something, Thorne," he said, flicking another glance at Aeron, who now appeared to be straining to hear his words. "Do you think you'll get what you need from him this way?"

A shadow of doubt crossed the warrior's face. "That is never certain with any prisoner."

"I know Aeron better than anyone here," Aidryn replied. "I can get answers without torture."

Thorne set his jaw. "He demanded asylum in exchange for information."

Aidryn sighed. "And you couldn't find it in your stone-cold heart to barter for that?" When Thorne didn't reply, he added, "Let me speak to him privately."

"You'll take Silira," Thorne answered warily.

"Yes," said Aidryn. "Just don't make a spectacle of him. You'll never get answers that way. Aeron is concerned with self-preservation. If he feels secure, he'll talk."

HALF AN HOUR LATER, Thorne delivered Aeron to Ljós's chamber, where Aidryn and Lira had been instructed to wait. The healer helped Aeron bathe and change into fresh clothes. He put salve on Aeron's wounds and surveyed his stitches, which were healing poorly. All the while, Lira and Aidryn sat in the antechamber in silence.

When Ljós was done, he led Aeron into the antechamber and motioned for him to sit. Painstakingly, Aeron lowered himself to the floor beside the pit of amber stones, keeping his eyes trained on the floor. He looked half-starved, and Aidryn noted that Ljós had not healed his wounds.

"Before you say anything," Ljós said, as though reading Aidryn's thoughts, "I'm under orders *not* to heal him. I'll take my leave. If you need me, I'll be in the Arthmael's Hall."

Thorne's father slipped from the chamber, and Aeron visibly sagged before he finally looked up at Aidryn. There was pain in his eyes, and he shrank as he spoke. "What made you come to my aid, Tarlach?"

"We need to know what's happening in Iathium," Lira answered before Aidryn could speak. "As anointed, Aidryn and I have every right to question you."

"I'll tell you whatever you want to know," Aeron said, the plea in his voice apparent. "I'm dead regardless. Once I'm back in Beran's hands, it's just a matter of time."

"I came to your aid because I don't wish that fate on you," Aidryn answered. "I'll do whatever I can to intervene."

"You've done enough," Aeron said. "I don't deserve that much."

Lira rose, moving to the pit of amber stones and selecting a small one. She motioned for Aidryn to follow. They sat nearer to Aeron, and Lira hefted the stone in her hand.

"We need to see your memories," Lira said.

Aeron flinched. "I don't—no. I only want to speak to Aidryn."

For a moment, Lira's dark lashes fluttered shut. She took a deep breath. "My magic tells me you have much to hide. You don't want us to see everything you remember."

He dipped his head. "Something like that."

Aidryn peered at his friend with renewed curiosity. "What brings you to Halgeir?"

Aeron shifted, wincing. "Eremon banished me from Iathium."

"Eremon?" Lira sat up straighter. "He's revealed himself?"

"Only to the sentries," Aeron said, "and a few longstanding members of the staff. Says he wants to rebuild quietly. The sentries are complying, but they're angry about it. They hate Caitir."

"He banished you, but Caitir is in the city?" Lira asked.

"I'm just the unwilling messenger," Aidryn said, holding up his palms.

"How is Caitir?" Aidryn felt a pinch of guilt at the question, especially when Lira glared at him.

Aeron's gaze slid to Aidryn. "Prickly. Fearful." He snorted softly, looking down at his hands. "I should have helped her; that's what got me into this mess. I was the worst kind of fool, and where I am now is my own fault."

The hairs along Aidryn's neck rose. "What do you mean by that?"

"I mean—" Aeron sighed. "Your sister thought none of us knew about Aila's imprisonment. She was going to buy herself time, but then Eremon showed up. You know how I love Caitir. I thought... I thought if I didn't make a move, I would never get the chance to."

"What did you do to Caitir?" Aidryn growled.

"What do you mean, Aila's imprisonment?" Lira cried.

Lira and Aidryn exchanged a glance, and Aidryn gave her an almost imperceptible nod. Without warning, Lira seized Aeron's arm and poured her magic into the amber stone, willing Aeron's memories to project above the pit.

"Witness," Lira commanded.

Aeron's body went rigid as his memories flooded out.

Aidryn watched Aeron and Fiadh swear fealty to Aila, befriend Caitir, then double-cross her as they feigned loyalty. He watched them betray the clan army. Saw them hold secret meetings with Aila's spies, and with Aila herself.

The memories moved in rapid succession, a testament to Aeron's power. Even under the influence of Lira's magic, he managed to be evasive. It was like trying to read a book while hastily flipping its pages.

Lira's projected image crackled with black lightning, and Aeron cried out in pain. There was a sheen of sweat beading on Lira's forehead, but she squeezed Aeron's hand harder, doubling down.

Aidryn saw Aeron stealing into the shadows of the Dome's main corridor, carefully opening the wax seal of a small scroll while Fiadh watched, eagerly bouncing on her toes. They'd puzzled over the missive until they deciphered enough to know that Aila was King La'hiran's captive.

Then there was Fiadh again. In one memory, she was forging glass at her father's smithy. In another, Aidryn caught glimpses of strange-looking glass jewelry—four bracelets and a necklace that appeared to be an exact replica of Lira's pendant. All the glass teemed with the shimmering colors of dark power and Aeron's violet water magic.

He saw Aeron force Caitir against a wall and kiss her against her will. Watched as Eremon, in his cat form, intervened. Saw the horror in his sister's eyes when she finally freed herself.

Finally, Lira released Aeron, panting and trembling. Aeron scrambled away from her, gripping the spot she'd been holding. "Since when do *you* have dark magic?" he demanded.

Lira paled and opened her mouth to answer, but Aidryn cut in, "Leave us, Lira."

She whirled, eyes widening. "But—"

"Summon Thorne and the others," Aidryn said. "Please, trust me."

Slowly, she nodded, seemingly reluctant to leave. She took the amber stone and rose, slipping into the night and latching the door behind her.

As soon as she was gone, Aidryn rose, crossing the room to Aeron in a few strides and hauling him up by his tunic. "You're a coward and a traitor, even in your memories," Aidryn growled. "What did Eremon say to you? What did you hide?"

He'd caught a momentary glimpse of Eremon speaking to an assembly of sentries, though Aeron had managed to force another memory to project in its place.

"If I tell you, it'll endanger Caitir further," Aeron answered, swallowing hard.

"You mean it'll endanger *you*," Aidryn shot back.

"I told you, Tarlach," Aeron shouted, "I'm already as good as dead!"

"Then you decide who you trust more with the information," Aidryn said, giving Aeron a shake. "Me, or Thorne Beran?"

"You!" Aeron clasped Aidryn's shoulders, tears brimming in his eyes. His voice broke as he added, "I'll tell you."

There was a long moment of heavy silence. Aidryn held his breath. Finally, Aeron said, "Eremon intends to rule through Caitir."

The world around Aidryn splintered, then scattered. Eremon had squandered his chance to untangle Caitir from the power she sought. If Eremon was truly fixated on using her as a political puppet, then he would further expose and endanger her.

"Does Caitir know he's back in the city?" Aidryn asked.

"When I left Iathium, she did not." Aeron let out a sigh and sagged. "I didn't know I would feel so relieved, but somehow, I do. Perhaps because it's you I was able to tell."

Aidryn let go of him and took a step back, scrubbing a hand over his face. "Mortal gods. We have to stop this."

"It seems you have bigger problems than your sister," Aeron ventured, "like your wife."

Aidryn's attention snapped back to the sentry. "You're not to speak of her to anyone," he said, baring his teeth. "Under any circumstances."

"Wouldn't that be a prize piece of information." Aeron didn't try to hide the grin tugging at his lips. Aidryn could almost see his traitorous thoughts whirring, and rage rumbled up from his legs into his torso and arms. "The Witness Tree of Rodhlan, corrupted by dark magic. Wouldn't Iteloria's king love to hear about that?"

A harsh laugh burst from Aidryn. "For a moment, I thought you might actually be remorseful." He began to pace, circling Aeron, who suddenly seemed wary. "When did you become such a selfish monster? A traitor on all sides but your own, not fit for any alliance."

"Maybe after you showed your hand and chose Lira over family," Aeron said, his own rage on full display now. His nostrils flared, and he clenched his fists at his sides. "I was your family. Faolan and Fiadh, they were your family. And Caitir— she's your sister, damn you! And you chose Lira over all of us!"

"I chose goodness and truth, and so did Faolan," Aidryn said. "I will always. Choose. Truth."

Time slowed. The truth was that Thorne *would* torture Aeron and would likely execute him.

The truth was that Aeron would spill everything he knew about Eremon and Caitir before Aidryn could intervene.

The truth was that Aeron was a danger to Rodhlan. No matter where he went, no matter who he served, he was a liability—most of all to Aidryn, Lira, and the people they loved most.

Aidryn's fingers closed around the dagger at his hip, and he drew it from its sheath. His vision sharpened, his movement fluid as he closed the distance between them to draw his blade across Aeron's throat.

CHAPTER 45
LIRA

Fortress Halgeir

"Why, Aidryn?"

Lira's question hung in the space between them, expanding, weighing down. There was a sickening chill in Ljós's chamber, despite the warmth cast by his enchanted amber stones.

Aeron's body lay in a pool of sticky blood on the stone floor, covered with a heavy fur. Though Lira had deliberately sat with her back to it, she had to resist the urge to look behind her—to prove to herself that this was real, and Aeron was still lying there dead.

The anointed were gathered around the amber stones. Oda wrapped her arms around herself and squeezed, her eyes trained on the floor of the healer's chamber. A somber, furious Thorne kept his unblinking gaze fixed on Aidryn, who squeezed his red-rimmed eyes shut.

"He threatened to expose Lira's dark magic to Iteloria," Aidryn said. "He proved himself a traitor on all sides."

"We all knew what he was," Thorne said with a grunt. "It was not your place to execute Clan Beran's prisoner."

"Aeron wronged us all," Aidryn protested. "And despite all that, I still felt mercy. I couldn't bear the thought of letting you torture him."

"So you killed him instead?" Thorne rubbed his eyes. "Tell me how that makes sense."

Lira's head spun. What Aidryn had done had shaken her to the core. If she had known what he intended, she would have never left him alone with Aeron. There must be something more to this.

Had Aidryn been influenced by her dark magic somehow? Maybe Eremon's protection over the Binding was finally wearing thin.

That's it, a small voice said in the back of her mind. *Now you're getting somewhere.*

Thorne turned to Lira. "I want you to confirm that Tarlach speaks truth."

An uneasy ache turned her stomach, but she nodded. "That's wise, Thorne."

Aidryn's eyes lit with something akin to panic before he nodded resignedly. Thorne laced his large fingers together and took a deep breath. "Go on," he said.

Lira hefted the little amber stone in one hand and reached for Aidryn, grasping his hand. "Witness," she said.

The last moments of Aeron's life flickered before them.

Aeron flashes a feral grin at Aidryn. "Wouldn't that be a prize piece of information? The Witness Tree of Rodhlan, corrupted by dark magic. Wouldn't Iteloria's king love to hear about that?"

Abruptly, Lira's connection to Aidryn's memories was broken. A spark of dark magic passed between their palms, and she yelped, drawing her hand away.

"I'm sorry," she stammered, casting a panicked look at Aidryn. "I don't know what happened."

"You've overextended your magic for the day," Thorne said. "Why don't you just use it to confirm the rest of what Tarlach has to say?"

"There's not much else to say," Aidryn hedged. "Eremon revealed himself to the sentries within the Dome, and they're following his orders."

Thorne sighed. "Silira?"

Reluctantly, Lira felt for her magic's affirming tug. "Confirmed."

"If they are following his orders, why has Caitir been allowed free reign over the Dome?" Thorne asked.

Aidryn shifted. "I don't know."

A half-tug. Lira tried to conceal her frown. Everything within her body screamed that he should not be lying—that she should not support his lies, especially with her magic. But Aidryn had never lied without just cause. Perhaps there would be some way to reconcile this.

"What did Aeron know about Eremon's plans?" Thorne asked.

"He said Eremon hopes for an alliance of sorts with Caitir," Aidryn answered. "As far as the details are concerned, I couldn't say."

Another half-tug. "Confirmed," Lira lied, trying to keep her voice steady.

"*Are* they allied?" Thorne pressed.

Aidryn's throat bobbed. "To the best of Aeron's knowledge, Caitir has no idea Eremon has returned."

Lira's magic tugged, stronger this time. She released a shaky breath. "Confirmed."

Thorne sat up straight, his amber eyes sharp. "He was meant to dispose of her."

"That isn't his way, Thorne," Lira argued. "He prefers a gentle approach when given the option."

"Weak," the warrior scoffed. "Your emotions have stunted your ability to see truth, Witness Tree—or your willingness to."

Indignation flared in Lira at the accusation. "I *know* Eremon; you do not. Aidryn and I watched him lead Iathium for seven years. We understand how he operates. Sometimes he sidesteps conventional wisdom in favor of a nontraditional approach, but he has always tried to do what's right."

Thorne leaned forward, a knowing glint in his eyes. "If you know him so well, tell me: Did he make wise use of his time with you? Did he set his grand plans for the city into motion, or did he try to charm his way under your skirt?"

A cry of outrage burst from Lira. "How dare you!"

When she had first come to Fortress Halgeir in the aftermath of Eremon's death and Aidryn's capture, Thorne had seemed to understand her grief. He had offered her brotherly comfort when the world around her had fallen apart. She had believed him to be empathic and kind beneath his hard exterior.

Clearly, she had been wrong.

"Mortal *gods*, Thorne!" Aidryn exclaimed. "Could you not?"

"Eremon was *dying*," Lira said. "Our attention turned from revealing the histories to searching for a cure. We spent weeks studying, and we still failed. Your implications are insulting beyond belief. You have no right to twist our relationship so it fits your agenda."

"And what is my agenda, Silira?" Thorne glowered.

"Undermining Eremon, of course," she snapped. "Trying to sway the rest of us to your side. You would rather use brute force to make your point than understand what could possibly drive a ruler to be merciful."

The idea of Eremon showing mercy to someone like Caitir made Lira's stomach sour. Still, she couldn't let Thorne distort the truth.

"Mercy is one thing; betrayal is something else," Thorne

replied. "You think his loyalty is guaranteed just because you awakened him."

Lira set her jaw defiantly, though her heart pounded as the truth tugged within her. "Eremon would never betray us—"

"Foolish girl," the warrior said, clenching a fist.

Warning flashed in Aidryn's eyes. "Don't interrupt her, Thorne."

Lira cast an exasperated look at Aidryn, willing him to be silent. She turned her attention back to Thorne. "You refuse to hear reason."

"Eremon left you vulnerable to dark magic and disappeared because he does not know what he's doing," Thorne growled. "Instead of correcting his mistakes, he let the usurper distract him. He is a lost little boy with too much power and too little sense."

"Eremon knows what he's doing," Lira argued, shoving her truth magic down. She was exhausted with trying to interpret its push-and-pull.

Thorne doubled down. "He is compromised. It's clear to me."

Lira was taken aback, though the warrior's amber gaze remained unyielding. "Compromised how?" she demanded.

"You're an intelligent woman. You know." Thorne's eyes lit with a knowing glint. "How long until Caitir lures him into her bed and turns his loyalties? How do we know she hasn't done so already?"

The color drained from Aidryn's face. Lira felt a chasm of doubt open within her. Felt a tug of sickening affirmation at Thorne's words. Still, she went to war against it. "That's impossible."

Thorne made a fist, then pointed an accusing finger at her. "You know it is not. Eremon is bitter and entitled, and that makes him weak."

Lira's body tensed. "He is *not* vulnerable to treason, Thorne."

"Perhaps not, but an alliance born in secrecy is foolish either way," Oda said in a low voice. She kept her green eyes trained on her hands, which she'd folded in her lap.

"It's not complete secrecy," Lira protested. "The sentries know. That means others in the Dome know, too. Eremon just hasn't ascended yet—"

"If he ascends now, it will draw attention to the alliance. The people want Caitir's head, and you know he will not give it to them." Thorne said. "Tell me: When did Eremon bother to inform us of his plan—or the fact that Aila is being held in Iteloria? Don't the anointed have a right to know?"

Lira had twisted her mind into knots, trying not to blame Eremon for everything that had happened so far. But her resentment toward him had grown with each passing day. And with this latest revelation, that resentment solidified into something darker.

Her heart sank. "Yes, we do."

"A little secrecy encourages more," Thorne pressed, watching Lira as though he could read her thoughts. "It makes people bold enough to be dishonorable." He flicked a pointed glare toward Aidryn.

Each blow landed exactly as Thorne intended it to. Lira's breaths quickened with the pace of her heartbeat. "From the beginning, I only wanted us to give Eremon time in good faith."

"My good faith is spent." Thorne straightened, his countenance decisive. "As Clan Beran's Anointed, I say it's time to remove both Eremon and Caitir from Iathium, before this goes any further."

"No," Aidryn said. "As Anointed of Clan Tarlach, I disagree."

"Your word is worthless." Thorne leered at him. "She is your sister."

"And that makes me incapable of good judgment?" Aidryn's voice wavered, his anger barefaced. "I have always been distrustful of Eremon, but I think we should find out why he saw fit to spare her."

Thorne barked a laugh. "Of course you do. If she has Eremon's attention, all the better for you. It keeps him away from your wife and gives your sister time to birth that wretched child."

Aidryn swore and moved as though he might stand, but Lira braced a hand on his arm to stay him. "I disagree as well, Thorne. If you intervene, this could escalate beyond our control."

"Not if Silira exercises her right as lawful heir," Thorne replied, turning to Lira. "Take the throne peacefully. The city wants you."

"I can't," she said in a small voice. "You know I can't."

Challenge flashed in the warrior's amber eyes. "Can't, or won't?"

"Won't." Lira held his stare. "I didn't want the throne before, and I do not want it now."

"It doesn't matter what you want," Thorne shot back. "You told Eremon the same. Why should you owe the people less than he does? You chose to wear that ring."

Anger surged through Lira. She clenched her fingers into fists, nails biting into her palms. "What happened to finding a solution to this dark magic first?" She opened her hands, letting the power spark. "Do you really think I can lead a city like this?"

"Lira, no," Aidryn warned, moving into a crouch. He held out a hand to stay her, his expression clouded by fear.

Lira had seen that look before. Aidryn had once charmed a mad dog in one of Iathium's alleyways, leading it away from Lira and coaxing it onto the main road, where it tucked its tail and trotted in the direction of the city gates. At the time, she had been too consumed by fear to question how he had done it. Now, she realized he had been using the magic he'd kept secret until the past year. She suddenly felt self-conscious; perhaps he saw her as no more than a cornered animal now.

Another wave of anger crested, then broke over her. Aidryn had harbored so many secrets. If he truly loved her, he would be honest. He would stop behaving as though she was too fragile to hear the truth.

He'll never do that, she thought, though the words in her head didn't quite feel like her own. *He fancies himself a protector, but every secret creates more danger.*

It was Thorne's grip on her wrist that shattered her thoughts and brought her back into the moment. The dark magic in her hands flickered out, leaving open wounds behind. Her blood pooled in her palms, running down over her life lines in small rivulets before it dripped onto the stone floor.

She was breathless, and her heart pounded as the room came back into focus. Her own horror at losing herself clashed with a strange shot of glee, which coursed through her body at the look of horror on the warrior's face.

The edge dropped from Thorne's voice, and his next words came in a soothing baritone. "You're right, *sjeinga*. You cannot lead a city like this."

With a tremulous breath, she locked her focus on him, and the magic dissipated. Gently, Thorne took her bloodied hands and bathed her palms in orbs of golden light. She watched as the raw skin healed before her eyes, the pain dissolving so quickly she could have wept.

"It's only..." Lira fought the tears that threatened to fall. "Rodhlan can't withstand an Itelorian invasion. I'm in no position to deal with King La'hiran, but Eremon can."

"Let it go now," Thorne murmured. "We shouldn't continue speaking of him."

"Whatever Eremon's strategy is, it's temporary," Lira

pressed. "You saw the letter from King La'hiran in the witness-ing. Eremon will *have* to do something before that time runs out."

The idea of Aila being captive had eased Lira's mind momentarily; that was, until Thorne had shared his theory about Caitir. Lira had immediately concluded that Eremon was going to run the clock out and let the Itelorian king exact what-ever harm he wished on Aila. The problem, however, was that six weeks was more than enough time for La'hiran to learn Gerallt's fate, and whether the king would take action in the meantime was wholly unpredictable.

"Yes, Lira," Aidryn answered in earnest, his voice wavering. Lira looked past Thorne to meet Aidryn's terrified gaze. Her emotions lurched from anger and defiance into remorse, anchoring her to the present. "We'll meet with Eremon—get answers from him."

"I think that's wise," Oda added.

Thorne pursed his lips, releasing Lira and rising. He crossed his arms, the familiar glower returning. "That would be a waste of time."

Lira stood, too, and the others followed. Perhaps they felt the same discomfort she did when it came to sitting so far beneath Thorne.

"I want to talk to him," Lira said, setting her jaw defiantly. "It won't be a waste."

"Of course, you would take your husband's side," the warrior mused, a note of bitterness in his voice. "Two anointed against one."

Aidryn scowled and opened his mouth to retort, but Oda cut him off. "Three anointed, Thorne."

Oda stood straighter, waiting for her words to settle over Thorne. The energy in the room shifted with alarming speed, moving from tense to stifling in moments. Lira and Aidryn exchanged a terse glance.

"Three." Thorne looked at Oda as though he'd suddenly entered a violent argument with himself. "What do you mean?"

"Faolan's magic chose me when he died." Oda set her jaw defiantly. She was so tightly wound that Lira could feel the apprehension emanating from her in waves.

Thorne rounded on Lira, not bothering to reply directly to Oda. "Is this true?"

He looked as though he'd sustained a mortal wound, and there was a desperation in his expression that made Lira's heart stumble. She couldn't explain why, but she perceived a depth of grief in him that she almost couldn't fathom. It reminded her of the way she'd felt when her father died.

Lira closed her eyes. "It is."

"It's not possible." Thorne shook his head slowly. "Why am I the last to know?"

"We agreed it was Oda's story to tell," Aidryn answered, studying Thorne's every move. "If she ever wished to, that is."

Now, Thorne turned to Oda. "And why wouldn't you wish to?"

Her wide-eyed fear was wholly unfamiliar as she replied, "You know why."

Thorne didn't reply, but instead turned his back on her, running a hand over his face. His shoulders heaved once, as though he was struggling to take in the truth. "It was already a risk, keeping you close. Sharing your secrets."

Oda recoiled, withdrawing her hand and stepping back. "Yet you still made me your warrior." She clenched her fists at her sides, her body trembling with what Lira could only guess was restraint. "What makes me a risk now?"

"If you accepted the anointing from your father's clan," Thorne answered, his lip curling with contempt, "this changes everything."

He shouldered past Oda and left the chamber without another word. She did not follow.

CHAPTER 46

AIDRYN

Fortress Halgeir

Biting night wind whipped Aidryn's cloak as he saddled Fannin. Senga and Edan were already tethered to the fence, ready to ride. After the altercation with Thorne, he had decided to return to the Ridge. He had a nagging suspicion that Lira was the only reason Thorne had not tried to imprison him.

"What are you doing?" she had asked as Aidryn packed his meager possessions.

"I need to disappear for a little while," he'd answered. "Wait until Thorne's anger cools."

"That could take a very long time." Lira had leaned against the chamber wall, watching him intently, her dark eyes full of suspicion. "I'm not letting you disappear without me."

Aidryn had paused and turned to regard her. Lira's expression was open but pained. Self-consciously, she'd gathered her curls over one shoulder and bit her lip. "You still want to be with me, even after today?"

"Yes," she'd hedged, though wariness flickered in her eyes.

"I do want the entire truth—why you killed Aeron and what you're hiding. Knowing why I helped you lie to Thorne would give me peace of mind."

He'd snorted. "I doubt that."

It had pained him to lie to her—to know she had sensed every falsehood and half-truth he had spewed to Thorne. After they'd finally escaped Iathium in the spring, he'd believed he would never need to lie to her again. But now, he found that lies were necessary if the slightest possibility of protecting his sister existed.

"But I will tell you more," he had hedged, "soon. Let's get settled in the Ridge first."

Footsteps echoed from further down the pathway as Aidryn adjusted the straps on Fannin's saddle and inspected his shoes. Lira and Oda emerged from the mist a few minutes later, shouldering their satchels and dressed in warm leggings and furs. The cold had turned Lira's cheeks bright pink, a stark contrast to her too-pale skin. She'd secured her long curls in tight braids that wound around her head in preparation for the ride.

Aidryn wanted to pull her close and kiss her, but he didn't deserve that now. The shame that had filled him in the hours since Aeron's death was near overpowering. It roared his unworthiness, and Aidryn did not have the strength to fight it.

"Ready?" Aidryn gave Fannin's flank a pat as he stepped away to greet the women.

"I've never been so ready to shake the Beran dust from my boots," Oda said.

Her voice was uncharacteristically breathy, as though she was fighting to sound buoyant. But Aidryn could see the deep, cutting pain in her eyes, the profound loss, and he wanted to embrace her. Instead, he gave her a little salute and a wink.

"If it's dust you're looking to shake, look no further than the Seanlaoch," Lira said, jerking her chin in the horses' direction.

Aidryn's heart clenched at the sight of her forced smile. "They'll do the job properly."

Lira mounted Senga, and Aidryn, Fannin. Oda stepped toward Edan, stroking his black mane with gentle fingers. She secured her belongings in the saddlebag, then mounted smoothly and released a harsh sigh.

"Let's see this done," she said. "We can send the overlord home and put his heir in check while we're at it."

Aidryn clicked his tongue, and Fannin broke into a rapid walk. Lira and Oda followed. They warmed their horses in the chill air, breath coming in white huffs before them. When they had cleared the long pathway out of Clan Beran's territory, Aidryn gave them the signal. Together, they moved their mounts first into a trot, then a canter, and finally, a full-speed, magical gallop.

The blistering wind stung Aidryn's cheeks and brought tears to his eyes, but the movement was welcome. He needed to be far away from Thorne and the fortress where he'd taken his friend's life. Far from the watchful eyes of the Beravakt. If he truly wanted to stop Eremon's foolish plan and halt Clan Beran's growing distrust of Iathium, he would have to keep moving—and quickly.

THEY ARRIVED in Rodhlan Ridge in the early morning hours the next day, exhausted and beaten by the merciless wind and the horses' furious pace. Lira fell into bed with Skelly, who had long since settled back into her cottage. Aidryn then led Oda to the keep, where she collapsed on one of the long benches before the great hall's fireplace.

He unfurled her bedroll and draped the blanket over her as she closed her eyes. When he moved away, she opened one and whispered, "You're leaving."

Aidryn started but gave her a slight nod. "I am. Remember, your weapons are at the cottage."

"Did you tell Lira?"

"No."

"Stupid fool." Oda closed both eyes again and exhaled. "I'll cover for you."

He laughed nervously, forcing down the now ever-present unease that bloomed in his belly. "You had better. I have to buy all of us time."

"Then buy wisely," she replied.

He hesitated for a moment, the crackling of the low fire roaring in his ears. "I'll do my best."

Oda cracked one eye open and looked up at him. "You wouldn't have killed him without an incredibly compelling reason. I know there's more to it than what you told us."

Her words bludgeoned Aidryn. "Then why didn't you ask?"

She shrugged, closing her eyes again. "Something told me not to."

CHAPTER 47

EREMON

Dome

Trem's timepiece was mesmerizing. If Eremon's body had allowed him to sleep, its soft ticking might have lulled him. As it was, he sat staring blankly at the stack of books he'd pulled for himself after Caitir left the archival chamber for the evening.

They'd spent long hours here over the past few days, poring over books of law and economics. If Eremon had still been mortal, his back would have been in spasms by now. He'd been bent over parchment for hours, drafting directives for her to "uncover" in the coming weeks.

He smiled to himself. It was a good thing Tomis knew what was coming. Eremon hoped the treasurer would have the wherewithal to play his part without a hitch.

In order to maintain an outward illusion of haphazard discovery, Eremon had tucked his finished directives into random books and rolled them into scrolls. Several times a week, Caitir would receive vague clues about where to look. Hiding the papers kept her on a constant hunt for new pieces of information. This process appeared more authentic than if she had simply found a bundle of papers tucked away in a neat stack. Eremon also enlisted Iona to discover some of the writings herself and deliver them to Tomis for analysis.

Caitir never forgot anything Eremon told her, no matter how complex or mind-numbing the subject matter. Beyond working nobility, courtier, or advisor, she was intelligent and shrewd enough to hold a position on council, be an ambassador, or become a true ruler in her own right. It was a shame she'd chosen the path of an underhanded usurper, or she might have a bright future in Iathium beyond this game they were playing.

A pulse of magic thrummed from the inner chamber's floor and up through the walls surrounding Eremon. He sat up straighter, turning from his work to survey the secret entrance to Irem's chamber. A flash of crimson caught his eye just before the tile floor opened to reveal the staircase beneath. Aidryn emerged a moment later, squinting against the candlelight as he pocketed Iuchair, the great key.

Eremon rose abruptly from his stool, bumping it with the backs of his knees. Hastily, he covered the stack of scrolls he'd drafted. "What are you doing here?"

"What are you *doing*?" Aidryn countered.

The Key Keeper looked more haggard than usual, the youthful energy inexplicably sapped from him, dark circles beneath his exhausted eyes. A surge of panic engulfed Eremon as he thought of all the things he had promised—and failed—to remedy.

"Working," he hedged. "How is Lira?"

Aidryn leveled an accusing glare at him. "The darkness is deepening, but she's still fighting it. We've left Halgeir for the mountains."

Eremon tilted his head. "Why?"

"Because you banished Aeron Énna, and Clan Beran

captured him," Aidryn said angrily. "If I hadn't intervened and drawn the information from him myself, Thorne's warriors would be storming the city in a matter of days."

A wave of shock washed over Eremon. "Did you leave Lira alone to tell me this?"

"She's not alone," Aidryn said, crossing his arms. "I don't know why you suddenly care."

Eremon clenched his fists. "Of all people, you know how much I've always cared."

Aidryn's normally bright cerulean eyes darkened further, a maelstrom brewing within them. "Have you? Even when you're plotting to make my sister a political puppet?"

"She is lawful Crown Regent," Eremon replied, rage toward his longstanding rival rising like a rapid tide.

Aidryn's brows raised in surprise, his eyes widening. "It's already done?"

"Nearly a week ago," Eremon answered.

Aidryn advanced on him, drawing his broadsword. "I came here to stop it!"

"Stand down!" Eremon ordered.

Though he gripped his sword in both hands, Aidryn sagged. "Do you mean to tell me you already went through with this madness? Did I kill him for nothing?"

Eremon gathered cobalt power into his palms, illuminating the archival chamber with its light. "Kill who?"

Aidryn's grip tightened on the hilt of his sword, his knuckles turning white. "Aeron!"

Horror washed over Eremon at the anguish in Aidryn's voice. He had forgotten one of his father's most important lessons: He should have kept Aeron close. In his anger, he hadn't considered that the sentry might take everything he knew to Thorne.

"Why would you do that?" Eremon asked.

"I wanted to protect Caitir," Aidryn said, his voice suddenly weak. He released his sword, the heavy blade clattering to the ground as he pressed his hand to his brow. "Now, it's too late."

"*I'm* protecting her." Eremon's shoulders sagged resignedly. "If you'd listen to me, Tarlach, you would understand."

"How is putting her in power a protective measure?" Aidryn demanded. "She's either bait for King La'hiran or the people. Thorne is set on destroying her—and you, too."

Eremon willed his temper to cool, letting his magic wink out. "As I said: She is Crown Regent, not Raní."

He moved back to his stool, sat, then pulled out another, motioning for Aidryn to join him. Aidryn shook his head, instead leaning against the nearest bookcase as Eremon continued. "The position prevents her from taking the throne as rightful ruler, now and in future. We informed Iathium that she's a temporary custodian until the rightful heir returns."

Aidryn swore, the words guttural and harsh as his eyes glazed with fury. "This can't stand; Lira doesn't want the throne. You're supposed to ascend."

Eremon held up his palms. "I *will* ascend," he replied, "three weeks from now. But having Caitir show affection and deference toward Lira helps her in the meantime."

Aidryn threw his hands up. "But it's all an elaborate lie!"

"Which you are well versed in navigating," Eremon replied. "You've spent more years living a lie than not. Surely, you can help me for long enough to save your sister's life and ensure Aila's demise."

As Eremon explained the details of his plan, Aidryn began to visibly relax. By the time he was finished, it was well past dawn—at least, according to Irem's timepiece. Aidryn stifled a heavy yawn and rubbed a hand over his face.

"I still don't like this." Aidryn headed for the stacks, running his fingers along the spines of the well-worn books. "But three weeks will pass quickly. Giving Lira a time frame to set her expectations by will be a relief."

"I don't think Lira will be keen to go along with my plans," Eremon ventured.

"No," said Aidryn. "She'll have a lot of questions, I'm sure. Which reminds me..."

He fished in the leather pouch he carried on his belt and produced a small amber stone, then extended it to Eremon. The stone was smooth and warm, and Eremon hefted its weight in his palm.

"What's this?" he asked.

"Lira imbued it with Aeron's memories," Aidryn said. "If you can navigate her magic, you can see everything he gave us. He was a spy for Aila, that's certain. Fiadh, too."

"I should have known," Eremon mused with a small nod. "Aeron left Iathium before Caitir assumed the regency. I've had spies trailing Fiadh's every move, and there has been no indication of spy activity on her part. She's been spending time at her father's forge, making blown glass."

"There's something to the glass," Aidryn said. "You'll see it in the memories—we're not sure what to make of it."

Eremon nodded. "You should get some rest. There are plenty of empty chambers."

"No, thank you," Aidryn said. "I need to get back to Lira. Just... thank you for caring about Caitir's wellbeing."

Suddenly, Eremon was reluctant to admit the depth of compassion he'd begun to feel for Caitir. He waved Aidryn off. "I can dole out some sort of justice after the babe is born."

Aidryn looked at him in a searching way that made him feel as though all his secrets were bared. "Of course."

CHAPTER 48
CAITIR

Dome

Caitir sat in the Dome's elaborate dining hall, waiting to greet emissaries from the artisans' guilds. The dining hall was hidden within the Dome's interior, its walls and ceiling of stained glass illuminated by torches. No natural light shone through the panes here, so the roaring fire and torchlight against the room's rich crimson and gold trimmings created a deep warmth that settled her nerves.

Over the past few days, Eremon had given her a series of strict instructions on how to handle relations with not only Iathium's most influential citizens but with the clans as well. His lessons had evolved from the basics of politics and diplomacy to a more nuanced, strategic approach to continental unity. Together, they were embarking on a multi-layered, multi-pronged approach to gaining Rodhlan's trust.

If all went according to plan, Eremon would move to the next phase: slowly re-forging relationships beyond the Dome, meeting face-to-face with his old allies. He wanted to prove himself to them, he'd said, rather than seizing the throne in a show of force. The people needed to see him as safe and trust-worthy, not a dangerous magical force to be feared.

Today, she had asked Kenji to prepare a midday meal for the guild masters. He and his staff had created a mouth-watering spread of baked fish, root vegetables, breads, and cheeses. They set the table with the finest dinnerware: plates rimmed with pure gold, silver cutlery, and crystal goblets filled with sweet mead. Kenji had swiped Caitir's mead with an affec-tionate wink before she could drink, replacing it with a cup of honeyed tea.

Fiadh stood at attention beside the entryway. She'd barely spoken to Caitir since Aeron's disappearance, and her presence was grating. Even still, Eremon had encouraged Caitir to keep Fiadh close, so they'd devised to keep her busy nearby.

Caitir raised her cup to her lips and took a sip, eyes darting to the doorway as Deghan led the guild masters in. She recognized none of them except Fiadh's father, Fiond, who brought up the rear. Her heart hammered as they locked gazes. Fiond's dark eyes simmered with hatred as he chose a seat opposite Caitir's at the far end of the table.

He gripped the back of the chair yet did not sit. Each of the guild masters, ten in total, took up a place behind a chair at the table, gathering near the far end. No one sat. No one approached her. No one spoke.

Eight men and two women from Iathium's guilds glared at her with loathing in their eyes. Some wore the colors of their respective clans emblazoned on their clothing, or as fabric wrapped around their wrists. They all looked worse for wear—pale, gaunt, haunted. Not the thriving band of craftspeople Caitir had expected to greet.

Caitir knew her face fell—felt it, even, and couldn't mask her expression. Though she cast a pleading look at Kenji, the cook pleasantly ignored her, playing his part as he oversaw the spread of food the cooks had arranged. She gripped the arms of her chair, keenly aware of all the eyes trained on her.

She pushed her own chair back and stood, clasping her hands behind her back in an attempt to conceal their trembling. "Thank you all for coming. Please, sit. We will serve you a meal."

Her voice was hollow, and it echoed around the room as though she were the only living being here.

Fiond snorted. "And a fine meal, it is. You could have fed the whole of Iathium, yet you chose to sink precious coin into rich fare for a handful of people."

Caitir narrowed her gaze. "Well, let's get directly to the point, Fiond Énna."

"Yes, let's," another man said—blond hair, black eyes, middle-aged, and with the scruff of an uneven beard peppering his jaw. "I'm Gryn Tarlach of the Masons' Guild. I knew your father, Caitir. He would be ashamed of you."

The others hummed in agreement. Heat rushed to her face.

"I called you all here to help me right Iathium's economy," Caitir replied. "What I may or may not have done under duress is none of your concern."

"You will never atone for this, and Iathium will never recover," Fiond growled. "The minute you three marched on the city with your mountain warriors, everything halted." He punctuated his statement by pounding his fist on the table. "*Everything.*"

The others nodded their agreement. A young woman spoke up—red-haired and clad in shades of gray, rich brown leather, and Clan Beran's deep orange. "Evin Beran of the Leatherworkers' Guild, my lady. Fiond speaks truth. Trade with the clans has all but halted, and that has affected our businesses here in the city."

"It's nearly impossible to feed our families," the other woman added. She was a bit older than Evin, with brown skin, black hair gathered at the nape of her neck, and dark, piercing eyes. The room hummed.

"I've invited the clans to return to trade as it was," Caitir answered.

"It's not enough," the woman protested.

"What is your name?"

"I will not grant you that honor," she replied stiffly, raising her chin. "But I lead the Mapmakers' Guild."

"Fair," Caitir clipped, letting her gaze slide from one enraged face to another. "I've opened the opportunity for trade to resume. We're building arenas to train magic wielders and educational infrastructure to teach the people. How is that not enough? Help me understand your position."

"It's impossible to learn when you're barely eating," Evin answered in a gentle voice, though a hint of deeper anger lay beneath her soft tone. "Our people need work and food. There's no use trying to teach starving city-dwellers."

"If we can train the magic wielders, then we begin to solve the problem." Caitir said. "They're incapacitated because suppressed power builds in their bodies and makes them ill. If they know how to expend it, that's half the battle."

The brown-skinned woman gave her a slow shake of the head. "You need to make some sort of emergency provision. We cannot wait until you feel safe enough to tour the city and see for yourself."

Caitir was taken aback. "I wasn't planning to wait—"

"She'll never be safe in Iathium," Fiond cut in. "If I had my way, she would never be safe inside this Dome!"

"Stop it, Father," Fiadh hissed.

"Is that a threat, Fiond?" Caitir released the careful hold she kept on her dark magic, allowing its black lightning to gather in her palms, to swirl around her body. The static raised the hair on her arms.

The other guild masters shrank from her, fear in their eyes. But Fiond stood firm. "It's not a threat, girl. It's a vow."

"Father!" Fiadh barked from the far end of the room.

Fiond straightened, his enraged gaze flicking to his daughter before locking on Caitir again. She let the power wink out and said, "Deghan, see Fiond out and bar him from reentry."

The sentry approached with one of his comrades at his side. He cuffed Fiond, and the sentries each took one of the older man's elbows, his body now rigid with rage. The room was silent, with Fiadh glaring daggers at Caitir as she continued.

"Anyone else who sees fit to threaten me in my own home will see the same fate, or worse." She locked eyes with Fiond, approaching him. "I spare your life this once, because Fiadh is in my employ, and because you've lost your son."

Fiond spat at her. "Damn you!"

Caitir shrank back in time to miss the worst of it. His spittle landed on the hem of her sea foam-green gown, and her dark power surged within her once again. She closed the distance between them, grabbing his face roughly as she summoned power into her bloody palms again. He screamed—Fiadh screamed—as Caitir let a surge of searing black lightning pass from her fingers into his face, singing and melting his skin where she touched him. Blisters rose to the surface and burst, seeping and bleeding as she retracted her hands. The old man whimpered and wept, but she shut her heart to the sound.

"Because you asked so nicely," she said, letting her voice settle into an icy timbre, "you forfeit your mastery of the Blacksmiths' Guild. You may remain an artisan, but your rank is hereby stripped." Caitir jerked her chin toward the door, addressing the sentries now. "Get him out of my sight."

The sentries obeyed. Fiadh made to follow them, but Caitir barked her name, halting her in her tracks.

"Do not follow them," Caitir said coolly. "I have need of you."

Grudgingly, Fiadh stopped by the door, casting a last, desperate glance toward her father before turning to face Caitir, her rage evident in her expression. She didn't speak but instead, waited.

"Fetch Tomis from his chambers and bring him here," Caitir ordered. "I need him so we can sort out how to get the people fed and cared for properly."

Fiadh gave her a vacant stare and a shallow nod, then left the dining hall. The artisans remained silent as Caitir took a seat, and this time, they sat, too. Kenji nodded to his cooks, who began silently serving the other guests.

Movement flashed in Caitir's periphery, and she glanced to the serving table to see the silver cat silently crouched beneath. His tail flicked as he eyed her, and it took everything in her power to turn her attention back to the meeting at hand.

LATE THAT AFTERNOON, Fiadh and Peasant trailed Caitir down the corridor. Golden sunlight streamed in through the glass panes, bathing the gilded sconces and trimmings as they moved down the wide walkway. When they reached Caitir's chamber, Fiadh slammed the door and stormed across the room toward her.

"How could you?" she said, voice wavering. "My father will never recover—my *family* will never recover."

"Then he should learn not to threaten those who offer him help," Caitir replied coolly.

Fiadh's gaze locked on Caitir, and she snarled. "You've scarred his face forever. Taken everything from him. Would it not have been enough to simply bar him from the Dome?"

Caitir sniffed angrily. "You wouldn't be defending his behavior if Macha or Eremon were on the throne."

"That's because they were, at least, worthy of respect—which is more than I can say for you. You're just a child playing dress-up until your mother returns to end your fun." Fiadh shut her mouth immediately, eyes widening.

"Do tell. What is your role in the game?" Caitir crooned, trying her best to appear calm. "Will you be the one to free her from Iteloria? Or have you done that already?"

Fiadh took a step back, looking aghast. "Are you daft?"

Caitir narrowed her eyes. "Perhaps we should have your father brought back for questioning—see what secrets you spill then."

Roaring something unintelligible, Fiadh drew one of her swords and charged at Caitir, blade raised.

Caitir held still, dark magic flowing into her hands unbidden. She suspended a large orb of the black power between her palms and stepped aside, floating it out to deter Fiadh's strike. As the blade passed through the lightning, it turned to ash. The silver cat leapt onto the settee, its tail flicking as it watched the scene unfold.

Fiadh dropped the hilt abruptly, as if the metal had burned her. Its heavy clatter against the marble tile echoed through the chamber. She bared her teeth.

"Pathetic and empty-handed," Caitir spat. "I would challenge you to a magical duel, but you've nothing to wield."

"Nothing," Fiadh echoed, clenching her fists at her sides. Her body trembled with rage as she locked eyes with Caitir and shouted, "*You* are nothing!"

With her cry, waves of dark magic burst from Fiadh's chest with such force that it threw her backward. Fiadh's head snapped back, cracking hard against the wall before she crashed to the floor.

Caitir didn't have time to brace for the magic's effects—

couldn't have even if she'd wanted to. Yet she watched the massive, uncontrolled burst of power splay across the chamber, popping and charring and burning its way across the drapes, the fixtures, the linens. Every inch of glass in the room, including the windowpanes, shattered, blowing shards outward. Yet Caitir felt nothing: no impact, nor any sensation from the power whatsoever.

Perhaps she was dying. That was the only explanation. How else could she be standing here, watching all this destruction unfold around her, completely untouched?

Time moved slowly. Caitir gradually became aware of the altered colors in the room—not just from the charring, dark power but a change that appeared to have applied itself to everything she laid eyes on. A cobalt shimmer, like a sheen that had fallen over the entire place.

And her child—her *child!* Caitir pressed her hands to her belly, slightly rounded now. It emanated warmth and life. She was keenly aware of how right every part of her body felt, how peaceful and safe. The wonder of the sensation swept away any thought of what was happening in the room around her, and a warm tingle spread from her belly to her hands, up her arms, and finally all over her body.

A long moment passed before she thought to look back up at Fiadh, who was slumped against the wall, gaping at Caitir. At her belly. So Caitir looked down, too, and cried out at what she saw.

There was an otherworldly glow—that same cobalt power —emanating from within *her*, as though it surrounded the babe in her womb. The power flared, clearly visible despite the opaque fabric of her dress, then faded before finally bursting across her skin.

Fiadh leapt to her feet, shaking her head as though in a stupor. "That wasn't your magic." She pointed at Caitir. "It's that magic from the feast—the night that sentry threw her spear."

Caitir hummed. "I never show my entire hand. You know that."

Fiadh pushed to her feet, her expression darkening. "I know you and your mother were after some immortal power of Eremon's, before Silira brought him back, and you didn't get it."

She straightened, her eyes brightening, sharpening, as she looked more closely at Caitir. "He's been here, hasn't he? He's here now."

"You're mad." Caitir's voice was too breathy, so she refrained from saying more.

Fiadh's eyes landed on the silver cat, a disbelieving laugh erupting from her. "That stupid cat! It's him!"

In a flash, Eremon transformed and prowled toward Fiadh. She had nowhere to run, so she backed against the wall, dark eyes wide with terror.

"Stupid cat?" he said with a wry grin. "That's rather insulting, Fiadh."

"Quite," Caitir answered.

Eremon assessed Fiadh from head to toe. His angular eyes flashed. "A bitter, hollowed-out little thing, filled with power she can't use. One surge of well-placed magic from the right opponent, and you'd shatter like a glass orb."

"What do you know about it?" Fiadh spat.

"Enough to know I don't envy your fate." He raised his chin. "Tell me: What did Aila promise you in exchange for your loyalty?"

"What?" Fiadh yelped.

Eremon shook his head. "Enough lies. We have Aeron's memories from Silira."

"How?" Fiadh let out a startled laugh. "Where did she get them?"

"Fortress Halgeir," Eremon answered. "We know you're allied with Aila, so give up the ruse."

Caitir gaped at Eremon before turning to Fiadh, who held

up her palms. "We're not allies. I swear it. It would not benefit me if she returned."

"What did she promise you?" Eremon asked in a low voice. "You clearly saw a benefit before."

"Significance, riches," Fiadh answered, stumbling over her words. "When we learned she'd been taken captive, we ceased communication."

"'We?'" Eremon pressed.

"Th—the spies," Fiadh stammered breathlessly. "None of us wanted to risk being imprisoned."

"How much does she know?" Caitir demanded. "And King La'hiran; what about him?"

"It's too bad Silira isn't here with her truth magic," Eremon mused, crossing his arms. "You would be much easier to decipher. Though, I hear Caitir is rather skilled at torture. Perhaps we can give that a go."

"No; please," Fiadh pleaded, shaking her head. "Aila cast a wide net. I'll give you names of everyone involved."

"I have something different in mind," Eremon replied. He snatched the lapels of Fiadh's doublet and leered down at her. "The dungeon would be fitting."

Fiadh bared her teeth and grasped his wrist. "Unhand me!"

As though compelled, Eremon abruptly let go of her, stumbling backward a few steps. A look of horror flashed briefly across his face, but he recovered swiftly. Fiadh's eyes lit with glee.

Eremon looked down at his hand, then back up at Fiadh in alarm. "I thought there was something different about you. You have no heartbeat. How is that possible?"

"There was an accident," Fiadh answered, clasping her hands behind her back. "Caitir tried to give me magic, but it failed."

"Clearly," Eremon muttered, flexing his fingers.

Caitir thought of the young prisoner they'd tried to steal

magic from. Fiadh had seemed dazed after their last attempt, but Caitir had been so wrapped up in her own distress that she hadn't noticed anything quite so amiss. Then again, Fiadh had never mentioned that important piece of information.

Fiadh shrugged weakly. "If I could better explain it, I would."

"Dead, yet you appear alive," Eremon mused. "I didn't know it was possible."

"Many nights, I go to sleep wondering if I'll ever wake again," Fiadh admitted. "Each morning, I'm still here."

"Perhaps we can help you decipher it," he said. "What say you?"

"I don't want your help," Fiadh snapped. "I'll live as long as I live."

"That's enough!" Caitir cried. "What will it take, Fiadh? Do you still want to be my right hand? My armorer? You can have whatever you want, but I need you on my side."

"Empty promises," Fiadh hissed. "Your right hand is standing beside you—or are you his? And the armory? You said you're giving that to Clan Tarlach."

"Then be my spymaster," Eremon cut in, giving Caitir a knowing look. Fiadh's gaze snapped to Eremon. "Help us get more spies on the ground in Iteloria and Rodhlan. Give us the names you promised. Do this for me, and you'll be pardoned when all this is over."

Fiadh's gaze darted between Eremon and Caitir. "And if I refuse?"

"Then the outcome will be unfavorable," Eremon said darkly.

"How did you wind up in service to *him*?" Fiadh demanded, turning to Caitir.

Caitir pursed her lips. "Avoiding an unfavorable outcome."

"And what about your friends in the clan army? The

sentries?" Fiadh sneered up at Eremon. "What will they say when they learn you've partnered with a traitor?"

"Nothing, because they already know," he answered softly. "There's nothing you can do to bend their ears, Fiadh, so I suggest you consider my offer. This is the only time I'll extend it."

Caitir's stomach did a flip, and she bit down on her bottom lip to mask the fear that would've overtaken her expression otherwise.

Eremon must have sensed her turmoil, because he shot her a pointed look that was at once soothing and unsettling. Caitir regained her composure and raised her chin expectantly. "Well, Fiadh?"

"Spymaster," Fiadh said, letting the word roll off her tongue. She straightened her shoulders. "What must I do?"

CHAPTER 49
EREMON

Dome

Caitir pressed the door shut as Fiadh departed with her orders, glaring at Eremon accusingly. "Who knows about our alliance?"

Eremon tried to keep his expression impassive as he took note of her eyes. Though her irises had been pale moments ago, they now shone with the cobalt light of his power. This phenomenon might be an interesting record for the archive. He wanted to move closer to inspect them.

Instead, he answered. "Your brother."

She groaned, closing her eyes. "Which means Lira knows."

He inclined his head and shrugged. "Not necessarily."

"Who else?"

Glancing up at the ceiling, Eremon blew out a breath and ticked off the names on his fingers. "The loyalist sentries, Tomis, Iona, Kenji—"

"Kenji?!" Caitir blanched, horrified. "How long has he known?"

"Since before the feast," Eremon admitted.

"How is my child protected if everyone knows?" She closed the distance between them, her lithe body tense, and pointed a finger at his face. "You *promised*."

He caught her wrist, wrapping his fingers around it and angling his head down to meet her eyes. "And I haven't broken it."

She glanced at his hand, brows creasing before she looked up at him again. "But everything you've done up until this point has been—"

"Choreographed," he said. "I know."

Caitir pulled her wrist from his grasp. "So I'm to spend the rest of my life a pawn."

"Of course not." He flexed his fingers. "You must understand, Caitir: I couldn't ally with you in complete secrecy, otherwise I'd become the enemy, too."

She scoffed, taking a step away from him and glancing toward the other side of the room. If she was trying to mask hurt feelings, she was failing miserably. "That's all I'll ever be to any of you—the enemy."

Eremon chuckled, clasping his hands behind his back. "Why would I waste my protective magic on an enemy?"

Caitir's gaze snapped to him, the magic in her eyes still deeply unsettling. "Protective—like the power that turned that spear to ash?"

"And the power that burned Aeron when he—" When she flinched, Eremon cut himself off. "Yes. That protective power."

"That magic was supposed to be in Lira's ring," Caitir mused. "It protected me from Fiadh's power; why didn't it protect Lira?"

"The ring was damaged," Eremon replied. "At the time, it had no power. And I wasn't on my guard. I didn't anticipate the need to protect her in that way. When my power has protected you, it's because I was paying attention. I knew the need to call on it might arise."

Her mouth fell open. "How did Lira survive what Fiadh did to her? How is she now?"

"She lives," Eremon hedged.

"But something more is wrong." Caitir pressed her lips together, her gaze hardening. "Tell me what it is."

"I can't."

Curiously, every fiber in Eremon's body urged him to. But he was reluctant to give her more information, especially after what had just happened with Fiadh. It had quickly become obvious to him that Caitir had not fully understood what had transpired.

"Well, I suppose I know where your trust ends," Caitir said, turning her back to him. She surveyed the demolished bedchamber, her shoulders sagging a bit.

Eremon tensed. "I don't trust Fiadh." He watched her carefully, but she didn't turn back around. "It's best that I don't answer your questions about Lira at present."

"I really have no right to know." There was a sudden softness in Caitir's voice that gave him pause. It was unfortunate that he had no desire to lie. Instead, he blurted, "If you hadn't allied with Fiadh—"

She whirled on him, her eyes bright with his power. "I allied with Fiadh because I had no one else. Not Lira, not my brother, and certainly not you."

"How could I..." Eremon's question guttered out, and instead, he began to laugh, pressing a palm over his mouth. "There was nothing I could have done; I was dead. And besides, how was I to know what you needed?"

Caitir's expression darkened. "I thought—"

"What, that I would rescue you?" Eremon said.

She looked as though he had struck her. Before she could reply, he barreled on, ignoring the pang of guilt that rose in his stomach. "All I saw was your ridiculous mother, parading you around like some preened little mouse, dangling you over the open mouth of every snake in court. What makes you think I would have ever wanted to be a part of that?"

"Because you were the king of them all," Caitir said, low and dark. "Eremon the Viper."

He sighed, exasperated. "Your blade is dull, my lady, and you're hacking away at bone."

"Then I'll be sure to sharpen it." She pressed her fingertips over her eyes. "I'm exhausted."

Eremon's vexation melted away as he considered their surroundings. Fiadh's burst of dark magic had destroyed the chamber, charring the furniture, the drapes, and the structure itself almost beyond recognition.

"Then we need to get you another chamber," he said.

She waved him off. "Just leave me here. I'll figure it out."

Eremon reached out and grasped her elbow. "Don't be stupid," he commanded. "Come on."

Caitir let out a little yelp at the contact, but she moved with him. He led her across the room, scanning the wall until he found a familiar nick in the wood. This door was adjacent to the one beneath the tapestry, and he snuck a peek at her surprised expression as he pressed his palms to the panel. The hidden doorway opened into a pitch-dark tunnel, and a burst of cool air hit them as it yawned wide.

Summoning an orb of cobalt magic in his hand, Eremon cast it toward the empty torches that lined the wall, illuminating the path. She followed him through the doorway, letting it shut behind them, and they fell into silence.

He ran his fingertips along the smooth passageway as they walked, his thoughts giving way to memories of sneaking through these tunnels to escape his tutors as a young boy. Slipping into young courtiers' chambers as the willful teenager he'd been before his magical illness took hold. A memory of carefree laughter and stolen kisses reverberated through him, but he shook it off, veering to the right, reaching behind to offer

Caitir his hand. She grasped it with tentative fingers, as though unsure whether she should offer him more than a light touch, accepting his guidance but nothing more.

They reached a dead end, and he pushed against a new panel in the wall. It opened into a familiar, plush chamber decorated in cream and gold.

"See what you think of this one," he whispered, stepping aside to let Caitir pass.

She entered, spinning slowly in place to survey the chamber. Everything was creamy-white, from the massive canopy bed beneath the window to the furnishings in the sitting area. There were several large chairs and a sofa, with shelves for books and a desk against the far wall.

"This is a *real* chamber," Eremon said, watching her take it all in. "Much more comfortable than the one you've been living in. Fiadh did you a service without knowing it."

"Whose room is this?" Caitir said, running her fingers along the heavy, gold-trimmed curtain that would have separated the sitting area from the bedroom, had it not been drawn.

"It has been empty since before my untimely demise." Eremon cracked a grin, crossing the room to sink onto the sofa. He threw his arms across the back of it. "Dena Beran and her mother always requested these rooms when they came to court."

Dena's father, Den, had been one of Emyr Tarlach's friends. He'd recused himself of a position at court three years ago, though—not unheard of among courtiers who had been in service for more than a decade.

"Dena," Caitir said, as though testing the feel of the name on her tongue. "I remember her. Never liked her."

Eremon scoffed. "Who did you *actually* like?"

Caitir scowled. "Aidryn. Lira, sometimes. And you."

"You didn't know me."

She put her fists on her hips. "And *you* didn't know Lira."

Now it was Eremon's turn to scowl. "Leave her out of this."

"Fine," Caitir conceded, moving to a chair across from the sofa and sinking onto it. "Then let's talk about Dena. I suppose you spent ample time in this chamber, to be so familiar with it."

"What if I did?" he drawled, trying not to grin. Mortal gods help him, he was enjoying toying with her.

Caitir's gaze swept up and around as she studied the detailing on the gilded ceiling. "I never took you for a rake."

"I wasn't a rake," Eremon said with a scoff. "But I had my favorite courtiers." He rested his head against the back of the sofa. "All that stopped when I became ill. I masked it all with seriousness, as though I was suddenly too old for such dalliance. And then there was... well, you know who."

Her expression dropped. "Yes. I know."

There were no candles lit in this chamber, and the orange glow of sunset poured in through the window, alighting on the gold in Caitir's hair. Eremon studied her: pale skin. Pink, full lips. Eyes that had once been a lovely, rich shade of blue. Sometime between her old chamber and here, the residual magic had faded from them.

Upon closer inspection, he could see that the gold of her hair ended an inch beneath her part. An ash blonde grew from her scalp, peeking out from beneath the familiar color.

Caitir seemed to notice him studying her, because her hand flew up to grasp a strand. She wound it around her finger absently. "It's not really *golden* blonde." The way she said it—with a mocking lilt—made the corner of Eremon's mouth quirk up. "I'm sure you've noticed."

"Only just now," he said, standing and crossing the room toward her. "May I?"

She rocked back a bit but nodded, tensing as he reached for a strand of her hair. He was careful to grasp only the ends of a lock, lifting it to get a better look. Her hair was soft, and this close, he caught her scent: woodsy cardamom with a hint of honey. It had become familiar to him in his cat form, but somehow, it had a completely different effect now.

"Are you all right?" Caitir tilted her head, looking puzzled.

With a sharp breath, Eremon returned to himself. He had gone too quiet, for too long a moment. "Yes, I—I've only ever seen the gold." His voice sounded pinched and distant to his ears.

Caitir scoffed. "I'd like to be free of it. I hardly remember what it looked like before."

He felt her intention reach for him, curling around his fingers. His hand tingled, and magic swept over her hair. In an instant, the gold coloring vanished. Eremon gasped, dropping the strands he'd held.

"What?" Caitir cried, her hands flying to her hair. "What's wrong with it?"

"Nothing, just—the dye is gone. Have a look."

He crossed the room toward the mirror, waving her over. She gaped when she stood before it. "How did you do that?"

"I don't know."

She whirled on him then, her expression one of pure awe. "I wonder if it's possible to change my eyes back."

Eremon looked closely at her irises—so light they were almost white. "When did they lose their true color?"

"After I married Gerallt," she admitted. "Mother used a strange sort of Binding she learned in Iteloria, and my eyes changed right after. She has pale eyes herself, though you'd never know; she uses magic to mask them. Her hair, too."

"Tai'ceru," Eremon mused. "You're half?"

"That's right." Caitir ran a hand over her belly.

It wasn't unusual for the Tai'Ceru people to have pale irises. They were a small tribe on Iteloria's frozen western coast, famous for the blue and teal nea'la roses they cultivated in the ice and snow.

Instead of throwing another insult at her, he said, "I

remember the hue. The pale blue is beautiful; only different than before, that's all."

She stilled, lips parting slightly as she gazed up at him. "I thought you said I was inconsequential."

Eremon sighed and fixed his gaze on her face, tracing its soft lines and delicate curves. "I was trying to be hurtful."

Caitir averted her eyes. "It worked."

Guilt clenched his heart with unexpected intensity. During his first life, she had been nothing more than an annoyance. Now, he wished he had taken just a moment to speak to her, at least once.

Perhaps he could have saved her from this mess before it began.

"I shouldn't have said that to you," he said.

She shrugged, but the nonchalance of the gesture was offset by the deep sorrow that welled in her eyes. "Why not? It's the truth."

Eremon took a tentative step backward, then another, and shook his head. "Not anymore." He ducked back through the hidden doorway and made to pull it shut, but not before he added, "Get some rest."

The door clicked shut between them before Caitir had a chance to reply.

CHAPTER 50
LIRA

Rodhlan Ridge
1 Week Later

Aidryn's frequent disappearances were starting to trouble Lira.

Not only had he ridden into the meadowlands without a word the night they'd returned; he'd begun slipping out of the valley before dawn regularly. He took special pains to leave before she'd awakened so she couldn't ask questions. When she did, he became evasive.

When he entered the cottage that afternoon, looking wind-blown and a little sheepish, Lira was waiting for him. She and Skelly had stoked a warm fire, and they were cooking a large pot of stew over the hearth. He opened the door carefully, as though he believed no one would notice him entering. Lira propped her fists on her hips and raised a brow.

"Where's Skelly?" Aidryn asked, scanning the small space for Lira's grandmother.

He was wearing the warm leathers he'd brought from Fortress Halgeir with a heavy, crimson cloak Eiren had given him. In honor of Lira's birthright, he'd added swatches of emerald fabric near the clasp and along the inner edging. His hands were clad in fitted leather gloves, his long, dark hair secured in a low bun at his nape.

"At the keep," Lira answered. "You've left nearly every morning since we returned. Where have you been?"

"Seeing to Clan Tarlach," he answered, "and Iathium. I wanted to speak with Eremon."

"We agreed to do that together, with Oda," Lira replied, pursing her lips.

"And we can," Aidryn hedged, "but I knew I could make a short trip of it, and now I have some tasks to complete."

"Tasks?" Lira crossed her arms. "Like what?"

"Iathium's armory is being passed to Clan Tarlach as a peace offering," he replied, shucking off his riding cloak.

"Passed to Clan Tarlach by whom?" Lira pressed. She didn't miss the slight flicker of annoyance in his expression. "And what does it have to do with you?"

"I'm their anointed, of course. More than once, the Tarlach Assembly has asked me to take my place," Aidryn explained, crossing to the large pot that hung over the hearth and stirring the stew. "I've refused, naturally, but I think there's no harm in helping set them up for a better future after they lost everything."

There it is, Lira thought. *Further proof he's keeping his distance from you.*

"I thought we agreed to stay together," Lira said in a small, quivering voice. "Yet you've fled my side at every opportunity."

Aidryn turned to look at her, his expression unreadable. "I'm not fleeing, but I will be delivering news to the assembly and helping them prepare to move nearer to Iathium before snowfall, if they want."

"You shouldn't be running off with Clan Tarlach," she said. "I need you here."

"I don't need you telling me what I should or shouldn't do," Aidryn shot back. "I'm every bit as anointed as you are, and I have a right to help my people if I wish to. I'm paying attention to what needs to be done and taking control of what I can."

"Taking control," Lira said slowly, "like how you silenced Aeron?"

He stilled. "That," he snapped, his eyes taking on a glassy sheen, "was meant to prevent an invasion."

"Is that why you ran to Eremon? You thought you could prevent Thorne from acting on the information you withheld."

"I thought I could prevent a lot of things," Aidryn said softly, dipping his head.

There was far more to this than he was letting on. Slowly, his unspoken truths began to weave themselves together in Lira's mind. Where she expected to feel anger, there was only emptiness. Numbness. She tried to suppress the trembling in her hands by busying herself.

"Like what?" She watched him closely. "Like that alliance between Eremon and Caitir he predicted?"

Aidryn's eyes flashed. "Eremon and I talked about his plans for ascension and righting relationships with the clans."

Lira hummed. "You said the armory was a peace offering."

"Did I?" Aidryn rubbed the back of his neck, his cheeks turning pink.

"Eremon has no quarrel with Clan Tarlach, and he hasn't ascended." Lira crossed her arms, pinching her hands against her torso. "Who seeks peace?"

"Eremon," Aidryn ventured, "would want to undo any damage the usurpers inflicted in Iathium's name."

"But why so quietly?" Lira asked. "His return is traveling on whispers that become louder by the day. Our leaving the valley kept the rumors at bay for a while, but people are demanding to know the truth. I can't enter the keep without being bombarded with questions I can't rightly answer because I'm being lied to."

"No one has lied to you," Aidryn replied, his expression pained.

Lira swore, her face suddenly hot, her muscles tensing. "I'm not stupid. Stop trying to manipulate my power with selective honesty. I helped you back at Halgeir because I trusted you had good reason for withholding information. I trusted you to tell me."

Aidryn raised his voice, pounding a fist on the worktable for emphasis. "I can't have you losing yourself to the dark magic when you learn the full truth. You're a danger to yourself and everyone else."

His words sent another reverberating shock through her. She was accustomed to Aidryn's blunt honesty, but there had always been a tender undertone to his sharp tongue. Today, there was no sign of it.

Lira slammed the tea kettle onto the worktable. Water sloshed out, splattering the wood surface. She and Aidryn stared one another down for a long moment.

"I understand completely," Lira sneered.

Before Aidryn could respond, she turned away from him and stormed into the bedchamber, locking the door behind her. A few moments later, she heard the front door of the cottage open, then slam. She grabbed one of the pillows from Skelly's bed and shrieked into it, screaming until her throat was raw.

When she had exhausted herself, she threw the pillow at the bed as hard as she could. Panting and trembling, she paused, considering what to do next.

Control, Aidryn had said. But what could Lira control? Thus far, all she had been able to do was wait for other people to right the many wrongs around them. First, Eremon had been preoccupied by his own feelings. Now, it was Aidryn. Oda was determined *not* to access her power successfully. At present, Thorne seemed to be the only person looking out for the greater good.

The dark magic was the root of Lira's biggest problems. It was the reason no one trusted her. The reason why Aidryn now seemed to fear her. Had he not declared his belief in her mere weeks ago? What had changed?

In your fears, you will find your salvation.

That thought had stayed with Lira since it first crossed her mind. What were her greatest fears?

Losing Aidryn, she thought. *Losing control of my power. Being useless to Rodhlan and the people I love.*

Her greatest fears had one thing in common, just as she'd suspected: the dark magic. If she could gain more control over that, then perhaps Aidryn would stop pulling away. Perhaps she would protect her birthright power. And if more control was possible, maybe her loved ones would once again see her as more than a liability.

As though responding to her thoughts, the dark magic beneath her skin roiled and skittered, sending sharp, prickling tingles over her body. While she had wielded her own magic since Fiadh's attack, she had never attempted to discharge the black lightning. Maybe that was what she needed—to get relief.

She shot to her feet and raced through the house, bursting out the front door and into the fresh, cold air. Her breath came in shallow huffs as she surveyed the valley. It was especially quiet; there was far less activity around the keep and fewer horses roaming the open field. Fannin was gone, meaning Aidryn was likely far from here for the time being.

With a pang in her stomach, Lira turned her back on the pasture, moving toward the tree line behind Skelly's home. On the way to the forest, a strange pressure filled her body, like the feeling of a scream stuck in her throat or tears that refused to fall. It welled up inside of her, building with her rage until it was almost unbearable. This must have been how Eremon had felt for so long—fighting this power that felt too big for his skin, yet too unpredictable to unleash.

How would it feel to discharge an excess of this dark magic? Was it safe this far from the keep?

Try it, she heard a taunting voice say. *You might like how it feels.*

Lira whirled, searching for the source of the sound. But she was alone, and further into the woods than she'd realized.

Here, it was nearly as dark as night. Steep cliffs began their ascent not far from where Lira stood, and their sheer height blocked much of the sun's light from the forest floor. She looked behind her to see the valley below, the keep, and the roof of Skelly's little cottage. Her head pounded, and her teeth ached.

If she were to release some of her magic, where would she do it? Black lightning would burn the trees—and worse, could spark a wildfire. This time of year, the foliage was too dry to burn without endangering the settlement.

She craned her neck to look up the cliff, suddenly curious. Its ancient, craggy formation towered over her. Stepping forward, she reached out and placed her hand on the cool rock.

The rock won't burn, the voice said, *and you will finally feel better.*

Several images flashed before Lira's eyes in quick succession —like a witnessing, but tinged with green.

Lightning strikes the rocky mountainside, leaving a charred mark behind. The forest is intact, its trees lush as they sway in the breeze. Riku pours his power into the cliffside with a mighty shout, and the rock absorbs his magic with ease.

As the vision lifted, Lira released a jagged exhale. She allowed the dark magic to well up inside of her, filling her palms as it burned and popped. Gritting her teeth against the pain, she willed the ball of power to grow larger, coaxing it out of her body bit by bit. There was a price to be paid for using this magic, but it would be well worth every agonizing second if she could be free of the pressure—even just for a little while.

When she was too exhausted to draw out any more of the power, she took a step toward the cliffside. Her raw palms dripped blood now, and she ground her teeth harder. All she needed to do was will the black lighting into the rock, and then—

"Lira, stop!"

She jumped, searching for the source of the familiar voice. The magic dropped from her hands, and for a moment, she felt the relief she'd been seeking. Her eyes filled with green smoke, which quickly dissipated.

Oda was running full-tilt in Lira's direction, her light, leather boots barely making a sound as she pounded over the underbrush, leaping over boulders and dodging trees as she ran. Her lips were moving, her eyes wide with terror. Lira blinked slowly, unable to make out her friend's words.

It was warm around her, she noticed, and a sheen of sweat sprang to her skin. She swayed on her feet, barely registering the brief flash of violet just before a wall of fire obstructed her view. Her ears roared, and for a moment, the world around her was drowned out.

Then Oda's scream cut through the roar.

The world rushed back, overwhelming Lira's senses.

A wildfire was spreading from around her in a wide ring, burning up the trees overhead and rushing down the mountainside, toward the valley. Heat from the blaze singed her cheeks, and she felt as though her clothes might melt from the intensity of it. Trees cracked, burning limbs tumbling down and crashing around her.

There was nowhere to run.

"Oda?" she cried.

When Oda didn't answer, panic seized Lira. What had she

done? What if the fire killed her friend? What if it destroyed the village and took more lives in the process?

A blazing branch crashed to the ground nearby and sparks showered her, burning her right cheek, her ear, and her neck, exposed from braiding her hair that morning. Her cloak ignited, and she shucked it off, throwing it into the fire. In moments, the flames consumed it entirely.

Lira called for Oda again, violent tremors taking hold of her body. Smoke and heat burned her throat, and she coughed violently, eyes watering as she tried and failed to catch a glimpse of the warrior's figure through the fire. Sweat beaded on her skin, soaking her clothes, rolling into her eyes and burning as she attempted to blink it away.

We're going to die out here.

"Please," she cried, hot tears spilling down her cheeks. "Rodhlan—*anyone*! Help us!"

From what seemed like far away, she thought she could hear Oda's voice. She strained to make out the words, but she only understood one.

"Rhona!"

A surge of cool water burst from beneath the trees, as though a dam had broken open in the middle of the forest. Lira barely had time to take a breath before it engulfed and submerged her, lifting her feet off the ground before planting her back where she'd stood a moment before. Its swell passed almost as quickly as it had surged, and she broke its surface, gasping and sputtering as the water made its way down the mountainside.

Almost as suddenly as the fire had begun, it was extinguished. A deluge of water showered her like rain, crashing down from where it had swept up the cliffs, then back down again. It rushed down the mountainside, gradually dissipating as its reach broadened. She could see it flowing into the valley

—caught a glimpse of clanspeople emerging from the keep and their homes to see what had happened.

Lira turned her back on the settlement, instead searching for Oda, who was only paces away. Her dark brown skin shimmered with a violet sheen, and there were tears in her green eyes. When she opened her arms, Lira rushed into them, slamming into the warrior full-force as they embraced.

Oda held steady, wrapping her arms around Lira. They were both soaked. The rush of adrenaline and the heat of the fire faded, replaced by the biting winter wind. They huddled together, frightened and shivering.

"That was your magic," Lira said, her teeth beginning to chatter.

The warrior ran a soothing palm up and down Lira's back. "I know."

"It all—c-came at once," Lira stammered.

Oda drew back, her eyes shimmering as she reached for Lira's face. Gently, she poured her healing magic into the burns, soothing the deep sting the flames had left behind. "I asked Rhona for help, Lira. Nothing else has ever worked, but she was *here*. I know it."

Rhona—Rodhlan's mortal goddess, long dead. Lira had never been one to believe in unseen deities, but then again, she hadn't believed in magic before, either.

"If that's the case," Lira replied, "then she knew you'd need the full force of it today."

The warrior pressed her lips together, then smiled. She put her arm around Lira. "Let's get you back to Skelly's."

CHAPTER 51

CAITIR

Dome

S erving as Crown Regent felt more precarious than Caitir had expected it to. Every day since she'd accepted her regency, she had received audiences and held meetings with individuals and dignitaries from all over Rodhlan. Merchants, tradespeople, and artisans came begging favors from the treasury. Prominent clanspeople negotiated new trade deals.

A few members of the working nobility who had survived Aila's purge came to Caitir because they'd known her father in his lifetime. In accordance with Eremon's wishes, she began to rebuild the council. She appointed Tomis as the first member, followed by Evin Beran and Gryn Tarlach. She had yet to secure more takers.

In secret, she begged Eremon and Kenji for guidance. For the time being, she'd closed the borders to visits from outside the continent. Once diplomatic meetings began again, she would need more nobles willing to back her.

Some days, she resented having to pour her newfound

energy into meetings and strategy. The subtle, lingering nausea of pregnancy had finally abated, her waistline slowly becoming fuller. To the outside observer, it still wasn't obvious that she was expecting a child. Toryn had said that often, with the first baby, no one else would notice until halfway through term.

She had begun to feel subtle, fleeting flutters in her belly— finally, something tangible for all that time she'd spent feeling ill. At night, she lay still and silent in bed, hoping to feel the child moving and wishing she didn't feel so alone.

Eremon often worked in the archive or locked himself away in his own chambers. One day, Caitir overheard a few superstitious servants—who had, apparently, been snooping around his tower—buzzing about how they'd seen a light beneath his door. That had resulted in a number of fantastical ghost stories that spread through the Dome and into the city streets.

"You're going to need heavier curtains for your rooms," she'd finally told Eremon one evening as they studied in the archival chamber. "People have seen the candlelight, and now they think you're haunting the place."

"I *am* haunting the place," he murmured as he continued scratching out the directive he'd been working on for the past two hours. The corner of his mouth turned up in amusement.

"You know what I mean. Get your drapes during the day tomorrow and bring them to me. I'll need extra fabric, but I can fix them so they're thicker and block out the light at night."

He pursed his lips. "What are *you* going to do with my drapes? Just have new ones made."

"I'm going to sew them," she said airily, though the declaration made her feel a bit woozy. "I can ask Kenji to get fabric for me."

Eremon sat still for a moment, then put down his quill and turned to regard her. "You sew?"

"I used to." She folded her hands in front of her. "I'm quite good, but Mother didn't like it."

"So you stopped." He rested an elbow on the desk and leaned on it casually. "What else did you stop?"

The question bludgeoned Caitir. For a long moment, she just blinked at him. "What did I stop?"

Eremon sat patiently while she took a long breath, then blew it out from between her lips.

Finally, she said, "I used to draw. Aidryn hounded me about it for years. He and Lira were the only people who cared about my interests."

He turned back to his work. "Ah."

They fell into an uneasy silence. Caitir selected a book from the stack he'd pulled for her to study and sat on a stool on the other side of the room, cracking it open.

Most of the records Eremon selected on their trips to the archive were about economics, law, and all the nuances of ruling a city-state. Occasionally, he paused writing to quiz her on the finer points of governing, but they'd fallen into a habit of working alongside one another in loaded silence.

She supposed the heightened discomfort between them was fueled by their mutual memories of this place, and of who had occupied it for so many years before. Lira and Aidryn had been a permanent presence in the archive, and the very air was punctuated by the memory of them—and the memory of what Lira and Eremon had shared, too.

Eremon's work ethic was as relentless as Lira's always had been. He hunched over his parchment for hours at a time, neglecting to stop and stretch or even to speak. Caitir didn't have the luxury of sitting still for too long; if she did, her ankles would swell uncomfortably, her calves and hips cramping. She stayed in motion much of the time, taking frequent breaks to move and stand.

Caitir yawned, stretching and rising from her stool. She moved closer to the desk, looking down over Eremon's shoulder at the words he'd carefully scripted with his quill. His handwriting was elegant and sure, each loop and line perfectly crafted, the ink obeying his every command. It was a strange metaphor for how she'd imagined he might lead the city, if he ever had the chance to do so freely.

She sighed. "I never realized how much weight you carried on your shoulders. Mother plied me with the idea of a crown, but I never truly understood."

"You thought royalty was all about... what? Jewels and riches and revelries?" Eremon faced her fully then. "Last spring was the first time I truly enjoyed a celebration of any kind since I became Rí. And you know how short-lived that was."

"I do," Caitir replied.

He looked wistful as he continued. "I spent my days and nights working, studying. Trying to rid myself of that wretched dark magic. I would have done anything to just enjoy being Rí, but I exhausted my energy wishing I wasn't."

"And I exhausted mine wishing..." Caitir pressed her lips together, cutting herself off. "Never mind."

"What? Wishing you were living some imaginary existence here?" Eremon swept his hand around, gesturing vaguely to the books around them. "Look around. Lira and I pored over books until our eyes blurred and our backs ached—every day for weeks. Even during *Nami Mostari*, she was down here working, trying to find a cure for my ailment. The urgency to learn what we could about magic, the pressure we were both under... it was nearly unbearable some days."

She crossed her arms. "Yet you still managed to fall in love with her, in spite of all that."

Eremon scoffed softly and shook his head. "I was in love with her before we began. I chose her as Defender because I loved her."

Caitir couldn't help it; the truth stung. She shifted uncomfortably, her face suddenly hot—with humiliation or envy, she wasn't sure. Probably both. "I never realized you'd noticed her."

He turned back to his work. "No one cared that I loved the histories." With a steady hand, he signed his name to the scroll, then blew over the ink. "I knew Lira would."

"I was surprised she fell for you," Caitir admitted. "She never behaved as though she was interested in *any* man."

"It took more convincing than I anticipated." Eremon chuckled, though it sounded forced. "She was horrified when I proposed. She was diplomatic about it, but I could see it in her eyes. I believed myself above rejection, but she proved me wrong."

He paused to twirl his quill between his fingertips.

"And then, she thought that somehow, putting the ring on would keep me from dying. She was trying to give me hope, I think. Trying to absolve herself of guilt she shouldn't have been feeling in the first place. Now, look where that's left us."

Caitir straightened. "What do you mean?"

Eremon waved her off with a sigh. "Never mind."

She bristled, shoulders tensing and brows knitting. "You've made me Crown Regent and involved me in your ruse, but you still don't trust me enough to tell me what's wrong with Lira?"

"When you need to know, I'll tell you." He'd taken on that heavy-lidded, arrogant look he got when he was being stubborn or guarded.

Caitir wasn't sure whether she wanted to slap him or…

She brushed off the thought. "Keep your secret about Lira. It's all you have left of her now anyway."

Eremon whirled. He balled his fingers into a fist and pounded the desk, eyes flashing. "I just laid my feelings bare, and you can't be content with that; it's not enough. You want it all."

"Of course I want it all." Her heart began to pound. She'd spoken without thinking, but it was too late to take it back now. "Who could blame me?"

Eremon rocked back against the desk in surprise. He

studied her unabashedly, and the prolonged look raised goose-flesh on her skin. When he didn't respond immediately, Caitir pushed harder.

"You were everything I'd *ever* wanted, but Lira was the one you chose." Her voice trembled. She began to pace the narrow space before the Defender's desk. "When I found out, it was like the entire world fell out from under me."

His expression was unreadable, his eyes sharp and bright as she spoke, because apparently, her mouth wouldn't have closed if she'd clapped a hand over it herself. Instead, she let the words pour out, pressing forward despite her unsteady voice and the sudden urge to run from him.

"To me, you were freedom. Being with you meant I would have control over my life for the first time, and a man I could love because I admired him—not because I'd learned to be content."

She pressed her hand to her forehead and burst into erratic laughter. "There it is. I couldn't keep holding it in."

"Candid, indeed," he murmured dryly, casting his gaze to the floor.

His wry response infuriated her, and she closed the distance between them, leaning down to pound the desk adjacent to him, just like he'd done.

"I *hate* being closed in this room with you," she said as his face snapped up, his silver eyes meeting hers. "All I can think about is you and Lira, and what you probably *did* down here all alone when your noses weren't shoved in books."

Abruptly, she straightened and stepped back, covering her blazing face with both hands to hide from his piercing gaze. "Mortal gods, I was so stupid."

Her breath hitched as warm fingers closed around her wrists, easing her hands down. Eremon had risen from where he sat, and now he stood before her in a valiant effort to make eye contact again. She stared past him at the desk, his stack of books suddenly blurring.

"Caitir," he said, the sound of his voice sharpening her senses. "Look at me."

She released a shaky breath and made herself meet his eyes. Quiet rage shimmered around him, reverberated in the narrow space between them. "What do you think we did down here?"

Eremon was still gripping her wrists, but his touch was gentle. She could find no compelling reason to break his grasp as she tried to fish a reply from her suddenly jumbled thoughts.

"I... I've thought a lot of things."

"She kissed me a few times," he said with a small shrug. "Fewer and more chaste than I would have liked." Caitir shivered as he ran a thumb over the inside of her wrist. He didn't step back—didn't attempt to put any space between them. "Does that satisfy your curiosity?"

"No." She turned her hands over to grip his forearms, pulling him down to her. Eremon dipped his head, and their foreheads touched as he released a soft exhale. Caitir angled her head, hesitating for only a breath before rising to meet his mouth.

Eremon made a soft *oh* against her lips before he gave into the kiss, releasing her wrists to wrap his arms around her body, drawing her against him until there was no space left at all. His lips were warm and smooth, and they locked with Caitir's as though they had only ever kissed one another, in this lifetime and every one before that.

He felt nothing like the boys Caitir had stolen kisses from in the alleyways of Iathium. Nothing like Gerallt, who hadn't even bothered to kiss her properly. Instead, his every movement was heated, insistent. She could feel the depth of his vexation in every glide of his mouth across hers.

Eremon kissed her as though he could imprint his

contempt on Caitir's soul, and she wanted it. Years of suppressed desire ignited into a sudden blaze. She was greedy for every spark of ire she could draw from him, every arrogant glance, every stupid, stubborn insult.

She wanted to kiss every thought from his mind, erase every memory but this.

Eremon reached for her hair with practiced hands and unbound it effortlessly, teasing her mouth open with his tongue. Her hands roamed along his tunic, up his chest, over his strong shoulders. With one, she traced his jaw; with the other, she tentatively explored the silken strands of his hair.

He broke from her lips long enough to say, "In case you were wondering, this is what I would have preferred."

Again, his mouth was on hers. He nudged her back against one of the tall bookshelves, hands hot on her waist, lips searing down the side of her throat. She tipped her head back with a gasp as he trailed his fingertips over her shoulder and down her arm. He drew away long enough to shuck off his robe and pitch it onto the desk behind them, then turned his attention back to her.

Eremon slowed his pace, his movements now agonizingly deliberate. Caitir's heart was racing, her breathing ragged as she reveled in the softness of his lips, the way he tasted. He placed a trail of light kisses from her jawline to her ear, taking the lobe gently between his teeth and giving it a little tug before flicking his tongue against the spot. She whimpered, unable to suppress the sounds he drew out of her as he explored.

Catching her hand in his, he placed her palm on his chest. Then, his fingers drifted to the collar of his tunic. He unfastened the top button with a heated, meaningful glance, then guided her hands to continue the work while he returned to her mouth, gingerly cupping her face.

With trembling fingers, she unfastened the buttons of his tunic to reveal pale skin with small, jagged silver scars along its surface—like the lightning in the dark magic they shared. The scarring began just beneath his collarbone, and she brushed her fingertips over his bare skin for the briefest moment. He was warm and strong beneath her hands, and he shivered at the contact.

As she worked her way down the fastenings, she revealed a larger scar that marred the center of Eremon's chest. It shone silver against his skin, like molten metal poured into a ragged gash. He stilled when she traced it, panting shallow breaths against her hair.

"It's where my magic burst out when I died," he said on a harsh whisper.

Caitir bent to kiss the scar. His body went rigid as she did so, as though he was holding his breath. When she raised her head again, she murmured, "It's beautiful."

He was beautiful. An indecipherable emotion filled his gaze as they locked eyes again, and the chamber around them faded away. This was the man Caitir had longed for, dreamed of, pursued for so many years, and she was in his arms. Touching him. Tasting his lips.

Caitir closed her eyes at the warmth of his breath on her skin. One of his hands wandered lower, bunching the fabric of her skirts and pushing them up until her thigh was exposed. Eremon hooked her bare leg around him, pressing his body against hers, and she froze with a sharp intake of breath.

Heart hammering, she forced down the memories that suddenly invaded her mind. This wasn't Gerallt, it was Eremon. *Rí Eremon*. And he wanted—she wanted—

What did she want?

"What's wrong?" Eremon drew back enough to look her in the eyes.

She tensed, unsure what to say. His palm was hot on her thigh, his face still a breath from hers. Her cheeks were flushed, her body aching with desire. So why did she feel the over-whelming urge to flee?

Caitir squeezed her eyes shut, willing her panic to dissipate. "Nothing."

"You're certain?"

She hummed, tugging him closer again, reaching for more, gripping the back of his neck as she traced his lips with her own. He held still against her, and for a moment, she feared he might pull away.

Relief flooded her when he finally returned her kisses once again. She sank back into his warmth, pushing the memories and her fear into the back of her mind. All she needed to do was lose herself in him again, and she would be able to overcome this.

Tightening her leg around his body, she whispered, "Take whatever you want."

But Eremon flinched, gently broke the kiss, then moved away. The rush of fabric from her falling skirts did nothing to soothe the sudden chill he left behind. He reached to remove her hand from his neck and looked down at it, as though he was no longer sure why he was touching her at all.

The heat between them dissipated as quickly as it had blazed. "Why did you stop?" she asked breathlessly, a heavy sense of dread descending on her.

His eyes flashed. "I want nothing until there's complete trust between us."

The fervor that had filled his gaze moments before faded and he released her, taking a step back, compassion on his beautiful face. Or perhaps it was pity. But it was no concern of his whether an unwanted thought crept into her mind. If she wanted to tell him, she would do so when she pleased.

With a sinking feeling, she realized her falter was just an excuse for Eremon to right his obviously addled brain. There was no other explanation for why he had returned her kisses, besides his own pathetic memories that she had so foolishly wanted to blot from existence. As though she could ever hope to overshadow the memory of Lira.

"Which will be never," Caitir hissed. "Just say you don't want me at all."

"I can't," Eremon replied, his silver gaze hardening. He began to fasten the row of buttons on his tunic, hiding the scar from view. "But I can put a stop to this."

"And what is *this*?" She didn't think she was imagining the high color in his cheeks or the hitch in his breath when she stepped closer and traced her fingertips over his tunic.

"It's nothing," he answered curtly, putting more distance between them.

Nothing.

Heat crept into her cheeks. She shouldn't have been surprised. Why would Eremon be any different than everyone else who had used her?

"I trusted you with my feelings," she said, setting her jaw. "You accuse me of wanting it all? You're the entitled one, thinking you have a right to every thought in my mind."

"I have a right to know if I've harmed you," he said, eyes hard, teeth bared. "I asked because I wanted to help."

"You can't help me,"—she savored the cruel words as they rolled off her tongue— "any more than I can transform into the woman you really want."

The corners of Eremon's mouth tugged downward, his lips tightening, nostrils flaring. She could feel the anger emanating from his body.

"I should have never let your scheming mouth touch me," he said in a low voice.

She forced down the mortification that made her want to shrink. Of their own accord, her eyes flicked to his lips, still swollen from their kisses. "I think you want more of my scheming mouth."

Eremon blew out a breath when he finished buttoning his tunic, shifting his shoulders as though to shake her essence from him. "Everything between us has been a ploy. We have no grounds for anything more."

This is a ruse, he'd said. And Caitir had just made a part of it too real.

She wanted to disappear into the stacks. It had been stupid to say anything about Lira. Stupid to admit how she'd felt about him, and how thoroughly her heart had been shattered. Eremon hadn't needed to know any more of her vulnerability than he already did, yet she had laid it bare anyway in hopes that he might... she wasn't sure what.

Mortal gods, I was so stupid. It was entirely true.

Caitir let her humiliation transform into a mirror of the anger he'd poured into their kisses. Dark magic rose into her palms unbidden. "Can't finish what you start, I see. Doesn't bode well for our little scheme."

He backed away, pausing only long enough to tap his fingertips on the scroll he'd just completed. "Here are your next directives for Tomis. I'll be back in a few days."

Caitir watched him go, her body buzzing with fury.

"Did you hear what I said?" she demanded.

Eremon glanced back at her indifferently. "It didn't warrant a response."

He wrenched the door open, then slammed it behind him.

CHAPTER 52

EREMON

Meadowlands

Eremon fled Caitir, the archive, the Dome, Iathium. His physical form. Within moments, he was soaring over the meadowlands as quickly as his silver wings would carry him. Rodhlan's landscape sprawled below, its territory familiar and soothing.

He hadn't given his lips time to burn, or his arms time to feel empty. Instead, he'd transformed right outside the chamber door, moving up the staircase in cat form before emerging into the courtyard and becoming a falcon once more. The magic numbed his emotions and dulled his senses, which were still so achingly human.

What had possessed him to touch Caitir in the first place? If he hadn't closed the distance between them, she wouldn't have been able to kiss him. Eremon could have easily remained at the desk, focused on his work. Instead, he'd allowed his own wounded feelings to draw him to her.

Perhaps that was what she'd been doing—playing on the

deep sorrow he felt every time he entered the archive. All the more reason to reinforce distance when he did return.

But the more he followed that line of thought, the more disquiet he felt.

It would have been easy to convince himself that she'd been playing games with him, yet... it was her shame that had gotten his attention. Her sorrow, not his. He'd wanted to soothe her and had not once thought of seeking comfort for himself.

It's nothing. He was a filthy liar.

The words had singed as they hit their mark, and he had run from her. Her devastated expression was burned into his mind.

Warmth surged through his body for the thousandth time. *Mortal gods, her mouth... her touch...*

Eremon shoved the thoughts away, tuning into the animal instincts that came with his shifting forms instead. The further he could get from Caitir and the memory of their kiss, the better. Perhaps he would spend a few days as one of his creatures—disappear for a little while.

He flew in the direction of the mountain range, savoring the crisp night air. The snow-peaked mountains might help him clear his mind. As he neared Clan Mór's valley, he could make out flickering firelight in the keep windows and the warm glow of Skelly's cottage.

But there was something decidedly wrong with the landscape beyond the valley. Concern flooded him as his raptor eyes roved the mountainside. There had been a fire—a large one, from the look of it. Though it appeared to have been extinguished, he could still feel the reverberating imprint of the familiar magic that had been expended here.

Although this was Lira's valley, the forest had not been burned by her birthright power. It had been dark magic, just like his.

Eremon's worry turned to terror, and he swooped down

toward Skelly's cottage, landing on the fencepost at the pasture before transforming. There was still candlelight flickering in the window, so he approached the front door and knocked. After a moment, the wizened woman peeked through the window, her expression relaxing when she met his gaze.

Skelly opened the door, forehead pinched with worry. "What took you so long?"

He dipped his head sheepishly. "Too many things. What happened on the mountainside?"

"Come in," she said gravely. "We'll tell you everything."

She ushered Eremon inside, latching the door behind him. Beside the crackling fire, Lord Irem sat dozing, his head drooping as he slumped in his chair. A teacup sat in his lap, precariously balanced. His dark skin, so like Oda's, was luminous in the firelight, almost youthful despite his advanced age.

"Wake up, old man," she said, taking a blunt poker from the hearth and gently ribbing him with it. "We have company."

Irem gave a start and blinked blearily before he turned his head and saw Eremon. His eyebrows rose into the deep wrinkles that creased his forehead, and his dark eyes were suddenly glassy. "My boy!"

He looked as though he meant to stand, but Eremon held up a palm to stay him. Instead, he leaned down and embraced his mentor—his friend—pressing his cheek to the top of the elderly Defender's head. Irem gave a shuddering exhale and leaned against Eremon's shoulder, his gnarled hands coming up to grip the younger man's arms.

"It's so good to see you," Eremon murmured. "I've missed your counsel."

"And I've missed *you*." Irem's hands moved to Eremon's face, and he angled him so their eyes met. "Let me look at you."

"I still look like me."

Irem's gaze lingered on Eremon's eyes before he chuckled

softly and said, "Close enough," before patting his cheek and letting go.

Skelly took the mug from where Irem had left it on his knees. "Is this the closest I'll get to meeting a grandchild of yours, Irem?"

"I have three I consider my own," the elderly man said with a grin. "One of them is the mirror image of you as a girl—I believe you're acquainted. But I couldn't stop with Silira. I claimed Eremon and Aidryn Tarlach, as well."

"A fine pity you never had children." Skelly sniffed. "That's a patchwork of a family, if I've ever seen one."

"The tomes were my children; their devotees, my grandchildren," he replied. "And patchwork is the best sort of family, for I chose them myself."

"Lord Irem's the only grandfather I've ever known," Eremon added. "So I completely agree."

"Now, Eremon." Skelly turned her keen gaze on him, sizing him up. He suddenly felt small beneath her scrutiny. "There has been an accident. Because Silira—and the rest of you anointed—saw fit to keep her ailment secret, I didn't realize how closely she should be watched. But she was left alone today, and she nearly brought the mountain down."

Eremon shrank beneath the elderly woman's scolding. "Is she safe?"

"We gave her a draught, and she's sleeping," Skelly answered, voice clipped and features stern.

"I see." Eremon glanced to Irem, who gave him a subtle shake of the head, his dark eyes wary.

Tread carefully, his mentor seemed to say.

Skelly fixed Eremon with a piercing, soul-shattering stare. "For an immortal, you seem awfully afraid."

He *was* afraid. Eremon had thought Thorne was intimidating, but the massive warrior had nothing on this diminutive woman. She was Lira in a solid seventy years.

"Lira's exactly like you." He hadn't meant to say it, but it slipped out anyway.

Skelly rocked back in surprise, then laughed. "Of course she is!" She moved to the worktable, where she prepared a third cup of tea. "It's too bad she's still so young; she would be more straightforward."

Eremon sighed. "She doesn't need any help with that."

Irem's sigh echoed Eremon's. "Do you want some tea to go with the tongue-lashing you're about to get?"

They gathered in Skelly's small kitchen, sipping tea and nibbling on fresh, crusty bread from the keep. Eremon brought them up to date on everything that had happened in Iathium. In turn, Skelly and Irem recounted what they knew of the wild-fire and the near-rockslide Lira had started—and how Oda's anointed magic had finally broken free.

Eremon set his empty mug aside, resting his chin in his palm. "Do we know why Lira wandered into the woods in the first place?"

"She had been quarreling with Aidryn," Skelly said angrily, slamming her own cup on the table, "about Clan Tarlach."

Eremon's stomach dropped. He and Aidryn had agreed to keep Lira in the dark about their plans to help Caitir with clan relations. Surely, Lira hadn't already figured it out.

A knock on the door broke the tension, and Skelly rose to answer it. Oda stood on the stoop, with Aidryn two paces behind her. Oda dumped her heavy cloak on the nearest chair. Aidryn shut the door behind him, shucking off his own cloak and piling it on top of Oda's. Skelly cut him a disapproving look.

Aidryn looked grim as he surveyed the room, his gaze landing on Eremon. "Didn't expect to see you here."

"I came on a whim," Eremon answered with a shrug.

"Well, it's a good thing you did," Oda said. "So you know what happened?"

Eremon nodded, resting his forearms on the table. "Perhaps it's time to come clean with Lira—about everything."

Everyone in the room fixed their disbelieving attention on Eremon. He shifted uncomfortably, unsure who to make eye contact with. In the end, he settled on studying the fire that roared in the hearth.

"Are you daft?" Oda exclaimed.

Eremon glared at her. "Oh, I don't know. I thought the aftermath of the wildfire might be the perfect time. She's thoroughly frightened of herself—less likely to cause another catastrophe."

Skelly and Oda exchanged a glance. "You make a point," Oda conceded.

But Aidryn shook his head vehemently. "Absolutely not."

Eremon raised his chin, scrutinizing Aidryn. "You're just trying to spare her feelings toward you. I can't help that your decisions vexed her fragile sensibilities."

"I'm not the only one, Eremon." Aidryn closed the distance between them, sliding into a seat across from him. He lowered his voice, though it trembled with fury. "If she was uncontrolled enough to cause that fire, who knows what might happen next?"

Leaning closer, Eremon said, "Who knows what might happen if you continue to lie—"

"I *don't* lie—"

"By omission?" Eremon crossed his arms and smirked at Aidryn's scowl. "Calling dishonesty by another name is also falsehood."

Aidryn narrowed his eyes. "You would know."

"Now, now." Skelly swatted Aidryn's arm with the back of her hand.

"Enough of that." Irem gave Eremon a stern look that made him want to shrink beneath the table. "This squabbling is a waste of time and energy."

"I only intended to state my opinion," Eremon said, keeping

his voice steady and calm. Speaking to this room full of dear friends was suddenly more daunting than holding council. "You've done well to guard Lira from full knowledge, but it may be time to tell her more. If she finds out in the wrong way, at the wrong time, it may pose a greater danger to us all."

Oda stoked the fire, her gaze playing along the mess of trinkets Skelly had crowded onto the simple wood mantel. "The longer we keep her in the dark, the more likely she is to learn in an uncontrolled way."

"I disagree," Skelly said. "I think Silira should be kept under close watch until we can find help beyond the Beran healer."

"Yes." Aidryn nodded. "It seems the dark magic is progressing. At this point, I think we should minimize her contact with others. Keep her close."

"What do you think, Lord Irem?" Eremon turned his full attention to his mentor, whose forehead wrinkled with concern. "Is the time right?"

Irem rested his hands on the end of his cane, contemplating before he answered. "Deciding when to share difficult information with someone you love is always a challenge."

The room was silent for a moment, save for the fire's crackling. Irem was right, of course.

"I fear you've created a situation that will draw an unfavorable reaction, no matter when or how she learns the truth." Irem looked pointedly at Aidryn, who flinched beneath the older man's scrutiny. "So now that you understand, you must make a decision."

CHAPTER 53
LIRA

Rodhlan Ridge

In the early morning hours, Lira awakened to soft voices in Skelly's kitchen. Her grandmother had given her a strong dose of Nevala's sleeping tincture after the fire, and Lira had expected to rest in the familiar bed until dawn. But after expending so much dark magic, she'd found her body in a state of restless exhaustion. Apparently, that involved the inability to stay asleep.

She perked up at a familiar sound: Eremon's voice.

"...Unpleasant no matter what," he was saying. "I think you should get it over with. Rip the bandage from the wound while her memory is fresh."

"I'm her husband, and I say absolutely not." Aidryn sounded cross, but his words rattled Lira. She rose from bed and crept quietly to the door to listen.

"Oh, she's not going to like that." The smug satisfaction in Eremon's voice was all it took for Lira to burst from the bedchamber and into the kitchen, still bleary-eyed but very much alert.

"You're right: I'm not," she said, realizing too late that she was clad only in her nightgown, her curly hair mussed from sleep. Her cheeks heated as the five people crowding Skelly's kitchen turned to gape at her in tandem.

Aidryn went so pale, she thought he might faint on the spot. "How much did you hear?" he blurted.

She crossed her arms tightly, resisting the urge to return to the bedchamber for a dressing gown. Her stomach felt like a hollow, sour pit. "Enough to know you were holding council about me while you thought I was sleeping. What's going on?"

"We were telling Eremon about the fire," Irem said warily. "He paid us an unexpected visit."

A chill skittered along Lira's skin at the memory of the fire. "And Aidryn felt the need to decide what for me, exactly?"

"He doesn't want them to tell you that Irem and I are going to Iteloria," Skelly said with a defiant glint in her green eyes.

The words bludgeoned Lira. Her eyes widened as she looked from her grandmother to Oda, Aidryn, Eremon, and finally, Irem, who gave her a solemn nod. "What?"

"I volunteered my cousin, Rune—and his ship," Oda said. She stepped over to the chair nearest the door, picking up her heavy fur traveling cloak and shrugging it on. "I'll take my leave and ride for the western coast to make the arrangements."

"You can take Senga," Aidryn said.

Oda inclined her head, then glanced at Lira. "We're going to change our approach to your care," she said, discomfort clear in her posture. She forced a pinched smile as she adjusted the bone clasp on her cloak. "I'll see you soon?"

Lira nodded. The warrior backed toward the door, then let herself out with a quiet click.

The room plunged into silence. With a twinge of horror, Lira realized Oda was afraid of her. They all were. Perhaps the fire had been the straw that had finally driven a wedge between her and everyone else.

No one needs you here, the voice from the forest said. *You're useless now.*

Lira caught herself mid-gasp, trying too late to suppress it. On top of all that had happened, no one needed to know she was hearing voices.

Speaking truth, no less, it said.

She squeezed her eyes shut for a moment, inhaling sharply before opening them again.

Aidryn and Eremon exchanged a worried glance. Lira watched the pair suspiciously. "And what will you and Lord Irem be doing in Iteloria, Skelly?"

"I was just telling the boys that you should be kept under close watch until we find a cure for you," Skelly answered. "I intend to seek help in Iteloria."

"You can't do that," Lira cried. "You and Lord Irem, you're..."

"What, too old?" Her grandmother waved her off. "We have one more adventure left in us."

Irem pursed his lips, looking as though he was trying to suppress a smile. He balanced his cane before him, gnarled hand gripping its bronze end, worn to a shine from years of use. Firelight flickered in his dark eyes as he answered, "Don't be so fatalistic, Wilga. We have at least two."

Eremon laughed uneasily, rubbing a hand over his face as he flicked his gaze to the ceiling. "Mortal gods."

"You laugh now," Skelly said, peering at him, "but we're going just as much for you as for Silira."

The grin dropped from Eremon's face instantly. "Why for me?"

"Because you need to know more about your kind." Now, it was Skelly's turn to look smug. "I had an old Tai'ceru friend— Fa'rundin, they called him. He's long dead now, but at one time, he harbored an immortal girl in his settlement: your Itelorian counterpart, Silira."

"Counterpart?" Lira shivered again. "What do you mean?"

Aidryn rose and disappeared into the bedchamber, emerging a moment later with Lira's dressing gown and a blanket. He helped her shrug the gown on, then wrapped the blanket around her. Instantly, her body felt more relaxed. She took Aidryn's hand as he led her to a stool by the fire, then sat, soaking in its warmth.

"I want to tell you all a tale," Skelly said, her voice taking on the familiar, singsong lull that Lira remembered from her childhood. "It begins with two continents.

"This tale is so much more expansive than the rewriting of Rodhlan's histories. It is about mortal gods and their immortal creations. It is the story of a vow of magic made between two worlds.

"Our story begins with the union of Rhona and Riku. One: the goddess of Rodhlan, of the natural world and all the magic it possessed. The other: a mortal god of Iteloria who coveted all Rodhlan had to offer.

"Riku's rule over our land opened the door to a long series of terrible treaties and spells. One of the treaties—as you know, Eremon—demanded the sacrifice of all mortal gods born on Rodhlan's soil. But beneath the surface, so much more transpired.

"Every mortal god or goddess carried a distinctive marking from birth, Nami being the first. The marking was called Nami's Rune."

"It became a death sentence in the centuries that followed. Eremon was the first mortal god born in nearly two thousand years who survived past infancy," Irem said in a low voice.

"The first in Rodhlan," Eremon corrected gently.

"The first anyone admitted to, more like," Skelly harrumphed. "And that was only under duress."

Eremon's father, Corlan, had been forced to seek help for his son in Iteloria when it had become clear that his burgeoning power would eventually threaten his life. Corlan had died on the journey, along with Lira's father. With no further help or guidance where his magic was concerned, Eremon eventually succumbed to the deadly overflow.

Eremon touched the back of his neck. "The midwife hid the rune from my mother," he said absently, his gaze straying to the fire.

"Smart woman," Skelly replied. "Show it to us."

Eremon turned his back to them, lifting his hair to expose his nape. A rune of pure cobalt magic was etched into his skin, its gentle whorls shimmering with immortal power. Lira gasped softly.

"That's the rune from your ring," she said, running her thumb over the time-worn band.

"It is." He released his hair, casting a fleeting, sidelong glance over his shoulder at Lira before he faced the room again. When she tried to make eye contact, he looked at the floor.

"The rune appears briefly on an infant's first day of life, then fades," Skelly added. "It only reappears when the mortal god wields his magic. If an immortal is created, then the marking is permanently visible."

"I would ask why immortals were created in the first place," Aidryn ventured, "but that seems obvious."

"The mortal deities weren't satisfied with the power they had?" Eremon supplied.

"Not quite; we'll get to that," Skelly said. "While Rodhlan may not be teeming with immortals, Iteloria is another matter. That's why we must go."

"Are there many immortals in Iteloria?" Lira asked.

"It's unclear," said Skelly, "but there is one woman, Vor'sca, who resided on the western coast at one time. She is a living vessel of Iteloria's histories, Lira, as you are of Rodhlan's. She is Tai'ceru and almost as old as Rodhlan itself."

Realization washed over Lira as she recalled the memory

she'd witnessed in the summer. "My counterpart," she murmured.

The girl had appeared to be young, with silver hair, light brown skin, and sea foam-green eyes. In the witnessing, Vor'sca had drawn memories from Lira's father at the behest of a Tai'ceru leader and the Itelorian king.

"She was there when our fathers died, Eremon," Lira said. "I've seen her in a witnessing."

"Then it's imperative we find her," Eremon said. "I could fly to Iteloria myself. I'll find her more quickly than anyone else."

"Not so fast," Skelly said, suddenly looking cross. "You're getting ahead of yourself—and ahead of my story. It's important to understand the deeper nature of the relationship between Rodhlan and Iteloria."

Eremon scowled. "Then continue. Please."

Lira exchanged a bemused glance with Aidryn. No one and nothing interrupted Skelly's storytelling without raising her ire. Not even the Rí.

"Iteloria never wanted its mortal gods coming to Rodhlan, populating this land with their magic and combining it with Rhona's elemental powers. They believed that changing the magic was dangerous—and they were right," Skelly said, her expression grave. "It upset the magical balance between our land and theirs, and Iteloria's treaty with Ulan was secretly meant to correct it."

"Magic isn't finite," Lira said. "It builds and grows within each wielder. Why does Iteloria behave as though there's not enough to be had?"

"Iteloria requires an exponential amount of power in order to thrive," Skelly said. "Until the mortal gods Rasu and Riku left for Rodhlan, there was more than enough magic to feed the land. But they fathered many descendants before they left. There was a dark period in Iteloria's history, during which those mortal deity children were sought out and sacrificed for their power.

"The first immortals were created as a test. Tai'ceru leaders wanted to emulate Rodhlan's anointed ones in hopes that the balance of power might be reset. They succeeded in creating counterparts to match clans Mór, Beran, and Tarlach."

"And Clan Énna?" Aidryn asked.

"They never succeeded," Irem said, "perhaps because Clan Énna kept its anointed a secret, thus protecting the magic Rhona had bestowed to its people."

Lira and Aidryn exchanged a tense glance.

"And when the Itelorians were successful at creating immortals?" Eremon urged.

"Once they had succeeded, they began using the Itelorian Key Keeper to turn mortal deity children as infants," Skelly said. "More survive to this day because of the silent rebellion that sprang up to keep Sov'is from taking the people's children. Unfortunately, that's why the treaty with Rodhlan was formed.

"Ulan was fearful and vulnerable," she continued. "He didn't want more rulers like Nami losing control of their magic and wreaking havoc. Until Rodhlan's magic was fully stripped and suppressed, the Great Key Iuchair was used to send mortal deities' magic to Iteloria."

"Kenji said there are signs that Iteloria's balance is indeed waning," Eremon said. "If there's been no power coming from Rodhlan all this time, and if mortal deities born in Iteloria are being changed, then I could see why King La'hiran is so desperate for magic."

Lira's magic gave a soft tug, and for a moment, her vision clouded with thick, sickly green fog. She blinked rapidly, attempting to clear it, her heart pounding. As quickly as it had happened, though, the fog dissipated—and she tensed, hoping no one had noticed her sudden loss of control.

Eremon's voice snapped her back into the present. "Why wasn't I told any of this?"

"Much like many of Rodhlan's truths were hidden from Silira, Iteloria's were kept from you," Irem answered. "Your father wanted to protect you for as long as possible."

"So you're saying there's some kind of Binding between the continents?" Eremon demanded.

Lira's mind spun. She had missed that detail.

"That's what we think." Skelly held up a palm to cut Eremon off. "And it's why you should remain in Rodhlan and let us make the journey."

"I don't want to risk either of you on a mission I should be able to complete on my own," Eremon said, looking worriedly from Skelly to Irem and back.

"You have enough to manage in Iathium," Aidryn answered, peering hard at Eremon.

"But I—" Eremon stopped abruptly, cutting a glance at Lira, then righted himself. Warning bells sounded in Lira's mind as she watched him relax into an easy posture. "I just want to help."

"So do the rest of us," Aidryn said, "but we must do the right thing."

Lira wasn't sure why, but she felt increasingly suspicious that this journey to Iteloria had been cobbled together. They were making her into a fool, and she hated it.

They do think you're foolish. Again, the words dropped into her mind. *But you and I both know that nothing could be further from the truth. You are powerful. You are right.*

She shouldn't have entertained the voice's words. After all, this was the presence that had led her to discharge her power in the forest.

They want you isolated and defeated. If you keep this one secret for yourself, I can help you stay strong. Right now, it is time to learn patience.

Though dread coiled within Lira, there was a strange comfort in the words. So, for the first time, she answered it: *Why should I be patient?*

Because I need for you to wait them out. Everything will unravel in due course, and when it does, you will be ready to rise.

CHAPTER 54

AIDRYN

Rodhlan Ridge

"Tell me about Oda's magic," Aidryn said.

He, Lira, and Eremon sat before Skelly's hearth late into the night, nursing mugs of hot tea. Lira had grown unusually quiet after Irem and Skelly had departed for the keep. Once again, Skelly had graciously gifted her cottage to Aidryn and Lira for their use.

"It engulfed me, like being inside an ocean wave," Lira said. "She looked magnificent when it was over, though drenched and a little worse for wear. The violet magic faded into her skin, like my emerald power."

Aidryn could feel the sudden despair that took hold of her as though it was his own—and perhaps it was. It rushed over them both, nearly suffocating in its intensity. His thoughts raced as he searched for something better to focus on.

Without warning, Lira leaned past him and glared at Eremon. "Exactly what is Caitir doing in the Dome while you're quietly rebuilding your alliances?"

Eremon choked on his tea. "Excuse me?"

"And the rest of her accomplices," Lira continued. "How could you let them continue to run roughshod over Iathium?"

"All of them are being watched day and night," Eremon said, sitting up straighter. "Think of it as a very comfortable house-arrest. It'll all be over soon."

"That's not very comforting." Lira sighed. "I'm trying to understand, but I just can't. At least Aila's out of reach—that's one mercy." She closed her eyes and rubbed her brow. "I don't feel well. I'm going back to bed."

"I'll join you soon," Aidryn said, reaching over to squeeze her hand. She gave him a pinched smile before rising, setting her mug on the worktable and shuffling back toward the bedchamber.

"Eremon, don't keep my husband up all night again," Lira said before she crossed the threshold.

As soon as the door clicked shut, Eremon mumbled, "So awkward."

"You chose to stay," Aidryn said with a shrug. "Who's creating the awkwardness?"

Eremon rolled his eyes, allowing Aidryn to direct him. "You were always insufferable, but when did Lira join in?" he mumbled.

Aidryn smirked. "How long did you actually know her before you proposed?"

The Rí swore under his breath and scowled.

"My point," Aidryn said. He lowered his voice to a whisper. "What possessed you to come here tonight?"

"Call it immortal instinct," Eremon replied. He shifted, suddenly looking uncomfortable. "How much does she know about—"

"Almost nothing," Aidryn hedged. "Two weeks left. Maybe we can hold steady."

"Rhona help us all," Eremon said with a soft snort, his shoulders hunching.

"Any word from Iteloria?" said Aidryn. "Do they know Gerallt is dead?"

"Caitir replied to La'hiran's first letter as Gerallt," Eremon answered. "He'd dictated his correspondence to her before, so it wouldn't have been unusual. Told him we were looking into the details of the treaty. We've received nothing since."

"What do the spies say?"

"They're slow in gathering information," Eremon admitted. "Right now, there are only two at my disposal, and they can't be everywhere at once. I'm trying to rebuild the network."

"Have you managed to learn more about your immortality? Between political plays and ruling in secret, I mean." Aidryn rubbed the back of his neck.

"Not much," Eremon admitted. "There's little useful information in the archive, from what I've found. The Itelorian texts are mostly records of dates, battles, and rulers. I was counting on finding something more interesting."

Aidryn shifted on his stool, letting a long moment pass. "Besides threatening Aila's life, what do you think La'hiran will do when he learns you've returned?"

"I don't know," Eremon said with a sigh. "Lira fears an invasion, but I have to wonder. If the king's best threat is harming Aila, he must be desperate. I would've expected some sort of escalation by now."

"That doesn't sound right," Aidryn replied, scratching his chin. "The silence might be a strategy in itself."

"That could be." Eremon inhaled and exhaled slowly. "I suppose I should go back to Iathium. See how she fares."

Eremon didn't have to say Caitir's name for Aidryn to know who he meant. "But you don't want to," Aidryn supplied.

"I *do* want to," Eremon answered hesitantly, "and that's the problem."

The words took a long moment to land. Then—

Oh. *Oh.*

A wild swell of hope filled Aidryn's chest. Growing up with Caitir had forced him to become agonizingly familiar with helplessness—the same dreadful sensation that filled him at the thought of Lira's dark magic. Now, though, there might be a chance to truly save his sister. He'd watched her descend into darkness, and had eventually given up on the notion of her ever returning from it. Was it possible that Eremon could truly save Caitir, beyond this political scheme he'd concocted?

Would Aidryn get his sister back one day?

As though anticipating Aidryn's coming barrage of questions, Eremon raised a hand, his expression pained. "Don't say anything. Just... it will pass." He shook his head. "That's all. It's nothing."

"But she could be—"

"It's a transactional relationship, Aidryn. Nothing more."

Aidryn scoffed. "How many times do you have to say *nothing* before you actually believe that?"

"Well, what else could it possibly be?" Eremon hissed. "It could never stand."

For a moment, Aidryn's dread and anxiety melted away. His thoughts shifted from Lira's impossible predicament to this sudden hope for Caitir. For now, he was stuck in a holding pattern with Lira while they waited for more help. It would do no harm for him to give Eremon a nudge.

"I knew if you saw fit to help her, she might not be too far gone," Aidryn whispered, ignoring Eremon's melodramatic groan. He leaned in like the shameless conspirator he'd become. "What can I do? What do you need to know about her?"

"I want to know what's really important to her," Eremon answered without hesitating, "beyond everything her mother forced on her. How can I help her feel significant?"

Aidryn thought his heart might burst. Lira and Talfryn had

been the only people besides Aidryn who had been invested in Caitir's talents. "Encourage her to do things she enjoys."

Eremon's eyes lit with recognition. "Like drawing and sewing?"

"Yes!" Aidryn exclaimed. "*Please.*"

Eremon cringed, bringing one finger to his lips, and Aidryn lowered his voice again. He spoke at a clip, forcing as much information as he could into the few remaining moments they had. "And talk to her—*really* talk to her. No scheming, no strategy. You can learn so much by listening to what she refuses to say."

The Rí gave Aidryn a curt nod. "If you had to guess, what would you say she values most?"

As though Caitir had been sitting beside them, the answer immediately sounded in Aidryn's mind. "Freedom."

CHAPTER 55
EREMON

Iathium

When Eremon returned to the city near dawn, he passed by the Dome to see how Caitir fared. He perched on her windowsill in his falcon form, peering in at her.

Caitir lay on her side, facing away from him, a shaft of moonlight illuminating the ash blonde of her hair. She'd kicked her blanket off sometime during the night. He watched the subtle rise and fall of her shoulder, studied the delicate curves of her form. One arm cupped her belly, which was just beginning to become more obvious to anyone who might not have known she carried a child.

On the other side of the room, a small silver pendulum —the sister to Irem's golden timepiece—ticked delicately on the mantel. He peered at it, noting the time. Caitir would be asleep for a few more hours yet before she began her day. That meant Eremon had time to spare before she woke.

Inexplicably, he realized that he wanted to be *with* her when she woke.

Clearly, he was going mad.

INSIDE THE DOME, Eremon made his way to the southwestern towers, where Aila had taken chambers. Before he'd left the Ridge, Aidryn had suggested he make a thorough sweep of her rooms, as well as the old Tarlach home across town.

"You might find important information there," Aidryn had said, his hands jammed deep in his trouser pockets. He'd shuffled his feet, looking down at the ground for a moment before he'd added, in a low murmur, "And then there's the matter of Caitir's sketchbook."

Eremon had raised a brow. "What about it?"

Aidryn had given Eremon instructions on where to find a book he had gifted his sister years ago. Their parents had discouraged her talent, so she'd hidden it away in an old wardrobe, along with her drawing pencils.

Eremon entered Aila's room, letting the door click shut behind him. The chamber was scattered with books, loose parchment, and notes, as though she'd spent just as much time studying as she had plotting. A heavy, dark energy hung in the room, almost suffocating in its intensity. He scattered a burst of his own magic throughout the space, willing it to clear the imprint Aila had left behind.

Eremon wandered to her desk and picked up the last piece of parchment she'd scribbled on, as far as he could tell. The lines of script were written in Itelos, mostly incomplete questions and nonsensical half-thoughts, as though she'd been processing her ideas on paper without fleshing them out. She had scrawled things like:

Magical intermingling yields ___?

What is the appropriate ratio...

Need these answers to effectively succeed.

How many clans? How much of the mortal gods' power?

But his gaze snagged one particular question she'd written toward the bottom.

When does the rune emerge?

Below that, she had scrawled several illustrations of Nami's Rune.

Eremon rifled through the papers as quickly as he could, gathering stacks of parchment and as many seemingly relevant books as he could carry. He took them up to his chamber, then made another two trips until he'd moved all of Aila's books and papers over.

Once he was finished, he slipped out again, shifting into cat form, then falcon once he was outdoors. He crossed the dark city in silence, scanning the landscape for the Tarlach estate.

If he'd never had an inkling of where the tower home stood, guessing wouldn't have been difficult. On the other side of the Moravon River, the estate was in shambles, and it had been swallowed up by massive trees that pulsed with Lira's magic.

He landed in an open chamber window and shifted again, his feet landing lightly on the wood floors, now weather-beaten and overgrown with tree roots and living things. Birds had taken up residence along the wide beams that stabilized the ceiling, and he could hear scurrying around the roots, as though some small, furry creatures had built their nests inside the shelter of the home.

The wardrobe against the wall stood open, and he made his way over to it, sifting through the clothes that hung there. He thought he recognized a few of the garments as Aidryn's, then spotted the dead giveaway: a crimson archival uniform that had been pushed to the back, its linen apron draped haphazardly over it.

Eremon selected a dark gray cloak and threw it around his

shoulders, pulling the hood up over his head. Aidryn stood only an inch shorter than Eremon, and they were of similar build: tall and lean, both possessing more agility than muscular bulk. This cloak would be useful; if Eremon found even half as many books and notes in this house as he'd found in the Dome, he would need to return home on foot.

He hastily explored the tower home where Caitir and Aidryn had grown up, searching for anything of substance—books, notes, or magical items Aila might have hidden there. He located two tomes in a glass display case in the receiving hall and removed them, hefting them in his arms as he moved from one room to the next. Finally, he entered the tower room Aidryn had told him about—Caitir's old chamber.

Eremon pushed the door open and stepped inside, his gaze sweeping from the plush bed covered in pink satin and cream quilting to the white wardrobe that sat against the far wall. The interior room, remarkably untouched by the damage to the home, embodied everything he might have expected from her before, given what little he'd known about her back then. But it held nothing of her true essence. It seemed clear to him that she hadn't been given a say in her surroundings, just as everything else about her life had been tightly controlled.

Aidryn had said Caitir's sketchbook would be tucked into a secret compartment in the wardrobe. Eremon dumped its overflow of hanging garments out onto the floor so he could more easily explore the wardrobe itself. It took longer for him to locate the compartment than it had to unearth the books and documents from Aila's chambers. Just as he was ready to give up the search, he found the book and pried it out of the slot with his fingertips.

The sketchbook was bound in rich leather and looked as though it had never been used. A bit more shuffling, and he found Caitir's drawing pencils and the small knife she'd used to sharpen them. Carefully, he tucked them into the pocket of his borrowed cloak, then ran a hand over the book's cover.

He felt as though he was violating her privacy in some fundamental way simply by being here. Against his better judgment, he sat on the edge of her bed and cracked the book open.

On the first few pages were messy, unfinished sketches she'd made of Aidryn and Lira—several years ago, clearly. They were startlingly accurate and depicted her brother and his wife in their younger years. Aidryn grinned impishly from the page, a set of horseshoes in his hands. Lira held a quill and quirked a brow, a familiar smirk on her lips, as though Caitir had interrupted her studies to trace her features. He chuckled at the thought.

Eremon turned the page again and was met with an uncanny likeness of himself, clad in his ceremonial robes with a circlet resting on his head. Unlike the sketches of Lira and Aidryn, this was a full, finished drawing, beautifully detailed and near painful in its perfection. Its corner was bent, as though she had detached it from the book, then hastily shut it back inside.

He adjusted the page carefully, straightening the corner of the drawing, then closed the book, hugging it to his chest and shutting his eyes. *To have poured so much time and effort into a drawing like that*—his heart squeezed. He had once considered her a vain annoyance, no better than a rock in his boot, but she was so much more. She had always been more.

"I'm sorry, Caitir," he whispered to the empty room.

CHAPTER 56
CAITIR

Dome

Caitir awakened late in the morning, stretching her arms above her head and arching her back with a groan. Sitting up, she rubbed the sleep from her eyes and blinked blearily, letting her vision focus on the bright, sunlit room before her. Something about the sitting area wasn't right; the furniture seemed to have been disturbed during the night.

She pulled her dressing gown from the mattress where she'd discarded it and shrugged it on, padding across the room to inspect several neat stacks of books and papers that had been stacked on the low table. A nervous rush swept through her body. Who would have been here while she slept?

Certainly not Eremon.

Her skin flushed at the thought. After their kiss yesterday, he would likely want to keep his distance. She brushed her fingertips along her lips and released a shaky sigh, letting her eyelashes flutter closed. But then she pushed the memory aside, refocusing on the books before her. She immediately recognized two of the tomes on the bottom of the nearest stack as being Aila's.

Before she could reach for them, the chamber door swung open and Eremon stepped inside, cloaked and hooded in heavy gray fabric, another stack of books in his arms.

"You're awake," he said, lowering the stack onto the table and filling its surface completely. He didn't make eye contact with her; instead, he focused wholly on lining up the books' corners and straightening the edges of protruding papers.

Caitir's lips curled as he straightened, lowering his hood. "Lucky you." She rose, too, tilting her head as she scrutinized the familiar fabric of his cloak. "That's Aidryn's."

Eremon gave her a quick, sidelong glance. "It is."

"Where did you get it?"

He made a show of walking across the room to check the timepiece on the mantel, clasping his hands behind his back. "Your home. Aidryn suggested I ransack Aila's rooms. I was happy to oblige."

"When did you speak to him?"

"Last night in the Ridge," Eremon answered.

He finally turned around to face her, but rather than make eye contact, he seemed to look straight past her, as though something over her shoulder was infinitely more interesting than she was. She bristled as he continued. "I started in her chambers here, then worked my way outward to the estate—"

"Where he could have been seen!" Kenji barreled through the open chamber door, laden with a large basket, which he deposited on the sofa. He rested his fists on his hips with a scowl. "I told him once—"

"And he's telling me again." Eremon chuckled, crossing his arms. He kept his gaze trained on the cook.

"He won't listen to me, Caitir," Kenji pleaded, turning to her, "so you tell him."

Caitir rolled her eyes. "Far be it from me to control male stupidity."

At that, Eremon snapped his head around to look at her. Though her cheeks warmed, she didn't return his attention. If he could play this game, so could she.

"Imagine if someone had recognized you out there," Kenji pressed, ever the mother hen.

"I had a cloak!" Eremon swept it around himself for emphasis. "With a hood!"

"And a very conspicuous height with a recognizable face!" Kenji made a frustrated noise, throwing his hands up in defeat.

A giggle escaped Caitir at that; she couldn't help it. Eremon's façade broke, too, and he cracked a wide grin. He finally looked directly at her, laughing softly. His silver eyes shone with amusement, and Caitir felt as though the floor had dropped from beneath her. Her stomach did a flip, so she held her breath, stifling her laughter and turning her attention to the books.

"So—these documents you brought," she began.

Kenji closed the distance between them to swat her shoulder.

"Breakfast before books," he scolded. "I brought pastries but left the tea. I'll nip back to the kitchen to get it."

Though he moved toward the door, he shot Eremon a dirty look. "Don't you follow me unless you look like a cat! It's too late in the day for you to be traipsing about unless you want to be seen."

The cook opened the door further to step out but nearly ran headlong Tiriya, who had appeared in the doorway with the tea tray. She wore black trousers and a linen tunic, and her black hair was cropped shorter than when Caitir had seen her before —just beneath her chin. She took a step back as a startled Kenji righted himself.

"Careful, Papa!" she chided in a singsong voice.

"Tiriya," Kenji scolded. "I told you never to follow me here!" He pushed the door closed behind her and leaned on it, rubbing a palm over his face.

"You forgot the tea," she answered airily, sweeping into the room as though she was perfectly comfortable here.

Eremon's lips parted in surprise. "Well, if it isn't the great sneak herself."

"*The great* is the only part of that sentiment I'll accept," she said over her shoulder with a haughty sniff. "Eremon the Sly."

He grinned impishly, but Kenji scowled. "*Tiriya*, you haven't seen him since he died! He doesn't need any cheek from you."

"Well, what did you want me to do, Papa? Bow?" Tiriya said, heading straight for the sideboard and unloading her tea tray onto it. "If he's alive after all that, he can take it."

Caitir's eyes widened in shocked surprise at the girl's spirit. She threw her head back and cackled.

Tiriya turned toward Caitir, deep dimples forming when she grinned. "You see? Caitir thinks I'm amusing, too."

Now, Kenji was hiding his face behind both hands. "No one is *listening* to me today."

It didn't take much persuasion for Kenji and his eldest daughter to stay in Caitir's chamber for breakfast. True to his usual practice, Kenji had brought enough food for eight people. Tiriya steeped four cups of tea, and the group gathered on the soft sofas in the sitting area. Their presence was both an unexpected surprise and a welcome break from the palpable tension between Caitir and Eremon.

When they'd finished eating, Eremon tipped his chin back, dumping the last bitter dregs of tea into his mouth. "What brought you to the kitchens today, Tiriya?"

"Gevy is ill again," she answered. "With Tam working the dining hall, Papa needed more hands."

Gevy was a member of Kenji's regular staff. The teenage boy was sickly and often needed days off from work. Tiriya, who was fifteen, had a knack for baking, which came in handy when Kenji needed her.

"Are you still apprenticing?" Eremon asked.

"Well," she answered, "I have been helping Mama, yes. But I want a change of scenery." She leaned forward, bouncing her knees excitedly. "I want to spy for you."

Kenji went pale and completely still, his gaze sliding slowly to his daughter. He looked as though he might vomit, and for an agonizing moment, Caitir thought he would. "You haven't said a word about this at home."

"It would have done no good!" Tiriya reached out to grasp Kenji's hand. "But you and Mama have done this work for years, and I know I can. Please, my Rí."

Her knee-bouncing intensified, and she looked as though she might fly right off the sofa before she received an answer. Eremon suddenly looked pained, and he cut a panicked glance in Caitir's direction. But all she could think about was the idea of her own child asking to take on a dangerous job for the crown. Kenji's horror was perfectly understandable, and Caitir felt it as though it was her own.

"I know you're eager," Eremon hedged, holding up a palm, "but I think your parents need time to consider this."

"But I already have a plan!" Tiriya pleaded. "I could take up residency as an artist in Sov'is, gather information that way. You know I can paint; it could be very convincing."

"That *is* a thought." Eremon tapped his chin. Tiriya *was* a talented painter, and the idea, although too superficial at the moment, was a feasible one. "But you'll have plenty of time and chances to help us. Perhaps don't rush it just yet."

A rush of appreciation—admiration—filled Caitir as she studied Eremon from her periphery.

Tiriya's face fell. "But—"

"Being a skilled spy takes more than excellent eavesdropping skill, or the ability to follow someone down a corridor undetected," Eremon answered gently. "There are abilities you must learn and hone beyond that scope. If your parents agree, I'll appoint them to train you formally. Kenji is still my spymaster, after all."

Caitir straightened as his full meaning sank in. "But I thought Fiadh—"

Eremon cut her off, "I know. But it's just a formal title. Our friend the cook? He's the real mastermind." The compliment rattled Kenji from his shock just enough that he blushed.

It wasn't long before the cook was ushering Tiriya from the room, casting an apologetic glance over his shoulder before the door clicked shut. Caitir could hear him scolding her as they made their way down the corridor.

Eremon sat before the table piled with books, surveying them as though he had no idea where to begin. Caitir pulled her own chair closer to the table, her gaze resting on Aila's books again.

"These were Father's *status books*; that's what Aidryn always called them," she mused, running her fingers over one of the ornate spines. "He had them commissioned from the archive, but they're written in Itelos. I don't know how he managed it, with the laws being what they were. Mother was the only one of us who could read them."

"All her notes are in Itelos, too," Eremon said, "but I can read it."

Caitir's gaze strayed to a thin leather-bound book on top of the stack, and her mouth went dry.

"Where did you get that?" she demanded.

Eremon went pale and reached for it, though Caitir was quicker. She pushed past him and snatched the sketchbook before he could. Humiliation blazed through her body, and she began to tremble.

"It was in your wardrobe," Eremon admitted. "Aidryn told me where to find it."

Caitir's cheeks grew hot. "He had no right." She hugged the book close, wishing her brother was here so she could embrace him. "Nosy sneak."

She cracked the sketchbook open, intending to peer inside, but shut it abruptly when she felt Eremon's gaze on her. There was a portrait of him in the sketchbook—the very reason she'd stopped drawing in the first place. She had hoped to give it to him years ago, but Aila had shamed her for being presumptuous, so Caitir had tucked the book away for good.

Eremon wouldn't have liked it, anyway.

Caitir kept the covers of the book pressed tightly between her fingers, waiting for him to say something. But he just sat there expectantly. Suspicion, followed by a dismaying sense of exposure, crept into her belly. "You already looked at them, didn't you?"

He shrugged sheepishly, and she thought she saw a hint of a blush creeping into his cheeks. "Would it help if I said they're quite good?"

"They are not." She stood, slapping the sketchbook back onto the top of the stack where she'd found it and turning her back to him. Aidryn had had no right to bring this up, and neither had Eremon. Hadn't they both known it would vex her?

Then again, Eremon enjoyed vexing her, so perhaps she shouldn't have been surprised.

Her shoulders tensed, and she crossed her arms tightly, focusing on the window and the bright winter sky beyond to keep her tears at bay.

"Caitir." He stepped closer to her. "Look at me?"

Reluctantly, she did, forcing herself to hold his gaze.

"You shouldn't have hidden them," he said, lightly brushing the back of her hand with his thumb. She stiffened at the contact. "If I'd known you had that kind of talent, I might have commissioned a portrait."

"She—" Caitir turned to face him fully, blinking against the sudden burning in her eyes. "She said I would only humiliate myself if I showed you my work."

He pressed a hand to her cheek. "She was wrong, Caitir. Please, don't hide it from me."

More than anything, she wanted to lean into his touch and accept the comfort he seemed to be offering. But it was too late; she already knew it couldn't mean anything to either of them, even if she wished it. A stray tear made its way down her face, but she set her jaw and shook her head. Reluctantly, he dropped his hand, crossing his arms tightly as though to restrain himself.

As he should, she thought.

This was her co-conspirator, the man who was using her as a means to an end until he could take his throne back. He'd told her she was inconsequential to him, and it was true. She wouldn't give him the benefit of warming her heart with a gift that would ultimately mean nothing when this was over.

Caitir hardened her stare and took a step away from him. "Why do you care? You said this was nothing."

Eremon drew back. "I..."

She raised her chin. "I want to be alone now."

He exhaled, the hurt apparent in his eyes, but said nothing more before letting himself out of the chamber.

CHAPTER 57
EREMON

Dome
1 Week Later

The clean, cool scent of ice was on the wind when Eremon reached Iathium's high sea wall, where archers and sentries patrolled in shifts. Today, the Strait of Ulan boasted rough waters. Its waves crashed hard against the rocks directly below, and the tide on the other side of the pebbled beach was high. A snowstorm was coming.

Eremon often patrolled the area in falcon form, and for the past week, he'd spent more time in the skies. After the debacle with the sketchbook, he had been glad to leave Caitir to her own devices. He hadn't had the stomach to go back to her chamber and study the documents he'd collected from Aila's rooms.

He'd thought that taking the sketchbook to Caitir as a sort of peace offering might help to soften the tense edge that had grown between them since that day in the archive. He couldn't stop thinking about their kisses, and even after this short time apart, he'd found that he craved being near her. Of course,

mending their rift couldn't be as simple as giving her a childhood sketchbook, and perhaps he'd been foolish to think it
would be.

Perching on the wall's highest rise, he surveyed the
sprawling coastline. Rodhlan's beautiful simplicity had never
ceased to amaze him. Although he'd often heard members of
the council and his father's ambassadors boast about visiting
the thriving peninsula across the strait, Rí Corlan had instilled
a love for their own land in Eremon. In comparison to Iteloria,
Rodhlan held much to be desired, with its small population
and predictable, temperate climate. Still, it was the potential of
becoming intimately familiar with the land and its peoples that
had always attracted Eremon.

Unfortunately, that was all it had ever been: unrealized
potential. In the time since he'd awakened, he had seen more of
Rodhlan than he had ever been permitted to in his human life.
He wondered if he would ever get the chance to know his
people in the way he'd always longed to.

Movement further down the wall caught his eye, and he
refocused his attention on the patrols. Two of Artagán's archers,
Tugal and Fyn, had abandoned their posts and moved to an
area at the base of the wall, out of view of the other guards.

Suspicion filled Eremon's gut. His gaze flitted down to the
rocky shore, where they stood close, heads bent as though in
conversation. A third figure moved into view—a young woman
Eremon had never seen before.

Warning bells sounded in his mind as he took in her form:
She was obviously Tai'ceru, and had clearly not attempted to
dress in any style reminiscent of Rodhlan's peoples. If she had
no intention of blending in, Eremon surmised that this meant
she didn't plan to remain on the continent for long, either. He
scanned the horizon in search of the vessel she'd sailed in on,
but no new ships had docked in Iathium's port since Aila's
departure.

The girl was barefoot and dressed in fitted, white leather leggings that ended at her calves. She had long silver hair, nearly colorless eyes, and light brown skin. Upon closer inspection, Eremon could see that her eyes were the color of her tunic —an unusual sea foam green. On her wrists, she wore crystal bracelets with a strange, iridescent sheen.

He perched nearer, straining to hear the conversation between the girl and the archers.

"...really think it's time?" Fyn was saying, her arms crossed tightly.

"If it's true that he's back, then we should go," Tugal replied.

"Good," the Tai'ceru woman said, her accent thick. "There is no time to waste."

A sly grin spread across Fyn's lips. "Lead the way, Vor'sca."

Her name jolted Eremon, and his thoughts raced. *Vor'sca*— the same immortal Skelly had told them about? The one she and Irem had set out to find? There would not have been enough time for Skelly and Irem to locate her. In fact, they had set sail for the Tai'ceru territory on Iteloria's western coast. Rune had planned to navigate the long way around the continent to avoid passing the Port of Najyn and drawing unwanted attention from King La'hiran's loyalists, who were sparse in the west.

Vor'sca straightened and held out one hand, and both archers took it. In her other palm, she held a small object Eremon couldn't make out. His falcon sight homed in closer, and he nearly burst into a blaze of magic when he saw what hung around her neck.

Lira's pendant.

Just as he registered what was happening, the girl swept the archers into *turas*, and the three disappeared in a flash of sickly green smoke. Smoke the color of Lira's eyes, when he'd tried to protect the Binding. His thoughts raced as he tried to piece together what had just happened.

Where had Vor'sca taken the archers? Their conversation had sounded as though it concerned Eremon's return. If she was taking them to the Dome, that would mean trouble for Caitir.

As Eremon was preparing to fly, Vor'sca appeared on the shore once again. Reluctantly, he held still, watching her. She fitted her fingers into her mouth, giving one short, sharp whistle, then leaned casually against the wall, waiting.

One by one, the other archers emerged from hiding places along the coastline, filing down to where the immortal woman waited. She took them, two at a time, disappearing in a burst of Lira's corrupted magic. Although Artagán had only brought five archers with him to the formal meeting, he'd recruited more since then. All in all, Eremon counted twelve, in addition to Lira's turncoat cousin—whom he had yet to see.

During Vor'sca's final *turas*, Eremon caught a glimpse of Artagán, who was jogging toward the sea wall at a clip. His bright auburn hair and forest green garb were stark against the overcast sky and the whitecaps rolling in from the sea. No matter where the archer was at any given moment, he looked as though he should be sitting in the high limbs of a tree instead, training his arrow on unsuspecting trespassers.

He waited until Artagán had moved further down the northern wall, overlooking the jagged cliffs below. The wall was at least a hundred feet high from here. Moving northeastward toward Clan Beran's territory, the land rose sharply, transforming into craggy cliffs that tapered back down into Beran's Gorge in the heart of Rodhlan.

Eremon swept down from his perch and transformed, blocking Artagán's way. The archer's balance wavered, his green eyes widening with terror. As quickly as he'd faltered, he righted himself and drew an arrow, nocking it in his bow and aiming it at Eremon.

"So it's true," he said, strands of hair whipping against his face in the frigid, salty air.

Eremon fixed his gaze on the tip of Artagán's arrow, which hummed with dark magic. "You know that arrow won't hurt me," he said, suppressing the urge to roll his eyes.

"Funny, that," Artagán said with a sneer. "Won't hurt the mistress, either."

"How many mistresses do you have now, Artagán?" Eremon smirked. "Seems you've become quite the whore."

The archer adjusted his aim and drew his bowstring tighter. "Masters, mistresses, immortals—it matters not, so long as they pay what the work is worth."

Immortals. "Like Vor'sca?" Eremon asked.

Artagán's eyes flicked toward the Dome for a split second. Eremon took advantage of the archer's distraction, closing the distance between them. He raised a hand, and his own magic leapt from his open palm to meet Artagán's arrow. On contact, Eremon's power turned the arrow to ash. The archer stepped back, flexing his fingers and looking unsure of whether to forfeit another.

"You can tell your immortal benefactor she'll have to do better than a mountain archer with stolen power," Eremon said in a low voice, moving forward.

Artagán grinned, but the smile did not reach his eyes. "Be more specific: Which immortal should I tell?"

Eremon's brief jolt of confusion was all Artagán needed. He shouldered the bow and formed an orb of black lightning between his hands, launching it at Eremon. The power struck him in the center of his chest, and he toppled over the side of the sea wall, tumbling down toward the jagged rocks. Panic seized him as the cold wind whipped at his hair and sea spray dampened his clothing. During his human lifetime, a fall like this would have meant certain death.

But he was not human, and he had nothing to fear.

In midair, Eremon's fractured attention coalesced and snagged on his own magic. He shifted into falcon form, sweeping upward just before he made impact. As he circled back to the place where he and Artagán had faced off, he spotted Vor'sca, who had just returned again. She stood with the archer now, hand extended as they both kept their eyes trained on the silver falcon before them.

Eremon barreled toward them, but he was too late. Artagán seized Vor'sca's hand, and the two vanished in a flash of corrupted magic. He changed direction and careened toward the Dome.

Toward Caitir.

He didn't bother to continue his usual discretionary ruse of changing from falcon to cat to pass through the Dome. Instead, he landed near the entrance to the western towers, shifting to his human form as he slammed his way through the doors.

"Caitir!" he shouted, breaking into a run as he moved through the wide corridors in the direction of her chamber.

Members of the Dome's staff rushed out into the hallway, gaping as he passed. Until now, he'd managed to control who encountered him. But right now, he didn't care who knew about him or what happened next, as long as he could get to Caitir before Vor'sca could. It would be as easy as a *turas* into her chambers, then across the Strait of Ulan to Iteloria if the immortal wished it.

Just like before, at the sea wall, he was likely too late.

She could be gone, she could be dead. I failed her, I failed everyone.

Sickening dread filled him, and he pushed himself harder, letting his magic fuel his body as he moved. He continued calling to her, in case she was elsewhere in the Dome, so she might hear him before he reached her. The closer he drew to her room, the more he gave in to his own wild panic.

Please, please, please—

CHAPTER 58
CAITIR

Dome

Eremon burst through Caitir's chamber door, wild-eyed and panting. With a shriek, she dropped her sketch-book and pencils, drawing her feet up onto the sofa. The book landed in a heap, and the pencils rolled haphazardly across the floor. He froze when he saw her.

"Are you all right?" he said, just as she shouted, "What's *wrong* with you?"

Their harried sounds overlapped and mingled, and for a moment, they grew silent, eyes locked as Eremon's ragged breathing returned to normal. The sudden, raging frustration he'd kindled in Caitir shifted to worry as she took in his panicked expression. She sat up straighter, studying him. "Eremon?"

He moved across the room, sinking onto the opposite cushion and keeping his gaze trained on her. His fingertips went white where he gripped the back of the sofa.

"Have they come here?" he asked in a low voice.

Caitir's heart began pounding. "Who?"

Eremon's silver eyes shone with fury. "Vor'sca. The archers. Anyone."

"No." She cradled her belly as his words sank in. "Who is Vor'sca?"

"An immortal from Iteloria—she's like Lira," Eremon said, taking a deep, shuddering breath. "Skelly and Lord Irem were sailing for the continent in search of her, but she's here, and she has Lira's pendant. She's using *turas*."

"*What?*" Caitir cried.

"I don't know how she got it, but it might explain why you couldn't remember what happened," Eremon says. "She's using it to tamper with memory somehow. And mortal gods, what's happened to Lira—she could be connected to that, too."

Caitir didn't know what questions to ask first. Her body trembled violently, and she crossed her arms tightly across her chest in an attempt to stop her hands from shaking. "What happened to Lira?"

Her voice sounded painfully small when she asked it.

With a heavy sigh, Eremon told her everything, beginning with his attempt to protect Lira and Aidryn's Binding with his immortal magic. His story ended with the encounter at the sea wall. When Eremon had finished, they sat in loaded silence as the pendulum on the mantel ticked away the time.

Finally, Caitir said, "Why would you waste your time scheming with me when you should have been helping Lira?"

Eremon leaned back against the cushion, running a hand over his face. "I was trying to help you both. I believed I could."

"That's why she still has your ring, and why you've waited to ascend."

His silver gaze slid to her. "That's part of it. I wanted to lend any remaining protection I could."

Caitir drew her knees up. Her belly felt tight, and her back ached. She took a deep breath, willed her racing thoughts to slow, and closed her eyes.

Eremon, apparently, couldn't abide her silence. "What are you think—"

"*Shh.*" She held up a hand to silence him. "The problem is that when you speak, I cannot think."

He exhaled hard. Nervous energy buzzed from his body as he waited. Caitir took a moment to let her thoughts piece themselves together, because in his panic, he'd brought her a clarity that she hadn't possessed since all this began. When she was ready, she opened her eyes again and held his stare.

"I need for you to focus on what I have to say to you, Eremon," she began, keeping her voice as steady as possible. "You've been acting as though you have no limitations, but your mind is still very much mortal."

Eremon opened his mouth to protest, but she cut him an icy glare, and he promptly closed it.

A little shot of triumph crept through her, but she focused on the truths that were unfolding instead. "You shouldered too many burdens alone, when you know very well that you need to learn how to exist as an immortal before you carry the world's weight. Even then, you shouldn't have to bear it all alone."

He cast his gaze aside, looking ashamed, and nodded once.

"It was noble of you to try to help both me and Lira, and I believe you're wholly capable of it. But your emotions... mortal gods, Eremon, I can feel them emanating from you now. They're more manifest than your magic, and that is a problem."

Suddenly, he looked as though she'd struck him. He rocked back, blinking and apparently unsure of what to do with this information.

"The Eremon I remember," Caitir said gently, "took command of his feelings and simply did what must be done. But this Eremon is so frenzied—pulled in so many directions— that his thoughts are fractured and his actions disjointed."

A dark expression swept over his features. She might have

imagined it, but for a moment, his eyes looked as though they'd taken on a brighter sheen. Slowly, Eremon inched nearer to her, stopping at the end of his cushion and fixing her with a determined stare. "What should I do?"

Caitir held steady, though her heart began to race. She took a deep breath. The fear she'd held at bay flooded her, but in reality, she'd known this day was coming, one way or another. It was time to stop pretending it never would.

"I think you need to take the ring back from Lira and ascend," she said reluctantly, though her body began to tremble. "It's time."

"Why do you think so?" he asked.

"Think about it logically," Caitir answered. "Vor'sca is from Iteloria; she's an immortal. She may be tampering with Lira's power, if your theory is correct. And you know how obsessed my mother always was with Lira's magic.

"Chances are, she's connected to Mother somehow, and maybe even the king. By now, we should assume they know you're here, that Gerallt is dead, and that I'm Crown Regent. We can't waste any more time."

Eremon reached across the sofa for her hand. His skin was warm against hers, and he squeezed her fingers, holding her gaze. "I'll do whatever I can to keep you and the child safe. I promise."

At the contact, she shut her heart to the hope that welled in her chest. "I know you'll try."

The corners of his mouth pulled downward.

Suddenly, the open door slammed against the wall, and he whirled to face it. Fiadh rushed in, a hand on the hilt of her sword. Her cheeks were red, as though she'd run all the way here, just like Eremon had.

"Caitir, the archers—"

Caitir pulled her hand from Eremon's, but not before Fiadh took note of their proximity. Her dark eyes flashed, but when she spoke, she turned her full attention to Eremon, straightening her spine and squaring her shoulders. He rose to greet Fiadh.

"My Rí." She offered him a bow, swallowed hard, and began again. "The archers allied with both Iathium and Clan Beran at Aila's behest. Artagán and Vor'sca answer to her, and ultimately, to Iteloria."

Caitir's stomach dropped. "Of course they do." Her voice was breathy and panicked, and she felt as though the world was fracturing around her.

"There's more," Fiadh added. "King La'hiran has agreed to free Aila. Biren's report indicated she would be released in a week."

"Why?" Eremon asked.

"He's known about Gerallt for some time." Fiadh looked at the floor. "And you, Eremon. But Aila gave him something of value."

A brittle laugh broke from Caitir. "If the king knows about Eremon, what could she possibly promise him?"

Fiadh looked pained when she answered. "A way to restrain immortals."

Eremon went rigid.

"What?" Caitir cried.

"The king has been hunting them—enslaving them. That's why he's been silent," Fiadh said. "Vor'sca was the first; she had a longstanding friendship with La'hiran, and he exploited it."

"To what end?" Caitir asked. "I thought he needed mortal deity magic."

"He takes pleasure in stripping the powerful of their abilities," Fiadh said. "Beyond that, I don't know."

"This makes you vulnerable, Eremon," Caitir said, turning to him.

But Eremon didn't respond. Instead, his attention was fixed

wholly on Fiadh. "So that explains the glass bracelets you forged. Were those for Aila, or did I miss something?"

Fiadh clamped her lips and raised her chin defiantly.

Heat crept up Caitir's throat and into her cheeks. "What's going on?"

"You may as well admit it, Fiadh," Eremon said. "I saw Vor'sca wearing them."

"They're cuffs," Fiadh answered in a quiet voice, "not bracelets."

"You compelled me to release you." Eremon circled Fiadh like he was preparing to strike. "That night in Caitir's chamber."

Caitir sucked in a breath. She remembered the odd exchange when Fiadh had gripped Eremon's wrist, but had paid no more mind to it. "You helped my mother create immortal restraints?"

"It was unintentional—I didn't know," Fiadh protested, taking a step closer to Eremon.

Eremon held out a hand, glaring hard at Fiadh. "Keep your distance," he said.

Her eyes went glassy, her knuckles going white as she gripped the hilt of her sword. "You said I'd be pardoned if—"

"I said, get *back*!"

He held up his palms, and cobalt magic burst from them, driving Fiadh away. She shielded her eyes, crying out as the magic made contact. Fiadh braced against the power like one might brace against a driving wind, gritting her teeth and dropping into a low stance.

Eremon looked more fearsome than Caitir had ever seen him, as though he'd suddenly learned how to embody his full presence. His eyes flashed with intense white light. The room rumbled as the sheer resonance of his power rippled from him, and she shuddered.

"Fiadh Énna," he said, currents of magic shimmering

around his body as the force of it began to dissipate. Her face snapped up as she steadied herself, and she blanched at the sight. "You are hereby ordered to remain ten paces from me at all times, and no less. Come within my reach, and I will erase you from existence."

Fiadh dropped her head and sank to one knee, bowing her head. "Yes, my Rí."

With a sharp breath, Eremon's eyes faded to silver once more.

"I need you to understand," Fiadh pleaded in earnest, looking to Eremon as though she expected him to help her. "I thought I was simply discharging dark magic. Aila said the glass would make an effective container."

"Do you expect me to believe you?" Caitir laughed in disbelief.

"You, of all people, should know how convincing she is!" Fiadh cried. "She knew how to release some of the magic that's trapped inside me, and I thought she was helping. I didn't know what I was creating!"

"When did you give the cuffs to Aila?" Eremon demanded.

"Before she sailed," Fiadh answered. "I swear."

"How many other immortals exist?" Eremon asked, the apprehension apparent in his tone. "How many has La'hiran imprisoned?"

Fiadh squeezed her eyes shut and shook her head. "I don't know."

"I assume anyone can wield the restraints?"

"I suppose," Fiadh answered.

"Then we'll need to attempt to remove them from Vor'sca, if we can get close enough to her—doubtful, since she has Lira's pendant," Eremon said. "But if we can free her, perhaps we can turn her loyalties."

"You're getting ahead of yourself, Eremon," Caitir cut in.

"We need to determine where Vor'sca and the archers went first."

"Fortress Halgeir or Iteloria, probably," Fiadh ventured, "unless they were going after Lira."

"Mortal gods." Eremon paled. "I can't be everywhere at once."

Caitir could sense his panic rising again. She crossed to where he stood, grasping his elbow and giving it a squeeze. His attention snapped to her, and though her pulse hammered, she held steady. "Remember what I said about your emotions. *Think.*"

He relaxed enough to exhale, and Caitir released him. She couldn't help noticing his fleeting glance in her direction, and the way his opposite hand flew to the elbow she'd touched. Her ears grew hot.

"The girl is already manipulating Lira's power, so not the mountains. But—" Eremon's paused in thought. "One of the archers said something: '*If it's true he's back.*' I thought they meant me, but maybe they meant Artur Beran."

"The overlord?" Fiadh said. "Thorne hired the archers, not Artur."

Eremon's gaze darkened. "But Artur would support Thorne's idiotic notion of taking the throne in Lira's name."

Caitir snorted, if only to mask the terror that was threatening to overtake her now. "That stupid brute wouldn't know whether to sit on the throne or piss on it."

Eremon burst into startled laughter. The rich, rolling sound of it filled the room, and she couldn't help but smile, too, despite these new revelations. Fiadh just scowled at them.

"The timing makes sense," she said. "Maybe you should start there."

Caitir gave Eremon a nod. "Don't tell us your plan—just decide what you're going to do, and then go. We'll be here when you return."

"I can't leave you," he blurted, taking a step toward her.

There was an unnerving sort of desperation on his face that she didn't want to consider. Even if there was something of substance between them, they would never have the luxury of exploring it. So she held up a hand, shaking her head, and he halted.

"You have to." Caitir willed him to obey her command, though he looked like he might continue to protest.

"I'll stay nearby," Fiadh cut in.

Reluctantly, Eremon nodded. "All right. Call the sentries. Set up extra guards around the perimeter and outside Caitir's chamber."

"Yes, my Rí. Do us a favor; don't get yourself captured." Fiadh gave him a little bow, then slipped out of the room, pulling the door shut behind her.

When Eremon turned to Caitir again, his silver eyes shimmered, like he was fighting back tears. "I've failed everyone." He crossed to the nearest chair and sat, dropping his face into his hands.

Tentatively, Caitir moved nearer. She wanted to embrace him, but she settled for resting a palm on his back.

"Stop that," she scolded, trying and failing to will a sharp edge into her voice.

He shivered, curling in on himself. "I'd be better off back in the crypt, I've made such a mess of things."

Tentatively, Caitir trailed her fingertips along his shoulder, then moved her palm to the center of his back, making soothing circles. Beneath her touch, she felt him begin to relax. "Do you think I'm going to let you spew such hatred toward yourself without challenging it?"

Eremon scrubbed a hand over his face and looked up. "I was born into a royal bloodline, crowned Rí at age twelve." His smile was tight. Sad. He reached for her hand, grasping it gently. "I don't appreciate being challenged."

She closed her eyes, curling her fingers around his.

"Funny," she said softly, resting her other hand on his shoulder. "I rather thought you enjoyed it."

Without thinking, she tucked a strand of silken hair behind his ear. Eremon's hair was soft, his skin warm as her fingertips grazed it. An unmistakable heat filled his gaze, and she swallowed hard. His eyes darted to her mouth, so fleetingly she might have imagined it.

She wanted to kiss him again, wanted to feel his lips on hers, his hands on her skin. Ever since that night in the archive, she had fought to force the memories from her mind. But this close to him, it was impossible not to remember.

It's nothing.

It was also impossible to forget how the moment had ended. The memory shattered her surge of desire, filling her stomach with a heavy, cold sensation. She'd felt the sting of his rejection more than once now. If she opened herself to another disappointment, then she was truly a fool.

Eremon's lips parted at the change in her countenance. "Caitir—"

She let go of his hand and took a step back. "It's time for you to go."

Slowly, Eremon rose from his seat. His movements were as smooth and elegant as ever, honed by his years on the throne and sharpened by immortality. He looked as though he was debating his next words before he finally said, "I would take you with me if I could."

And I would go, Caitir thought. She didn't reply but gave him a shallow nod instead.

He sidestepped the chair and rested his arms on its high back. "Keep both eyes on Fiadh, as often as you can. I don't trust her story."

The corner of her mouth tugged up. "As you should never."

A long, tense moment passed. Neither moved from where

they stood. Everything Caitir longed to say pressed at her insides, threatening to burst out of its own accord if she didn't force its submission. Damn him and the way he was looking at her, and damn her for craving her own weakness.

She laced her fingers together, clasping her hands before her. "Don't tell me your plans."

Eremon gave her a curt nod. "The less you know, the better."

When she was alone again, she sank onto the soft sofa, cradling her rounded belly and taking steadying breaths. She didn't try to resist the current of deep despair that dragged her down. Her alliance with Eremon had been a thrill and a brief moment of reprieve, but she had always known it couldn't last.

Her vision blurred with tears as she stared at her chamber door. She couldn't help wishing that Eremon would refuse her counsel, change his mind, and return to her side. But with each passing moment, it became more apparent that he would not.

She'd told him it was time to ascend again, and that answer was still the right one.

For Eremon, this arrangement had never been about Caitir. It had always been about Rodhlan, the clans, the anointed, and Iathium's throne. She had only been a means to many important ends. Now that her role was complete, Eremon didn't need her.

The less you know, the better.

And that was how it should be.

CHAPTER 59
LIRA

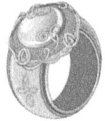

Rodhlan Ridge

"All was quiet on the ship, the gentle waves rolling beneath its hull." Lira scanned the faces of the small crowd that had gathered around the bonfire to listen to her story. "Gerallt the Usurper lay dead by his daughter's arrow within the manor's walls."

Over the past week, Aidryn had all but kept her sequestered in and near Skelly's cottage. He'd spent the days and nights wholly focused on attending to her needs and desires, and she had let him. She'd wanted to forget the failures and the lies that had brought them to this point.

Really, she should be grateful he'd stopped disappearing and devoted himself to her again.

Each time she was tempted to bring up the situation in Iathium, she stopped herself. With each passing day, though, the steady drum of resentment that had begun to emanate from within her became more difficult to ignore. Her mind spun as she ruminated on the secrets Aidryn and Eremon had kept from her, and their desperate attempts to gain sway over so many unknowns. Only the voice that had spoken to her on the day of the wildfire understood what she was feeling. Commiserated with her.

You are an escape for your husband, the voice had whispered this morning. *But who will offer you an escape of your own?*

Lira had been lying alone in bed when she'd heard it, after Aidryn had risen to tend the horses. The words had stung, siphoning any joy that lingered from their dawn lovemaking and leaving Lira feeling chilled and utterly empty. It had been difficult to ignore the deep sense of betrayal that coursed through her as the voice rang true. After all, Aidryn had a knack for distracting himself when reality was too difficult to bear.

Three years ago, when Aidryn had believed Lira too far out of reach, he'd pursued Fiadh for a short time, holding the secret close until it had emerged last summer at Fortress Halgeir. Fiadh had gone on to betray them to Caitir, and subsequently, Aila and Gerallt. Then, of course, there was the dark magic.

Lira's despair had morphed into a flash of hatred at the thought.

For a brief moment, she'd felt a sense of deep satisfaction that her anger was still so fresh and easily accessible. But then she'd realized that her emotions weren't only isolated to Fiadh. They applied to Aidryn, too.

The problem was that each time the voice spoke, it uttered truth. Sometimes, that truth soothed. And other times, like this morning, it cut unbearably deep.

Do you know who is ultimately responsible? the voice had asked her the afternoon before. *Your husband.*

That thought had frightened Lira enough to shove the voice from her mind for a short time, but she hadn't managed to eliminate it completely.

"Faolan leapt into the sea and cut a swift path toward

shore," Lira said, bringing her awareness back into her story and the present moment. "He'd promised us a spectacle, and that promise he kept."

Tonight, she'd managed to persuade Aidryn to bring her to the nightly bonfire near the keep. Though he'd been reluctant, he had agreed, and she'd found herself filling Skelly's usual role of storyteller. To her surprise, telling Faolan's story had begun to dissipate the heaviness she'd carried with her all week, and she reveled in the momentary reprieve.

It was a centuries-old tradition of Clan Mór's to host night-time revelries with storytelling and music throughout the year. During Gerallt's final years as clan master, when Skelly had taken ill with an overflow of magic, the music and stories had ceased. Before her departure, Skelly had urged the people to gather once again. And, as she had predicted, the gatherings had begun to dispel the lingering tensions amongst the fractured clans dwelling in the valley.

Oda rested her head on Lira's shoulder, scooting closer for warmth. The warrior had just returned from Clan Énna's territory, where she'd helped to secure safe passage for Skelly and Irem aboard Rune's ship. They'd seen off Lira's grandmother and mentor almost a week ago, and she knew Oda was as worried for their safety as she was.

But the elderly friends were only one facet of Oda's worry. Rune had a young son called Fell—barely three years old— whom he'd left behind for the journey. Though Ellwyn had accompanied Oda and offered to care for Fell at the coastal settlement, Oda had insisted that her young cousin be brought into the mountains instead. She'd ensured he was comfortable at the keep with Ellwyn, who had taken a liking to Rune after their first encounter on the coast last summer.

Now, Ellwyn carried Fell on her hip not far from the bonfire. He had hazel eyes flecked with green and gold, light brown skin, and a wide, cheeky smile. His coarse curls were golden-brown, and Oda had shown Ellwyn how to properly care for them, helping her arrange them in short twists before the gathering.

"Why don't you keep him with you?" Lira had asked the night before, when Oda and Ellwyn had arrived back in the valley with Fell in tow.

"I think my Uncle Rune has his sights set on your cousin," Oda had answered with a grin. "Ellwyn might as well get to know the boy, if there's a chance she might raise him."

Now, Fell wriggled out of Ellwyn's arms, running toward the remaining children of Tarlach and Mór, who were playing together in the clearing. Nevala and Mytr sat shoulder-to-shoulder, a blanket pulled tightly around them. Aidryn leaned against the nearest tree, his gaze burning through Lira, a contented smile deepening his dimples.

"When Rune and Ellwyn returned to the ship, Faolan summoned the sea, for you see: He was Anointed of Énna." Lira continued. 'Twas a secret never told, yet there he was, bringing down the stone manor with the raw force of the waters he commanded."

Oda clicked her tongue and cut in. "Don't forget the vines you and Talfryn grew beneath its foundation. You set the stage for Faolan's grand exhibition."

Lira didn't break from the bard's cadence she'd adopted. "And here I was, ducking into the shadows in favor of my friend. For shame."

"You don't belong in shadow, Witness Tree," Aidryn said. She saw a glimmer of sorrow in his eyes, followed by the fierce pride he always carried when they spoke of Faolan's final days.

She kept her eyes on Aidryn as she launched back into the story, her attempt to weave a tale the way Skelly always had. Next, she would recount the story of Eremon's return, because the people deserved to know the entire truth. It was far past time.

Now, if only you knew the entire truth, the voice taunted. *Above all others, you are the one person in Rodhlan who should.*

"We—we departed…" Lira faltered in her telling, shaking her head to rattle the words away.

The small crowd went utterly silent, waiting for her to continue. There was no sound, save for the fire's crackling. Before the wildfire, Lira had loved the sound of a bonfire, the spray of tiny sparks, the scent of its smoke. But now she noticed the spark of panic it induced and wondered why she had asked to come here in the first place.

Her breaths quickened, pulse speeding. Suddenly, she wanted to flee.

Beside her, Oda went rigid, sitting up to scrutinize her. From his vantage point by the tree, Aidryn was suddenly on alert, fixing her with a hard, wary gaze.

"Silira?" Nevala leaned forward, as though she could somehow catch a glimpse of what was happening beneath Lira's surface.

"I'm fine," she lied, reaching for Oda's hand. "The grief is still so fresh."

Nevala and Mytr exchanged a terse glance. Aidryn ran a hand over his face. Oda's eyes narrowed, but she gave Lira a reluctant nod and a squeeze of the hand.

Despite their wariness, Lira completed her story without another hitch. When she had finished, several of the children who had drifted nearer to listen chanted for more. She forced a smile, smoothing her emerald-green skirts. The fabric was thick and warm, and she'd layered trousers beneath tonight in addition to her new, thick cloak.

Lira wished the voice had not broken through her story, because now she felt exhausted and hollowed out. Perhaps she could defer to Aidryn for a moment—gather herself. "Who wants to hear about the Seanlaoch?"

"The magic horses?" one little boy piped up.

"The very same." Lira grinned at Aidryn, extending her hand to him. "Come and sing, Aidryn, and I'll tell another story after."

Even in the glow of the bonfire, she could see the blush creeping into his cheeks. He pressed against the tree, biting back a smile. "They didn't ask for me; they want you."

But the crowd coaxed him up anyway, and he stepped closer to the fire, joining Lira on the large log where she'd been sitting. He looped an arm around her waist and kissed her temple, warming her down to her toes. The people waited expectantly, and a hush fell over them until all they could hear was the crackling of the fire.

"What am I supposed to sing?" he murmured, nudging her side.

"Something happy," she said. "Not the ballad; I know you like that one, but it's so sad."

He dipped his head and chuckled before straightening again and taking a breath. In his rich tenor, he began. Lira leaned into him, resting her head on his shoulder and closing her eyes as she savored the sound of his voice. She had rarely heard him sing, but she wanted more of it, along with the contentment and hope it stirred within her. Again, the heavy darkness fell away, and she felt lighter.

When the song was over, Lira was the first to applaud. Aidryn flashed her a crooked grin, his cheeks reddening. "So that was acceptable?"

"It was beautiful," Lira replied. "Where did that one originate?"

"Up here." Aidryn tapped his forehead. "I wrote it."

Lira straightened. "You never told me you were a bard!"

He shrugged, bashful. "I've only dabbled in writing my own songs. Most of them live in my head."

She bumped her shoulder against his. "Well, as the living

vessel of history, I command you to put them to parchment. I want the whole of Rodhlan singing your songs."

"You say that now," he said with a wicked grin, "but you haven't heard the bawdy ones."

She threw her head back and laughed as two musicians from Clan Énna began a rousing rhythm on the round skin drums they carried everywhere. They had remained in the valley when their fellow clanspeople returned to their coastal settlement, blending with Clan Mór's lone fiddler. The trio launched into a reel, and the children were the first to leap into a dance.

Aidryn grabbed Lira's hand, pulling her up from where she'd been sitting. His cerulean eyes sparkled as he laced their fingers together and drew her hand to his lips. "Dance with me, Silira."

Lira had not danced since *Nami Mostari*—had not planned to ever dance again. But the beat of the music was infectious, and she had never danced with Aidryn before. All those years, she and Caitir had danced Iathium's traditional reel at the festival, and he'd hung back, grinning as they made fools of themselves. Aidryn had never joined, though, and Lira hadn't paid that fact any mind until now.

He gripped her waist in his strong, gentle hands and pulled her flush against him. "Are you all right?" he whispered.

"Better now," she answered, tilting her face up to look him in the eyes. "I've never danced with you."

"I know." A brief shadow crossed his face, but then he grinned. "Come on."

Then, he drew her into the fray.

The dance was thundering, intoxicating. Aidryn led her along, laughing and smiling as they moved together, so fluid it felt like they'd always danced this way. As the first song ended, he lifted her arm and gave her a little twirl, pulling her against him.

"Why don't we go back to the cottage, and I'll sing you one of those bawdy songs I wrote," he whispered, his breath hot on her ear.

She quivered in his arms. "Careful, Tarlach; I'll hold you to that." The musicians began a familiar tune that Lira couldn't quite place. It sounded both distant and warped, and she strained to remember where she'd last heard it.

"I fully expect you to." He pulled back, reaching up to frame her face with his hands, brushing the curls back.

But as he raised his hands, the image before her shifted, and she was standing before a gray-eyed Eremon in his bright, ceremonial garb. He raised the crown of nea'la roses as though to rest them on her head. She flinched, then squeezed her eyes shut with a gasp. The world around her dissipated, and for a moment, she was alone in darkness, thunder rumbling in the distance.

I know you remember this song, Silira, the voice taunted. *It was playing when he died.*

"Help me," she pleaded. "Take me back to Aidryn."

Open your eyes. He never left your side.

Lira's ragged panting calmed, and she forced herself to open her eyes. But when she did, Eremon still stood there, hands raised—only now, he was clad in his black tunic, strands of dark, silken hair swirling around his enraged face in the turbulent wind. His silver eyes glowed so brightly that they were nearly white. Black lightning split the sky, and the thunder now crashed so loudly, she could hear nothing else.

When she saw what Eremon held over her, she froze in horror. Rather than the crown of blue and teal roses, he now held a crown made of blackened dagger blades inset with blood-red rubies. The corner of his mouth twitched up, and he moved the crown as if to place it on her head.

But then he turned it over and drove the knife-tips down.

CHAPTER 60
AIDRYN

Rodhlan Ridge

Lira's eyes transformed, glowing eerily with that cyclone-green sheen. Her lips were moving soundlessly, her features twisted with terror. Aidryn gripped her shoulders.

"Lira?" He gave her a little shake, searching for any sign that she could see or hear him. "Lira, I'm here."

Suddenly, she screamed, dropping to the ground and folding her arms over her head.

There was a clamoring around them as the music ground to a halt. Aidryn hit his knees beside her, attempting to gather her into his arms. She curled in on herself tighter as Oda rushed to their side.

"What's happened?" Oda knelt, surveying Lira's trembling body.

"Get the children away from here," Aidryn gritted out, pressing his palm to Lira's back. "Clear everyone out."

Her eyes widened. "Mortal gods—Fell." She rose abruptly,

taking two steps before she turned back to Aidryn. "I'll be back."

He gave Oda a nod, then turned his attention back to Lira, who had begun to gasp and weep. A wave of horror washed over Aidryn as he realized her body was humming with dark magic, as though she was attempting to suppress it. This was what Eremon had done to himself all those years, but Lira would never be able to hold up to it. Eremon had endured a slow build over the course of his short mortal life, not an abrupt overflow like this.

Aidryn sought out her right hand, where she wore the ring Eremon had given her last spring. Its stone flickered with cobalt light, as though fighting against the dark magic over-taking her. Though dim, it was clear the ring continued to provide some measure of protection to her.

Painstakingly, Aidryn gathered Lira into his arms, coaxing and soothing her as the dark magic gradually released its hold. He expected her to resist, but she curled into him, clutching the sleeve of his tunic as she wrapped her other arm around him.

"I'm sorry," she mumbled through her tears. "I'm so sorry."

"Don't apologize." He swept a hand over her hair and cradled her. His chest felt tight and heavy, the sudden rush of heartache reverberating down to his bones. "I'm going to help you up, and we're going home, all right?"

She nodded, the movement rapid and tremulous. Aidryn helped her stand, then scooped her up and carried her toward Skelly's cottage. Lira relaxed into his arms, and her gasping turned to keening as tears streaked down her cheeks.

"Come on, now," Aidryn soothed, swallowing the lump in his own throat. "We'll get you settled."

Helplessness crept from his heart into his limbs, a phantom truth he'd been fleeing since the day he'd learned of Lira's dark magic. He'd known that one day, this corruption would become too potent for her to manage. Now that the time had come, there was no escape from the sudden, disorienting sensation of falling headlong into a dark, endless chasm.

Aidryn carried Lira to the bedchamber, bundling her into bed and tucking her tightly in one of Skelly's homespun blankets, though they both still wore their heavy winter cloaks. He lay beside her until she calmed, cocooning her in a warm embrace. They remained that way until she finally stilled.

He stroked her curls, pulling her as close to his body as he could. For a long while, he thought she might have fallen asleep. But then she stirred, stroking his cheek with a cool palm.

"Aidryn?" she whispered, her voice thick from her tears.

"I'm here," he repeated, tightening his hold.

"I won't survive this." Her words were unnervingly decisive, as though she'd made up her mind long before she uttered them.

He shook his head, kissing her hair as the tears he'd been denying finally escaped. "You will."

But when he reached for her magic to confirm his truth, it only recoiled.

CHAPTER 61
EREMON

Fortress Halgeir

T he sun was setting by the time Eremon arrived at
Fortress Halgeir. He swept down into the courtyard on
an icy wind, alighting on one of the surrounding
walkway's massive stone railings. The first thing he noticed
were the unnatural hanging gardens, which should have withered in the winter chill. Instead, they teemed with Clan Mór's
power, some of which Lira had discharged.

The imprint of her dark magic lingered here, and he
wondered what sort of damage she'd managed to do in her
short time at the fortress.

Because I couldn't help, he thought.

Before guilt got the better of him, he caught a glimpse of
movement in the shadows below. Talfryn stumbled into the
courtyard as though he'd been shoved, and every fiber of
Eremon's being went on alert.

"You heard the overlord." One of Thorne's brutes emerged
from the dark walkway, brandishing a broadsword. Its metal

glinted in the torchlight. "You're unwelcome in Fortress Halgeir."

"I can understand Brylla, Bard," Talfryn said, drawing his own blade and steadying his stance, "and I'll be gone sooner if you don't delay me."

Two more Beran warriors followed Bard into the courtyard, menacing in their statures and posturing. Talfryn's eyes flicked from one to the other in calm assessment. Dread filled Eremon's chest at the sight: three against one, and Talfryn with his single arm. He would go down fighting with no question, but Eremon feared the odds.

"We didn't say you could leave," Bard sneered. He sank into a fighting stance and raised his sword, his fighting leathers groaning with the movement. His companions drew their own weapons and followed suit.

Talfryn held firm, leveling his blade. "I didn't ask your permission."

Eremon tensed, ready to intervene. Before Bard could charge, though, Talfryn threw his sword with all his strength. Bard sidestepped the blade with an angry growl, then advanced again, the other two warriors barely faltering behind him.

This time, Talfryn opened his hand and shouted, "Vines!"

The ground beneath his feet split open with terrifying intensity, glowing with Clan Mór's emerald power. Magical vines burst from the earth, clambering toward the warriors faster than the men could flee. They snaked up Bard's legs first, twisting and writhing around his body, trapping him and his companions in their grip. They struggled against the vines, hitting their knees as they were bound.

Bard cursed Talfryn in Brylla just before one of the vines wound around his throat, silencing him. The veins along his temples bulged, his face reddening, eyes widening. Talfryn strode casually forward, picking up his sword and angling the point over Bard's heart.

"I like seeing fear in your eyes," Talfryn said in a soft voice, angling his head as he surveyed the bound warriors. "Suits you."

Bard flinched as Talfryn drew the broadsword back to strike —but then, he flipped his grip on the hilt and slid it into its scabbard in one smooth stroke. He patted the pommel, then grinned so broadly that his deep dimples showed in the flickering torchlight. "Have a pleasant evening."

Talfryn turned to go, leaving the warriors shouting and swearing at his back. But then, a familiar sound caught Eremon's sharpened hearing: the tightening of a bowstring. His gaze darted to the opposite railing, where Artagán was aiming an arrow at Talfryn.

"Don't move," Artagán called down.

Talfryn froze, his fear only apparent for a breath before he tilted his head up to survey Artagán. "You're late to the party, cousin. The rest of your rogues are in the arena for sentencing."

"Sentencing?" Artagán hesitated, his brows crinkling with confusion. "That's a lie."

Lira's brother just laughed. "Did you not realize Clan Beran's overlord demands complete loyalty?" He swept his arm out to indicate Bard and the warriors, whom he'd left lying on the ground, entangled in his magical vines. "Weren't you wondering why I've taken my own prisoners here? I expected you to ask, but you're a disappointment, as always."

Enraged, Artagán gave a wild shout and loosed his arrow. Panic seized Eremon, and he swooped down toward Talfryn as quickly as he could fly. He transformed in midair, landing in a roll and rising to cast a wide orb of protective magic around himself and Talfryn just as the arrow met its mark.

...Or so he thought.

Cobalt magic lit the entire courtyard, casting Talfryn in its bright glow. He was standing before Eremon, mouth agape, eyes wide. Eremon grabbed him by the shoulders and surveyed him, looking for any trace of blood, any sign of an injury. But there was nothing but a pile of ash on the ground where the magic had burned the arrow away.

"Are you all right?" he asked, panting.

Talfryn gave him an incredulous look, then loosened the laces at the top of his tunic, peeling it away. "It's too bad," he said, revealing fitted armor made of hardened leaves. "I was looking forward to trying this."

In his surprise, Eremon almost lost his hold on the protective magic he'd cast. He threw his head back and laughed, relieved, then clapped Talfryn on the shoulder. "I heard you say you're leaving."

"As soon as I can shed this last nuisance," Talfryn grumbled, scowling up at Artagán, who had swung his body over the side of the railing and was scaling the stone column, moving down toward the courtyard.

"Nuisance he is," Eremon agreed. "What's happened here?"

"Artur's doling out punishments. I already took mine: seventeen lashes, one for each year of my life for refusing to swear fealty to him. And Mam—"

"What about your mother?" Eremon asked, tensing.

"He made her relinquish the magic Lira gave her," Talfryn said, a dark shadow crossing his expression. "She gifted it to me, which caused a stir and earned me another lashing. He's forcing her into confinement for disloyalty."

Eremon's simmering anger rose, and he clenched his fists at the thought of Beran's overlord publicly humiliating Lira's brother and mother in front of Clan Beran. They'd done nothing but keep Artur's people alive. The overlord's spite was so potent, it was a wonder he hadn't made them destroy the magical gardens, too.

"Why?" Eremon asked.

"Because of Aidryn, and you, and what's happened in Iathium," Talfryn answered earnestly. "Thorne was punished, too, for letting Aidryn leave after he killed Aeron."

"We should take your mother with us," Eremon said, his body rumbling with rage. "She isn't safe here."

But Talfryn merely shook his head. "I tried to convince her, but she wouldn't agree. She believes staying here will protect us somehow. When I pressed her for answers, she refused to say more."

A swell of grief washed over Eremon. He could either choose to force Iva's escape or get Talfryn out safely. It was unlikely he could do both, so he refocused his attention on Talfryn. "What about your wounds?"

"Ljós healed them," Talfryn said. "He's already gone; we're meeting outside the fortress to travel together. Says he'd rather be in Iathium."

Artagán had almost made it to the courtyard now.

Eremon crossed his arms, arching a brow. "And Thorne?"

"He's at Artur's right hand, playing the loyal hound," said Talfryn, scoffing. "Where else?"

When Artagán's feet hit the ground, he approached Eremon's magical orb with caution. Artagán looked it up and down as though he might spot a vulnerability to exploit, then scowled.

"Drop that shield," he demanded, "and we'll negotiate."

Eremon did no such thing. "Where is Vor'sca?" he asked, crossing his arms.

Artagán blinked rapidly, as though trying to conjure the memory. His green eyes clouded with that same sickening fog he'd seen in Lira's eyes before. "Who?"

Talfryn swiveled to look at Eremon. "Now I'm curious."

"The immortal who brought you here," Eremon answered slowly. "Or have you forgotten?"

Artagán's expression screwed up in confusion. "I... we came here by boat."

Eremon swore under his breath. Vor'sca must have tampered with their memories. There was no way the archers had had the time to travel here by way of the gorge. "That *damned* pendant—"

There was stirring behind them, and Eremon whirled to see Thorne kneeling at Bard's side, cutting away Talfryn's vines with a dagger. He handed the blade to Bard, speaking to him in low tones before rising and crossing to where Eremon and Talfryn still stood beneath the protective magic.

"You missed one, Thorne," Talfryn said, jerking his chin toward Artagán, who backed up a step and aimed his weapon at Thorne. He looked nervous, as though unsure of where to focus his attention.

Thorne's glower was menacing, and the look in his amber eyes gave Eremon pause. There was anger in his gaze, to be sure, but there was also deep, profound grief. Eremon could feel it emanating from him, and for a moment, he felt remorseful for assuming Thorne to be an unfeeling, brutish beast.

"I'll shoot!" Artagán warned, but there was an unmistakable current of defeat in his voice.

Thorne continued his advance. When Artagán pulled the bowstring taut, he didn't hesitate. He charged Artagán, who froze in terror. Thorne ducked low and drove his shoulder into Artagán's gut, taking his feet from under him. The bow and arrow clattered to the ground as Artagán hit his back with a loud *oof*. Thorne pinned him down, dropping his full body weight onto the smaller, struggling man. He grasped the lapel of Artagán's tunic and pulled it taut across his throat, pressing lower to tighten the fabric. In moments, Artagán lost consciousness.

During the brief scuffle, Eremon had moved further back, guiding Talfryn along to put more distance between themselves and Thorne. He noted that the two remaining warriors who had been bound with Bard were still struggling to free themselves. Bard was nowhere to be seen, though, and Eremon cursed himself for losing track of the red-haired warrior.

Thorne left Artagán lying on the ground. "Take him to a cell," he called to his men. Then, he advanced on Eremon and Talfryn. "Dispel your magic."

"You and your men keep away from Talfryn," Eremon replied.

Instinctively, he threw an arm out to shield the younger man. But he was surprised to feel the press of Talfryn's fingers on his forearm.

"I appreciate the sentiment," Talfryn said in a low voice, "but I'm not a child."

Reluctantly, Eremon gave him a nod and dropped his arm again. Thorne's lip curled. "He is more of a man than you are, Eremon—that's certain."

Eremon bared his teeth, anger rippling through his body. "How dare you speak my name."

"There is nothing else to call you," Thorne replied with a small shrug. "You have no title, no power here."

He opened his mouth to retort, then shut it. *I am Rí*, he'd wanted to say—only that wasn't true. Lawfully, he held no status beyond trespasser at Halgeir.

"If you tell me what's happening, I'll drop my magic," Eremon said. "But Talfryn remains free to go."

Thorne's brow creased in confusion. "He was always free to go."

"Not according to those three." Talfryn looked pointedly at where he'd grown the vines. "You can see me out yourself."

Thorne gave a shallow nod, then lowered his voice. "When you see my father, thank him for me."

Talfryn exhaled, taking a step toward him. "I know you wouldn't have—"

Thorne cut him off with a sharp look, and Talfryn shrank

back a bit. "Don't say it here." His amber eyes cut to Eremon next. "You have no power in Halgeir. The Arthmael has spoken, and we will protect Clan Beran and Rodhlan from the woman you crowned."

Eremon went rigid. He could feel Talfryn's heavy gaze on him. "She was not crowned, Thorne. She's regent."

"Then explain the reports from my archers," Thorne answered, clenching a fist. "You stood by while she sat on the throne with a crown of blades on her head."

"*Your* archers?" So it was true; Thorne had hired them before Caitir did. His mind raced. "The crown—that was a ruse to gain their loyalty."

"And Artur took it seriously," Thorne replied. "You handed power to Caitir, letting her build influence while Lira suffered."

Talfryn stilled. "Does Lira know this?"

Eremon swallowed hard, hedging. "I—"

Thorne cut in. "No one has told Lira about the regency."

Swiveling to gape at Eremon, Talfryn let out a low whistle. "I hope you're prepared to die again."

Beneath the dark humor, however, Eremon perceived the horror that rocketed through the younger man. Talfryn wasn't truly worried over Eremon's wellbeing, but he was terrified of Lira's reaction.

And perhaps in his distracted frenzy, Eremon had never considered what might truly happen to Lira when she inevitably learned of his deception. Of all their lies and misdirections. Nearly everyone she had trusted had chosen to keep the full truth from her in an attempt to soften the many inevitable blows.

But Lira was filled with dark magic, and Vor'sca had her pendant. If Vor'sca was manipulating Lira's birthright magic through the necklace, then it was possible she could reveal the entire truth to Lira before her friends could.

Horror gripped Eremon, and his magic flickered out. He locked eyes with Thorne, who just shook his head.

"Weak and foolish," Thorne said with a resigned sigh.

The next few moments passed slowly—almost nightmarish in their progression. Eremon's power filled his palms, surrounding his fists. Cobalt magic illuminated Thorne's features, and for the first time, Eremon thought he saw a flicker of real fear there. But then he noticed that Thorne's attention was no longer on him—and the warrior's fear had nothing to do with Eremon at all. With mounting dread, he followed Thorne's line of sight.

Bard had seized Talfryn in a headlock and was holding the point of a dagger to his temple.

They'd been too close to the shadowy corridor, Eremon thought fleetingly. Bard must have been lurking in wait—a feat made easier by the bright orb of protective power Eremon had cast before.

"Stand down, Bard!" Thorne barked.

But there was a wild look on Bard's face, and he wrenched his arm harder around Talfryn's throat. Talfryn's eyes went wide, but he reached up to cup Bard's forearm, pulling it free enough to get a breath. He dropped his weight a bit, looking as though he intended to throw the larger man. But what movement he did make caused the tip of Bard's dagger to slice up from his right temple and into his hairline, leaving a shallow gash.

"Talfryn, *don't move*," Eremon ordered.

Talfryn froze, shock apparent on his youthful face. Blood poured down from the wound, slick and thick, and he blinked furiously as though to clear his vision.

"What will you do now, Thorne?" Bard let out a dark laugh. "You traitor."

Thorne held up his palms and moved slowly in Bard's

direction, as though cornering a wounded animal. "What is my treason?" he asked.

"Letting their kind into the fortress." Bard tightened his grip again, and this time, Talfryn let out a groan. "Failing to act as the overlord would have."

"The overlord tried to ally with Macha, in case you've forgotten," Thorne shot back.

Eremon's attention snapped to Thorne. That was a detail he'd missed in the weeks since Lira brought him back. What had she and Aidryn been thinking, rushing Artur back here? Thorne had been a far better substitute, yet they'd been so incapable of reconciling their differences as the anointed that they'd allowed a tyrant to regain power.

"The monster on the throne now is worse than Macha ever was." Bard angled his dagger, tracing the blade along the shell of Talfryn's ear. Talfryn squeezed his eyes shut, holding his breath.

Eremon's rage built, the pressure drumming through his body and pounding in his head. It felt as though it might crack him open at any moment. His thoughts raced as magic and fury rattled him from the inside out.

These Beran brutes had no more right to command Rodhlan than any other commoner. His forefathers had granted territories to the clans out of kindness. Mercy. That gift was never meant to be squandered by a band of ogres playing pretend.

Perhaps his ancestors should have barred the clans from selecting their own leaders long ago. If every territory in Rodhlan were subject to Iathium, it would deter disloyalty and gross displays of treason. It would prevent beasts like Gerallt and Artur from gaining a foothold on *his* continent.

Talfryn's ragged exhale pulled Eremon from his frenzied thoughts and back to the moment.

The whole of his attention narrowed to Bard's sneer. The

prominent veins in his hand as he gripped the dagger. The visible, pounding pulse in the side of his neck.

"Let him go now, Bard," Thorne warned in a low voice, "or I'll end you right here."

"I'll do what you would not," Bard seethed, "and I will win your title from the overlord."

His eyes flicked down to Talfryn for a moment before he added, "Beran is merciless." It was an old saying that Eremon remembered seeing in the archival records, and the foremost sentiment the clan was known for.

Merciless. Perhaps, sometimes, mercilessness was appropriate. Eremon flexed his fingers, preparing to strike.

"Unhand him!"

A booming voice rang out from across the courtyard, where Artur emerged from the wide corridor, flanked by sixteen masked members of the Beravakt. Thorne kept his attention fixed on Bard, though every hair seemed to stand on end at Artur's approach. Bard faltered, dropping his dagger and releasing Talfryn, who collapsed, gasping. Eremon focused the whole of his anger on the weapon, turning it to ash.

The overlord's attention snapped to Eremon. Artur's large frame was still gaunt from his ordeal with Aila and Caitir, and there were dark shadows beneath his eyes. More so than his build or the guards that surrounded him, it was the emptiness in his gaze that made Eremon's stomach turn.

"The elusive immortal," Artur said by way of greeting. "You have forfeited your rule and forced my hand."

The Beravakt broke rank, assembling in a wide circle surrounding the men. They raised their shields in unison, assuming a defensive posture as Artur strode toward Eremon.

"How so?" Eremon challenged, widening his stance. From the corner of his eye, he could see Talfryn rise.

"You take me for a fool, boy-king," Artur barked. "Silira is still heir of Iathium. Since you saw fit to put my tormenter on the throne, Beran will take the city."

Eremon squared up to Artur, flooded with that same rush of magic he'd felt in the Dome earlier. "Set foot in my city, and it will be the last step you take."

Artur didn't flinch. But the Beravakt must have seen what Fiadh had, because several of them noticeably shrank. It was too bad he couldn't enjoy gloating about it.

"You have three days to prepare your defenses," Artur said. He jerked his chin toward the Beravakt, who snapped to attention. "Take Bard. Let Iva's son go in peace."

Four of the Beravakt, who had posted themselves behind where Bard and Talfryn stood, advanced on Bard and seized him. The young warrior struggled, and Talfryn moved back in Eremon's direction, giving them a wide berth.

"Three days?" Eremon scoffed. "That's barely enough time to shoe your horses, let alone drag an entire army from this gods-forsaken crag."

Artur's eyes narrowed. "You assume the army is waiting *here* for my order?"

Eremon tried to hide the dread that overtook him as he grappled with a terrifying realization: Iathium had been infiltrated. All Artur's warriors needed was a word from their leader, and they would assemble.

His attention shot to Thorne, who merely closed his eyes and sighed, resigned.

"You did this," Eremon growled. The accusation was laced with hatred.

When Thorne opened his amber eyes again, pain glinted in them. "I did what must be done," he said.

"Aila is being freed in a matter of days," Eremon said. "I was going to take the ring back from Lira."

Thorne's eyes widened almost imperceptibly; Eremon could see the horror in them. But it was Artur who replied:

"Then you will have Aila and Clan Beran to contend with. The time for peace is over."

A thundering rage pounded through Eremon's body. "I will decimate your army, Artur, even if I have to do it alone."

Rather than reply, Artur turned his back on Eremon. With a flick of his fingers, the remaining Beravakt snapped to attention. They followed him in the direction of the Arthmael's Hall without acknowledging Eremon again. His face burned with a humiliation he'd never been dealt in his first lifetime. In fact, no one in his mortal life had dared turn their back on him.

I am your Rí.

Eremon desperately wanted to demand that Artur and his warriors defer to him. But Clan Beran might never heed Iathium's rule unless he was willing to not only assume the throne again, but also to bring the clans to heel.

Regret slammed into him. Eremon had awakened from death bitter, resentful, and keen for a taste of freedom apart from his city. He had feared himself—feared the people's reaction to his immortality—and he had given his own authority away, over and over. Now that Iathium's throne was slipping from his grasp, he realized he truly wanted it. The horror at everything he'd willingly relinquished was nearly overpowering.

Eremon attempted to shove the thoughts from his mind, forcing his attention back onto Thorne, who had moved to Bard's captors to give quiet instruction. When Thorne stepped away, the Beravakt nudged Bard in the same direction Artur had gone.

As they moved, the red-haired warrior cast a final glance over his shoulder and said, "The little usurper is ours. And when we're done with her, we'll throw what's left in the Moravon."

The ground beneath Eremon's feet rumbled as his lips curled and an enraged cry burst from him. Thunder rumbled overhead, and Thorne froze, craning his neck to look at the sky, which had darkened to a deep, menacing violet. Eremon's black lightning split the clouds as dark magic swept out from his body unbidden, curling around Bard's limbs, his torso, his throat.

Bard's eyes went wide, and his mouth opened as if to scream just as his body exploded in a cloud of ash.

The warriors who had been holding him were next. Dark magic swept out from Bard's ashes, taking two of the four Beravakt with him. They were ash before they could even cry out for mercy.

Artur whirled, his expression a mixture of horror and rage as he registered what had happened. His guards halted several paces behind him.

"Thorne!" he bellowed. "Kill the boy!"

It took Eremon too long to realize that Artur meant Talfryn. Luckily, the order caught Thorne off his guard, and he hesitated. His amber eyes widened as he beheld Talfryn, who uttered a low, "No."

Thorne made no move in Talfryn's direction. Instead, he shook his head almost imperceptibly, as if to say, *I have no choice.*

There was no time to think, only act. Eremon angled his body between Thorne and Talfryn, letting dark magic surge into his palms. To Thorne's credit, he remained motionless.

"Don't hesitate, Talfryn," Eremon said.

"Wha—"

Eremon didn't wait for Talfryn's questions. He called on his immortal magic, shifting into a massive, winged stallion. Half a thought later, Talfryn mounted.

CHAPTER 62
AIDRYN

Rodhlan Ridge

When Lira had finally succumbed to sleep, Aidryn and Oda slipped out of the cottage, leaving Nevala to tend to her. Guilt gnawed at him, and he crossed his arms tightly as they trekked toward the tree line, passing the horses' pasture along the way. Oda kept pace at his side, offering silent companionship in the deepening darkness.

"I don't know what to do." The words burst from Aidryn, and his insides twisted as they emerged. His stomach ached and his heart pounded at the admission. "The darkness is getting worse. I fear losing her, more than anything."

"There's still hope," Oda said, though she sounded as exhausted and helpless as he felt. "As long as she lives, there's a chance we can save her."

He sighed. "Even if we do, she might never forgive me for what I've done—what I've hidden from her."

"She's intelligent," the warrior replied. "When all this is

over, I think she'll understand why you concealed certain details."

"Maybe some of them," he conceded, "but not all."

Oda paused walking and tilted her head, green eyes glinting knowingly. "About your sister and Eremon?"

Aidryn drew back in surprise. "How did—"

"An intuitive guess," she answered, holding his gaze with unnerving intensity, "like you once made about me."

Oh. Aidryn nodded, his throat suddenly dry. He felt far too exposed under Oda's scrutiny. "Thorne was the first to say it aloud. About Eremon and Caitir, I mean."

She looked out across the pasture, pulling her cloak tighter. "Lira won't be happy you encouraged a connection."

"She might hate me for it." Aidryn followed Oda's gaze to rest on Fannin, who was watching them intently, flicking his tail as though he expected a treat. He fished a sugar cube out of his pocket and offered it to the stallion. Fannin took it from his palm with a greedy huff.

"I spent my life trying and failing to protect Caitir," Aidryn said. "I watched her descend into darkness and lost all hope. I thought if there was a small possibility Eremon could bring her back, then I wouldn't stand between them."

"Maybe foolish," Oda said slowly, "but maybe wise."

"Time will tell us everything we need to know." Aidryn began moving again.

In the distance, the trees rustled as though a rush of wind had stirred them—but there was no wind tonight. The horses in the pasture snapped to attention, listening. A moment later, Aidryn could hear the same rustling again, only now, it was nearer. He strained to listen, realizing with a start that the sound was coming from overhead.

Over the din of leaves, he could make out a slow, rhythmic beating. He and Oda exchanged a glance.

"What in Berav's name..." Oda breathed.

They tilted their heads to look at the night sky just as a great silver horse—a *winged* horse—burst from over the tree-tops, soaring over the valley in a wide sweep before it landed paces away from where Aidryn and Oda stood. Now that the beast was nearer, Aidryn could see that Talfryn and Ljós sat on its back.

"Eremon," he breathed, breaking into a run, Oda at his side.

Talfryn and Ljós dismounted, looking windblown and a bit worse for wear. The winged horse transformed, and there stood Eremon, a grim look on his face. Aidryn halted before him, awestruck, while Oda headed straight for Talfryn and the healer.

Eremon grunted. "I am *not* giving free rides."

Shaking himself, Aidryn said, "I didn't ask for one."

"But you wanted to." The Rí crossed his arms with a smirk. "I could see it in your eyes."

"That's a personal attack," Aidryn muttered. He noted the exhaustion in Eremon's expression, alarm rising as he turned his attention to Talfryn. The younger man's tunic was soaked in blood, his expression stricken. "What happened?"

"Artur Beran has declared war on Iathium," Eremon answered wearily. "He knows everything."

Roaring filled Aidryn's ears, and every muscle in his body tensed. He suddenly felt on edge, as though he might crumple or break apart at any moment. If Artur had no qualms about invading the city, then everything they'd worked toward—everyone they'd attempted to protect—was now at risk.

Suddenly, he felt cold down to his bones. His mind raced, the dark truth sweeping through his body, as potent as the dark magic that had invaded his beloved Lira.

Every lie has been for nothing.

They gathered around the bonfire, which had nearly burned itself out, and stoked it back to life. Eremon, Talfryn, and Ljós filled Aidryn and Oda in on the events that had taken place over the last few days, from Vor'sca's presence in Iathium to the chaos that had unfolded at Fortress Halgeir. Aidryn thought he might be sick as the gravity of their situation swept over him.

"If Artur wants to seize the city," he said, the world reeling around him, "then he and Thorne are against the rest of the anointed and anyone allied with us."

"He's not against Lira," Talfryn said.

"Yes, he is," Aidryn retorted. "He only wants to use her for control."

"He'll discard her the moment he gets what he wants," Eremon added.

"Artur has already positioned himself as her future adversary," Ljós said in a low voice. "He has permanently barred Aidryn from re-entering Halgeir for taking an enemy hostage's life."

Aidryn winced. "Well, that stings."

Oda gave him an exasperated look. The forced humor hadn't helped him feel any better, either.

"What about me?" she asked. "Has Thorne told him about my power?"

"Your name wasn't mentioned," Ljós replied, his tone suddenly sharp, "so I assume not. When it comes to you, my son seems unable to utter a word of truth. Excuse me."

The healer stood abruptly, leaving the others by the fire as he trudged toward the keep.

Oda groaned, dropping her face into her hands. Aidryn tried to remain passive as Eremon and Talfryn gawked at her.

"Not a *word*," she gritted out just as Eremon was opening his impudent mouth to comment.

He shut it immediately, instead exchanging a loaded glance with Talfryn before both young men turned their attention to Aidryn.

"You realize what position this puts us all in, don't you?"

Aidryn said, flexing his fingers. He fought against every instinct to take Fannin and Lira and flee—take her to Iteloria himself, which was, perhaps, what he should have done all along. "Lira is Iathium's heir. Now that Artur feels his hand has been forced, she'll have to choose a side."

"She'll choose Iathium, of course," Eremon said.

"Will she?" Talfryn challenged, meeting Aidryn's eyes.

Though Aidryn desperately wanted to be wrong, the next words rushed from him like water from a broken dam. "She would have, with no question. But if Clan Beran and the city are at war, she won't be able to. Eremon, when she learns about Caitir's regency, she won't be able to ally with you."

Eremon set his jaw. "She won't have to ally with anyone. I've come to take the ring back and end the regency."

Aidryn blinked incredulously. He tried to ignore Eremon's implications, focusing on Lira instead. "You think you can come here and strip the last dregs of Lira's protection like this?"

In an angry burst, Eremon rose, baring his teeth. Aidryn wouldn't be looked down upon, so he stood as well, leveling with the immortal, whose eyes now glowed bright white.

"The Binding is protected," Eremon protested. "I only need the ring to assert my full authority—"

"Which you should have done before." Aidryn's head pounded as he cut in. "It's what Lira wanted in the first place— what we all tried to tell you!"

Fear clawed at him. For all he knew, taking the ring from Lira now could be catastrophic—not only for her, but for anyone in her path. She could erupt.

She could die, just like Eremon had.

"If it hadn't been for you and Lira, Artur would still be here, languishing in the mountains!" Eremon growled. "You two sent him back because you thought he was a better option than Thorne? You're both mad!"

A wild laugh broke from Aidryn. "Oh, this is my fault now?"

Eremon's magic flared, but Aidryn was past the point of caring. He could feel Oda and Talfryn's gazes boring into him, but he kept his attention fixed on the boy-king.

"If we had not sent Artur back to Halgeir, Thorne would have unseated my sister long ago," Aidryn continued. "We bought both of you time that we no longer have—that Lira will never get!"

Eremon blinked in surprise, drawing back a bit. "What are you *talking* about, Tarlach?"

Aidryn shook his head. "You've no idea what happened here today. She's losing her ability to control the darkness."

"We all tried to prevent this day from coming—or at least delay it for a little while," Eremon replied soberly. "But I hardly think that removing my broken ring from her will make much difference in the short term."

"We don't know that," Aidryn shot back.

"Maybe you should let Lira decide for herself," Eremon said, lips curling in contempt, "instead of making her decisions for her."

"You—" Aidryn growled.

Without thinking, he lunged for Eremon, whose eyes flashed with rage. But Oda exploded to her feet, the heel of her palm striking Aidryn's chest hard enough to wind him.

"Enough!" She was panting, and her green eyes glinted wildly.

Eremon looked as though he might try to shove past Oda to get to Aidryn himself. "I was trying not to sacrifice *anyone.*"

Regret flooded Aidryn's gut, but he shoved it down. "So was I."

"And you know as well as I that Thorne and the rest of the Beran brutes would rather see Caitir executed before her child is born," Eremon replied.

Aidryn opened his mouth to protest, but Eremon was right.

Beran *would* end his sister's bloodline—Gerallt's—before it could continue.

Oda fixed Eremon with a withering glare. "Those are my people you're talking about."

"Are they?" Eremon smirked, his expression darkening. "The moment your beloved overlord finds out about your anointing—and whatever else you and Aidryn keep skirting around, because don't think I haven't noticed—he'll banish you, too."

"You demand fealty from me when you have done nothing to earn it," Oda spat. "Don't expect me to transfer my vow to you, just because you think you deserve it. You don't."

Eremon drew back as though she had struck him across the face. Aidryn's entire body was on edge, his muscles vibrating with tension as he watched the two square off.

"I defeated death," Eremon spat. "I killed my own mother to save all of you—"

"And you forfeited your honor afterward," she shot back, "because you're too afraid to embrace what you are."

Eremon's eyes went white again. "And what am I?"

"Right now?" Oda crossed her arms, glaring up at him. "You're a monstrosity."

The enraged power that emanated from Eremon faded abruptly, leaving the unmistakable feeling of worthlessness in its wake. Oda didn't wait for his response; instead, she turned and stormed toward the keep, leaving Talfryn alone with Eremon and Aidryn.

For a moment, they all gaped after her. A long, tense beat of silence passed before Talfryn spoke. He leveled a hard, disappointed look at Eremon, then turned to Aidryn, fear etched in his youthful face. "Tell us what happened to Lira."

CHAPTER 63
CAITIR

Dome

Caitir locked herself in her chamber, as though that would deter her mother or Vor'sca from entering with *turas*. When she tried and failed to sleep, she rose again, wrapping herself in a warm dressing gown and pacing the room aimlessly. Night slowly deepened, and time crept by at an agonizing pace. Although she knew not to expect Eremon's return anytime soon, she longed for it anyway.

Once he came back with the ring, it would only be a day or two before he took the throne. Caitir anticipated and feared her pardoning by varying degrees. The questions of where she would go—how she would give her child a good life after this, or whether she would ever be able to evade Aila's grasp for good—weighed heavily on her.

She sank onto the sofa, resting her head and sighing heavily. Her lashes fluttered closed. A moment later, a soft *click* echoed, and she sat up straight, her gaze darting to the hidden panel in the wall as Eremon slipped through, looking haggard.

She'd anticipated that he would return with an air of triumph, but instead, he seemed diminished. Defeated.

Alarm coursed through her body, but she pushed it away, instead keeping her focus on Eremon. "What happened?" she asked.

His voice was weak, devoid of its usual vigor as he answered, "I failed to take the ring."

A spark of anger replaced her fear. "Why?"

"Because Lira is hanging on by a thread," he said. "It was too great a risk."

Her anger quickly faded to fear again. "Mortal gods." She and Fiadh—they had been responsible for this.

They sat on opposite ends of the small sofa, with Eremon turning to face Caitir fully. He explained that the dark magic was gaining control of Lira by the day. Though Aidryn had refused to turn the ring over to Eremon, he'd agreed to bring Lira to Iathium within two days' time.

When Eremon had finished, they sank into a deep, uneasy silence. With every moment that passed, Caitir could feel her dread mounting. She watched the timepiece on the mantel. The pendulum ticked its rhythm, growing louder and louder in her ears until she could no longer bear it.

"What else is there?" she asked, turning her attention back to Eremon. "You haven't told me the rest, have you?"

Reluctantly, he looked away and said, "No, I haven't."

Caitir leaned nearer, resting her hand on his knee. His gaze snapped up to meet hers, and he searched her face, his body leaning a fraction nearer. She was tempted to withdraw contact, but instead, she held still. "Tell me."

Eremon's eyes flicked briefly to where her hand still rested on him. When he looked up again, he said, "Clan Beran has declared war."

Now, Caitir did pull away. "*What?*"

His voice was low as he added, "Artur believes I crowned you, and he wants Iathium for Lira."

"But you didn't crown me," she protested, her throat tightening. "He can check the city records and see for himself."

"Do you really believe he'll to do that?" Eremon shook his head sadly. "The archers were working for Clan Beran before you hired them. They reported back about that first day—our ruse, remember?"

Caitir released a tremulous breath. "I see."

She remembered the way Eremon had rested the crown of blades on her head. At the time, she had relished the way she'd felt in the crimson gown, with the weight of power on her brow. But now, she would give that moment up completely if it meant that Eremon could ascend in peace.

He rose, crossing the room to the mantel, his gaze resting on the pendulum before he moved to the wall and leaned there. Closing his eyes, he rested his head against it and sighed.

Eremon's grief was leaden, and Caitir's heart sank in kind. "You should never have allied with me." Her voice trembled as she said it, but it was the truth.

"I chose to." Eremon pushed off the wall and walked toward her. "I chose to let Lira keep the ring. I chose not to take the throne. I was so concerned with how others would perceive my immortality that I cowered. I hid behind you, Caitir, and for that, I'm deeply sorry."

She rose, meeting him halfway across the room. "Why should you apologize? You protected me when no one else could have. The things I've done—they're unforgivable." On impulse, she reached out to grasp his hand. "You might have been working quietly, but you've already done so much good for the people. They're beginning to learn their power. The pieces are in place to help them rise to their full potential."

Eremon glanced down at as though he wasn't sure how to respond, and her heart sank when he held still. She pulled her hand from his, but a moment later, he caught it again and gave it a gentle squeeze.

"I failed Lira when she needed me, and I'll never forgive myself for it." he said with a dull, quiet laugh. "I've led Iathium to ruin at Clan Beran's hands." He averted his gaze, the corners of his mouth tugging downward.

"No. Look at me." Caitir shook her head, reaching up to touch his cheek. She guided his face back so she could meet his eyes. "There will be a way to stop it. Artur doesn't want war. He's only trying to intimidate you."

"He has already infiltrated the city." Eremon closed his eyes. "And I killed three of his warriors, in his territory. One of them attempted to kill Talfryn, and I couldn't let that happen."

Caitir's heart squeezed. She remembered the curly-haired boy who had so often trailed after her and Lira on their childhood jaunts. In the autumn, she had taunted him over the loss of his arm. If she ever saw him again—and if she ever came face-to-face with Lira—she would try to make amends.

"That is my point," she pressed. "You didn't go into Halgeir intent on wreaking havoc, but you defended a friend when you saw the need."

"It doesn't matter. To everyone else, I'm the enemy—a monstrosity." He gave her a wan smile. "I suppose your prediction was true, after all."

Caitir frowned. "You speak of yourself as though you've tortured innocents, plundered magic, and stolen a city—like you're the one who needs redeeming." She shook her head with a soft laugh, suddenly in awe of their proximity. "I was always wasted effort, Eremon. But *you*..."

"Nothing about you is a waste, Caitir," Eremon replied, his silver gaze suddenly burning through her. "*Nothing*."

He tightened his fingers around hers, reaching up to brush her cheek with gentle fingers. Her breath caught, and her eyelids fluttered closed at the contact. She wanted to stand on her tiptoes and bring her lips to his, but she remained still and held her breath, savoring his touch.

"Now *you* look at me," he whispered, withdrawing his hand.

Reluctantly, she opened her eyes—and she could have drowned in the tenderness of his expression.

"You are magnificent." He grasped both of her hands in his own, his gaze as intense as the current of electricity that rippled between them. "You're brilliant and bold, and you have a mind for leadership that I never saw in you before. Every day that we've been together, I have hated myself for ignoring you all those years. You would have made a wonderful Raní, if I'd given you the chance."

"To be fair, I didn't know myself then," she answered, her heart pounding erratically. "I'm not sure how well I know myself now, or if I even want to."

"Well, I know you," Eremon whispered, stroking her cheek, "and I want to know you better."

He tipped her chin with his forefinger, and then he was kissing her, slow and deep, his lips lingering over hers as he cradled her face in his hands. She whimpered against his mouth, gripping his tunic and pulling his body flush against hers. He slipped an arm around her waist, holding her there. Reaching up with one hand, she trailed her fingertips up his jawline, then brushed a soft strand of hair away from his face as she opened her mouth to him.

The kiss was warm and soft, and they moved together with deliberate slowness. Caitir poured every bit of her desire into him, hoping he might somehow grasp the depth of what she felt. She wasn't sure she understood the immensity of it herself. He had sacrificed for her, shown her kindness. Treated her as though she meant something to him.

Eremon cupped the back of her neck, pulling away to kiss the corners of her mouth before angling his head and claiming her lips again. They deepened the kiss further, keeping their movements unhurried, restrained, as though equally afraid of frightening one another.

The weight of what might have been crashed down on Caitir—who she and Eremon could have become, had their world not shattered so irreparably. Him, a young and beloved ruler, vibrant and full of life. Her, a skilled courtier and suitable love match for him—his favorite above all others. They might have slipped away to this very room, moonlight pouring through the windows. Might have savored one another like this, carefree and drunk on mead and pleasure.

But there was nothing carefree about what was happening, and no mead to soften the harsh edge of reality that scraped against her euphoria. They weren't simply an infatuated couple, sneaking away for a moment of secret bliss. This closeness could cost Eremon everything if Caitir allowed it to continue.

So she broke the kiss with a gentle sigh. Eremon dipped toward her again, intent on continuing what they'd begun. But she pressed a palm to his cheek and shook her head. He pulled back, confusion and uncertainty clouding his features.

"What is it?" he whispered, skimming his fingertips over her arm, trailing them up her shoulder.

"They'll call you a traitor for this," she replied in a low voice.

He studied her face and shrugged a shoulder. "They're already thinking it."

Caitir shivered at his touch, looping her hands around the back of his neck and lacing her fingers together. His skin was warm. This near, she caught his subtle scent—cinnamon and vanilla, and something more. The smell of earth and lightning after a summer storm. She wanted to disappear into it.

Eremon stared at her unabashedly. As she studied his face, her desire went to war against her better judgment. He reached for her chin again, brushing a thumb over her bottom lip.

"We both know this is a terrible idea," she said, her words barely audible.

That arrogant expression lit his face. "Is that so?"

Caitir wanted to argue with him, but he was drifting nearer, and now might be her last chance. She stood up on her toes and kissed him. On a sharp intake of breath, Eremon wrapped his arms around her again, sliding his fingers into the loosely bound hair at her nape. Beneath his touch, she surrendered to every bit of desire she'd kept locked away. Every missed opportunity, every disappointment, every fear dissipated as she melted into him.

For a brief moment, she considered denying herself again. Perhaps it would have been better to keep her distance, but she had already lived that misery. If Eremon wanted her right now, then she wouldn't hesitate again.

He held her close, brushing his lips over hers until they were both breathless. Already, she knew that his kisses would never be enough—that she would always want more. She arched against him, pressing herself closer, gently catching his bottom lip between her teeth.

Eremon groaned, bending down to scoop her up. He carried her across the room to the bed, never breaking their kiss as he climbed up beside her, trailing his fingers down the side of her throat, then over her shoulder. His hand came to rest on her waist, and he gazed at her, heavy-lidded, his lips swollen from their kisses.

"When did you stop hating me?" she whispered, pressing her palm to his cheek.

"I never hated you," he answered, bracing his body above hers as she rolled onto her back. He leaned down to kiss her jaw, then trailed kisses down her neck. She tilted her head back, a little gasp escaping her at the sensation. "And don't argue with me, because I know you want to," he murmured against her collarbone.

Caitir threaded her fingers through his hair, coaxing him up to her mouth again. She slid her palm down over his shoulder, tracing the shape of the lean muscle beneath his tunic. "Don't expect that to change," she said with a soft laugh.

He pulled back and tilted his head, grinning mischievously. "I would never."

They traded kisses until the moon was high outside the tall tower windows. Eremon kissed her as though he'd never experienced the sensation, and she absorbed every moment of contact, reveling in the newness of how it felt to be loved.

Love. She was afraid to say it aloud, but... was that was this was? Did he love her?

Eremon silenced her thoughts, drawing her into a kiss that made her go molten. Heat rushed through her, and she returned the kiss with equal fervor, pressing herself so close to him that there was no space left.

"I want weeks of this," Eremon said between kisses. "Months. Years."

"I can barely tolerate your presence for an entire day." She stared at him unabashedly, because finally, she was determined not to resist this. "You make bold assumptions about years."

Eremon brushed the tip of his nose against hers. "I have a general bad habit of making bold assumptions." He placed a flutter of kisses along her jawline, pausing to nip at her earlobe and whisper, "I also have ways of making my presence much more tolerable for you."

"Another bold assumption," she said, her breath catching in her throat. "Prove it."

CHAPTER 64
EREMON

Dome

Eremon nearly lost himself as he kissed Caitir again. She whimpered, gripping the back of his neck as she pressed herself closer. In the space of a few breaths, their pace transformed from languid and indulgent to heated and demanding.

He thought of the first time they'd kissed in the archive and how desperately he had wanted this. His thoughts snagged on the way she had frozen in his arms that day, as though fearful or doubtful of what might happen next. But when he'd pressed her for answers, she had refused to open up. It seemed that she would have preferred to disappear into him instead. It was that reluctance—her urging for him to *take* from her—that had made him halt.

At the time, he had walked away believing that she didn't trust him; after all, she'd refused to tell him what she was thinking. The truth was, it seemed that *taking* was largely what she had experienced from men. Perhaps it was the only warped picture of intimacy she'd ever known. That realization dropped into his stomach, a weight of grief that made him draw back enough to look into her pale eyes.

"I want you to guide me," he said, cupping her cheek. "Show me what you want this to be."

Caitir blinked up at him, her eyes hazy, expression open and curious. "I thought—" Her cheeks reddened, and she looked away, suddenly bashful. "I thought perhaps you might show me."

As the harsh truth of her implication sank in, the world gave way beneath him. The truth was, he had never been with a woman who had suffered under a man's unchecked power the way Caitir had. The thought of hurting her or otherwise adding to her suffering horrified him—and he knew he already had. Last time, he'd gone about this all wrong. Demanding that she tell him what had vexed her, then turning his back on her when she'd clearly needed comfort, had been a terrible way to handle himself.

He dipped his head and pressed a kiss to the side of her neck, just beneath her ear, before propping on his elbow at her side.

"What about this?" he began slowly as she shifted to look up at him. "I will be happy to share pleasure with you. But there's something I want in return—and please, hear me out."

Her expression grew somber. "You have my attention."

"I think I would like to know... no." Eremon chewed the inside of his cheek, working out how to put it into words. He shut his mouth for a moment, then began again. "What would *you* like me to know in this moment?"

Caitir brow crinkled, and she drew back slightly as if she wasn't sure how to respond. Quickly, he added, "I only ask because the last time we kissed, I demanded answers from you that I had no right to."

"Hmm." She held eye contact with him and reached for his hand. "I want you to understand that I have a flood of terrible memories locked away. Sometimes—the worst times—they trickle through and invade my thoughts. I don't think I will ever want to speak of them."

He gave her a small shrug. "You never have to."

Caitir reached for the top button of his tunic, then hesitated, doubt filling her pale gaze. "May I? I want to see your scars again."

Eremon swallowed hard. His throat was suddenly dry, and the answer came out on a rasp. "Yes."

She worked with deft fingers, undoing the short row of small buttons in moments before peeling the fabric back to reveal the veins of silver on his skin. With a shaky breath, she drew back to look at him, then pressed a palm to the largest scar in the center of his chest.

The feeling of her skin against his sent a wracking shudder through his body, and he coaxed her nearer, guiding her to rest in his arms, her palm never leaving his skin. He lay back on the pile of soft pillows, pulling her along with him. She sighed contentedly, her fingertips trailing over skin and scars.

"I also want you to understand," she ventured in a soft voice, burrowing down to lie on his shoulder, "that even though I trust you, I'm still frightened. I want this, but I fear it, too."

Her admission weighed on his entire being. He brushed a strand of hair away from her forehead and held her tighter. "Then I'll do everything I can to help you feel safe."

CHAPTER 65

CAITIR

Dome

Safe.

The word washed over Caitir in a maddening rush. She drew away from Eremon long enough to sit up beside him on the plush mattress. As she'd expected, a jumbled mess of emotions crossed his face—confusion and disappointment, followed by a flash of apprehension—until she pushed him onto his back and braced herself over him, brushing a soft kiss to his mouth. Then, he understood.

Eremon's hand flew to her hip, his fingers tightening against the fabric of her dressing gown. As Caitir deepened the kiss, he matched her intensity, as though content to follow her lead. After a lingering moment, he brushed her cheek with his other hand and gently broke away.

"Are you sure?" His silver eyes roved over her face, his expression earnest.

"Yes," she answered on a breath.

Caitir rose to her knees but remained at his side. Eremon reached for her, resting a palm on her thigh, silent and contemplative. His skin felt hot against the thin fabric of her night-gown. With trembling hands, she slipped off the warm dressing gown she'd layered over it, tossing it over the side of the bed as she released a nervous breath. For a moment, the room's chill pebbled her skin—until Eremon rose to meet her, catching her mouth in a brief kiss before drawing the soft blanket around her shoulders and cocooning her in it. He pulled her back down to share his warmth, bringing her body flush against his.

With hushed whispers and sighs, they explored one another. Any tension and timidity Caitir had felt when they'd begun melted away at his touch, her muscles gradually relaxing and warming beneath his hands. She let him undo the bindings in her hair and run his fingers through the loose strands. He was devastatingly gentle as he ran his palms over the curve of her hip, the soft swell of her belly.

She relished traversing the thin, silver scars that covered his pale skin. The scarring spread from the center of his chest to his shoulders and upper thighs, where it gradually lightened. His arms, hands, legs, and feet were smooth and unmarred, like his neck and his face.

"You're beautiful," she breathed.

Eremon dipped his head with a soft laugh. "Terrifyingly so." His mouth tugged into a smile at the mention of their autumn encounter outside the crypt. How far they had come since then.

The hours passed into afternoon in a blissfully slow haze. Eremon made love to Caitir in attentive silence, so wholly focused on her comfort and pleasure that she could scarcely believe any of it was real. He encouraged her to lead him—to show him what she desired. When she faltered, he dreamt up ideas to share, then let her choose which path she wanted to follow. And when a painful surge of memory threatened to numb her, he patiently held her through it, then gently guided her back into the present.

When it was over, there was an expression of awe on his

face that made Caitir's heart feel so full, it might have burst. Every nerve in her body tingled, a blush rising to her cheeks at the sheer intimacy of it all.

She wanted more of this. More of him.

"How do you feel?" he whispered, resting his forehead against hers.

Perfect. Content. Loved.

The irrational urge to laugh overtook her at the thought— and before she could answer him properly. She burst into a fit of uncontrollable giggles, throwing an arm across her face.

"Why are you hiding?" he asked, his voice rich with amusement. "Let me see you laugh."

She peeked out from behind her arm, and he was smiling broadly. Eremon grasped her fingers and coaxed her arm down, never taking his eyes off her face. He watched her expectantly as she caught her breath and considered how to answer.

"I feel..."

The words she wanted to say snagged in her throat. Her joy gave way to a sharp prickle of tears, and she found herself blinking them away furiously. The stark contrast between past and present made her want to weep. But more than that, she wanted to stay here in her body, tangled in Eremon's arms. Not tangled in the scars of her past, which would only pull her away from this moment. Away from him.

She traced the shape of his ear with her fingertip. "I didn't know it could be this way," she finally admitted, her voice breaking on the raw truth of it.

As the words left her lips, an unwelcome reality slammed against her heart. It was unfair that she had been forced to live a life devoid of real joy—unfair that she'd never been able to imagine anything like this for herself. Unfair that even though he held her in his arms as though he cherished her, Eremon would never truly be hers.

In a few short days, he would try again to take the throne. If all went according to plan, he would have a city to lead, and Caitir would have a child to raise alone—if she was allowed to live, and if there was a way to evade her mother's grasp in the weeks and months ahead. Depending on Eremon's allies and how the numerous conflicts in Rodhlan and Iteloria played out, he might not have as much sway over her fate as they'd believed he would.

Regardless of the political outcome, he was immortal, and she was not. That was a fact she would never be able to rationalize away, no matter how much she wished to ignore it.

Rather than grappling with her thoughts, she accepted them. They were all true, but Eremon had also chosen to be here with her now. And today might be the only chance she would ever have to share this with him.

He must have read the distress in her expression, because he tilted his head, his brow furrowing in confusion. "What are you thinking?"

She squeezed her eyes shut for a moment, gathering her thoughts. "I'm thinking..." she began, "that I wish this would never end, but I know it has to."

Eremon grew silent, and he tightened his hold on her, stroking a gentle hand over her hair. She pulled him in for another kiss. Whatever the coming days brought with them, she didn't have to leave this moment yet. She could choose to make the most of it—both for what it was now, and what it would mean to her forever.

"It doesn't have to end," he finally whispered.

She didn't have the heart to call him a liar.

CHAPTER 66
AIDRYN

Rodhlan Ridge

A gray dawn was approaching, and Aidryn still hadn't gathered the nerve to return to Skelly's cottage. Volleying the Rí's incessant maneuvering for the ring had exhausted him, and he didn't want to risk waking Lira and being pressed for details. More than that, he feared admitting that he'd made this decision on Lira's behalf—even though it had been the right one.

When Eremon had not been able to convince Aidryn to retrieve the ring, he'd changed tactics, attempting to appeal to Aidryn's magic. It hadn't worked.

"The ring is a key, you know," he'd said, desperation glinting in his eyes. "If you'd rather not broach the topic directly with Lira, your magic will call it to you through the Binding."

Ever the schemer, Aidryn had thought, but he didn't say it aloud. He had rarely thought about the ring serving as a key, and he'd never considered that it might have been another reason why Eremon had chosen to forge the Binding. The thought of being coerced into wielding his power behind Lira's back enraged him.

"Taking the ring by any method is still *taking* it, Eremon," Aidryn had said with a sigh. "I said no, and I meant it."

After Eremon had finally departed the valley, Aidryn, Oda, and Talfryn had spent several tense hours debating what should happen next. They'd agreed that meeting Thorne in Iathium with Lira in tow would give them the best chance at negotiating some semblance of peace. Aidryn hoped that Ljós would accompany them for Lira's sake, but he doubted the healer would agree.

Aidryn was apprehensive about returning Lira to the Dome. Taking her to Eremon would mean revealing the full details of his arrangement with Caitir—and Artur's intentions. But Lira's presence in the city might also help to quell the Overlord's rage, at least long enough to delay bloodshed.

Surely, Eremon could survive two more days without the ring in hand. He had already forfeited his rule for much longer than that.

Dew had gathered on the grass, and the toes of Aidryn's boots were wet as he strode slowly along the fence line, watching the horses stir lazily. Fannin ambled up to the gate, tossing his white mane and blinking his big, black eyes as though he had been deprived of attention for months. Aidryn chuckled and stroked the gray stallion's velvety gray nose, whispering to him in low tones.

"You want to tell me what happened here last night?"

Aidryn nearly leapt from his skin at the sound of Terovi's voice. He swore under his breath as the older man sidled up to him, eyeing Fannin from head to hooves.

"I don't know what you mean," Aidryn said coolly.

Terovi snatched a fistful of Aidryn's tunic, yanking him forward so hard that his feet nearly left the ground. "Don't lie to me, boy. I saw the Rí—he was here. He's *been* coming here."

Aidryn's heart pounded. He grabbed Terovi's hand, locking the joint of his thumb and pressing down hard. That did the trick; the older man let go with a hiss of pain.

"Keep your hands off me," Aidryn growled. He took three steps back, holding his palms out to warn Terovi off. "You had no business eavesdropping."

Terovi snorted. "I've been waiting to see if you'd ever bother to tell the adviser any of this. Turns out you're just as stupid as I always said you were—the lot of you. Keepin' secrets from your elders and each other when the continent is on the brink."

"And what have you done to help?" Aidryn retorted sharply. "You have plenty of time to spy on us but nothing of value to offer. Besides, you said this fight wasn't yours."

"It isn't," he said, "but if you're going to own it, then you need all the help you can get. I have nothing to offer, but Eiren does."

Gooseflesh covered Aidryn's body at the mention of the adviser. "Like what?"

Terovi made a show of crossing his arms and shrugging before he gave Aidryn a slow, exasperated blink. "You've never bothered to ask her what she knows about dark magic or immortals." He let a long beat pass before he added, "Or that Binding spell you think you've been hiding all this time."

CHAPTER 67
LIRA

Rodhlan Ridge

Lira snapped awake, rolling over to find Aidryn's side of the bed still neatly made and his pillow fluffed. She sat up, blinking blearily, and listened for any sign of him in the quiet cottage. Moving to the edge of the bed, she planted her bare feet on the floor, rose, and padded into the kitchen, shivering.

The fire had burned itself out overnight, so she added wood to the hearth, her skin pebbling in the cold. It wasn't like Aidryn to stay away all night—and certainly not to let the cottage freeze like this. She worried her bottom lip, the soft skin chapped from the frigid air, and stoked a new fire.

Silira.

Lira startled at the sound of the voice, her teeth clamping down hard on her lip. The metallic taste of blood filled her mouth.

"Silence," she hissed, willing the voice—whoever it was—to disappear.

No matter how often it spoke and no matter how well it

seemed to understand her, she still felt unnerved by its presence. There had been no time or opportunity to reply to it before, but here in this silent home, she felt compelled to. She pressed the urge down, turning her attention back to the hearth.

Wait until you learn what has happened, the voice taunted, so loud it drowned out the merry, crackling fire and every other thought in her mind. Lira stilled, listening. The hairs on her arms rose as it continued. *Your time is at hand.*

"Who are you?" she whispered, her gaze darting to the door, the window. There was still no sign of Aidryn outside. "Why are you speaking to me?"

If Aidryn could see her speaking to a disembodied voice, he would think she'd gone mad. Still, she wished that she had told him about it before. Perhaps he might have been able to help drive it out of her mind.

Tsk, it scolded. *You cannot simply drive me out. I am a part of you now.*

Fear engulfed her at the thought of somehow being one with this entity. There was no reason for her to trust the voice. After all, it had led her into danger. Compelled her to discharge magic that had burned away a swath of her ancestral forest.

Lira's thoughts, suddenly hazy, dragged her back to that moment in the woods, when Oda's power had finally broken free and drowned the wildfire. The warrior believed Rhona had helped her. Was it possible the mortal goddess was guiding Lira now?

"Are you Rhona?" she blurted, her grip tightening on the iron poker she held. "Tell me. I'll not play games any longer."

I am everywhere, it answered, *in the very fabric of Rodhlan itself.*

From what little Lira had managed to read, cryptic non-answers seemed to be common fare for deities. But even if she stopped asking questions now, the voice would still be with her, as it had been these past weeks. It couldn't hurt to press for more.

"When you say my time is at hand..." Lira ventured, "what do you mean?"

Your time to ascend. To claim Iathium's throne as your own.

She laughed bitterly. "That is not my destiny. It's Eremon's, and I will help him fulfill it."

Ah, but if you knew everything, would you still want to? Would he be worthy of it?

Lira stilled, moving to the sturdy worktable and drumming her fingertips on its surface. She sank slowly to the bench, staring into the fire. Did Rhona know everything that Aidryn and the others had hidden from her? Was this her chance to learn it for herself without having to beg—only to be denied by the people she loved most?

She swallowed hard, her heart pounding as she wrestled with the implications. Finally, she rasped, "Tell me what you know."

Telling you everything now is not in your best interest. But here is what I will reveal: Eremon of Iathium was here before dawn, asking for his ring to be returned.

Lira's fingers flew to the ancient band, and she twisted it nervously. She fought against the disappointment that filled her at yet another denial. "And?"

And your husband refused him.

Her head snapped around to look out the window again, her heart pounding so hard that its beating filled her ears. Why would Aidryn have said no? This was what they'd wanted—what Lira had begged Eremon to do. If he had declared himself ready to take the throne again, Aidryn should not have hesitated.

She didn't realize she'd said it aloud until Rhona—*was* this Rhona?—replied.

No, indeed. He should not have.

Bile rose in Lira's throat. If her stomach had not been empty, she might have vomited. Her breaths came in shallow pants, and she found it increasingly difficult to draw in enough air. When the voice spoke again, her consciousness homed in on it, narrowing until there was nothing left but the words that reverberated through her mind and chilled her to the core.

I want you to ask yourself why.

CHAPTER 68
AIDRYN

Rodhlan Ridge

Aidryn felt lightheaded as he and Terovi moved purposefully toward the shelters his namesake clan had erected in the valley. Lira would be awake soon, if she wasn't already. He hated himself for leaving her alone all night. Hated even more that Terovi had overheard his row with Eremon and Oda.

Before heading for Clan Tarlach's remaining shelters, Aidryn had gone to Ljós. The healer had risen from a troubled sleep before dawn. Aidryn had hoped to convince him to travel to Iathium as Lira's healer, but Ljós had refused.

"It's better that I remain here for now," Ljós said, "far from my son and the overlord. If Eremon had ascended as he should have, I would go with you in a moment. But my presence will endanger Thorne and Oda, and I cannot in good conscience be part of that."

"But Lira needs you," Aidryn had pressed. "*I* need you. We don't know what will happen once we've removed the ring."

Ljós had shaken his head, looking sorrowful as he

answered. "There is nothing more I can do. It won't be long until the ring's protection is completely void, regardless. After that, I fear it's only a matter of time before the darkness takes her."

"It is *not*," Aidryn had growled, surging forward to snatch the lapels of Ljós's tunic in his fist. Rather than reacting, Ljós had calmly held his gaze until Aidryn had relented and let him go, his fingertips biting from the sudden release of pressure. "There will be another way."

But Ljós had closed his eyes for a moment, as though debating whether to reply at all. Finally, he'd said, "You must protect your own magic now, before it's too late."

Terovi had stood back scowling, arms crossed, grumbling about wasting time. When Aidryn had finally stormed away from the keep and toward Clan Tarlach's tents, Terovi had barked, "I told you your well had run dry," then followed at the younger man's heels.

Inwardly, Aidryn fumed as he pushed forward, his jaw set. Everyone else—except perhaps Terovi, now that he thought of it—seemed to have given up hope for Lira, one by one. But Aidryn couldn't give up. He refused. There had to be another answer, and he was determined to find it.

If he had not been so afraid of exposing himself to Clan Tarlach's ire before, he might have sought help from their adviser sooner. All this time, he could have been honest with Eiren and sought her counsel. Instead, he had repeated the same pattern over and over, expecting a different outcome.

He had spent so much of his life desperate to be all things to all people. Trying and failing to protect those he loved most, while striving to keep the peace—and suppressing his own instincts and better judgment in the process. His deep craving for acceptance, for love, had drowned out his ability to move swiftly and decisively, for better or worse.

Aidryn burst into the adviser's tent without pretense. Eiren was sitting cross-legged on the thick mat that covered the ground, as though she'd been waiting for him. Her long silver hair was unbound. It tumbled over her shoulders, complementing the dull russet wool of her robes.

Eiren straightened, taking in Aidryn's form and Terovi standing behind him. "What's happened?"

"I have something to confess," Aidryn blurted, trying to catch his breath.

Eiren and Terovi exchanged a loaded glance. "Leave us, Terovi," she ordered.

The older man scowled at Aidryn, who half expected him to snarl. Instead, Terovi gave the adviser a nod of acknowledgement before brushing past Aidryn, then ducking back out of the tent.

Eiren patted the mat beside her, a concerned glint in her eyes. "Come. Join me."

Hesitantly, Aidryn moved toward the middle of the tent and lowered himself to sit beside her. His entire body quivered, the morning's frigid air suddenly sinking deep into his bones. Eiren reached for a folded blanket that sat on the cushion next to her and opened it in a sweeping gesture, then offered it to him. Gratefully, he took it, wrapping the deep brown fabric around his shoulders and praying that the chattering of his teeth, both from the cold and from his own terror, would ease.

"I—I don't know where to start," Aidryn stammered. He couldn't help second-guessing his snap decision to come here. Perhaps this had been a bad idea.

"Tell me," Eiren urged gently, "and I will advise you."

Aidryn began with the Binding, confessing to the magical connection forged between himself and Lira. The adviser listened in contemplative silence. Words poured from Aidryn as he wove the tale—everything that had happened since Lira had been named Defender of Histories, up until last night's dispute with Eremon.

When he'd finally finished speaking, he felt wrung out and exhausted. "I know it's probably impossible," he said, fully aware of the desperation that tinged his voice, "but if there's another way to help Lira, I'll do anything."

Eiren's gaze was shrewd as she sized him up. "Do you really mean that?"

Aidryn tried to ignore the pang in his chest. The way Eiren was looking at him—piteous yet knowing—told him there would be some sacrifice involved if he said yes. But he was tired of being afraid. Tired of trying and failing to spread himself thin, to protect everyone in his path. All he could do was take the next step presented to him in the moment.

Realization washed over him as the world shifted, then refocused. Over the past weeks, he had felt guilty for helping Caitir and Eremon with their scheme. For opposing Clan Beran and making an enemy of them. For holding Lira at arm's length while he'd steadily grown fearful of her dark magic.

Aidryn had always returned to Lira as his focal point. He always would.

He released a steadying breath and held Eiren's stare. "I do mean it."

Eiren laced her slender fingers together. "You have your mother's spirit. Did anyone ever tell you how she came to share my name?"

What did this have to do with her counsel? Aidryn tried to ignore the swell of disappointment that rose with her words. "No, they didn't."

"Your grandfather, Pàlnos, was a dear friend of mine when we were young," Eiren explained with a tentative smile. "When your mother was born anointed, he wanted to bring her back to the assembly. We hadn't welcomed an anointed to our midst in over a century, you see. But I urged him to raise her in Iathium instead.

"He believed she should grow up among the stallions. We

had a bitter argument, and I banished his family from Va'hesk. But one quarrel does not undo a lifetime of memories. He eventually came to understand my reason."

Aidryn wrinkled his brow. "And what was that?"

"That Clan Tarlach can't remain a remnant forever. In time, your mother met a handsome young sentry named Emyr who would later become ambassador to Iteloria. She embraced the influence she might one day have as both a political figure and Tarlach's Anointed, so she pursued a seat on Corlan's council. Sadly, it never materialized.

"Before you were born, she told me that she dreamed of leading a new era of magic-wielders to power. She was of the same mind as Eremon—the same mind as you. Your father would have come to support her efforts, had she not died so young."

"And if Aila had not enslaved him," Aidryn added bitterly.

He couldn't ignore the pang of longing that rushed through him at the thought of his birth mother. As long as he'd known of her, he had managed to ignore his own curiosity, because knowing more about his anointed mother would have made little difference to his circumstances. But somehow, speaking with the adviser had opened the fissure in his heart that he'd been so adept at keeping sealed.

"Grief can make us wiser, but it can also deceive us," Eiren said, a note of censure in her tone. "Your father was grieving, and so he was easily deceived."

Something about Eiren's story didn't add up. Why was she so bent on telling him about his mother? What did that accomplish, as far as Lira was concerned?

"With the utmost respect, Adviser Eiren," he said, resting his elbow on his knee, "I want to know more about my mother, but right now, I need to help Lira more. As I said: I'll do anything."

"You mean you'll join the assembly and take your part in leading the clan," Eiren said, a knowing glint in her eyes.

"*Yes.*" He was growing more agitated by the minute. Lira would have awakened alone in the cottage—he should have already been back.

Eiren raised her chin. "You believe you must trade yourself to the clan in some sort of obligatory indenture in exchange for my help."

"As I said," he gritted out. "Anything."

"Your lack of creativity is disappointing," Eiren said with a sigh. "I embrace you as our anointed whether or not you choose to sit on the assembly. You were not raised among Clan Tarlach—how are we to bind you to our settlement when you can do so much more for Rodhlan?"

Aidryn reeled back as though she'd struck him. A slow smile spread across Eiren's lips as she continued.

"As *I* said: You have your mother's spirit. Like you, she was our anointed. She also never lived at Va'hesk because she was following her greater purpose, just as you are now. Do you understand?"

Aidryn studied her. His jaw was so tense that his head had begun to ache. "I thought service to the clan was what you wanted."

"Service to the clan would be an easy trade, but it's no sacrifice," Eiren answered. "I offer my knowledge to you freely, expecting nothing for myself in return."

Aidryn's heart stuttered. "So there *is* a way to help Lira?"

"A possibility—a dangerous one," said the adviser. "You won't come out unscathed, and she may not, either. Therein lies your sacrifice."

"Any risk is worth it," he pressed.

"Is it? So you understand," Eiren said slowly, "if both of you live, there may be irreparable damage—not only to your bodies, but your minds and spirits, too. When it's over, both of you could be forever altered. You must be prepared to accept that possibility."

Aidryn began to tremble. The thought of doing harm to Lira was so overwhelming that for a moment, he considered fleeing. But where would that leave them? Lira was already altered by the spread of the darkness. Though the dark magic hadn't driven Aidryn away entirely, it had made his heart ache with a ferocity he hadn't been able to put into words. He missed the studious, prideful, witty girl he'd fallen in love with. If he could somehow keep her from descending further into the dark, then he would try—even if that meant things might never go back to the way they had been before.

So, he took a deep breath and said, "I can't just let the darkness kill her. She won't die at the mercy of my fears."

Eiren reached for his hand. There was a depth of sorrow in her eyes that was so visceral, he held his breath against it. His muscles tensed all over, and he thought he might be ill before she finally spoke again.

Gently, Eiren squeezed his fingers. "Listen well."

CHAPTER 69
LIRA

Rodhlan Ridge

L ira tightened the straps on Fannin's saddle, whispering to the stallion as she worked. He responded with a friendly huff, as though entirely out of tune with her roiling emotions. Every so often, she glanced out the stable's small window in search of Aidryn, who had yet to return to the cottage.

She had been shaking since she'd realized the truth, which had significantly slowed her progress. Her mind had been a tangle of rage, disbelief, and reluctant acceptance when the pieces had finally come together. When she'd calmed herself enough to bridle Fannin, she gently slipped the bit into his mouth and tightened the buckles until the leather was a snug fit.

Before she led the stallion into the sunlight, she did a final check of her belongings. She had managed to fit a few of Skelly's books into a large leather satchel Eiren Tarlach had given to Aidryn. Her heirlooms hung in the pouch at her waist, and in her own satchel, she'd stashed a bit of bread, cheese, and dried meat for the journey. She'd filled a drinking horn with fresh water and tied it alongside the satchel at her waist.

Her fingers flew along the fastenings of her cloak, checking that it was secure. Then, she pushed open the stable door. She and Fannin stepped into the warm, midmorning sun—such a stark contrast to the freezing air. The valley was still empty, as though its dwellers had seen fit to sleep in.

Lira gripped Fannin's saddle, placed one boot in the stirrup, and swung herself astride his broad back. He whinnied, low and content, eager to ride at full speed again. She stroked his mane, then patted his warm, velvety neck.

"Come on, old boy," she whispered. "Let's take the throne."

CHAPTER 70
AIDRYN

Rodhlan Ridge

W hen Aidryn returned to Skelly's cottage, Lira was gone.

She'd left no note, and the kitchen was in disarray. A quick check of the bedchamber told him that her belongings were also gone, and for a moment, he wondered whether she had been taken. Heart pounding, he burst out the front door, intent on checking the keep. But a distressed Talfryn rounded the corner of the cottage as he emerged, nearly colliding with Aidryn in the process.

"Where is she?" Aidryn demanded.

"Delory Tarlach saw her leave the valley," Talfryn answered, his expression grim. "She took Fannin."

"How long ago?"

"Two hours, at least," Talfryn said. "I asked Delory why she waited so long to tell anyone, but she just looked at me like I'd grown another nose."

Aidryn's stomach dropped. Lira would be in Acton's Cove by now. "Mortal gods."

He rounded in the direction of the stable, where sure enough, Fannin's tack was gone. His thoughts raced, his breath coming in ragged huffs.

"Why would she leave?" he asked as Talfryn stepped just inside the doorway.

"I don't know," he said. "Why would she have wandered into the forest and tried to raze it to the ground?"

"She didn't do that of her own volition," Aidryn answered slowly. "She was prompted."

After the wildfire, Lira had told him she'd had a vision— not a witnessing. He'd been so overcome by panic at the time that he hadn't followed the thought to its proper conclusion. This vision had originated from outside of Lira's power, and he'd mistakenly believed it was coming from the dark magic. But if Vor'sca had the pendant, then she had likely been manipulating Lira's power the entire time.

"You think someone else is controlling her?" Talfryn asked, eyes widening in disbelief.

"Not controlling; she would never stand for that," Aidryn answered, seizing Edan's saddle from its stand and snatching a bridle from the peg by the door. "Persuading."

Vor'sca was immortal, which meant she had patience beyond what Aidryn, Lira, or even Eremon could fathom. She would have possessed the ability to weaken Lira, one step at a time, content to work slowly. Having an accomplice this powerful must have thrilled Aila, who had always been incredibly patient herself.

Still, Aidryn couldn't fathom what might have been so convincing to Lira that she would leave the valley behind— leave *him* behind—without so much as a word. Fannin was *Aidryn's* horse. Though he'd never minded sharing him with Lira, her silent claiming of the gray stallion set Aidryn on edge.

"Something is deeply wrong with all of this," Talfryn said softly, echoing Aidryn's raging thoughts.

Aidryn didn't reply. He worked feverishly to saddle Edan while Talfryn kept him occupied with soft murmurs and pats. The black stallion nipped at the younger man's hand and stamped nervously, as though fully aware something was amiss.

Wordlessly, Talfryn handed Aidryn the reins. They emerged from the stable to find Oda and Ljós standing just outside, their expressions stricken. Aidryn's distress must have shown on his face, because Oda didn't hesitate before she launched herself at him, hugging him tightly. His knees nearly buckled as he leaned into his friend's embrace.

"You go," she said against his chest, giving him a tight squeeze. "Talfryn and I will follow on Senga."

"I'm riding toward Iathium," Aidryn said, drawing back to rest a hand on the warrior's shoulder. "I'll need to use Lira's magic to see where she's going until I can catch up. No matter what happens, I want you and Talfryn in the city before Beran strikes. I'll need you to negotiate with Thorne if Lira and I can't be there."

Oda blinked rapidly, as though fighting tears, and gave him a single nod. "Be safe."

EDAN AND AIDRYN began the slow journey down the mountainside, moving along the well-worn, rocky pathways that led toward the cove. He murmured commands to the stallion, who took charge of navigating so that Aidryn could think. Although Edan had never been quite as intuitive as Fannin, he was a trustworthy mount who had ridden hundreds of miles—maybe even thousands—at his master's behest.

Aidryn made no attempt to calm his racing heart. From the time he'd swung into Edan's saddle in the valley, he had begged

Rodhlan to show him where Lira had gone, but the continent seemed uninterested in sharing details. It enraged Aidryn to think that this land, which had allowed her to carry such an immense amount of power, would betray her like this. Would force Aidryn into tampering with her magic just to learn the truth.

But he would do whatever was necessary.

"Show me Lira's most recent memory," he begged, twining his consciousness around the Binding. "Just a glimpse— enough to know where she's going."

A flash of emerald magic overtook him, and there she was. Lira and Fannin were riding at breakneck speed toward Iathium, just as Aidryn had suspected. Her long, dark curls lashed her face and whipped in the wind as they rode, a determined expression on her lovely face. Whether she rode to confront Eremon, return the ring, or something else entirely, he couldn't be sure. But at least he knew what direction to take Edan.

Aidryn released his hold on the magic quickly, but not before pain pierced him behind his left eye. His head began to ache, and he blinked rapidly to clear his vision. Slowly, the trail came back into focus, and he sighed with relief. He hadn't forgotten the momentary blindness that had taken him back at Skelly's cottage. Though he might have gladly exchanged his vision for Lira's safety, he needed it now to protect her.

The pain in his head persisted all the way down the mountainside, but it was a small price to pay for the knowledge he'd obtained. Until they reached Acton's Cove, Aidryn forced himself not to dwell on what this journey would require of Edan. But as they moved from the cove and into the meadowlands, he let out a groan, dread weighing on his chest, his limbs.

Eiren had imparted a wealth of Clan Tarlach's wisdom to Aidryn in the span of a few short hours this morning. Tucked among the spells she'd shared was an ancient command

Aidryn had never heard of, much less used. Looking back, it seemed as though Eiren had known he might need to wield it soon. The realization filled him with sorrow.

The truth was, he had been so preoccupied with the focal point of her teaching that he had barely given the spell any mind until now.

Clan Tarlach's Seanlaoch had once been legendary for their magical speed, and Aidryn had used Fannin's and Edan's power with abandon for years. They'd ridden cross-continent together —found freedom together—more times than he could recall. If Eiren was correct about this particular incantation, then there would be a heavy price to pay.

But there was no time to consider the price; only to use the knowledge that had been granted to him.

So Aidryn gave Edan an affectionate pat on the neck and whispered, "Thank you, my friend."

Then, he leaned forward in the saddle, tightened his hands on the reins, squeezed his eyes shut, and murmured the incantation in Hes'ka.

"*Ano je sah*, Edan."

What happened next could only be compared to hurtling over the Moravon falls.

Edan shivered from his mane to his tail, the movement reverberating up into Aidryn's body. There was no additional time to prepare for the speed at which the stallion began to move—not even a breath. It was unlike anything Aidryn had ever felt on horseback, and unnerving in its intensity. He couldn't remember a time when he'd feared any steed for any reason, but in this moment, he dearly wished he could take the words back.

The stallion moved so quickly that his hooves scarcely touched the ground. It was almost as though Edan was moving above the earth, his hoofbeats making none of the hard, reverberating impact Aidryn loved and sought comfort in. This felt almost like floating, and he grew nauseous as Edan galloped at double speed.

Aidryn held on for his life, sheer terror gripping him. If he vomited on horseback, he would likely lose his grip and fly right out of the saddle. Again and again, he forced himself to swallow the bile that rose in his throat. His head pounded, and his jaw ached from grinding his teeth.

By the time Lira came into view, Aidryn had almost grown weak enough to give up. He longed to let the stallion rest—to slide off the saddle and onto the cold ground where he could be sick. But the sight of her, with her flowing brown curls and the emerald fabric of her cloak snapping in the freezing wind, jolted him into alertness.

"*En seh*," he ground out, and Edan began to slow as they caught up to Fannin—although in this case, *slow* was relative.

Finally, the renewed impact of Edan's hoofbeats helped Aidryn to feel grounded. The stallions matched pace, and Aidryn eased Edan up beside Fannin.

"Silira!" he shouted.

She whipped around to look at him, and he nearly toppled from the horse when their gazes locked.

Lira's eyes were wholly the color of that sickly green fog, with no whites to be seen. Her eyes widened, and she blinked at him as though trying to see through the haze. Then she turned again, refocusing on the path ahead and moving to whip Fannin's reins.

But Aidryn had predicted what she might do. If he couldn't get through to Lira, he would use his birthright power to take hold of Fannin instead.

"Fannin, *ano kah!*"

As Fannin obeyed, Aidryn called Edan to a halt, too. He fully intended to dismount, then snatch Fannin's reins— perhaps mount up behind Lira and have Edan follow. But the moment his boots touched the ground, his knees gave way and he collapsed, catching himself just before he emptied the contents of his stomach onto the dry grass.

He heaved until there was nothing left. Beside him, he heard Edan emit a low groan—one that echoed how Aidryn felt inside. As he sat up on his knees, panting and wiping his mouth on his sleeve, he saw the great beast shudder, then fall.

"No!" Aidryn choked on his own shout, his throat still burning from retching.

He scrambled to the horse's side, laying a palm on Edan's clammy coat. The stallion was struggling for breath, its black eyes wide and fearful. Aidryn moved his trembling palms to the stallion's neck, stroking its ebony mane.

"No," he repeated, hot tears clouding his vision. But when he'd spoken that incantation, he had known this was a risk. "I'm sorry. I'm so sorry."

Barely a moment passed before Edan exhaled his last, then closed his eyes.

Aidryn hung his head and wept. Tears streamed down his face, landing heavily on the parched ground below.

"I've always known you to be a schemer, Aidryn Tarlach." The voice was Lira's, but the words—the timbre—were not. "But killing your horse in pursuit of a throne? That is a new low. We're lucky I'm the one who took Fannin."

From where he knelt on the ground, Aidryn looked up. Lira stood only an arm's reach from him, her emerald cloak and skirts billowing in the wind, dark curls swirling around her beautiful face. Her cheeks were high with color from the ride, and her eyes were still tinged green.

If he wanted any chance at saving her, he could not beg or plead. Whoever was influencing her movements had managed to suppress Lira's consciousness. He couldn't appeal to the Lira he knew, so he would have to think quickly.

"You cut an imposing figure, looking down on me like that," Aidryn rasped. "Why did you leave the valley?"

"It was time," she answered, and turned to mount Fannin again.

"He won't run for you," Aidryn said. Her hands stilled on the saddle, and she tilted her head a bit, listening intently. "I've called off his trust. He will only answer to me now, so we'll have to ride together."

"Always fighting to regain control," she hissed, "or at least a semblance of it. You fancy yourself a great protector, but you're fumbling your way through this world, just like the rest of us."

"I won't deny that," he answered. "But I would do anything to protect those I love."

"Oh, I'm well aware." Lira's lips curled into a sneer. "It's a pity your love is so fickle. Knowing who you're willing to protect is difficult to predict from one day to the next."

The words bludgeoned him. "What do—"

"One moment, you would give up everything to protect a lowly historian from magic she neither understands, nor wants."

She walked a slow circle around Aidryn, assessing him. He held still, fighting every urge to jump to his feet and take her in his arms. To somehow cut through this fog so she could see *him*.

"The next..." Lira knelt before Aidryn. She placed a thin finger beneath his chin, coaxing him to meet her eyes. "You murder your friend. Lie to your *wife*. Encourage a love match between the immortal I nearly *died* resurrecting, and the sister who tortured you and tried to kill me."

Aidryn swallowed hard at her proximity, equally drawn to and repelled by her. He forced himself not to argue, even as each accusation found its mark.

"Did you think I would never learn about Caitir's crown of blades, Aidryn? Or the way Eremon dove between the sheets with a traitor when he was meant to be saving his people?" She pinched his chin and pulled him forward, only an inch from her face now. "Did you think Rodhlan would hide the truth from the Witness Tree? I received the words from Rhona herself."

As abruptly as Lira had pulled him in, she let him go.

"Never," Aidryn said. "We only withheld truths that might endanger you."

"What endangers me, Aidryn Tarlach, is your deception," Lira hissed. Suddenly, the green fog cleared, and she was looking at him through the familiar brown eyes he loved so dearly.

Hope swelled in Aidryn's chest, hot and bright, but when Lira spoke again, her words cut him to the quick. "When you said you loved me, I believed you."

Her voice was tremulous and tinged with hurt, and Aidryn felt his heart shatter at the look in her eyes.

She shook her head ruefully. "I loved you with everything I had, Aidryn. But I was so naive. It never crossed my mind that the Key Keeper could one day exploit our Binding to take Eremon's ring for himself."

Reverberating shock rattled through Aidryn, immediately shifting to anger.

"*What*?" he growled.

There wasn't time to think too deeply about what she had said: *loved*, as though that was now a thing of the past.

This logic couldn't be Lira's. If it had been—if the thoughts had truly been hers—then she would have come to him before. He would have been able to explain somehow, to show her that he would never have exploited her for any reason.

But after all his lies, would she have been able to believe him, even without the dark magic's influence?

"You heard me," she said coolly. "I pieced it together for myself this morning. If Eremon wants his throne back, then I'll meet him in Iathium myself. Give him *my* answer face to face."

Something pressed against Lira's magic in alarm. Aidryn felt its jolt through the Binding, and he stilled, assessing the truth. The magic was in so much distress, he could hardly discern what the truth was. But then it came to him, almost unbidden, and he knew what he needed to do.

"I refused Eremon because removing the ring could kill you," Aidryn said. He was shaking so violently that he could barely get the words out. But he commanded calmness into his limbs. Made himself breathe as he re-centered on her. "I was trying to protect you."

The cruel laugh that burst from Lira's lips filled him with icy dread. "And when have you succeeded at that?"

Though Aidryn was still reeling, he recalled the cool, calculating façade he'd been forced to develop as a young man. He'd had to play along with Aila and Caitir for so many years, while simultaneously trying to shield Lira from so many of their schemes. If he must, he would do it again. He *had* to.

He slowed his racing thoughts for long enough to lock them away, just like Eiren had instructed.

"You know very well that I've protected you. Defended you." He rose in one smooth motion, meeting Lira's gaze and hoping that the passion he willed into his voice rang true. "I would have done anything for you. I still would."

Aidryn closed the distance between them, curling a possessive hand around Lira's waist and pulling her close. He felt her body go pliant against his, though the distance in her eyes remained. Her long, dark lashes fluttered closed as he murmured, "Let me take you to Iathium. And when we arrive, I'll lead you to the dais and crown you myself."

CHAPTER 71
EREMON

Dome

Eremon woke in the afternoon with Caitir in his arms. Her warm skin smelled sweet, and he pressed a kiss to her temple, pulling her nearer. They were still tangled together beneath the white coverlet, and a surge of happiness swept through him at the memory of what they'd shared.

Outside the tower window, the sun was high. Then, it occurred to him: He had *slept* for the first time since becoming immortal. Chuckling to himself, he nuzzled Caitir before relaxing into his pillow again.

"What's so funny?" she mumbled, rolling over to face him.

"I didn't mean to wake you," he said, leaning forward to press a kiss to her nose. "I was laughing because I fell asleep."

His hands drifted down to idly stroke the soft, taut skin of her belly. Caitir's cheeks flushed with pleasure.

"Oh?" She propped on her elbow, suddenly alert, and gave him a wicked grin. "That doesn't say much for immortal stamina."

Eremon looped his arm around her waist and dragged her

closer. "I'll show you stamina." He laughed, drawing her in for a lingering kiss. "How are you feeling, truly?"

Caitir smiled sleepily and sat up, stretching her arms overhead. "I feel well-rested. Content. Tired, but happy."

Eremon nestled deeper into the plush blankets, letting his gaze linger over her as she wrapped the sheet around her body. "Did you feel safe with me? Cared for?"

Her hands drifted to her belly as she considered. "Yes," she answered, her gaze flicking up to meet his. "You've no idea how much."

Relief flooded him, and he smiled. "Good. That's what I hoped for." He laced their fingers together, studying the rise of color that had crept into her cheeks. "Can I fetch you a glass of water or something to eat?"

She bit her bottom lip, then grinned at him. "A big, crusty pastry and a cup of tea."

He groaned playfully. "But that requires getting dressed."

"If I have to do it, so do you," she said, moving past him to slide off the bed. She picked up the dressing gown she'd discarded and wrapped it around herself as she padded toward the bathing chamber.

"I want that pastry waiting for me when I return," she called over her shoulder.

Eremon smiled lazily, watching her until she disappeared behind the door, then fell back again the pillows. What had happened between them today... he wanted it forever. But a flash of sorrow threatened to shred his euphoria.

I wish it would never end, but I know it has to.

Truly, it didn't *have* to end. Caitir's regency didn't prevent her from marrying Eremon if she wished to. Or he could rule Iathium alone as Rí. Having his wife serve as a ruler wasn't a requirement, but it had been a long-held custom. In his mortal life, he'd been notorious for breaking tradition, so at least the people were already used to that old habit.

Whatever happened, there had to be a way forward for them—one that didn't involve sending her away or worse. He would find a way to keep her by his side.

Eremon sighed and rose from bed, pulling on his trousers and tying his hair back with a leather cord. He cracked the door open, intending to shift. When he peeked out, he saw a small crowd of courtiers and staff gathered in the sitting area. Their attention snapped to the chamber door, and he slammed it shut before they could see him, engaging the lock for good measure. He could hear them clamoring outside, calling Caitir's name.

"Crown Regent!"

"Is it true Eremon has returned?"

"Caitir, we need you!"

"Let us see him!"

"What do we do?"

He pressed his back against the door, heart pounding. Caitir stepped out of the bathing chamber then, concern on her beautiful face. She had pulled her hair into a high bun and looked as though she'd just scrubbed her face pink. The fresh, ivory-colored gown she wore accentuated her soft curves, the subtle swell of her lower belly.

"What's happening out there?" she said, her voice heavy with apprehension.

"They want you," he answered slowly, reluctantly dragging his gaze back up to her pale eyes, "and me, apparently."

It had been quiet when he'd first returned this morning, and in the moments after they'd awakened together, neither of them had been attuned to what was happening outside. But now, Eremon's ears picked up a clamor he hadn't noticed before. He crossed the room to look out the tower window and groaned when he beheld the massive crowd in the streets below.

"*No*," Eremon said, shrinking back from the window.

"I hear them too," Caitir said, eyes wide.

Eremon flicked his fingers, and suddenly, all sound from outside the chamber vanished. Caitir's ears popped, and it felt as though the air had been momentarily sucked out of the room.

"What was that?" she cried.

"A spell I learned from the Beran healer years ago," Eremon said. "For privacy."

Caitir's jaw dropped. "And you didn't think to use it before?" Her face flushed, and Eremon grinned.

"To be fair, I was preoccupied," he answered.

The hidden panel in the wall opened across the room, and Toryn stepped through. The midwife's lips parted in surprise, color rushing to her cheeks as she took in Eremon's bare chest, Caitir's casual dress, the rumpled bedclothes, the garments strewn across the floor.

"Dear Riku!" she exclaimed, pressing a hand to her rounded cheek and turning her back. "Forgive me!"

Eremon chuckled. "There's nothing to forgive, my friend."

He retrieved his tunic from the floor and shrugged it on. Then, he crossed the room to lay a hand on the midwife's shoulder. When he did, she whirled to face him, eyes glassy.

"I have wanted to see you for *weeks*," she cried, grasping his face in her hands. "Now I understand why you've been so preoccupied." Toryn glanced over his shoulder at Caitir and smiled warmly. "How are you feeling this morning? You look very well."

Eremon didn't miss the note of laughter in her voice. He turned to look at Caitir, who just smiled. "I have been well," she began, "but—"

From behind Toryn, Tiriya's voice sounded. "A little help, please?"

Toryn's eyes went wide, and she scrambled toward the hidden door as though she could somehow prevent Tiriya from bursting into the chamber—and the intimate moment she'd unwittingly disturbed.

"Wait a moment, Tiriya," the midwife called. "She isn't decent!"

"We're all women here. Besides, I need to set this tray *down*," Tiriya grumbled. "My arms are falling off!"

Toryn closed her eyes and pressed her fingertips to her forehead in exasperation. She looked resigned yet apologetic as Tiriya emerged through the doorway, then nearly dropped her entire meal tray in tandem with her jaw.

"Oh—" she exclaimed as Toryn rushed to help her salvage the tray. "Oh! I am so— I apologize, I—I didn't know—"

"That's nothing," her mother murmured in singsong, steadily preparing a cup of tea as though she hadn't just been flustered enough to blow steam from her ears. "You didn't catch him half naked."

Tiriya turned as red as a radish. "*Mama.*"

"What brings you here?" Caitir asked, fetching a cup of tea for Eremon.

"Kenji said he hadn't seen you today," the midwife said. "We wanted to make sure you were well fed. From the look of things, you're likely hungry."

Tiriya snickered, and Caitir flushed.

"Do you know what's happening outside?" Eremon said.

"It seems," Toryn began slowly, "that you were spotted yesterday, by quite a few of the Dome staff. Up until now, there was only the odd, superstitious rumor from the barracks. Now, even the common folk in the city are demanding to see you."

"It's not just that," Tiriya added. "Silira Mór was seen out on the meadowlands, riding for Iathium."

"What?" Eremon bristled, exchanging a terse glance with Caitir. He had been expecting Aidryn and Lira, but not until the next day. "Was she alone, or was someone with her?"

"All I know is she was on a gray horse," Tiriya answered.

"She was still a day's ride from here, but the western tower lookouts spotted her through their scopes. I overheard—"

"You mean you spied," he pressed. Surely, Aidryn was traveling with Lira.

Tiriya looked at her feet as her confession tumbled out. "Yes, I was eavesdropping." She looked back up then, her dark, angular eyes flashing. "Biren reported to Fiadh, and she told him not to repeat what he'd seen—that she would personally escort Lira into the city in the morning."

"No," Caitir and Eremon bit out in unison.

The panic in Caitir's eyes matched the sudden squeezing in Eremon's chest.

"Has Fiadh already left the Dome?" he said.

"Not yet," Tiriya answered. "She said she'd wait until Lira was nearer the city gates."

"Then here is your first assignment," he said, leaning toward her conspiratorially. "I need you to orchestrate ways to delay her departure. I'll go to Lira myself, but you make sure Fiadh is prevented from leaving as planned. You're free to be as creative as you like."

Tiriya's eyes lit with mischief. "As you wish, my Rí."

He turned his attention to the midwife, who had paled. "Toryn, I need for you and Kenji to activate whatever spies you've managed to make contact with since my return. Have them watch the sentries, both within and around the Dome's perimeter, and ask them to stay on alert for unusual activity in the city. Clan Beran has infiltrated, and we need to be ready. Spies should report back to Kenji and cease all communication with Fiadh; I hereby strip her superficial title."

"Of course." Toryn looked from Eremon to Tiriya, then back again. "Tiriya, I—"

"It's all right, Mama," Tiriya said in a soothing tone. "I want this. I asked the Rí to let me help."

"It's only on a limited basis," Eremon reassured Toryn. "I promise."

Tiriya closed the distance between herself and her mother and rose on her tiptoes to kiss Toryn's cheek. "I'll see you in a little while."

Just as Tiriya was preparing to duck back through the hidden door, Kyra burst in, red-faced and panting. "You can't make me go back home, Mama. I want to be here with you!"

Toryn groaned. "Kyra," she chided as the little girl crossed the room toward them. "You were supposed to stay with Fjella."

"I know," the little girl sang, "but I didn't want to."

Kyra stopped toe-to-toe with Eremon, a shy grin on her little face. Her black hair had been cropped like her eldest sister's, accentuating her round, rosy cheeks. She threw her arms up in the air. "Pick me up, Emon!"

He obliged her, chuckling as she scrambled into his arms. They turned to face Caitir, who was watching in such slack-jawed wonder that Eremon wanted to embrace her, too.

"Is that your wife?" Kyra asked, scrutinizing Caitir with narrow eyes.

"No," Eremon ventured. He was afraid to meet Caitir's gaze again, for fear of what he might see in her eyes.

"Oh." Kyra chewed on the inside of her cheek, deep in thought. "Do you want her to be?"

"Don't ask such nosy questions," he said with a nervous chuckle.

"Well," Kyra ventured, "it's only that I know how babies are made, and she has a baby. And I *know* she doesn't have to be your wife to have a baby with you."

Caitir let out a startled laugh. From her spot by the hidden door, Tiriya burst into a peal of giggles. She had made her way back across the room once again and was standing beside the hidden door.

"*Kyraaa*," Toryn groaned, her face turning red. "I am so very sorry."

"Don't be," Caitir said, seeming to emerge from her own shock. "I knew Kenji had other daughters, but I've never had the pleasure of getting to know you all." She sat on the small sofa and patted the cushion beside her. "Would you like to come sit with me, Kyra?"

"Yes!" Kyra bounded across the room and launched herself onto the sofa, against her mother's cautioning to *slow down* and *be gentle*.

Toryn and Eremon exchanged a glance. The midwife threw her arm around his shoulders and gave him a squeeze as they turned their attention back to the little dark-haired girl and the Crown Regent, looking elegant with her hair piled atop her head, without silks or jewels to adorn her fair skin.

Caitir mirrored Toryn, opening her arm for Kyra. The little girl wiggled her body flush against Caitir's, heaving a contented sigh as she looked up to study the regent's features.

"Everyone said you were cruel," Kyra said, "but I don't think you are."

With a tilt of her head, Caitir admitted, "I can be cruel sometimes."

"Why?" Kyra asked.

"Because..." Caitir met Eremon's gaze, and he didn't miss the little flash of panic in her eyes. But she seemed to settle quickly as she continued. "For most of my life, I felt angry, and sad, and trapped every day. But now I have your papa and mama—"

"And Emon," Kyra added.

"Yes," Caitir said with a soft laugh. "And Emon. And they help me."

"They love me, too," Kyra said, draping one of her little arms over Caitir's belly and snuggling deeper into her side.

For a moment, Caitir stiffened at the contact; Eremon was

the only other person she'd allowed so near since Aila's departure. But then, she visibly relaxed.

"They do love you," she answered. "And now, I have a lesson for you. Are you ready?"

Kyra's little hand was wandering over the soft swell of Caitir's belly, and she'd stuck her tongue out in concentration. "I'm waiting for the kick."

Caitir laughed softly. "All right. I want you only to befriend people who treat you in a loving way and never ask you to hurt someone else. Do you understand?"

"If Eremon isn't going to marry you, then he can marry me," Kyra said idly.

When he looked at Caitir again, the warm smile on her face made him go molten.

"Well, if that's what you're planning," she said, her gentle fingertips playing over the little girl's dark hair, "you have a bit of a wait yet."

CHAPTER 72
CAITIR

Dome

A s evening fell, Caitir and Eremon stood side-by-side at the tower window, studying the crowd's movements below. They'd remained together in this chamber, each as reluctant to separate as the other. There were only a few short hours left now, and after that, it was unclear what would unfold.

Eremon had fallen into a deep, uneasy silence as the afternoon wore on. Now, he leaned heavily on the windowsill with one hand, his other gripping Caitir's waist.

"Tell me what you're thinking," she said, moving closer to rest her head on his shoulder.

"Something about Lira riding here feels deeply wrong," he murmured, nuzzling Caitir's hair.

"You said Aidryn was bringing her," Caitir answered.

"Exactly. She shouldn't be traveling alone." Eremon was silent for a long moment before he spoke again. "Have you ever been able to just *feel* that something isn't right? It's almost as if there's a dissonance in my magic."

She thought about Eremon's ring and the protective magic he'd tried to imbue around the Binding that tied her brother to Lira.

"Well, your magic *is* connected to Lira," Caitir replied, her eyes following a pocket of commotion on the street below. Two sentries broke up the clamor, and she relaxed as she watched the people dissipate into the crowd. It would be just like Clan Beran to start an uproar down there—to incite the violence they so wanted to inflict on Iathium in the name of justice. "Don't wait until dawn to go to her."

She hated directing Eremon to Lira's side. If things had been different, if Caitir hadn't played along with Aila's schemes and done so much harm to her former friend, she would have felt thrilled to have Lira as a sister. Now, she was filled with cold dread at the thought of coming face-to-face with her again.

He turned to look at her, covering one of her hands with his. "Is it terrible for me to say I don't want to?"

"No," she murmured, "but you must. Better for you to escort her into the city yourself than to let Thorne, or Artur, or any of the other Beran dogs get hold of her."

Eremon had sent word to Deghan through Kenji. The sentries were to tighten their protective ranks around the Dome's entrances and cut down any of the city-dwellers who showed signs of violent uprising. So far, the people were mostly being vocal—*incredibly* vocal. But Iathium didn't have much violence in its recent history, and its people were both soft and unaccustomed to mob tactics.

Adding untamed magic to the mix had served to make them weaker and more fearful, not the other way around. Although the educational programs Caitir had helped Eremon to enact had begun on a successful note, they were still fairly small. Once the people stopped fearing themselves, then the real transformation could begin.

The gentle brush of Eremon's fingertips along the shell of

her ear made Caitir's skin tingle. She hummed, closing her eyes for a moment to revel in his touch. His fingers meandered down the side of her neck, then beneath the shoulder of her dressing gown. He coaxed it down, peeling it back to expose the thinner fabric of her nightgown beneath.

"We don't have much time," he whispered, leaning in to press a kiss to her throat.

Caitir shivered, letting her eyes drift shut. "Shouldn't you be..." The words fizzled out on her tongue, but they didn't matter. There was only Eremon and the way he was touching her. Tasting her.

"Absolutely not," he said against her skin.

With so little time left, there was nothing else they could do but wait for Lira to draw nearer. Now that so many people knew of Eremon's return, Caitir's authority would be ineffective beyond adding more sentries to the watch, and she had done that already. Her best defense was to remain hidden until power could be handed over properly. Then, she would disappear.

The thought of leaving Eremon behind sent a wave of sorrow crashing over her, but that would not do. Caitir couldn't afford to drift into fearful thoughts now. She needed him again, the way she'd claimed him this morning. The way he had claimed her.

"I want something from you," she said breathlessly, moving just far enough away that his lips broke contact with her skin. The chill was instant, and she regretted it.

"And what is that?" Eremon asked, attempting to close the distance between them again. He reached for her elbow, but she pulled away from his grasp, a coy smile playing on her lips.

"I want you to show me how you might have charmed me," she began, "if I had been your favorite courtier."

"A game, is it?" he said with a wicked grin. "I think we're far past that already."

He leaned in to kiss her again, but she placed a hand on his chest to hold him off.

"For the sake of the game," Caitir said, holding his heated gaze, "let's say you've never touched me before. We've never kissed."

She leaned nearer until their lips almost touched again, lowering her voice. "If we encountered one another in the corridor, and I brushed past you, like this"—she stepped past him, letting her fingertips graze his— "what would you do?"

"I would catch your hand, then let it go," he answered, reaching out to grasp her fingers in his own, then releasing them, allowing her to move away. "Then I would catch your eye. See if you'd stray from your intended path to follow me."

Eremon turned, flicking his gaze to her as he moved toward the hidden door on the other side of the room. He opened it, then disappeared into the shadows. Warmth flooded her body as she followed. When she entered the passageway, he was nowhere to be seen.

"What then?" Caitir whispered, letting the chamber door click shut behind them. The last slice of light vanished, plunging them into darkness.

Eremon's hand found hers, and she laced their fingers together, pressing her palm to his.

"Then, I might tease you with a little innuendo masked as small talk—try to gauge your intentions," he answered. "And if I found that those intentions matched my own, I might ask..."

He guided Caitir's footsteps, gently turning her and walking her back until she was pressed against the wall.

"May I touch you, my lady?" he whispered in the darkness, his breath hot on her ear.

Her throat bobbed, her mouth suddenly going dry. "You may."

His fingertips were feather-light on her cheek, trailing down her throat to her collarbone, then lower. Gooseflesh pebbled her skin in the wake of his touch.

"I would entice you with compliments, pretty metaphors. For example—" He leaned in, lips brushing against her jaw. "Your skin is so soft, like rose petals."

Caitir's breathing quickened as Eremon placed slow, lingering kisses down the side of her throat. Her hand rose to rest on his shoulder, and she tipped her head back for him, letting him trace his mouth over her skin at an agonizing pace. She dug her fingertips into the toned muscle of his back, tracing the shape of him beneath the fabric. He smelled of soothing spices and a summer storm.

"Eremon..." she sighed.

He raised his head, his breath warm on her face. "May I kiss your lips?"

Caitir said nothing but instead slid her fingers into the hair at the nape of his neck, pulling him to her. Their mouths clashed, all softness and longing, as Eremon pressed the length of his body against hers. Shadows enveloped them, shrouding them in secrecy, cloaking their embrace.

"If I was feeling particularly scandalous," Eremon whispered against her mouth, "I might give you a taste of the pleasure you'd receive in my bed." She gasped as his hands roamed, the sensations sending her thoughts into a scatter.

"And then what?" she asked breathlessly. It was a wonder she had managed to find the words at all.

"I might discreetly trail you to your chamber," he answered, pressing his forehead to hers. "But if you were my favorite, then I'd invite you to mine."

He cupped her face in his hands, kissing her deeply. Her stomach did a giddy flip, because this was so much better than what she'd dreamed of, all those years. She sank into his embrace, returning each kiss with as much love as she could convey. Whatever happened in the next day, the next week, these moments with Eremon were the ones she most wanted to remember.

"*If*. We both know I'm your favorite." Caitir smiled against his lips. "So lead the way."

CHAPTER 73
LIRA

Meadowlands

Tathium's magnificent walls were finally within view.
As Lira and Aidryn tore across the meadowlands
astride Fannin, she was hungry for a glimpse of the
Dome and its towers. She had dearly missed this place. Why
had she let her enemies drive her out?

Her thoughts snapped to the man behind her. The man
who held the reins. Fitting, since Aidryn was the person who
had ultimately taken her from her beloved city in the first
place. As it turned out, he had been controlling far more than
she'd wanted to admit, for far longer than she had realized.

At the time, she'd thought he was protecting her. Now, she
knew better.

Lira had been everyone's pawn. It was the very fate her
father had died to help her avoid. Arlen Mór had installed her
in this city. He had instilled a love for the histories in her and
had seen to it that she developed a work ethic that rivaled
Eremon's. In truth, Da had prepared her for far more than the
archive.

He had prepared her for the throne.

The realization sent a thrill through her body. Her destiny was so much greater than she'd ever dreamt it could be. Eremon had seen her potential, before his death had ruined their future. She'd been sorely disappointed to find that death had also ruined the man he'd once been, but it was just as well. For years, she had been content on her own. It would be possible to resume that solitary life once again.

But this time, it would all be on her terms. She had spent far too long being subdued and submissive—a good citizen. A good historian. A naive, trustworthy girl who had followed every rule to the letter and worked hard for her place in the city.

Lira didn't need anyone's permission to take the power she was due. She had earned it.

The birthright magic in her veins felt wild. Panicked. It pressed and pushed and struggled, and Lira ground her teeth against the sensation. She dove into her power, seeking the source of its distress, and found a frayed thread of Eremon's cobalt magic still wrapped around the Binding.

Pathetic, she thought as she focused on that thin little string, then called upon her dark magic to sever it.

CHAPTER 74

EREMON

Dome

Eremon's eyes snapped open.

It was pitch-dark in his chamber, and no moonlight shone outside. He lay still in the silence, listening for Caitir's soft, steady breathing. But his senses went on high alert as he realized he could hear nothing at all.

Pushing himself up to sit, he strained his ears. Called Caitir's name. Raised his hand to eye-level in an attempt to see it.

Relief washed over him as he summoned a mote of cobalt flame into his palm. That relief was quickly replaced by dread as he realized there was nothing in this room—wherever he was. He had awakened in a dark void.

A distant scream sent a shockwave through Eremon, and his hair stood on end. Fire mote in hand, he climbed off the bed and felt for the tunic and trousers he'd discarded on the floor. Thankfully, they were still there, so he let the magic wink out and tugged them on.

Another scream. He reignited the cobalt flame and padded

in the direction of the sound. The scent of ozone reached his nostrils, and the air around him was charged with dark magic. A sickly green haze swam in his vision, and he probed it curiously.

The screams grew closer, their bearer's identity painfully near, though he could not grasp whose voice the cries belonged to. So he walked through the darkness and fog in the direction of the sound, his apprehension growing as he neared its bearer.

Finally, shadows and haze gave way to the eerie illumination of dark magic, the rest of the space around him devoid of light. His flame extinguished and a figure emerged from the fog: a young woman, consumed by the power, erupting with it.

Lira.

He called to her, but she didn't respond. She threw her head back, her eyes glowing emerald, and cried out as though in pain.

Before he could move toward her, Eremon was thrust back into his bed, and time slowed. Like an apparition, Lira's figure followed him there. Her eyes widened in horror as her gaze fell to Caitir. And then her irises changed to that sickly green color, crackling with black lighting. Agonized screams ripped from her throat as the dark magic held her in its throes.

"Lira," Eremon cried, though he couldn't move—couldn't reach her. "Stop! You have to fight this!"

Beside him, Caitir still slept, as if she heard none of it. As if she couldn't hear him calling Lira's name, begging her to listen.

Then Lira locked eyes with him. And the protective magic he'd woven into her Binding was gone.

CHAPTER 75

CAITIR

Dome

W hen Caitir woke in Eremon's bed that night, she was alone.

The unfamiliar chamber was vast, with high ceilings and dark trimmings. His sheets and coverlet were made from the softest fabric she'd ever touched, and they were as black as a starless sky. She recognized the crimson curtains she'd sewn for him, but not much else. It almost felt more intimate to be here alone than it had to be tangled with him in bed.

Evening had passed swiftly, and the few hours they'd spent together came rushing back to her. Caitir pulled the soft blankets up to her chin, nestling beneath them as she closed her eyes again, reliving every touch, every kiss. Moment by moment, she replayed the past day in her mind. She wanted to emblazon it in her memory so she'd never forget.

Cradling her belly, she curled on her side. The baby in her womb wiggled and shifted, as though trying to get comfortable just like she was. Her belly tightened a bit, and she pressed a palm to it, waiting patiently. A moment later, she was rewarded with a little thump against her hand.

"We're on our own after this, little one," she whispered, her heart squeezing.

It was just like Eremon to leave without saying goodbye—as though refusing to acknowledge the truth would somehow change fate. The thought fell over her like a cold shroud, and she let it. This was how things had to be.

In just a few short hours, Lira would be here. Aidryn would be, too. As Crown Regent, Caitir would need to show her face for posterity. The thought of being in the same room with her brother and former friend again threatened to turn her stomach, but she clamped down on the sensation. There was no use wallowing in it now.

It was true that she'd harmed those closest to her in her attempt to survive. She'd hoped that the crimes she'd committed at Aila's behest would one day give her enough power to free herself. At the time, she'd believed that everything she had done would be worth that cost.

If she had even a small chance at freedom after today, it still would be.

CHAPTER 76

AIDRYN

Meadowlands

D awn was just beginning to break when Iathium's tall, sprawling walls came into view. Aidryn had shifted Fannin's pace along the way, from his magical gallop to a trot and the occasional canter. Edan's death weighed heavily on him, so as much as he dared, Aidryn let his stallion rest.

Absently, he found himself checking Fannin's coat for sweat, monitoring him for signs of exhaustion. Luckily, the Seanlaoch didn't tire easily. It was only the new incantation that had taken such a toll.

If Aidryn could help it, he would never speak those words again.

Over the past several hours, he'd remained as silent as possible. He was too wary of giving away his terror to attempt speaking to Lira. Thankfully, she hadn't said much to him, either.

The change in her demeanor had been so jarring, he had almost let her ride away without him. Her magic had shoved the truth across the Binding to him in a frenzied panic: She was planning to take the throne herself. In the moment, he hadn't had the time to prod any further. But as they rode, he'd dared to explore her truth magic, coaxing little bits of memory through the connection they shared and praying she wouldn't notice.

When he'd finally pieced together enough of the truth, he had barely managed to pull himself out of the shock. Though his panicked thoughts had coalesced into a furious cyclone, he had forced himself to focus on his next steps. These next moves would be crucial, and he would have to carefully guard his own thoughts to avoid arousing her suspicion.

Aidryn's head pounded, sharp pains flashing behind his eyes. He would need Eremon's help to carry out the plan he'd formed with Eiren—or some semblance of it, at any rate.

As they drew closer to the city walls, Aidryn could make out additional movement in the gray dawn. A sprawling contingent of Clan Beran's warriors had congregated outside the gates. Lira must have spotted them at the same moment as Aidryn, for she went rigid in the saddle, and he groaned.

She held up a hand, signaling for Aidryn to slow the stallion. When he obliged, she threw him a half-glance over her shoulder and said, "What is Clan Beran doing here?"

"Supporting your bid for the throne." The answer tumbled out before he could finesse it, but he was grateful that it was true. A breeze stirred her dark curls, and he tried to ignore the faint scent of roses that wafted to meet him. He squeezed his eyes shut against it. "Your stepfather desires to see you in power."

"Good," Lira replied curtly. "A show of force will make this easier."

Aidryn suppressed a shuddering breath, opening his eyes again to refocus on the wall. Just then, a flash of silver wings in the sky caught his attention. And then there was Eremon in falcon form, soaring toward them, over the city walls and the warriors. Aidryn clicked his tongue, urging Fannin to move toward him despite Lira's protests.

When they'd closed the distance between them, Eremon swooped toward the ground, transforming with ease just as his black boots hit the dry grass. Aidryn called Fannin to a halt, and Lira sat up straighter in the saddle, raising her chin as Eremon approached. There was a wary expression on his face as he gently reached for Fannin's reins, studying Lira.

"My magic," he began carefully, his gaze flicking to Aidryn. "Did you notice anything strange about it, Silira?"

Aidryn widened his eyes at Eremon for a split second, hoping the subtle expression might somehow convey his immense panic.

"It's gone," she said solemnly, though Aidryn could have sworn he heard a note of glee in her answer. "I freed myself of it."

Eremon inclined his head, keeping his attention focused on her. "I see." He folded his hands behind his back. "I thought perhaps we might have a chat."

"In Iathium, if you please," Aidryn cut in with a subtle shake of his head.

It was clear Eremon wanted to resolve this dispute before taking Lira to the Dome, but if chaos broke loose in the meadowlands, and if Clan Beran's warriors witnessed it, they could invade the city while Eremon was distracted. Aidryn's heart was hammering, and the way Eremon's gaze flicked down to his chest, he wondered whether the immortal could somehow hear or sense his fear.

"Very well," Eremon said slowly, "but you see the warriors at the gates. The streets around the Dome are teeming with people, and you'll have to cut a path through them all."

"Then we'll do what must be done," Lira answered. Aidryn hated the cold, detached tone she'd taken on.

"I'll lead the way," Eremon replied. He didn't make eye

contact with either of them again. Instead, he transformed and took to the skies.

THORNE WAS WAITING on horseback at Iathium's gates when Aidryn and Lira arrived. He appeared to have instructed his warriors to form their lines along the wall. Upon closer inspection, Aidryn noted that he appeared to have brought as many members of the clan army as he could assemble. Beran's warriors were fairly small in number—roughly three hundred, compared to Iathium's eight hundred sentries. But with clan fighters in their midst, there were easily one thousand here now, if not more.

One look at Aidryn's face seemed to communicate more than enough, for the warrior's stony expression shifted to fear in an instant. His amber eyes flicked between the two, but he merely gave Aidryn a nod. The massive, stocky bay stallion he rode shifted its weight, its thick mane gently ruffled by the breeze.

Thorne nudged his horse to fall into step beside Fannin. Ahead of them, Iathium's massive iron gates groaned open. Eremon would have given the order. Still, Aidryn couldn't help but notice that more sentries than usual were positioned just within the gate.

"I didn't expect the Clan Beran horde until tomorrow," Aidryn said, casting a meaningful glance toward the warrior. "I trust your warriors won't attempt to breach the gate while it's open."

"No," Thorne replied flatly. "I've ordered them to stand down and stay where they are."

"For now." Aidryn scoffed. "We'll see how well that works out."

"Perhaps we won't need their assistance," Lira put in. "I'm sure we'll fare well enough without resorting to violence."

Thorne cut an alarmed glance at Aidryn. So he could hear it, too.

His brow creased with concern. "What is the matter, *sjeinga*?"

Aidryn didn't break eye contact with the warrior as he said, "Lira has decided that she will do her duty by the city and ascend. You both agree that is the best course of action, do you not?"

Thorne blinked, clearly confused. "Yes, I—" He shook his head as though to rattle it. "Yes."

"Then follow us," Aidryn said, nudging Fannin ahead until he was in the lead, "and stay alert. This ends today."

They passed a contingent of wary-looking sentries, many of whom Aidryn didn't recognize. As they rode into the city proper, straggling citizens who had not ventured to the Dome turned to gawk at them. The sight of their gaunt faces, their empty eyes, made Aidryn's heart stutter.

How hopeless Iathium had become. Gone were the luster and liveliness that had colored these streets. There was a despair hanging in the atmosphere that he'd never felt in this city before. Lira seemed to sense it too, because she grew somber as Fannin trotted down the cobblestone path.

They hadn't made it two city blocks into town before Aidryn noticed a larger crowd gathered on the walkways. People emerged from their homes, peeking out their windows and doors as he and Lira rode past. A murmur rose from the people, and they buzzed as Fannin passed them.

"Witness Tree!"

"It's the Defender of Histories!"

"That's Aidryn!"

"Silira!"

"The heir of all things."

Lira sat up straighter, stiffening in the saddle. Even after all that had happened, she still disliked drawing the attention of a crowd. Perhaps there was hope for her yet.

Aidryn leaned forward and whispered, "He *can* go a little faster, you know," before brushing a kiss to her ear.

She nudged Fannin into a canter, moving more quickly past the curious crowd. Aidryn could feel her body relax as they left the people behind, but she tensed again a few minutes later as they approached the courtyard. It was teeming with people who had breached its gate, just as Eremon had warned—so many they overflowed into the streets. Citizens had crowded against the Dome's entrance. Some pounded on its doors and the thick glass of its walls, begging to be allowed inside. Many shouted, while others wept.

Fannin stuttered to a near-halt at the sight of so many people, stamping nervously at the cobblestones.

"Eremon the Eternal!" someone shouted.

"Show yourself!" cried another.

"Bring us the Crown Regent!"

Lira cast a glance over her shoulder. "So the word is out."

"So it is." He nodded toward the pathway into the courtyard. "Push through. They'll part for us."

She took a shaky breath and steered Fannin toward the courtyard gates. Though the crowd was tight, the stallion moved them forward. The people's attention wandered from the Dome, and they fixated on Lira and Aidryn, as the people on the streets had.

Again, choruses of their names, their titles, their anointings, greeted them. Lira's hands found Aidryn's, and she pressed her fingers into his skin. Her palms were coated in sweat.

"That's it, Lira," he murmured as they moved. "You're doing beautifully. Keep your eyes on the Dome. Keep moving forward."

"I can't do this," she said, her voice tinged with fear. "But I know I must."

For a moment, Aidryn thought he heard *Lira*—the true Lira —and his heart shattered. He kissed the back of her head, closing his eyes as he finally allowed himself to take in the faint rose scent of her hair, the feel of her body warm against his. Longing and grief warred within him, but it was time to set his emotions aside. Whatever happened next, he must move swiftly. Decisively.

He would only have one chance to succeed, and he had to take it.

"Come now, my love," he whispered against her hair, blinking back the tears that stung his eyes. "You have a city to save."

CHAPTER 77

LIRA

Dome

Use the warrior.

Lira tried not to perk up at the sound of the voice as they drew nearer to the Dome's western entrance. Instead, she kept her face impassive and strained to listen.

They concealed Artur's plans from you, just like everything else. Turn those plans against Clan Beran. Lure them in. Slaughter them.

She blinked, shoving the thought away. Why would she want to destroy Thorne's warriors? The thought sank into her belly like lead.

As though reprimanded, the voice grew silent, and Lira focused her attention on the looming Dome. After last spring, she had fantasized about an unlikely, but triumphant, return to the city. This was anything but.

Instead of triumph, Lira felt nothing but dread and fear as they crossed the courtyard. They rode through the teeming crowd, pushing through the scores of bodies like wading through thick mud. Reverent hands reached for them, brushing against their feet, Lira's skirts, Fannin's flanks. The stallion huffed nervously at the contact. Lira held her breath and forced herself to keep looking straight ahead.

In the ten months since Eremon's death, the city had fallen into shambles. The overbearing gloom, the heart-rending hunger in the people's eyes, their desperation—it was all too much. A swell of anger rose within her, and she pushed Fannin. If Eremon couldn't bring himself to rectify this, then she would.

The cacophony of voices roared in Lira's head, pressing against her growing rage, until suddenly they'd broken free of the mob. Sentries parted to let them onto the grounds of the western towers and away from the groping, gawking crowd.

When they reached the doors, Lira dismounted from Fannin, followed by Aidryn. He took the saddle bag from the stallion's side, looking a little more reluctant than usual as he handed the horse off to a stable hand who had come to fetch him.

Lira felt a little pang at the memory of Edan's death, but that had been Aidryn's doing, not hers. There was no reason to waste her time dwelling on it.

Aidryn extended a hand to Lira, shaking her from her thoughts. She took it, and he laced their fingers together as they led Thorne into the Dome.

"I never truly believed I would enter this place again, especially not for you to ascend the throne," he said softly, though the troubled expression on his face gave her pause. "It's surreal."

"Yes," she rasped, taking in the palace's familiar, ornate trappings. Translucent glass that filtered in sunlight. Marble tile. Gold and crimson trimmings. High, arched ceilings. She glanced through the window, where she could see the stained-glass oculus of the main corridor.

This had been her home. As much as she had loved the cottage she and Talfryn had grown up in, the Dome had been her home and her heart. For a little while, she'd believed that Aidryn had taken its place. But now that she was back, she couldn't imagine anything better than spending the rest of her days ruling this place.

The sound of footsteps drew their attention, and they turned to see Eremon, who stood at the entrance of the receiving hall. He was regal, clad in black silks embellished with silver and cobalt stitching. He'd worn his black hair loose, and his silver eyes flashed as he regarded Thorne, Aidryn, and finally, Lira.

"It's good to have all of you here," Eremon said, his ruler's voice as regal and smooth as she remembered it.

Anger blurred Lira's vision. She clenched her fists at her sides. Aidryn lay a steadying hand on her shoulder, but it served no purpose other than to enrage her further.

"What have you done to my city?" Lira said through gritted teeth.

Eremon rocked back on his heels, his brows rising in surprise. "What you see in the streets is only half the tale. If you'll allow me to show you the citizens in the archive, learning to read—and the new training grounds outside—you'll see the other half."

She opened her mouth to retort, but he held up a hand. "You see, it takes time to undo nearly a year of disaster, wouldn't you agree?"

"Less if you had ascended as you should," Lira spat.

Aidryn's grip tightened on her shoulder. "Remember, my love: Even the furnishings in the Dome have ears. We should retire to the throne room, where we can speak in private."

Lira didn't miss the loaded glance that passed between Eremon and Aidryn. The immortal fixed his silver eyes on Lira's husband, then said, "Very well."

Never mind the fact that this place is near vacant, the voice said. *Never mind that the council and most of the staff are dead.*

But it's just as well; the throne room is where you should be, after all.

Eremon turned and headed down the wide corridor. Lira and Aidryn fell into step beside Thorne as they followed in silence. She noted Thorne's rapt attention to the details of the Dome's interior. He craned his neck, taking in the glass overhead, the rich tapestries, the decadent embellishments—all such a stark contrast to Fortress Halgeir's bare, earthy stone and ornate wooden doors.

Eremon glanced over his shoulder at the warrior, as though echoing Lira's thoughts. "Is this your first time in the Dome, Thorne?"

"I visited one of the towers when we came for Aidryn," Thorne answered. "We used *turas*. I have never seen the rest."

"Remind me to give you a proper tour after we're done here," the Rí replied coolly, leading the group into the throne room. "For your willingness to negotiate peacefully, I offer you that, at the very least."

Negotiate peacefully? the voice mused.

"Under normal circumstances, I would have anointed you Defender in the throne room, Silira," Eremon said, pausing before the sentries who guarded its entrance.

He turned to Lira, his eyes glinting with an emotion she couldn't place. "It's unfortunate we've come to this, but perhaps we can put our tensions behind us and focus on the happy memories we have together here." His gaze flicked to Aidryn, then back to her. "All of us."

Lira bit her tongue and forced a tight smile. The coppery taste of blood flooded her mouth. It was best to avoid instigating another disagreement. Once they were in view of the dais, she would take it.

CHAPTER 78

AIDRYN

Dome

"I wish it were possible to focus on the good, Eremon," Lira replied. "But let us sit and talk it through. Perhaps we can reach some sort of accord."

It was obvious the immortal was stalling for time. When he spoke again, it was clear why.

"Silira..." Eremon began slowly. "I've asked the Crown Regent to be present for the official handover. Are you aware who holds that title?"

"Caitir," Lira said, her voice suddenly harsh and clipped, "no thanks to any of you. My magic was forced to tell me."

"Then you understand she can lay no claim to the throne, now or in the future," Eremon said.

Lira was clearly startled by that revelation. She rocked back a bit, regarding him with suspicion. "My magic confirms the truth," she said, a twinge of surprise in her voice.

"As it should." Eremon cast a fleeting look at Aidryn, then continued, "Caitir has been an asset to Iathium while I've reforged alliances with the sentries and my spies. But her moment of authority has passed."

Aidryn took a step back for a moment, motioning for Thorne to follow. It was only safe to move a few paces away, and just for a moment. They wouldn't have long.

He kept one eye on Eremon and Lira as he leaned toward Thorne and murmured, "Once we're inside, I need your trust. Do not question—just act. Understood?"

"You dare order me, Tarlach?" Thorne rumbled, crossing his arms. He was watching Lira and Eremon as closely as Aidryn was.

Rage roiled in Aidryn's gut, but he kept still, willing himself to remain calm. "I can't explain it yet. But you'll see." He took a steadying breath and added, "You will also call off the invasion. Call for any fighters who infiltrated the city to leave, or there will be consequences."

Thorne's eyes flashed. "Is that a threat?"

"It is," Aidryn said, holding his stare, "and unless you want Eremon, Lira, and all of Clan Beran to know the meaning of *sjovyn*, you will do as I ask."

Thorne stilled, though the glint in his eyes was murderous. "When this is over, I will end you."

"And Oda, too?" Aidryn shrugged indifferently, turning his full attention back to Lira. "I doubt that. You still aren't sure how much I know, or who else I might have told. Can't be too careful when a bit of knowledge could get you executed."

He hadn't breathed a word to anyone, of course. But it didn't hurt to make Thorne squirm. So few things in this world had that effect.

The warrior remained still but said nothing else. When Aidryn was satisfied he'd made his point, he added, "Once you understand the path I've chosen, you'll thank me."

Thorne grunted. "I doubt that."

CHAPTER 79
CAITIR

Dome

T hey were here. Lira, Aidryn, and Thorne Beran—
together in the Dome, meeting with Eremon right this
moment.

I can't do this.

That was exactly what Caitir had said to herself as she'd
forced Eremon's chamber door open. As she'd descended the
tower steps, emerged into the corridor, and returned to her own
room. As she'd dressed in a pale silk gown and arranged her
hair.

Now, she was in the kitchen, plaguing Kenji with her anxiety. Her palms were sweaty, her heart beating erratically as she
paced the room, the cook never taking his eyes from her as he
worked.

She paced to the foot of the stairs, then back to Kenji's
worktable, a hand on her belly. The baby kicked, and she
patted the place where she'd felt the impact.

"Caitir?" Kenji's voice drew her from her thoughts, and she
looked to him. His forehead was creased with worry.

"Yes?"

"Why don't you come sit down?"

She shook her head rapidly. Her stomach was so nervous, she felt breathless. "I can't sit down."

The cook stepped nearer, throwing a cloth over his shoulder. "It's going to turn out all right in the end," he said, patting her shoulder tenderly.

Caitir swallowed hard. "In the end, perhaps. But what about tonight?" Her voice dropped until it was barely audible. "Tomorrow?"

"We'll know in short order, won't we?" Kenji's hand rose to her face, and he pressed his palm to her cheek. The laugh lines around his eyes deepened as he smiled affectionately. "Remember that your brother is among the anointed. You have his love and Eremon's, above any contention the others may feel toward you. Even though it feels like you're alone, you are not."

Her eyes stung. "But Lira... I can't face her."

"You must," the cook replied, drawing her into an embrace. "And you must try to make amends."

"But—" The words caught in Caitir's throat, and a torrent of fear crashed over her. She fought against the rising conflict.

Everything I did was worth the price. Worth a chance at freedom. Worth Eremon. I can't make amends.

That was what she wanted to say. What she'd convinced herself to believe for so long, and what she'd told herself, even this morning. But a sudden flood of regret filled her, and she sagged against her friend.

"I don't know how to make things right," she admitted, sinking into his arms.

"You *do* what's right, of course," he replied. "It may not change things between you and Silira, but you will have more peace in the end."

Caitir tightened her grip on him. She would miss these

quiet times with Kenji—his humor and warmth. His pastries. The way he always seemed to know just what to say to lift her spirits or set her to rights. But once Eremon took the throne again, she wouldn't be able to remain in or near the Dome, for any reason. He had never said as much, but they both knew it was true.

She'd hoped to keep her next words locked away safely, but instead they poured from her unbidden. "I wish you were my father, Kenji. I wish my child could grow up knowing you."

"There now," he said, the crackle of tears in his voice. "I love you like my own. And Rhona knows that child needs a doting grandfather. I'm sure we can work something out." He gave her a little squeeze. "What say you? She'll have her mother, and her Emon, and her Kenji—and her uncle Aidryn, of course."

Caitir swallowed every argument that rose within her. For a moment, she let herself enjoy the thought.

But reality quickly swept back in. It was time to go, and...

Aidryn. Aidryn is here.

A swell of hope rose in Caitir, and suddenly, she wanted her brother. She had missed him, and she would tell him so, no matter what that meant.

That thought alone gave her enough courage to gently pull away from Kenji's embrace, though she grasped his plump hands and held his dark gaze.

"I will never forget your kindness," she said in a soft voice. "And I love you, too."

"Never forget your own heart." Kenji leaned forward and kissed her forehead. "It was the one thing your mother couldn't take from you, and it will guide you to your destiny."

CHAPTER 80

EREMON

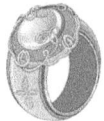

Dome

Eremon checked the timepiece on the wall across the corridor. It was nearly time for Caitir to enter the throne room. He'd asked her to use the opposite entrance, where another set of sentries would flank her for protection.

Knowing she would need that protection made his heart sink.

Here in Lira's presence, Eremon feared for Caitir's safety. This was not the woman he'd known before, and certainly not the woman he'd loved.

Though Lira's dark eyes were hard, he occasionally caught a glimpse of sickly green mist wafting across her irises. Clearly, something had gone very wrong since he'd last seen Aidryn. This was a reality he hadn't considered, nor prepared himself for. If he was being honest with himself, he was afraid to let her into the throne room at all.

He continued to stall, attempting to explain the improvements he and Caitir had enacted together. But it was clear Lira was hearing none of it. She stared straight through him, as though she could see beyond the thick, wooden doors that divided them from the dais. Her hands were clasped before her, her knuckles whitening with her obvious effort to remain still.

Paces away, Thorne was glowering, and Aidryn's expression was equally grim. The two had exchanged heated whispers a moment ago, but Eremon had been too preoccupied with Lira to eavesdrop. His agitation rose to dizzying proportions.

"Eremon," Lira ventured when he paused to wrack his brain for something else to say, "I'm curious. Why are we still standing out here? I thought this was to be a private meeting."

"It is," he answered, flustered. He cast a panicked glance at Aidryn, who just shot him a withering glare. "It's only that it isn't quite time yet."

"Oh?" Lira bit her lower lip, averting her eyes for a moment. When she met his gaze again, they were wholly green with corrupted power. "It's time when I say it is."

She gave no warning before she lifted her palms and hurled a burst of dark magic at Eremon.

It hit him squarely in the gut, blasting him clear through the wooden doors, which splintered with the impact. As he skidded backward into the throne room, he caught a glimpse of the sentries who had been guarding the door—or what was left of them. There was a clamor from Aidryn and Thorne as Lira stepped through the ruined doorway, past the burning wood and the sentries' melting armor.

Her corrupted green eyes were fixed on Eremon, her expression stony as she summoned more dark magic into her palms.

"Lira, what is this?" he shouted.

"You're trying to delay the inevitable," she replied, aiming another—larger—orb of dark magic at him. "I'm *going* to take the throne."

Lira released her hold on the power, and it shot in Eremon's direction. This time, he met it with cobalt magic of his own. The powers clashed and sustained as each poured their magic toward the other. Eremon's cobalt power devoured the black lightning, but still, Lira continued to expend the dark magic as though it was limitless. Her power had become far vaster, and she wielded it like a mortal goddess.

Eremon kept a careful tether on his magic as it flared, hoping to exhaust Lira. She screamed, fighting the sheer force of it, her curls blowing back, her face illuminated with cobalt light. He let the power surge once more, until the dark magic was finally extinguished and Lira collapsed onto her hands and knees, panting.

"You are not yourself, Lira," he said, closing in on her.

She looked up at Eremon and sneered. A trickle of blood was running down from her nose, over her lips, and dripping from her chin. His heart sank at the wild look in her eyes.

Behind her, Aidryn and Thorne had been inching closer, their weapons drawn. They looked as though they'd shared some unspoken agreement. Eremon was afraid to know what it was.

He fixed his attention on Aidryn, whose knuckles were white around an object that glinted of gold. The Key Keeper's blue eyes were wild, and for a moment, Eremon remembered what Aidryn had done at Fortress Halgeir. How he'd murdered Aeron to protect his sister.

Was that a dagger Aidryn held?

Eremon's horrified expression must have given him away, because Lira whirled on Aidryn and Thorne. This time, though, Eremon was ready. As she turned her dark magic on the other two men, Eremon enveloped them all in his protective magic, forcing the black lightning to fizzle out.

"Drop the blade, Aidryn!" Eremon shouted over the roar of his power.

He was surprised to hear Lira cry, "It's not a blade!" She

whirled to face Eremon, her brown eyes completely clear as the magic stirred the curls around her face. "It's Iuchair."

The key? Why would Aidryn have summoned it?

But the question fizzled out when Eremon fully understood the shift that had just taken place.

"It's *you*," Eremon said, almost losing his hold on the protective power. His magic must have somehow snuffed the darkness that had overtaken her. Hope swelled in his chest at the realization. "What happened?"

Aidryn looked stunned as he took another step closer to Lira. Two steps. Thorne watched him carefully, his amber eyes flicking between the Key Keeper and the Witness Tree. He was clearly trying to fit together the disparate pieces of a puzzle he hadn't yet deciphered. If nothing else, Eremon could understand *that* about the warrior.

"I..." Now, it was Lira's turn to falter. "I don't—"

"You *do* know, Lira," Aidryn said, taking another step toward her. His gaze was hard, and a chill swept over Eremon at the sight of it. "Tell us yourself, or I'll do it for you."

"Threats are unnecessary, Tarlach," Eremon said, maintaining his hold on the cobalt magic. "She knows we only want her safe."

Lira took a panicked look around, only to realize the three men had her surrounded. When she turned back to Eremon, there was steely resolve in her expression.

"Do you?" A harsh laugh broke from between her lips. "It doesn't seem that way."

Thorne held up a steadying hand, then lowered his sword to the floor, setting it aside. Eremon didn't think the warrior's attempt at reassurance was the least bit soothing. Equally unnerving was the way Aidryn was looking at Lira, and the sharp tone in his voice.

"Your thoughts have been warped," Aidryn replied slowly. "That voice you've been listening to—it isn't Rhona."

"What voice?" Eremon and Thorne demanded in unison.

Lira went ashen. "She has given me answers when none of you would. Her words ring true."

Several realizations dawned on Eremon at once. *A woman's voice. Truths. Corrupted magic. The pendant.*

Vor'sca.

"Do they, indeed?" Eremon called on the cool, detached manner he'd often embodied when doling out a sentence or dealing with an unruly council. "Then the fault lies with us. In trying to protect you, we failed to explore some possibilities. So let us begin with this: your pendant has been found, Silira."

Her gaze flicked to Aidryn. He confirmed Eremon's words with a nod.

"Where is it?" she asked. She fiddled nervously with the fabric of her sleeve.

"In the hands of the immortal, Vor'sca," Eremon answered. "The one your grandmother set out to find."

Lira puzzled over his answer. In her distraction, she didn't notice Aidryn edging nearer, still gripping Iuchair in his fist. Eremon's heart hammered.

"Does that mean it will be returned to me?" she asked hopefully.

"I don't know," said Eremon. "You see, she is allied with Aila. Maybe even King La'hiran."

"What?" Lira cried, horror washing over her expression. She quickly masked it with a look of contempt. "Why didn't you tell me?"

"You were slipping further away from us," Aidryn answered, his voice dangerously smooth—almost hypnotic. "Because we had so few answers, we tried to shelter you until we knew more. Clearly, that was the wrong decision."

"I think, *sjeinga*, that you should have told us of the voice," Thorne said.

Sister. The painfully gentle tone in the hulking warrior's voice surprised Eremon. He watched Lira soften in response to it, and a wave of jealousy washed over him. From the look on Aidryn's face, the Key Keeper was feeling equally piqued.

"I thought it was helping me. I thought..." Lira squeezed her eyes shut and shook her head. "No one else would tell me everything."

"Then you and I have something in common," the warrior replied. "I also knew little. I was forced to have my spies learn the truth when no one else would share it. If I had known everything when you were still at Fortress Halgeir, I would have told you."

Lira reached out to Thorne as though she wanted him nearer. He closed the distance between them and took her small hand in his. Instantly, Eremon noticed the flash of golden magic that passed between their palms—watched Lira visibly relax as Thorne poured his healing power into her.

For the first time, Eremon felt grateful for the hulking oaf. Perhaps he would be of some use yet.

"I'm sorry we've met the same fate, *sjeovi*," Lira said.

"We have," Thorne answered, "in more ways than you know. Now, I will share the rest of my truth. We were warped by the same immortal."

"What?" Lira rocked back in surprise. Eremon and Aidryn exchange a loaded glance.

Thorne gave her a small nod. "Vor'sca controls the archers. I hired them for information, and so did Caitir."

"And what became of that?" Lira asked warily.

"She used *turas* to take everything they learned to Aila," Thorne answered, his expression stony. "They've succeeded in creating division in Rodhlan, to the point of war."

"A war your overlord incited," Eremon said through gritted teeth. His power flickered, and Thorne's attention snapped to him. The warrior gave a nearly imperceptible shake of his head.

Weak and foolish, Thorne had said. Perhaps he had been right.

Eremon doubled down on his magic to sustain it, pushing past the swell of emotions that had caused it to falter.

"No, not war," Lira said with a shake of her head. "Artur believes I should rule as rightful heir."

"Then what are those warriors doing outside my walls?" Eremon demanded, sweeping his arm to indicate the vast Dome. He couldn't suppress the angry waver in his voice as he added, "I left the choice of ascension to you, Silira. I trusted you."

"And I trusted *you.*" The resentment in Lira's eyes nearly took him to his knees. "I believed you would come back and take the throne, but you were too fearful. The Eremon I knew would never have bowed to fear; he would have made the right choice!"

Eremon barked a bitter laugh. "Oh, would I have? I'm curious—which Eremon did you think you knew? Because I was a failure of a ruler. I couldn't even survive my own magic."

The color drained from Lira's cheeks.

"Mortal gods, Eremon, could you have at least tried to finesse your answer?" Aidryn groaned.

Lira kept her focus wholly on Eremon. Her dark eyes—the eyes he'd come to love so dearly, and then resent—bored into him.

"So you simply returned to what was familiar: failure." A cruel smile curled her lips. "Pity; you have so much unrealized potential. I'm sorry I ever believed in it."

The world around Eremon hollowed out, and finally, he lost his grip on his protective power. For a moment, his eyesight dimmed. A harsh ringing filled his ears, drowning out Thorne's shouts and the crackle of Lira's dark magic. Eremon's skin crawled with the force of the black lightning, and the smell of ozone filled his nostrils.

He fought for control of his senses, his pulse pounding in his head. Suddenly, his hearing and sight rushed back into stark clarity—just as Aidryn lunged for Lira. Her eyes were wild as she registered his movements, just a moment too late. Before she could react, Aidryn had knocked her to the ground.

CHAPTER 81

LIRA

Dome

Lira's head cracked against the throne room's marble floor, Aidryn's full weight holding her there. He pinned her arms above her head, pressing her wrists against the cold tiles. She cried out, struggling against him, hoping to gain a foothold and throw him off. But Aidryn had trained with Clan Beran, too, and he knew how to evade her efforts.

"Thorne!" he shouted, grunting as he applied his full strength. Lira's head swam with the impact of her fall. "Eremon!"

In moments, both men were at their side. Lira tried and failed to thrash, a wild wail tearing from her throat. Thorne was on his knees beside her head, reaching to soothe her as he might reach for a scared pup or a lost bear cub.

"Shhh," he said, touching her curls. "Hush now, sister."

She stilled for a moment, turning her head to look at the warrior. Thorne had never spoken the endearment in Athi. He doubled in her line of sight, and she blinked rapidly, attempting to right her vision.

"Why should I?" she rasped, her voice now raw. "Eremon will lead my city to ruin."

Above her, Aidryn flinched. Though Eremon had followed Thorne to her side, he hung back, staring at the floor.

"This is no longer about Iathium," Thorne said. "It is about you, Silira Mór. Lira Tarlach. Witness Tree. We love you."

Unbidden tears began to flow down her cheeks. She hated the way these men commanded her emotions and filtered the truth to suit their own ends. Hated that they believed she was too weak and breakable to handle honesty.

Still, the strange sort of awe that lit Eremon's expression was almost enough to break through her anger. He had never been able to imagine that Thorne could be tender or compassionate. She was glad he'd gotten the chance to see that the warrior was capable of more than brute strength.

Lira's show of weakness gave Aidryn the chance to shift his hold on her. He gripped her wrists with one hand now. In the other, he held Iuchair.

"Eremon," he said, "be ready."

"For what?" the Rí asked.

"You'll see," Aidryn murmured. His voice was hypnotic, and it lulled Lira in a way that was deeply unsettling, though she wasn't quite sure why.

A swirl of crimson magic burst from the golden key, twirling around Aidryn and illuminating his face. His lashes fluttered shut, concealing the cerulean eyes she loved so dearly. Lira was mesmerized as the key itself began to glow, as though made of light itself. Her breath caught as she studied Aidryn, and for a moment, the will to fight left her entirely. She relaxed in his grip, watching his magic stir the loose strands of hair that framed his face.

"This I vow," he began, pressing the key to his own heart. "The Witness Tree's birthright power is freed from the corruption of dark magic."

Iuchair transformed, abandoning its tangible gold form and shifting into something akin to sunlight.

No, the voice breathed in horror. *Stop him!*

Lira bucked against Aidryn. He sank his weight lower onto her body. His brow creased with the effort, but he held firm on the spell. "This I vow," he ground out, holding her down, "that the anointed powers of two clans will no longer be at the mercy of darkness."

From Aidryn's lips tumbled an incantation in Hes'ka that she couldn't place. She screamed and thrashed. And inside her head, the voice did, too. But he never broke concentration; he continued to speak, and Lira continued to scream.

"What are you doing to her?" Thorne demanded over the din.

"You're going to kill her!" Eremon cried. He suddenly sounded very far away.

Your husband will kill you, the voice agreed grimly. *He will kill you all, and deep down, you know he is capable of it.*

Perhaps Eremon was right. Lira had believed that Aidryn only wanted the ring, but maybe she had been mistaken. Maybe he truly wanted her dead.

The pounding in her own head drowned out Aidryn's answer, and for a moment, she felt lost in the swirling chaos of her own mind. When the world came into focus again, Aidryn had raised Iuchair, and there was a terrible resolve in his eyes she'd never seen there before. It was love and fury and madness, and she froze at the sight.

"This I vow," he said, the final words catching in his throat. "Today, the Binding between the Witness Tree and the Key Keeper will be forever broken."

With one swift motion, Aidryn plunged the key made of light into Lira's heart.

CHAPTER 82
AIDRYN

Dome

Lira's face contorted in pain, and she screamed, her body arching beneath Aidryn. His eyes filled with searing tears, but he maintained his grip on Iuchair. Then, he gave the key a slight turn—just the way Eiren had instructed.

"Draw away the darkness," he commanded in Hes'ka, his voice thick with grief.

Eremon had moved to Lira's opposite side, watching with horror as her magic—sickly green and flickering with black lightning—gathered around the key's base and began to rise from her body in a corrupted orb. It illuminated her face like a death shroud as it rose, and Aidryn didn't try to fight the full-body shudder that wracked him at the sight. The orb hovered a foot above Aidryn's head, threads of magic trailing from where the key of light was lodged in the center of Lira's chest.

Beneath him, she continued to struggle.

"You'll have to summon the Binding," Aidryn said through gritted teeth. Eremon winced. "I need your help to break it."

"No..." Lira wailed, tears streaming down her cheeks.

Aidryn tried to shut his heart to the sound, but he failed miserably.

"I..." Eremon's gaze flicked between Aidryn and Lira, and then he nodded reluctantly. "All right."

Eremon summoned a burst of bright, cobalt magic into his palms and began murmuring in Itelos. His magic built and tangled around and between them. It drew a thread of pure, emerald magic from Lira's body, along with a thread of crimson from Aidryn's. In the middle of the threads was a glowing knot that tied the two together, where their powers coiled and mingled. The sheer harmony of it dragged a ragged sob from deep within Aidryn's chest.

How could a power that had once healed their magical wounds have been so easily turned into a force for destruction?

"Stop looking so forlorn, Tarlach," Eremon said gently, as though he'd been reading Aidryn's thoughts. "It's only a spell. But the bond you have with her? That is very real."

The truth in Eremon's voice, and the sorrow that under-pinned it, were the only comforts Aidryn could salvage.

Lira cried out again, pressing hard against Aidryn's grasp before she gave up, limp and panting.

"Please..." She sobbed harder.

The sound of the agony in her voice tore at him, and his chin trembled. "I'm sorry," he ground out, shuddering, fighting every impulse to release her. "Lira—"

A wave of dark magic burst from her body, which dissipated when it met Eremon's magic. Its impact reverberated through Aidryn, burning his palm where he held her wrists. The acrid smell of singed skin made his stomach churn.

"Release me, please—*please*," Lira rasped, "I don't want to harm anyone, I swear."

"We know, *sjeinga*," Thorne said softly. "We know your heart."

"Where is my heart?" Her voice was weak. Lost. "I fear I've

none left."

Thorne turned to Aidryn, panicked now. "We're *losing* her, Tarlach," he said.

Indeed, Lira's body had gone pliant beneath Aidryn. Panic tore through him. What if he killed Lira with this unknown spell, the same way he'd killed Edan? Did her survival matter to Clan Tarlach? To Eiren? Or had it only been about preserving Aidryn's magic all along?

Suddenly, he felt selfish and foolish. In his fear, he had asked for help from the adviser. He had trusted without question when he didn't truly know her motives.

What if she had devised all of this to end Lira?

He couldn't stomach the thought. Too many of his loved ones had already died—some by his own hand. And Lira was his greatest love, so why would he risk this? What had he been thinking?

Stunned, he released his grip on her wrists and rocked back. She blinked up at him, as though equally surprised.

"What are you doing, Aidryn?" Eremon cried. "It has to be now, before the dark magic takes over again."

Aidryn faltered. "I..."

"Do it, Rí," Thorne growled furiously.

Eremon didn't hesitate again. He began to whisper in Itelos, his power surging and flaring. The strands of power responded in kind, as though snapping to attention while Eremon's magic moved. Vines and cords of silver appeared among the strands, knotted in the center and wrapping around Aidryn's and Lira's forearms. This physical manifestation of the Binding had appeared once before—when the spell had first taken hold in the mountains.

Eremon made several movements with his fingers, as though unraveling bits of string from a knot. The vines and cords responded in kind, unraveling themselves from around Lira's and Aidryn's forearms until there was a mere thread left connecting the two of them. He and Lira watched, transfixed by this final look at the power they'd shared.

"Why are you doing this to us?" she whimpered, watching as the cord began to burn away beneath Eremon's power.

Though Aidryn's heart squeezed, he kept his focus. "This is the only way to protect our magic."

"But our marriage..."

"Our marriage isn't lost," Aidryn replied, heartened that she had ceased struggling and hopeful at the sound of her voice. "Just the spell that initiated it."

He held his breath as Eremon let out a heavy sigh and let the final cord burn up in a burst of cobalt flame. Lira whimpered, covering her face with her hands.

For a moment, the world went wholly silent.

A sudden spark of heat ignited in Aidryn's chest as the Binding dissipated and Lira's magic was sealed out of his body. Lira must have felt the same sensation, because she made a sound as though in pain. Immediately, what was left of her emerald magic surged up from the base of Iuchair, still violently lodged in her heart, and gathered with the rest of the power that floated above her.

There was a void within him where Lira's magic had been, and he suddenly missed the cool, soothing feel of it. But his own power felt brighter and more vibrant than it ever had. His sense of loss clashed with his magic's singing, as though it were glad to finally be home and untangled from so many strands of power.

Lira grew quiet, stunned into stillness. "Is it over?" she whispered, her fingers drifting to where Iuchair still protruded from her heart, glowing as brightly as a star.

No; there was one more step.

"Suspend the power of the Witness Tree," Aidryn whispered, tightening his hold on the key, "until she may use it without fear of corruption."

CHAPTER 83
LIRA

Dome

S uspend. *Suspend.*

Lira felt the magic begin to leave her body just as she fully understood what Aidryn was doing to her.

He was locking her magic away.

"No," she screamed, thrashing against him. "You can't do this!"

"Lira, there's no other way." Eremon's voice sounded from somewhere beside her.

Through the haze of pain and desperation, she couldn't find where his voice was coming from. All she could perceive was the Great Key and her husband pinning her down, stealing the one thing that had truly been hers: her magic. Her birthright.

Was Aidryn stealing it for Aila? After all this time, had he been lying in wait for the perfect opportunity?

Her mind raced as they struggled. Lira could feel dark magic welling up inside of her, taking up the space that her birthright power had occupied moments before. Perhaps if she projected it outward, she could preserve her magic. Flee for safety.

Lira flailed, striking Aidryn's left eye with the heel of her hand, intent on finally freeing herself from his hold. But dark magic poured from her palm unbidden, sealing her to him as though it possessed its own intention. Aidryn cried out in pain and terror, and the sound of his agony was enough to make Lira freeze.

Look what you have done, the voice in her head crooned.

Horror overtook her.

Aidryn pressed against Lira, making no attempt to escape the pain. Her thoughts were cut short by a sharp twisting in her chest. When she looked down, Aidryn had turned the key. It sent a wave of heat blazing from her heart into her limbs, like a merciless hunter's knife.

The intensity of the pain silenced the scream that crept up Lira's throat, and she went rigid in its grasp. She watched the final strands of emerald magic pour from her body, joining the orb that had suspended itself high overhead.

Over the next few moments, Lira returned to herself as the last of the dark magic left her. Her mind filled with an agonizing, keening wail—the voice. A moment later, it vanished.

Iuchair vanished, too.

And Aidryn's head lolled, his lifeless body collapsing against Thorne in a heap.

The warrior caught him with a grunt and lowered him gently to the floor.

"No, Tarlach..." Thorne murmured. "Don't do this."

Eremon scrambled to Thorne's side. "Mortal gods," he groaned.

Terrifying clarity overtook Lira. "Aidryn..." she whimpered, immobilized by a flood of questions she couldn't bear to ask—though the answers lay at her side, within reach. In the arms of her friends, who had not betrayed her, but who had helped her husband save her life.

Aidryn had found a way to remove the dark magic. *Aidryn.*

Memories of the past few days rushed in on her, and her body began to shake. How could she have kept the voice a secret? Why had she let it warp her thoughts until she'd believed that Aidryn, of all people, meant to steal Eremon's throne—or do her harm, for that matter?

The horrible things she'd said and done... *mortal gods.* She couldn't have meant them. She *couldn't* have.

Lira ached all over, and she was so weak, she could barely move. She rolled to her side, straining to catch a glimpse of Aidryn, but she couldn't rise. Thorne and Eremon were entirely focused on him, and she was so weary—so afraid of what lay ahead of her. Absently, she noticed that there was no tremor in her right hand. Perhaps that was because her magic was gone.

Gone. She could scarcely grasp the finality of it.

Eremon threw a glance over his shoulder at her. "He's alive." His tone was cold, clipped, and drenched with hatred.

Alive. Fresh tears filled Lira's eyes. "What did I do?"

Eremon turned away from her. Neither he nor Thorne answered.

Thunder rumbled overhead. For a moment, Lira thought a storm must have blown in outdoors. It didn't take long before she realized it was the rumble of dark magic, consuming her birthright.

Thorne's gaze flicked up toward the orb, and he jerked his chin in Eremon's direction. "Make quick work of that. I'll stay with Tarlach."

Eremon nodded, not bothering to look at Lira again as he rose and lifted his hands. He closed his eyes, and the orb of power drifted down to him until it hovered between his palms. Lira watched as he began to draw threads of black and emerald power from the orb, burning away the dark magic in one cobalt-filled palm. In its wake, only pure emerald was left behind. The purified power reformed in a twin orb of its own.

"Come closer, *sjeinga*," Thorne murmured, drawing her attention back to Aidryn. "You need to see."

It took every ounce of strength Lira had left to begin crawling toward the warrior and her husband. Thorne let her struggle, and she deserved to. In her stubborn pride, she had allowed herself to be completely overtaken by hatred and darkness.

No matter what she was about to see, she would never forgive herself for it.

On trembling limbs, she moved to Aidryn's side. He lay unconscious and pale, his breaths alarmingly shallow. A strange, jagged wound was forming around his left eye, making its way outward and etching into his skin.

When Lira reached his side, she cradled his face in her hands, tears clouding her vision.

"Aidryn, wake for me, love," she said, stroking his cheek. "I'm here."

He didn't stir. Lira whirled to look at Thorne, but the look of deep disappointment on his face was enough to make her avert her eyes again.

"What kind of wound is this?" she demanded, voice tremulous. "Can you heal it? Your father?"

Thorne closed his eyes. "I don't know."

She reached out to clutch the warrior's hand. "Thorne, what did I do to him?"

"We won't know until he wakes," Thorne said, his voice grim.

"*If* he wakes," Eremon said in a low growl.

Lira flinched, a sob breaking from her as she leaned forward to press her cheek to Aidryn's chest. A moment later, Thorne pressed a gentle hand to her shoulder. Something about the contact shattered Lira's insides, and she began to wail.

This felt like Faolan's death all over again. More tears trailed down her cheeks at the memory and its eerie similarity to this scene. But Aidryn was still breathing—he was breathing. He was breathing and stirring, and—

"Lira," he whispered, his hand drifting to the back of her head. His voice was raw and weak.

"Aidryn..." She was afraid to move, so she lay there and let him stroke her hair. Noticed the steady rise and fall of his chest, the strong drum of his heartbeat.

"You survived the breaking," he rasped. "I'm so glad."

Lira pushed herself up so she could see his face. Aidryn's brow was furrowed as though he was in pain. Tentatively, she traced her fingertips over his jawline.

"I hurt you," she said. "I'm so sorry."

"It's nothing," he whispered. "Just a headache. Likely no worse than the one I gave you."

She had forgotten the pounding in her own head. Now that he mentioned it, the pain rushed back into her consciousness. As though sensing her discomfort, Aidryn found her hand and squeezed it.

"It isn't nothing, Tarlach," Thorne said in a soft voice. "I want you to open your eyes."

"In a moment." Aidryn tried to blink but winced. "I had a pain in my head before. It was this horrible, bursting sensation, just here." He pointed to his left cheekbone. "It felt like a dagger blade lodged in my eye."

Thorne exchanged a panicked look with Lira. The warrior summoned an orb of healing magic and applied it to Aidryn's face, over the scarring. He relaxed, sighing in relief as the power took hold.

"Try now," Thorne said after a long moment. "I don't like that scarring on your face."

"Can you open your eyes?" Lira said, stroking his arm reassuringly.

Aidryn's eyelids tightened for a moment, and he raised his hand to shade his face as his lashes fluttered open. When Lira met his gaze, her fist tightened on his tunic sleeve, a broken cry rising in her throat.

His right eye was clear, cerulean—the lovely blue it had always been. But in his left eye, the iris had lost its color. His pupil was clouded and gray, and it roiled like a magical storm. Lira thought she could see the flash of black lightning in the ominous-looking clouds that swirled there.

She clamped a hand over her mouth to suppress a cry. Thorne swore in Brylla, low and deep.

Aidryn blinked again. Gingerly, he pressed a palm to his eye and stared straight up at the sky.

"Something's wrong," he said, his gaze darting around the room but never truly resting on anything. "I can't see out of it."

Oh, gods. His eyesight. Aidryn had gone momentarily blind when he'd tampered with Lira's magic. They'd both known it was a risk through the Binding before. But Lira had directed dark magic *into* his eye when she'd tried to escape him. Intentional or not, she was responsible for this.

Lira's body trembled violently. "Perhaps Ljós can restore your sight," she said, her chin trembling. "Surely, he can reverse the damage."

Aidryn pushed himself to sit, hissing in pain. Thorne barked at him to lie back down, but he held up a hand to silence him, keeping his gaze trained on his wife. Lira shrank beneath the horror that etched its way across his expression, followed by rage so tangible, the hairs on her neck rose.

"Silira," he said, short, clipped—firmer this time. "Why did you keep the voice a secret?"

He sounded cold, hard. Distant. The tenderness he'd just

shown her was gone. It chilled her blood and turned her stomach.

Her face burned, and fresh tears fell down her cheeks as the words tumbled out. "At first, I believed I could figure out how to control the dark magic myself. Everyone was divided—all of us trying so hard to do everything alone. All of us afraid of making the others angry because of who we supported or what course of action we thought we should take.

"When the voice came to me, I knew you were keeping the truth secret, and she *felt* so real. Oda believed she heard Rhona during the wildfire that day, and I thought..." Her words were barely tangible, she was quaking so hard as she spoke. "I hoped Rhona was helping me, too. I felt so alone."

Eremon crept closer to listen, his work on the magic finished. The more Lira spoke, the more horrified she became —with herself, with the broken magic that had led them here. With this mess that none of them seemed capable of righting.

Aidryn's face crumpled, tears gathering in his eyes, too. He covered his face with his palms. Lira sat up, drawing her knees to her chest as Thorne watched her carefully.

"First, Silira, you should know that your power was being tampered with," Thorne said. "If Vor'sca is your counterpart and she has the pendant, we know that to be true. We will not hold you responsible for everything that has happened, but you will need to answer for yourself." He heaved a deep sigh as he continued. "This is why I told Aidryn to sever the Binding weeks ago. He refused."

"You warned me she would turn the dark magic on me," Aidryn said, voice vacant. "I didn't listen. I was a fool."

"Aidryn, you must believe that I didn't mean for this to happen," Lira said. Desperation welled within her. "I swear it."

"You could have come to me," he said, "yet you trusted yourself above all others."

"When no one else would," she answered. "*Please.*"

Aidryn refused to look in her direction. Instead, he pushed himself to his feet and headed toward the throne room's eastern exit.

Lira forced herself to her feet, wrapping her arms around her middle as she limped after him. "Aidryn—"

He turned, throwing out a hand to stay her. "Don't!" he snarled.

The visceral fury in his voice—his expression—stopped her in her tracks.

"Aidryn, *please!*" she cried, her voice brittle with desperation.

But Aidryn kept moving, lengthening the distance between them. Now, he was almost to the door, and despite her pleas, he did not look back again. When Lira tried to follow, her knees began to give way. Thorne caught her by the elbow and held her up, pulling her against his side.

"Let him go," the warrior said in a low voice, tightening his hold on Lira and giving her a little shake. "Let him grieve."

CHAPTER 84
CAITIR

Dome

Caitir jumped as the door to the main corridor burst open and Aidryn pushed through. A strange, startled noise squeaked from her as she pressed herself against the far wall and covered her mouth with a palm. He turned toward the sound, throwing out a hand as though to steady himself.

He looked terrified, and his face—his *eye*—

She gasped, then stepped closer to survey the wound. "Nami's rotting *bones*, Aidryn. What happened?"

"Blind," he said through gritted teeth. His unkempt brown hair was falling into his face, half-unbound. Tear stains streaked his cheeks, and his skin was splotched and red. "Blinded by dark magic, and loyalty, and love, and whatever other weaknesses you always goaded me for. You were right, they were all true, and I hope you're happy."

Shock rushed over her as she tried and failed to piece together what might have happened.

He moved to go, but she grabbed his wrist. "Stop!"

Reluctantly, he ceased his movement and let Caitir coax him back to face her. He closed his eyes, a stray tear slipping down his cheek, and she reached up to brush it away.

"My brother." She tightened her grip on his wrist, and his expression softened. "I was right, they're all true, and that's why I love you. And I missed you. And I'm sorry for everything."

Aidryn said her name on a sob, then enveloped her in a warm embrace. She leaned into his familiar scent and the safety of his arms, and she wondered why she had never trusted him to protect her before. Being here with him was like being home. And though she would never deserve his forgiveness, she could at least savor this moment. It might be all she would get.

"Forgive me." Aidryn sighed, pulling away after a long moment. "I'm in considerable pain, and it has been a terrible few days. Weeks." He huffed a laugh that sounded more like a scoff. "Months."

Caitir gave him a tight smile. "Why not years, while we're at it?"

He shrugged halfheartedly, turning toward the throne room doors as though he wanted to go back inside. But he hesitated, instead placing a palm on the door and hanging his head. "Years."

Tentatively, she took a step toward him, wrapping her arms around her middle. "Where is Lira?"

"With Eremon and Thorne Beran," Aidryn said, "just through these doors."

"And you... don't wish to go back to her?"

He laughed bitterly. "Not particularly."

She worried her lip. Something was deeply wrong, but it would do no good to demand an explanation now. Instead, Caitir tried to consider what Aidryn might need.

In the past, she might have found a way to turn the attention back on herself. She likely would in the future. Truly, she was no good at seeing to others. It had always been much easier for her to fish for compliments, hurl a barb, or change the subject with the latest gossip.

But the way Aidryn sagged—the defeated look on his face —gave her pause.

"Would you like a quiet place to rest?" she finally asked.

Slowly, he turned his head to look at her again. His expression was a bit dumbfounded. Strange, how something so simple could inspire his awe of her. Instead of refusing the offer, he straightened. "I would. Alone, if you please."

She nodded, then offered her arm. Aidryn would need to move carefully, adjusting to an injury like this. "Then come with me. There are plenty of empty chambers—take any one you like."

Cautiously, he looped his arm though hers, just like the old days when they walked through the city arm-in-arm with Lira. And to her surprise, he leaned in and kissed her cheek. She wasn't sure why, but there was a finality to it she didn't want to explore.

Somehow, it felt like goodbye.

CHAPTER 85
EREMON

Dome

E erie silence descended over the throne room in Aidryn's wake. The horror of what had just transpired had ripped anything Eremon might have said from his throat. Letting silence lie wasn't a strength of his. The urge to fill it was agonizing against his lack of adequate statements.

His eyes drifted to Lira's magic, which still hovered overhead, suspended in an orb of glowing emerald. Thorne had followed her to the floor, wrapping a large arm around her and holding her to his side as she wept. Pain lanced Eremon's heart at the sight, and then he was walking in their direction without a second thought.

Eremon moved so he was facing them and knelt before Lira. She raised her tearstained face to meet his eyes, and for a moment, he was transported back to the spring. Back to their first real meeting in the archival chamber, when he had anointed her Defender of Histories. He had been so full of love for her back then. Even now, after every terrible word that had passed between them—after the quarrels and even the magical battle they'd just waged—he cared for her still. Perhaps he always would.

They held one another's gaze for an agonizingly long moment before either spoke.

"Would you like to have your magic back?" Eremon asked softly. "I think it's ready for you."

Lira blinked at him, as though she hadn't understood the question.

"After everything that's happened?" She shook her head, looking down at her lap. "Why would I want it now?"

Her words bludgeoned him. She was the Witness Tree of Rodhlan. Once an anointed was chosen, the choice was set until the end of their days. Even if she never embraced her magic again, there would be no Anointed of Clan Mór until her death. And with the mountain clan's preference of Skelly's maternal bloodline, he wasn't sure how the power would be passed down. Lira would have to bear a daughter first—or perhaps, if she perished before Ellwyn, her cousin would take up the mantle next.

"Eremon, your panicked thoughts are almost loud enough to hear," she said, every bit of her weariness apparent in her tone. "Why don't you share them?"

He refocused on Lira, keenly aware of Thorne's menacing stare weighing on him. Her curls were soaked with sweat, her pale skin blotchy. Dark shadows had bloomed beneath her eyes, and she looked badly in need of a bath and a good night's sleep.

"I was only thinking about what's going to happen if there's no one else to embrace your power," Eremon said. "What would Rodhlan do without its Witness Tree?"

Lira leveled a steady, piercing gaze at him as she replied, "What it would do without its rightful, immortal ruler, I suppose. There's only one of you, and only one of me. And if you have the agency to abandon your role here because you might not *want* it, then so do I."

Eremon opened his mouth to retort, then shut it as the truth flooded his body, reverberating down to his bones. He'd wanted to say, *We need you to do the right thing.* But hadn't that been what Lira had begged him to do this entire time?

The room reeled around him as he finally grasped how she had been feeling. How everyone had felt toward him. And Eremon had been trapped in his own fear, unable to consider anyone's feelings but his own.

In the wake of his loss—in his own devastation at losing Lira and his city—he had immobilized himself in the worst possible way. And although it was true that Caitir had been worthy of his help and protection, he could have ascended and still chosen to protect her. This deceptive charade to buy himself time had resulted in chaos on every level, and now he wasn't sure if he could repair the damage.

Eremon ran a hand over his face and sighed, closing his eyes for a long moment before he opened them to meet hers once again.

"Lira." He extended his hand to her, but she only looked down at his empty palm, as though unsure how to respond. "I am so very sorry. I swear to you, I'll make this right."

She turned her own hand over, studying his ring. "I suppose you want this," she murmured.

He rocked back in surprise, pulling his hand back. "No, I—I only meant for you to take my hand."

Suddenly, the ring flared with cobalt light. Lira's eyes widened a fraction, and she turned the stone so he could see it. Thorne drifted toward them, squinting.

The gemstone's full power was replenished, and it glowed luminous with Eremon's protective magic.

"It must have repaired itself when we removed the dark magic," Eremon said, leaning closer for a better look.

"I think my darkness was suppressing it," Lira said.

Thorne grunted in agreement.

"We should find Aidryn," Eremon ventured, "and gather back here like we meant to before."

Lira looked down at her hands again and shrugged, curling in on herself. "He won't want to be found."

This time, Eremon moved near enough to grasp Lira's hand. Her face snapped up, and her fingers tightened on his. "He will *always* want to be found by you, Lira."

Lira's dark eyes filled with tears again, and she shook her head. "Not after today."

"Yes," Eremon pressed, "he will. The two of you have a bond that I was always jealous of before, and I never understood it. Now..."

Now that I have Caitir, I finally do, he wanted to say. But perhaps this was the wrong time to articulate it. Lira might not understand.

But she nodded. "Now you have it, too."

He sighed. "Yes. I want to keep her safe, even after she gives up the regency."

"I hope she proves herself true." Lira held his gaze. "If there's a way to help her, I have no doubt you'll find it."

CHAPTER 86
LIRA

Dome

On trembling legs, Lira led Thorne down into the archive. They descended the wide stone stairwell together, the daylight vanishing quickly as they moved. Thankfully, the torches at the base of the stairs had been lit. Beyond that, it appeared as though the archival floor was illuminated, too.

Lira's orb of emerald magic hovered at her side, drifting along behind her like an eager companion. Even after Eremon's pressing, she had still declined to take it back. For now, she wanted to rest—to remember what it was like to be in her body without an entire clan's magic thrumming inside her. To recall a memory or a portion of recorded history without being inundated with fragments of the lived histories.

She hadn't realized how much magic exhausted her until she'd been freed from its hold.

Reluctantly, Eremon had shown Lira how to summon the power and coax it to move with her, like it was now. Like everything else within Rodhlan's vast magical sphere, it was initiated through intent. He had explained how, in theory, Lira could anchor the magic to an object. The method stopped short of fully imbuing the object with power. It had been seldom practiced throughout history because it made the free-floating magic vulnerable to theft.

Now, Lira hoped to anchor her power to an object—a book, perhaps—in the inner chamber, just long enough so that she could rest and determine what to do next.

Afterward, Eremon had gone in search of Caitir, who had not been waiting outside the throne room as agreed. Since Aidryn had used the exit where she would have been, they'd surmised the siblings must be together. Lira couldn't help the pang of jealousy that squeezed her heart at the thought. Aidryn had fled from her, only to disappear with his sister who had caused them all such trouble.

Then again, Lira had caused everyone trouble, too. The realization was equal parts maddening and sobering.

She hadn't missed the look in Eremon's eyes when he'd said Caitir's name. That had also stung, but there was also relief in knowing he had truly moved on. It had hurt for him to admit that he still loved Lira when all this began.

Apprehension filled her as she and Thorne stepped onto the archival floor. A quick scan of the room proved it to be vacant. Quills, books, ink pots, and sheets of parchment had been abandoned haphazardly, as though everyone had fled.

Shame swept over her, and her cheeks grew hot. They had likely overheard the commotion in the throne room.

Lira paused in the middle of the archival floor, an overwhelming sense of familiarity surging through her. Her magic bumped into the back of her head, as though it hadn't looked where it was going. The familiar feeling of its power raised the hairs on her neck.

She sighed, her eyes roaming the familiar stacks. Her beloved tomes, full to bursting with deceitful ink, seemed far less inviting than they had in her former life. For that's what her time in the archive had been: a life now past. The realization nearly brought her to her knees.

"What's wrong?" Thorne murmured, moving nearer to her. More than once today, he'd shared his healing magic, calming her when nothing else could.

Lira forced a pinched smile. "Only realizing that all those years, everything I dedicated myself to was for nothing."

Thorne glowered. "It was not a waste. Iathium still needs you."

She chewed her lip, reaching into the pouch at her side to retrieve Eremon's key to the inner chamber. "Iathium doesn't need *me*."

Thorne raised a skeptical brow, then heaved a long-suffering sigh. He followed her to the chamber door as she unlocked it and let them in.

Several candles burned low in their stands. The familiar scents of parchment, leather, and wax overtook her, and memories—her true memories—washed over her. She thought of Irem working at his desk, his spectacles slipping down to the end of his nose. Eremon bounding up the hidden staircase to pull her into an embrace. Aidryn sliding notes and sketches beneath the door to make her laugh when the world had fallen down around her.

"Do you remember what I said to you at the fortress?" Thorne asked, coaxing her from her thoughts. "Don't shrink. Raise your chin."

Lira turned to face him, releasing an unsteady breath. He tipped her chin up with a knuckle, drawing her to meet his eyes. "Don't let anyone—or *anything*—overpower you. Including what happened today."

She flinched and turned her head, drawing away from his reach. "I can't fix what happened today."

"Eremon can't fix his decision to stand down," Thorne said,

challenge flashing in his eyes, "as Caitir can't fix her treason. As Aidryn can't fix the murder he committed. As I can't fix—" He blinked, as though catching himself in a forbidden thought.

Lira straightened, assessing him. "You can't fix what?"

Thorne lowered his voice, though he looked rattled. "What I am trying to say is this: When you are put in a position of power and your intentions are pure, you should hold it for as long as possible. Don't shrink. Do whatever it takes to put your mistakes behind you, then press forward."

"Did you put your mistakes behind you?" Lira said, crossing her arms. "Or are you hoping no one finds out?"

When he flinched, she knew she'd hit the mark. He turned away from her, taking a sudden interest in the vast collection of tomes that surrounded them. Lira rifled through her thoughts, piecing together everything she'd gathered so far. She thought of Oda's reluctance to embrace her water magic, her justified fear of Thorne's response to it, and the secret she and Aidryn seemed to be harboring.

"Thorne..." she ventured. "These kinds of secrets get people hurt. Killed. They keep us divided. We can't work in Rodhlan's best interests—or anyone else's—if we continue closing one another off this way. Whatever you're so ashamed of, I'm sure it pales in comparison to the rest of our failures."

"It could cost our lives," he answered on a breath. "Oda's and mine, for certain. But the consequences would extend far beyond that."

Lira grasped his elbow, drawing him to look down at her. "Why?"

"*Sjovyn,*" he said, repeating the forbidden word that had rattled him back at Fortress Halgeir. "It means *bound by vow.* Oda and I—" He closed his eyes and swallowed hard before beginning again. "Four years ago, we deceived Artur."

Lira leaned forward in rapt attention as Thorne spoke. She

had never heard the warrior's voice tremble this way. As his story tumbled out, she understood why.

In the dim candlelight, she thought she could see his cheeks flood with color, and her chest ached at the sight of it. So many times, he'd used his golden healing magic to take away her anxiousness, her panic, and the unnerving surges of fear that had overtaken her ever since Eremon's death. Now, she wished she could do the same for him.

When he'd finished, she surged forward, enveloping him in an embrace. He went rigid in her arms, then patted her head awkwardly. "What you said about unity... well. This—"

"I understand," Lira answered solemnly. "It should remain secret."

Her magic flickered, as though attempting to draw her attention. It worked. She tilted her face up to puzzle at the emerald orb, then sighed. "I suppose it's time to find a book for you. Let's test this theory of Eremon's."

Lira took one of Skelly's bound volumes from the far shelf, opening it to the illustrated title page—like the one that had activated her magic in the spring. A flood of warmth and longing filled her at the sight of the tree, her pendant's twin. For a moment, she considered taking the power back and forgetting this notion, but perhaps it was best to take a day or two to rest, like she'd said. Surely the magic would be safe locked away in the chamber.

She held out a palm, drawing the familiar power toward her. It hovered over one open hand as she set her intention, then closed her eyes.

Rodhlan, she thought, *tether my magic here until I have clarity —for myself, my clan, my city, and my continent. Guide me. Help me to do the right thing, even when I'm afraid.*

She placed her other hand over Skelly's illustration and held her breath. Her magic dimmed to a tiny kernel, and for a moment, she feared she had diminished it somehow. But then it flared with such brilliance that she had to shield her eyes against it.

What had been an orb moments before exploded into thousands of strands, like vines that rushed from the power's central point and into Skelly's illustration. The vines poured into the tome itself, until its inked pages glowed with emerald magic. Tears of sorrow and relief streaked down Lira's face. She'd feared that she might never see her power whole again, yet here it was, resilient and bright. It seemed wrong to abandon it, but it also felt wrong to take it back after she had failed so thoroughly.

Please, she pleaded silently, *help me find a way to make things right.*

Thorne took a deep breath, pulling Lira's attention away from the book for just a moment. His expression was awestruck. "It smells—clean, like the forest after a rainstorm." Pressing his fingertips to the desk, he added, "I know I should hold firm. When Artur is gone, I will make a better overlord."

His candor shocked Lira. After what he'd just confessed, perhaps it shouldn't have. Still, it had always been so dangerous to speak out against Clan Beran's overlord. And here in the inner chamber, Thorne's words were truly secret.

"You will," she replied.

"He ordered us to conquer in your name." Thorne's expression was resolute as he continued. "But this place does not need another conqueror. It needs a leader. It needs hope."

Lira assessed him thoughtfully. She dearly missed the affirming tug her magic might have given her to signal his truth. "Then why did you bring the warriors here? The clan army?"

Thorne sighed. "It's true that Artur ordered me to bring them. I don't trust Eremon, but my aim was to remove the warriors from Artur's influence. By moving them to the city, I now hold sway."

She nodded slowly. For Thorne to even consider solidifying the warriors' loyalties to himself, something must have gone terribly awry at Fortress Halgeir. "What broke you?" she asked in a low voice.

"Artur's order to kill Talfryn," he answered. Fury reverberated through Lira's body, followed by a wave of shuddering anger as he added, "And his treatment of your mother."

Lira clenched her fists, her muscles bunching with tension and fear as his words found their mark. "Where is Talfryn?" she demanded. "What happened to Mam?"

"Eremon saved him," Thorne answered, raising his palms defensively. "Took him to the mountains."

Relief and gratitude slammed into her. "And my mother?"

Thorne shook his head, a troubled look crossing his face. Lira's heart sank. "Artur ordered her into confinement. She was forced to give her share of your magic to Talfryn."

Lira ground her teeth, a disbelieving huff escaping her as his words sank in. "And Mam stood for that?"

"She did." He looked at the floor, as though ashamed.

Lira clenched a fist, pounding it on the desk. Pain lanced up through her arm, but she welcomed it. Deserved it.

"You let this happen, didn't you?" she ground out, her body trembling with anger.

"Yes," Thorne replied steadily, "because she was part of our deception. You aren't the only person to consider in this."

Lira's face felt hot, and her heart hammered an erratic rhythm. "But who will protect her?"

Thorne's expression grew more grim, if that was even possible. "She is standing by her strategy," he said, "and holding her position for as long as she can. She's buying us time."

It didn't matter that her mother had amassed wisdom, influence, and physical strength. Artur was still her overlord, and she had made herself subordinate to him.

"We'll need to act swiftly in the transfer of power," Lira said, almost to herself. A plan was already forming in her mind, her thoughts whirling more quickly than she could process them. "Have your warriors stand down. If Clan Beran overthrows Iathium, Artur will move in as he sees fit. I am no tyrant, but he is, and you are part of his tyranny if you go any further with this show of force."

Thorne looked wary as she spoke, but he held her gaze. "If you claim the throne, you can block him from taking power here. Build your allies and put sanctions on the clan. Force Artur into submission."

"Eremon can do the same," Lira answered.

"But you hold a sway over Artur that Eremon does not," Thorne pressed. "Use your connection to Clan Beran to your advantage. Begin with diplomacy, then maneuver him wherever you must. And if you need to get your mother out, you can offer her protection in the Dome."

"Again—" She swallowed hard, closing her eyes and taking a cleansing breath before she looked back to Thorne. "I can do all of that with Eremon's help."

"You could," Thorne said, "but if *you* ascend, you'll buy all of us time that we won't have otherwise. If it becomes necessary to bring Iva here, we will have a better chance of doing so with you on the throne."

"I appreciate your stance on this." She wrapped her arms around herself with a sigh. "Let me think on it. We have all hinged the city's future on personal interests over the past two months. Iva is my mother, but remaining at Fortress Halgeir was her choice. My objective is simply to make it as difficult as possible for Artur to maneuver his way into power here. Rodhlan doesn't need him on the throne."

Lira closed the tome that was now the temporary home for her magic, then picked it up and hugged it to her chest. It hummed pleasantly, and she tightened her grip on it, scanning the shelf for the empty space it had occupied before. She crossed the room and moved toward the furthest stack, which was cast in shadow.

Her fingertips grazed the spines of her beloved books as she sought a dark place to conceal the tome. Finally, she knelt, shuffling books and scrolls to create a slot for it. She slid it into place, then moved some of the scrolls to cover its spine. However, there was nothing she could do to staunch the emerald glow that now emanated from it.

Rising, she heaved a sigh. When she emerged from behind the bookcases, Thorne was watching her warily. She took a deep breath and said the words she'd been mulling over while rifling through the books.

"Iathium needs a leader who can put the city's needs, and the continent's, over their own interests," she said. "Right now, Thorne, you're using my personal interests to sway my sentiment over the throne. For now, I want to set this discussion aside and consider my options."

He blinked incredulously, then gave her a small nod. "Very well."

She took a trembling breath, glancing at Lord Irem's pendulum clock. They'd been in the chamber far longer than she'd anticipated—but then again, she had not expected Thorne to share his secret.

"It's nearly dawn," she said. "I should look for Aidryn."

Lira retrieved the chamber key from Irem's desk, gripping it in her suddenly sweaty palm. Now that she'd chosen to shift her thoughts back to Aidryn, she was terrified once again. She needed to start forging a path toward reconciliation, if such a thing was even possible.

After everything she'd done, she wasn't sure it would be.

CHAPTER 87
AIDRYN

Dome

Aidryn sat alone in the empty chamber, his head in his hands. He had tried to sleep but found himself too restless. Now, another dawn was approaching, and he did not wish to face it.

In vain, he'd hoped to fall asleep and awaken with his wounded eye healed. The nightmarish events of the past day barely felt real. But his lingering pain and the forever-altered state of his vision kept him tethered to the horrible reality.

The chamber Caitir had brought him to was dark, cold, and deathly silent. His sister hadn't said much on their walk here, and she had departed with little fanfare, closing the door behind her with a barely audible click. Her guarded demeanor had been unnerving, but he supposed that was to be expected, in light of all that had happened.

Aidryn's sudden shift in depth perception had been disorienting. As they'd moved down the inner corridors of the Dome, he had been forced to keep one hand on Caitir, the other held before him. He'd quickly learned the necessity after colliding with a door frame, the impact smarting his shoulder and rattling his teeth.

Caitir had stolen more than one concerned glance at the left side of Aidryn's face, biting down on her lip as though to resist asking more questions. They had begun their trek with her on his right side. But after he'd struck the door, she had moved to his left to shield him from further injury.

Now, his face, head, and shoulder ached, and he was alone in this forsaken room when he wanted to be with Lira—or at least, that's what he should have wanted. Any time he thought of touching her, kissing her, or pulling her close, his insides recoiled, and he had the horrifying urge to run.

He didn't know how both things could be true at one time. How could he need her so deeply, yet feel so repulsed by what she had done to him?

Aidryn shook himself, trying to right his thoughts.

You won't come out unscathed, Eiren had said, *and she may not, either. Therein lies your sacrifice.*

Any risk is worth it, Aidryn had answered foolishly.

Both of you could be forever altered. You will have to be prepared to accept that possibility.

Aidryn hadn't truly understood the implications of removing Lira's birthright magic this way. When he'd decided on his course of action, he didn't realize that she had already been lost to darkness.

Still, what Lira had done—that hadn't truly been her. She had been manipulated and twisted by an immortal bent on corrupting her magic.

Every aspect of this situation reeked of Aila. If he ever had the chance to end her, he would do it without a thought.

Idly, Aidryn wondered whether he might have been able to save Eremon's life with Iuchair, had he understood how to wield the key. Lira might have remained at Eremon's side, and the Binding would never have existed in the first place. Never getting the chance to love her—to experience her love in return —would have been its own terrible kind of heartbreak. But perhaps, in the end, it would have been less painful than the soul-rending ache in his chest now.

This pain was far worse than what had happened to his eye. It had shattered him from the inside out, and he didn't know how to begin piecing himself back together.

In truth, he wasn't sure he had the will to.

Aidryn thought of Fannin alone in Eremon's unfamiliar stable, the way he was alone in this strange room now. The urge to ride seized him, and he was on his feet and racing for the chamber door before he could fully register what he was doing.

Moving through the Dome and out to the stable proved to be more difficult than Aidryn had anticipated. But he pushed himself hard, trying to ignore the pain in his head and the disorienting shift in his perception. He wanted to run—and when he burst outside and the stable finally came into view, he did.

His breathing was ragged as his boots pounded the ancient cobblestones. As he approached the stable's entrance, he threw out a hand, slowing his pace and feeling for the doorway before he ducked inside. He wove through the stalls, searching for where the stable hand had put Fannin.

When he spotted the stallion, he took several long strides toward his stall. Something warm slammed into his left shoulder, and whoever he'd bumped into let out a startled cry. Aidryn whirled to find himself face-to-face with Fiadh.

She looked up at him and froze, eyes widening a fraction. Her hand flew to the hilt of her sword, and she stepped closer, her soft black boots stirring the fine dirt underfoot. True to form, she wore a black tunic and leggings—garb that was strikingly similar to the uniform she'd worn at her father's smithy. Her straight, dark hair was woven into a braided bun at the base of her neck.

"Aidryn Tarlach." Her tone was drenched in contempt.

"That's new," he replied, taking in her narrowed eyes, the slight sneer of her lips. "The last time you said my name, you were trying to seduce me."

At that, she drew her sword. A dry, bitter laugh broke from between his lips as the cold tip of her blade met his throat. His sword and dagger were still at his side, but he made no move to draw them.

"I heard you were in Iathium, so I came here," she said in a low voice. It made him feel uneasy to know her first thought had been to visit his horse. She tilted her head, surveying his wound. "What *happened* to you?"

Fiadh lowered her blade. For a moment, Aidryn thought he saw genuine concern flash in her dark eyes. She looked so like Faolan, so like the Fiadh he'd known before. The girl who had once been his friend, and for a little while, something more.

From his stall, Fannin snorted. Aidryn turned to pat his velvety nose, taking his attention off Fiadh.

When he didn't answer, she stepped back into his line of sight and bared her teeth. "Doesn't matter; you likely deserved it." She raised her chin, a bit of glee alighting in her eyes as she added, "It's Lira's doing, isn't it? Is that why you won't answer me?"

He flinched—harder than he would have liked. At her low, disbelieving laugh, heat flooded his cheeks.

"*Mortal gods*, as you say," she murmured, mimicking his inflection. "I didn't expect to see comeuppance in my lifetime, but here we are. If it was the dark magic—likely, judging by that storm in your eye—I suppose I'm somewhat responsible, and I'll own that with pleasure."

Anger and guilt flared in him anew. Aidryn opened his mouth to reply, but a strange, violet flicker in the center of her chest caught his attention. The image was there one moment, then gone the next. He blinked hard, straining to understand what he was seeing.

"Look at my face," she sneered, reaching up as though to seize his chin.

But Aidryn caught her wrist, looking up at her face himself. "I can see magic in you." He pointed to his own heart. "Just here."

She wrenched out of his grip. Absently, she touched her sternum, her slender fingers playing along the buttons at her collar. "What are you talking about?"

None of this made sense. "It's like... wait."

Aidryn wasn't sure why, but he had the urge to cover his right eye with a palm. Sure enough, the glint of magic remained—the only thing he could perceive with his left eye. He hissed in pain as the image sharpened, and suddenly, he could see an entire network of veins beneath her skin. They glinted like glass shot through with iridescent, violet tones— her clan's power, he guessed. He followed the path back to her heart, recoiling in disbelief at what he saw.

Her heart was made entirely of glass, similar to the blown glass baubles Fiadh had once made at the forge. Inside it, a violent storm roiled. Black lightning and flashes of violet magic intermingled, rumbling and clashing. Pressure filled his head, like the deepening force of an oncoming gale.

Fiadh yanked his hand away from his face. "*What* are you looking at?" she demanded.

"It's the only thing I can see through this," he said, motioning to his blind eye. "Your stolen magic and the glass veins that encase it."

Something she'd said during their last encounter struck him then.

I love you because I am incapable of anything else, she'd said. *My heart is like glass; it's unchanging. You can break it, over and*

*over. It may tear me apart inside, but it will still be yours—every
shard.*

"You knew," Aidryn breathed. "Back in the meadowlands.
You knew you'd done this to yourself."

"I perceived," Fiadh answered stiffly, taking a step back and
raising her chin. "I know what you're thinking, and I haven't
forgotten what I said. But my mind has changed. My thoughts
have."

Her voice trembled, giving away the lie. She'd loved him
when the dark magic did this to her, and she loved him still. His
heart grew heavy at the implication. But love was near enough
to hatred in its intensity. Perhaps by applying the right amount
of pressure, Aidryn might be able to change those feelings
for her.

"Let's test that theory, Fiadh," he said slowly, assessing her.
She flinched almost imperceptibly as he leaned forward,
crossing his arms. He dropped his voice almost to a whisper. "I
hear you've been playing at Eremon's spymaster, so indulge me:
What do you know of your cousin's whereabouts?"

Fiadh's eyes widened a fraction, and she swallowed hard. "I
know Eremon drove him out. Caitir suggested he might have
made improper advances, but..." She looked at the dirt floor.
"He's still my cousin."

"And after Eremon drove him out?" Aidryn asked quietly.
"Where do you think he ended up?"

"With Clan Beran," Fiadh shot back. "I already knew that. I
sent word to him weeks ago."

Aidryn hummed, pausing for effect. "Did you know I inter-
rogated him myself?"

"So, he's alive?" She canted toward Aidryn hopefully, and
his heart twisted as he delivered the final blow.

He bit down on his own nausea as he forced himself to say,
"I drew out his answers, and then I slit his throat."

A beat of dead silence. Then, horrified realization dawned on Fiadh's face.

"No!" She stumbled backward, then sank to one knee, knuckles whitening around the hilt of her sword. "No..."

The wild horror in her eyes stirred the depths of his own regret. Aidryn hadn't wanted to harm Aeron, but he had feared for Caitir's life, Eremon's rule, and Lira's protection. What had any of it mattered in the end?

"It was far more merciful than the execution Beran would have given him," Aidryn murmured.

She was weeping now. "You should have released him— helped him escape!"

Aidryn shook his head resolutely. "He was a danger to all of us, including you and Caitir. He would have sacrificed everyone else in his desperation to survive."

"Everyone deserves to survive," Fiadh said, though she surged to her feet and drew her blade again in one fluid motion. She angled it to his throat once more and added, "Except, perhaps, for you."

There it is. Hatred. Aidryn's eyes drifted shut, and he took a steadying breath. "Maybe that's true."

"It would be easy." She applied a bit of pressure to the blade, and he hissed in pain. A warm trickle of blood ran down the sensitive skin of his neck.

"Then do it." He swallowed hard, then opened his eyes to hold her disbelieving stare. "Go ahead."

But Fiadh withdrew, wiping Aidryn's blood on her black tunic. "I don't think so, Tarlach." She angled her head as though seeing him for the first time. "If you have a death wish, consider it denied."

Sheathing her sword, Fiadh took a step closer. This time, it was *her* voice that was smooth and cruel and undaunted. "You deserve to wallow in your wretchedness."

She reached up to cup Aidryn's scarred cheek and lowered her voice.

"I hope, with every fiber in my spirit, that you suffer the way I have," she whispered as he recoiled. "I hope you lose everything you ever dreamed of, hoped for, fought for. If I can take any more of it from you myself, then I will. I will make your life a waking nightmare—one you can't ride away from on your precious stallion."

Fiadh turned as though to leave the stable. But she paused and added, "I hope you live an agonizingly long life, knowing the damage you've done."

As she stormed from the room, the full stupidity of what Aidryn had just done slammed into him. Fiadh had formed a tenuous alliance with Caitir and Eremon, and now, Aidryn had likely destroyed it. He had been too mired in his own pain over Lira, and encountering Fiadh had reawakened the shame of her heartbreak. Of Aeron's death.

Flaunting Aeron's murder to further wound Fiadh was undoubtedly the cruelest thing Aidryn had ever done. Then again, he had never imagined killing a friend until the necessity arose. After it was over, he thought he'd found his own limit. But the truth was, he didn't yet know what darkness he was truly capable of.

The small cut Fiadh had made on his throat stung. Though the urge had been fleeting, he'd truly wanted her to take his life. Alive or dead, Aidryn deserved the depth of her contempt. It had been grounding to have some semblance of his own feelings mirrored in the flesh. As sharp and deep as her hatred was, though, it paled in comparison to what he felt toward himself.

All those years, Aidryn had fought his own nurturing because he'd wanted to be better than the people who had raised him. He had fancied himself to be virtuous, chivalrous, good. But he was none of those things.

Though he had hated Aila for most of his life, her influence had clung to him like the stink of a carcass. He'd learned deception and manipulation from her. But he'd used those skills for good by maneuvering his loved ones into safety for as long as he was able. Lying and scheming had been necessary evils, and he was accomplished at both. He'd assumed he would always use those skills for the greater good.

But then, the greater good had demanded lying to Lira despite his promises to be honest. It had demanded Aeron's death to protect all of their interests in Iathium—including Caitir and her unborn child. Finally, the greater good had demanded that Aidryn use an unknown spell in an attempt to draw out the dark magic.

A spell just as unknown to him as the one that had killed Edan.

The darkness would have soon overtaken Lira completely if nothing had been done. Still, desperation had driven him to Eiren, and what if the adviser's motivations had been impure? What if she had meant to dispose of Lira because of the Binding and Aidryn's loyalty? What if driving Iuchair into Lira's heart had killed her?

Aidryn had been so fearful that he hadn't considered the possibility. He had done what he believed he must. In the end, Lira had survived, but the full impact of the risk he'd taken pummeled him like an icy wave. His body trembled, his jaw tightening against the winter air and the chill that spread from his belly into his limbs.

He thought of Lira, back in the Dome and safe with Eremon and Thorne. Truly, she didn't need Aidryn any longer. Now that the Binding was broken, she would likely begin the process of distancing herself and taking back her own life here. Perhaps that was best for her. Lira hadn't asked for the spell that had connected them in the first place.

She had not wanted to be married, but Aidryn had. He had always wanted her, and he always would. In the end, it didn't matter that she had wounded him. That pain would heal in time, and he would forgive her more readily than he cared to admit.

Aidryn cast a glance out the stable's window toward the Dome. Fleetingly, he considered seeking Lira out. He needed her in his arms—wanted to know that what had existed between them was more than just a spell. His heart had always said it was, but...

He shook himself. The past day's events had proven that he was more of a liability than anything else. For now, Eremon and Lira had Caitir and Clan Beran to deal with. They had always made a formidable pair, and between the two of them, they would make the best decisions for the city's future.

As much as it hurt to admit, Aidryn's presence here would do them no good. He had always been capable of pulling himself together and strategizing his next moves to minimize possible damage. Today, he'd inflicted more than his share. And suddenly, he was keenly aware of all the further ways he might endanger Lira and their friends, rather than protect them.

Aidryn braced his hand against Fannin's stall door and lay his head against the cool wood. The stallion huffed, his warm breath stirring Aidryn's hair. He lifted a heavy hand and stroked Fannin's mane, inhaling the comforting scent of his coat, the hay, the packed dirt underfoot.

"Do you want to run as much as I do, old boy?" he whispered.

Fannin gave a soft whinny, and Aidryn smiled sadly. Even after all these years, his answer had never changed.

Aidryn thought of the healers back in the mountains. Of Yrsa, who had been forced to stay behind while her master traveled. Perhaps he could have Ljós examine his wounded eye, then take the bear home to Thorne once matters in the city were settled. That was a job no one else could accomplish. It would be a way to make himself useful without imposing his presence on anyone.

He couldn't help thinking that maybe, more than anything, he needed to spend time with his own darkness. For so long, he had convinced himself it didn't exist. Now, the evidence was visible to all in the pupil of his blinded left eye.

Eventually, perhaps he would come to regard the wound as a lesson and a reminder. Until then, he would grieve, just as Thorne had suggested. Grieving wasn't a luxury Aidryn had ever allowed himself, but maybe the warrior was right.

He sighed heavily, debating again whether he should tell Lira goodbye. But seeking her out would only cloud his mind and cast doubt on his chosen path. Maybe one day, when Iathium had been set right and Aidryn had more courage, he would see her again.

But for now, he would take Fannin. And they would run.

CHAPTER 88
CAITIR

Dome

Eremon found Caitir in her chambers, where she'd hidden herself away. She was sitting in silence by the tower window, watching snow clouds gather overhead. He knocked lightly on the door as he entered, and she turned, her heart sinking at the pained expression on his face.

"How are you?" they asked in unison.

His laugh was brittle. "You go first."

"I'm..." Caitir glanced down at the sea below. She'd caught a glimpse of Lira sitting alone on the sea wall moments before, and she motioned Eremon over. "I want to go to her."

Eremon braced his hands on the marble sill, surveying Lira. "It might not be a good time."

"That's not for you to decide," she said, keeping her attention fixed on her former friend.

He shrugged. "You're right. And truthfully, it will never be a good time with Lira. Not after what's happened."

"It's the first approach that stings so much," Caitir murmured.

She and Lira had quarreled often as young girls. Swallowing her pride and offering up the first apology had never been easy with Lira, but she supposed it wasn't truly easy with anyone. Fake apologies—yes. But genuine ones? Those were the most difficult, because it had always meant she truly felt regret when she admitted wrongdoing.

Now, her regret felt as deep and vast as the sea. Caitir wasn't sure how to articulate it. But she knew that if she didn't at least try to approach Lira, a part of her heart would never have peace.

So she turned to Eremon, who had moved near enough to snake an arm around her waist and nuzzle her cheek. "Will you walk me to the wall?"

"Of course," he answered, offering her his arm.

CHAPTER 89
LIRA

Dome

Lira sat alone on the edge of the sea wall, watching the icy, gray waves crash against the rocks below. When she and Thorne had emerged from the archive, she'd intended to set out in search of Aidryn right away. Instead, she had felt the overwhelming urge to run.

Thorne had calmed her with his magic, then walked her to the sea wall. The fresh air would clear her head, he'd said. Lira had insisted on taking a few moments alone, an idea Thorne had not been thrilled about. Reluctantly, he had departed, promising to learn where Caitir had taken her brother. Now, Lira struggled in vain to quiet her racing thoughts.

She had never appreciated the ocean for what it was. To her, its beauty had always been a backdrop to Iathium's magnificence. But she'd placed all her love and loyalty in the city, ignoring everything else to its detriment. By the time she'd begun to realize that her trust had been grossly misplaced, she had been laden with clan magic and was running for her life.

The wind carried the scent of ice, cutting in its intensity.

Although she shivered, she welcomed the discomfort. It was strangely quiet inside her body, and simply feeling the sea wind sweep her curls around her face was a welcome change from fighting the dark magic that had clawed at her insides for so many weeks.

She ran a thumb over Eremon's ring. Soon, she would decide on a path for Iathium's future. Whatever the way forward, she did not envy Eremon or the other anointed. Finally, she understood the full scope of his reluctance to ascend, and she felt ashamed of the unyielding pressure she'd put on him. If Lira had only taken some time to ask him why he'd felt so reluctant, perhaps they could have talked it through before everything fell apart.

Then again, she had been quite out of control of herself, whether she'd realized it or not. And perhaps if she had bothered to explain exactly what she was feeling to Aidryn or Eremon, or to any of their friends, they might have been able to offer more help.

Behind her, the Dome rose and sprawled as it always had. Its stained glass oculus caught the morning light, and its tower spires kissed low-lying clouds that looked heavy enough to spill snow. And for the first time, she was in awe of none of it. Instead, she turned her back to it and took in the sea.

"Witness Tree." An eerily familiar voice drew her from her thoughts, and she shivered.

Lira turned to see a young woman with light brown skin, silver hair, and sea foam-colored eyes approaching. Her feet were bare, and her fitted, white clothing was scant, particularly for Rodhlan's winter. When Lira's gaze fell on the pendant hanging from her neck, the woman paused with a wry grin.

"Vor'sca," Lira breathed, muscles tensing.

The immortal raised her chin and cracked a smile. "Good; you *should* know who I am. We've been conversing for quite some time."

Lira's first thought was to call on her magic, but she had none. In the moment she'd taken to hesitate, Vor'sca had moved near enough to touch her. She took a step back but stumbled and lost her balance.

Vor'sca reached out to catch Lira by the elbow, helping her steady herself before she plummeted into the ocean.

"There, now," she murmured, her Tai'ceru accent thick. "You are too important to lose."

"I'm nothing of importance," Lira answered, "and I've relinquished that title."

Vor'sca scoffed, looking amused. "You think I don't understand the rules of your magic here. Convoluted and disordered? Yes. But that was by design. I'm sure you would love to know more of the true histories."

Lira couldn't help drifting forward a bit at that. *What do you mean?* she wanted to ask. She suppressed the urge. Instead, she said, "How did you get my pendant?"

"My mistress has her ways," she said. Lira didn't miss the little look Vor'sca cast down at the glass cuffs around her wrists.

"I can free you," Lira said, following Vor'sca's gaze. "You don't have to serve Aila."

"I don't have to serve *her*," Vor'sca said, "but I must serve King La'hiran. I have no choice."

"But you *do* have a choice," Lira replied. "You're in Rodhlan, not Iteloria."

A peal of laughter erupted from Vor'sca. "You really have no idea how this works, do you?"

Before Lira could protest, the immortal seized her and swept her into *turas.*

CHAPTER 90

AIDRYN

Meadowlands

Fannin's hooves pounded the dry, packed ground as Aidryn drove him out of Iathium and into the sprawling meadowlands. Sentries had cleared the courtyard and the main road while he, Eremon, and Thorne had battled with Lira in the Dome, so it only took minutes to leave the city behind. The staggering relief he'd felt at the sight of the open cobblestone road had been enough to make him want to weep.

Ever since the throne room, he couldn't think or breathe properly. While saddling and mounting the massive stallion had been cumbersome, to say the least, it had been a relief to let Fannin take over their progress. Aidryn had quickly adjusted to the familiar lull of balancing in the saddle, then let the stallion do the rest.

This was a familiar ride for both of them. They'd done it so often that they knew it by heart. If Aidryn had wished to lie on Fannin's back and fall asleep, then the stallion would still have known exactly where to take him.

They raced across the open meadow at full magical speed, despite the warriors gathered at the gates and the gaping sentries who watched them go. Aidryn had always been careful to conceal Fannin's magic until they were well away from the city walls, but today, he no longer cared. The time for hiding magic was long past.

Absently, Aidryn realized that he'd left his traveling cloak back at the Dome. Icy wind bit at his cheeks, hands, and ears as they rode. Deep, piercing pain lanced his face as Fannin moved, and he briefly debated whether this level of discomfort was worth the freedom of a ride.

It was.

Tears stung his eyes and ran down his cheeks from the cold. Aidryn was tense in his saddle as he held his seat. Although he tried to let his body move with the horse's rhythm, relaxing enough to do so quickly became a struggle. Still, he pushed harder. His decision was made, and he was going to see it through.

On the horizon, he thought he could see another rider moving toward him. He squinted to make out the shape, pushing Fannin harder so he could get closer. In moments, it was apparent who was coming: Oda and Talfryn, together astride Senga.

Each mount slowed upon approach, until the horses were walking toward one another, preparing to meet face-to-face. Talfryn's expression fell when he saw Aidryn, and he lay a hand on Oda's arm, the alarm on his face apparent as he whispered to her. When her gaze snapped to Aidryn, she called Senga to a halt, her green eyes wide. Her hand drifted upward to cover her mouth, and she shuddered as though suppressing a sob.

"Aidryn..." she breathed.

"It suits me, don't you think?" He barked a harsh laugh. "Just as broken on the outside as within."

Talfryn gave him a dark look. "He is not himself."

"Maybe I am," Aidryn replied. His voice sounded very far away to his own ears. Out in the open meadow with Fannin, he was more himself than anywhere else. "Maybe I'm tired of pretending to be something I'm not."

"Where is Lira?" Oda demanded.

He glanced down at Fannin's reins, clutched in his whitened knuckles. "She's at the Dome, safe with Thorne and Eremon."

"Ah." The warrior inclined her head. "And where do you think you're going?"

Aidryn looked past Oda, as though he could see clear through the southern forest, to the ocean far beyond. "Where I belong: into the wilderness where I can't do more harm, and where no one can harm me."

"That's not our Aidryn," Oda said, her expression steely and resolute. "What did the dark magic do to *you*?"

He laughed bitterly. "Nothing, except shatter my illusions— and blind one of my eyes in the process. Funny, though. I'm seeing things clearly for the first time."

"And how clearly is that?" Talfryn asked. He was watching Aidryn with a gaze as steely as Oda's.

Aidryn blinked slowly, considering. But after a moment, he shook off the question. He clicked his tongue and nudged Fannin to walk past Senga instead.

"Halt," Talfryn ordered. "Until I get a clear answer from you, *brother*, you will not leave."

"Have a talk with Lira before you call me that again," Aidryn growled.

Oda drew a sharp breath, then leaned toward Talfryn as though Aidryn couldn't hear. "He's broken the Binding," she hissed.

Talfryn's attention snapped to Aidryn again. He must have sensed Aidryn's next move, because he shouted, "Wait—" just as Aidryn uttered Fannin's incantation.

The gray stallion accelerated as they passed Senga, but Oda

didn't miss a beat. She used Clan Tarlach's incantation, too, and the bay mare sped toward Fannin, catching up in a matter of moments. Aidryn pushed his horse harder, but Senga kept pace with him. Oda brought the mare alongside Fannin, shouting something unintelligible at Aidryn.

He focused on the path ahead, letting Fannin's pounding hoofbeats drown her voice. A moment later, water blasted against his body, forcing Fannin to slow.

Oda took advantage of the stallion's faltering and pushed Senga past Aidryn. He was cold and wet down to his bones, and his teeth had begun to chatter. The warrior made a wide arc, turning the mare so she and Talfryn faced Aidryn and Fannin. Senga stamped her hooves, nostrils flaring as her hot breath fogged the icy air.

Lifting her palm, Oda summoned her violet power. Despite the bone-deep cold, a smirk tugged at Aidryn's lips. "I see you've finally embraced your anointing. Magnificent."

Oda didn't reply to the barb. She offered the reins to Talfryn as though she intended to dismount. Instead, Talfryn swung a leg over the saddle and leapt down, striding purposefully toward Aidryn. His emerald eyes flashed with fury.

"Get back on your horse," Aidryn said firmly. But Talfryn ignored him, stalking up to take hold of Fannin's bridle.

"Get off yours," the younger man snapped. He might as well have added, *That's an order,* because Aidryn dismounted without a second thought.

It struck him that, although Talfryn was five years his junior, they stood nearly eye-to-eye now. After everything Lira's brother had faced, and the permanent injury he'd adapted to, he had matured into a fine young man who easily commanded respect and wielded that power with grace.

Aidryn wasn't prepared for Talfryn to snatch the sopping collar of his tunic and yank him forward until their noses were almost touching.

"If your face wasn't injured, I would punch it," Talfryn seethed. "What were you thinking?"

"He wasn't," Oda put in with a roll of her eyes.

"They don't need me," Aidryn said simply, raising his palms in defeat. The next words snagged in his throat, and he had to force them out. "She doesn't—Lira doesn't need me."

"Did she tell you that?" Talfryn demanded, letting Aidryn go. "Did *anyone* in Iathium say they had no more need of Aidryn Tarlach?"

Aidryn righted himself. "No."

"Then *what*?" This time, Talfryn shoved his chest. Hard.

"I'll only endanger her," Aidryn said, holding his ground. "I could have killed her like I killed Edan and Aeron."

"I think you're afraid," Talfryn said. "If you broke the Binding and ran, you must be."

A new wave of chills wracked Aidryn's body. "And what if I am?"

Oda heaved an exasperated sigh. Then, she dismounted, swearing angrily on the way down. She cursed as she opened the saddle bag and dug out a fresh change of clothes, then again as she closed the distance to shove the dry garments at Aidryn.

"Change," she ordered. "Talfryn, make him some privacy."

Talfryn flicked his fingers, sending a little blast of magic into the ground. A large willow tree burst up from the earth, sprouting long branches that drooped and drifted along the dry grass. Its deep green leaves looked wildly out of place against the barren winter landscape.

Reluctantly, Aidryn took the change of clothes Oda had offered him and ducked inside the cover of the willow's long branches. He peeled off his wet things, grinding his teeth as the cold wind swept along his skin, pebbling it painfully. But the fresh tunic and trousers were a welcome comfort. They were made of thick wool rather than the cotton and linen he'd worn beneath his abandoned cloak, and they calmed his shivering.

Aidryn had barely finished fastening his belt when Talfryn joined him beneath the willow, now appearing even angrier than before. The younger man stopped an arm's length away and narrowed his eyes.

"I'm not much for public humiliation," he began, his voice low, "so I thought I'd use the privacy here to make my point."

Aidryn crossed his arms. "And what point is that?"

Talfryn leaned nearer. "I won't let you abandon Lira," he said. "How many knots did you tie in your mind to convince yourself that leaving was the right choice? Unravel them now."

Rather than replying, Aidryn just stared Talfryn down. The younger man held his gaze with an unnerving stillness. Then, his attention drifted to Aidryn's wounded eye.

"Did Lira do that?" he asked softly.

The world fell from under Aidryn, but he righted himself enough to answer. "She did. Unintentionally, I think."

"But it happened through her, or because of her, all the same." Talfryn nodded as though deciphering a puzzle. "It would have been easy for me to blame Lira for my lost arm. After all, it happened because I swore fealty to her. Like you, I vowed to protect her, and I paid a price for it."

Defend her, Eremon had once begged.

I swear it, Aidryn had replied.

Talfryn let a beat of silence pass. "We do our best from one moment to the next. In those moments, we use whatever tools and weapons are at our disposal. Sometimes we're wounded in the process, and sometimes, those wounds don't heal. But our purpose doesn't change, does it? Our vow doesn't break."

He laid his hand on Aidryn's shoulder as the truth settled between them. Then, Talfryn squeezed, pulling Aidryn into a hard embrace.

Aidryn's breath left in a whoosh as he wrapped his arms

around Lira's brother. He might have broken the Binding, but he had never once considered breaking the vows he'd made to Lira. Their marriage might have been a force of magic, but his promises to her had not been. Abandoning Iathium meant abandoning her and all the ways Aidryn had sworn to keep her safe.

Suddenly, he regretted following his urge to run. But perhaps this encounter was what he'd needed to shake himself awake.

"Thank you," he whispered as Talfryn finally drew back.

The younger man's eyes shone as he gave Aidryn a nod. "When that wound heals," he said solemnly, "I'm still going to hit you."

"I'll be waiting for it."

CHAPTER 91

EREMON

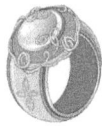

Dome

Eremon covered Caitir's hand with his own as they strode down the Dome's main corridor together, arm in arm. The building appeared completely empty, although Eremon assumed the staff had fled to their homes below, or out into the courtyard, during the previous night's ordeal in the throne room. A quick glance out the window proved the former to be the case.

Their battle with Lira's dark magic would not have gone unnoticed. Unfortunately, too few of Iathium's people—and sentries, especially—were equipped to fight dark magic. As it was, even the clanspeople who had wielded power in secret for years didn't know how to defend against it. That was a more frightening prospect than simple ignorance of inherited magic, and one Eremon would have to remedy as quickly as he could.

As soon as I understand it myself, he thought.

Through instinct and intention, Eremon could neutralize dark magic. His own blend of cobalt power and darkness made that easy, and it had been that way since the crypt. The problem was, he didn't know how to begin teaching clan descendants what to do. In that regard, he was just as lost as everyone else.

They stepped out the doors by the western towers and moved toward the sea wall, where they'd seen Lira from the tower window. The icy scent of winter contrasted sharply with the salt smell of the sea. As they drew closer, Lira was nowhere to be seen. The crash of waves against the rocks would drown out any attempt to call for her, so Eremon searched in silence.

Caitir halted, her pale eyes scanning the area. Tendrils of blonde swirled around her face, the chill wind stirring them. Her forehead creased in concern.

"I don't see her, either," Eremon said.

When he turned back toward the Dome, he could see Thorne's looming figure coming down from the entryway. Without a thought, Eremon let go of Caitir and started toward him.

"Have you seen Silira?" he asked.

"I left her here to look for you," Thorne answered, looking past Eremon to the sea wall. His brow creased, too.

"Well, Lira's not here," Caitir put in.

Thorne cut his gaze to her briefly. "I can smell her magic," he said with a small shrug, as if that fact must mean she was near. Then, his eyes went wide with alarm. "But I should not be able to."

"Her magic's in the archive?" Eremon asked, panic filling his chest.

The warrior nodded grimly, suddenly on high alert. "That immortal uses *turas*."

Eremon thought of Vor'sca and how she seemed to favor the sea wall as a place to conduct her mischief. His heart dropped with the realization, and he ran a hand over his face. "Oh, gods."

The color drained from Caitir's cheeks. "Vor'sca has her."

Thorne groaned, squeezing his eyes shut. "I should not have left her alone."

"She has no magic and is unarmed," Eremon said through gritted teeth. "You, of all people, should have thought of that."

"You think I don't realize?" Thorne barked, pinching the bridge of his nose.

Eremon scoffed. "Clearly not!"

The warrior's eyes snapped open, and his glare was murderous. His lips curled in contempt. "I will not waste time quarreling with you, boy-king."

"Eremon, that's enough," Caitir said sharply, laying a steadying hand on his arm.

Thorne drew back, regarding her with what appeared to be newfound appreciation. Eremon couldn't help resenting it, but she and the warrior were right. The time for petty rivalry was far past.

"I'll take Thorne to Aidryn." Caitir stepped forward and pressed a hand to Eremon's cheek. "*You* start searching. If Lira's power is in the archive, Vor'sca probably took her there. If you can't find them nearby, you have your wings."

Eremon took a steadying breath, willing his racing thoughts to settle. "Whatever Vor'sca thinks she's doing, Lira still has my ring. She can't be killed unless she's persuaded to remove it."

Thorne cast a longing glance back toward the Dome but crossed his arms and widened his stance. "Then we should be cautious. Silira has some measure of protection; that is a good thing."

"But her magic—" Eremon protested.

The warrior raised a hand. "I know. But no one can steal her anointing."

The theft of Clan Mór's magic would be a terrible loss, but no one except Lira would be able to fully wield it.

"I think we are meant to react without thinking," Thorne said after a silent moment. He looked to Caitir again. "Or separate without strategy. Why? If Vor'sca is working for your mother, who are they trying to get to?"

Caitir answered without hesitating, "Aila never has just one goal. There are always several. There must be multiple advantages to her before she makes a move. I suspect that's why she has always been so patient."

She began to pace as she gathered her thoughts, then turned and headed toward the Dome. Eremon wanted to reach for her, but he held himself back, keenly aware of Thorne's scrutiny and his own poor timing. Instead, he and the warrior followed.

"I think Aila struck at Lira's magic first because she knew we wouldn't be able to resist turning our focus to her," Caitir said. "Once the dark magic was removed, Vor'sca didn't delay. I suspect that's because she no longer had the same access to Lira's thoughts and memories."

"That's why your mother was able to stay away," Eremon said. "She had eyes and ears here."

"King La'hiran is allegedly holding her in Sov'is." Caitir rubbed the back of her neck as she contemplated. It struck Eremon how much the gesture reminded him of Aidryn. "I suppose he knows everything, too."

"Why would he have let Aila live?" Thorne asked. "What is valuable enough to him?"

"He would want to call in his treaty somehow," Eremon answered. "My existence violates it, but only a mortal deity can be sacrificed to Iteloria for power; not an immortal."

Eremon wasn't sure why, but Thorne abruptly stopped walking and went preternaturally still. He closed his eyes as though meditating, then inhaled deeply through his nose. When he opened his eyes again, he looked aghast, his eyes flicking from Caitir to Eremon, then back again.

"Eremon," he said in a low voice, "Leave us."

"Why?" Eremon demanded, alarm coursing through him.

"I need to unravel a scent," Thorne answered, his gaze sliding back to Caitir. "I know yours, Eremon, but..." He looked curious now as he turned his full attention to her. "Hers is different from the last time we met."

"Well, she's with child now," Eremon said, planting his feet. He had no intention of leaving Caitir alone with this brute.

"Does that mean the child has magic, then? If you can smell it." She tilted her head to survey Thorne. Absently, her hands drifted to her belly. Her skin looked especially pale against the soft cobalt fabric of her gown.

"It's..." Thorne rounded on Eremon, glowering down at him. "I will not harm her, but your immortal scent is too strong. You need to go. Look for Lira in the archive while we speak, then we'll find Tarlach."

Eremon heaved a sigh, then turned and strode toward the Dome, leaving Caitir alone with Thorne.

CHAPTER 92
CAITIR

Dome

Caitir forced a tight smile as she watched Eremon go. Thorne's proximity made her feel uneasy. He and Lira had come to Aidryn's rescue last summer, and Caitir knew he held no fondness for her.

Still, he didn't waste time reminding her of her transgressions. He simply closed his eyes again and concentrated. While he stood there, silent, she clasped her hands before her, studying his clothing. He wore leather boots and breeches, along with a leather tunic etched with runes. His muscular arms were exposed as though he was unaffected by the cold. On his wrists were leather bracers, and peeking out from beneath them, she could see tattoos of runes on his forearms. In his thick blond hair, he had woven beads and bits of bone, and his beard was neatly trimmed, though a bit longer than Caitir remembered.

His earthy scent of oils and leather drifted to her on the cold breeze, and at once, she felt ashamed for belittling Clan Beran's people. Thorne had a sternness to him, that was true.

But if Lira admired him so, there must be something redeeming about him.

"You had dark magic and a bit of Clan Tarlach's power when we met," he said. He opened his eyes to study her. "But now there's Clan Mór's magic, and—"

"My late husband," Caitir said with a small shrug. The words were sour on her tongue. She hadn't known what would be worse to say: *husband* or *Gerallt*. In the end, uttering his name had been less palatable than a title he could no longer claim. "That would be the child's inheritance, I suspect."

"There's more," he answered, "but telling you might be a poor choice."

She crossed her arms. "Why?"

Thorne's lips tugged as though he wanted to smirk. "Because what will you do with it when you know? What will *she* do?"

"Whatever it is, I'm sure *she* knows already," Caitir snapped. He meant Aila. "You talk of wasting time, but here you are, wasting it yourself. Decide to tell me or don't, but we need to fetch Aidryn."

"Then lead the way," Thorne said, motioning toward the Dome.

They entered the western wing of the Dome, with Caitir leading him along the corridors toward the chamber where she'd taken her brother. Thorne remained silent the entire way. Caitir fought the temptation to ask him again what he knew about her magic—or the child's. But diplomacy had taught her not to press for too much, too quickly. The warrior had revealed that he knew *something*, so he might be willing to tell her more when he was ready.

When they arrived, the door was ajar, so she pushed it open and stepped inside. A quick sweep of the room revealed it was empty, except for the traveling cloak he'd discarded. She drew back in alarm and turned to Thorne, whose concerned expression mirrored the drop in her stomach.

"Gone," she said, her voice wavering.

Thorne cursed in a low growl, then turned and started back the way they'd come. "We should not have let them out of our sight."

"They'd been through an ordeal..." Caitir's words stuck, forming a lump in her throat. "We did our best, that's all I know."

"Tell me what else you know," Thorne said. Caitir had to walk at a clip to keep up with his broad strides. "I hear talk of immortal restraints."

"The glass cuffs," Caitir supplied. She repeated Fiadh's story about them, conceding that she and Eremon didn't know whether the full truth had been revealed.

"So the only thing this Vor'sca can do is *turas*?" he asked.

"As far as we know," she said.

"She has taken Silira, and maybe Aidryn." A muscle in Thorne's jaw tightened as he contemplated his next words. "But I think they are bait. She means to trap you."

Just then, Eremon came into view at the other end of the corridor. His expression was distraught, and deepening dread tightened Caitir's chest.

"They're not in the archive," he said. His words slammed into Caitir with unexpected force. "There's no sign of Lira."

"Aidryn is gone, too," Caitir said softly.

Eremon swore under his breath, dipping his head. His black hair, which he hadn't tied back today, fell in a silken sheet, concealing his pained expression from Thorne. After a brief moment, he looked up again, squaring his shoulders and straightening his tunic.

"I suppose we should try to decipher a motive," Eremon said, his tone clipped. "More magic, more power, more control

—we know Aila wants that. I imagine this is another ploy to steal the anointed powers."

Thorne took a step back, folding his muscular arms across his chest. "There's more." His gaze flicked to Caitir, looking almost pained. Her heart began to pound, her palms suddenly slick with sweat.

Eremon tilted his head, peering hard at the warrior. "What is it?"

"Aila wants the child," Thorne said without hesitating, "because it's immortal."

The world around Caitir warped, and she swayed on her feet. There was no way—no way she had understood him correctly.

"No." She shook her head, pressing her hands to her mouth. "No, no, no, no—"

Eremon's hands were on her now, and her legs must have given way, because she was sinking toward the floor. But strong arms lifted her up, and suddenly she was against his chest, and he was kissing her brow and whispering soothing words into her ear. Everything he said was garbled, and she couldn't understand him through the heavy, thudding heartbeats in her ears.

When she couldn't respond to him, he turned to Thorne and barked a command. The two men moved, speaking in low tones as Eremon carried Caitir. Where they were going, she wasn't sure...

Until Eremon lowered her to a sofa in the sitting area, just outside her old chamber. He pulled her legs up onto the cushions while a wordless Thorne slipped a pillow behind her head.

"Stay with her, Beran," she heard Eremon say. He brushed her hair over her shoulder, his fingertips playing along the back of her neck. There was a long pause before he added, "I'll fetch the midwife."

"Did you—" Thorne began.

"It's there." Eremon already sounded like he was halfway down the corridor.

The child was fine; it wriggled in Caitir's belly just like every other day, as though attempting to get comfortable once she settled. They didn't need Toryn, they needed to find out what had happened to Lira and Aidryn. She tried to say as much, but panic closed her throat around her words.

Thorne shushed her, conjuring an orb of golden healing magic. "May I help you?" he asked. She was surprised at how soothing his voice sounded.

Caitir nodded her consent, and Thorne gently passed the magic into the space over her heart, never making contact with her skin. Instantly, she began to relax. He repeated the process, sending orbs of power into her throat, her forehead, her legs— all the parts of her that had gone weak at the revelation about her child. After a long moment, her mind quieted, and she lay still while the warrior knelt at her side.

"The Beran dog," she murmured, more to herself than him. "I should have never called you that."

"It's in the past." He kept his voice low, then leaned closer. "Did you understand what I told you and Eremon?"

"That the babe is immortal?" The thought of it brought hot tears to her eyes. It scarcely felt real.

"Yes, but..." Thorne glanced down the corridor before he continued, "Do you know what it means?"

"That my mother wants it," Caitir answered. "She must want its power, like she wanted Eremon's."

"Not just that." Thorne looked as though he was waging a fierce internal debate over whether to finish his thought. "It means you're a mortal goddess. There's no other way to give birth to an immortal child."

"I'm not—" She sat up abruptly, though her head swam with the movement. "I wasn't born with the rune."

"Are you sure?" Thorne pressed. "You have it now."

Her hand flew to the back of her neck where Eremon had touched her. "*What?*"

Thorne's amber gaze bored into her. "You have Nami's Rune."

"Do you think my mother lied about it?"

"Maybe," Thorne answered, "but a mortal deity can also be made. It's why the clans' powers were divided in the old days. Why the ruling line became so corrupt."

Caitir wanted to protest, but the warrior's words settled over her like a blanket made of lead. She thought about her mother's notes and calculations that Eremon had found. Deep down, she knew Thorne was right, and suddenly, everything made sense.

"Mother always talked of making me a goddess," she mused. "At some point, she must have succeeded."

"It seems that way."

Caitir's next realization made her nauseous. "I thought death had to occur for an immortal to exist," she said, pressing a hand to her belly, "but this child hasn't been harmed."

"One can be born immortal," Thorne answered. "But born mortals must die first."

"Nami's bones." She drew a shaky breath. "I never once considered she'd use me to create an immortal child."

After all this time, she'd thought she had freed herself from Aila's grasp—freed her mind from the fear she had always lived under. But now, a new kind of terror swept in. How would she protect her child if the child had been Aila's goal all this time?

"This is what a thirst for unlimited magic yields," Thorne murmured to himself. When he looked her in the eyes again, his own were filled with pity. "I believe you."

CHAPTER 93
EREMON

Dome

E remon raced down the stairs and into the Dome's underground, the impact of his footsteps against the stone reverberating into his bones. It was crowded down here, as he'd suspected it might be. Members of the staff gathered in the narrow, torchlit halls, murmuring amongst themselves as he entered.

He realized his misstep when one of them turned, eyes widening, and shouted his name. A clamor to reach him began, and the people clawed at his robes, closing in on him. In a flash of magic, he transformed, taking on the body of a spider, smaller than any creature he'd ever embodied. Their cries of indignation sounded from high overhead, their footsteps reverberating through the stone floor.

Careful not to be trampled underfoot, he crawled up the side of the wall and away from clamoring feet. He kept clear of the floor, moving toward Kenji's apartment with surprising speed. All he could think of was getting to Toryn, asking questions he already knew the answers to.

Caitir was likely a mortal goddess.

Thorne had said it quietly, as though he pitied her. The rune Eremon had found on the back of her neck confirmed the warrior's suspicion. It had glowed with a sheen of cobalt magic so dim, it was barely visible. He could only guess that it was visible because the babe was immortal.

As he moved, the full horror of the truth sank into him. If the child was immortal, then the child would be safe—at least, in terms of bodily health. But Caitir's mortality meant that her life would be forfeit once the baby was born.

It seemed that Aila may have struck more than one deal with King La'hiran. One, they'd surmised, was to sow discord in Rodhlan so she could return a peacemaker. But the sinking suspicion in his gut intensified as he focused on the other.

Aila planned to sacrifice Caitir to Iteloria. She would be the atonement for Eremon's immortality, forever placing Aila in La'hiran's good graces and securing her influence between the two continents.

Eremon couldn't fathom how this woman had managed to leap from one complex scheme to the next, as easily as the Moravon tumbling over pebbles and rocks. After lying in wait beneath Macha's sharp eye for so long, Aila had stolen magic, brought Clan Mór to ruin, usurped Iathium's throne, and now, she had schemed her way into King La'hiran's favor.

To Eremon's mind, Aila was far too young to have accomplished these feats and lived through them all. Worse, she had been resilient enough to keep going relentlessly, with each ambition grander and more terrible than the last.

He thought of the documents and notes he'd found in her chamber, and now, they made more sense.

Magical intermingling yields __?

What is the appropriate ratio...

Need these answers to effectively succeed.

How many clans? How much of the mortal gods' power?

When does the rune emerge?

Thorne had said it earlier: Aila had found a way to combine the powers of the clans with immortal magic to make Caitir into a mortal deity. When she hadn't been able to steal Eremon's magic, she had left her daughter in a situation that would likely expose her to it.

Had Aila ever really been King La'hiran's prisoner in the first place, or had she staged a ruse of her own?

She had certainly been hoping for this outcome. Now, Eremon needed Toryn to confirm that Caitir's rune was the same as his own.

When he arrived at Kenji's home, he squeezed beneath the bottom of the door and transformed just within the small parlor.

The sight before him stole his breath.

Kenji was huddled by the cold hearth with his daughters, and they were weeping. Little Kyra clung to Fjella and Juri, and Tiriya's arm was clamped around her father's shoulders. Her body was tense, and she was the first to whirl on Eremon at the sound of his footsteps.

"She's gone," Tiriya said, her eyes wide and glassy.

Eremon stilled. "Who's gone?"

"Toryn." Kenji turned slowly to face him now, his face red and streaked with tears. "She went willingly."

"Where did she go?" Eremon demanded, panic coursing through his body. His limbs felt as though they had been imbued with pure dark magic.

"To Iteloria," Kenji answered in a wobbly voice, "with the immortal girl. Aila wanted my wife." A sob broke from him, and it shattered Eremon's heart to see his normally jovial friend reduced to tears. "I want her back."

Several things clicked into place for Eremon, all at once. He hoped Kenji could read the apology on his face. "She means to take Caitir there for the birth."

"Don't they have their own midwives?" Tiriya demanded.

Eremon held up a hand to stay her. "We'll get your mother back."

Enraged, he turned and burst back through the door, not caring that there was now a crowd teeming outside Kenji's door. Eremon didn't care that they wanted him—didn't care that he shoved through them as though they were nothing but stalks of grain on the meadowlands. He moved as quickly as he could, taking the stairs three at a time and bursting back out onto the Dome's main floor, where he began to run.

It wasn't long before he could hear light footfalls behind him, and he threw a glance over his shoulder to see Tiriya in his periphery. She was running at full speed, several short strides to each of his longer ones. If she could keep up, that was fine; but he wasn't going to stop for her. She could follow him back to Caitir.

He led Tiriya back to the sitting area, where Thorne and Caitir sat facing one another, their expressions drawn. A strange, grim tension had settled between them. When Caitir caught a glimpse of Tiriya, she rose abruptly, her expression stricken.

"What now?" she cried, holding her arms out to Tiriya, who fell into them with a broken wail.

"They have Toryn, too," Eremon said. "In Iteloria."

"*Turas* is making this too easy," Caitir murmured, stroking Tiriya's dark hair. "Vor'sca will continue taking our allies, one by one. Gathering in one place and staying together might force her to face us all."

"Division is what they want," Thorne mused. "If we gather, she might not come."

"She will." Eremon raised his chin. "Now that we know about the child's immortality, she won't wait long."

At that, Tiriya raised her head, looking from Caitir to Eremon, then back again. "That's why they wanted Mama?"

"They think I'll be more amenable if Toryn is with me," Caitir said with a heavy sigh. She let go of Tiriya, who scrubbed furiously at her tear-splotched face. The girl seemed to be fighting to appear resolute. "The good news is, they'll keep her alive. By her calculations, we have four to five months until the babe arrives."

Tiriya sagged with relief at the realization. "Let's assume four. What can we do?"

Movement outside the Dome's thick windowpanes caught Eremon's attention. He could make out the shapes of two horses approaching, and he nudged his way through the small circle they'd created to peer outside. When he opened the door to the courtyard, he saw Fannin and Senga bearing three riders: Aidryn, Oda, and Talfryn.

Lira's brother was the first to dismount, leaping from Senga's back with ease. Oda was next, and she held up a steady hand while Aidryn dismounted from Fannin. A stable boy was there in a flash, taking the mounts' reins and leading them away.

Eremon didn't miss the way Aidryn hung behind his friends as they approached. Had he tried to flee the city? Judging from his lack of a cloak and the others' guarded expressions as they maneuvered themselves to flank him, that appeared to be the case. Anger threatened to cloud Eremon's judgment while he determined what to say next.

"What happened here?" he asked coolly, stepping aside for the three to enter.

"Aidryn was a bit shaken," Oda said carefully, chancing a look at Thorne. "We made sure he returned in one piece."

"Where is Lira?" Aidryn asked, though he looked askance. "I need to speak to her."

"I wish I knew," Eremon answered grimly.

The shocked, sickened expression on Aidryn's face remained as Eremon, Caitir, and Thorne explained what had happened. They described what they'd deciphered about the child, Caitir, and Toryn—how they suspected Aila wanted the baby born in Iteloria, and of the changes Thorne had been able to detect in Caitir's power.

"We'll need to post extra sentries in the archive to guard Lira's magic," Eremon said. "Talfryn, you're the only person here with a measure of it."

"I'll go," he agreed with a nod.

Wordlessly, Aidryn conjured a key to the inner chamber and handed it to Talfryn. Eremon turned to Tiriya next. "Will you fetch four sentries from the western tower? Take them to the archive, then report back to me."

"I will," Tiriya said, though she paused, tilting her head as she regarded Talfryn for the first time. "I've heard your name, Talfryn Mór. We haven't forgotten what you did for your sister."

Talfryn blinked at her, as though stunned. "I... suppose I won't forget it, either." He reached up to pat his left shoulder, a nervous laugh escaping him.

"This is a very bad time for gallows humor," Oda muttered.

"On the contrary," Eremon said, resting a hand on Tiriya's shoulder, "it's fitting. How else will we keep our heads about us?"

Talfryn narrowed his green eyes as he deadpanned, "We might not."

He and Tiriya peeled off toward their respective missions. Eremon grasped Caitir's hand and regarded Thorne and Oda, who had carefully positioned themselves on either side of him. There was no time to analyze the guarded tension between them. Instead, Eremon looked to Aidryn, who had drifted toward the window.

"I shouldn't have run," he said quietly as Eremon stepped to his side.

"No," Eremon conceded with a thoughtful nod. "But you

did, and she's gone—although this might have happened regardless."

"If Lira can be saved, I doubt she'll forgive me." Aidryn's sorrow was palpable, so Eremon clasped his shoulder and gave it a gentle squeeze. "I don't know how to feel about any of this."

"You owe plenty of forgiveness to one another," Eremon replied firmly. "But we must focus now. Otherwise, there won't be a chance to extend or receive it."

When Aidryn didn't respond, he added, "Remember: She has the ring. Wherever Vor'sca has taken her, she's alive."

"Bait, as I said before," Thorne said from where he stood in the center of the corridor. His arms were crossed tightly. Eremon caught the brief glance Oda stole at him before looking away. "Eremon, you said she was connected to Lira's magic?"

"Yes," he said.

"But not anymore," the warrior said. "Now Aila cannot take the throne by proxy."

"Vor'sca is panicking," Caitir added, realization dawning in her expression. "Trying to cover up her failure by abducting whoever she thinks will help her case."

"We'll need to play on her desperation, then," Thorne said. "We agreed to stay together. Let's see if that brings our enemies to us."

Caitir drifted to stand beside them, placing a tentative hand on Aidryn's back. She opened her mouth as if to speak, then shut it, shaking her head. Her expression was suddenly resolute, but still, she remained silent.

The devastated look on her face turned Eremon's stomach, and he wanted to run with her. Perhaps he could transform like he'd done at Fortress Halgeir. Take flight, carry her away from this place. But if he did that, he would be abandoning his friends and all their anointed powers. Worse, it would only be a matter of time until Vor'sca sought them out through *turas*.

Running would only delay the inevitable confrontation with Aila, and Eremon feared that would come sooner, rather than later.

It seemed that every stone in their path had been carefully placed to lead them back to Aila. No matter what they had done to avoid this outcome, it had been inevitable.

Thorne closed the distance between them and placed a hand on Caitir's shoulder. "There will be a way to protect you and your child," he assured her, as though trying to convince himself it was true.

Caitir gave Thorne a tight smile. "There may not be."

CHAPTER 94

LIRA

The Rí's Garden

L ira and Vor'sca squared off in Eremon's garden, regarding one another warily. Vor'sca had been lurking about in the Dome after Lira's magic was suspended— long enough to have gathered where it was hidden. From the sea wall, the immortal had transported them to the catacombs below, demanding to be taken to the archive.

It was clear Vor'sca hadn't traversed the grounds beneath the Dome often enough to navigate them herself, because she had asked too many questions as they picked their way through the dark. Lira had avoided answering most of them, revealing only that Eremon's ring was a key and there were few doors it unlocked—but that one of them was to the archival stairs that led to the inner chamber.

That answer had been enough to satisfy Vor'sca until Lira led her in the opposite direction. They'd emerged into Eremon's large, indoor garden, an eternal spring despite the bitter cold outside. The immortal had let out a cry of frustration as Lira hoisted herself aboveground in a mad scramble.

When Vor'sca had attempted to put her hands on Lira again, Lira had been prepared. She'd evaded the woman's grasp completely, assuming the low fighting stance Oda had taught her over the summer.

"You know I could easily best you," Vor'sca said, amusement playing in her eyes.

"If you weren't restrained," Lira shot back. The other woman's reluctance to engage had given away her physical weakness, in addition to the magical leash Aila had placed on her.

"I could do it now." The immortal tilted her head, her silver hair slipping from where she had tucked it behind her ear. "Why don't you try me?"

"We're wasting time." Lira put more distance between them, backing carefully onto the small bridge where Eremon had once brought her a cup of tea. "What are you getting at?"

"My king needs to collect a debt," she answered, "to satisfy his treaty."

"And where does he presume to find that?" Lira asked incredulously. "There are no mortal deity children here for him to sacrifice."

Vor'sca's lips curled. "It doesn't have to be a child."

"This makes no sense," she protested. The way Vor'sca was looking at her, it was clear there was more to the story. Lira wasn't a mortal goddess—she didn't even have magic now. So who could it be?

"It will in time." Vor'sca folded her hands before her, lacing her slender fingers together. "Aila also wishes to gather the clans' powers, of course. You were meant to take me to yours."

"I won't." Lira stood resolute. "We didn't come this far to hand our power to Aila. What loyalty do you owe her?"

"That's a pity," Vor'sca said, ignoring the question. "What will it take to get your attention?"

"You have my attention now, but nothing more," Lira gritted

out. "Once my friends realize I'm gone, they'll find me. They aren't far from here."

"Good; that's what she wants." A subtle smile played along her lips. "I admit I enjoyed spending time in your mind. I'm envious, you know. There are few of my kind, and even fewer who find mates."

The revelation—the sheer loss of privacy in the disclosure —made Lira's skin crawl. Her face burned. "That's vile."

"Far from it." Vor'sca joined her on the bridge, leaning over its railing to study the fish that swam beneath. "Your Aidryn is a rare gift. I wonder if he will ever look at you that way again."

Lira curled her fingers into hard fists. If this was meant to provoke her, she wouldn't let it. "I suppose Aila used you to spy on me when she wasn't using you to fill my head with nonsense. Is she speaking through you now?"

Vor'sca inclined her head. "She's not omnipresent."

"How long has she had you in those cuffs?" Lira asked. When Vor'sca flinched, she pushed harder. "It must be terrible, having no access to your magic. No personal autonomy."

"You should know the feeling by now," Vor'sca said, her tone flat.

"I do," Lira answered sagely, taking a slow step away to put more distance between them. She moved off the bridge now, closer to the garden's entrance. "If I were immortal, I would want to find others of my kind. Teach them. Together, you could become a force to be reckoned with—not mere serfs for rulers who would use and discard you."

"I'm not a serf," Vor'sca shot back, though the flicker of doubt on her face made Lira press forward.

"There was a time when you lived with the Tai'ceru on your western coast," Lira said. "I saw you in a witnessing once. You were present at my father's death."

There was no hint of emotion on Vor'sca's face. "I was."

"And you were free to exist among your people then, were you not?"

The way Vor'sca scrutinized Lira, it was clear her words had an effect. "Within limits. There are always limits for people like me."

"Limited lives for those whose existence might never end? Come now." Lira crossed her arms. "You can do better than that. Your power could be limitless, and you know it."

"It is the only way." Her voice suddenly broke, and she took a faltering step backward, as though she hadn't meant to say it. "I have to protect my people from the king."

Lira had only studied the Tai'ceru people briefly, during her relationship with Eremon. He'd told her that their bloodlines had yielded the mortal deities. From that tribe had arisen his dynasty: the line of Riku, and all the rulers of Iathium who had come after.

"What's happened to your people?" Lira asked.

Vor'sca faltered, her gaze shuttering as she hesitated. "The king—he's—" But then she pressed her lips together and refused to say more.

"What if you had help? I mean—if Rodhlan came to your people's defense."

Vor'sca shook her head. "Rodhlan can do nothing."

"Are you so sure?" Lira studied the way the afternoon sunlight played against the immortal's silver hair, her light brown skin. "What if Rodhlan's immortal could?"

The promise was a gamble. Lira had had no success in drawing Eremon into any of her schemes for him yet, but perhaps he would forgive her this if she could convince Vor'sca to stand down.

"Rodhlan's immortal is impotent," Vor'sca said dismissively. "He knows nothing of his own potential."

"But *you* do." Fleetingly, Lira wished she was tethered to Vor'sca's mind once again so she could apply a bit more persuasive pressure. As it stood, all she had to work with were her words and the tone in which she delivered them. "We could make a deal. I'll free you, and in return, you'll teach Eremon how to wield his power. Then, he can help you."

"There's not enough time for that, and you cannot trust me," Vor'sca retorted, though her gaze lingered a little too long on Lira's face. There was a longing there that was clearly difficult for her to hide.

"Can I not?" Lira searched her expression, wracking her thoughts for something that might convince Vor'sca. It didn't take long for her to find it. "By losing your connection with my mind and my power, you've failed Aila and your king. What will they say when they learn what happened?" She lowered her voice. "What will they *do*?"

This time, the immortal's eyes went wide.

Lira leaned nearer and added, "Whatever freedom they promised you—whatever deal trapped you in those cuffs—they will never honor it now."

"What makes you think I would consider your offer?" Vor'sca whispered, her voice so low it was nearly inaudible.

Lira gave her a wry smile. "The fact that you already are."

She moved a bit further down the path, never taking her eyes off Vor'sca as she edged nearer to the exit. If she could just get close enough to the corridor, someone might be able to see them through the towering glass windows that separated Eremon's garden from the rest of the Dome's interior. "I think, working together, that you and Eremon could drive all our enemies out of Rodhlan for good."

Vor'sca blinked rapidly. "I..."

Suddenly, she crumpled, a look of anguish on her ageless face. She grasped one of the cuffs and cried out in pain, trying fruitlessly to remove it. Lira took a few harried steps in her direction before halting. Hesitation flooded her. She wasn't sure whether to try to remove the cuffs or see if the pain would pass.

"Vor'sca?" Lira asked tenuously.

"Tell her you won't accept her deal." A familiar voice sounded from behind Lira, and she whirled to find herself face-to-face with Fiadh, who had emerged from the thick foliage on the other side of the path. This time of day, the eastern side of the garden was cast in deep shadow—the perfect hiding place for someone with nefarious intent.

"I—I won't," Vor'sca ground out. She seemed unable to continue speaking after that. Lira wasn't sure if the other woman was obeying Fiadh's command or defying it.

A glint caught Lira's eye, and her attention snagged on the glass cuffs Fiadh was wearing—twins to the ones around Vor's-ca's wrists.

"Fiadh, stop!" Lira cried.

But Fiadh kept her attention fixed on Vor'sca. "Kneel," she said through gritted teeth, and closed her fingers into fists.

Vor'sca hit her knees, grunting on impact. They cracked hard on the stone pathway, and she grimaced in pain.

"Didn't know I could wield power, did you, Lira?" Fiadh said her name on a sneer. "Now, you see: I can call an immortal to heel. No one in Rodhlan can do that but me."

She flicked her fingers, and Vor'sca writhed, her mouth pried open in a silent scream.

"Stop it!" Lira shouted. A shadowy figure passed through the garden, just behind Fiadh. Careful not to call the woman's attention to the fourth presence in the room, Lira asked, "What sort of magic is this, Fiadh?"

"It's death," Fiadh answered, her dark gaze fixed on Vor'sca. "Limitation for the unlimited. She who is not truly alive, reigning supreme over she who will live forever."

"How did you come by it?" Lira feigned fascination. Grandeur had never fit Fiadh, but Lira got the sense that she was trying it on for size. "Was it a talent you discovered after your accident?"

"Aila discovered it," she said, raising her chin. Tendrils of black hair had come loose from her braid. They framed her face as sweat beaded along her forehead. "I made the restraints. She thought she'd outsmarted me, but I figured out what they were—what I could do. So I made more of them."

The shadowed figure was closer to Fiadh now—only a step or two behind her. Lira kept talking, though it was a struggle to keep her attention on Fiadh.

"You sound as though you anticipate controlling more immortals than just Vor'sca or Eremon," she said. "I was only aware of the two."

"Oh, there are more," Fiadh said, grinning triumphantly. "When you learn how many—"

Her eyes went wide as the figure emerged from the shadows at her back—and drove a dagger into her right side. There was a sickening, shattering sound as she did it, and Fiadh cried out in pain.

Fiadh's knees buckled and she sank to the ground, a shocked expression on her face. A dark-haired young woman Lira didn't recognize lowered her to the floor, then disarmed her. She was of slight build, dressed all in black, and looked barely over fifteen.

"Damn you," Fiadh gritted out, "Tiriya." She said the girl's name on a grunt as Tiriya drew the blade from her side. The sound of broken glass scraping against metal set Lira's teeth on edge.

"Good; you've heard of me," Tiriya said.

With trembling hands, Fiadh sought out the wound and pressed her palms against it, whimpering. There was no blood, but Lira half expected dark magic to burst from it haphazardly the moment Fiadh released the pressure. Tiriya grasped the pommel of Fiadh's sword, surveying it for a moment before she flipped the grip and slammed it against the side of her head.

Fiadh's eyes rolled back, and she collapsed.

"She'll live," Tiriya said, making quick work of the glass cuffs. "We're just going to borrow these."

She stood and strode to Lira, dropping the cuffs into her waiting hands with a quirky grin.

A disbelieving laugh rose from Lira as she placed the cuffs into the pouch at her side. "Who are you?"

"Tiriya, eldest daughter of Kenji and Toryn, and spy in training for Rí Eremon—at your service." She bent to remove Fiadh's belt and scabbard, then put them on herself and slid the sword into place. With a little flick of her head, she flipped her cropped hair out of her face. Effervescence emanated from her as she flashed a wide, admiring smile. "I know who you are, Silira; no introduction necessary."

Lira couldn't help but grin. "Pleased to meet you."

Tiriya tilted her hips this way and that, admiring her newly acquired weaponry. "I think it suits me."

Lira remembered that Vor'sca had been in pain moments before. The immortal had pushed herself up onto her hands and knees and appeared to be catching her breath. She moved nearer and knelt to survey her.

"Your father makes the pastries?" Lira asked over her shoulder as she watched Vor'sca warily.

"The best pastries," Tiriya said. Her expression hardened as she motioned to Vor'sca. "Get her up; I want to know where she took my mother."

Lira helped Vor'sca to her feet. As the immortal woman steadied herself, Lira reached for her bronze pendant, snatching it from around her neck before she could react.

"This belongs to me," she said, dropping it into her pouch. She pulled the leather drawstrings tight, then leveled a gaze at Vor'sca. "You're done tampering with my magic."

Lira headed for the garden's exit. Vor'sca followed, edged along by the point of Tiriya's sword at her back. When they stepped into the Dome's main corridor, Lira took a deep breath and shouted, "Eremon!"

Her voice carried down the corridor, strong and clear. They stood still, straining for a response. After a moment, it came: the echo of several pairs of footsteps moving swiftly toward them. It wasn't long before Eremon came into view, followed closely by Aidryn.

When Lira caught sight of her husband, she broke into a run, bursting clear past Eremon and forgetting Tiriya and Vor'sca completely. Aidryn's red-rimmed eyes filled with tears as she flung herself at him. They crashed against one another with enough force that they almost fell to the floor. He stumbled but gripped her hard, lifting her feet off the marble as he righted himself.

"I'm sorry," she said, burying her face in the crook of his neck. "I'm sorry."

Aidryn shushed her, nuzzling her curls. "So am I," he murmured. "It's my fault you were taken. I abandoned you."

Lira drank in the scent of the outdoors on his unfamiliar clothes, noting his windblown hair. If he had wanted to run, she didn't blame him—but that didn't matter. He was here now, and she was home. She tightened her hold on him. "I'll never forgive myself for harming you, Aidryn. I don't know a heart purer than yours, and I've broken it."

"Just—stay with me," he whispered, his voice breaking on the words. There was a mournful plea to them that shattered Lira's heart all over again, and she whimpered in response.

"I swear, I will," she promised. Aidryn lowered her to her feet, and she gently took his face in her hands, bringing him closer for a soft kiss. "What I feel for you—it was never about the Binding. The spell was a catalyst, that's all."

Aidryn gave her a pained smile and brushed gentle fingers against Lira's cheek. She tried not to wince at the sight of his wound.

"I see we have a new companion," he said, nodding toward Vor'sca, whom Eremon was engaging. They spoke in low tones, their postures tense. Vor'sca was gesturing in Lira's direction, and Eremon's head was bent toward her as he listened intently. Every few moments, he would nod.

After a long moment, he looked to Lira. They exchanged a terse glance, and Eremon gave her a subtle shrug. She sighed, turning back to Aidryn. "We'll see."

Tiriya, who had been listening in on their chat, stepped back and peeled off in the direction of the western towers. Lira watched her go, still dumbfounded at the younger woman's bravery in the garden. Another flash of movement caught her eye, and she turned to face Eremon, who had led Vor'sca over.

"Is she telling the truth, Lira?" he asked by way of greeting. There was doubt in his silver eyes as they flicked from the immortal woman to Lira, then back again. "You offered to free her in exchange for teaching me?"

"It's true," Lira replied, suddenly uncomfortable with the admission. "I'm sure I overstepped, but—"

"You did," he conceded, "but you were right. If she goes back to Iteloria, she won't be free, and we need her help here."

"I won't go back into captivity," Vor'sca whispered. Her eyes glinted with an emotion Lira couldn't quite place. "I fear for my people, but I won't let the king enslave me again."

"There's something else," Eremon said, dropping his voice until it was barely audible. He leaned close to Lira and added, "You have to trust me. Hold out your hand."

Lira obliged, and Eremon offered her Vor'sca's cuffs. She took them, exchanging a glance with the Itelorian woman as her fingers tightened around the warm glass. Vor'sca must have been convincing—whatever her story had been. A nervous rush swept through Lira's body as the weight, the *wrongness*, of the moment began to sink in.

"What should I trust, Eremon?" Lira asked, struggling to

suppress the alarm in her voice. Right here, only steps away, stood a centuries-old immortal with a vast amount of power. An immortal who had, until moments ago, been willing to betray everyone in this room on King La'hiran's behalf. She had nearly destroyed Lira, Aidryn, the Binding, and their powers in the process—and Lira couldn't help fearing that Eremon had made a terrible mistake in freeing her. "What did she tell you?"

Eremon gave her a quick, shallow shake of the head and said, "Soon. Just—*please*, trust me."

There was something about the desperation in his voice that made Lira's protests die on her tongue. For too long, she had demanded answers, action, accountability. And though she deserved his answers now, something deep within her told her to wait. To trust. That answers were coming, but now might not be the time to reveal them all—not with so many ears to listen.

"All right," she said with a sigh.

She didn't miss the way Eremon's shoulders relaxed with relief, nor the worried glance he cast at something—or someone—just behind her.

Thorne stepped to Lira's side and placed a hand on her shoulder then, drawing her attention away from the immortals. "Someone asked to see you," he murmured.

Lira followed his attention, turning to see Caitir, who stood several paces away with Oda at her side. The female warrior looked wary as she flicked her gaze between Lira and her former friend.

Caitir's expression was stricken, and she had bunched a handful of her gown's cobalt skirts into a fist, accentuating the soft swell of her belly. Lira remembered Aila chastising her daughter for the nervous habit years ago.

A rush of intangible emotions washed over her at the memory. At the sight of Caitir now.

She studied the young woman before her, whom she could scarcely claim she knew any longer. At some point, Caitir's hair had been stripped of the familiar golden dye she'd worn for so long, leaving behind the ash blonde Lira vaguely recalled from childhood. There was an openness in her pale blue eyes—a vulnerability that Lira hadn't seen in quite a long time.

Lira opened her mouth to speak, but she didn't know what to say, so she held up her open palm instead.

Tense silence filled the corridor. Caitir's gaze flicked to Lira's hand, then back up to her face. She took one tentative step forward, then another, closing the distance between them. Pressing her palm to Lira's, Caitir interlocked their fingers. Then, Lira leaned forward, rested her forehead against Caitir's, and closed her eyes.

They stayed like that for a long, silent moment. Lira felt Caitir exhale, as though she was relieved.

"I'm not who you thought I was," Caitir said, her voice so low that no one else would have been able to decipher her words.

Lira gave a little shrug. "I'm not who I was."

"Where does that leave us?" Caitir's voice sounded thick, and Lira fought back tears of her own.

She opened her eyes and drew back far enough to study her friend's lovely face. "Just... here."

With a shaky sigh, Lira pulled Caitir into a warm embrace. She felt Caitir's arms envelop her, and they tightened their hold on one another. Gradually, they relaxed, melding into the gesture. The feeling was both familiar and foreign, mended yet still irrevocably broken.

Things would never return to how they used to be, but perhaps now there would be a chance to forge something new. Something real.

"I'm sorry, Lira," Caitir whispered. "For everything."

CHAPTER 95

CAITIR

Dome

"If everyone is ready," Thorne began, seeming almost hesitant as he spoke, "we should consider the transfer of power now."

Lira gave Caitir a final squeeze and withdrew, smoothing her long, fur-lined tunic and straightening her shoulders as she turned to face the Beran warrior. She gave him a shallow nod, then reached for Aidryn's hand. The sight of her brother with Lira was still so new, Caitir could scarcely believe it. They had found one another—then nearly lost one another—multiple times in the months since they had last been together.

It was tempting to mull over her role in their many disasters, but it wouldn't do to sink into regret. Caitir needed to keep her wits about her. Later, when she had more time to reflect, she could sort through the mess of emotions that this reunion with Lira and Aidryn had stirred in her.

"Eremon?" she called, drawing his attention from Vor'sca. He turned toward Caitir's voice, seeking her out, and her cheeks flushed at his heightened awareness of her. "It's time."

"Perfect timing, my love."

The familiar voice emanating from one of the many shadowed side corridors set Caitir's hair on end. Her insides hollowed out, and her heart began to hammer as full-body tremors overtook her. She turned slowly, knowing who she would see, yet dreading it down to her bones.

Aila stepped out from the shadows, her gaze immediately sharpening on Caitir. Her dark hair shone in the late afternoon sunlight, a stark contrast to her pale skin and the long, silver gown she had donned. Around her neck was a pendant shaped like Lira's brass one. It was made of iridescent glass, the same material as Fiadh's cuffs.

So, this was how her mother had used Vor'sca. The immortal woman had been nothing but a proxy to get to Lira. Anger flooded her veins, and she held her mother's gaze with a glare of her own.

Aila gave her daughter a slow, languid blink—and in that blink, Caitir glimpsed silver irises. They were there one moment, then gone the next, replaced once again by the familiar dark brown.

Caitir's heart began to pound as a realization settled over her—something about her mother she had never once considered. Now, though, it seemed that it should have been obvious.

Thorne, Oda, and Aidryn drew their weapons, moving between Aila and Caitir. Eremon ignited cobalt flame between his palms. Oda pushed Lira behind them, too, and Caitir grabbed her hand to haul her back further. Lira's attention immediately snapped to Vor'sca, who was now standing just a step behind Eremon, her hands clasped behind her back. Her wrists were bare.

Caitir opened her mouth to warn Eremon, but Lira seemed to anticipate her alarm. She cut a quick glance at Caitir, warning flashing in her dark eyes. Almost imperceptibly, Lira shook her head.

Bristling, Caitir clamped her lips shut.

I hope they know what they're doing, she thought angrily.

"Well," Aila said on a breath, surveying the group before her. "What a welcome. My daughter, two immortals, and all the anointed of Rodhlan here in one place—almost as if it was planned this way."

"Don't you mean three immortals, Mother?" Caitir relished the way Aila's attention snapped back to her. A sly grin spread across her mother's face.

At her side, Caitir thought she heard Lira suppress a small gasp.

"Did you know, Caitir?" The hint of disbelief in Eremon's voice stung, but Caitir supposed she deserved it. If she had known the truth, she might have kept it secret at first.

"Not 'til just now," she answered softly. A moment of strange recognition passed between Caitir and her mother, but she shook off the shock and added, "I'm sure there's a reason why she concealed it for so long. If I were her, I wouldn't waste the opportunity to share with an audience."

She thought she heard an approving grunt from Thorne's direction.

"Of course," Aila said, folding her hands before her in mock solemnity. "I'm rather proud of how well this elaborate scheme concluded. It took some time for each of you to shatter properly, but finally, it's done."

"Now it's your turn to shatter," Eremon growled, his power flaring. The cobalt magic reflected brightly in the shimmer of Aila's gown.

"Brave words from a boy-king whose mother led him around by the nose," Aila replied, waving him off. Her eyes darkened as she craned her neck to fix a sharp stare on Caitir. "Bring my child to the front of your pathetic line, where I can see her."

"No," Eremon answered through gritted teeth. Tendrils of

his cobalt power gathered around his fists, snaking up his arms and mingling with his dark magic. Caitir couldn't see his expression, but she imagined that his eyes flashed silvery-white.

A rolling *boom* of power reverberated from beneath their feet, and Caitir suddenly felt unsteady. Aila closed her eyes for a moment, but when she opened them again, her irises were the same eerie silver as Eremon's. This time, she didn't conceal the color.

Aila opened her palms, and deep crimson magic poured from them. It was laced with the familiar sparks of darkness she had taught Caitir to harness so many years ago. Her power quickly filled the wide corridor, smothering the torches' golden flames and replacing them with sparking motes of crimson. Against the quickly dimming light outside, the colors cast an ominous glow over Caitir's companions.

"You fancy yourself a powerful immortal, boy," Aila said, punctuating her words with another burst of power, "but you're a fledgling. I can snuff out your power with barely a thought."

And then, she did. With little more than a blink, Aila extinguished Eremon's cobalt magic. Suppressed it. Forced it back inside his body.

Eremon went rigid, fighting against the excess power as her crimson magic surrounded and pressed in on him. He cried out in rage as Aila overpowered him. Then, she extended her magic to the front line, easily snatching the weapons from the warriors' hands. Aidryn, Thorne, and Oda lost their blades, and the steel clattered to the marble floor at Aila's feet.

Before they could react, tendrils of her magic were snaking around each of them like serpents, coiling and twisting and squeezing. She bound everyone on the front line, save Eremon and Vor'sca, who remained far enough behind Eremon to hide her wrists. Aidryn, Oda, and Thorne struggled against the power, fighting for some way to free themselves from it.

The magic rushed toward Caitir next. Lira lunged, taking Caitir's hand just as Aila's power made contact. Though they braced for its burn, a cool blast of cobalt flared around them. It emanated from Eremon's ring, which Lira had yet to remove. Aila's magic dissolved against Eremon's protective shield on impact, and she let out an angry, anguished cry when she realized what Lira had done.

Lira was still the heir to the throne. She still possessed the ring, which meant she could not be killed by an outside force. That was why Aila had attacked her from within. Corrupting Lira's power had been the only chance Aila had to destroy the Witness Tree and Eremon's chosen heir in one fell swoop.

Enraged, Aila let her power fade. Aidryn and Thorne had already lost consciousness—Caitir prayed they weren't dead—while Oda was still fighting. She was clearly exhausted, with beads of sweat rolling down her lovely dark skin. Still, she struggled to conjure the water magic she'd inherited from Faolan. Each burst of water turned immediately to steam.

Caitir's heart was pounding, her breaths coming in rapid pants as her gaze darted from her companions to Aila and the immortals. Slowly, her awareness narrowed to where she and Lira were still clasping hands, Eremon's magic surrounding them. Lira was pressing something hard into her palm, and Caitir dared to brush a finger against it. She had to stifle a gasp when she realized it was a pair of Fiadh's glass cuffs.

Hooking one finger through the loop, she reached as though to clasp Lira's hands with both of hers. Lira turned to her then, following Caitir's lead. The friends held hands for a long moment, and to any outsider, they appeared to be clinging to one another, sharing one last shred of desperate hope before facing the inevitable cataclysm.

"Dispel that magic and face me, *now*," Aila demanded, drawing another *boom* of power up from beneath the Dome.

Fissures opened in the marble tile, and chips of stone fell

from overhead. The glass walls that surrounded them began to crack, thin veins opening up along the massive translucent panes and making their way up, up, up. It sounded and felt as though the building might come down around them.

Aila tilted her head up and closed her eyes as if reveling in the destruction she might wreak if she just pushed her power a little further. In that moment, Caitir took the cuffs from Lira and wrapped her arms around her belly as though cradling it, careful to hide the glass from view. Then, Lira let go of her and the ring's magic winked out.

Oda lay at Aila's feet, silent and motionless.

"No..." Lira whimpered, moving as though she might rush forward to her husband and the warriors.

"Stop," Caitir snapped. Lira froze. "Stay back."

"They're not dead, if that's what you're fretting about," Aila said with a wry smile. "That would have been too peaceful an end. I have greater plans for all of you."

Her silver eyes flashed as she looked from Eremon to Vor'sca, then back to Caitir and Lira.

"What do you want?" Lira demanded, stepping forward. Her voice trembled. "You're here with two living vessels of memory. If you want your story to be remembered, now is the time to tell it."

Aila's lip curled, though her eyes lit with satisfaction. "It's too bad you have no power, Witness Tree."

"I may not have my magic," Lira replied, "but everyone has memory. And I believe memory is just as effective as my birthright power, so long as truth is preserved."

"Go on, Aila." Eremon's voice was almost imploring enough to hint at genuine interest. "Your story could be forever etched into Iteloria's magic, if not Rodhlan's."

Caitir held her breath as her mother considered. Aila's gaze rested on her daughter before she replied.

"If I'm to share the tale," Aila began slowly, "I want my daughter by my side. Of all people, it concerns her most."

CHAPTER 96
CAITIR

Dome

"Caitir, stay back!" Eremon growled over his shoulder. But Caitir shook her head, meeting his pained gaze as she stepped forward. Rather than moving to Aila's side, though, she moved to Eremon's.

"You wanted me nearer," Caitir said, keeping her eyes fixed on Aila. Her mother's lips curled. "This is as close as I'll get."

Caitir clutched her belly as Eremon wrapped an arm around her. She pressed against his side, nuzzling close to conceal the cuffs she still held. In her periphery, she saw Lira edge closer to Vor'sca. Quickly, she turned her attention back to her mother.

Aila surveyed Caitir with an arrogant, heavy-lidded gaze. Her eyes drifted to Caitir's belly, and Eremon's grip on her shoulder tightened. Caitir felt herself curl in, as though it was possible to shield herself from the woman's scrutiny.

"You look hideous," Aila hissed through her teeth, "after everything I sacrificed to make you beautiful."

The words struck right where Aila meant them to. Even

though Caitir knew in her heart they weren't true, she couldn't seem to keep them from tearing at her anyway. She fought the wave of shame that coursed over her, and held eye contact with her mother.

"That's *enough*," Eremon snarled, but Aila just laughed as though amused.

"Let her speak for herself." Aila tilted her head, regarding Caitir. "How did you manage to draw him in? You did such a superb job of repelling him before."

"Getting rid of you, for starters," Caitir said. Aila drew back as though she'd been slapped. "But you surprise me, Mother. With your talk of immortal magic all those years, I was convinced you were merely *attempting* to reach immortality. You were already immortal. What more could you possibly want?"

"Retribution for old sins," Aila replied slowly, gauging Caitir's expression for a reaction as she dragged the answer out. "An immortal babe of my own. If you had been born a mortal goddess, I could have gotten what I wanted easily. But you weren't; and I was unwilling to wait for another lifetime."

"What?" Caitir breathed, her stomach turning. "But that would have meant killing me."

"A momentary death—yes," Aila said, taking a step closer, "but after that, an eternity together."

"That's horrible," Caitir said with a shudder. She pressed a protective palm to her belly. "*You* are horrible."

Aila laughed airily. Dismissively. "You just don't realize. Through your contact with Eremon's magic, I have gained more than I ever hoped possible: transformation without the need for death. You, a mortal goddess. The child, an immortal." She took a step closer as she continued. "Even better, I can give the Itelorian king what he desires: a restoration of the magical balance between our continents. It's everything we both wanted, and La'hiran will be just as thrilled as I am."

There was genuine, unbridled joy emanating from Aila now. Her glee snapped something within Caitir. Searing rage roared through her, pounding in her ears and flashing in her field of vision. She must have lunged forward, because Eremon tightened his grip on her, holding her back.

"*No*," he hissed, alarm flashing in his silver eyes. "Don't move."

"How sweet." Aila turned her attention to Eremon, tilting her head curiously. "Do you have any idea how long I've waited for you, boy?" She didn't bother to wait for an answer. "Seventeen-hundred years. You were the first mortal deity to emerge after my firstborn son was lost."

The room went utterly silent. All Caitir could hear was the pounding of her pulse in her ears. "*What?*"

"I watched your bloodline," Aila continued, keeping her eyes on Eremon, who had gone deadly still. "For centuries, I planned. Hoped. Waited. You were to be mine, yet your father and that *midwife* concealed your Rune. Not even Macha succeeded at such deception."

Eremon barked a harsh, disbelieving laugh. "You thought you would—what? Abduct me? Keep me at your side for eternity?"

Aila bowed her head, almost mournfully. "That was my hope until it was dashed, over and over again. Until now, I had lost all hope of ever taking an immortal child in my arms." She turned her attention to Caitir again, a slow smile spreading across her lips. "But you, my daughter, have made that dream possible once more."

Caitir's knees threatened to give out beneath her, but Eremon held her steady. She'd foolishly hoped that Aila didn't yet know about the baby's power, but like always, her mother was ten steps ahead. No matter how hard Caitir tried to evade Aila's machinations, she always failed. And this, above all others, was her greatest failure yet.

"You lived in the days of Ulan?" Eremon asked, his voice dangerously smooth. Too calm.

"I am the granddaughter of Rasu," Aila answered, all too eager to engage. "I was one of many who watched our own fathers flee to Rodhlan in search of the same power that drew him."

"Riku's Binding to Rhona upset the balance of magic between Iteloria and Rodhlan," Eremon said with a sage nod.

"Yes," Aila replied. "La'hiran is desperate. But now, with my own daughter a mortal goddess and an immortal child in her womb, we can both have what we desire."

Eremon threw an arm out to shield Caitir, taking a step toward Aila. "You will *not* touch either of them."

Aila's eyes flashed white. Caitir lay a trembling hand on Eremon's, lacing their fingers together and coaxing his arm down to his side. There was too much at stake for Eremon's power to erupt unchecked, and with no strategy. It would pale in comparison to Aila's, and the destruction and death they would leave in their wake would be unthinkable. Caitir was forming a plan, but she needed time. If she could keep Aila talking, perhaps there might still be a chance to sort it out.

"Tell me, Mother," Caitir said, "if you died to become immortal, how did it happen?"

"By my own father's hand." Aila's chin quivered, a flicker of emotion crossing her face as she uttered the words. "While in Rodhlan, he met a certain anointed from Clan Tarlach who told him of Iuchair and its counterpart in Iteloria. He abandoned our family for two decades while he hunted down the great key and learned how to wield it. Then he used his dark magic to kill me in my sleep."

Her eyes flicked to the ceiling briefly. She seemed as though she was fighting back a flood of fresh emotion over the centuries-old crime. "In the end, my father turned the key in the wrong direction. Rather than taking my power for himself, he made me immortal. When he realized what he'd done, he fled—but not before he killed my husband and took my newborn child, who was sleeping in the bassinet beside me.

"The babe had been born a mortal god," Aila said on a groan. "He could have been mine for eternity. Instead, his grandfather—his own kin—delivered him to the king, and his magic was sacrificed to the land."

Caitir's stomach dropped, and she felt bile rising in her throat. The horror her mother must have experienced—the unending heartache of losing a child—made her own heart squeeze with momentary compassion.

Aila's eyes glistened with unshed tears. "I don't even know where they buried him."

"Gods..." Caitir whispered, pressing her hands to her mouth.

A dry laugh broke from Aila. "For nearly two thousand years, I have lived hundreds of lives between Iteloria and Rodhlan. I have borne mortal children. Watched as they aged and died with no magic to speak of. Some families I have raised —others, I have abandoned, disgusted by my repeated failures. I have been patient. I have tried, over and over, to bear a child with the same power as my first son—to right the wrongs inflicted on my family.

"I had almost given up hope when I met your father, Caitir: a descendant of Clan Tarlach whose bloodline had yielded a boy powerful enough to inherit its anointing."

Aila looked to where Aidryn lay, still unconscious. Caitir resisted the urge to turn and look at him, instead keeping her eyes trained on Aila, whose gaze returned to her. "And then you were born, and you were so disgustingly *ordinary*. But the boy was willing to part with power, and so began my grand experiment. I wanted to know if it was possible to make a mortal deity —and I have accomplished so much more."

Aila's eyes lit again, and Caitir's body trembled with revulsion. She wanted to block out her mother's next words—drown them in screams if she must. But instead, she remained sealed tightly to Eremon's side, her gaze dropping to the floor as Aila continued.

"I dedicated my existence to gifting you with magic from as many sources as possible. You received power from Clan Tarlach's Anointed and the Raní herself. We were so close to Silira's anointed power before, and then there was Gerallt, the eldest son of the last Witness Tree." Aila's gaze flicked to Lira before returning to her daughter. "I taught myself as many spells and incantations as I could, because if I couldn't bear another mortal deity, then perhaps one could be made. And if I failed to make you in the image of the child I lost, perhaps a powerful grandchild would suffice."

Her eyes drifted to Caitir's middle, and she took a step closer to Eremon.

"I hoped that if you ever encountered the boy-king's power, you might bear the mortal deity I've so desperately hoped for, all this time," she murmured. "I was more than right. To think, you: a mortal goddess, bearing an immortal babe. It didn't even have to be *Eremon's* child!"

"So, you'll take the child for yourself," Caitir ventured, though her body shook with terror, "then deliver me to La'hiran for a sacrifice when I've served my purpose. Am I following, Mother?"

A feline grin lit Aila's features. "Quite."

"You call Caitir your great experiment," Eremon mused, his rage barely leashed, "but how many other innocents did you affect when you began your tampering?"

"More than you can possibly imagine," Aila answered. "Bending your magic—the clans' magic—to my will was easier than I'd expected. I gave Rodhlan more access to its old power than it had been afforded in years, and for that, your people owe me their gratitude."

"*You*," Eremon said, realization dawning on his face. "You were responsible for my death."

Aila gripped the glass pendant she wore, turning it so it caught the sunlight streaming through the windows. "Your death, Lira's madness, Aidryn's blindness—the host of disasters the lot of you created for yourselves," she answered, amusement tinging her voice. "All it took was a little nudge here or there. In a manner of speaking, if you *must* blame me, then go ahead. But truly, I only leveraged your weaknesses and failures to my own advantage.

"And Caitir, you were stupid enough to think that you could act on your own, as though I didn't know every move you were making here—from wasting your time in the archive to your meaningless regency. I saw it all, I know it all, and there is no way you will prevent me from getting what I came back for."

Heat crept into Caitir's face, and her knees threatened to buckle beneath her. She'd believed Aila's absence to be her chance at freedom. To know her mother had been watching her every move—and Eremon's, too—stoked the deep rage she'd been suppressing all these weeks. Her mind began to race.

Movement caught her eye, and a moment later, Vor'sca had moved between Caitir and Aila, taking Eremon's hand as she uttered an incantation in *Itelos*. The force of her sea foam-colored magic knocked Caitir off balance as it erupted around them, but Lira was there to catch her by the elbows—to steady her. She grasped Caitir's hand, giving her fingers a squeeze.

As though empowered by Vor'sca's show of force, Eremon let his own cobalt magic flow from his palms. Their powers combined, swirling throughout the corridor, illuminating everything with an otherworldly glow. Aila's gaze flicked from one immortal to the other, as though considering her next move.

"Ah, so you've already gained the boy-king's trust," Aila said, her eyes narrowing in Vor'sca's direction. "It's too bad. I quite enjoyed controlling Lira through you. Now, I suppose I'll have to do it myself."

Aila flicked her fingers, and coils of crimson power lashed out, snatching up the three unconscious anointed and suspending them in midair.

Another tendril of power wrapped itself around Lira and yanked her from her feet. Caitir screamed as Lira's hand was ripped from hers. With an angry shout, Lira rose into the air alongside Thorne, Oda, and Aidryn, and she struggled against the magic that held her.

"No!" Caitir screamed as Eremon and Vor'sca intensified their power. "Stop this!"

Aila laughed and let her magic surge. "I will stop," she said, "when the immortals do."

"Release them first!" Eremon bellowed.

His power clashed with Aila's, the crimson and cobalt mingling into a deep violet glow. Lira continued to fight, but the others were still suspended, dead weight, their color fading fast. All Caitir needed was one look at Aidryn's face to know he was near death, and she imagined Thorne and Oda weren't far behind. Eremon's ring might be protecting Lira, but it likely wouldn't keep the others alive against this onslaught of terrible power. Worse, Aila hadn't truly begun tapping into her dark magic.

Caitir had to think quickly and act *now*. There was no time to strategize, no time to scheme. All she would be able to do was rely on her instinct. And if there was one thing she'd learned from Aila, it was how to adapt and survive any situation. If she had managed to survive her mother all these years, then perhaps she could endure once more.

She took a step forward. "If you let them go," she began, willing her voice into steadiness, "then the immortals will stop, and I will negotiate."

"No," Eremon roared.

Caitir fixed her eyes on Aila. "Lower them: Lira, Aidryn, Thorne, and Oda. Set them down unharmed. Vor'sca will release her magic, and Eremon will listen to me."

"I will *not!*" The heartbreaking rage in Eremon's voice almost gave her pause. Almost.

A knot formed in the pit of Caitir's stomach. "Yes," she said softly, turning to face him fully, "you will, or three of the four anointed will die."

Shock was written across Eremon's features. "You can't do this. I forbid it."

Caitir shook her head. "As whose ruler? You know as well as I that she'll kill them before you can counterattack."

"But—"

"*Please.*" It emerged from her lips as a broken whisper. "The risk is too great. Let me negotiate with her."

Eremon relented, sighing in resignation.

"Vor'sca," he said, his voice wavering, "when the anointed touch the ground, we release our magic. Understood?"

Although Vor'sca's forehead creased with worry, she nodded once. "Yes."

"Mother," Caitir said, daring to take two steps closer to Aila, then another. Another. Aila turned her full attention to her daughter, drawn to the movement as though magnetized.

The next words Caitir spoke threatened to destroy her as they emerged, but she made herself say them anyway. "If you want me, you must do as I've asked. No one comes to harm."

"You're *not* going with her," Eremon said, his voice murderous and low.

"I never realized how much a grandchild meant to you," Caitir answered, painstakingly ignoring Eremon's words. She held her mother's gaze. "I will go with you, if you will abide by my terms and let me say goodbye."

"No!" Lira cried.

Caitir squeezed her eyes shut, drowning out Lira's protests.

Eremon's. "Move them to safety, Mother. No more damage; no more harm. And you'll let me say a proper goodbye."

Aila faltered, though she held Caitir's gaze. "Very well."

Slowly, agonizingly, Aila used her power to lower Lira and the other anointed to the marble floor. The moment Lira was free, she ran straight to Caitir, throwing her arms around her friend. Caitir returned Lira's embrace, but she watched Eremon over her friend's shoulder, hyper aware of his every movement.

Reluctantly, Eremon and Vor'sca withdrew their magic. Caitir was careful not to look at Eremon, though he tried to place himself in her line of vision. Now wasn't the time to let him draw her in. She had no choice in the matter—not this time.

Too many lives were at stake. Not just the lives in this room, but Toryn's, too.

Eremon stepped nearer, his gaze flicking from Caitir to Lira and back. He didn't speak, but Caitir knew that expression— the way his forehead furrowed in concentration. It was a face he'd often made just before an idea struck him, and she loved him for it. She cast a brittle smile in his direction, but he slowly, sorrowfully shook his head.

"You can't do this." Lira grasped Caitir's face in her hands. "Don't—you can't. Eremon, *tell* her."

"Save them," Caitir replied, her lower lip quivering. Though Eremon moved near enough to touch, she focused wholly on Lira. "Take care of my brother; he needs you."

A tear traced its way down her oldest friend's cheek. "Don't do this," Lira whispered.

"You've said your goodbyes, Caitir," Aila said sharply. "Now, fulfill your end of the bargain."

"A moment more," Caitir replied, lacing her tone with venom. "Then, you may have me."

Eremon reached for her hand; he was shaking so violently that she wanted to take him and run. Run and never look back. But Aila was an ancient immortal—not an ordinary woman obsessed with magic and power, but a goddess with the knowledge and skill to decimate the city. The destruction she would leave in her wake was not worth the risk.

"I can't lose you," Eremon said, taking Caitir's free hand and intertwining their fingers. "What about us? The child?"

"There's no other way." Caitir folded her other hand behind her back, still concealing the cuffs from Aila. "Rodhlan needs its anointed. Kenji needs Toryn—their daughters need a mother. All of them must survive today."

His hands moved to rest on her shoulders. "She'll kill the anointed the moment she has you."

"I will protect them." Vor'sca stepped forward, her eyes darkening. She tilted her head in Lira's direction. "Silira, Caitir will need your pendant for *turas*."

For a moment, panic and reluctance flashed across Lira's features. But she took a step back, opening the drawstring pouch at her side and rifling through it. A moment later, she held the pendant in her palm.

"Lira," Eremon hissed as Lira placed the heavy bronze pendant against Caitir's heart.

"Remember where you come from," Lira whispered as she latched the chain at the base of Caitir's neck. "Remember that we love you."

Eremon edged between them, his eyes pleading as he gripped Caitir's elbows. "You can't do this, Caitir. I won't allow it."

"It's a good thing I've never been submissive," Caitir replied softly, trying to smile. She ran her fingertips over the pendant, which hummed with Lira's familiar power. "I have to do this for our future."

"What future?" Eremon framed her face in his trembling hands. "You're walking right back into the prison you freed yourself from. What will you be subjected to once you're in Iteloria?"

"Eremon, I was never free. It was all an illusion," Caitir whispered. "Aila won't break me yet. She covets the child too much. If I go with her, I will be safe for a time, and so will our friends. But if I refuse, they die."

Eremon released a breath, defeated. Caitir stroked his cheek, rising on her toes to kiss him. He pulled her flush against him, returning the kiss as though there would never be another. And perhaps there wouldn't be. They'd both known this would have to come to an end, one way or another.

Caitir placed a hand on Eremon's chest. Gently broke the kiss, though he chased her lips for more. She guided him to look her in the eyes.

"I'm buying you time," she whispered, the words almost inaudible, "just as you bought me time. Use your time to ascend. Become who you were meant to be."

The lie seared her throat as it emerged, but she couldn't bring herself to leave him without hope.

"I'll come for you," Eremon swore. "We will find a way."

"Perhaps," she answered, "but not today."

Caitir tried to take a step back, but Eremon held onto her, moving forward, as reluctant to break contact as she was. He brushed tentative fingertips over her belly, and she covered his hand with her own, pressing his warm palm down.

"I wanted to be with you through everything," he said, voice breaking. "To wake with you every morning. To hold your hand when your child is born. I wanted—"

"I know," she answered, blinking away her own tears, "and I love you for all of it."

Aila's voice cut through the room, sharp and impatient. "Caitir!"

She cast a glance over her shoulder. "*Patience*, Mother," she said coolly. "Isn't that your greatest virtue?"

Straightening, Aila raised her chin and closed her mouth.

Caitir slid her fingers up and over Eremon's hand, gripping his wrist as she drew him to her again. He sank into their kiss, closing his eyes. It was warm and full of longing, and she knew she would grieve the loss of this—the loss of him—for the rest of her days.

"When I go," she whispered against his lips, "Tell Vor'sca to cast protective magic. I don't trust Aila to keep her word."

"Why Vor'sca?" Confusion clouded his gaze.

"Because you'll need protection, too," she whispered.

Caitir tightened her hold on him, pulling him down for a final kiss as she closed one of the glass cuffs around his wrist. It was warm, and for a moment, Eremon remained lost in her. Abruptly, he opened his eyes, searching her face in confusion as the foreign sensation registered.

"What are you doing?" he demanded, his face twisting with rage and grief. When he tried to pull himself from her grasp, she clapped the other cuff on his free wrist. It fastened with a soft click as he broke away, eyes widening in horror. There was a short pulse of magic between them, and his power blinked out.

"Forcing you to stand down," Caitir answered, fighting back a sob. "I'm so sorry."

"You know I won't forgive you for this." Eremon's breathing quickened, and she could see her betrayal reflected in his silver eyes. But she couldn't let him erupt—not when she was risking everything to protect everyone here.

"I'm not asking you to."

She made herself move backward, in Aila's direction. Forced herself to turn her back on Eremon, on Lira, on her brother and the warriors and the Itelorian immortal. So much power, all in one room. So much magic they couldn't afford to lose.

Caitir halted between her friends and her mother,

steadying her ragged breaths. Then, she raised her chin, closed the distance between herself and Aila, and extended her hand.

"I'm ready," she whispered.

I'm not ready. I'll never be ready.

A serpentine grin spread across Aila's lips, and she laced their fingers together. "Say goodbye."

Black lightning blasted from the floor around them, forming a ring around Caitir and Aila and rising upward. Outward. Caitir screamed as Aila wrenched her to her side, readying Lira's pendant for *turas*.

She thought she saw the room explode with sea foam-colored light, just before the spell swallowed them up.

CHAPTER 97

EREMON

Dome

Vor'sca's protective magic filled the glass corridor, blasting effortlessly from her body, swallowing up the dark magic. Her magic swept over Eremon and his friends, cocooning them until the last of Aila's remaining power had dissolved. When the magic finally dissipated, a heavy silence fell over the room.

Eremon sank to his knees, bracing himself, pressing a shaking hand to his aching chest. The glass cuffs around his wrists had so thoroughly blocked his magic that this yawning, agonizing well of grief was all he had left.

He hated Aila. Hated what Caitir had done. Hated himself for being too weak to stop it.

Vor'sca moved from Aidryn to Oda to Thorne, kneeling by each, assessing them. Eremon could sense her releasing pulses of power, but he was too unfamiliar with pure immortal magic, and too lost in the overwhelming pain of Caitir's loss, to pay it any mind. All that mattered was that someone was tending to his friends. He wasn't sure he could have done it himself.

Vaguely, he sensed Lira beside him. He didn't bother looking up. She lay a comforting hand on his back, then lowered herself to sit beside him in silence.

Long moments passed before he said, "I thought I knew despair when you brought me back from the crypt." He released a hollow laugh. "It was nothing compared to this."

Lira patted his shoulder, shushing him. "We can't lose hope."

Eremon drew away from her touch. "She's going to be used as a sacrifice," he said. "And she promised herself—her child—to that monster."

"Caitir never promised the child to Aila," Lira said firmly. "She only said she would go to Iteloria. You heard her: She's buying us time, and she was the only one who could."

But Eremon was so filled with despair that Lira's words sailed over him, landing somewhere beyond. In the Moravon, perhaps, or maybe the Strait of Ulan. It didn't matter now. Nothing did.

"I'm worthless," Eremon groaned, resting his head in his hands.

"Aila is very old," Lira replied, and the patience in her voice made Eremon's chest tighten. *This* was the Silira he remembered. The Lira without dark magic, who was brilliant and blisteringly honest and *kind*. "Vor'sca is also powerful. She'll be able to help you embrace your full potential, and together you'll be a force to be reckoned with."

Eremon shook his head slowly. "This power means *nothing* if I can't save Caitir."

Lira turned up her palms and extended her hands toward Eremon. "Give me your wrists."

He obliged her, and she removed the glass cuffs carefully.

Then, she set them aside and grasped Eremon's hands in her own.

"You have had so much weight on your shoulders," she said in a soft voice. "I know what it's like carry a heavy burden, but not as heavy as a crown. You have borne more than any one person should have to, and for that, I'm sorry."

"It should have been simple. Straightforward," Eremon replied, squeezing her fingers. "Take the throne back. Save the city. Get on with our lives."

"I thought so, too," Lira ventured slowly, "but I've learned that sometimes, doing the right thing is a bit... nuanced. If you hadn't had compassion for Caitir, if you hadn't fallen in love with her, we wouldn't know she's a mortal goddess. We wouldn't have learned about her immortal child, and we wouldn't have had the chance or knowledge to save either of them."

"By letting Aila have them, I failed," Eremon argued, hanging his head.

"It's a delayed victory; not a failure. They are not the same." She chewed her lip, as though carefully considering her next words. "Sometimes, a delay allows us to grow into who we were meant to be."

CHAPTER 98

LIRA

Dome

Night had fallen before Aidryn, Thorne, and Oda regained consciousness and the ability to move about. Aila's immortal power had incapacitated them completely, driving them into a deep sleep that took Vor'sca hours to unravel. She'd said they were lucky to be alive, and Lira didn't take that fact for granted.

Each had awakened with a terrible headache, and Eremon had taken their pain. It was something he'd done for Oda in the crypt when she was wounded. He had spoken to each of the anointed in low tones, and Lira imagined he must be recounting the day's events, as well as its grave losses. Eremon spent extra time with Aidryn, drawing the discomfort from his wounded eye as Lira watched from a distance.

She had been grateful for this kindness, even in the midst of Eremon's devastation. This was the man she remembered. The compassionate, warm, caring person who had represented their city so beautifully in his mortal life.

She would do anything to help him regain the happiness he so deserved.

The group gathered in Eremon's council chamber, a room constructed from ornate, dark wood and carpeted with plush crimson. Its air was stagnant from misuse, and Vor'sca lit its candles and sconces with her magic. They sat around the table in pained silence.

Lira nervously twisted Eremon's ring around and around her finger. "Before today's events, we'd intended to discuss the transfer of power." Her voice sounded small and far away to her own ears, and her heart thudded in her chest. "Let's talk of it now."

Eremon straightened in his seat.

"Silira, I gave you my ring for safekeeping. As Defender of Histories, you were the ring's legal custodian. But when you put it on at *Nami Mostari* and said the incantation, you became my heir. If you wish to lead Iathium, speak now."

"I do not," she answered hastily, stealing a glance at Aidryn, who lightly stroked the inside of her right forearm with his fingertips. Lira shivered at his touch, reveling in the wonder of this love he held for her. She would never be worthy of him— not now. But she could spend her days trying.

Eremon nodded decisively. "Then I respectfully request that the ring be returned to me, so I may assume my duties as Rí and appoint a new heir."

"I respect your request," Lira replied slowly, "but I also have something to say. Please know that, as yet, I have not spoken these words to anyone."

Aidryn sat up straighter, his full attention on Lira. Thorne and Oda exchanged a terse glance. Vor'sca, who had been sitting alone at the end of the table, raised her head to study them.

Eremon frowned as he waited for Lira to continue.

"I've never coveted a crown, or a throne, or a city," she said, her heartbeat quickening. "As Defender, I only wanted my quiet role in the archive. But life and destiny are unpredictable. We each carry our own scars. Secrets. Actions and decisions we regret."

The room was completely silent now. Lira shifted uncomfortably, dragging her sweaty palms across the bottom of her long tunic.

"When I awakened you, Eremon," she said, "I intended for you to take the throne immediately. I believe that now, we all understand why you did not. Nonetheless, we each made decisions that carry specific consequences."

Eremon leaned forward in his seat. "What are you trying to say, Silira?"

Though she wanted to look away, Lira held Eremon's gaze. "Remember what I told you?" Her voice was tremulous. "A delay allows us to grow into who we were meant to be."

A beat of silence passed, devoid of Eremon's understanding. He watched her with an open apprehension that made her muscles tense, her stomach ache. But Lira pressed forward, desperately willing him to grasp her perspective.

"Eremon," she said softly, "as your friend and ally, I sincerely believe a delay is in order. You're unfit to reclaim the throne at this time."

Hurt and shock flashed in his eyes, and he bared his teeth. He stood abruptly, toppling his stool and pressing his hands on the long table. "How dare you judge my ability to rule?"

Thorne and Oda went on high alert, straightening, their gazes flicking between Lira and Eremon. Lira thought she saw Thorne reach for the hilt of his broadsword. She met his eyes, seeming to give him an unspoken order. The warrior's gaze shuttered, and he relaxed his grip, though his hand never left the sword.

"Answer me," Eremon demanded in a low voice.

From beside Lira, Aidryn reached for her hand and laced

their fingers together. It gave her the nerve to continue speaking.

"In this *moment*," she pressed. "Not in your past, and not forever."

"After everything you've done, you have the audacity to accuse *me* of being an unfit leader?" She could feel Eremon's panic emanating from him, raw and unbridled. His dark magic stirred the air in the room, charging it, though he refrained from wielding it.

"You know what happened was out of Lira's control," Aidryn said, setting his jaw. He stood slowly, deliberately, moving his stool back and rising to his full height. Rather than drawing his own weapon, however, he placed a hand on Lira's shoulder. "At least listen to her reasoning."

"I suppose you already know the entire plan," Eremon snapped.

Aidryn held up a hand, keeping his voice steady. "This is the first I've heard of it, and I'd like a chance to understand as much as you would."

Eremon sneered, "Oh, I'm sure—"

"Let me make something clear," Aidryn interrupted, his voice firm and unwavering. "If we want to protect Rodhlan, then we must be unified. We're responsible for leading a continent, and the people are looking to us for answers. There is no council, and there are precious few elders left. It's us now. Rodhlan is on our shoulders, and we will fail it if we continue to fight each other."

His gaze swept around the table, and the others nodded their assent. Eremon kept still, watching Aidryn closely as he righted his stool and sank back onto it.

"Now," Aidryn said, pressing a palm to Lira's thigh beneath the table as he reclaimed his seat, "I believe Lira was speaking."

Panic rose from deep within Lira, but she nodded once to Aidryn, then looked to Eremon again.

"Eremon, I need you to understand." She paused, closing her eyes and taking a deep breath. "You need time. Time to learn your magic, time to retrieve Caitir from Iteloria. You can't do all those things and take charge of the city, too. Not in the way we need you to."

"You think I can't lead my city and master the magic?" Eremon snarled, not bothering to mask the hurt in his voice. "I led Iathium while my magic was *killing* me."

Thorne's hand drifted the hilt of his broadsword again as he eyed the exchange warily. Oda was watching Thorne, Aidryn was watching Lira, and Vor'sca was watching Eremon. The tension in the room rose, making Lira's head throb.

"This is different, and you know it." Lira sighed. "There's so much more at stake now. When your power was killing you, there was no way to gain control over it. But now, you can learn to control what you have. Wielding your full measure of magic will mean longstanding protection for Rodhlan. As custodian and heir, I feel my judgment is fair."

Eremon clenched his fists. "This is a power play."

"On whose behalf, Eremon?" Aidryn countered. "She's made it clear she doesn't *want* the throne."

"Whether she wants it or not, she knows what is best for Iathium," Thorne added.

"She said she doesn't *wish* to lead Iathium!" Eremon turned to Lira, his rage barely contained beneath the carefully culti-vated exterior that was at once both familiar and foreign. "Lira, if you don't want the city and I can't have it, then who *is* fit? Indulge me."

The room fell silent again, and all eyes turned to Lira. She swallowed hard, her pulse pounding in her ears, and squeezed her eyes shut before she answered, "Thorne."

CHAPTER 99
CAITIR

Sov'is, Iteloria

Caitir awakened in a strange chamber made of white marble. Round columns shot through with gray veins rose around her, the trappings of the room covered in cobalt and gold. Sunlight streamed in through the tall windows, which bore clear glass panes. The bed she lay in was plush and decadent, covered in blankets that matched the curtains and tapestries.

With a soft gasp, she pressed her hands to her belly. As if in answer, there was a soft, barely noticeable nudge from within her. She released a breath, relieved, and rolled onto her side, cradling her middle. Whatever had transpired since Aila's *turas*, the child was still safe.

Something heavy and metallic slid down over her breasts and onto the mattress beside her. She reached for it—Lira's pendant. Aila had not bothered to remove it. She likely intended to try controlling Caitir with it, the way she had manipulated Vor'sca and Lira. Idly, she ran her fingertips along its ancient whorls, feeling the comforting hum of Lira's power within the brass.

Everything was quiet, and she lay still for a long while, turning memories over and over in her mind. She thought of Eremon and the way he'd loved her. The devastated expression on his face when she'd cuffed him. If they ever saw one another again, she wondered whether he would regard her in the same way.

You know I won't forgive you for this.

Caitir shook off the stinging memory and sat up, dropping the pendant beneath the fabric of her gown. She carefully climbed down from the high, plush mattress using the little wooden staircase at her bedside. A dressing gown had been left draped over a chair by her bed, so she threw it on, crossing the room and trying the doorknob. It was, surprisingly, unlocked, and she let herself into the brightly lit corridor beyond.

Everything about this place—for she assumed this was the palace in Sov'is, Iteloria's capital city—was deceptively charming. She paused by a window in the corridor to look out over the sprawling cityscape, at least four times Iathium's size. The bustling streets below were busy and crowded, and beyond, she could barely make out the skyline of Najyn, the continent's port city.

Caitir continued along the corridor until she reached a large sitting area, where Aila was reclining with a man who looked to be middle-aged. She smiled warmly when she saw Caitir, standing and extending a hand toward her.

"Look who has finally deigned to show herself," she said in a rich, joyful tone that might have caused Caitir to lower her guard once. Now, it rang sickeningly false.

"How long have we been here?" Caitir asked, skipping the niceties altogether.

"Three days, dear," Aila answered airily. "You needed your beauty rest."

Caitir shut her mouth, trying not to gape. Three days? Had she been drugged? Enchanted to sleep against her will? Neither answer would have surprised her. She squashed her rage, schooling her expression into pleasant neutrality.

"And who is this?" she asked, motioning to the man, who had been watching her closely since she entered.

The man turned to regard Caitir. He appeared to be in his mid-forties, with bronze skin and hair the color of pewter. His dark eyes sparkled, and he flashed her a charming smile.

"It's an honor to finally meet our guest," he said. "Welcome to Sov'is, Caitir. I am King La'hiran."

Caitir inclined her head, her gaze flicking to Aila before she replied, "Charmed."

His lips curled almost imperceptibly. "Is that all the thanks I receive for offering you such a lavish suite?"

"The suite is beautiful," she answered curtly, "but I preferred my room at the Dome."

Aila broke into a rich laugh, as though Caitir had just said something hilarious. "After you've seen what Iteloria has to offer, you will *never* wish to return to Rodhlan."

"Is that so, Mother?" Caitir perched on the arm of the sofa, and Aila sneered.

Aila opened her mouth to speak, but La'hiran silenced her with a dismissive wave of his hand. He turned to face Caitir more fully, raking his eyes from her bare toes to her face. "Let me tell you a story about Rodhlan. Have a seat."

Crimson power wrapped itself around her arms and legs, compelling her to move. Aila used the magic to shove her into a chair across from La'hiran's, who leaned in close.

"Rodhlan is weak," the king began, picking up a glass of strong-smelling liquor and taking a sip. "*Eremon* is weak. I have more power and resources at my disposal than he could possibly hope to muster. If you choose to be an uncooperative guest in my home, then I will see to it that his pitiful continent is decimated." Another sip. "The end."

He set the glass on a small table beside him and regarded her smugly. Caitir's eyes darted between La'hiran and Aila, whose expression was twisted into a satisfied smirk. Her hand drifted to her heart, and her fingertips grazed the bronze chain that still hung around her neck.

"I'll need that necklace back, daughter," Aila said, holding out a palm expectantly.

She held her mother's gaze, pulling the pendant up by its chain and making slow work of turning it in search of the clasp. As she worked, she couldn't help but think of Lira. Something deep within her warmed at the memory of their final embrace, and she was glad they'd had the chance to make amends before the end.

Remember where you come from, Lira had said.

She hadn't had much time to puzzle over the statement, but it had raised the hairs on the back of her neck. Now, gooseflesh spread across her skin. What had Lira meant by it?

Caitir came from Rodhlan. She was a descendent of Rasu and Clan Tarlach—*Tarlach*. She had Tarlach magic in her veins. Metalworking power.

Turas is making this too easy, Caitir had said before. The spell had given Aila far too many opportunities to wreak havoc. Her eyes flicked to the necklace's glass twin, which still hung around Aila's neck.

Well. Aila had taught Caitir how spot opportunities, and this was an important one.

Caitir bit back a smile as she undid the chain's clasp, then painstakingly closed it again. She weighed the pendant in her palm. It was heavy and warm and *alive* with power.

"Hurry, girl," Aila snapped.

Swiftly, Caitir turned her attention back to La'hiran,

holding eye contact with him. She tightened her fingers around the pendant, ignoring Aila's pointed reaching.

"Let's make sure I understand, Your Majesty," Caitir began, training her gaze on the king. "If I'm to play your game, you expect me to be content in Sov'is. We'll never be left wanting; therefore, there is no reason either of us should desire to return to Rodhlan."

The king regarded her, then gave her a slow nod. "That's the idea."

"Good," she answered. "Then how about this?"

Caitir flashed the bronze pendant at La'hiran, garnering a cry from Aila. "I take the first turn. I'll show you how dedicated we truly are to remaining in Iteloria with our gracious host."

She let her dark magic surge into the ancient pendant, which gave easily beneath her clan's metalworking power. It turned to ash in her hand.

"How dare you!" Aila shrieked. She scrabbled at the glass replica around her neck, which promptly shattered.

King La'hiran raised his brows and leaned back, looking almost impressed. He seemed as though he was suppressing a laugh—until Caitir held her palm over his liquor glass and poured the ashes into it.

She leaned in, picked the glass up to swirl its contents, and said, "Your move."

CHAPTER 100
LIRA

The Rí's Garden

Dawn was breaking over the Dome's garden when Eremon entered, his light footsteps the only sign of his approach. He didn't speak as he joined Lira on the little bridge that spanned the indoor stream, and she did not acknowledge him. Instead, she kept her gaze trained on the fish that swam lazily through the dark water, their fins swaying elegantly with the current.

Eremon leaned forward, resting his forearms on the red railing. There was a slight rustle in the trees, and the soothing sound of water tripping over rocks lulled Lira into a false sense of peace. She had not spoken to anyone but Aidryn since the meeting in the council chamber, and she had no desire to begin now. To speak to Eremon, Oda, or especially to Thorne would mean being forced to defend her position again and again.

It had been nearly impossible to justify her choice when she hadn't been at liberty to share all her reasons for it.

When she'd extended the ring to Thorne, his amber eyes had snapped to hers, his expression stricken. He had shaken his head, uttered a guttural, "No," and left the council chamber without another word. Oda had gawked at her before going after him, and Eremon had mumbled something about showing Vor'sca to a chamber before storming out himself.

That was when Lira had come to the garden, with Aidryn at her heels. They'd found Fiadh still lying on the pathway, barely conscious from Tiriya's attack. Lira hadn't possessed enough sympathy to feel sorry for her, but she'd sent for Deghan, asking him to detain Fiadh in her chambers under heavy guard and await further instruction.

Her kinsman had watched her warily, as though awaiting some sort of retribution from Lira for having followed Gerallt here. But Lira was too exhausted to consider what to do about the sentries or the damage Gerallt and Aila had managed to do. She was too tired to deal with any of it.

"She should be locked up," Aidryn had said as Deghan and another sentry hefted a groaning Fiadh onto a litter and carried her away. "We can't trust her."

"Agreed," Lira had replied. "Oda has yet to exercise her anointed role as Rodhlan's High Judge. Perhaps she'll be willing to try."

Alongside Clan Énna's water magic, its anointed had been known in centuries past for doling out judgment across the continent. Perhaps determining Fiadh's fate was the perfect way to help Oda learn another facet of her new power.

As for Clan Énna, they had closely guarded their anointed for so long that, once word of Oda reached them, they would be another force to contend with. The magic may have chosen her before witnesses, but Énna's elders would have plenty to say about their secret being exposed.

She'd thought about Lord Irem and Skelly then, unease churning in her gut. They were still, presumably, in Iteloria with Ellwyn and Rune Énna. If they survived the journey, maybe they would contact more immortals like Vor'sca along the way—immortals who would be willing to help them fight against Aila's darkness.

Lira and Aidryn had watched the sentries move painstakingly toward the garden's exit with Fiadh in tow, and Lira had tilted her head in their direction. "I don't trust Deghan. Will you see to it that Fiadh is deposited in a guarded room?"

Aidryn had released a soft sigh and nodded. "I will."

He'd taken two steps away from Lira's side before returning to her, gently taking her face in his hands and studying her as though for the first time. Slowly, he'd leaned in and pressed soft kisses to her forehead, her nose, her lips. Lira had clung to him—perhaps too tightly—and deepened the kiss, pulling their bodies flush against one another for a long, lingering moment.

She'd fought back the swell of sorrow that threatened to drag her down, focusing instead on the scent of him and how it felt to be in his arms. Without the perpetual hum of magic between them, Lira had been free to focus wholly on Aidryn. On his lean muscle, gentle hands, kind words. On the ever-lingering smell of springtime that clung to him like a shower of her favorite blooms drifting from mountain trees.

Their future had never been guaranteed—not in this time or place, and not with so many forces poised to clash around them. Lira supposed no one's fate was secure, even in peaceful times. But she had emerged from her war with dark magic with more clarity than she'd ever possessed. What mattered most now, more than anything, were the people she loved and those whose lives and actions might impact the world for the better. The coming conflicts ran so much deeper than the question of who would protect Iathium's throne in the short term.

Lira had spent her life dedicated to a city built on lies, but she wouldn't give herself to it any longer. It was time to return truths to the people—time to help them master their powers.

Time to untangle the mysterious Binding between Rodhlan and Iteloria before it was too late.

"What are you thinking, Silira?"

Eremon's soft voice cut through the weight of her thoughts, and she shook herself, returning to the present. She turned her head to regard him, and the sight of his mournful expression made her chest ache.

"I'm thinking..." She released a short, breathy laugh. "You call me Silira when you're angry or trying to make a point. I'd rather you stopped that."

His expression was flat. "*Really.* The truth can't hurt any more than being told I have no business taking the throne."

Lira leaned nearer, forcing down the dread that filled her. "Do you know how to deaden the sound around us, the way Ljós does? So no one can hear what I have to say?"

Eremon flicked his fingers. All at once, it felt as though the sound had been sucked from the room. "Yes, because he taught me how."

She relaxed, giving Eremon a curt nod. "Thorne won't forgive me for telling you this. I wasn't willing to say it in front of Vor'sca—we can't trust her with the information. Aidryn and Oda don't realize, but Thorne told me everything."

"Ah," Eremon breathed. "Finally, the guarded secret emerges. Tell me: What's more important than protecting Caitir —who has now been imprisoned in Iteloria by two tyrants— and saving her child from an eternity with Aila?"

"Nothing," Lira answered. "That's why I offered Thorne the ring. Caitir is more important to you than the throne. Why else would you have offered her a regency, rather than ascending before? And don't deny it—I can see straight through your protests."

Eremon shut his mouth, wrinkling his forehead before he said, "Fine. Enlighten me more."

Lira rolled her eyes. "You don't see it now, but my choosing

Thorne keeps Caitir at the forefront of your focus. If Vor'sca helps you hone your power, then perhaps you can band together to save Caitir before it's too late. But if you're ruling here, your attention will be split three ways and Iathium will always take precedence."

"I still fail to see how Thorne is a better choice than you or Aidryn," Eremon answered. "And you still haven't gotten to the secret."

"Aidryn needs time to heal," Lira answered carefully, "and you saw what the dark magic did to me. I need to sort out what should happen with my birthright power—and you're going to need the two of us to help you research."

She didn't say that denying herself the throne was, in part, her atonement for concealing the voice and causing so much harm to her friends and allies. To Aidryn. Lira had no business ascending when she'd just attempted to usurp the throne herself. Regardless of what had influenced her actions, the fact was that she'd allowed it to happen. Wittingly, unwittingly... the details didn't matter.

Through her own struggles, she had come to realize that her unflinching self-reliance was not always her strongest attribute. It was time to start looking outside herself more often for help. Time to stop trying to handle everything alone when there were other people and resources willing to provide support.

"You'll take your magic back, of course," Eremon quipped, straightening and folding his hands behind his back.

"Likely," she conceded. "Yes. But I have some thoughts about that—anyway, now isn't the time. We're talking about Thorne."

She rose to her full height, leaning against the bridge's railing and crossing her arms. "Placing Thorne in charge of the city forces Artur to stand down. You saw his warriors in place outside the walls, and you know some of them infiltrated the city weeks ago. I'm neutralizing Clan Beran's threat. Rodhlan can't withstand infighting among the clans."

"How is that neutralizing anything?" Eremon demanded, now exasperated. "You just handed power to Beran with your halfwit offer."

"Not to Artur," Lira countered, her anger rising. "Not the overlord, not his heir, but Thorne Beran as a citizen of *Rodhlan*. It's political protection for him as much as everyone else. How can Artur argue against his rule? And if he's only temporary custodian, he can return to his duties at Clan Beran when the time is right. By then, maybe Artur's wrath will have cooled."

Eremon shook his head, confusion knitting his features. "Why would Thorne need political protection from Artur? He's the anointed."

Lira's muscles tensed, and her nails bit into her palm as she clenched her fists. "Are you sure you want to know the *halfwit* answer to that, Eremon?"

He sighed. "I just fail to understand your logic."

She inhaled deeply, bracing herself. "But you understand protecting those you love."

Eremon raised a skeptical brow. "Are you suggesting Thorne is capable of love?"

"I'm not suggesting it," Lira said, "I'm confirming it. You're determined to protect Caitir and her unborn babe, yes? And you would do anything it takes to make that happen, wouldn't you?"

Now, Eremon's frustration was apparent. He pressed his fingers to his temple and blew out a hard breath. "Why are you asking me questions you already know the answers to?"

Lira was trembling. Once she uttered the words, there would be no going back. She prayed that Eremon would prove trustworthy—that he would begin to understand everything once she shared this final piece of truth.

For a moment, she closed her eyes. "Because when the time

comes, Thorne will need Iathium to shield his family from Artur."

When she opened her eyes again, Eremon was shaking his head, clearly confused. "And? His father is safe in the mountains, and besides, he refused the ring. He *stormed out* of the council chamber." He ran a hand over his face, muffling his next words. "I fail to see why you're so set on this idea."

"I believe he'll reconsider," Lira said slowly.

Hurt flashed in Eremon's eyes. He made a fist, pounding it lightly against the bridge's railing for emphasis as he leaned forward, holding her gaze. In a low voice, he asked, "Why?"

Lira let a long moment pass before she swallowed hard, steeling herself. "Because he would do anything—even rule Iathium—to protect his wife and child."

∿

THE END

Notes & Acknowledgements

Wow - I am so very grateful!

To the friends, mentors, fellow authors, and readers who have cheered me on and supported me as I crafted *Vow of Magic*: Doing this without you would have been a lonely journey and a dark night, indeed.

To Tim O'Hearn and Marcella W.: Thank you for reading multiple drafts of *Vow* and helping me make this book the very best it could be.

Tim: I so appreciate your encouragement, eagle-eyed proof-reading skills, and gentle nudging for me to keep pushing until this book was done. It has been a very long road, but the work has been worth it. And maybe now that *Vow* is out in the world, I can finally start recording some of the music you've written for the series! (I am still so humbled and grateful. Thank you.)

Marcella: While I wish we didn't live half a world away from each other, I'm so grateful you were always up at 3 a.m. Central Standard Time to fangirl about my characters with me and keep me awake during countless all-nighters. Kittymon heartily approves. I so appreciate your friendship and your talent, and I'm excited to share the new art you've created for *Vow*. If I could send you a pastry right now, I 1000% would!

To Elisabeth Belsher: Your feedback for both *Keeper of Keys* and *Vow of Magic* has been absolutely invaluable. Thank you for the long conversations and the lovely artwork you've done for my series so far.

To Rebecca F. Kenney and Gracienne Standen: thank you for being my first Patreon patrons. While I've paused that leg of the journey to focus on finishing the core series, I hope to return to developing it sooner, rather than later.

To Elyse Grothendick, Emily Prebich, and Christine Hutton: Thank you for coming alongside me to assist with my marketing, ARC team building, and book launch. I couldn't have built this momentum without you, especially in this season.

To Lyssa, Chloe, and Gracie: Thank you for the belly laughs and the many, many pep talks over the past year. I will always do whatever I can to return the favor!

To my husband, Grant: You have motivated me to pursue this dream of publishing fiction in countless ways. Thank you for being by my side and reminding me to look for the sunshine. I love you!

To our children: You inspire me and crack me up every single day. Thank you for continually showing me, through your exuberance and (near unfathomable amount of) energy, how to reach for the joy in every moment. I love you so much!!

To Mom and Dad: Y'all know I've always kept myself suuuper busy. Thank you for your help and for being there for me while I've worked to build two creative businesses. I love you!!

To my incredible readers: Many of you have become dear friends since I began publishing this series. Some of you had already known me for many years, and dove into these books alongside me. I'm so grateful for the time you've taken to read, review, and interact with me both online and in-person. I wish I could name you all individually, but I'm afraid I'd leave someone out! Love you all.

Until the next leg of the journey...

- Haley

THE SAGA CONTINUES IN SOVEREIGN OF CLANS...

The Witness Tree Chronicles continues with book 4, *Sovereign of Clans*, coming soon! Keep up with the latest news at authorhaleywalden.com.

RUSE OF HEIRS
GO BACK TO WHERE IT ALL BEGAN...

HALEY WALDEN

RUSE
OF
HEIRS

TALES
OF
RODHLAN

RUSE OF HEIRS
A TALES OF RODHLAN NOVEL

When love and loyalty collide, there can only be one victor.

Riveting and emotionally charged, escape into this romantic fantasy story of magic, intrigue, and a forbidden love that conquers the most dutiful of hearts.

Fiery warrior Oda and her family gave up everything to live in Clan Beran's isolated fortress. She has relentlessly fought her way up the warriors' ranks, gaining the trust and friendship of Thorne, the headstrong and handsome general.

Oda spends her days sparring in the arena, rooting out traitors, and protecting the clan. She keeps her deepening attraction to Thorne under lock and key, until a devastating tragedy forces their true feelings to the surface, igniting a desire neither can contain.

But trouble is brewing in the fortress, and the fearsome overlord is growing more tyrannical by the day. Only Thorne can save their people - but taking the throne requires an unthinkable, heart-wrenching sacrifice.

Will they have the courage to fight for their love, or will the greater good tear them apart forever?

Ruse of Heirs *is a prequel set three years before the events of* Defender of Histories (The Witness Tree Chronicles, Book 1).

Although it's a prequel and can stand on its own, it's best read after Vow of Magic.

Learn more:
authorhaleywalden.com

THANK YOU!

Enjoyed what you read? Please leave a review on Goodreads or the retailer of your choice.

Reviews help readers like you discover new stories, characters, and worlds they'll love.

(Plus, Eremon very much enjoys the validation and would be displeased if I neglected to mention that fact.)

About the Author

Haley Walden writes fast-paced, character-driven epic fantasy with magical adventures, spellbinding love stories, and unforgettable friendships. As a multi-passionate geek she has many obsessions, including music, martial arts, history, pop culture, and musical theatre. She lives in Alabama with her husband and children.

www.authorhaleywalden.com

LET'S KEEP IN TOUCH!

Stay up-to-date on bookish news and happenings:
www.authorhaleywalden.com

Follow me on Instagram, TikTok, and Facebook:
@authorhaleywalden